GIDEON'S DAWN

IN A WORLD WHERE WORDS *Can* KILL,
THE LANGUAGE YOU *Speak* DETERMINES
THE DESTINY OF *Your* SOUL

MICHAEL
D. WARDEN

BARBOUR
PUBLISHING

© 2003 by Michael D. Warden

ISBN 1-58660-725-1

Acquisitions and Editorial Director: Mike Nappa
Editorial Consultant: Stephen Parolini
Art Director: Robyn Martins
Cover Design: UDG/DESIGNWORKS

Published by Barbour Publishing, Inc., P.O. Box 719, Uhrichsville, Ohio 44683, www.barbourbooks.com

 Member of the
Evangelical Christian
Publishers Association

Printed in the United States of America
5 4 3 2 1

Contents

To Don, James, Jonny, and Sky,
whose noble lives continually remind me
that the Remnant is real.

And to Mark James Furaus,
who proves beyond doubt that there is
a friend who sticks closer than a brother.

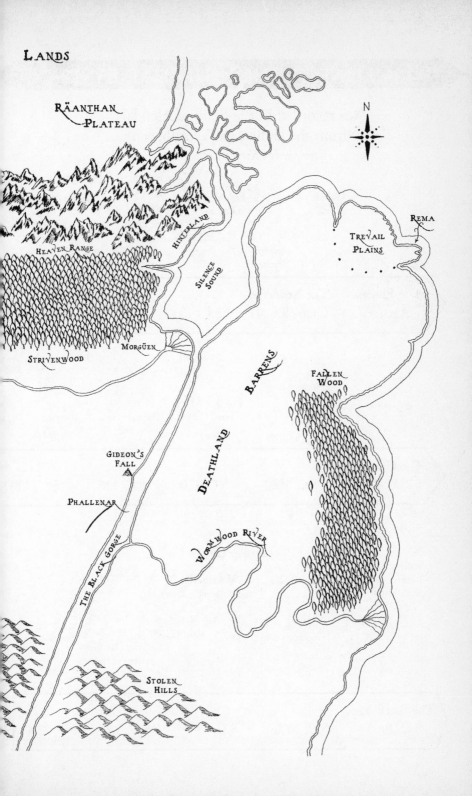

TIMELINE OF THE INHERITED LANDS

(as recorded in the Seltan Calendar;
from the archives at Wordhaven)
compiled by Kyrintha Asher-Baal

Gideon's
Fall

Enlek's
Sojourn

Naron's
Sojourn

Makela's
Sojourn

Basrea's
Sojourn

Machim's
Sojourn

Akhill's
Sojourn

The Endless Age (??)	The New Age (Starts S.C. 1)	S.C. 100	S.C. 200	S.C. 300

Prophet Mikail
born (1086)

Prophet Bari
born (1217)

Prophet
Silmar
born (1277)

The Grey Ages S.C. 900	S.C. 1000	S.C. 1100	S.C. 1200	S.C. 1300

Sky
Rebellion (2060)

Society of the
Remnant
established
(1858)

Laudin Sky
born (2026)

Wordhaven
rediscovered (2096)

Laudin
slain (2139)

Gideon Dawning
arrives (2150)

The Black Ages S.C. 1900	S.C. 2000	S.C. 2100	S.C. 2200	S.C. 2300

Larell's
Sojourn

Marin's
Sojourn

Catrine's
Sojourn

Natel's
Sojourn

Cala's
Sojourn

Kih's
Sojourn

S.C. 400　　S.C. 500　　S.C. 600　　S.C. 700　　S.C. 800

Prophet Endimnar　Prophet Shikinah　The Slaughtering
born (1430)　　born (1564)　　(1605–1608)

Palor dies,
Council rule
begins (1610)

The Black Ages

S.C. 1400　　S.C. 1500　　S.C. 1600　　S.C. 1700　　S.C. 1800

PROLOGUE

Two thousand years before the Visitation

High Lord Gideon, *Batai* of Wordhaven, stood motionless on the emerald plains and glared up at the quickly graying sky. His stoic, aging face shone with the determination to hold his sense of dignity, even now as he faced the greatest peril of his life. But the small tendrils of sweat on his forehead betrayed his anxiety.

He knew his path would lead him to this; he'd even planned on it for decades. But all the years of forethought and dreams had failed to fully prepare him for the finality of his predicament or for the unexpected feelings of remorse for betraying those who named him High Lord.

From behind him, Gideon felt the first chilled breezes of the Storm of Deliverance coming from the west. Even now, at this distance, its winds cut through his regal blue robe with ease, prickling his skin with the threat of vengeance to come. The storm's multicolored lightning bolts danced across the distant fields, taking aim, gauging the distance until they could reach him—a fragile white-haired man standing so solemnly with the Staff of *Dei'lo* at his side. He did not bother turning around.

Beneath the rumblings of distant thunder, he could just make out the sound of hundreds of people—the ranks of Guardians coming to retrieve the Pearl he had stolen from Wordhaven only hours before. But he knew they would not come in fury like a common mob, brandishing weapons of destruction and hate. They would come with no weapons at all, save their voices.

They were singing. The song was beautiful, heavenly. But in the Words, Gideon could hear their rage breathing down upon him in pulsing chords. And somehow he could hear their sorrow too.

Without warning, the High Lord sensed a presence around him, a living phantasm so tremendous that he could not comprehend its depth or expanse. But within it resonated a power so beautifully alluring that he hardly noticed the hate that fueled it. His body shuddered involuntarily, despite the hundreds of times he'd felt its coming.

"Sink the staff into the earth, Lord Gideon. . . ," the voice, so vile it seemed to dim the sky, whispered above the sounds of the storm and the song of the Guardians, ". . .and stand away."

There was no face or body with the voice; there never had been. But its reality was sure in Gideon's mind and heart—sure enough that he'd gradually given up everything Wordhaven and the Pearl could offer him for the chance to have what only the voice could promise—dominion over all, even—no, *especially*—over the Pearl itself.

Gideon paused a moment, silently debating one last time whether the path he had chosen was the one he really wanted. The people who pursued him were once his friends. Now they would feel nothing for him but an appalling hatred or perhaps in their arrogance a sort of condescending pity. And the voice would certainly be no ally in the future. It meant to use Gideon as its puppet once the deed was done—he was hardly fool enough to believe otherwise. When this day ended, however, whatever baleful favors the voice demanded would prove irrelevant. Its insidious whispers would soon be silenced under the potent force of the Pearl, the supreme power that would reside in Gideon from this time on.

Only then would Gideon no longer be consigned to live in the shadow of the Pearl's glory—ever the reflection of power but never its source. Then everyone—from the Lords of Wordhaven to the lowliest soundenor—would be forced to acknowledge what Gideon had come to realize for himself, that the Pearl was not their deliverer as it claimed. . .but rather their keeper.

The High Lord raised the staff high overhead and thrust it deep within the plain. The huge Pearl crowned at its end continued to glow, still as eerily silent as it had been all day and seemingly oblivious to Gideon's malice. *Perhaps it is not so all-knowing after all*, he mused smugly. Still, as he backed away some twenty paces, he was careful to keep his gaze averted from its glow.

"Now, lend me your mind," the voice hissed in the wind. "Just as before—quickly."

Obediently, Gideon closed his eyes and faced the thickening blanket of clouds overhead. Around his feet, dark shadows began to swirl. They slowly writhed their way up his legs and torso, filling his body and thoughts with an overwhelming oppression of dread mixed with ecstasy. His body trembled under the tingly flow of the rich darkness around him. The shadows slowly coiled around his neck like a snake, hesitating ever so slightly before slithering into his ears.

Instantly, his eyes flew open in horror, like the eyes of a child awakening from a nightmare or the eyes of a man beholding the darkness of his own soul for the first time. He realized he had forgotten to breathe and wondered for a moment whether he should, whether in releasing his breath he would uncontrollably utter the horrid Words that now spun raging in his mind. Cautiously he allowed his breath to escape, holding his lips tight to keep from speaking, and then quickly took in another. His robes now reeked with the fetor of death—the inevitable result of the formless one's touch.

But the stench didn't bother him. Nothing mattered now. . .now that he had the power of life and death in his thoughts. Now that he could destroy the world if he chose. The Words ripped through his mind, tearing slivers of his sanity, cursing the good within him wherever it hid. He felt himself severing inside, cleaving apart, as though the Words were blades and his soul a shroud of thin-spun cloth. He was overcome by the dominion of the Words, losing himself in the magnificent insanity of its pure malevolence. It no longer occurred to him to be afraid.

"High Lord Gideon, hail there!" a deep voice called from behind him as the singing suddenly ceased. "Stop where you are. You have taken the Staff of *Dei'lo* from its proper chambers. We know not your intentions in this matter, but many suspect them to be foul. In either case, the Pearl must be restored to Wordhaven. We come in force, High Lord. Turn and do not speak, and no harm will befall you. Return now, *Batai*, or the storm will consume you where you stand."

"Never!" The High Lord turned on the Guardians, numbering in the hundreds before him, his eyes ablaze with an unearthly fury not fully his own. "You think me so easily moved by your petty storm. I shall soon show you who will be consumed! *Damonoi shalon nietan richt!*"

At Gideon's Words, the storm cloud began to mutate. The lightning stopped, the wind subsided, and from its dark center a rain of acid began to fall.

Without hesitation, as though linked in heart and mind, the Guardians began to sing again. This time their song was different. It bore in its melodies a holy vengeance, like the rage of a son avenging the murder of his beloved father. The dark cloud churned and shifted once again and coalesced into a tornado towering more than three hundred feet into the air. But there was no wind around it. It was as though all the wind of the Inherited Lands had been sucked into that one churning vortex, forcing all its fury into a cone of pure destruction. No sooner had it taken shape than it raced toward the *Batai*.

But Gideon had already turned his back on the throng. His mind was filled with other matters, other Words.

The Words!

They tore at his heart, ripped through his thoughts, raping him of sanity. He felt he must speak them before they destroyed him altogether, before he lost the capacity to speak at all.

He outstretched his arms toward two horizons and set his glare on the Pearl that yet rested so placidly, so meekly, atop the Staff. Even in the fury of his growing madness, he wondered why it did not speak, why it did nothing in its own defense. Perhaps what Abaddon said was true. Perhaps the Pearl was not so mighty as it claimed.

Drawing in the deepest breath of his life, he lifted his head and yelled the Words that had ripped his mind away.

"Lusifen vadestro shon ak Jeo Perlein! Vadestro shon ak Jeo Perlein sic atros et accustros! Damonoi terradestro shon ak todras veot!"

The world fell silent as the Words echoed toward the east. Then the world was black. The vortex was gone. The people were gone. The plains had turned to nothing. Gideon closed his eyes and forced his breathing to slow—calming his thundering heart. The Words were gone now, expelled in the fury that had ravaged his sanity, and he felt a measure of peace return to him.

After a moment he opened his eyes, but saw only blackness. He felt suspended in a shapeless void, his Words having torn away the world—or having torn him away from it. He didn't know which. There was no sound save the rasping of his breath and the incessant pounding of his heart.

Deep in his mind, he questioned whether by some chance he were dead. Perhaps the voice, the voice of Abaddon the Destroyer, had tricked him, convincing him that the Words he spoke to destroy the Pearl and draw all of its power into himself might actually have done nothing more than end his own life.

Or worse yet, the Words might have banished him to some netherworld existence, a place that is not a place.

Deep-stirring rage surged in Gideon as he thought of this. It would be just like the Destroyer to gain a victory through such deceit. But the High Lord wasn't Abaddon's true enemy; the Pearl was. So long as the Pearl lived, Abaddon would be forced into subjection to it. That vile spirit wanted the Pearl destroyed, probably even far more than Gideon could conceive.

Then, quietly, gently, a light appeared within the void, looking like a distant star in the night sky. He focused on it, and his heart leapt in recognition. This was the power coming to him—the power Abaddon had promised in return for the Pearl's destruction. The power of the Pearl itself.

The light began to move toward Gideon, slowly at first, then racing, faster and faster, growing ever brighter until it silently filled his whole world. As it drew nearer, he leaned forward and stared into its immeasurable brilliance. He wanted to see the power, the limitless power, coming to reside in him, coming to be his alone.

It *was* just as the voice had promised, he assured himself. Just as Abaddon had said.

But as the light came close, it changed. What was a distant star took on the shape of a flaming sword, emblazoned with pure fire that burned hotter than even the world could bear. But there was something else. Gideon could see something more than the sword. Someone was holding it. Someone more brilliant than the sun and far more terrible.

And that someone was coming. . .for him.

"Noooo!"

CHAPTER I

FOUNDATIONS

*He was nothing like what we expected, what anyone
expected. But then, saviors rarely look or sound the way
we envision that they should. They are far too real to be
so casually defined by our poor imaginations.*

—THE KYRINTHAN JOURNALS, BEGINNINGS, STANZA 1,VERSE 73

Gideon Dawning glanced westward just in time to see the final rays of amber sink behind the old limestone buildings of the university's West Mall. It was sunset. And that meant Gideon was late.

"Stink!"

Palming sweat off his eyebrow, he whipped his bike around and shot off like a madman, pedaling frantically toward the geology building on the other end of the campus. There was only one thing he hated more than his frequent—and absurdly boring—meetings with Dean Powell, and that was arriving late for one of them.

The man was a certifiable idiot, no question about it. All lard and pomp and pipe smoke. But as dean of geology, he was powerful all the same—especially over Gideon's much-envied status at the university. And the dean was a stickler for time like no one Gideon had ever known. If his star assistant were so much as a half-minute late to the meeting, the belligerent reprimands would drone on for weeks.

With a quick glance at his watch, Gideon knew he had only a few minutes before Dean Powell started making calls to find him. Ignoring the "keep off the grass" sign, he cut across the greenyards near the tower and recklessly plowed his bike down the long multiple sets of granite stairs, ignoring the angry complaints of the students who shuffled awkwardly out of his path.

How the dean ever got his position in the first place was a mystery to Gideon—he was certainly no expert in geology and even less of one at people skills. But he'd held the chair for more than a dozen years and clearly relished the dominion it gave him with the fervor of a rottweiler in a cage full of kittens. And for whatever reason, Gideon had become one of his favorite kitties to bat around.

Not that Gideon saw himself as the dean's hapless pawn, of course. If anything, the situation was really the other way around, although Dean Powell would certainly never recognize it. After all, it was the dean's personal recommendation that had allowed Gideon to pursue his master's degree in geology without cost. And it was the dean who had given Gideon the position of head graduate assistant and later granted him a substantial stipend so he could "attend to his duties without needless distractions." You didn't get those kinds of perks without knowing how to work the system—or, in this case, the fat bureaucrat at the top of the system.

Gideon pedaled faster, absently plowing through several clusters of flowers that blocked his path. Actually, he had no idea why Powell wanted to see him this time. It wasn't one of their scheduled meetings. The dean had called his apartment just after lunch and left a message detailing the time and place—with no question as to whether Gideon was available, naturally. That was assumed. As to the reason, all the man said was, "It is a matter of great urgency and sensitivity."

With wording like that, Gideon might have thought the dean had uncovered some foolhardy thing he'd done—except he never did anything foolhardy. Not of the common variety, anyway. He lived his work and his studies and allowed time for little else. Alcohol turned his stomach, ganja gave him an out-of-control feeling he readily despised, and as for women. . .well, there was none of that either. He had stopped believing long ago that he would ever fall in love. Really, he no longer believed he was even capable of it. Maybe once upon a time. But not anymore.

He shook his head in frustration. No point in thinking about that now. Pondering his childhood accomplished nothing, except to arouse his anger. And the last thing he needed was to walk into the dean's office with a scowl on his face, especially since he was late.

Gideon pedaled hard onto the East Mall. The geology building sat close to the eastern edge of campus, next to the transit circle where the commuter buses made their final stops. Thundering his way down one final set of stairs, he wheeled up to the doors, locked up his bike, and stormed into the building.

This had better be good, he fumed silently, suddenly annoyed at the dean's presumption in expecting him to rearrange his schedule without so much as a "could you please?" and even angrier at himself for acquiescing to the demand without the slightest protest.

Without thinking, he slammed the elevator button with his fist—so loudly that several students in the hall turned to see what had happened. He glared at them with a look that said if he wanted to rip that stupid little button right off the wall, what business was it of theirs? They all looked away.

Frustrated, Gideon roughly ran his hands through his sweaty black curls. *Why am I so angry all of a sudden?* he wondered impatiently. *It's not like the dean hasn't pulled this kind of stunt before.*

It wasn't the right question to ask, though, and he knew it—just as he knew the dean wasn't really the source of his agitation. The truth was he was always angry—had been for as long as he could remember. The real question—the million-dollar question that had plagued him for years—was why.

He could guess at some of the reasons, all of them coiled in one way or another around the image of his father. Gideon had always been high-strung, but his anger didn't come to stay until his father left. Gideon was eight then, when he learned to hate for the first time.

Later, after his dad was long gone, the hatred gradually lost its focus and became a fog of undefined rage that grew up with him. Eventually he mastered it, after a fashion, by keeping it shoved away in the darker corners of his soul. Over the years it had become familiar, even comfortable. Like a man limping from childhood, Gideon grew so accustomed to it that he hardly noticed it at all.

Until the rages began.

The first one occurred when he was eighteen, and, like all of them, it came in his sleep. A nightmare, he supposed, though he remembered none of his dreams. He even considered it possible that someone had broken into his room in the night, ripped the pictures off the wall, and gouged the bed stand with a knife. But he could not imagine how he could have slept through something like that. All he really knew was that his room had been vandalized, and the knife was in his hand when he woke up.

On several occasions since then, he had awakened to find his bedroom wrecked, but with no memory of having performed the act. He had tried to recall what happened, but the memories eluded him. They seemed to escape his consciousness like gases through the cracks of a volcano. All that remained after those episodes was a lingering sense of loss. Then the steel doors would close on his thoughts, and the sense would drift away like smoke.

The elevator doors finally parted, and he stomped in. By the time he'd reached the third floor, however, Gideon forced himself to assume a more relaxed posture, running his hands through his curly, raven black hair and consciously releasing the tension in his brow. He wiped the remaining sweat on a kerchief he kept in his backpack, using the moisture to slick his hair out of his eyes. As quickly as it had come, all the anger now was gone; he hardly remembered it. He looked quite confident now and hardly in a rush.

Such comportment was a farce, naturally—all a part of the Game, as Gideon privately named it—but it had become his way of life. "Control" was his continual mantra and isolation his prime defense.

Show people what you want them to see, and only that. All the world's a game, right? A big, merciless, competitive game. So the trick to winning is to be the best player out there.

That was how Gideon saw it. Really, he believed that's how everybody saw it, even though most people weren't honest enough with themselves to admit it. But Gideon was. If anyone were to ask him, he would say he was one of the best players out there. But naturally, no one ever did. No one ever got that close.

With a coolness that belied his ill humor, he approached the dean's office and knocked. The dean's gruff mumble drifted through the heavy oak door. So he walked in.

The first thing Gideon noticed were the curtains. The entire back wall of the dean's office was tinted glass, affording a generous view of the law school campus and the East Mall fountain. The view had never been blocked before, but now dusky orange drapes hung like sentinels over the room, forbidding even a hint of natural light.

Dean Powell sat at the head of the conference table. That too was unusual, since Gideon had never known him to sit anywhere but in the overstuffed leather chair behind his expansive oak desk. That seat had always made the dean look like something of a judge in high court—a fact that the man clearly enjoyed. But on this occasion the dean had opted to leave his seat of power and sit, rather awkwardly it seemed, in one of the simple chairs that ringed the table.

Gideon frowned despite himself. Without his austere, university trappings, the dean was just a rotund, blotchy old man with a pipe and hardly seemed worth all the trouble Gideon had gone to in order to appease him over the years.

"You're late, son," Dean Powell said, looking up from his seat. "You know how I feel about promptness." Gideon nodded, but said nothing. He hated being called "son." With a sigh, the dean gestured for Gideon to sit. He obliged.

"We'll be here awhile," said the dean. "I hope you already ate."

Gideon hadn't eaten since breakfast. But, of course, that really didn't matter to the dean. Without another glance in Gideon's direction, he began unstacking a formidable pile of papers and printouts that sat on the table in front of him.

After a moment he began to talk. And talk. And talk. Before he finally pushed aside the last stack of data printouts, graphs, and geologic reports, he'd refilled his pipe three times and downed almost two pitchers of Perrier. Supper had come and gone, as well as one of Gideon's evening undergrad sections, which the dean absently informed him was being taken care of. Through the entire affair, Gideon dutifully took notes and did not say a word.

"Well, that's about it," the dean said finally, leaning back. "I don't have to tell you how sensitive this information is. I only trust you with it because I have to. One slip of the tongue, and it'll cost you your assistantship."

Gideon nodded dully. He'd heard the threat before and promptly dismissed it as unnecessary. Who would he tell? His cat? Gideon squeezed his writing hand to stop the throbbing ache in the muscles, then slowly stood to leave.

Even if I did tell someone, who would believe me?

He walked out without saying good-bye, his face awash with a combination of shock, hunger, and general fatigue. Under his arm bulged an ordinary brown paper satchel—the kind with the string closures tied around two buttons. The satchel contained all the information Gideon would need for his special assignment. He'd have to study it fast and well enough that it became a part of him. He could do that, of course, but it meant more than a few sleepless nights in the weeks to come.

Once outside, Gideon carefully stuffed the satchel in his pack and headed over to the all-night cafe just south of campus—Katz, it was called.

He didn't leave there until five the next morning. During those seven hours (except for one hour he couldn't remember), Gideon pored over the contents of the brown satchel. Though he had learned over time to see the world through eyes of gritty realism, what he found in the satchel shocked even him.

Earthquakes were on the increase worldwide. That wasn't news, of course. Quakes had been showing up in unlikely places across the globe for the past decade. Thousands had died, especially in Third World countries, where the buildings were less stable and adequate medicine was a rarity. What shocked Gideon was that the situation was apparently far worse than was commonly known. Where the international media had reported hundreds of deaths, there were more often thousands or tens of thousands. And the severity of the earthquakes was increasing at an alarming rate—so much so that the U.S. Geologic Survey and its sister agencies around the world had collectively made the unprecedented decision to "suppress" the actual strength of the earthquakes in their reports to the media. In other words, they lied about the data, apparently to keep from sparking any more of the violent outbreaks of panic that had already begun to erupt in several nations around the globe.

The scientific agencies weren't acting autonomously, of course. They were more or less pressured into suppressing the information by their respective governments, which had been meeting together in several top-secret summits in Geneva over the past five years. These summit meetings had led to the formation of a huge and most unlikely alliance that encompassed over fifty nations. It included all of the major military powers and—remarkably—all the nations of the Middle East. What permitted this unlikely coalition to exist was its narrow and singular goal—to create an international treaty that allowed for the free flow of resources and earthquake-related research among member nations and set international policy related to the earthquake problem. The treaty, which was called the All-Earth Accords, had gone into effect more than three years ago.

Gideon set the report down. Now that he thought about it, he vaguely remembered hearing something about the Senate ratification of the All-Earth Accords treaty some years back. At the time, it was touted as a rather innocuous agreement to cooperate more openly with scientific agencies in other nations. Clearly, it was much more than that.

Gideon returned to the report. As a result of the treaty, scientists around the world had been commissioned to work together on solving the quake mystery—combining genius and scientific research in a way that was unprecedented. The results had been promising; but, as often happens in science, every new discovery had led to a thousand new unanswered questions.

Just recently, the latest satellite telemetry revealed a truly disturbing development: A crack was forming in Antarctica. Not a crack in the ice shelf, but in the continent itself. This crack was so dimensionally vast that it threatened in time to split the continent. The scientists believed the plate Antarctica rested on could be splintering apart. In fact, geologists and geophysicists across the globe had already begun testing that same theory in other "quake-rich" areas. "In-plate rifting," it was called. Scientists believed the phenomenon could be occurring in over thirty places across the globe, with new rifting patterns potentially being added every few months.

That was where Gideon came in. Teams of researchers were secretly being requisitioned by the government to set up seismic tests all along the Rocky Mountain range. Some highbrows in the USGS believed a new rifting pattern might be forming in the Rockies—an unlikely place, Gideon figured, since the Rockies were formed mostly by plate compression, not expansion. Nevertheless, that's what they believed. And they needed teams to set up stations that would measure any unusual fault activity along the range. They hoped to record the pattern as it emerged and in that way learn more about its cause.

Good old Dean Powell thought with his wallet. Three teams were requested from the university, and the dean knew that no professor with tenure would just up and take off for two weeks without considerable compensation from the department. A lowly assistant, however, could do the job just as well and for next-to-nothing in pay. And even though no mention of it was made in the report, Gideon had little doubt that the government had also made a juicy contribution to the department in exchange for its silent cooperation. That was money Gideon would never see, even though he would do the work.

So, for the next four weeks, Gideon's job was to select five to seven top-level undergrad students and train them to assist him in the project. They'd all have to sign nondisclosure agreements. But all their expenses would be paid, and they'd receive an automatic A in their plate tectonics course. All the while, of course, they would be told nothing of the real nature of the project. Even the test results would be altered if necessary to keep them ignorant. For them, it would be just a glorified field trip to measure fault movement in the Rocky Mountains. For Gideon, it promised to be an unending headache.

Stuffing all the research back into the satchel, he paid his bill and walked out the glass doors. The predawn air hit his face like a curtain of warm mist as he stepped outside. The morning hadn't yet arrived, but enough light crept around the earth to cast pale shadows over the campus buildings and make the sky look like a pinkish-gray dreamscape.

The very thought of morning approaching made Gideon realize how exhausted he was. Rubbing his swollen eyes, he draped the satchel over his shoulder, then pedaled lethargically northward, up the drag toward his apartment.

Whatever plans he'd had for this morning were forgotten now. He didn't even try to think about it. He just rode on up the drag, absently wondering how it would feel to be caught in an earthquake.

CHAPTER 2

REVELATIONS

Cutting into an alley off Guadalupe, Gideon coasted down a dirt path to his home. He rented a small one-bedroom place over the garage of an elderly couple who'd retired from active life some years before. Mostly now they just sat idly in their dingy white house, deteriorating right along with the paint job.

Like the house, the paint on the garage was dull and peeling, and the water inside had turned rusty in recent years. But it was private, and his landlords didn't ask many questions.

As Gideon hauled his bike up the creaking stairs to his door, he heard his owner step outside for his brief morning walk. *Why do old people get up so early?*

"Hello, Mr. Finch." Gideon tried to make his voice sound light. "How are you this morning?"

"Fine, fine," grumbled the old man without looking up. He hobbled down the stairs on his own porch and shuffled out toward the front of the house to retrieve the paper.

"Nice to see you too," Gideon grumbled back, then fumbled with the lock on his door. It took at least a minute before he was able to find just the right "click" that caused it to unlock. Inside was dark and smelled of cats and bad fruit. He stumbled over the mail on the floor as he rolled in his bike, and part of the contents of the satchel fell out as he tried to regain his balance.

Mumbling a curse, he set the bike in the corner, then collected the spilled papers and stuffed them back in the satchel. He also grabbed the mail and plodded into the kitchen to open a window. He glanced through the letters as he walked, just in case there were any surprises that he wouldn't want to wake up to later.

There was. Amid the usual junk from scientific societies, bills, and ad sheets, he found a letter from his mother—she'd FedEx'ed it to him two nights before.

He dropped the rest of the mail on the counter, then eased himself onto the couch in the living room. *Why would Mom send a letter to me by FedEx?* he wondered. He opened the seal, then leaned back to read:

Dear Gideon,

I am so sorry to have to try to reach you this way, but I've been trying to call for over a day, and I began to wonder whether your answering machine was recording my messages. Something has happened that you need to know about, although I'm not sure how you'll feel about it.

Abe is dead. He was killed a few days ago in a head-on collision. Both your father and the other driver had been drinking, but the other driver survived. They tell me Abe was probably killed instantly and that he didn't suffer much. I know you haven't seen your father in nearly twenty years, but I thought it best that you know what happened as soon as possible anyway.

The funeral will be at Ridgeway Community Church up in Dallas at 10 A.M. on August 13. I believe I'm going to attend, though I don't expect you to come unless you want to.

I just thought you should know. Call me if you need anything.

Yeshua be with you,
Mom

Gideon sat motionless, staring at the letter. He read it again and again. Then just one sentence: "Abe is dead. . .Abe is dead. . . Abe is dead."

The letter fell out of his hands. *My father is dead. He was killed in an auto accident. He is finally dead.*

Gideon shook his head. It just didn't seem real. He'd wished his father were dead a thousand times over the years, but now that it was true. . .no, it couldn't be true. He read the letter again. *Abe is dead. The man who beat my mother and cheated on our family, the man who abandoned us and took all the money, the man who hated the fact I was his son. That man is dead.*

He tossed the letter on the coffee table. "Well, good," he whispered. "That's one less jerk in the world to worry about."

Gideon didn't move for a long time. His face registered no

emotion, no thought. His eyes focused occasionally on the letter, but mostly on a picture on the far wall. It was a photograph of Gideon as a child with his family on their vacation to the Grand Canyon. It was the only picture of his father he had, but that wasn't the reason he kept it. He told his brother once that he kept it because he could never remember Mom looking so happy as she did on that trip. He said he wanted to remember her the way she was back then, before everything happened.

And although he never told his brother more than that, he also kept the picture for another reason. . .because of the older little boy he saw in it, the black-haired kid who knew how to smile and loved to be tickled. He wanted to remember him too.

Gideon thought back on the days of his childhood, recalling random snippets of memories of the few happy times he had before his father betrayed them—building forts with his brother Jacob in the woods behind their house, helping his mother in kitchen, laughing and playing in the free-spirited way all children do. And, in between these thoughts, absently wondering if his father's death would make any difference in his life now. . .now that the damage was already done.

Eventually he lost track of time. Exhaustion and emotional numbness slowly overtook his thoughts. Gradually, he slumped over on the couch and fell asleep.

The forest runs wet tonight under the moon. White moon. Wet leaves brush my eyes on the run. I run silent, I run alone. Why am I running? I'm looking for him. Through the night forest canopy, I weave through the trunks and under dripping branches. I'm looking for him.

He hunts alone. He hunts, me. But I will find him first. I will.

A howling! Is it him? No, a pack. They are other wolves on the trail of some small bite. He is not there. They do not hunt alone, like him, like he has cursed me to. . .Wait!

On the ridge above me, there he is! I crouch. He will not see me. He must not see me! Don't breathe! Don't breathe!

He sniffs the air; his black coat glistens in the moonlight. He is coming toward me, silent, aware. His head swerves, his lips curl. He sees me!

Fight? Will I fight? He pads closer, black hairs rising on his shoulders. I will fight! I will. He is old now. And I have grown strong.

"Why are you hiding in the bush, Gideon?" The black wolf speaks.

I look down, and now I am a man, a naked man. But he is still a wolf.

"I'm not hiding from you. I've been waiting for you."

The wolf's lips snarl so his teeth glisten in the moonlight. "Well, here I am, boy."

I step out from the bush. "I'll kill you for what you did."

The wolf howls, as though in laughter or anticipation. "You don't even know what I did, little man. Come closer, Gideon. I haven't seen you in so long."

"Don't try to change the subject! I do know what you did to Mom. She told me everything after you were long gone!"

The wolf pads a few steps closer, his black eyes sparkling. "I wasn't talking about her, Gideon. Don't you remember? Step closer. I want to see you."

"I'll kill you."

The wolf's snarl deepens, and his growl pierces the night with an eerie fear. I feel it too, but I will not run. Not this time, not ever again. My heart pounds in terror, but my anger has made me brave.

"C'mon, beast! Or are you afraid of me after all these years?"

The wolf growls again, then crouches as if to spring at my throat. I reach down and grab a fallen branch from the forest floor. I hit it against the ground.

"C'mon! Take me if you can!"

The wolf lurches, but just as its feet leave the ground, it is sideswiped by another. A wolf whose jaws lock around its throat. It is the pack.

The two wolves roll across the forest floor, white teeth glistening amid quivering black fur. No sooner has the lone wolf thrown off his attacker than another four take its place. They are on him, tearing his hide, ripping flesh from bone. He howls into the forest night in anger, but I can tell he would soon be killed.

"No!" I scream. I run toward the pack madly swinging the branch in my hand. "Stop it! Get away from him! He's mine! Leave him alone!" I thrash at the mound of wolves with my branch, beating their backs until the wood cracks, but they ignore me. I kick them and swing the branch at their blood-soaked faces, but they only shake off the sting and return to the kill.

"No!" I scream again. "You can't take him away yet! He's mine! Mine!"

I swing the branch madly around him, striking the trees, the ground, even. . .

"Augh!"

The knife was trimmed with blood. Gideon looked down at the blade in his hands. He was in the kitchen, standing slightly crouched, with his arms spread as though ready for a fight. Glasses, silverware, and appliances lay strewn all over the floor. He was panting, sweating, and his shirt was off. He had no idea why he was standing that way. He remembered nothing of the dream.

Slowly, his senses began to return to him. His feet felt the floor. He turned his head slightly. The window was still open. He immediately wondered if anyone had heard him. He turned to walk toward the window and felt a warm bead of sweat trickling down his stomach. Reaching down with his free hand, he wiped it off. The hand came back red.

He started panting again. Looking down, he saw the gash—on his chest, just above his heart. It was five inches long and pouring blood down to his pants. Panicked, he grabbed his shirt from off the floor and pressed it to the wound. Forcing himself to move slowly, he walked down the hall and into the bathroom.

Cautiously, he turned on the light and lowered his shirt. He felt no pain, but that only frightened him more. Probing gently with his fingers, he pressed through the blood to the base of the cut.

It was deep. To the muscle.

There was still no pain. Gideon pressed the shirt back over the cut as a wave of tingly warmth spread over his body. His expression slowly turned icy calm. Something automatic within him began to take over, directing his thoughts, planning his movements with streamlined efficiency. He didn't know what was overtaking him, but it made him feel somehow removed from himself, like an actor watching himself in a play. It was. . .comforting.

With slow, deliberate steps, he moved into the living room and sat next to the phone. Keeping his left arm still, he used his free hand to call a cab.

While he waited for the cab to arrive, he straightened the living room and kitchen, being careful all the while not to aggravate his wound. He kept his shirt in place over the cut by holding it under both his armpits. Then, slowly, he draped another shirt on over it. By the time he changed pants and washed the blood off his hands, the cab had arrived.

Moving easily down the stairs, he slipped into the backseat.

"Hey, how ya doin'?" asked the old man in the driver's seat.

"Seton Hospital, please," Gideon said.

The driver didn't say anything else after that, much to Gideon's relief. He could feel the wound beginning to clot, so he tried to keep his breathing shallow to keep from starting the flow again.

Ten minutes later the cab pulled into the Seton parking lot. "Which entrance you need?" he asked.

"This is fine," said Gideon and handed the driver a twenty-dollar bill. "Keep the change."

"Thank ya, sir," said the driver. "Ya have a fine day, now." But Gideon had already walked away.

━━━━━

Finding the emergency room was easy, but getting someone to help him was more of a challenge. His cool composure made it difficult for the nurses to believe his wound was serious. Finally he got a nurse to help him remove his outer shirt so he could show her the cut. Moments later he was flat on his back staring up at a bright light and into the silhouette of a woman's face.

She asked him his name and when the accident happened. She explained she was a doctor and that she would have to use stitches to seal the wound. Someone next to her said there would definitely be a scar. That person also kept telling him to relax, that he was too tense. The doctor needed him to relax so she could seal the wound.

Of course I'm tense, he cried from behind his icy gaze. *I've cut open my own chest! I've never cut myself before, don't you understand? This is madness! I can't even trust myself anymore. I think I'm going crazy.*

But he said nothing and forced his body to relax.

Three hours later he was back in his apartment. His chest was wrapped in tight gauze. His left arm would have been immobilized too, but he argued with the doctor until she gave in—on the condition that he wear a harness when he slept at night.

Although it was after noon, Gideon left the curtain closed and all the lights off. He wanted to protect himself, if from nothing else than having to look at himself and the world in the full light of day.

After slowly and carefully cleaning the blood off the floor and the countertops, he scanned the house for any remaining signs of the rage that had consumed him. When he was finally satisfied, he gingerly lifted the brown satchel and set it on the coffee table. His chest throbbed now. Carefully lowering himself to the floor, he leaned back against the couch, wincing with every move until he finally felt settled.

He sat there for hours, ignoring the throbbing in his chest and staring blankly at the research reports, the graphs, and the charts pulled from the satchel. He made no sound, but absently listened to the distant hum of traffic and the rhythmic ticking of the wall clock in the kitchen. Dusk came and went, and he continued to stare, never turning on a single light. His eyes were glazed, his face empty. The only sign of life within him was an ambiguous twitch that occasionally flexed the fingers of his right hand.

It wasn't until after midnight that he finally lowered his head and began to cry.

CHAPTER 3

PROVIDENCE

Six weeks later,
somewhere in the Mummy Range of Colorado

"Do you believe in God, Professor Dawning?"

A moppy-headed student squinted up from the outcropping about six feet below where Gideon stood. Here in the mountains, something seemed different about the prof she had only known in a classroom. There, he had seemed little more than a curiosity. He was one of the youngest professors in the department. But with the wind whipping through his black, curly hair and the mountain clouds swimming around his wind-blown black sweatshirt, he looked strangely ominous, like an angry prophet from the pages of an Old Testament book.

"Professor Dawning?"

Oblivious to her presence, Gideon continued to lose himself in the rugged beauty that surrounded him. Reaching out with his eyes, he tried to drink in the miles of evergreen forest that blanketed the slopes below him and imagined himself back in his favorite dream—one he'd escaped to from time to time since he was a boy. In the dream, he was Robin Hood and lived deep in the secret places of Sherwood Forest. He was master of the wood and preferred the comfort of treetops to the chill of the ground—far from anyone except his merry men. In that place he could live in peace. He could live forever.

"Professor?" The student shaded her eyes to get a better look.

"Huh?" Gideon still didn't look away.

"Do you believe in God?" This time she spoke more forcefully, as if to scold him for not paying closer attention.

Gideon reluctantly turned from his dream and looked down at the young lady. She had been the first student assigned to this trip—her other professors all raved about her quick mind and willingness to work. Unfortunately, they said nothing about her annoying tendency to ramble on and on for no reason whatsoever.

Her name was Shelley something. *Langley? No, Langston*, he thought. She'd been in one other class Gideon taught, if he remembered correctly. As she looked up at him through hair-shrouded eyes, her expression conveyed an almost comic fear—as though she was simultaneously amused by Gideon and a little afraid to be near him.

"Why?" Gideon responded finally as a thundercloud rumbled behind the peaks to the west.

"Why believe in God or why am I asking the question?" Shelley sounded a little frustrated with the whole interchange now.

"Well, both," he repeated.

The girl stroked her hair to reveal her face at last. She had the look of a naturalist—no makeup, short-cropped dark brown hair, simple beauty—but with an overly dramatic smoothness of motion that projected an arrogance oddly out of place with her image.

"Oh, I don't know," she answered. "It just struck me, I guess. I mean, you look around at these mountains. . . ," she took in a deep breath as her eyes swept the horizon, "so much beauty, so pristine, you know? It just makes me wonder about where it all came from. Do you know what I mean?"

"Huh. . ." Gideon had turned back to the mountains while the girl spoke. "Yeah, I know what you mean. Sure." But his mind was already fixed again on another, different land.

"Professor Dawning?" Another voice came trailing over a small ridge some twenty yards away. Gideon sighed. From behind the ridge appeared a young man, another member of the team Gideon had trained. His name was Shane McClanahan, a native of Ireland who'd come to the university on scholarship.

"Professor Dawning, there's no more work to be done on the receiver," Shane called in his Irish lilt. "Wouldya mind verifying the settings before we seal her down?"

"Sure," Gideon said, taking one last look at the mountains before traversing the rocks toward the ridge. Shelley bobbed along only steps behind. Over the ridge, he found the five other students he'd brought with him on this project from the university. Three of them, two guys and a girl, were diligently checking over the global positioning receiver and other equipment, which was precariously secured on a tripod among the rocks. The other two, both guys, were roaming off on the slope to the south.

Gideon grimaced. He knew he should've brought only five students instead of seven. He'd only brought them to spite Dean Powell, whose incessant reminders to "keep the cost at an absolute minimum" had driven him to find subtle ways to make the trip as expensive as he possibly could.

He ignored the two roaming students. "Do we have confirmation from the other teams?" Gideon asked.

"Yeah," Shane responded. "We've already done three test measurements. We should have no trouble recording any movement over the next five days."

The only other girl in the group besides Shelley stood up to face Gideon. She had long, black hair and a slender, well-proportioned figure camouflaged beneath a frumpy gray sweatshirt and baggy jeans. But it was her petite nose and clear hazel eyes that made Gideon have to continually watch his reactions around her. He didn't want to let on how attracted he was.

"Professor, I still don't understand how this is supposed to do any good," she said, brushing her hair behind her ear. "A major earthquake has never been reported in Colorado. The biggest quake ever reported in the state was a magnitude 6.6 in 1882 just west of Fort Collins. Other than that, the only one of consequence was in 1967, and it came out of the fault lines running through Denver—not way up here in the Mummy Range."

"Well, Miya," Gideon replied, trying not to notice her eyes, "who knows what we might find during our time here? We're just here to gather what information we can."

Miya and Gideon had been through this conversation twice today already. She wasn't buying his explanations, and he was running out of new excuses.

"Are you thinking there might be a connection between these minor fault lines and the earthquake epicenters near, like, Atlanta, Boston, or Baton Rouge?"

"I don't know, Miya." Gideon shrugged his shoulders. "But that's what we're here to find out. Is everything set?"

Miya didn't respond right away. She just looked at Gideon, who kept his eyes on the receiver. "Yeah, it's ready," she said finally.

Gideon glanced nervously up at the afternoon sun. He didn't like her staring at him that way. "C'mon, let's get the equipment secured for the night," he said. "I don't want to be caught on the mountain after dark."

Gideon supervised as the team secured the receiver and packed up the loose equipment. Then the team members strapped on their backpacks and began the two-hour hike down the mountain to their van.

This was only the second day of the trip, and Gideon knew Miya would be pressing much harder for more plausible answers before week's end. It was his fault for choosing someone with such street smarts. She knew the Game too, he could tell. And she didn't like to be played any more than Gideon did. She might not have the answers right now, but by the end of the trip, she might just figure out what was really going on. He would have to decide what to do about that when the time came; but for now he just avoided her as much as he could, which wasn't easy in such a small group or with her hazel eyes flashing around him all the time.

The university had arranged for the team to lodge in a second-rate hotel in Providence, Colorado, about thirty miles from the trailhead. Providence was a one-stoplight mining community that had tenaciously hung onto life long after the copper mines had died. There weren't many people left now. Mostly retired folks who'd lived out their best years working the mines or minding the businesses around the town. Now, much like the mines, most of those establishments were empty shells. And yet, the people stayed on. There was only one grocery store, one restaurant, and one hotel—the Dream Spin Inn. It didn't take five minutes to survey the town from end to end.

By the time the group hiked down, traveled to Providence, grabbed some dinner, and arrived at the hotel, it was nearly ten o'clock.

Despite Dean Powell's obsessive need to control every penny requisitioned out of his department budget, Gideon conned him into approving payment for one extra room at the hotel. That way Gideon could stay by himself. It wasn't just a convenience. He hadn't allowed himself to sleep in anyone's presence since he first started having the rages almost ten years ago. Of course, they didn't happen very often; but he was terrified of anyone finding out about them or, worse, becoming a victim of his anger. His last rage, several weeks before, had only caused his fears to deepen. He simply would not allow himself to let his guard down around anyone. He had to sleep alone.

Of course, having his own room hardly made him feel secure. The walls between the rooms were paper thin; and if he destroyed something, he had no way of explaining his actions to the hotel management. No, even alone, he didn't expect to get much sleep this night. Or, for that matter, any night that week.

After he got everyone settled, he entered his own room and locked the door. He unloaded his stuff, stripped down to his boxer shorts, and turned on the news.

◆━━━━◆

"A new wave of earthquakes struck several cities today worldwide. The worst of the quakes shook Budapest just before dawn this morning. Scientists say the quake measured 6.8 on the Richter scale. Officials are working this hour to try to estimate the loss in lives and property.

"Early reports estimate the death toll could reach as high as three hundred, with property damage reaching well into the hundreds of thousands.

"Another quake was reported near Sydney, and a third struck off an isolated coast in northern Greenland. Both quakes measured around 5.7 on the Richter scale. Damage was moderate in Sydney, but there was no loss of life. No damage was reported in the Greenland quake.

"More now on the earthquake rage from our science reporter, Trey Sel. . ." *Click.*

◆━━━━◆

Gideon tossed the remote control on the bed and plopped down on his back. He knew, of course, that the numbers he'd just heard were most likely lies. Who knew how strong the earthquake really was in Budapest today? Maybe 7.8. . .or higher. And what about the death toll? They can't fake those numbers, can they? He wondered. Brownout or no brownout, people would eventually figure out the truth.

What is going on?

Gideon's thoughts drifted back to the scene in his apartment six weeks earlier, when he'd gotten word that his own father had died. He wondered if anyone in Budapest today was reacting to death the way he did. He'd hardly thought about his father since that night. He wasn't sure why, really. Maybe he was afraid of what might happen if he did. Besides, he was so busy preparing for this trip that he didn't have time to think about much of anything else.

He absently reached inside his shirt and felt the lumpy scar on his chest. *It's better not to think*, he told himself. At least, it was safer.

For a time, Gideon stared at the light on the ceiling and thought of nothing. The long hike and the stress of working with his students all day had left him exhausted. He dreaded the thought of another day on the mountain with the team, especially dealing with Miya's questions and Shelley's constant chatter. It would be so much nicer just to be alone, without the hassles, without the people. Gideon closed his eyes, telling himself he wouldn't go to sleep. He just wanted to stop thinking for awhile and rest his eyes.

The forest is soundless and still. I know it is full day, but I can find no sun. The trees, awesome spires, jab into the sky's heart like spears, their leaves acting as canopies to make the forest floor dark and damp.

There are no signs of animal life. No bird, no insect. Only me. And I walk, looking about me like Alice in Wonderland. I am fleeing from something. . .what? I can't remember. But I walk, waiting for my mind to clear, waiting to remember.

I look down at myself. I am wearing white—all white. It is an outfit like a priest would wear, or a judge. On my breast there is embroidered the emblem of a sunrise, with bright spectrum-color beams shining from my shoulders to my waist. But the sun is not a sun. It is more like a pearl, woven from silk. And I am still walking. . .looking. Looking for what?

"Do you know why you are here, Gideon Dawning?"

A Voice. Terrible. Booming. Where did it come from? I see no one. Only the trees. They must be over three hundred feet tall.

"Do you know why you are here, Gideon Dawning?"

"No!" I yell, covering my ears. "What do you want? And how do you know my name?"

One that looks like a man stands before me. His eyes are fire. His hair is whiter than any white I have ever seen. He wears a robe like mine, but it is torn. It is torn across the chest.

"You are here to die, Gideon Dawning. Indeed, you have already died

that your life may be saved. This land will die too that it may also live again."

"Die?" I step away. "But I don't want to die. Not really. Not now. Who are you? I don't want to die."

"I will not slay you, Gideon Dawning. But you are here. Do you know why you are here?"

I try to dash behind a tree and run away, but my feet won't move. "No. I mean, I don't understand. What are you talking about?"

"You are a sojourner in a land not your own, Gideon Dawning. You always have been. But now you have come here to make a way for me. Speak pure, and you will not fail."

"Fail? Fail at what?"

The light from the man's eyes floats away toward the sky, farther and farther until. . .

Gideon awoke and found himself staring at the light on the ceiling of his hotel room.

With sudden awareness, he shot up off the bed. In a panic, he checked the room for signs of a rage, but nothing was changed. Every lamp was in place, every mirror unbroken.

A dream! That's it.

He had been dreaming. The experience startled him, not just because he feared the rages. It was the first dream he'd remembered in years. And he remembered it all in vivid detail.

But something still wasn't right. The dream was over, and he was standing next to the bed. Why, then, did the room feel damp? And what was that smell? Honey! He was sure he smelled honey.

"Oh my God," Gideon said aloud. "Wake up, Dawning. Wake up." Gideon rubbed his face. "C'mon now," he chided himself. "Don't be crazy. It was just a dream." Gideon sat on the bed and forced a chuckle. "That's what you get for thinking."

Slowly, Gideon shuffled himself back up the bed and reclined against the headboard. He closed his eyes again, not to rest this time, but to try to calm the thoughts in his mind. The man was so vivid— who was he? His features were solid and real, carved in his face like someone who had seen the painful side of life.

Where have I seen that guy before? The image was too exact for his subconscious to have made it up. It must have been someone from his past.

Gideon rolled over, clutching the pillow underneath his head. *What was it that he said?* Gideon thought. *"Speak true, and you will not fail." Fail at what? Speak what "true"?* The whole dream was making less sense the more Gideon tried to figure it out. Whatever had triggered it, Gideon couldn't bring it to mind now.

Irritated by his inability to silence his thoughts, Gideon changed his strategy. He tried to think of other things—things that would help him forget about the man.

Almost automatically, his mind turned to Sherwood Forest. Or, more precisely in this case, the piney woods behind his childhood home in East Texas.

Gideon and his younger brother, Jacob, were only three years apart, and they did everything together growing up. They even looked alike, with the same black, curly hair and deep blue eyes. While their mother was away at work, the boys would often sneak off into the pines behind their house and pretend it was Sherwood Forest. Gideon would be Robin Hood, since he was older, and Jacob would act as one of his merry men. They'd sneak out of the forest into their neighbors' backyards and steal whatever "riches" they could find there. A water sprinkler here, a rake there. One time they even stole a lawn mower, but returned it when they realized it was busted and didn't have a blade. Most of the items they found, however, would be smuggled back to their secret camp and hidden away under pine needles until even the boys forgot they existed.

Many times since those days, Gideon had wished he could go into that forest again, lose himself in it like he used to, and never come out again.

That was all before the "bad time," when Gideon's father went away forever. He'd destroyed them all before he left. Gideon was only eight then, but he never had a childhood after that.

As the years passed, Gideon and Jacob spent less time together. Jacob was shielded from most of what happened with his father, so he never developed the hatred for his dad that Gideon felt. And, sadly, that one fact alone eventually drove a wedge between Gideon and his brother. Jacob couldn't understand Gideon's rage, and Gideon couldn't accept his brother's apparent apathy over what their father had done.

The final blow to their relationship had come when Jacob decided to move in with his uncle Thomas in order to go to college in Dallas. "Uncle" Thomas was Abe's brother, and Gideon could think of nothing so cruel as for Jacob to move in with a man who still believed Abe was innocent. At the trial, Uncle Thomas had claimed Gideon's mom was insane—a "religious nutcase who believes God actually talks to her" were his exact words—and that Abe was just a victim of her religiously inspired imagination.

Gideon didn't say good-bye to his brother when he left for college seven years ago, and he hadn't spoken to him since.

Still lying on his bed, Gideon sullenly realized his thoughts weren't helping him relax. He sat up and turned the television back on. *Planet of the Apes* was on, so Gideon watched it numbly, forcing himself to focus on the story to quiet his mind. He watched two shows on horticulture that came on back-to-back after that. He tried not to focus on anything besides the television; but in the back of his mind, he cursed the dream he'd had for making his mind spin, and then he cursed himself for thinking about his brother.

Eventually, he turned off the television, looked out the window, and waited for the sun to come up.

CHAPTER 4

THE BURIAL

When morning finally arrived, Gideon and his crew grabbed a quick breakfast, then loaded the van and took off for the trailhead. On the way, the team members all excitedly discussed the possible causes of the earthquakes they'd heard about on the news the night before. Their conversation was mostly a low rumble to Gideon, who was still caught up in the torrent of thought from the night before. He'd managed to forget about his brother; but as he dully watched the winding road to the trailhead, scenes and words from the dream kept buzzing around like a persistent fly inside his head. And every time they came around, one question continued to echo in his thoughts.

Fail at what?

As the van neared the trailhead, Gideon scanned the sky for signs of bad weather at the top. The sky was clear blue everywhere except directly over the range they were heading for. But Gideon couldn't tell if that was a storm or just a quiet white backdrop for the mountains.

He never said anything to the students, but decided to carry on as though he'd never had a second thought about making the climb. He figured none of them would be thinking enough to question the weather, and he was past caring.

Once the crew was on the trail, conversations quickly died down. No one was used to the altitude, so breathing got more difficult the higher they went. Only Shelley continued to ramble. Though irritated, Gideon was inwardly amazed at the enormous volumes of air she could take in—just to keep her tongue wagging.

"Wow, these trees are so awesome, don't you think?" she panted, turning briefly toward Miya. She didn't respond. "Next to geology, I just love environmental science. Trees really are like the lungs of the earth, you know? I think they just provide so much beauty in addition to giving us life. A prof I had last year talked about how trees are like people in a lot of ways too. There are different kinds, but each one functions in pretty much the same way, you know? And no two trees are alike, just like people. My professor said that trees are like diagrams of humans' souls. He said, 'Show me a tree, and I'll show you a man or a woman whose life reflects that tree.' "

She glanced again at Miya, who was trying very hard to look off in the other direction. Shelley, oblivious, continued, "He'd project slides of different trees—giant redwoods, pine, oak, twisted trees, straight trees, fruit trees, and barren trees. And after each one, he'd project a slide of, like, a man or a woman that matched that tree. Some of the connections he made were really thought-provoking. Ever since then, I've been fascinated with trying to discover what kind of tree best suits me. And others too.

"Professor Dawning, what kind of tree do you think best suits you?"

Gideon was at the front of the line and continued walking without turning around. He winced at the question, but saw no way he could avoid responding. At last he said, "Well, since I'm a geologist, I guess I'd be a petrified tree."

The group laughed at Gideon's sarcasm.

"Well, yeah." Shelley smiled along with the others, but she didn't get it. "But, you know, a petrified tree isn't a living thing at all. It's just stone. No, I meant what kind of *living* tree do you. . ." Her voice abruptly stopped. For a moment, Gideon thought the hundred or so prayers he'd offered since the hike began had finally been answered; but when he turned around, she was still there. But she was quiet at least and looking off to the side as though examining a puzzle with missing pieces.

"What is it?" Gideon asked.

"That's so strange," Shelley said. "That shouldn't be here."

"What?" Gideon backtracked to the girl, suddenly aware that the clouds overhead were looking more ominous now.

The girl took off into the woods, talking as she went. "This tree shouldn't be here. Almond trees aren't indigenous to this part of the country. They could never survive at this altitude. But here it is. I wonder how it got here." She reached the tree and began to walk around it. "And look. It's been hit by lightning."

This tree theme was really wearing thin on Gideon. He followed the girl so he could quiet her down and so the team could get back on course. But as he followed her off the trail, he saw the almond tree and immediately found himself also intrigued by the sight.

It was situated in the middle of a small clearing, surrounded by towering pines. It reminded Gideon of an orphan, standing away from the rest of the world, never quite having a place to belong. It reminded him of himself for all the same reasons.

The almond tree was small as trees go. One side was charred black from what appeared to be a fairly fresh lightning strike. But the rest of the tree was green, a more vibrant green than the dark hues of the pines that surrounded it. And there were buds on it. Simple, greenish-white blossoms clinging to the limbs. Gideon marveled at the scene, though he couldn't figure out why. It was just a tree in a clearing.

But there was something about it. Something that didn't seem natural.

Off to the side Gideon saw a limb in the grass. It had apparently been severed from the tree in the strike. One end was charred, but the other still bore some green and even a few white blossoms. He picked up the stick, broke off the branchy end with his knee, and wiped the soot off the other end in the grass. The limb was relatively straight; and without its extra branches, it made a fine walking stick. So Gideon took it and tested it out around the almond tree.

That's when he noticed that Shelley had returned to the group and that she and the rest of the team were now quietly watching him, trying to figure out what he was doing and where his mind had gone.

Without a word, Gideon turned and hiked toward the group, testing his new walking stick as he went. He didn't care what they thought. He liked the stick. It felt good in his hand, almost like it had been made for him.

He hadn't taken five steps when he stopped again. Turning his ear up toward the sky, he listened. Had he heard thunder? But what direction did it come from? Then it clapped again—a thunder, yes, but not from the sky. Gideon felt it in his bones, in his chest, as if the rumbling was coming from within his own body.

Suddenly, the leaves on the trees and the grass began to quiver as though chilled. From the ground came a roar that sounded like the churning of a thousand waterfalls and felt as if someone had grabbed the earth and started to shake it like a rattle. He could feel the vibrations resonate up his legs, into his chest, his arms, and his eyes. Everything was moving too fast for him to follow.

For a quick moment, he stood still, as though his own resolute stance would somehow calm the earth around him. But then the trees began to sway; he knew their roots wouldn't be deep enough to hold.

Everything after that seemed to happen all at once. Gideon yelled to the group to follow him into the clearing with the almond tree. But the students had already returned to the trail, and they were huddling around each other, hiding their faces from the trees that had begun to creak and fall. They couldn't hear Gideon anyway now. The roar of the quake was deafening.

Seeing that they wouldn't follow, he turned and ran into the clearing alone. With one hand, he grabbed the trunk of the almond tree; and with the other, he jabbed his walking stick firmly in the ground. He told himself not to fall down, no matter what. *If you fall, you can't run. And your control is lost.*

Without warning, the ground under Gideon's feet began to swell and recede, churning the grass and causing the almond tree to lean almost horizontally. In an instant, the earth became water, and Gideon found himself helplessly drowning in it.

Waves of earth split open the ground beneath the tree and Gideon's feet. It gaped wider and wider, like a hungry mouth swallowing tons of soil in its spread—hungrily devouring the tree and sucking Gideon into its throat.

With the tree gone, Gideon stabbed the walking stick deeper into the soil and held on for stability. But the ground itself betrayed him and began to carry him toward the crevasse. Panicked, he struggled to run away; but the earth was a conveyor belt beneath him, drawing him into the heart of the mountain.

A new ground wave hit the slope, and Gideon fell, still gripping his walking stick as though welded to it. He stabbed the earth with it, trying to find a spot solid enough to hold him, if only for a second, just enough time for him to regain his foothold. But the earth had surrounded his legs now, up to his knees, and he couldn't find the strength to pull free. From the crevasse now directly below him, he could hear the sounds of rocks grinding together into dust; and all around him the smell of damp earth and crushed grass filled his senses.

As he slipped into the chasm, he thought he heard a distant voice calling out a prayer.

"Oh my God! Oh my God!"

Then there was just the roar and the remote sounds of falling trees.

For a moment that seemed to last an eternity, Gideon saw only blackness and hacked up the clod of dirt in his mouth. He couldn't breathe; soon the oppressive weight of the earth would crush him like a papier-mâché doll. Desperately, he prayed for unconsciousness.

Then, quietly, a wind began to blow. It enveloped him, just as surely as the earth enveloped him, and filled his lungs with air that held no taint of damp soil. Rather, the air was sweet like honey and familiar. The earth that had been crushing Gideon now seemed to cradle him. He felt as though he were being carried or simply embraced—he couldn't tell which. As he cuddled there, the wind grew warm, thawing his mud-covered body, making his breathing easier.

Absently, he noted that he still held the almond branch, though he couldn't tell how much of it was left. He thought about working up the courage to open his eyes.

Gently, a firmness came against his back. He felt as if something were pushing him, but it didn't seem dangerous or painful. Then he realized it was his own weight he felt. He was lying down, and he wondered if the earth might have spit him back up to safety. All around him, he began to hear voices, people yelling and running about, but he couldn't understand what they were saying.

It must be a rescue team, he thought. *Or the kids. It's probably the kids. I wonder how much time has passed. I wonder if they know I'm here.*

Slowly, purposefully, he let go of the almond branch, wiped the mud away from his eyes, and opened them. The sky above was blue, but it was more the blue of the ocean than of the sky. The air was rich with the smell of honey. And there were no clouds.

What mattered more to Gideon, however, was that there were no mountains.

Cautiously, he propped himself up on one elbow so he could see where he was. No sooner had he turned his head than he was nose to nose with a dirty, round-faced little girl. She made no sound as she knelt next to him, clutching her heart as though trying to hide it. He was black with mud from head to toe, but she only looked at him, waiting.

And slowly, sadly, her eyes began to fill with tears.

CHAPTER 5

THE VISITATION

During the years of my imprisonment in the Wall,
I would in some more quiet moments allow myself to dream of
a gallant and powerful champion who might break through
my parents' defenses to deliver me from their horrors. I naturally
imagined such a man would be a highly born lord of some
distant country, a noble prince who would come to our land in
all the finery his wealth could afford. How ironic it is, then, that
my deliverer came not in royal robes, but in a cloak of humble
dirt. And now, of course, I see this is exactly as it should be.

—THE KYRINTHAN JOURNALS, SONGS OF DELIVERANCE, STANZA 4, VERSES 151–153

Gideon opened his mouth to speak and gagged from wads of dirt caking in his throat. In spasms, he coughed up chunks of mud coated with saliva. The rotting taste sickened him. Soon the gags turned to heaves, and he emptied his stomach onto the ground.

Slowly, his breathing eased, and he raised his hand to wipe the drool away from his mouth. To his surprise, his arm, like his face, was coated in mud.

He looked up. The girl hadn't moved.

Gideon spit. "Where's your daddy?" he asked, unable to think of anything else. She didn't answer. It seemed odd to him that a member of a rescue team would bring his little girl on a search following an earthquake, but nothing about his circumstance made sense yet.

Where are the mountains?

Gideon looked around him for signs of his team from the university. If any of them survived, they'd probably be helping in the search. But he saw no one around, just smooth, rich grass. No sign even of an earthquake. It didn't make sense.

Gideon turned back to the girl. She was still crying, though she made no sound. It was apparent she was waiting for Gideon to do something, but what, he had no idea. She looked at him with a hopeful expression that said, for whatever reason, she had chosen him as her protector and guide. She wasn't going to budge.

Ignoring the girl, Gideon tried to stand. His body ached. He felt like he'd been tossed in the back of a cement truck, then hung out to dry. The mud caked on his legs cracked and pulled his hair as he slowly shifted his weight onto his knees. It wasn't until he was nearly upright that he realized he was naked.

"What the. . .?" He quickly crouched back down on the grass.

Using one hand to help cover himself, he reached the other around to feel if any shred of clothing remained. There was nothing—only damp, crusting mud. Even the almond staff, which he discovered lying next to him intact, was encased in a mud cast. He picked up the branch and laid it across his lap. It didn't help, but he did it anyway.

Gideon turned again to the little girl. She seemed more frightened now than before.

"Listen, little girl," Gideon said, smiling. "Can you help me?"

"Hide," said the girl softly.

"Okay, now, listen to me, okay?" Gideon tried to look nonthreatening, as if that were possible in his present state. "I want you to go get me. . ." Gideon stopped. He hadn't thought about what to ask the girl to bring to cover him. "I want you to go get me a blanket, okay? I'm cold, and I need a blanket. Can you tell your daddy? Can you ask him to bring me a blanket?"

"Hide?" she said again.

"Yes, that's right," Gideon said, smiling, "I want a blanket so I can hide. Can you go get Daddy to bring me a blanket?"

"No," the girl said. Her eyes began to well up with tears again. Then she pointed off in the distance. "Hide!" she said.

His eyes looked behind him in the direction she pointed. "My God," he said, "where am I?"

The grassy plain Gideon sat in was situated in a shallow valley surrounded by deep green hills. No mountain pines or aspen. No mountain peaks. Just clean grass. Small hills. And a village.

At least, that's what he assumed it was, though it looked like nothing he'd ever seen. Hundreds of perfectly round cottages set in perfectly spaced rows. They were all identical. Bark-covered walls with red-curtained doorways and windows. It looked like a picture out of a children's book—sloping fields of neatly arranged tree stumps with cone-shaped, leafy roofs.

Gideon sat at the base of the hillside village in a large grassy area set off by four stone towers, each about six feet across and twenty feet high. Beyond the grassy area, to the west, stood a wall of trees so massive that Gideon first thought them to be redwoods. But the color of the bark was a deep chocolate, and the leaves, those he could see from the ground anyway, looked more like fig leaves than anything else— except they were much bigger.

Suddenly he heard a roar, like several men yelling in chorus, then a woman's scream. It wasn't a scream of fear or terror, but of pain. Awful pain. He looked up toward the sounds just in time to see one of the round cottages burst into flames.

From around its perimeter ran several men and women, all in black. They raced together to the cottage just below the one that burned. Gideon figured they must have found it empty, for no sooner had they run in than they were out again, running to the next cottage down the hill. The line they followed would soon lead directly to him.

"Hide!" the little girl said urgently, tugging on Gideon's arm. She must have seen them too.

"Okay, okay," Gideon said in a whisper. "We'll hide."

Seeing no other place to conceal themselves, Gideon decided to move toward the giant woods. Perhaps one of the supersized leaves might have fallen too, giving him a way to cover himself.

Gideon got up slowly, trying not to expose himself any more than necessary. He hoisted the girl up in one arm and grabbed the almond staff in the other. He wasn't sure why he needed the staff, really, but he gripped it like it was his only hold on reality. Nothing was making any sense.

Maybe this is all a hallucination, he thought. *I probably got banged on the head in the quake, and now I'm hallucinating.* That at least sounded plausible.

But everything around seemed too real to be a mental mirage. The clear air, the mud on his body, even the warmth of the girl in his arms. And what was that smell? It was honey. He smelled honey again.

Is this a dream?

If it was, this dream was scaring him. After another quick glance at the burning cottage, he hastily turned and headed for the wall of trees.

Gideon's steps abruptly stopped when, out of nothing, several men suddenly appeared in his path. Now he knew he must be dreaming or hallucinating. That was the only explanation. People just didn't appear out of nothing. Unfortunately, the explanation didn't make his heart pound any slower.

There were five of them, all in layered leather uniforms of black. Each man carried a sword at his side, but not one was drawn. They just stood there, looking at Gideon, then at the girl, then at Gideon again.

And they laughed. At first, Gideon chuckled too, hoping they would all see how ridiculous he looked, get a good laugh together, and go on their merry way. But their laughter wasn't the laughter of mirth. It was the laughter of disgust. And of hate.

"Hold there, rot! What sort of perversion is this?" A tall man smiled thinly as he stepped out from the group. "You bring new meaning to your name, rebel filth." His face was angular, his hair brown and thin. His frame was thin too—so thin that Gideon absently wondered how he could ever make it as a soldier. But the question quickly dissolved with one look at the man's eyes. Where whites and pupils should have been, there was nothing but blackness.

"Did you think to disguise as the land itself? Or do you come as the emissary for the whole of the Inherited Lands, to speak in its favor and plead its case before me?"

Gideon stammered. "No. . .I don't know what you mean."

The man pursed his lips as he shook his head. "Fool," he said. "Your cause is dead, just as all you rebels will be soon." The man stepped closer to Gideon. The lines on his face became scars. "Why do you cling to this little girl? Do you think she can prevent the anger of the Council from striking you down?"

"No," Gideon said. "She was scared."

The man grunted, then turned his face toward the little girl in Gideon's arms. He held her close, for his own reassurance more than for hers.

"Little girl," the man said with a sickly smile. "Little girl, look at me. Do you know who I am?"

The little girl poked at her mouth with her finger. "Bad people," she said.

The man smiled. "No, little girl. I am a Guardian, the Firstsworn. It is you who are the bad people." Then the man stood tall and glared at the girl as a man might glare at a demon. And he said, *"Demoi blassht!"*

Instantly, the girl burst into flames in Gideon's arms. She screamed, as did Gideon, and she fell out of his arms to the ground. He dropped to the ground too, rolling quickly away from the heat. His entire right side felt as though it had been seared with a hot iron. Only his mud covering protected him from being seriously burned.

The girl's cries didn't last long, nor did she. It all happened so fast that there wasn't even any smell of burning flesh.

Gideon jumped to his feet and glanced around for a way of escape. How did that happen? He saw no weapon. Not even a torch.

Wake up, Gideon! C'mon, wake up!

The thin-faced man turned his attention from the ashes and focused on Gideon. Just as he did, Gideon took off in a blur toward the nearest cottage.

"Demoi brun."

Gideon collapsed in a heap, cradling his stomach and feeling as though he'd been kicked by a horse. For several moments, his world became pain. All other thoughts died away. The pain was red and hot, like someone had reached inside him and lit a torch. He rocked himself on the ground to calm the fire inside. He didn't even notice the men as they surrounded him. The thin-faced man smirked at the contorted expression on Gideon's mud-covered face.

"Foolish of you to run away, rebel," the man said. "Now we must make sport of you—for conscience' sake. *Demoi hacht trell!*"

Gideon's head flew back, spinning his body around on the ground. A gash appeared on his head beneath the mud, and the blood mixed in, creating a metallic rust color on his scalp.

Gideon's mind spun, his thoughts jumbled like popcorn in a pot. *Men. Black, words. Stop. Run away. Must get away. Must stop.*

"Demoi hacht learon!"

Gideon screamed at the pain that shot through his legs. Again the force of the impact spun him on the ground. When he became still again, he tried desperately not to move his legs, wondering if a tree had fallen on them, wondering whether they were broken. But the pain instinctively drove his body to writhe and squirm in an effort to find release from the intensity of the agony.

All his thoughts became engulfed in the pain. Like a red swirling flood, the agony rose in his mind, drowning thoughts of escape, drowning questions, drowning even his identity under the swell. Gideon opened his eyes in an attempt to hold on to consciousness. But the angry images of the soldiers spun around him like a centrifuge. He couldn't focus—and he began to forget why he wanted to stay awake at all.

"Enough toying," the thin-faced man said. "Our task here is finished." He knelt beside Gideon and yanked his ear up in one hand. "You're a pathetic dreamer, rebel. But the truth has turned your dream into a nightmare. Sleep forever, Remnant—*Damanoi brun sol!*"

Gideon felt a churning in his gut, like a drill boring holes in him from the inside out. Just before he faded into unconsciousness, his hand reached down and felt the warmth of blood spilling from his stomach onto the grass.

"Speak pure, and you will not fail."

The words came echoing down from the heights of darkness, spilling down, down into a blackness without form, a room with no walls. But there was an echo. Gideon listened and looked up, but couldn't find the man again. Only the man's voice.

"Speak pure, and you will not fail."

Down, down from the darkness, into. . .into Gideon's room. His bedroom back home in East Texas, when he was a boy. There was his baseball glove, hanging on the wall, and his poster of Reggie Jackson. And there, on the far wall next to the window, was a picture of a rose. Gideon's grandfather had given him that on his first birthday; at least that's what Mom had told him. At the bottom corner it said,

"A man's heart is like a rose,
and forgiveness, its only sun.
For any hand, of God or man,
that would cuddle its bloodstained petals,
must first be willingly crucified by its thorns."

Mom had asked Gideon about that quote lots of times. She always wanted to know what he thought it meant. He never really gave her an answer because he never really had one. And when he finally moved out of the house to go to college, he left the plaque hanging there on the wall.

"Mom!" Gideon called. "Mom, where are you?"

"What is it, dear?"

"Mom, I'm hurt. Some men hurt me. I think I'm dying." Gideon thought his voice sounded shaky.

Gideon saw his mother come into the room. She was wearing an apron, like she always did around the house. And she was carrying a dishtowel. When she saw him, her eyes welled up with tears, and she ran over to the bed where he was lying.

"Oh, Great Yeshua," she cried. "What happened?"

"I'm hurt, Mom," Gideon said weakly. "Please. I'm hurt."

Gideon's mom scooped him up in her arms and laid his head on her breast. She cradled him there and rocked him. And through her tears, she began to sing a prayer.

It was a Messianic Jewish prayer she'd sung a hundred times before. Gideon remembered she used to sing it to him every night before he went to sleep. It was all about God coming like a storm to protect His chosen ones from harm. He felt so comforted with her, so safe. Her voice seemed to soothe away the pain that throbbed through every muscle and joint. For a moment, he forgot about his injuries and began to sing along. . . .

Thunder boomed in the azure sky. Without warning, black clouds invaded the skies over the village, announcing their arrival with a fury of claps that shook the ground. No sooner had the sound reached the valley floor than mighty winds barraged the village and the surrounding hills. The giant woods began to creak and moan as the tops of the trees bent under the force of the gale.

The Guardian soldiers turned a confused stare toward the skies. The clouds had come from nowhere, but now they hung over the village like a lion over its prey.

Immediately, the thin-faced man called for three of his side guards to join him. They huddled together for a moment, yelling in each other's ears to be heard above the wind. Then they formed a circle with their backs toward the center and faced up toward the storm.

From out of the black cloud struck a blue bolt of lightning, then a green, and finally a red. They each struck three of the four men, leaving nothing behind but a pile of ash. At this, the thin-faced man dove to the ground, and the other Guardians turned to run. But the storm lashed out at them with almost a tangible wrath, striking like a machine gun with bolts of red, blue, green, and yellow—never missing its mark. The villagers who had been in hiding now peeked out from their cottages, their curiosity overcoming their terror. In the end, only a handful of soldiers escaped the storm and ran off to the east. No villager had been struck. With the Guardians gone, the cloud vaporized as quickly as it had appeared.

Gideon lay curled in a ball on the grass, his blood spilling, his eyes glazed from shock and semiconsciousness. He was only vaguely aware of the storm. And when it passed, he was only vaguely aware of the arms that lifted him and carried him away.

CHAPTER 6

THE REMNANT

Donovan Truthstay, ever the skeptic of the human soul,
did not believe in Gideon Dawning. In part, that was the
reason Paladin Sky had chosen him to go and find the man—
so Donovan could see the prophecy fulfilled with his own eyes
and so be convinced. But, then again, prophecy is a fickle
thing—it rarely fulfills itself the way we expect.
That was the other reason Paladin Sky sent Donovan.
For if Gideon actually turned out to be an imposter,
as Donovan suspected, Paladin could not have sent a more
skilled and eager assassin to deal with him.

—The Kyrinthan Journals, Beginnings, Stanza 2, Verses 147–150

Gideon awoke in a silent room with no windows.

He felt groggy; his head seemed to weigh a hundred pounds. But the pounding inside it had already begun to fade as he opened his eyes and took his first tentative look around.

Despite the lack of windows, the room was far from dark. Every nook was bathed in a golden hue—not terribly bright but rich with color like the glow of a tropical sunset. The light came from a trough, plainly situated in one corner of the room and filled with water. The glow emanated from what looked to be a branch floating on top.

That wasn't the only odd thing about the room, however. Rather than being "built" in any ordinary sense, the room seemed to have been carved from the inside out. The walls, the floor, even the ceiling all appeared to be sculpted out of a single block of wood. Every surface was smoothed and polished with such meticulous care that Gideon could see his reflection everywhere, even in the ceiling.

Despite his growing curiosity, he wasn't ready to move right away. He closed his eyes as he remembered the Guardians and the beating they had given him. Nothing hurt right now, but the slightest shift in position could bring all that pain rushing back to his battered body.

From the reflection on the ceiling, he could tell he was lying in a large red bed. He was wearing something white on his torso, but red blankets covered his bottom half. There was little else he could tell about the room. Besides the bed and the strange glowing stick, there was only a little stool at his bedside.

The lack of windows seemed a bad omen. It made his new quarters seem a bit too much like a cell. Perhaps the Guardians had made him their prisoner.

How much time has passed? he wondered. There was no way to tell whether it was day or night. Why had they put him here? Why wasn't he dead? The room was simple but seemed eerie, almost alien. He didn't like the feel of it. Still, he was warm and clean; and however strange the room was, it didn't really have the look of a prison, despite the lack of natural light.

And even if the Guardians weren't holding him prisoner, what did they want? What did they call him? A rebel?

Maybe he was still hallucinating. For all he knew, this could be a private room in a hospital, and he was just imagining it was something else. Maybe he had a head injury and simply had all his brain connections jumbled in the quake. Maybe.

As if to test this theory, he slowly moved his hands over his midsection to touch the bloody wound he'd mysteriously received there.

He found nothing. No punctured skin. No pain. It wasn't even sore. More quickly now, he threw the blanket back and checked his legs. No bruises, no broken skin. He felt his head for signs of the gash he'd received—but again, he found nothing.

Alarmed, he leaned back on the bed again. *How is this possible? Am I crazy?* Perhaps the rages had come again, and he'd totally snapped this time, leaving reality buried somewhere in the mountain ranges of Colorado.

No, no, no! he told himself. *Don't think like that.*

Maybe he was still just unconscious. It could all just be one big dream. He could still be on the mountain, out cold. Or, who knows, he could be dead. He glanced again at the oddly glowing stick.

Until now, Gideon hadn't noticed the door just to the left side of the bed. But he did when the red curtain that covered it whisked to the side and in walked a blond-haired young man carrying a tray of fruit.

The boy immediately noticed that Gideon was conscious, but he made no effort to call anyone, nor did he seem at all surprised.

"Blessings, nobleman," said the young man. "You are welcome in the sounden. Peace has been restored because of you. Are you restored?"

Gideon slowly sat up and eyed the boy for a moment. He wore a simple white frock, similar to Gideon's, only his had no sleeves. He looked about seventeen and was well muscled, like he was used to heavy labor. Despite his brawny frame, the young man bore a definite innocence. His eyes especially, big and grayish-blue, seemed filled with an eagerness to trust.

"Are you a nurse?" Gideon asked, unsure of what he was seeing.

The boy gave a puzzled look, then slowly set the tray on the edge of the bed. "No, nobleman, I am Lairn," he answered. "Are you well?"

"I'm not sure," Gideon responded, then remembered his missing wounds. "Was I injured?"

"Oh, yes, sir." The boy's eyes grew wide. "I heard the Guardians' Words. They took you to death. Only the healer was able to bring you back. That is why you have been in sleep these three days—a healing from death takes at least that long, or so we are told."

"From death!" Gideon exclaimed. "I'm not dead. . .am I? What are you talking about? What happened to me?"

The boy took a step back, his face revealing a mixture of confusion and remorse. "Please pardon, nobleman," he said, bowing slightly. "I see I have upset you. I will leave." The boy turned to go.

"No, don't," Gideon said. "Please. I just don't know what's going on." He paused to rub his forehead. *Think, Gideon, think! This has to make sense.* "Listen, uh, could you get me a doctor?"

The boy cocked his head to the side and furrowed his eyebrows, apparently gauging what his response should be. It seemed odd to Gideon that one so large should be so timid.

"I am not crafted to talk with one such as you," the boy said. "Is Adoktor your friend?"

Gideon shook his head. "No, you don't understand." He closed his eyes and sighed. "I must not be speaking clearly," he added to himself.

"Perhaps these refreshments will help you gain clearer thought, sir," suggested Lairn, gesturing to the fruit.

The tray was piled with assorted fruits and dried meats. Some things looked familiar to Gideon—grapes, apples, nuts. But a few of the other fruits he had never seen before. He wasn't sure how to eat them. So he avoided them and reached for a bunch of grapes instead. He didn't realize until that moment how famished he felt.

"Okay, just tell me this," said Gideon as he chewed. "Is this a hospital?"

"I think it is not, nobleman," began the boy. "You are in Calmeron sounden, at the edge of Castellan Watch. It is not known how you came to be here or where you came from. But the Guardians found you here during the raid. They took your garments and covered you in filth—for sport we presume, though it is hard to fathom their motives." Gideon smirked at that. But Lairn's face grew more serious, even sad. "And they beat you. But we are grateful that you have traveled among us, for you stopped the. . ." The boy stopped short and dropped his gaze to the floor. His lips tightened to keep his chin from quivering.

"What?" asked Gideon. "What's the matter?"

"Lairn." The deep voice resonated from the doorway. Gideon turned to see a huge man standing there, right in the room, though Gideon never heard him enter. He was watching the boy, seeming for the moment to ignore Gideon altogether. He stood well over six feet tall, with broad shoulders and a thick chest. He wore a brown leather drape that looked something like a shortened poncho, with a dark green sash tied high on his waist and a leather bag hung across one shoulder. Around his head was a thin leather band. He looked like a soldier—perhaps a Guardian, though his clothes weren't black. The thought made Gideon shiver, and he shook his head to banish it.

He could be a simple woodsman, he said to himself. *Just that. . .but then again, he looks more like an assassin.* Gideon frowned. Perhaps he was all of these. Perhaps none. It was difficult to tell.

The man's hair was nut brown and hung loosely around his shoulders in subtle waves. His jaw was hard and pronounced, like a stone. A noticeable scar ran down the left side of his face, from the outer edge of his eye to the edge of his mouth. The mark was not made by the random lash of an enemy, Gideon realized. The gash had been cut slowly, with deliberate malice.

But all these qualities were shadowed by one that made Gideon's blood turn cold. The man's eyes. Pitch-black orbs—with neither whites nor pupils—that seemed capable of seeing through anything, even a man's soul. Just like those of the Guardian who had attacked him.

The big man's dark gaze followed the boy as he walked around the bed and passed quietly out of the room. Gideon sat quietly as well, now convinced that this imposing stranger meant him no good.

"Please pardon the boy," the man said. "He is in mourning over his sister, who was slain in the raid."

"The little girl." Gideon suddenly remembered. Her face, her hair. The fire. Gideon felt a wave of nausea rise in his gut. *But that was just part of the hallucination, wasn't it?*

"I am called Donovan," the man said, ignoring Gideon's comment. "Purity to you, nobleman, and blessings. Are you restored?" The man's morbid eyes were completely unreadable, but his body language betrayed his words. He looked to be anything but pleased at Gideon's presence.

"I'd be a lot better if you'd tell me why I'm here," Gideon responded flatly.

"Of course," responded Donovan. "I will try to assist you as I am able." He walked over to the stool and sat down. His bulk dwarfed the little seat, but sitting on it seemed as natural to him as a recliner might to Gideon. With a calm that seemed chilling, he looked at Gideon and waited.

"Well, first of all," Gideon began, trying to sound unafraid, "where am I?"

"You are in Calmeron sounden, in the house of Cimron. You are safe."

"Where is Calmeron sounden? What's it near?"

A confused look flashed across Donovan's face, but it was gone as quickly as it came.

"The sounden rests on the eastern edge of the Castellan Watch—the great wood from which the sounden gains its life. West of the Watch are the Barrier Mountains, and the great Castel Morstal, the mountain keep. To the north lie the Scolding Wind Hills, and to the east are the Deathland Barrens. Does that help you?"

Gideon frowned. "No, not really. How did I get here?"

"Cimron and his son, the boy Lairn," Donovan inclined his head briefly toward the door, "carried you here after the passing of your storm. Shortly thereafter I was sent to restore you as best I could. That was three days past."

"You healed my wounds?" Gideon asked. "How?"

Donovan hesitated for a moment, as though trying to decide whether to answer Gideon's question. Finally, he said, "I am of the Remnant."

"The what?" Gideon shot back immediately.

"The Remnant."

"What's that?"

Again a flash of confusion. "It is odd that you do not know of these things," Donovan said. "Are you truly restored?"

"I feel fine, really," replied Gideon impatiently. "Please, explain."

Donovan eyed Gideon for a moment, then responded. "The Remnant are those who hold some truth of the distant past—before the present Council Lords came to be. We have gained some knowledge of *Dei'lo*, the Tongue of Life, which has been hidden from the people for generations. It was *Dei'lo* that brought you back from death."

"No. No, wait a minute." Gideon leaned forward on the bed, paused, then shook his head. "You're telling me that I died, and you spoke some magic words over me and brought me back to life?" He laughed, albeit nervously. "Now that's just crazy!" Then he added to himself, "I have to be dreaming."

"The Words are true, nobleman," Donovan replied, his black orbs as smooth as ice. "Do you claim it was not a Word of *Dei'lo* that brought your storm to disperse our enemy?"

"*My* storm?" Gideon frowned and shook his head. "What storm are you talking about? I don't remember any storm."

"You called the storm while you lay dying from the Guardian's Words. The storm lashed at the Guardians and harmed none of the soundenors. You do not remember this?"

"No. I had nothing to do with any storm." Gideon leaned back and closed his eyes. "Why are we talking about this, anyway? Why don't you just tell me what I'm really doing here?"

Donovan's deep voice grew instantly cold and heavy, like frozen steel. "I do not lie to you, nobleman. Several of the Remnant were watching you in stealth, waiting for the opportunity to come to your aid. They heard you call the storm, though they could not discern your Words."

"Oh, sure," Gideon replied sarcastically. He leaned forward again to get his face closer to the big man's. "Listen, man, I was out, okay? Even if I was some kind of wizard, which I'm not, how could I have conjured up a storm while I was totally unconscious?"

Donovan hesitated a moment, as though he didn't understand Gideon's words. Then he shrugged his shoulders slightly. "You sang," he said.

"I sang." Gideon stared at the man flatly. "Of course. How could I have been so stupid?" His sarcasm was blatant, but Donovan didn't perceive it.

"It is understandable," he said. "You have been many days in recovery."

Gideon sighed and closed his eyes. "Whatever."

Immediately and for no apparent reason, Donovan stood. "I have a weighty matter to discuss with you if your strength permits it." His voice sounded deep and strained, like a soldier following orders he didn't want to obey. Gideon sensed his uneasiness, and it made him even more wary. Whatever the truth of this situation really was, Gideon could still recognize the Game when he saw it. Donovan was being played—and trying to play Gideon at the same time. He knew he would have to get his wits back on line if he hoped to play this situation to his advantage. Even in an alleged hallucination, that might count for something.

Sitting up straight on the bed, he reset his face into a look of calm confidence. "Sure," he said. "I feel okay. And, just so you know, my name is Gideon. Gideon Dawning."

Donovan's black eyes widened and his hands clenched into fists. He almost spoke, but didn't.

"What?" Gideon asked. "What is it?"

"Do you speak the truth?" asked Donovan threateningly. "Are you mocking our cause?" For a moment, Donovan's eyes seemed to glisten in the golden light of the room, alive with the anger that rose in his voice.

"Yes, I mean, no, of course not," replied Gideon, now with timidity. "That's my name. Is that a problem?"

Donovan looked down at the polished floor. Gideon could see the muscles flexing in his jaw. After a moment, he spoke without looking up. "You are named after Gideon Truthslayer. Is your cause to follow him or redeem him from his Fall?"

"Uh, no," Gideon replied simply. "I don't have a cause. None that I know about anyway."

Donovan's gaze instantly shot toward him. Menacing. Calculating. He stared at Gideon that way for almost a minute before responding. Gideon said nothing and tried to hold Donovan's gaze for awhile. But he found it hard to look at those eyes for long and eventually gave up and busied himself with the tray of fruit on the bed.

"I shall call you Gideon Dawning, then," Donovan said at last. "But be warned. Though you say you have no cause, one may soon be attributed to you because of your name."

Gideon didn't understand what he meant, but Donovan went on before he had the chance to ask.

"Your words and appearance are strange to me, Gideon Dawning." Donovan pronounced the name slowly. "I perceive that you are a stranger in the Inherited Lands. Will you return to your homeland soon?"

"I don't even know where I am," said Gideon. "My team is gone— dead for all I know. And I apparently can't even see the mountains from here. Until I know more about where I am, I have no idea how to get home from here."

Donovan's eyes softened a bit. "Then you are a sojourner," he said quietly. "That would explain much."

"If you say so. Either that or hallucinating," Gideon responded. Absently, he finished off the grapes from the tray. He didn't realize he'd eaten just about everything else Lairn had brought in as well.

"I want you to journey with me," Donovan said solemnly. "I want you to come to my home."

Gideon shifted on the bed uneasily. This guy was definitely acting against his will. "Why?" he asked.

"You say you called no Storm of Deliverance. But you were heard singing while you were weighted with the blow of the Guardians. Perhaps the Words you spoke came from a vision. A vision you may not remember now in your health. There are those among the Remnant who are crafted in the revealing of dreams. I would like you to journey with me to. . .to Wordhaven that we might have the opportunity to gain from your knowledge."

"But I've already told you I don't know anything," Gideon replied. "And I don't understand this 'word' stuff you keep talking about."

"Even so," Donovan said. "I would be pleased for you to journey with me to Wordhaven. It is an honor offered to only a few—especially in these times."

Gideon wasn't impressed.

"The Guardians will return within a day or two at most," Donovan added, apparently sensing his hesitation. "They will be looking for you. If you remain here, they will slay you. Or worse."

That caught Gideon's attention. "What do they want with me?"

Donovan smiled. Clearly, a most unnatural act. "A few of them also heard you call the storm," he said.

Something wasn't right. Gideon was aware of Donovan's hesitation to trust him, yet he sensed no signs of deception in the big man. He genuinely believed Gideon knew something about some storm, even though he was unconscious through the entire episode. It didn't make sense. But then, nothing did. For all he knew, this could all still just be a dream. And if it was, then it didn't really matter what he chose to do.

Gideon shrugged. "Okay, why not?" he said. "Maybe things will become clearer if I get out and move around."

Donovan gave no response, but only nodded.

"So, how far is it to this Wordhaven?"

Donovan turned and headed for the door. "About seven days' journey," he said. "We leave at first light tomorrow. I'll return for you then." And with that, he was gone.

"Seven days," Gideon sighed. "If this is a dream, I hope I wake up soon."

CHAPTER 7

◀ JOURNEY TO SONGWILL ▶

How could they have known Songwill's destiny? It came as a
nightmare comes to a child's peaceful sleep—a violation of inno-
cence. But, perhaps, we should not have been so surprised, so
filled with horror after all. Perhaps deep in our souls we already
knew what had to be. We all hoped for a resurrection of the land.
But there can be no resurrection where death is not complete.
Songwill had to die, as it represented our last desperate clinging
to the life we once had.

—The Kyrinthan Journals, Canticles, Stanza 7, Verses 31–33

Sleep didn't come easily for Gideon that night, despite his surprising
exhaustion. Although he had been unconscious for three days, his
body was still recovering from shock and the lack of food. He probably could have slept another three days if he could've just relaxed. But
he couldn't—or wouldn't. He wasn't sure which it was.

For one thing, eating so suddenly and so much after three days had
made him nauseous. He couldn't close his eyes without feeling the
room spin like a carnival ride. And the ever-present honey smell made
his gut wrench.

But there was something more, though Gideon fought not to think
about it. The trouble first started when he noticed the scar on Donovan's
face. It was thin at the top and grew a little thicker toward the bottom,
around his mouth. And though it was mostly straight, there was a minute jag in the line about an inch from the eye, as though Donovan had
flinched slightly or winced in such a way to cause the blade to tear a little to the side before continuing down his face on its slow progression.

In short, the scar was brutally real—far too detailed to be a dream,
a hallucination—*anything* but real. But that meant that Donovan was
real, and the room, and Lairn. That meant there really was a village—a

sounden, or whatever they called it—and real Guardians, a real little girl. Most of all, it meant that Gideon really had. . .

He felt the bile rise deep in his throat. Slowly, he stood and leaned against the polished wall, cool and smooth as ice. "It can't be true," he muttered under his breath. "That doesn't make sense. It has to make sense."

After a few moments, his stomach settled a bit, and he eased himself back into the bed. He wanted to sleep, to dream, anything. Anything to make him wake up back in the real world, the world he knew. The world he hated. But, despite his mental objections, he was beginning to realize this "place" was not a dream at all.

The implications of that reality were too frightening to consider. And too terrifying to ignore.

Several hours later, long after Gideon had finally collapsed from exhaustion, he was awakened by a gentle handgrip shaking his shoulder. He slowly rubbed his eyes, then stretched out his arms. For an instant, he thought he was back in his own bed, in his garage apartment back home. He almost expected to open his eyes to find his cat nudging his face with her cold wet nose.

But when his eyes finally did open, there was the polished room, the stick still giving off its curious glowing. And there was Donovan's face, scar and all, looking strangely golden in the light. His foreboding eyes peered down at him like pitch-black chambers, denying others the opportunity to see into their mysteries.

"It's time to rise, Gideon Dawning," he said quietly. "The journey is long today, and the Guardians are heard not three hours distant." Gideon blinked widely to clear the fog of sleep and sat up in the bed. Donovan straightened, and for a moment his dark eyes softened just a bit. "I hope your rest was restoring." With that, he produced a bundle of clothes and set them on the bed. Then he walked out, moving with a silent grace that seemed incongruous with his bulky, muscular frame.

Once he was gone, Gideon quickly rose and shuffled through the bundle Donovan had left on the bed. The clothes seemed much like Donovan's own. A frock like the one he already wore, along with a leather vest and a fur-lined leather poncho with a green sash. The brown pants felt like linen on the inside where they touched the skin, but on the outside they felt more like sandpaper.

Donovan also provided a pair of lightweight boots. There were no socks, but the boots were lined with soft fur. In addition to the boots, there was a full-length dark brown cloak with a hood. The cloak was slightly torn in one corner.

This is real.

After perusing the items a moment longer, Gideon stood up and walked around. The nausea was mostly gone, thankfully. In fact, he felt. . .good. Almost giddy. He didn't understand why he felt that way, but he chose not to question it. He was tired of questions.

He removed his frock, put on the fresh one, and quickly slipped on the rest of the clothes. To his amazement, they fit perfectly. In fact, they felt more comfortable than any clothes he could ever remember wearing. The leather was warm to the touch, yet breathed enough not to feel suffocating. Once he had donned it all, he looked in one of the polished walls to check his reflection. And laughed.

"Robin Hood," he said aloud. "I look just like Robin Hood." He turned to the side. "No tights, though. . . Hmm. Too bad."

Gideon bundled the cloak and used the extra frock to tie it off. This was all too weird. Robin Hood? A coincidence. Maybe. Or maybe dreams do come true.

A shiver danced down his spine. He didn't know what to feel. Terrified, excited, trapped, free, cautious, bold, insane. He felt it all in opposing waves that spilled against each other with each new thought.

A new world. An unknown world. Like Nottingham. And I look like Robin Hood.

He was beginning to accept the fact that what was happening to him was real. But if so, then there were dangers here that must be considered. There were still games people played. Donovan played a game with him. And someone else was playing him. That could be dangerous. And deadly.

Gideon grabbed the bundled cloak, then checked his reflection in the polished walls one more time, brushing his hands through his black curls. Despite his fear, he still couldn't help but grin a little.

Sherwood Forest, here I come. . . .

Tentatively, Gideon drew back the red burlap curtain that hung in front of the door and slowly stepped through. The doorway opened to a large, round chamber—polished like his—with a high, cone-shaped ceiling. The ceiling was polished too, smooth as glass, except for the highest part surrounding an open hole. That part was covered with soot from the smoke that even now rose from a round hearth in the center of the room. Black cooking pots and utensils hung from the hearth's sides on rusty iron hooks. There was only one pot on the fire itself, and it was being tended by a plump woman dressed in gray with a long, honey-colored braid of hair running down her back. She didn't turn around.

The chamber was set in three sections, or so it seemed; there were no walls. In one sat a simple wooden table made from thick slabs and polished just like the floors and walls. Alongside the table were four wooden benches. Another part of the room was filled with bright red pillows. The third part was empty.

Quite suddenly, the woman turned from her stewing pot and saw Gideon standing just inside the doorway. Quickly setting aside her cooking spoon, she bowed her head and extended her arms toward him in a peculiar fashion. It wasn't an embracing gesture, exactly. Her wrists were turned up and her fists were clenched. It seemed more a gesture of submission. Or a threat.

"Lord Gideon, blessings to you," she spoke without looking up. "Forgive me, I did not hear you enter. You are welcome in the sounden. And the house of Cimron."

Not knowing what else to do, Gideon bowed toward the woman. "Thank you. Blessings to you as well." *Lord Gideon?*

Whatever Gideon said seemed to be enough, for the woman relaxed a little and let down her arms. Slowly, she looked up.

"I am called Mara, a breadmistress of Calmeron. Cimron is my bondmate." Upon seeing her face, Gideon realized she was quite a handsome woman. Her round features and soft gray-blue eyes gave her a look that was at once guarded and generous. But her expression was genuine, guileless. Gideon could sense no hidden purpose behind those eyes, no falsehood. All he saw was reverence, and. . .what was that? Sorrow. He saw sorrow.

"My name is Gideon Dawning," he nodded. "I'm. . .just visiting."

"We knew the Visitation was close," Mara said. "The *Bian'ar* eyes have come many times this year, many more than the year before. And that year there were more sightings than were ever recorded."

"Hmm," he nodded, pretending to ponder the implications of what she'd just said, none of which made any sense to him at all. It wasn't hard for him to pretend, though. He had done it all the time with his professors. "Is Donovan here?" he asked politely.

The voice that responded was not Mara's. "He has gone to prepare the mounts," the voice said. A deep voice, resonate, but soft. Gideon looked beyond the hearth to see a man enter the chamber from a curtained room like his own. He was bald, in his middle years. He wore a simple gray tunic, with pants and boots like Gideon's own. His face reminded Gideon of Lairn, so he guessed it must be Cimron. He didn't possess his son's strong appearance, but his gray-blue eyes exuded the same gentleness as the boy's.

With a gesture identical to Mara's, the man stepped toward Gideon. "Blessings to you, Lord Gideon. May your shoulders bear only peace under my roof."

Again Gideon bowed. He wasn't sure he could mimic their gesture accurately. "Thank you. The same to you."

"I have wronged you in not welcoming you into my home before now," Cimron continued, his eyes fixed on Gideon's, "but I and my bondmate are in deep mourning for our lost child. I have not been the host to you that you deserved. Today I will strive to do better."

Gideon winced at the mention of the girl. How could he have forgotten about her so quickly again? It all still seemed like a dream.

"I'm sorry," he said, unable to stop himself from shifting uneasily in their presence. He felt guilty that she had died that way, in his arms. He threw her down when she caught fire. *I threw her down!* He wondered if they had seen that. Of course, it was automatic. He didn't even think about it. But now, with her parents standing there. . . What else could he have done?

Cimron smiled. "Please," he said, "be refreshed for your journey." He took a step back and gestured toward the table. Gideon followed Cimron's lead and walked over and sat down. Mara said nothing, but went to the fire and returned with a wooden bowl filled with bread, fruit, and dried meat. She set it before Gideon along with a wooden mug filled with some kind of juice.

The sight of food instantly reawakened his nausea, but Gideon masked his reactions and determined to eat what he could. He didn't want to offend anyone—not until he knew more about them anyway.

The fruit was unfamiliar to him, as was the juice, but both had a flavor somewhat like mango. The dried meat was too salty to tell what kind of animal it might be, but Gideon didn't really want to know. He pretended it was beef. That made it easier to swallow without throwing up.

Despite his efforts at control, however, a few bites of the meat proved to be too much for his system. He could feel the gorge rising from his gut even as he forced down the second salty chunk. Beads of sweat dotted his forehead as he tried to master his nausea.

Quickly, he reached for the bread, hoping it might settle his stomach. His hand quivered slightly as he tore off a chunk of the dark loaf, but neither Cimron nor Mara seemed to notice. They just watched him in silence, with that same mixed look of reverence and sorrow and. . .fear?

Forcing his hand to be steady, he nibbled on a corner of the bread. It was heavy and moist and tasted of honey. It wasn't warm, yet it burned his throat as it went down. Quickly, the warmth spread outward from his chest to the rest of his body, adding strength, calming nerves. It felt like being flooded with warm jets of water, washing out weariness and worry and leaving only strength and peace. The nausea left him.

"The bread is good," he told Mara. "Real good."

Cimron and Mara both smiled and sighed as though they'd been holding their breath for some time. "May it please you as much as the giving pleases us," said Cimron.

"May it please you," echoed Mara.

"That which is wrought in weakness is now revealed in strength. No tear is lost," said Cimron.

"No tear is lost," echoed Mara.

Gideon said nothing, but took a second small bite of the bread. He couldn't remember feeling so alive since. . .since he was a boy.

"Mara is one of the mightiest breadmistresses in the sounden," said Cimron. "The *bian'ar* melds strong with her. This is the third bread she has made since your arrival. The first two are stronger by far."

"It feels wonderful," Gideon agreed.

"You are too modest, bondmate," said Mara. "Cimron is crafted in the harvesting of the *bian'ar*," she added. "In that, his weakness is added to mine. Our bonding makes the bread strong, and in the making, our bond is strengthened. That is the gift of the Watch. I am thankful."

"I as well, bondmate," added Cimron, putting his arm around her. "I as well."

Just then another red-curtained doorway flew open. Donovan entered, looking as ominous as a bear, moving as silent as a cat.

"It is time, Gideon Dawning." His deep voice echoed through the chamber. "We must go."

"Okay," said Gideon. He hated to leave the bread behind, but forced himself to put it down as he stood. "Thank you," he said to Cimron. "And thank you, Mara," he glanced at the bread, "for everything."

Gideon retrieved his bundled cloak and headed for the door where Donovan stood waiting. He felt a gentle touch on his arm from behind.

"I ask that you take this on your journey, Lord Gideon," said Mara. "It is *Ja'moinar*. It will strengthen you for the trials that await you." Her eyes held even more reverence now as she spoke. She placed the loaf in Gideon's hand. It looked like the other bread—only smaller. But it felt much heavier.

Donovan took a step toward the woman. "Blessings to you, Mara," he said with a slight bow. "Your gift comes from the treasure of your heart. We will strive to help Gideon Dawning use it wisely."

Gideon wasn't sure what to say, so he just nodded to the woman with a smile and placed the loaf in the folds of his bundled cloak. It took all his effort not to bite into the bread right then. He felt so—powerful.

Abruptly, Donovan turned and walked outside. With one more brief nod to the couple, Gideon followed him.

Once through the curtain, Gideon found himself on a small natural ledge looking down a hill on the rest of the sounden. He gauged the home to be about one hundred meters up the hillside. His senses were at a peak. He could feel every stirring of air around his body, detect every minute odor carried on the cool morning breeze. He could even sense the small crevices of earth beneath the grass at his feet. Peering off to the west, he could see the edges of the Castellan Watch as clearly as if he stood at the foot of those mighty trees. He could feel the animals begin to stir or settle to sleep. He could even feel a rainstorm building on the mountains beyond the wood. The sky was clear now, but in a few days' time, there would be rain here.

Stretched out below him were the semicircular rows of round cottages, all with thatched circular roofs—like an orchestra of musicians wearing Chinese hats. Beyond them Gideon could plainly see the grassy field and the four stone towers, where he had *allegedly* died three days earlier. He still didn't quite accept that part as true. Even with his heightened senses, the only visible sign that anything at all had happened there was a single scorched circle of earth in the grass. He suddenly realized he didn't even know the little girl's name.

The sun still hadn't risen above the hills to the east, but its glow gave the clear sky a deep purple shade. The air was sharp and filled with the smell of honey. For the first time he could tell the smell didn't come from the sounden itself, but from the great wall of trees to the west.

Without a word, Donovan led Gideon down the hill toward the towers. At the bottom, three figures waited next to five horses. One was a stout young man with a sleeveless leather vest whom Gideon immediately recognized as Lairn. The other two he didn't recognize, but one stood like a woman, though her face and body were concealed by a hooded cloak.

"Are they going with us?" he asked Donovan. The big man didn't respond.

"Donovan. . ."

"Hail, sojourner!" Gideon looked beyond Donovan's bulk to see one of the two strangers hold a fist to his heart in salute. "Be welcome with us as we travel this day. The Giver's canopy is wondrous today." He looked up. "He shall cover us."

For a moment the stranger's eyes lingered on the coming sunrise. He had to be one of the most impressive men Gideon had ever seen, though he wasn't sure exactly what it was about the man that caused him to take notice. He was tall, like Donovan, but not as heavily muscled. His clothing matched Donovan's exactly and his own, for that matter. His strong, angular face was handsome, though not so beautiful as to be distracting. Free-flowing blond hair fell in a gentle wave down the back of his neck and fluttered slightly in the morning breeze. His eyes, too, were striking—deep blue, like portals to an ocean. But even that couldn't account for the impact of the man. Gideon couldn't figure out what it was. Maybe it was just an effect of the bread.

The man's eyes finally turned back to Gideon as he and Donovan reached the bottom. "I am called Ajel, the Windrunner."

Hmm. The name fits. "Gideon," he nodded. "Gideon Dawning."

If Gideon's name had surprised the man, he didn't show it. "Blessings to you, Gideon Dawning. I think it is more than chance that we meet this day. I shall look forward to speaking with you on the journey."

Gideon nodded slowly, his own blue eyes locked on Ajel's. There was something foreign about this man. No, not foreign, exactly. Deep. Very deep. Too deep for Gideon to read right away. But he would—in time, he would. He always did.

Suddenly Gideon was distracted by the presence to his left. It was the woman. "Hail, sojourner," the woman said. "I am called Kair, of the Songtrust. I was the one who heard you call the Storm of Deliverance."

Unlike Ajel's friendly tone, the woman's smooth voice was hesitant, as though it carried a subtle challenge. He immediately felt defensive, though exactly why he wasn't sure. She certainly didn't look imposing. She was petite, with delicate alabaster skin and flaming red hair that kept spilling out of her hood faster than she could tuck it back in. The hood was attached to a deep green cloak that covered her all the way to the ground. The cloak made her true shape a mystery, but it could do little to conceal her intriguing eyes. They were the same gray-blue as Cimron and his family, though hers revealed a fierceness and wariness he'd not seen in theirs.

She held the reins on two horses, a white mare and a larger gray stallion. They were clearly mountain horses—bred for stability and not for speed. But they looked strong and healthy as far as Gideon could tell.

"Nice to meet you," he said at last.

There was some small commotion behind him, and Gideon turned to see Cimron and Mara embracing Lairn, with Donovan standing by. Cimron was crying.

"The Guardians return this day, Cimron," said Donovan. "You must have your people leave the sounden until they pass."

Cimron wiped his tears slowly. He didn't seem to hear Donovan at all. He only looked at his hands.

Mara's eyes widened as she looked at her mate. She grabbed his wrists in alarm. "You must not waste your tears, bondmate," she pleaded. "Will you disgrace your son by leaving your tears in the grass?"

"Forgive me, bondmate," he said, his head bowed. "Forgive me, Lairn. I do not mean to disgrace you. The sorrow is too much in the moment. First my daughter and now. . .my son."

"You bear no shame, Father," said Lairn. "No one saw but us. And I will not remember."

"You are brave, son."

"Cimron," Donovan interrupted. "You all must leave before midday."

Cimron turned to face the big man. "I will not let them destroy my home too."

"Better your homes than your lives," responded Donovan. "Homes can be replaced. But to lose hearts such as yours would be a curse on the land. Seek shelter in the hills or in the Watch."

Cimron didn't respond.

"Which way are you bound, Donovan Truthstay?" asked Mara, still holding her husband's wrists, but more gently now.

"Forgive me, Mara. . .but it is best you do not know." Donovan paused a moment, eyeing the woman solemnly. "Do not fear for the boy, Mara," he said. "He is in my charge."

"I have great confidence in your heart, Donovan Truthstay," said Mara. "The boy is safer with you now than he could be with us, wherever you are bound." She glanced sideways at Kair, who seemed preoccupied with a tuft of hair that had escaped her hood again. "Come, Cimron, we must go now," she added. And with that, she took his arm and they started up the hill. The boy watched them quietly as they went.

"Are you ready, Gideon Dawning?" asked Donovan.

"Sure," said Gideon, "just tell me where to go."

Donovan turned and walked away toward the horses. Kair still held the reins of two. The other three looked equally strong as horses go—Gideon was no expert. Besides the white mare and gray stallion, there was one other gray, a chestnut, and a black. The black horse had to be Donovan's. It stood a hand taller at the shoulder than any of the others, and its rich coat glistened in the morning light with the same imposing arrogance displayed in Donovan's eyes.

Kair handed Gideon the reins of the larger gray stallion. She said nothing and seemed glad to be rid of the horse, if for no other reason than it was the one he was riding. The woman clearly disliked something about him, and, unlike Donovan, she didn't try to hide her feelings.

By carefully watching the others prepare their mounts, Gideon was able to strap his bundled cloak to the gray stallion's back. None of the horses bore saddles—instead, they each wore two simple leather straps around their midsections. Down each strap dangled several leather strands, apparently used for tying on packs or supplies.

Since there were no stirrups, mounting the gray stallion proved to be quite a challenge. He'd never ridden a horse before, unless he counted the pony he rode each year at the school fair when he was a child. But after watching Ajel, Donovan, and Lairn mount their horses, he felt confident enough to try it himself. After only a moment of hesitation, he swung himself smoothly onto the stallion's back. He always was a quick learner, when he had to be.

"Mountriding is not known to you, Gideon Dawning?" said Ajel. It didn't really seem to be a question. Gideon shook his head slightly. He thought his mount had been very smooth. "The mount is called Orisoun," Ajel continued. "Speak kindly to him, and he may save you in trouble."

"I'll keep that in mind," Gideon said.

Once they were all ready, Donovan quietly motioned for the group to start toward the great woods, Castellan Watch. At first, they only walked the horses, careful not to disturb the sleeping soundenors. Gideon was thankful for that, for it gave him time to become more comfortable with the odd rocking motion of the horse. But once in the shadows of the great trees, the group turned north and began to run the horses along the forest edge—straight toward an expansive stretch of green, rolling hills that spanned the entire horizon to the north.

Without so much as a twitch from his reins, Gideon's horse took off in a full gallop right along with the others. In a panic, Gideon crouched low against Orisoun's neck and gripped the reins so hard his knuckles turned white. He'd never felt so wildly out of control in all his life, yet there was nothing he could do about it. All he could do was hold on. As time passed, however, he began to grow more comfortable with the smooth strides of the horse beneath him and with his own ability to grip the horse with his legs. He realized now why the pants he wore felt so rough on the outside. The fibers in the outer material clung to the hair like Velcro on felt. It was not long before he loosened his hold on the reins and looked up to let the wind pull his curly hair out of his eyes.

For as long as the horses ran, no one so much as looked around them. Or, if they did, Gideon certainly didn't notice it. All his energy was focused on staying upright.

About an hour into their trek, Gideon gave one final glance at the trees of the Watch as they disappeared behind them and turned toward the hills that now spread before him like the deep green waves of the ocean. The hills were not terribly high, but they were richly colored, carpeted masterfully in deep green grasses, and spotted with florescent blossoms and the occasional evergreen shrub. The rolling landscape seemed endless, wave after wave of green rising and falling on a peaceful journey to the horizon.

At first Gideon thought the beauty of the place was too stunning to be real. But the more his eyes swept across the gentle rise and fall of the hillsides, his opinion changed. The problem wasn't that the place seemed unreal—it was the opposite. The land before him, before his eyes, seemed *too* real. The deep greens of the grasses were too green, the flowers too bright, the shrubs too solid. Even the morning sky seemed too blue. Azure, like the color of deep ocean. The reality of what lay before him made his own real world seem like a dream—a world of grays and shadows, where nothing seemed certain.

Once the Watch was out of sight, the hills quickly surrounded the group, and Donovan slowed to a brisk walk as they rounded the knolls toward the north. Oddly, the horses didn't seem tired at all after the run. They weren't even breathing hard.

That wasn't all, however. Even after riding for over an hour, Gideon didn't feel the least bit sore. He should have been in agony by now, having never ridden a horse this long in his life. But he felt as fresh and loose as when he first began.

"Man, that *was* good bread!" he chuckled to himself. In fact, it wasn't just his body that felt good. He just felt good all around, calm, at peace with the world, that sort of thing—and his thoughts were sharp and perfectly clear.

As they traveled deeper into the hills, this sense of peace increased, until he began to realize the effect wasn't coming from Mara's bread anymore. In fact, what he felt now wasn't like the feeling Mara's bread had given him, but softer, deeper. More powerful in its own way. There was no breeze, but the still air cooled his skin like a splash of clear water. The life around him seemed vibrant like before, yet relaxed and free.

At peace. It was hard to explain. But it was wonderful.

"These are heavily Worded lands." Ajel's sudden words took Gideon by surprise. No one had spoken since they'd left the sounden. But without Gideon noticing, Ajel had drawn his chestnut stallion up beside him. "Do you know it?"

Gideon nodded. Despite the peaceful aura around him, he still felt a little uncomfortable next to the man. "The air is nice," he said. "I can't imagine why Donovan called this place 'Scolding Wind.'"

Ajel looked over at him. His azure blue eyes were deep as the ocean, as real as the sky that surrounded them. Gideon found them totally unreadable. "Where is your home, Gideon Dawning?" he asked.

"Uh. . .nowhere near here. . . . I don't think you've heard of it," Gideon responded awkwardly.

Ajel nodded. "Have you always been on sojourn?"

"No, uh, I. . .I'm from America."

Ajel smiled. "It has a beautiful sound, 'A-meer-iquah.' Why did you leave it?"

"I didn't mean to," said Gideon. "There was. . .an accident."

Ajel nodded as though he understood much more than Gideon had said. "I think I would like to see a place with such a beautiful name," he said. "Is it far?"

"You've never heard of America?" Gideon lowered his eyes and shook his head. "I can't believe I'm not dreaming."

Ajel laughed. "A dream! If that is so," he said, "then you are the giver of all of this wonder. You have done a fine job with the morning, small creator." He gestured toward the deep blue sky. It was too blue. Too blue.

"What is this place called?" asked Gideon.

"The soundenors at Calmeron call these the Worded Hills," Ajel said, still smiling. "But as you have said, most of the people know this place as the Scolding Wind. It is a powerful place—a force for good."

"No," said Gideon. "I mean, what is this whole land called? This country?"

"Ah," Ajel said. "This country has had many names, and not all are worth repeating. But within the Remnant, we call it the Inherited Lands. That was its name in the beginning."

Well, that was no help at all. Gideon grimaced. Then he said, "It sure would be nice to know where my home is from here."

Ajel tilted his head slightly. "But you are a sojourner. Have you not said this?"

Gideon sighed. "So you keep telling me."

Ajel sat thoughtfully for a moment, then smiled again. "Do not be concerned, Gideon Dawning," he said. "A sojourner's quest is his own matter. I will not try to learn yours. But perhaps in Wordhaven, answers may be found for a seeker such as you."

"I hope so," Gideon muttered. There had certainly been no answers so far, and his frustration was growing. Nothing made sense. Nothing. The sky was too blue, the land too green, and nothing had a name he could recognize. He needed more information. Something here had to make sense. Unless it was a dream, of course. But he had already dismissed that possibility. This was real. Weird, yes. Unexplainable, yes. But real. Definitely real.

And if it was real, he needed real answers to survive in it.

"Tell me about this place, Ajel," he said. "If you don't mind."

"You mean the Hills now?" asked Ajel.

Gideon shrugged. "Sure." There was a great deal he wanted to know, but his immediate surroundings were as good a place to start as any.

Ajel nodded and nudged his horse a little closer to Gideon's. "I will tell you what I know. As you can sense, it is a powerful place, strongly Worded in *Dei'lo* for good in the land. So it has been for more than two thousand years, from the time when Castel Morstal, the great mountain keep, was the prison home of the evil one. In that time, the Great Lords of Wordhaven spoke a mighty Word over this land to make it a natural barrier to resist him should he ever escape."

Gideon didn't understand. "The evil one—you mean a criminal or something?"

"I do not know this 'A-krem-men-ahl,' Gideon Dawning," said Ajel. "But the one of which I speak is not of the Inherited Lands, nor is he even a form like a man or woman. He came to the land long ago and brought with him the evil that now consumes both the land and its rulers. He is called by many names—Landspoiler, Destroyer, Barrenmaker, Father of Ruin—but in Wordhaven his true name is recorded. He is Abaddon, the Pearlslayer. Is this also the one you call 'A-krem-men-ahl'?"

"Not exactly." Gideon grimaced. "I'd be more likely to call that one something else." *If I believed in the devil*, he thought. But he didn't— despite his family's persistent attempts to convince him otherwise. Especially his mother, who had always taken her messianic Judaism too seriously as far as Gideon was concerned. She prayed to Yeshua every day to save her sons from the devil's influence. But to Gideon, the devil was just a mythical scapegoat people used to excuse their own vice. "So, the power the 'Great Lords' used on these hills, is it the same kind of thing the Guardians used against me?"

"No, Gideon Dawning," Ajel said, shaking his head just a little. "You truly know nothing of these things?"

This time Gideon smiled. "Like you say, I'm just a sojourner."

"And yet you called a Storm of Deliverance." For a moment, Ajel's brow furrowed, and he absently brushed a large hand through his gold-colored hair. Suddenly, those laughing blue eyes penetrated him like icy steel. "When we arrive at Songwill, you will need to speak as little as you may."

Gideon's horse whinnied, and he absently reached down and patted his neck. "Why?" Gideon asked. "I don't understand." *And, by the way, I didn't call any freakin' storm!*

Ajel waved his hand absently, his piercing gaze gone as quickly as it appeared. "That is a complicated matter, sojourner." He emphasized the title this time. "I will explain what I can later, perhaps. But you must do as I ask. It is important."

Gideon opened his mouth to speak, but Ajel kept speaking. "Now, let me answer your first question.

"*Dei'lo* and *Sa'lei*, the Languages of Power, are each borne of a different origin. *Dei'lo* was given to the people many millennia ago by the Pearl, the emissary of the Giver. *Sa'lei* is a different language altogether. It came with the evil one's escape from Castel Morstal, only a few thousand years past. The effects of the two tongues may appear similar at times, even identical. But they are each of a wholly different essence—like light and darkness. A man or woman who speaks one tongue is unable to speak the other, unless the heart can be turned. But that is very rare."

Gideon adjusted himself on Orisoun's back. Despite the magical effects of the hills, he felt his back beginning to get sore, and his rear was growing a little numb. "So the Guardian used *Sa'lei* to attack me, and Donovan used *Dei'lo* to. . .heal me."

Ajel nodded. "The power of one language can reverse the power of the other if spoken in time."

"Sounds like magic," Gideon said.

"There is no magic, Gideon Dawning," said Ajel. "Only words of Life and Death. Creation and Destruction. And the power of both is greater than our souls."

"Which language is stronger?" Gideon asked.

Ajel laughed. "Oh, *Dei'lo*, of course, for Life is always stronger than Death." He glanced at Gideon with a smile, then added, "The first encompasses the second. While Death means to destroy Life, Life simply transforms Death back to Life again."

Inwardly, Gideon moaned. *Why won't the man speak in plain English?* "So the Words of Life are more powerful," he concluded.

"Yes," Ajel nodded. "*Dei'lo* can both destroy and create, wound and heal. *Sa'lei* can only pervert and destroy."

Gideon grunted, shifting his weight to get the blood flowing to his legs and to give him a moment to take in what Ajel was saying. "Well, if you know this. . .language of power, why did your people hide when the Guardians appeared?" he asked. "And why does it seem like they're in charge, if they aren't as powerful as you?"

Gideon was hoping to see some reaction in Ajel, but the man's angular face didn't so much as twitch. "I fear you think too highly of us, Gideon Dawning," he said. "Our knowledge of *Dei'lo* is slight. What knowledge we have has been gleaned from the inner walls of Wordhaven. That is the only record that remains, that we can touch.

"The only other record of *Dei'lo*, a Book containing all the teachings of the Pearl, has been hidden away in Phallenar, where the Council Lords and their Guardians have locked it away for centuries. And for all that time they have striven to make the people forget the Book's existence."

"How do you know it still exists?" Gideon asked.

Ajel paused to look up at Donovan's position. Then he prodded his horse to go a little faster and motioned to Gideon to do likewise. Once the new pace was set, he continued. "My father, Laudin Sky, once lived in Phallenar, where he served the Council Lords as Chief Mentor—while secretly searching for proof of the Book's existence. He found more than that. In the midst of his search, he learned of the existence of Wordhaven, which for generations was believed to be merely legend. When the Council Lords learned that he had discovered the truth, they set their hearts to kill him. But he escaped with others who, like him, knew *Dei'lo* was real, and together they went on sojourn to find Wordhaven."

There was a pause before Gideon spoke again. Ajel's explanation made sense well enough, but it was a tad too dramatic for him to believe. "Well, that's quite a story," he said skeptically. "But why don't the Guardians, or these Lords, just destroy the Book?"

"I do not know," Ajel answered simply. "I can only hope it is because they lack the power."

"But that doesn't make sense," Gideon debated. "If they can't destroy the Book, then how did they gain power over it in the first place? You said *Dei'lo* is more powerful."

Ajel nodded. "Indeed, it is," he answered. "That is the very reason the Council keeps the Book hidden. They know it alone holds the power to destroy them.

"Long ago, things were not as they are now. In those days, there was no Council, no Black Gorge, no Deathland Barrens. In that time, the Guardians were noble men and women, fluent in *Dei'lo*, and sworn to the protection of the Pearl and the Book. Life in the whole land flowed from Wordhaven, not Phallenar. There was no Phallenar then. There was no war—no one in that day could have conceived of a language of death. Except one man."

Ajel fell silent and looked off to the horizon. He wasn't smiling at all now.

"What man?" asked Gideon.

Ajel turned on Gideon with a piercing gaze that sent shivers down Gideon's spine. It was all he could do not to shudder. "The man who shares your name," he said. "The Betrayer. The instrument of the Pearl's destruction, the servant of the evil one. He is called Gideon, the Truthslayer."

This time it was Ajel who seemed to watch Gideon for signs of reaction. But Gideon held his expression steady and kept his eyes locked on Ajel's.

"He held the title of High Lord of the Inherited Lands," Ajel continued, "the *Batai*, until he chose corruption and became the servant of Abaddon. The evil one taught him a Word of Death more powerful than any Word yet known in the Inherited Lands. Thankfully, it is lost to us now; but in its speaking, Gideon Truthslayer destroyed the Pearl and corrupted a great portion of the land.

"He himself was also destroyed, but that is only a small matter. The evil he released has festered and grown over the centuries and left us at the mercy of powers too great for us. Without the Pearl, without the Book, I fear all hope in the land will eventually perish."

Ajel looked up at the sky and took a deep breath. The few clouds that passed overhead were like bright cottontails floating against a deep blue backdrop. The sun was bright yellow, but its warmth was more reassuring than oppressive. Gideon didn't believe Ajel was lying to him, but his words didn't seem to fit here. The hills were all too beautiful, too strong. Nothing so dark and evil could ever touch these lands.

"There is so much to tell," Ajel said at last. "But perhaps now you can understand why you must stay quiet in Songwill. Much of the old knowledge is preserved there. They will know your name and who you represent. Those that do not wish to slay you on sight will likely wish to crown you as Kinsman Redeemer, according to the prophecies of Shikinah and Endimnar."

Gideon shook his head. "They want to kill me?" he asked.

"I cannot say what is in their hearts with certainty," replied Ajel. "Some may. And some may want to follow you. But if you truly know nothing of the Kinsman Redeemer or his purpose. . .if you do not claim that title, then know that it is best that you remain quiet."

Gideon's eyes darted up ahead toward Donovan. The big man had lied to him. In all his talk of dreams and travel to Wordhaven, he hadn't said anything about walking into a deathtrap. He was a liar. Gideon wouldn't forget that now. Not ever. "Great," he said with a smirk, "I guess I can look forward to dying twice this week. Once is never enough."

Ajel said nothing, but smiled.

For the rest of the day, Ajel stayed clear of Gideon, prodding his chestnut stallion up next to Donovan and talking with him quietly for hours. Kair and Lairn kept to themselves as well, falling several paces behind the rest and never seeming to utter a word.

Gideon didn't care. He still had more questions shooting through his head than he could hold onto at once, but he didn't feel like talking anymore. Perhaps Ajel sensed that. Or maybe the graceful man had more urgent business with Donovan. He wasn't sure. It was all so hard to read, still. He needed time. Time to think and time to get used to being. . .wherever he was.

"Hills of the Scolding Wind," he said under his breath. The hills seemed endless, as majestic as huge ocean waves, but glacial; peaceful giants that caressed rather than pounded. He couldn't remember seeing or feeling anything so beautiful. And there was absolutely no wind, he noted. There hadn't been so much as a gust all day.

Of course, why some idiot named this place "Scolding Wind" was the least of his questions. Every answer Ajel had given only served to raise ten more questions in its place. And, with each explanation, the questions they raised became more alarming.

He felt like this whole mysterious world was inexorably sucking him in, and there was apparently little he could do about it. At first, he was just a lost man trying to get his bearings. And before he barely knew where he was, he was attacked—though he still refused to believe he'd *actually* died—then healed and told he had miraculously saved the village. And that his name somehow pegged him as a cult figure. A Kinsman Redeemer, whatever that was. Maybe that was why Cimron and Mara had called him "Lord." Maybe. It could have just been a title of respect too. There was too much he didn't know.

And now he was riding toward another village—sounden—where the people wanted to kill him. Or at least some of them did. The rest wanted to make him king or something. All because they thought he was the fulfillment of some age-old prophecy that he knew absolutely nothing about.

How could this not be a dream? he wondered.

And yet, somehow, he knew it wasn't. He was certain it was real. It was crazy, he realized, but he also knew he had to deal with reality as it was now, not as it was before, not as he wished it to be. Not that he had ever "wished" it to be the way it was before either. No, he certainly never wished that.

In the peaceful quiet of the hills, time was difficult to measure. But the group continued calmly onward as the golden sun floated slowly down toward the west. In time, shadows lengthened across the hills.

Donovan allowed the group to stop only once, and then only briefly, to share food from their satchels and stretch their backs. But, really, they didn't seem to tire much at all—or hunger, for that matter. Even the horses seemed almost as fresh at day's end as they were in the morning and that without having ever stopped for a drink. Perhaps it was just another special quality of the hills.

Whatever it was, it made Gideon's first day of "mountriding" surprisingly easy. And, later in the night, it magnified his sense of wonder when they finally rounded the last knoll to behold a radiant golden city in the hills.

CHAPTER 8

SONGWILL SOUNDEN

Many believe that prophecy allows us to predict what
will happen. But after all that has transpired here,
I no longer think that is true. Instead, I believe prophecy is given
to explain the nature and origin of what has already occurred.
The prophecies of the Kinsman Redeemer were never designed to
show us exactly who that man would be or what he would be
like. Rather, after he came and did all that he was predestined
for, the prophecies were there to prove to us exactly who he really
was and reprove us for not being willing to see it.

—THE KYRINTHAN JOURNALS, MUSINGS, CHAPTER 9, VERSES 141–143

When Gideon opened his eyes, he found his body engulfed in a small mountain of soft feather pillows. He didn't remember lying down there the night before, but, well, it was late and he had been riding all day.

The last thing he remembered was watching Donovan scowl at him like a rabid mother hen. *Protect or kill? Protect or kill?* Gideon could see the mental Ping-Pong every time he looked at Donovan's eyes. So he tried not to look at him at all.

The walls in Gideon's pillowed chamber glistened like translucent alabaster in the sunlight streaming down from shafts in the ceiling. Scattered around the cavernous room were black stone tables displaying strange but beautiful artifacts. Odd-looking headpieces—sort of a mix between African and Native American, Gideon guessed—as well as lots of jeweled objects that resembled horns or cones. A few of the items Gideon couldn't begin to describe—crystalline sculptures of some kind? Whatever they were, they seemed to have been grown rather than carved. Not that it mattered. Just another minor unknown lodged in the belly of one big, fat, ongoing mystery.

The walls were another curiosity. Sparkling alabaster-white now,

Gideon would have sworn they were made of pure gold when he arrived last night. But then, he would've sworn the whole city was gold, the way it glowed in the darkness.

Besides the city's golden radiance, Gideon couldn't recall much about his arrival the night before. They were greeted, he remembered, by people in gold robes. Or maybe they were white too? Donovan made him put on his cloak and wear his hood, despite his argument that no one could possibly recognize him here. Someone took the horses, and then a handful of others led him here. There was some kind of singing—a welcome or a prayer, he wasn't sure—and then Donovan came and said something to him just before he'd lain down. He couldn't remember what.

He let out a yawn. Oh well. At least he'd been able to sleep through the night without destroying anything. He remembered wondering when he arrived just how thick those walls were and worrying about all the delicate-looking items displayed around the room. Whatever whirlwind of supernatural events had caught him in its throes, he still couldn't afford to forget about the more familiar demons that lurked within him. The last thing he needed was to be forced to explain how his bedchamber got trashed in the night—or worse, how someone got stabbed in the chest with a pointy, jeweled horn. Absently, he ran his finger along the scar across his chest and wondered whether his cat had run away by now.

When he finally stood up, which took some effort given the mushy nature of the pillows, he saw he was still fully dressed, except for his cloak and poncho.

That's odd, he thought. *Could I have been so tired that I didn't even bother to take off my boots?*

He also realized he was quite hungry. So he pulled on his poncho in preparation to go forage for food and to get a bearing on where he was.

Ajel had told him to stay out of sight while they were here, which he had reluctantly agreed to do. But he wasn't hungry when he said that. Besides, if there was real danger for him here, he'd much rather face it on his own terms, not just sit around waiting for some religious zealot to stroll in and kill him. If Ajel and Donovan had really wanted him to stay put, they should have left someone here to watch over him—or, at the very least, they should have informed him of where they all were. What if someone did attack him? He didn't even know which way to run. They certainly couldn't expect him to just sit here in ignorance while they went traipsing off who knows where.

Just as he reached for the door, Donovan opened it from the other side and stopped dead in his tracks at the sight of Gideon standing there. A look of alarm flashed across his face, as though he were looking at a ghost.

"You are awake," he said, a little too suspiciously for Gideon's comfort.

"Uh-huh," replied Gideon, a little sarcastically. *What's so weird about me being awake? Does everything I do shock this guy?*

Donovan quickly buried his reaction and strode past Gideon without another word, balancing two large bowls of food in one arm. He set them down on one of the black stone tables.

"How is your strength, Gideon Dawning?" he asked, his voice still sounding a bit wary.

Gideon only shrugged. "Where is everybody?" he asked.

"I did not expect you to have risen yet," Donovan continued. "Have you had other visitors before me?"

"I don't know, Donovan," Gideon said. "I was asleep. Besides, it must be nearly midday by now."

Donovan's black eyes seized on Gideon with unconcealed suspicion. *Protect or kill, protect or kill?* Gideon thought in a whiny tone. "I brought refreshment," Donovan said coolly.

Gideon glanced at the food. There was an assortment of fruits and nuts, along with a loaf of bread. With a fleeting thought of Mara's gift in his satchel, he walked over and grabbed the loaf and sat down at a nearby table. "You don't like me very much, do you?" Gideon asked.

"I think you may be a Guardian," Donovan said plainly.

"Excuse me?" Gideon nearly choked on the bread he'd been chewing. It wasn't special, like Mara's. "A Guardian?" Donovan stood motionless, like a rock. "What could possibly lead you to think that? I mean, those guys tried to kill me. They *did* kill me, according to you."

"You have no home in this land, no tribe," Donovan began, his deep voice resonating off the chamber walls. "You appear suddenly in the midst of a sounden that is not your own, in the middle of a Guardian attack. Even your clothes are taken to leave us no clues of your identity or your background. You call yourself by a name that can bring nothing but division among my people, and yet you claim no knowledge of the Inherited Lands. You claim no knowledge of the Words, yet you call a Storm of Deliverance, a thing that has not been done in a thousand years. And now you are awake, when last night I spoke a Word over you that should have caused you to sleep through the day. I do not know who you are, Gideon Dawning, but I see what I see. I will not deny it."

Gideon snorted derisively, then pointed the loaf of bread toward Donovan's face. "I think you've been in the war business too long, Donovan. I'm just an ordinary guy trying to muddle his way through a very weird situation. I don't know how I got to the sounden or how your 'Storm of Deliverance' or whatever got called. And I'm certainly not trying to spy on you." Gideon stood. "And just so we're clear, let me remind you that you're the one who asked me to come along with you on this little adventure. I didn't even know what Wordhaven was until you brought it up. Heck, I *still* don't."

Donovan said nothing in response. Gideon shook his head in frustration, then headed for the door.

"Where are you going?" Donovan asked.

"For a walk," he replied without turning around.

"You must remain here, Gideon Dawning," Donovan said. "It is Ajel's command."

"Is it really?" Gideon droned wearily. He stepped back from the door to face Donovan again. "Well, I'm not under Ajel's command, or yours." He spun away from Donovan and reached for the door.

"*Jeo di'*," Donovan whispered. And suddenly, Gideon's world went black.

———

Ajel stood on the portico outside the Elders chamber overlooking the rolling hills of Songwill and the blue waters of the lake on which the sounden was bordered. The ancients called the lake Severthrall; but since the time of the Slaughtering, it had been known as Palorfall, in honor of the only battle ever lost by the ancient false Redeemer, Palor Wordwielder. In his studies at Wordhaven, Ajel had sometimes wondered what it would have been like to be present at that horrid battle. In many ways, he wished he had been. In the entire history of the

Inherited Lands, it was the only battle ever fought in the Scolding Wind Hills, the only time men and women pitted sword against sword and Word against Word. King Wordwielder was never able to dominate Songwill; and the loss of that battle not only turned his kingdom against him, but set his mind on a course to madness.

No signs of that conflict remained now, aside from a few beautifully engraved murals here and there detailing the event. But Ajel worried that the choices he had made in recent days might once again cause blood to mingle with the peaceful waters of the sounden lake and be soaked into those emerald hills. He could not know. Unlike his uncle, Paladin Sky, his dreams tended to reveal secrets of the present, not the future. But he believed the course he followed was wise and that the faith he had placed in the sojourner would not prove false.

Even with his faith, though, he still wondered if he had made the right decision in bringing Gideon here without first seeking the Elders' permission. Songwill sounden presented itself to the Inherited Lands as a united people; but within its heart, factions and sects constantly bickered over the meanings of various prophecies.

Of all those, the prophecies concerning the Kinsman Redeemer were the most volatile. The prophecies about him were vague and at times seemingly contradictory. As a result, many thought him to be a messenger of Abaddon—as Palor Wordwielder had been—while others held that he would be the land's deliverance from Gideon's Fall. A few even thought he could be either or would be both. In any case, news of Gideon—"Stormcaller," they called him—had reached the sounden within a day of the Guardians' attack on Calmeron. Ajel was all too aware that bringing the sojourner here could incite a riot—or worse. But he saw no other way.

Kair stood at Ajel's side, once again garbed in her full-length green cloak. These last weeks had been difficult for her, Ajel knew. Though, as was typical, she never spoke of her pain. Kair's father had once been an Elder in Songwill, until he found in his heart the call to Wordhaven, to join the Remnant. It was there that he met and fell in love with Caram, a daughter of Calmeron sounden who had run away from home years before to join the rebellion. Kair became the offspring of their bonding. A half-person, not quite belonging to either tribe and therefore rejected by both.

For all their wisdom, the people of Songwill had the arrogance to match. They looked condescendingly on their southern neighbor, believing that the people of Calmeron sounden had squandered their Pearl-given Trust of knowledge in *Dei'lo*—essentially by prostituting themselves to King Wordwielder and to the Council Lords after that— by sending a tribute of knowledge to Phallenar every year in exchange for the right to live in peace.

This, of course, was far less true than the people of Songwill believed—or wanted to believe. Calmeron did reveal some of its Trust to the Lords of Phallenar in exchange for some measure of freedom in daily life. But Calmeron kept much of its Trust intact—and well hidden from the Council Lords. In some ways, in fact, Calmeron had maintained its Trust better than Songwill—and the people of Calmeron knew it. But they never tried to prove this to their neighbors in the hills. Their own pride kept them from it.

In the middle of all this silent condescension stood Kair. She knew the truth—about both soundens, being born from both. But no one would listen to her. Bearing the physical traits of both tribes, she belonged to neither.

Despite her struggles, Ajel was glad she was chosen to accompany them back to Wordhaven. He believed in her potential influence for good, even if she didn't. Kair's quiet strength and resolve had always served to create a calmness in any room she entered. And he hoped that would prove true here in Songwill as well. He needed her calm presence, especially in view of what he was about to ask of the sounden Elders.

Ajel and Kair continued to wait quietly outside the massive polished stone slabs that were the Elder chamber doors. The late morning sun sparkled on the glistening stone, casting deep shadows across myriad engravings and symbols. From out of the stone, artisans from the sounden had carved pictures and symbols that detailed the rich history of Songwill. Its battles, its great leaders, and, of course, its music. More than anything, Songwill was famous for its music.

Without warning, the great stone doors swung silently open. From behind them appeared two ivory-cloaked children, who gestured for Ajel and Kair to enter. Ajel smiled as he looked down at their innocent faces, so free from the concerns that now plagued him. *I wonder if I will be the one to tear that innocence from them.* He closed his eyes in an attempt to banish the thought, but it didn't work.

They followed as the children led them down a long corridor and into a large round chamber with a high domed ceiling supported by great alabaster beams. There were no other doors or windows. The room was lit entirely by staffs of glowood. The glowing poles cast rich golden shades upon the white stone walls and floor. The walls were filled with paintings and etchings, just as the doors were, but in much richer art and detail. In a downward swirl beginning at the top of the dome, the murals detailed the full history of the Inherited Lands, starting with the Giver's gift of the land itself, followed by the invasion of Abaddon, who had tried to take the Inheritance away. The murals illustrated the arrival of the Pearl, who captured and imprisoned the evil one in Castel Morstal. Farther down and flowing left to right, the paintings depicted Abaddon's escape, Gideon Truthslayer's treachery at Gideon's Fall, the loss of Wordhaven, the coming of Palor Word-wielder, the establishing of his capital city, Phallenar, the Slaughtering, and finally the establishing of the present Council of Lords. The bottom third of the chamber was blank, history waiting to be written. A history Ajel was creating right now, for good or bad.

Before him and Kair were seven elderly soundenors, seated behind a curved wooden table, polished until it glistened like refined gold in the artificial light. Unlike the people of Calmeron, all of these men and women gazed upon the twosome with deep brown eyes. But the years had turned their once-reddish hair white as fine cotton. All the elders wore ivory cloaks just like the children's, but these were gathered at the waist with a royal blue sash. Beyond that one sign of their office, they dressed and looked much like all the others Ajel had encountered since his arrival here.

In the center position on the table sat a woman whose deeply creased face was etched with an obvious dignity and determination. Ajel recognized her immediately as Elima conSeth. She was the *Nissirei*, High Elder of Songwill. Of all the Elders sitting before him, Elima was the only one Ajel had known before. He had talked with her several times on his travels through Songwill and had come to respect her as a wise and noble leader for her people. It was her brazen resolve alone that provided the glue that held the sounden together. She had found a way to embrace every faction of her tribe, and all of them claimed her as their own. The sounden would probably never break apart as long as she lived, if for no other reason than the fear of offending her.

Despite Ajel's relative familiarity with the High Elder, he had never been allowed to enter the Elders' chamber until today. And there was a reason for that. It was clear to him that Elima was not sitting before him as a friend, but as the protector and leader of her people.

"Windrunner Ajel, truthbearer from Wordhaven, blessings to you, and purity. You are welcome in the chamber." Elima conSeth spoke with confidence despite the shakiness age had brought to her voice. "Who is this one with you?"

"I am called Kair, of the Songtrust," she replied before Ajel could speak. "I come as does Ajel, bearing peace from Wordhaven to you and your people." Of course, Elima knew full well who Kair was. She had probably known her father years before. But her association with Songwill would not be recognized here because of her mother's heritage. In fact, her claim to be a member of the Songtrust under normal circumstances would incite any citizen of Songwill to violence, since it was one of the sounden's most revered societies. But these were not ordinary times, and the High Elder, thankfully, ignored the title.

"Blessings, Kair. I did not expect Windrunner to bring a companion with him to the chamber. Nevertheless, I say you are welcome here.

"These that sit with me are the Eldership of Songwill. Sita conTrell, Merca conMal, and Boroc conMata sit to my right. And these are Ruel conGad, Lorn conLorn, and Carell conDonari."

Ajel and Kair nodded greetings to each Elder in turn, but most nodded in response to Ajel alone.

"You say you come bearing peace to our sounden," Elima continued, her gaze also fixed on Ajel, "yet you have brought the Stormcaller with you without our prior knowledge. His presence here presents nothing of peace for Songwill. Why do you burden us with his appearance?"

Ajel raised his hands submissively. "Of all the peoples in the Inherited Lands," he began, "those of Songwill are fully aware of the critical days we live in. With the rediscovery of Wordhaven by my father and his companions over fifty years ago, a new hope and strength were born in the land. But also a new threat to the power of the Council Lords in Phallenar.

"You know how since the Council Lords realized Wordhaven was again inhabited, they have tirelessly hunted us like rabid animals. At this very moment, they search the land for the Stormcaller in hopes that they might destroy him and so destroy any hope for deliverance from their dark reign.

"But the news is even graver than this. We have learned that the Council Lords believe the Stormcaller to be one of the Remnant. Before his arrival south of the Hills, the Remnant of Wordhaven was a thorn in the Council's side. But with his appearance, we have become a spear. This was not by our own choice, but I know you can see how this endangers our efforts to free the land."

"Yes, yes," said Lorn conLorn, his wrinkled face laced with frustration at Ajel's lengthy speech. "You are not yet ready for a full confrontation with the Guardians. That is already perfectly clear. But that explains nothing that we have asked."

"I bless your indulgence, Elder Lorn," said Ajel. "But I feel my lack of brevity is necessary to understanding my purpose here." Lorn grimaced and looked away. Ajel could already tell that the man would not turn to support his request, even if he worked all day to convince him.

"The Stormcaller is like no man I have ever met," Ajel continued. "He claims no knowledge of the Guardians, nor even of the Inherited Lands. Yet we believe he did call the Storm of Deliverance. In truth, we do not know how to deal with his presence any more than you do. If he is as he claims—a sojourner who has no heart for *Dei'lo*—then we want no part of him. He draws too much attention from Phallenar. But if he is the Kinsman Redeemer, then we cannot ignore his presence. Whether for good or bad, his life would shape the destiny of every tribe in the land. As the Remnant, it is our duty to help shape his path for good rather than for evil."

"Ajel conLaudin," interrupted Merca conMal, a stocky old woman with a head full of white flowing hair, "we all know of the noble purposes set in your heart and the heart of your father before you. But the question remains before the Elders. Why do you bring the Stormcaller here?"

Ajel stood tall and thought silently for a moment. He wanted to prepare them more before he made his request. But it was clear now that their lack of patience would not allow it.

"We need your knowledge," he said at last. "We need the knowledge of the sounden to help us determine if this one might be the Kinsman Redeemer." He paused a moment, taking in a deep breath. "I am here to ask that you call a Gathering."

"A Gathering!" Lorn exclaimed. "Have you gone mad, Wordhavener? A Gathering in the presence of this Stormcaller would tear the sounden apart. I know of five leaders in the sounden right now who are ready to kill the Stormcaller on sight. They will certainly not let him stand in the midst of a Gathering."

"Peace, Lorn," said Elima soothingly. "No decision has been made—only a request given. Let us hear the Wordhavener completely before passing a judgment."

Ajel smiled at Elima, then turned to face Lorn. The other Elders remained quiet, but watched him intently. He knew the other Elders would make their decision based on how he handled himself with this one man. "I know of the factions within your sounden, Elder Lorn. And I know of the danger to the Stormcaller and to your people. But the question of the Kinsman Redeemer goes far beyond the borders of your sounden. It is a question whose answer will affect the four corners of the Inherited Lands. Already knowledge of the Stormcaller spreads throughout the land like a wildfire. If it continues unchecked, I believe it will lead to a new war—launched upon my people *and* yours. And at that time it won't matter if this man is the Kinsman Redeemer or not. The panic over the possibility of his identity will pressure the Council Lords to come down with an iron fist. If that happens, I fear that Wordhaven may be lost forever. And perhaps your sounden as well."

"This sounden has stood free since the founding of the Inherited Lands," cried Lorn. "You speak fear to our hearts to push us to do what we know is wrong for the sounden."

"I harbor no intimidation from his words, Lorn," said Boroc conMata. "But I do see the insight that they hold." Boroc was a plump man with a round face and an excess of color in his cheeks. Of all the Elders, he was the only bald man. Ajel remembered that Elima had mentioned him on several of his previous visits. She had chosen him to be her successor.

Boroc leaned his plump frame toward the Wordhavener. "You believe that by exposing this man now to be an imposter, that will quiet the forces in Phallenar that are building against him and your people."

"Your people as well," added Ajel somberly. "But you speak the truth of my heart. Nowhere but at Songwill can that manner of discernment be made about the Stormcaller. And in no setting other than a Gathering."

"But what if he is proven true?" asked Boroc. "What if the prophecies hold that he is the Kinsman Redeemer?"

"Then we will take him to Wordhaven and help him gain a pure heart for the Words of Life and the cause for freedom."

"Bah!" exclaimed Lorn. "The true Kinsman Redeemer is an imposter by definition. Even if he is proved true, that makes him all the more deserving of death."

"Not all share in your beliefs, Lorn," admonished Elima.

"Enough do, *Nissirei*, to give him only a slight chance to live through a Gathering."

"If one is called," replied Elima flatly, "I believe my word will be more than enough to keep the peace." She turned to Ajel and Kair. "We have heard your words, Windrunner," she said, "and we will now consider your request. You and your companion may leave us now."

Ajel bowed slightly toward Elima, as did Kair, and turned to leave. As they approached the huge stone doors, the two children that had led them in once again appeared out of the shadows and opened the doors. Ajel smiled at the one nearest him and rubbed the child's head as he passed.

Once outside, the doors sealed firmly behind them.

"What now?" asked Kair simply.

Ajel raised his eyebrows and sighed. "Now, we wait."

CHAPTER 9

THE GATHERING

The power of music lies in its capacity to create harmony out of chaos. Music can take words and rhythms and sounds that are dissonant and alone and combine them in such a way to create oneness, purpose, beauty, and direction. Now, apply this principle to Dei'lo, and you have discovered a weapon of limitless power.

—THE KYRINTHAN JOURNALS, CANTICLES, STANZA 3, VERSES 521–522

Gideon awoke late in the afternoon to the distant rumble of hundreds of voices outside. His mind was foggy. The last thing he remembered was snapping at Donovan on his way out the door. And now he was here, in bed. Again.

With considerable effort, he forced himself to stand. He was still fully clothed, as he remembered, except for poncho. But hadn't he put those on? It seemed too real to be a dream. Okay, insanity then. That would explain a lot of things.

Sluggishly, he walked to the door and opened it just a fraction to take a peek outside. All along the path in front of his chamber stood clusters of people—men, women, and children—all dressed in ivory frocks, like a city of clergy folk. They talked together in low rumbles, frequently glancing out beyond the path into an area Gideon couldn't see. He could hear music coming from everywhere—light, airy flutes and drums and something that sounded like a hammered dulcimer. Lots of people on the hillsides in the distance were forming circles and dancing around each other. *Like a good ol' hometown country festival,* he thought. *Well, if the festival were in Ireland. And if all the citizens were priests.* He sighed.

Out of the corner of his eye, Gideon picked out the comparatively dark form of Ajel easing through the crowd toward the chamber. Gideon slipped back into the room and quickly occupied himself by toying with a piece of fruit that looked suspiciously like an apple.

"Hail, sojourner," said Ajel as he walked in. "I hope your rest was restoring."

Gideon took a bite of the fruit. To his surprise, it tasted more like a strawberry. "Yeah," Gideon said, chewing. "I guess I needed more sleep than I realized."

"I would speak with you a moment," Ajel continued, more seriously. "And it would be best, I think, that you dress yourself as I talk. The hour is upon us."

There was a certain urgency in Ajel's voice that Gideon found uncomfortable. But he nodded nonchalantly and wiped his mouth, then began to pull on his poncho—*once again?*—as Ajel continued.

"The sounden has called a Gathering," he said. "The Elders have agreed to draw from the knowledge of the sounden to discover whether you could be the Kinsman Redeemer."

Gideon opened his mouth to speak in protest, but Ajel raised his hand to silence him. "It is our hope that you may be cleared of this association. For if you truly are not the Kinsman Redeemer, as you say, then your association with him will only call unwanted attention to the Remnant and its efforts to oppose the Council Lords.

"At sundown the Songs will begin, and the Elders have requested your presence on the Floor. Donovan will watch over you there, but you must be on your guard in any case. There may be those whose convictions concerning you are foul. We do not expect any danger to befall you, but neither do we want to move ahead as the blind."

"So is this a trial?" asked Gideon.

"Not at all. It is merely a pooling of knowledge."

"So what happens if they decide I am the Kinsman Redeemer?"

"Then perhaps there is more to your heart than even you know," Ajel replied with a grin. "The sun almost sets. Put on your hood and come."

Gideon draped his cloak over his back. "Wait, why do I need to wear the hood?"

Ajel didn't reply. He just grinned and deftly pulled the hood over Gideon's head. "This way," he said, gripping Gideon's arm to lead him out the door. Ajel was not an overly huge man like Donovan, but Gideon immediately noticed that his grip felt like steel.

Gideon was about to protest, but what he saw outside nearly took his breath away. The sounden covered not just a few hillsides like

Calmeron, but many. Domed cottages, all white except for windows filled with flowers, spotted the emerald hills in every direction. And all of these hillside cottages focused down upon the center of a placid blue lake. Or, more specifically, upon a large covered platform constructed in its waters. Gideon guessed that platform was likely the "Floor" Ajel had mentioned. Two arched bridgeways connected the Floor to the land, and already people were busily at work on it, preparing to remove the tarp that protected it.

Hundreds of ivory-cloaked people stood everywhere, blanketing the emerald hillsides in every direction. Ajel quickly led Gideon through the crowd. All eyes seemed focused elsewhere—either on the Floor, on the many dancers performing on the hillsides, or on the musicians that played along the shore—all of which made it fairly easy for Ajel and Gideon to slip past unnoticed. Gradually, they made their way down the hill toward the bridgeway closest to them.

As they drew closer, Gideon noticed several men and women moving to stand upon the arched bridgeways. They wore ivory cloaks like everyone else, but each also bore a blue sash around their waists. Six spread themselves along the bridgeways, while a seventh stepped onto the platform and directed the people there. All of them looked old.

"The Elders," Ajel spoke softly, as if hearing Gideon's thoughts. "The one standing on the Floor is Elima conSeth. She is the *Nissirei*—the High Elder of the sounden."

Standing along the shoreline to the left of the Elders, Gideon caught sight of Kair. She wore her full-length green cloak again, with her hood covering her abundant red hair, and was standing as motionless as a statue.

Just as the sun tipped the crest of the hills to the west, the workers on the Floor removed the tarp that covered it. What Gideon saw underneath made him stop short and gasp.

The platform glowed like molten gold. It looked like it was made of pure light, casting its hue down into the water and upon everything along the shoreline. Gideon recognized the effect. The platform had the same look as those odd glowing sticks he'd seen in Calmeron, only on a much grander scale.

When Ajel and Gideon finally reached the shore, Ajel directed him to wait next to Kair while he walked on toward Elima conSeth.

Gideon did as Ajel directed, though Kair didn't so much as offer a nod. Ajel and the High Elder exchanged whispers, then he left the platform, nodding reverently toward everyone he passed until he came to stand next to Kair. As he did, Gideon felt a presence behind him and turned to see Donovan and Lairn standing stoically at his back. He had no idea where they had come from. Donovan's face was stone—as always—but his black-orbed eyes seemed to scan the ivory-cloaked crowd warily, as though watching for any sign of danger.

In contrast, the people continued to dance, and the music played on, as though the possibility of danger in this place was all but inconceivable. But the chills running down his back told Gideon the danger was real. Despite the apparent merriment, he noticed that not everyone was dancing.

After several minutes, Elima conSeth glided to the center of the glowing platform, her flowing ivory cloak lightly brushing the polished Floor as she walked. Despite the obvious signs of age on her face, her movements were strong and full of grace and for whatever reason conjured images of silk.

When she reached the center, all the music stopped as if on cue. All eyes turned to her, waiting. She stood stoically for a moment, then slowly raised both arms toward the sky. As she did, the air around Gideon began to resonate with the low hum of thousands of voices, sounding as one. Elima closed her eyes and lifted her head, her silken hair now turning golden in the diminishing light of day.

Then, gracefully, unobtrusively, the entire sounden began to sing:

In the beginning was the Word,
That through the end remains untamed.
Past Gideon's Fall it yet endured,
past hate and vile death's stench—
its aroma is sweet.
Hail Mighty Word! Heart's Hope! Hail!
In you our hearts hold true.
Speak forth the Word that will prevail,
to let the land once more be new.

As the final tone faded from the amber, late evening sky, Gideon felt a chill run down his back. The song was beautiful, filled with a paradox of sorrow and hope. But it wasn't the melody that touched Gideon; it was the people. These thousands of people, who together sang this song as one voice. It spoke of their heritage, their hope, and struck at the very core of their collective soul. It was unavoidably moving.

The silence of nightfall returned to the Floor, and Elima lowered her arms, opening her eyes upon the throng of people blanketing the hills around her. All eyes fixed on her once again, waiting for her word. It was clear to Gideon that she held the respect and honor of the entire sounden.

"Before the Fall, the Lords of old gave to each sounden in the land a Trust," she began, her tremulous voice resounding despite her years. "For each sounden, the Trust became its charge, one portion of the Truth disclosed by the ancients.

"Over the centuries of treachery and negligence since that era, most soundens have all but forgotten the priceless Truths to which they were entrusted. Even here in Songwill, much of what was once entrusted has been lost, and for that loss we grieve.

"But we have been especially blessed to have found our home in these Worded hills. For they have served us as a fortress against the thieves of time and evil. So though we grieve our loss, the heart of our Trust remains whole.

"The power of song. Song adds to words as words add to silence. And so we sing—of triumph and tragedy, and in our songs record the drama of the times.

"Over the centuries beyond the Fall, when the Inherited Lands first grew dark with sorrow and pain, prophecies arose from the mouths of old men and young children. Prophecies of hope and destruction. So we added these to our songs and kept for posterity words long forgotten by even the aged among the tribes.

"There are those among us this day, visitors from a far place, who request a share in the collective knowledge of prophecy concerning the Kinsman Redeemer—the prophecies of these dark times. I and the Elders have called these travelers friends, men and women worthy of honor and peace from our hands. Hear them now, Songwill. And let your hearts guide your judgments in peace."

Elima conSeth turned and moved to stand next to Boroc conMata.

She never once glanced at Gideon or at any other of the Remnant.

In the graceful way that only Ajel could, he crossed the bridgeway and strode to the center of the Floor. His face was calm, but his blue eyes pierced the darkness like a knife in clay.

As he stood silently on the Floor, the last rays of the sun, now long set, at last faded from the deep purple sky. The people fell into deepening shadows, and Ajel stood like a lone castaway floating on an island of light in a sea of darkness. Just as Gideon began to wonder how Ajel would handle speaking into a darkness void of faces, staffs of golden light began to appear on the hillsides. At first there were only a few, but their numbers grew until the whole sounden, in every direction, looked like a rolling forest of golden, glowing trees. The golden hue flooded the valley, pouring down upon the Floor, making the night look, for all purposes, like an oddly golden day. The light poured down on Ajel's face as well, making his already golden hair blaze in the night, giving him the distinct appearance of a madman or a prophet.

Ajel grinned as he took in the beauty of the glowood that illumined the night, and, with only the slightest pause, he began to speak.

"Blessings to you, Songwill sounden, and purity." Ajel raised his hands, palms out, as if extending a blessing to the people. "I am called Ajel, the Windrunner, a visitor in your land, a seeker of peace and restoration. I and those with me are honored by your welcome and awed by your wisdom in the matters of prophecy and song. Indeed, it is for that reason that we have come to you, for we have encountered a matter for which we have no resolution.

"Six days past, a man came among us. He is like no man we have ever seen in all our travels—a man with hair as black as the night sky."

Black hair! Gideon thought. *What's that supposed to mean? There've got to be other people with black hair somewhere around here.* But of all the people Gideon had encountered, he couldn't remember a single one of them having black hair. But surely that didn't mean he was the only black-headed person in the whole country! Ridiculous.

Even so, he pulled his hood a little farther down over his face.

"He claims to be a sojourner in our lands," Ajel continued, "a stranger with no knowledge of the Words or even of the Guardians. Yet we believe he called a Storm of Deliverance while in delirium from the Guardians' recent attack at Calmeron—an act no one has been able to perform for many generations.

"This matter is too great for us to discern. That is why we have come to you, to gain from what you know and learn the truth of this stranger, who bears the name of the Gideon of old."

Suddenly, there was a rush of murmuring on the hillsides. Ajel continued, "Whatever your heart toward the Kinsman Redeemer, his coming is destined to change the face of the Inherited Lands. So help us know the truth of this matter, that we may dissuade the rumors that may be false or guide the heart that may be true."

The words echoed through the hills, fading into silence at last. Ajel stood still, hands at his sides, waiting. Waiting for what, Gideon didn't know.

Moments later, pockets of people stirred in several places around the hills. Gideon could just make out the forms all around the sounden making their way down to the Floor. Minutes later, a few reached the bottom and stood on the shoreline near the bridgeways. They spanned all ages; even children came. Strangely, none of them would look at Gideon. It was as though they were afraid of being somehow entranced by his stare. They moved around him as one might move around a snake or a king.

As the people gathered about the bridgeways, Ajel stepped down next to Kair, and the first of the people to arrive moved onto the platform. She was young, more child than woman from what Gideon could tell, with silky straight light red hair that fell to her waist. Calmly, she faced the throng on the hills around her as though it were as natural to her as looking in a mirror. And then she sang, her voice high and dainty like a flower, yet able to be heard on the farthest hill:

A light has come—rejoice!
A Word of might become a man.
His seed lived not within the land
'til from the land he was born.
From him shall spring a righteous race
as numerous as the stars.
In his death the seeds of victory rise;
in his pain the land with healing will flood.
And from his tears fallen mixed with blood,
shall spring up joy eternal.

The girl sang the prophecy like a dirge, in minor keys and piercing tones. For all her simple elegance, Gideon was disturbed by her song. It didn't sound like a prophecy for any kind of great "deliverer." She concluded by saying, "From the prophecies of Endimnar." And she walked off the Floor.

Suddenly, Donovan grabbed Gideon by the cuff of his cloak and pulled him back to where he and Lairn stood. "Lairn, take Gideon Dawning to the mounts. Wait for us there. Quickly!"

Without hesitation, Lairn's strong hand grabbed Gideon's arm and pulled him away toward the hillsides across from them, to the north. Gideon didn't even have time to speak before Donovan was well out of sight. *What happened?* he wondered. *Was someone trying to kill me?*

From behind them, a cry rose up into the night from what seemed like hundreds of voices. Gideon turned to see what Donovan had detected moments before. From over the hills to the east, hundreds of black-garbed Guardians poured into the Gathering, raising a battle cry as they came. Hundreds of long swords glistened in the golden light of the sounden. Before anyone had a chance to act, the Guardians were already cutting through ivory-clad soundenors on the upper hillsides along the eastern rim.

Without a word and with incredible strength, Lairn pulled Gideon past several stunned clusters of soundenors, beyond several cottages, and into a small corral on the far north side of the sounden, nestled in a small valley between two hills. They located the horses and pulled them all together, ready to ride in a moment's notice. Then they waited in silence, watching from their hidden vantage point within the corral.

After sending Gideon away from the Floor, Donovan had bounded up the nearest hill to the east in an attempt to reach the black lines of the Guardians. His sword, already unsheathed, glistened like gold in the night. By now the soundenors had realized what was happening. The children ran west, away from the attack, while the men and women faced the onslaught head on. They took up whatever weapons they could find—some had swords, but most found glowood staffs, wood posts, even rocks and chairs—and struck fiercely back at the advancing blanket of black uniforms.

Despite their determination, the Guardians continued to press through the mob, leaving piles of bloodstained bodies in their wake.

Donovan finally reached the encroaching line, his sword blazing in the golden light. He moved like lightning, dodging thrusts and swings at every turn, while his own sword rarely missed its mark.

Suddenly, Gideon saw Ajel and Kair not far behind Donovan. They split, one taking each side of the warrior, and faced the attack. But they bore no weapons.

"Idiots!" Gideon said aloud. Lairn shushed him.

Both Ajel and Kair extended their hands toward the advancing lines, now only feet away, and one by one the Guardians began to drop. Like dead men they fell, and they did not rise. Ten, twenty, forty Guardians piled in a heap as they came near the two Wordhaveners. Donovan left the twosome and moved north along the black line, forging his way through another advancing section of Guardians.

At this visible sign of hope, the soundenors once again took heart. They fought with renewed vigor, pounding away at the black-garbed soldiers, pitting sticks and rocks against swords.

Looking back onto the Floor, Gideon noticed that the Elders, led by Elima conSeth, had formed a circle facing outward toward the sounden. Together, as one voice, the Elders began to sing. It was a song of strength, a song of victory in battle, full of powerful rhythms and major chords. As the music reached the battle lines, it seemed to empower the soundenors even more. Slowly the battle tide began to shift, and the Guardians were pressed back, several falling to their death from wounds to the head and heart.

Gideon marveled as it seemed the soundenors might actually force the Guardians back altogether. But then a second wave rounded the hills to the east, this one on horseback. It was smaller, only about fifty strong, but the horses made one fighter equal to three on the ground. Donovan turned to press toward this new threat, but was blocked by a wall of foot soldiers opposing his blade.

From the fifty, five horsebacked Guardians cut through the ranks of fighters to come within earshot of the Elders on the Floor. Immediately Ajel saw the danger and called out a Word that Gideon couldn't quite make out. The horses stopped short, throwing the black-clothed riders over their heads and onto the ground near the Floor. Three were apparently knocked unconscious, but the other two quickly stood and charged on toward the Elders. Gideon recognized one as the thin-faced man who had attacked him at Calmeron sounden. Waves of anger and fear shot through him as he recalled the horror of that encounter. He did not envy the Elders at this moment.

Elima conSeth stepped out of the circle while the other Elders continued to sing. She raised her hand as though by such a simple gesture the Guardians would be forced to stop their advance.

"Do you think yourself so mighty that a wave of your hand can stop us, *Nissirei?*" demanded the thin-faced man.

"Hold there, Borin Slayer! Speak no more in this place!" The voice came not from Elima, but from Donovan, who had broken through the lines and now stood ten paces behind the Firstsworn of the Guardians, his long sword dripping with blood.

Borin spun around to face the voice. "Donovan Blade," he said with disgust. "How dare you show your face to me. Your name is a curse in Phallenar."

"Speak no more," repeated Donovan. "And take these blackened hearts back to the pit from which they came. You have no business here."

"The hills are Worded against you," added Elima. "It is vain for you to face us in these lands. Go while the hills remain forgiving."

"Don't threaten the Firstsworn, you old hag," yelled the other Guardian. "You think we fear your foolish legends? You should die in your delusion. *Damonoi blassht!*"

Instantly, Elima conSeth burst into flames. Her ivory cloak flared orange, then settled in the black of ash. In a moment, all that remained was a pile of black dust on the golden glowing Floor. The Elders stopped singing and stared in disbelief. Donovan too looked on in horror.

"There, you see, rebel," said Borin. "So much for your precious protection." And with that, he turned toward the battle lines on the eastern hills and called in a loud voice, "Guardians, hear me! To the Words! To the Words!"

Instantly, flames blazed out within the battle as the Guardians began to freely use the *Sa'lei* Words of death. Ajel and Kair retreated down the hill, calling behind them as they ran, causing still more Guardians to collapse lifelessly to the ground.

Gideon watched it all and fearfully wondered whether there was any hope that they would live beyond the night. He considered taking his horse and making a run for it. But where would he go? He had no idea where he was, much less how to get to Wordhaven from here. And, for all his suspicions about the Remnant, he didn't like the idea of facing the Guardians again. . .alone.

Suddenly, a strange sound came from behind him, out of the north. At first it sounded like a low howl—similar to the cry of a coyote in the night. But it grew louder as it approached, like the sound of mighty rivers flowing down a canyon floor. Gideon nudged Lairn to warn him to get ready for an attack from behind. If they needed to, they could mount the horses and take off for the west and hope their mounts were faster than the force behind them.

But just when the rushing sound seemed upon them, it passed like thunder overhead. It was invisible, but the sound of it was like a roaring train in a tunnel, hurtling toward some unknown destination.

Instinctively, Gideon and Lairn ducked as it passed, then watched as the invisible force reached the Floor, where Donovan and the Elders stood facing Borin and the other Guardian. Without warning, the great wind threw Borin's companion to the ground, pinning him forcefully against the grass. The Guardian closed his eyes against the pressure; but the wind was so powerful, it forced tears from his eyelids down across the temples. Then the wind increased, tearing off the Guardian's clothes like they were made of tissue. Seconds later, cracks formed in his skin from the chafing force that held him. Fissures erupted on his face, his arms and legs, even his chest. He gritted his teeth against the pressure; but the wind was relentless, tearing his skin apart, ripping at the flesh underneath, separating it from the bone.

Gideon watched in horror as the wind dissected the man, limb by limb, tearing away the flesh like the peeling on a fruit. Within mere seconds, the Guardian's face was gone, his arms, legs, and chest lay open, exposing the bones to the night sky. Then the wind lifted, almost gently, and shot off toward the front lines of the battle.

Ajel and Kair immediately ran after the wind, apparently unaffected by the gruesome specter they had just witnessed. Donovan turned back toward Borin Slayer, but he was not there. In the confusion of the wind's attack, he had slipped away unnoticed. Donovan shot a reassuring glance at the Elders, then turned and followed Ajel and Kair. The Elders began their song again.

The mighty wind ripped through the ranks of the Guardians, dispatching black-garbed soldiers left and right, more quickly now than at first. Those Guardians who saw what was happening, but had not yet used a Word of death, turned and fled back toward the east.

The booming howl of the great wind did not hinder the soundenors in their fight. If anything, the sound of it spurred them on even more. They continued to push back the Guardians and even chased after many bands that had turned to flee. The great wind cut down soldier after soldier, while the soundenors fought not three feet away. The wind fought against the evil, and the soundenors did not fear it.

With the battle turning strongly in favor of the sounden, Ajel and Kair turned their attention to the wounded that lay strewn across several hillsides. They each ran from body to body, surveying the wounds, then leaning to whisper something in the soundenors' ears. Without waiting to see the effect, they ran on to the next wounded, repeating the procedure. At first, Gideon couldn't tell if their efforts were doing any good. But soon, several of the wounded began to sit up, then stand and walk about. Tirelessly, Kair and Ajel continued, rushing to reach each person before it was too late. Within minutes, they had covered one entire hillside and were moving on to another.

Meanwhile, Donovan led the chase as the last of the remaining Guardians fled the sounden. No black-cloth remained to defy the wind, which also made chase, catching Guardians on the run and ripping them to shreds within seconds.

When it became clear to Donovan that the Guardians were fleeing for good and not regrouping, he turned back toward the sounden, calling men and women to follow him as he ran. Bloodstained Guardians lay strewn across the hillsides. Those that yet lived, Donovan pointed out, directing pairs of soundenors to carry the bodies to the Floor. Quickly, he and about twenty others made their way to the battlefront where Ajel and Kair had caused so many to fall by their Word. Several of the soundenors produced bands of rope. Donovan directed them to bind up the Guardians that lay in heaps all around. Apparently they were not dead as Gideon suspected. They were just unconscious.

Meanwhile, with amazing efficiency, Ajel and Kair had covered most of the eastern side of the sounden, speaking Words of healing to well over a hundred injured or dying soundenors—and possibly, he noted reluctantly, some that may have already died. Presently, they made their way down to the Floor, where the soundenors had brought the wounded Guardians. Without hesitation, Ajel and Kair began to heal their wounds and just as quickly speak the Word that put them into a deep sleep like the others. Soon after, several soundenors followed behind and bound up the sleeping Guardians.

Donovan had all the remaining Guardians brought to the Floor. Gideon counted well over seventy, but then gave up because of the number that kept being carried in. Once all the Guardians were accounted for, Donovan took a few steps toward the corral where Gideon and Lairn hid and waved for them to come out. Lairn hopped out from behind the horses and jumped the fence; Gideon followed closely after. Gideon noticed that Lairn hadn't said a word since this whole episode began, but then again, neither had he. Still, he felt something from Lairn, an emotion he couldn't quite pinpoint. Something like mistrust, perhaps. Or fear.

"Boroc conMata, do you have adequate holding for these black-cloths?" Donovan asked the Elder. For the moment at least, no one seemed concerned about Elima's death.

"We shall hold them," replied Boroc.

"Bind their mouths," said Donovan. "Those in desperate situations often do desperate things. We cannot be certain they will not speak."

"By your word, Donovan," replied the Elder.

"I fear that we have brought this evil upon you, Boroc conMata," said Ajel as he moved to stand next to Donovan. "I wish there was a way we could undo what has been done."

"The evil of the Guardians is upon us all," said Boroc calmly. "You did not cause it. Besides, your healing craft has saved many. Only a few did not survive." Boroc sadly looked down at the pile of ash that still rested on the grassy Floor. His eyes filled with tears.

"She stood as a bastion for the Truth," Ajel offered quietly.

"We will honor her in song," replied Boroc quietly. "She will not be lost."

Ajel turned to see that Gideon and Lairn had joined them. Then he said, "We will leave you this night, Elder."

Boroc lifted his head, his face suddenly full of concern. "You will not rest after such a battle?"

"Our presence here brings the Guardians," replied Ajel. "They are beaten, but they are far from destroyed. If we remain here, they are sure to return and in greater numbers."

Boroc nodded, his face still full of concern. Ajel turned and nodded to Donovan, who returned the nod, then walked away toward the corral. At news of their departure, Gideon said nothing, but inwardly thanked the stars that he had slept most of the day.

Minutes later, Donovan returned with the horses in tow. Gideon knew of few men who could lead five horses at once as this big man did. Gideon had seen a ferocious side of Donovan during the battle, and it had given Gideon a new respect for the Wordhavener. He was clearly not the sort of guy you wanted as an enemy.

As the company mounted their horses, Boroc had several soundenors bring supplies of nuts and dried meat, which they gave to Ajel to distribute to the others. Ajel stored as much as he could in the satchels that flanked his chestnut stallion. The rest he gave to Kair to keep.

Ajel and the others bade the Elders good-bye, again thanking them for their protection and hospitality. As the travelers turned to go, the Elders joined together in a song. Gideon immediately recognized it as the song he had heard when they arrived. It was a song of blessing and hope for deliverance.

The Elders continued to sing as Donovan led the company north into the night. As they rounded the hills that led out of the sounden, Gideon listened as long as he could, comforted by the music, until the song was just another distant hum in the night.

CHAPTER 10

THE PLAIN OF DREAMS

Many today would be amazed to learn that the Council Lords
were once good leaders—that is, that they had good intentions
when they took power after the death of Palor Wordwielder.
They truly wanted to use Sa'lei *for good—as Palor had*
promised but never did. But the power of the Words
turned out to be too much for them. After all, how much
evil can a leader safely embrace in the pursuit of good?
At what point does the evil he has done begin to infect his
thinking so that the good man he once was is slowly lost in a
sea of compromise? The Council Lords lost that battle with
evil centuries ago. And to this day they still do not know it.

—THE KYRINTHAN JOURNALS, CHRONICLES, CHAPTER 7, VERSES 196–199

The travelers rode north into the night. There was no moon, and the stars provided only a dim glow on the path, just enough for each rider to see only the shadowy outlines of those in front of and behind him.

For the first several miles, Donovan frequently doubled back in stealth, clearly expecting that the company would be followed. Once enveloped by the peaceful hills, no stray sound revealed the warrior's presence, as though the night blanketed everything in its dreamy quiet, even the noises of life. But, as mysteriously as Donovan would fade into the darkness, he would reemerge, usually in some unpredicted location, and continue as though he had never left. Occasionally he'd lead the group off in false directions, which they'd follow for awhile, then loop back to the original spot, carefully covering their latter tracks.

Donovan always bore an intensity about him. Gideon had realized that ever since their first encounter in Calmeron. But on this night, the gravity of the man's actions went beyond simple prudence. He was driven. If Gideon hadn't seen Donovan fight so bravely just a few hours before, he would have believed the man was simply frightened to the point of panic.

About two hours into their winding journey, Kair—who had been bringing up the rear of the line—screamed into the night.

"Giver of Life!"

In a blur that took Gideon by surprise, Donovan spun around and raced his horse back to where Kair's desperate voice had called out.

On first glance, she seemed unharmed. But even in the darkness, her face appeared pale and empty as a white wolf that had just lost its mate. She said nothing more, but only pointed back behind them. Far in the distance, over a seemingly endless array of hills, the horizon glowed a deep red hue. The stars above that place had disappeared.

"What is it?" Gideon asked Donovan, who didn't seem to hear him.

"Songwill!" Ajel cried aloud from the darkness. "The Guardians. . . have razed it!"

Slowly, the implications of Ajel's words sunk in. Gideon looked at Lairn, who had been riding next to him. But the boy just slouched over and stared emptily at his hands. Silently, tears formed and fell on his knuckles. He did not wipe them away.

Gideon wasn't at all sure why the young guy was so overcome. He had seemed as nervous and out of place in Songwill as Kair had. Or as Gideon himself had, for that matter. Lairn probably had no great affection for Songwill's people—however noble and beautiful they appeared to be. If anything, he seemed to fear them.

Maybe he is afraid his sounden will be next, Gideon told himself. *Maybe he cries for his parents.*

Beneath these explanations, however, Gideon knew the truth, although he didn't want to admit it. Like Lairn, his own mind saw the faces of hundreds of red-haired children, all running from the flames of death. And like Lairn, the image forced his thoughts back to another child killed in fire—a blond little girl with a sweet, dirty round face.

I didn't know, Gideon reminded himself. *How could I have known what would happen to her? And now Songwill too!*

Lairn's cries were silent. He just let his tears fall, never wiping his eyes or lifting his gaze toward the distant red glow. Timidly, Gideon rode closer to the young man, close enough to see the wetness on his cheeks even in the dark. For a moment, he lifted his hand, thinking to place it on the boy's shoulders. But then the hand fell, and Gideon simply fixed his eyes on the horrible glow in the distance.

Without a word, Donovan turned and moved back toward the group and away from the distant burning city. As Gideon watched, the big man's black gaze seized on him in the darkness. There was a tear tracking down the scar on Donovan's face—but his eyes were all icy hatred. He said nothing; he didn't have to. His look carried the message with perfect clarity: *If I find you had a part in this, I will kill you.*

Gideon looked nervously away. Donovan rode on and rejoined Ajel at the front of the group. Without a word, they continued.

Nothing more was said of Songwill the rest of the night. But Gideon could hear Lairn's occasional sniffle for miles as they rode, as well as Ajel's off in the distance ahead. Kair and Donovan were silent—such was their way, it seemed. But the weight of their sorrow nevertheless continued to bear down on Gideon, compounding the guilt he was already fighting to deny. How could they blame him for this? It wasn't his fault! Not the girl, and not this!

It wasn't his idea to go to Songwill. It wasn't his idea to hold a "gathering." It wasn't even his idea to have stumbled into this godforsaken place in the first place.

Angered by his thoughts and his lingering sense of guilt, Gideon pulled his cloak tight around him, wrapped himself in the night, and thought of turning into it and riding away—far away from these strangers and their silent accusations.

Donovan didn't backtrack anymore after that, nor did he lead the company on any more false trails. But from then on, Ajel held close to Donovan, sometimes arguing, but mostly just talking in hushed tones. Whatever their discussion was about, it went on for hours and seemed to come to no resolution.

As time wore on and the company rounded yet another unseen hill in the cool air of the pitch-black night, Gideon kept finding himself drawn to ride next to Lairn. He told himself it was just curiosity, to see whether Lairn was still crying. But even after he'd determined the young man was no longer weeping, he still remained beside him, glancing toward the boy whenever it wouldn't be noticed.

Lairn was the first person Gideon met in this strange land—except for his sister, of course. The boy had been full of talk and excitement at that initial meeting—but he had said hardly a word to Gideon since that first day. Even at Songwill, he spoke only what was essential to carry out Donovan's instructions.

Even the prospect of riding close to the sojourner seemed to make the boy tense. Despite the cloaking darkness, Gideon could tell that Lairn's youthful frame sat rigidly on his horse, his gaze never wavering from the dark path ahead of him. After several more miles of this tense silence, Gideon finally decided to speak.

"You're afraid of me, aren't you?"

The young man rode on silently, and Gideon began to think Lairn might not answer him. But a moment later, the shadowed figure turned his head toward him slightly.

"Yes, I fear you," Lairn said at last, his voice sorrowful and tired.

"Do you think I'm a murderer?"

"You have not harmed me," Lairn replied simply. "My parents say you are the Kinsman Redeemer. The hope of the Inherited Lands rests on you. That is why I fear you."

Gideon shook his head. "I don't even know what that is, Lairn. I wish. . .I'm just not what you think I am. I'm not. . ."

"By your word, Lord," said Lairn, then quickly prodded his horse and trotted up into the shadows.

"Don't hope in me," Gideon whispered. But Lairn didn't hear.

Just as the purple hues of morning began to color the wispy clouds along the eastern horizon, the travelers finally came to the last of the Scolding Wind Hills. Once past them, the group paused to drink in the lay of the land. In the predawn light, Gideon could just make out vast waves of velvet grasses sprinkled with gold on their tips. The Plain of Dreams, Ajel had called it. But to Gideon, it looked more like a peaceful ocean at sunrise.

To the west, the plain was abruptly cut short by three towering mountains. The land was still shrouded by night, but the tips of the snowcapped peaks already glistened in the light of the sun. Down the slopes, white turned to stony rust and purple and finally to black. Like three towering sentries, they watched over the plains with an ominous vigilance. They were breathtaking.

Donovan and Ajel didn't turn toward the mountains, but continued to push deeper into the plains. As the line of the sun crept down the mountainside, the view of the land became clearer. All the way to the horizon in two directions, grasses rippled like an endless bedsheet in the wind. Every inch of ground was carpeted with mint green grasses tipped with gold. They grew tall as well, reaching well above the knee on Gideon's gray stallion, Orisoun. A light and playful wind danced lightly over the land, making the ground seem fluid, like the rhythmic undulations of waves in a deep sea.

It wasn't until the wind came near that Gideon heard the music. They were lovely, almost mystical, tones emanating from the grasses whenever the wind blew over them. The rhythmic rise and fall of the breezes acted as a director's baton, composing all around them the corporate sound of hundreds of reed instruments, playing in concert.

Lost for the moment in the music of the plains, Gideon didn't notice that the rest of the group had turned northwest, setting their sights on the second of the three mountains. No one seemed to notice that he had fallen behind. It wasn't hard to figure out why. They had ridden almost nonstop through the night. Even in the "Worded Hills," that was enough to wear anybody out—even the ever-watchful Donovan.

Gideon too was exhausted. And the music of the grasslands, however beautiful, only made his weariness more profound. He wanted to collapse on the ground right there and let the grassland music lull him to a long, hard sleep.

But the rest of the group was getting away from him. And for all his weariness, he knew better than to let himself fall asleep alone in these unfamiliar fields.

It took several minutes for Gideon to catch up with the others, in part because the group was traveling faster now than they were out of the hills. Donovan obviously didn't like being out in the open either.

Not too long after the sun broke free from the horizon and spilled its fullness on the endless reach of singing grasses, the company reached the base of the second mountain. After traveling a short distance up the main slope, they came upon an outcropping of stones protruding from the rocky floor. It consisted of a rough semicircle of vertical slabs, dotted in places by gnarled trees and pale grasses. Off to one side there was a small, rainwater pond carved out of the rock. The water was clear.

Donovan and Ajel dismounted, then led the group across the shelf of stone to the pond. There, Donovan directed everyone to drink and to water the horses.

"We will rest here until evening," said Donovan. "We will need to make as much of the journey as we can through Dunerun Hope in the stealth and coolness of the night."

"What's Dunerun Hope?" asked Gideon. "I thought Ajel said this was the Plain of Dreams."

"That is true," said Ajel. "But we will not cross the plains on this journey. Tonight we head northwest into the desert of Dunerun."

"A desert?" asked Gideon in disbelief. "Here?"

"There is no other way to Wordhaven except through the desert," said Ajel. "Do not fear. We have made the journey many times."

"I do not 'fear,' " said Gideon, making quote marks with his fingers. "I'm just asking a question."

Ajel smiled wearily at Gideon, then motioned for the rest of the group to gather around. Then he spoke to them all, although his eyes rested most often on the sojourner.

"Donovan has indicated that, for a time now, we are safe from the Guardians' grasp."

"How do you know?" asked Gideon.

Ajel's eyes flashed at Gideon. But Gideon couldn't tell if the eyes held anger or simply an intense curiosity. "That the Guardians destroyed Songwill tells us that they did not find our trail and that none of the soundenors revealed our course. For some time now, the Guardians have believed Wordhaven to rest within these Barrier Mountains. They search to the south."

"How can you know that no one talked?" challenged Gideon.

"Donovan knows much about the Guardians that we do not," Ajel explained. "He assures me that they would not have taken the time to raze the sounden if they knew our course. They are ruthless and cruel. But they are also efficient. They razed the sounden as punishment for the soundenors' silence."

Ajel glanced briefly toward the ground and sighed. Then he continued. "We need rest for the journey ahead. And we shall have it. But we are on the edge of the Plain of Dreams. This is the land of dreaming—dreams of past, present, or future—that prosper or plague the sleep of all living souls.

"To ensure our rest, I will place all of you in a dreamless sleep to spare us the effects of the land. I will awaken you when it is time to depart."

"Uh-uh." Gideon quickly shook his head. "No way. You knocked me out in Songwill against my will. You're not going to do it again."

"I mean only to spare you from dreaming, Gideon Dawning," said Ajel. "It will aid your rest."

"I never remember my dreams," said Gideon dryly. "So, thank you. . .but no."

The two men locked eyes for a time, Ajel's piercing gaze seeming to probe Gideon's soul while Gideon fought to keep the man from seeing his terror at the prospect of sleeping at all with others nearby. He realized his exhaustion would probably soon overcome his will to stay awake. And if he slept, he might dream. It had been a long time since a rage had struck. He could never predict exactly when the episodes would occur. But he could tell when they were close.

And right now, they felt very close indeed.

"By your word, Gideon Dawning," Ajel said at last. "I offer the Word only as a service, not under compulsion."

"Right," said Gideon with a smile and a hint of sarcasm. He plodded over to his horse and grabbed his cloak from its back. Then he found a patch of grass at the farthest edge of the outcropping, spread out the cloak like a blanket, and sat down with his back to the group. Maybe he could stay awake, after all, he thought, staring off into the plains. It was just a matter of will.

Quiet movements continued to rustle behind Gideon's back for a time as various members of the group tended to the horses, checked supplies, and double-checked the trail to be sure it wouldn't be followed. When everything was secure, the rest of the travelers found grassy patches around the rock slabs and lay down. Gideon listened as Ajel spoke the Word to put Kair and Lairn to sleep, then Ajel himself lay down, somewhere near the pond from the sound of it. But there was no sound of Donovan—for all Gideon knew, the big man could be standing right behind him. With a deliberate casualness, he looked over his shoulder to see Donovan sitting on the edge of the farthest rock, scanning the horizon like a sentry guard.

About an hour later, as Gideon involuntarily trailed off into unconsciousness, he absentmindedly wondered whether Donovan ever slept at all.

"God help me! My arms!"

Gideon desperately cried out in the hollow muck-laden chamber, but his words just echoed up the stony walls and into the darkness above. In the near pitch-black of the dungeon pit, Gideon could see only faint indications of other things moving in the chamber. The floor, which was covered in water, rippled occasionally from the sudden movements of slimy creatures that apparently thrived there. It looked and smelled of sewage. The walls were stone, covered with wet growth built up from years of this cool, rancid dampness. The whole room reeked of waste and rotting flesh.

Gideon hung on a wall three feet off the floor. His body was suspended by chains bolted around his wrists that pulled his arms outward toward the corners of the ceiling—if there was one. Gideon couldn't tell. His legs were fastened to the wall, but he could not tell how.

Even in the cool of the chamber, his weakened body dripped from the humidity. His shredded clothes hung like rags from his waist and limbs. They were covered in blood, though he knew somehow it was not his own.

They want me conscious, *he thought.* They won't hurt me to the point that I might pass out. That's gotta be the only reason I'm not dead.

Gideon momentarily pulled at the iron band around his right wrist and immediately screamed at the awful pain that shot up his arm. The bonds were bolted so tightly that they cut into Gideon's flesh. He gritted his teeth in agony as he felt the cold iron rubbing exposed tendons in his wrists. But there was no way he could ease the pressure. His arms and shoulders screamed under the pull of his own weight.

"God, help, I . . . ," he cried again, stopping short because of the pain. He winced as he took in another breath. Even the motion of his lungs dug the iron deeper into his limbs. Exhausted, he hung his head down to his chest and watched sweat slowly drip from his drenched black curls onto the putrid floor. He prayed for unconsciousness.

In the distance, beyond the walls of the dungeon, Gideon heard a sudden clanging, like the sound of great iron doors closing. Moments later, muffled footsteps echoed in the chamber, made from leather boots passing on dry stone. Gideon raised his head and halfheartedly flipped his wet hair away from his eyes to try to see whatever or whoever was coming.

Somewhere in the void of the dungeon, the creaking of a massive iron door echoed through the chamber. Oily ripples sounded all at once all over the room as whatever creatures were there scampered into the safety of the corners.

For a moment all was quiet. Gideon squinted to try to locate the door that had opened to his hellish pit.

"Demoi fleur blassht," a woman's voice echoed through the room. Immediately, a torch came ablaze and floated on its own into the air about the center of the chamber.

Gideon winced, his eyes seared by the sudden brilliance. He blinked repeatedly in an effort to adjust and slowly turned his head back toward the voice.

"Oh, you poor thing," she said sadly. "You poor, poor thing." She shook her head, then sighed. "Well, let me get a look at you."

Carefully, she leaned in and tapped her index finger on her chin, as though Gideon were a piece of meat she was thinking about cooking for supper. "Hmm," she said. "So, you are the great threat." She sounded disappointed. "Well, I just had to come see for myself."

As Gideon's eyes adjusted, he began to make out a face to match the coarse, pinched voice. Standing under the arch of a doorway some thirty feet away was an older woman. Her abundant gray hair was pinned up in a pile on her head—in a way that Gideon supposed must have been the style of the day. She wore a purple gown, possibly velvet or silk, that pulled tight around her thin waist, then flowed to the floor in cascading waves of material. The sleeves of her gown draped almost to the floor as well, causing her to have to bend her arms to keep the fabric off the slimy surface.

Around her neck hung a great red stone, like a ruby, in a gold setting, surrounded by countless diamonds. Her neck plainly showed the wrinkles and sags of age, but her bony face was pulled as tight as the hair on her head. Gideon saw no wrinkles there. Her pencil-thin lips grinned. Her eyes, like black marbles, glistened emptily in the torchlight. If she hadn't been speaking, Gideon would have thought she was dead.

"Balaam has said that you could be the undoing of all we believe in," she said, folding her arms gracefully. "But from my view, you seem little more than a mouse caught in a trap." She chuckled lightly.

"What. . ." Gideon swallowed, trying to hide the pain in his voice. "What do you want?"

She smiled warmly. "You mean, dear boy, why aren't you dead yet? Oh, don't you worry about that, young man. You will be soon enough." She paused, considering him a moment. Then she added pleasantly, "But not with Words. The Words would kill you too quickly, and we need you to talk to us before you. . .well, pass on."

From behind the woman appeared a hulk of a man, his pale brawny arms glistening wetly in the torchlight. He wore black, a uniform similar to the Guardians Gideon had seen, though his had no sleeves. He towered over the woman, but she seemed to barely notice him. Extending her hand, he placed in it a wooden staff, polished so meticulously that it shimmered darkly in the torchlight.

"Young man, you do recognize this, don't you?" asked the woman.

Gideon forced his head up a bit more to get a look at the staff. "No," he said with effort, dropping his head again to his chest.

A fire lit in the woman's black eyes, but her tone remained pleasant. "Oh, come now, there's no reason to lie," she said with a wave of her hand. "It is your staff I hold, of course. The staff that collapsed that horrid chamber and very nearly ended my bondmate's life. My stars! I would just love to know how it works, you know. If you would just tell me that, then I just know I can get you out of this awful room and into a nice hot bath. With dinner to follow. You'd like that, wouldn't you? So tell me. What Word is used to give this its power?"

"I don't know," said Gideon weakly. "I don't know what you're talking about."

She waved her hand dismissively. "As I thought," the woman said. "You need a little coaxing. All right. I will return in a little while. But in the meantime, let me leave you with a little gift."

The woman turned to the pale-skinned man. "Bring the box," she said.

"Yes, Lord Asher-Baal," his deep voice groveled. Immediately he produced a wooden box about two feet square and set it inside the room next to the door. Once it was on the floor, he popped the lid and tossed it aside. Within seconds, large black rats began pouring out of the box and into the rancid mire on the floor.

"They're very hungry," said the woman with a smile. "And very good at smelling out food. When I return, perhaps you will be more willing to talk."

The woman looked up at the torch and opened her mouth to speak, but then stopped short. "No," she said. "I'll leave the light. It would be uncouth not to let you see what's coming."

Abruptly she turned and walked away, her regal gown flowing after her in waves of deep purple. The guard slammed the door and left Gideon alone to watch the black rodents, who were already sniffing their way toward him.

Within minutes, the first few reached the wall upon which Gideon hung *and sniffed the air. They smelled his flesh, but they weren't long enough to reach his feet, and the muck on the floor seemed to hamper their ability to jump.*

For a moment, Gideon breathed a sigh of relief, but then other rats joined the few that had found him, and slowly, almost purposefully, they began to crawl on top of each other, rat upon rat, until they could just reach the tips of Gideon's toes.

The first bites felt like pinpricks, not unbearable really, Gideon thought. But as soon as the first drops of blood hit the water below, the rats seemed to go mad. They clamored viciously over each other, latching their pointed teeth on Gideon's toes, then his feet. Gideon cried out at the pain and cursed the bonds that held him helpless against his attackers. Soon, some of the rats climbed up on his feet and began biting into his legs. The pain was nauseating, and Gideon screamed in horror as he felt small chunks of his flesh being torn away by the rodents' teeth.

"No!" Gideon screamed wildly, pulling at the bonds that tore into his arms. But the bonds wouldn't give, and all he heard in response to his call was his own echo coming back to haunt him.

DREAMS AND VISIONS

"No!" Gideon screamed wildly as he lurched up and began knocking off imaginary rats from his legs and feet. "Get off! Get off!" he screamed and rolled on the ground like a madman.

Donovan leapt from his perch on the rock and was on Gideon in a flash. He wrapped his great arms around him and held him fast on the ground.

"Peace, Gideon Dawning," he spoke softly in his ear. "Peace. It was a dream. You are safe."

Gideon struggled against Donovan's vise grip, fighting to get his hands free so he could stand. "Let go!" he said, his teeth clenched. "Got to get them off! Got to. . ."

At last Donovan's words sunk into Gideon's consciousness, and he stopped struggling and quickly looked around.

"All is well, Gideon Dawning," said Donovan.

"Let me go!" Gideon said harshly. Compliantly, Donovan released him. Gideon sat up on the grass and held his head in his hands, breathing deeply.

For awhile, no one said anything. Donovan returned to his lookout post, and Lairn and Kair still slept, dreamless under the power of Ajel's Word. Ajel himself was awake, standing off to the side next to a rock, watching the whole episode as if he had been expecting it. After giving Gideon a few moments to regain his senses, he walked over, his blue eyes filled with a mixture of intrigue and perhaps compassion.

"Gideon Dawning," he said, touching Gideon's shoulder with his hand. Gideon lifted his head from his hands and looked into Ajel's face. Only a remnant of the terror that had been evident remained.

"It was a dream," he said to Ajel, phrasing it almost as a question.

"Yes, it was a dream," said Ajel. "What did you see?"

Gideon took a deep breath, visibly relieved by Ajel's affirmation that it was indeed a dream. "Rats," he said at last. "Black rats, eating my legs."

Ajel frowned. "Where were you, Gideon Dawning? Did you see?"

"Yeah," Gideon said. "Um. . .I was in a dungeon, I think. The floor was slimy. My arms. . ." Gideon quickly felt his wrists and breathed a sigh of relief when he saw they weren't cut. "My arms were chained to the wall. I was hanging."

"Was there anything else?"

"It was dark," Gideon said, still trying to separate the present from the dream. "Then there was this torch in the air and this woman. Her guard put the box in the chamber."

"A box of rats," Ajel confirmed. Gideon nodded.

"Did you see the woman clearly, Gideon Dawning? Did she have a name?"

"Um. . .yeah," said Gideon, rubbing his eyes. He finally felt his head begin to clear a bit. "The guard called her Lord Asher-Baal."

Ajel stood back and sighed. "Lysteria," he said under his breath. "This is indeed a dark omen."

"Huh?" Gideon looked up at Ajel. He was frowning with his golden eyebrows furrowed—an uncommon expression for his typically calm face. "It was just a dream, right? That's all."

"I wish that were indeed all it was," Ajel responded. "The Plain of Dreams is Worded, just as the Scolding Wind Hills are," he explained, "though no one knows how or why it was done. Here people dream in the richness of full life. Sometimes they dream of their past, sometimes of the present. And sometimes, as in your case, they dream of the future. You did not know the woman, yes?"

Gideon stood up and brushed the grass off his pants. "Just what are you saying, Ajel?" he asked angrily. "Are you trying to tell me that the torture I just dreamed is really going to happen to me?"

"You have dreamed it in the Plains," said Ajel. "It will happen, though I cannot tell when. It is a matter that will need further thought."

"That's crazy." Gideon sighed and shook his head. "Who is this Lord Asher-Baal, anyway?"

"She is one of the Lords of the Council in Phallenar, second in power only to her mate, High Lord Balaam Asher-Baal."

"Great. . .Great!" Gideon nodded sarcastically. "You mean to tell me this witch is in charge of the Guardians? What the. . .?"

Gideon got up and stormed away from Ajel, his hands running

through his hair, inwardly surprised to find it dry. Suddenly, he spun back toward Ajel, who was still watching him. "I know what's going on here," Gideon said, shaking his finger at Ajel. "You're setting me up. You need a 'front man,' don't you—in your rebellion? You need an icon. Some kind of prophesied champion for people to rally around in your fight against the evil Council Lords. Right? That's the one thing you lack. That's the one thing that would give you and your movement *real* legitimacy. And I'm your guy."

"We do not know—" Ajel began, but Gideon ignored him.

"You think I don't know when I'm being manipulated, Ajel? All the talk about some kind of redeemer at Songwill, with me standing right there like a living, breathing fulfillment of prophecy for the masses to behold. And then you bring me here, where I just happen to dream about being martyred by your enemies. That wasn't really a surprise to you, was it? No, of course not. I'm sure you knew exactly what I would dream."

"I do not control your dreams," Ajel interjected coolly.

"How do I know what you can control? You can make people drop dead just by speaking to them. And if what Lairn says is true, you can even bring them back to life! Controlling a man's dreams would seem pretty easy compared to that. No, I'm just a pawn in your personal chess game. You're setting me up. And I don't like it."

"You misunderstand our intentions, sojourner," Ajel began. "We mean only to—"

"I see you and Donovan talking together," Gideon broke in again. "You think I don't know you're talking about me? You think I don't know you set me up to take the blame for Songwill and for. . .all the rest? I don't know exactly what you're trying to accomplish with all this, but it doesn't take a genius to see that sooner or later I'm going to end up dead."

Gideon suddenly realized he had moved closer to Ajel and was pointing his finger directly into the man's face. He quickly lowered his hands and took a deep breath, keeping his eyes fixed on Ajel's. Ajel, by contrast, stood stoically through the whole verbal assault, arms at his sides, face placid.

"We want nothing more than to discover the truth about your presence here," Ajel said in a tone that sounded a bit too controlled.

"Just as you do. We are taking you to Wordhaven so that we may find the answers we seek. And we must pass through the Plain of Dreams to get there. That is the only reason we are here. And, if you will recall, I offered to speak a Word of sleep over you so that you would be spared the effects of the Plains. It was you who refused. I did not force you to say no, did I?"

The tone of Ajel's voice took more of an edge as he spoke. He sounded almost like a scolding parent now. "You must reconcile yourself to the fact that, for good or bad, we are your best hope for safety and deliverance through this difficult time. And we mean to help you."

"How?" Gideon snapped. "How can you help me?"

Just then, Lairn screamed, tearing himself from his resting place near one of the stones, and ran toward the pond with his arms over his head as though trying to shield himself from something falling on him. His face was alive with terror.

"I will," he screamed at the sky. "Forgive me! I will give it!"

"Lairn!" the voice was Donovan's, booming in its authority toward the young man. Instantly Lairn stopped dead in his tracks and looked at the man. "Be at peace," Donovan added with a touch more softness. Without his gaze ever leaving the Wordhavener, Lairn slowly lowered his arms and stood up straight.

Ajel walked over to Lairn and placed a hand over his heart. "All is well, boy," Ajel said calmly. "What has startled you so?"

"A dream, Ajel," said the still panicked young man. "A message."

"You dreamed?" asked Ajel, visibly startled by the possibility. "While under the Word?" He turned to Donovan. "How can this be?"

"No, not a dream," Lairn said, his voice still raspy from screaming. "It was not about me, not my past or future. It was about him." Lairn pointed toward Gideon, who now stepped closer to listen.

"Perhaps you should begin at the beginning, Lairn conCimron," said Ajel.

Lairn nodded. "I was on an island in a great sea," he said. "And a man appeared before me. A man who shined like glowood, only far more terrible. He told me to give it back to him. That was all he said. Then fire began to fall from the sky like lightning in a storm." His eyes opened wide as he recalled the images. "Then I heard Donovan call my name."

"What are you to give back to the sojourner, Lairn?" Ajel asked.

"The staff," Lairn said sadly. "The staff of wood unlike any we know in the Inherited Lands. The staff he held when my sister died."

Gideon's mind lurched into remembrance. The almond tree in the mountains! The walking stick. The earthquake. With all that had happened after he had awakened in Cimron's house, he'd totally forgotten about the almond wood staff.

Slowly, he walked over to Lairn, who stepped back at his approach. "Please, forgive me," the younger one said.

"You have my staff?" Gideon asked. Lairn nodded and gestured toward his horse.

"It is here?" asked Ajel. "Then bring it."

Lairn walked away from the group and over to his mount. "My father and I found it next to the sojourner after the battle at Calmeron. It was my father's idea to gild it and present it to him as thanks for saving the sounden. He placed that task in my charge. I worked on it the three days he was recovering. It is a wood I have never encountered before. Nothing like the wood in the Watch."

Lairn unstrapped from his horse the long cloth Gideon had noticed when they first left Calmeron. From under the gray material, Lairn revealed the almond wood staff, now polished to perfection and sealed so beautifully that it seemed encased in crystal.

Lairn carried it back to Gideon and held it out for him to see.

"Why have you kept this from us, Lairn?" asked Ajel.

Lairn looked to the ground, avoiding Ajel's piercing blue eyes. "At first I intended to return the staff," he said. "But the sojourner didn't seem to be aware of its absence." He paused. "And I grew fond of it—as a remembrance of my sister in the land."

Lairn slowly looked up into Gideon's now guilt-ridden blue eyes. "Forgive me, Lord Gideon," he said and extended the staff toward him.

"Don't call me Lord." Gideon took the staff and abruptly turned and walked toward his cloak on the grass.

"Ajel," said Donovan, squinting at the sun in the west. "It is time."

Ajel nodded and walked over to Kair, who had slept peacefully through the whole experience. Ajel knelt down and whispered in her ear. Immediately she began to stir, opening her eyes and returning Ajel's smile of greeting.

At Donovan's direction, everyone gathered their things and prepared the mounts for the night's journey through the Dunerun Hope. Gideon watched everyone warily as he gathered his things and mounted his horse. He wasn't sure how they would treat him now, because of the dreams and the anger he'd thrown at Ajel. But they all seemed to carry on as if nothing out of the ordinary had happened. Only Lairn acted somewhat differently—he kept his face down and rarely looked anyone in the eye when he spoke.

When everyone was ready, Donovan led the company out of the outcropping and to the northwest. The late afternoon sun beat down on the Plains. Once out of the relative protection of the outcropping, Gideon could immediately tell the sun did not show the same kindness here that it had in the Hills.

The mountains that towered next to them were cut with deep angular shadows by the sun, which gave them an ominous severity that had not been there in the morning when they arrived. Within minutes, the crew began wiping their brows of perspiration from the heat and turning their faces toward the wind as it blew crisscross over the musical Plains.

Like before, no one spoke much as they rode, and that suited Gideon just fine. He preferred to ride on as though none of these people existed—at least for now. His lingering anger had now become mixed with confusion at the day's events. And more than a little fear. The last thing he wanted to do was talk.

A few hours later, as they cleared the last of the mountains and the last rays of the sun were falling below the horizon, Gideon saw it. A vast gray wall of churning dust sprawling out before them to the north as far as he could see. Here and there, in the brief seconds when the wind broke, he could just make out huge dune shapes shrouded in the fury. It was the desert of Dunerun Hope. And they were headed straight for it.

If the Worded Hills were heaven, he thought, *then this must be hell.*

CHAPTER 12

PALOR'S FINGER

*After his decisive defeat at Songwill, Palor Wordwielder
abandoned his army in disgust and headed northwest toward
the Heaven Range. It is not clear why he chose this course in
particular or where he was intending to go, but we do know he
created the Dunerun Hope to prevent anyone from following
him. He got only as far as the Delving Ocean, where it seems his
own inner demons finally overcame his arrogance and lust to
rule. For there upon the shores that now bear his name, legend
tells us he summoned a dragon to come and devour him.*

—THE KYRINTHAN JOURNALS, CHRONICLES, CHAPTER 5, VERSES 356–360

The grasses of the Plains faded from the ground, soon to be replaced by endless stretches of white gypsum sand. The winds grew stronger the closer they got to the storm; and as they reached the first major dune—a mass of white towering almost a hundred feet above them—they donned their cloaks, hoods and all, and plodded into the white wall of sand.

For the next several hours of the evening and into the night, they rode on slowly, weaving their way around dune after dune. Gideon had no idea how Donovan could possibly know where they were going—there was almost no visibility, and the dunes acted like a maze to confuse even the most adept. But Donovan plodded on with conviction, seemingly drawn by some unknown homing beacon toward their destination, wherever that was.

Nobody talked now, not even when Donovan gestured for everyone to dismount and lead his or her horse on foot. Really, nobody could talk, even if they wanted to. The winds blew so fiercely that opening a mouth meant filling it with grit. Even with the hood pulled tight around his face, Gideon still had to frequently clear the tiny white granules out of his eyes and nose. Ajel walked with his mount only a few paces ahead, but still he faded in and out of view depending on how the wind blew.

If there was any relief, it came a few hours after sunset, when the force of the sun no longer bore down on the sands and the ground had some time to cool. No wonder Ajel had wanted to travel at night. Dunerun was sure to be completely unsurvivable in the full light of day.

Early in the morning hours, while it was still quite dark, Donovan reached a break in the storm. Once the blowing sand began to die away, Gideon could see that they had come out upon a body of water. An oasis, perhaps. But the lake was too large, and there were no trees. Because of the moonless night, Gideon couldn't tell much about where they were. And really, he didn't care. He was just glad to be out of the blasted wind.

Donovan led the rest down to the shore's edge. Gideon hurriedly knelt at the shore to test the water's freshness.

"Do not drink the water, Gideon Dawning," warned Donovan. "It is the salt-laden water of the Delving Ocean. We stand at the edge of an arm of the ocean called Palor's Finger. We must restore the mounts with the reserves we carried from the Plains."

Gideon nodded mechanically and wiped his wet hands on his sandy clothes. Then he turned and walked toward Donovan, drawing his horse behind him.

After watering the horses and feeding themselves on dried meat and nuts, the company shook the sand out of their cloaks, spread out along the shore, and lay down to sleep.

Gideon, of course, had no intention of sleeping, despite his overwhelming exhaustion. After the incident in the Plains, he wondered if he'd ever sleep again. The day's travel hadn't afforded him much of a chance to think about the dream he'd had or whether what Ajel said about it was actually true. But in the last few days, he'd felt his control slipping steadily away—like a capped volcano, the pressures within him had forced new fissures, new cracks in his stony armor. It was hardly a new sensation, but it always provoked his hidden fears—and heightened the terror that, this time, the rage might lead him to permanent insanity.

He plodded wearily to the edge of the shore, away from the others, and stretched out his cloak on the sand. Lying on his side with his back to the group, he tried to content himself with the notion that the sound of the waters would calm his nerves. At least he wouldn't hear the others as they slept.

He listened to the waters for what seemed like hours and fantasized about sailing away to a deserted island where he could live in peace.

━━━━━

Just before dawn, Gideon bolted upright. Something had startled him, but he didn't know what. Slowly, he looked out across the stillness of Palor's Finger. The water was calm, placid in the stillness of the predawn. The only sound was the endless howling of the wind in the dunes behind him. He glanced around at the others. All were sleeping soundly. Even Donovan, whom Gideon had never seen take a rest, lay peacefully out next to the shore, still as stone.

Gideon shook his head and lay back down. *Must have been a fish breaking the surface*, he thought. Forcing his eyes closed, he drew his hands up under his chin and decided to try to lose himself again, this time in daydreams of Sherwood Forest.

Moments later Gideon heard a soft thud on the shore, like the sound of someone throwing a rock in the sand. A light, cool brush of wind tickled his cheeks, followed by a warm, moist, foul-smelling stench. Gideon opened his eyes, and his whole body froze at the sight that stood before him.

Not more than five feet away, looking straight at him with huge owl-like eyes, Gideon saw what he could best describe as a black lion. A massive black lion, with white fangs eerily gleaming in the predawn light. At first, Gideon thought he must be hallucinating; but the creature's hot breath wafting over him quickly dispelled that notion. The glowing owl-eyes stared right at him, almost seeming to dare him to move or call out to the others.

The creature had a mane, like a lion's, except it was jet black. Its paws were as big as Gideon's hands. He guessed that it stood about five feet high at the shoulder.

For a moment, the creature broke its gaze on Gideon and shifted its great body to the side a bit to look at the rest of the travelers. As it turned, Gideon's eyes widened even more. The creature had wings! Huge black-feathered pinions, like the wings of a raven, clung to the beast's sides as if they were a second skin. Gideon wouldn't have even seen them at all except that they extended far beyond the length of its body.

He froze in terror as the beast surveyed the group. Then, without warning, it turned back to Gideon and let out a roar like nothing he'd ever heard before—similar to the screech of an owl, only deeper and more haunting. It leapt at Gideon, its glowing eyes a blur in the night. Gideon rolled out of the path of the charge, but not before catching the rake of the beast's claw on his left shoulder. He screamed from the pain and fell to the side, landing next to the shore.

"Juron!" yelled Donovan, jumping to his feet and brandishing his sword in one fluid motion.

The juron saw the warrior flash his weapon in the air and turned to face the new challenger. "Everyone, behind me!" Donovan yelled as he stepped toward the beast to draw its attention. Ajel and Lairn stood behind Donovan as he moved past them. Kair ran to Gideon and pulled his good arm around her shoulders and carried him away from the shore toward the dunes.

The horses, which had strangely been unaware of the juron's presence, panicked at their first recognition of the beast and took off in a straight run for the dunes. Only Donovan's mount remained, its front hooves raised high in the air, whinnying its fear and challenge to the black creature.

The juron, meanwhile, didn't seem to notice any of this. It was entranced by the gleaming sword, which Donovan kept flashing to draw its attention. The creature didn't move but let out another eerie screech in challenge to Donovan's blade.

Just then, Kair pointed toward the dunes. "Look!"

"Quickly, get down!" Ajel ordered, and they all dropped to the ground. Seconds later a warm burst of air pounded down on the huddled group, along with a roar like that of the beast that stood before them.

Gideon glanced up. In the dim light of dawn, he saw the majestic forms of two more juron; their wings spread like eagles, soaring side by side out over the water. In the air, it became apparent to Gideon that in place of tails, these creatures had a fanlike spread of feathers, black like their wings.

The juron that still stood before them bared its awesome teeth at Donovan and snarled a low gravelly growl. Donovan took another step toward the beast, flashing his sword in the predawn light like it was a toy in his hands.

"More will come," Ajel said sternly. "We cannot fight them all. We must seek shelter in the dunes."

"They will follow," said Donovan, his steely black eyes fixed on the juron.

"No. They will not find us."

Just then the juron launched into the air and made an arc heading straight for Donovan. Donovan followed the creature with his sword and braced himself for the impact. At the last second, Donovan spun, moving just slightly out of the way of the beast, and flailed his sword upward into the creature's chest. Viciously, its claws ripped at the warrior as it hit the ground, tearing into Donovan's hand before he could pull himself free. The sword remained lodged in the beast's chest, though it had not killed it.

The juron landed on its back and rolled with amazing grace back to its feet. The hilt of the sword dragged roughly along the ground beneath it, but the juron didn't seem to notice.

Suddenly, the two airborne juron swooped past again, this time catching Kair's shoulder as they passed. They dragged her for several feet before she managed to rip her clothing from their claws. She fell in a heap well behind the injured juron. Within an instant, the injured creature turned on its new prey and stepped menacingly toward her.

With equally amazing quickness, Kair placed her hand over her wound and spoke aloud. . .something Gideon couldn't make out. Then she extended her hand toward the beast and spoke to it with a calmness that denied the terror in her eyes.

"*Jeo di'*."

The juron began to stumble, its head drooping to the ground as though it had been drugged. Within seconds, it had fallen on its side, dead asleep.

Suddenly, the juron in the sky were joined by five more, flying in from over the ocean. They joined the other two and began to form a circle in the air over the company, flying successively lower and lower with each rotation.

"They're surrounding us!" Ajel yelled. "We must hurry."

Donovan ran over to Kair and helped her back to the group, but not before retrieving his sword from the juron's chest. The juron stirred momentarily, but then fell quickly back into its dreamless slumber.

Ajel ran toward the dunes with phenomenal speed, and the others followed. Gideon was naturally quite fast, but it was all he could do to keep sight of the golden-haired man.

Seeing their prey moving out of reach, the juron quickly flew to the ground and began to chase after the travelers. Thankfully, they seemed incapable of flying in the winds of the Dunerun.

Ajel rounded a dune and waved the others after him. Momentarily hidden from the juron's sight, Ajel huddled them all together and held his hands up toward the sky.

"*Jeo 'haaven!*" he yelled.

Nothing happened.

Immediately, the juron rounded the dune and faced the company. Gideon began to cry out, but Donovan slapped his hand over Gideon's mouth.

For a moment the juron stood still in the wind, looking straight ahead. But then, one by one, they began to move stealthily off in different directions, sniffing the air and scanning the dunes with squinting, glowing eyes.

Everyone sat still for several minutes, avoiding even wiping from their mouths the buildup of grit that gathered in the creases of their lips.

Finally Donovan rose and plodded off into the dunes. Minutes later he returned from another direction but didn't look directly at anyone.

"It is safe," he called. "The juron have gone in the first light of the morning sun."

Immediately Ajel stood up, and Donovan looked at him as though he had just noticed his presence.

"Quickly!" Ajel yelled in the wind. "We must find the mounts."

Donovan directed Gideon and Lairn to return to the shore and hold Donovan's stallion while he and the others retrieved the four missing mounts. Horses didn't like the Dunerun any more than humans did. They wouldn't go far into the perpetual desert storm.

By the time Gideon and Lairn had shaken all the grit and sand from their clothing, the three Wordhaveners returned, leading three horses in tow.

"Where is the other?" Lairn asked.

"Kair's mount has been lost," said Donovan. "Ravaged by the

juron. She must share your mount for the journey ahead."

Lairn nodded numbly in response. Ajel took a step toward the sojourner.

"Gideon Dawning, you are injured," said Ajel with surprising compassion.

Gideon resented Ajel's concern. It made him feel guilty, especially after all Gideon had said to him in the Plains.

"It's just a scratch," Gideon lied. The juron's claw had torn into Gideon's shoulder. But it hadn't bled much, and there wasn't much pain. In fact, his whole left shoulder and arm felt a bit numb.

"*Jeo'rophe*," Ajel said quietly, almost under his breath. Instantly, Gideon felt a warmth spread across his shoulder and down his arm. It tingled on his skin and gave him goose bumps. Gideon pulled back the ripped section of his poncho just in time to see the gashes, one extremely deep, close by themselves, leaving nothing at all behind except smooth skin. Gideon felt no pain at all, just the warm tingling sensation. He watched this miracle as though it were happening to someone else or as he might watch the special effects in a movie. His brain just couldn't accept what he saw.

Nevertheless, the wound was gone. He gingerly rotated his arm to test what his eyes told him. His arm had never felt better. "Thanks," said Gideon to Ajel, his voice a little tentative. But Ajel didn't seem to hear him.

"We must leave now," said Ajel. "The juron were sent by the Guardians to find us. Soon the Guardians will search for us here."

"What do you mean 'sent by the Guardians'?" asked Gideon.

"Juron are mountain creatures," explained Ajel. "They would never venture near the dunes unless forced by power of Word. The Guardians already know we are here now, not in the Barrier Mountains. They will follow quickly."

"Their Words can do that?" asked Gideon.

"Yes. They can do many things." Ajel mounted his horse. "Come, we must reach Sacred Heart before the sun sets."

At Ajel's word, the rest of the company donned their cloaks, mounted their horses, and plowed after Ajel and Donovan into the perpetual winds of the Dunerun Hope.

The morning was young, but the sky was already obscured by the wall of sand that constantly pricked the riders' skin. Despite the cover of the storm, Gideon couldn't help stealing an occasional glance into the dull sky—watching.

CHAPTER 13

DUNERUN HOPE

*The Dunerun Hope isn't a real desert in any common sense of
the term, though that is how we think of it now. It is, in truth,
a massive deathstorm, created by the corrupted Word of Palor
Wordwielder and established in what was at that time a beautiful region within the Plain of Dreams. It only became a desert
over time as the deathstorm slaughtered everything within its
borders. Palor was, of course, thought to be mad by the time he
called the deathstorm into existence. But I have often wondered
if he created the storm not out of insane paranoia, but as a final
attempt at penance or self-redemption. Oh, the storm is a horror
to be sure. But I am quite certain that Wordhaven would have
been discovered and destroyed by the Council Lords years ago if
it had not been for the presence of that "horror" blocking the way.*

—THE KYRINTHAN JOURNALS, MUSINGS, CHAPTER 4, VERSES 34–40

Gideon was right. This was hell.

Donovan led on, plowing through the endless sandstorm of the
dunes, his apparent sixth sense moving the group ever closer to the destination, or so Gideon chose to believe. He watched Donovan occasionally, in the brief moments when the blowing sand allowed it, and
marveled as the dark figure plodded slowly and stoically forward, his face
lost in the folds of his hood. He never looked to the side, never checked
the position of the sun. Gideon thought he might as well have been riding with his eyes closed. There was, in fact, no way to tell he wasn't.

Time passed with excruciating slowness in this anguished landscape. Gideon knew it had been several hours since they left the shores
of Palor's Finger—only because they had stopped twice since then to
eat and countless other times to ration out one or two swallows of the

precious water they carried. Outside of those benchmark events, time grew vague—just an abstract concept that was too weak to impose itself on this defiant land.

The blowing sand continually stabbed Gideon's eyes like pinpricks. He felt the sand stings even through his cloak after awhile—or at least he imagined he could. No matter which way he shifted, the wind cut at him. The sand whipped around the folds of his hood, blasting his already swollen face, wearing his skin away one layer at a time.

Gideon had always considered himself to be pretty tough physically, but he honestly didn't know how long he could endure this sort of abuse. He'd already lived through one full night of the storm, and that had been enough to press him uncomfortably close to madness. Now, after many hours in the full sun of this second day, the sense of panic within him was getting harder to ignore.

It began with simple irritation, more or less—so much wind and grit and sweat all combined until it crusted around his eyes and made his lips sore and blistered. Then that irritation swelled and blistered through the hours of his thoughts until it finally erupted into what was now a continual urge to scream. The sand swarmed him and stung his flesh like bees. All he could do, all he tried to do, was *not* scream and keep Orisoun plodding forward—one step, then another, and another. All the while all he wanted to do was turn the horse around and gallop screaming back to the shore.

Back to the juron. Being killed by the juron would have been a lovely way to die, he realized now. Kind of glorious in a way. Daring Man Falls While Battling Killer Bird Thing. Much better than being pricked to death by a sandblaster.

For all practical purposes, time was dead. Gideon remembered exactly when it had died too—a fact that he considered paradoxical, though he couldn't think clearly enough to say why. It was about an hour after their last food break, when the sun was still high in the sky. Gideon remembered that he ate some of Mara's special bread and that it seemed to have no effect on him at all. And so he just grabbed Orisoun's reins and started plodding on through the storm, right behind Donovan. For awhile he knew he had been walking toward something, from here to there. But then it struck him rather suddenly, this notion that he wasn't really walking toward anything at all. He was just walking, without actually moving anywhere in particular. The sun continued to move, of course; he felt its heat shift on his shoulders, but it no longer gave any sense of the passage of time. The sun was just in one place and then quite suddenly appeared in another—as though Gideon had turned around and walked the other way on a whim. Who knows? Maybe he had. What did it matter? The storm was everywhere. The storm was all that there was.

It wasn't long after this realization that Gideon went blind. Or his eyes had swollen shut. He wasn't sure which and honestly didn't give it much thought. His hand still held the mane of his horse, who kept walking long after Gideon stopped leading him. So he didn't really need to see anyway. The horse still had eyes, he presumed. And, having no other apparent option, he was content to let Orisoun lead the way.

What had been a journey became an endless ordeal now—mindlessly walking, no vision, no hearing beyond the unrelenting howl of wind, no strength left in his body, and no purpose that he could remember.

There's no point to me, Gideon thought.

This realization seemed quite profound to Gideon, and he thought about it for some time. He wondered why he'd never considered it before, but then just as quickly realized he had thought about it all the time, actually, back home. Just about every day, in fact. He just never acknowledged the fact consciously before now, for reasons he could only guess at and didn't care to anyway.

"Why am I doing this?" Gideon heard himself ask aloud. But his words sounded garbled, and he wondered whose voice he was using. His mouth immediately filled with sand, but he was beyond caring.

The horse stumbled slightly in the sand and brushed against Gideon's shoulder. His coat was wet and smelled like horse. *I'm riding out of here,* Gideon thought. *This is meaningless. Absolutely meaningless.*

He scrambled to climb up on his horse, like a man trying to climb out of a pit. "Orisoun! Orisoun!" He couldn't hear himself scream above the wind. Why was he screaming out Orisoun's name? Orisoun shook his great neck, and Gideon tumbled backward onto the sand. Immediately he shot up and grabbed the horse's mane again. *Crazy horse,* he thought.

Some time later Gideon looked up with his blind eyes toward the heat of the sun. "I hate you," he said, but the words sounded to him like a weak groan. "What of it? I hate me too," he added and looked down toward the ground he could not see.

Maybe he'd just never thought about it openly until now. Nobody wants to admit that life is meaningless, after all. We all want to believe we matter, that what we do matters, that there's a purpose for all of it. But Gideon was ready to face the truth. He was never strong or honorable. All he had was tenacity and the will to survive. At one time he thought maybe that would be enough. That it was reason enough to. . .do what? He couldn't remember. It was a stupid line of reasoning anyway.

For a long time now his face and hands had grown numb. His feet lost their feeling too. They plodded through the sand awkwardly, like wooden stumps, barely able to hold him in balance. The flesh around his eyes and lips had chapped and swollen with pus. His throat was a dry and gritty fire. His tongue stuck to the roof of his mouth and had begun to swell. His dehydrated hands wouldn't work right anymore. He could barely force them to cling to Orisoun's mane under the folds of his cloak.

Gradually, despite all this pain, a surreal peace welled up within him. The sounds of the storm faded until in time they were no more frightful than the buzz of hummingbirds. Even the pelting grains became transformed, and it wasn't long before Gideon imagined the lashing of the sand was more like the gentle dance of spring rain on his cheeks. Gideon opened his eyes and looked around. The gritty blast bored into his pupils, but he didn't seem to mind. He saw nothing. And he thought it was beautiful.

There was no reason to go on now. He saw the truth at last. And, having found the courage to see it, he realized he could finally let go. He could finally stop fighting and give up.

Using his last reserves of strength, Gideon pulled back on the horse's mane. Obediently, Orisoun stopped, leaning into the wind to maintain his balance.

How odd, he thought. Images of Sherwood Forest passed before him. He'd just been pretending, the whole time. Just like everybody else. Pretending it all mattered, because he was too scared to believe the truth.

Death came walking through the trees, looking at him. It was the first truly welcome face Gideon had seen since he was a boy.

Then, without any warning at all, someone grabbed Orisoun's

reins and yanked the horse forward once more.

"No!" Gideon tried to scream, but the sound came out as less than a grunt. *I'm ready*, Gideon cried out in his mind. *I want the fighting to end. . . .*

The wind abruptly stopped, and the sand gave way to azure sky. Suddenly able to hear the labored wheezing of his cluttered lungs, Gideon stopped breathing just long enough to look out through his matted, swollen eyes. He saw blue and green and gray, all muted and mystical and cool.

I'm free, he grinned, thinking himself dead. And he promptly lay down and went to sleep.

———

At first his eyes wouldn't open. But he could hear the roar of the river current, exploding into his senses suddenly like a train emerging from a tunnel. In his mind, he tasted the cool, crystal waters and frowned. His throat burned. But it shouldn't. He shouldn't be thirsty. Dead people didn't get thirsty. Did they?

Gideon shook his head gingerly. His throat was on fire from thirst. Straining, he tried to force his eyes to open.

"Let them rest closed a moment," Ajel said. His voice was very close. "Open your mouth."

Slowly, Gideon found the muscles that worked his jaw and after some twitching managed to part his lips slightly. More senses awakened as he felt icy cold liquid trickle over his lips past his tongue, cooling the fire in his throat.

"The Word of healing can repair what is injured, but it cannot replace what is lost," Ajel explained. "The Hope stole away your life waters. You must try to swallow when you are able."

Gently, Ajel poured more water into Gideon's mouth, then lifted his head slightly. Gideon swallowed roughly, moaning from the effort, then let his head rest back on Ajel's chest.

"Whhh–Whher. . . ," Gideon rasped.

"Do not try to speak, Gideon Dawning," Ajel said, then held the water to his lips once more. Gideon received it and swallowed more easily this time.

"We have not moved far from where you collapsed," Ajel explained.

"We are only on the banks of the Narrows, at the base of the mountains of Heaven Range. Here, take more water."

Gideon obliged, again swallowing easier than before. Ajel laid his hand over Gideon's heart. "*Jeo'rophe*," he whispered.

Strength streamed into Gideon's limbs like rain down a desert wadi. His murky thoughts cleared a little. And he found he could open his eyes.

"Slowly, slowly," admonished Ajel. "The water is a help, but you are still weak. Here, take more."

Gideon slowly opened his eyes to see Ajel's face looking down on him. The Wordhavener was cradling him in his arms like a baby, holding a cup made of leaves to his mouth. Gideon would've sat up instantly, if he could, to get away from Ajel's embrace, but his body was not yet willing to move. It bothered him to be held like this, like a helpless child. But he could do nothing about it; and so, reluctantly, he took the water Ajel offered, then rested his head back against his chest.

"There is no sign of the Guardians," Donovan's voice boomed from somewhere beyond Gideon's limited range of vision. He didn't even sound tired. "But I did not venture beyond the mouth of the trail we shall take into the range. We could be watched from the slopes. We cannot stay here."

"We cannot move on," Ajel corrected. "You know we must remain until our fluids are replenished, as always."

Donovan lowered his eyes onto Gideon. "We are staying longer than is usual."

"Patience, kinsman," said Ajel placidly. "The Dunerun Hope is never such an easy trek, especially the first time."

"He was not properly prepared," Donovan said flatly.

"No," Ajel frowned. "In that you speak truly, as always. If only there had been more time in Songwill. But it is enough," he added, lifting Gideon's head to help him take another drink. "He is alive. The Giver knows the paths he weaves for us. And he is good."

Donovan gave a curt nod and walked away, but Ajel stayed fixed on Gideon's soiled face, searching every feature as though in them he saw hints of mysteries he could not yet unravel and signs of hidden pains his Words could not yet touch.

"There are injuries in your soul that even you no longer see, sojourner," Ajel said aloud.

Gideon, who had slipped again into a healing slumber, stirred rest-
lessly. "What?" he asked raspily. "What did you say?"

"I do not see how you could live in such a way," Ajel continued.
"But I have healed you enough times now to know they are there."
Gideon opened his eyes suddenly and glared up at the golden-haired
man. "Here." Ajel held the leafy cup to his lips. "Drink."

It was nearly two hours before Gideon was able to travel again. It
would have easily been more like two days, if not for Ajel's Words,
which added healing to the fluids Gideon drank.

Nevertheless, Donovan's irritation at the delay was clear. Gideon
had learned to read the man much better in the last several days. An
untrained observer would've thought Donovan to be a model of stoic
acceptance in their present circumstance. Hour to hour, he stood
placidly among a row of trees on the crest of a small ridge east of the
river. Though his eyes constantly swept the horizon, his body rarely
moved. But, about twice an hour, he would turn his massive shoulders
just slightly to the right, just enough to allow him a straight glance at
Gideon. It wasn't easy to notice, but Gideon had learned that for all his
bulk, Donovan was a man of subtle expression. Hard to read, but not
so impossible as he first thought.

After Gideon had washed the grit off his body and shaken out his
clothes, Ajel barely had to glance his way before Donovan came running back to the river. Kair and Lairn had already prepared the horses
after their rest, but Donovan checked them anyway, then mounted his
black stallion, impatiently waiting for the others to follow.

Gideon took the reins of Orisoun and patted him gently on the
neck. This horse had been the only thing that kept him from going
completely insane in the desert. He felt a new bond with the beast, a
faint sense that, for the first time, perhaps he was not alone in this
strange and unfamiliar land.

The land, or at least this particular stretch of it, was stunning.
Before him spread an expanse of mountains that stood in proud defiance to the sky all the way to the northern horizon. The snowcapped,
noble peaks looked similar to the mountains on the edge of the Plains
of Dawn, only larger and much richer in the colors of life.

There were no foothills. Knife-edged slopes shot up out of the flatlands as though they'd been set there by God as an afterthought, yet they added an astonishing beauty to the landscape that the Plains could not create alone. The whole scene conjured images in Gideon's head of crowns and kings and mystical kingdoms.

Along the base of the mountains, like a natural border between two worlds, ran a beautiful, clear river. Its waters were deep blue like the sky, and it was speckled all along its easy course by the cotton white rumblings of rapids.

In most places the river looked impassable. Its waters were deep and furious as they cut around the polished boulders that jutted out of the current. But Donovan quickly found a wider section of the river— hidden by lines of tall aspen trees—where there were no rapids and the water flowed smooth and cool.

Donovan crossed first. The blue current came high on the horse's legs at the deepest point, but the flow was slow enough so that the animal maintained its balance. Gideon frowned. He knew Donovan would allow no time for a swim but had hoped at least to douse his aching body once more in the refreshing waters. At least his feet would be refreshed, he conceded.

Gideon and Ajel crossed after Donovan. As they entered the shallows, Gideon double-checked the straps binding his almond wood staff to his mount. He had tied the staff there after regaining it from Lairn in the Plain of Dreams. The windstorm may have loosened its cords, and he didn't want to risk it falling into the current.

"This river is called the Narrows," Ajel said as they crossed, almost idly. "If it could be followed upstream, it would lead us almost all the way to Wordhaven."

"Why don't we follow it then?"

"The Narrows threads its way through Strivenwood Forest on its way up the Heaven Range. The river is too swift for travel upstream without touching shore. And the shores of Strivenwood are deadly."

The mounts climbed out the other side of the river, their coats slick and dripping from the water. Gideon felt a sudden cool rush of wind on his wet feet and ankles. The air was crisp, and everything around him smelled clean.

"Deadly how?" he asked.

"It is not fully known," Ajel replied. "But anyone who ventures far into the forest never returns. For centuries legend held that the forest was the home of ancient Wordhaven, and those who never returned had simply found a better life in the wood. Many of the Council Lords, in fact, still believe this legend, thank the Giver." Ajel made an odd gesture toward the sky. "Some records at Wordhaven suggest that the forest is blanketed with a certain madness. Those who enter lose their way, spending their remaining days trying to find the route to freedom."

"Like a prison," said Gideon.

"No," replied Ajel, "like a labyrinth."

"How did it get that way?" asked Gideon. "Or the desert. How did it get to be that way?"

"You mean the hope?"

"Yeah. Yeah, I guess you call it that," *though I can't imagine why*, he added silently.

Ajel pulled back the reins on his mount, then turned and watched as Kair and Lairn rode up out of the river and approached. "It is not known exactly how all of these things came to be so, Gideon Dawning," Ajel said. "There was a period in our history, a time called the Slaughtering, when the *Sa'lei* tongue was first wielded in battle by King Wordwielder. We know that Palor created the Dunerun Hope, though we do not know exactly how he did it. Horrors like that were commonplace then—more so even than now. The dignity of life was raped away from the living, and the Inherited Lands were. . .injured to the heart. The Slaughtering was almost seven hundred years past, yet many of the scars of those injuries remain. Strivenwood and the Dunerun Hope are examples. I cannot guess what horrors the injuries themselves must have held."

Kair and Lairn reached the place where they waited. Kair's petite frame made her look like a child next to Lairn, though she held the reins, with Lairn's comparatively bulky frame seated awkwardly behind her. She had finally discarded the cloak that had concealed her appearance since Calmeron, revealing her to be a woman of noticeable beauty. Blazing auburn curls danced off her shoulders playfully. Her small, stocky shape conveyed both frailty and strength. She was well proportioned for her frame. She wore the same leather tunic and breeches as all the others—only hers had been noticeably altered to fit her more feminine form.

Gideon would have thought her gorgeous, in fact; except for the hardened, bitter expression that never left her face—an expression that, for whatever reason, Gideon suspected was always directed at him.

This was nothing like Lairn, however. Though his broad, young shoulders dwarfed the red-haired woman, the look of awe that came over him whenever Gideon turned his way made the young man look every bit like a little child dumbfounded by a visit from a hero he'd only read about in comic books.

Even though Gideon didn't understand Kair's hate, it was Lairn's fear-laced admiration that bothered him more. In some ways, Lairn's attitude reminded him of his own when he was a boy—before his father betrayed the family. He had been so guileless then, just as Lairn was now. Gideon's father was his hero, and he loved him easily, with everything he had.

But that love and admiration only made the betrayal more impossible to bear. It was Gideon's naïve trust that had left him powerless, and in the end it was his own love for his father that destroyed him. Gideon didn't want Lairn to know the betrayal he had felt. He knew he could never be whatever Lairn believed he was. He wished the boy hated him now, as Kair did. That, at least, would save him from hurt.

Donovan appeared suddenly out of the vine-covered trees. Gideon hadn't even realized the big man had left. "Follow," he said, then turned back into the wood the same way he came.

Ajel prodded his chestnut stallion forward, followed by Gideon, Kair, and Lairn—their usual order. Within minutes, they were engulfed in a steep, rocky canyon that cut an easy path between the base of two mountains. The canyon's presence surprised Gideon. He didn't notice it was there until they were almost upon it.

In keeping with Donovan's wishes, no one spoke as they rode. Although Gideon had preferred the silence before, now he found himself wanting to talk. Traveling such a narrow trail between two walls of green-shrouded rock made him uncomfortable. There were too many things that could too easily hide in the deep green foliage around them. Still, he admitted, it was far better than the desert.

About three miles into the range, Donovan turned sharply up an obscure trail that appeared to lead straight into a wall of rock. The riders leaned heavily on their horses' manes to maintain balance as the animals struggled up the slope, their nostrils flaring out steamy breaths from the exertion and the thinning air.

The air also became noticeably moister as they climbed. Misty clouds rested among the slopes like blankets strewn on the sides of a cradle. The foliage around the riders changed. Evergreens and aspen groves gave way to an older, dense growth of vines and other jungle-like plants.

Once the path leveled out a bit, Gideon was able to sit up and look around. He filled his lungs with the richly scented mountain air and remembered the solitude he had longed for back in the Rocky Mountains. That all seemed like another lifetime, now that he was here in these mountains, riding with these unusual people. He wondered again if this might still somehow be a dream. In moments like this, he could almost believe it. Almost. But with every experience he'd had since the quake, his awareness of the reality of this place had become irrefutable. It was almost as if someone knew he would find all of this impossible to believe and had set up this odd sequence of events to make certain he was convinced.

Abruptly, the trail opened onto a vast grassy meadow cradled between several steep rocky slopes. The meadow wasn't visible at all from the lower elevations, but at this height it spread out its flower-carpeted beauty wide to the sun.

And in the middle of the meadow, nestled up against a mountain-ous rocky horn jutting out of the grassy floor, was a brilliant white city.

CHAPTER 14

SACRED HEART

In the time before the Fall, there were thousands of Lords living at
Wordhaven and in various places throughout the Inherited Lands.
But for every man or woman who became a Wordhaven Lord,
there were three thousand novitiates who had failed the tests
of the hearted cities. Of every three thousand who failed, one
thousand of them died in the attempt. Even those who physically
survived paid a severe price for the effort, though the nature of
the cost was unique to each person. The truth is that no one has
ever become a Wordhaven Lord without paying a terrible
personal cost. How wondrous it is, then, that so many have tried.

—THE KYRINTHAN JOURNALS, CHRONICLES, CHAPTER 2, VERSES 45–49

"Sacred Heart," Lairn said softly, his face alive with excitement. "The legends are true."

"Yes," responded Ajel from up ahead. "But legends often become laced with fiction where reality doesn't suffice. The city will not be what you expect."

Lairn nodded at Ajel, but his face continued to beam as he gazed across at the sunlit city as though it were a long-lost king returned from the grave.

In truth, it was an impressive sight. Like an alabaster crown on the mountain, the city circled a horn-shaped plateau with clusters of jewel-shaped structures. All were white, but each sparkled differently in the sun—some topaz, some opal, and others ruby and blue sapphire. The city was encircled by a low white wall, split in places by great spiraling archways. These archways were clearly the gates, though there were no doors. For that matter, the wall couldn't have been more than four or five feet high. *Obviously decorative*, Gideon decided. *Or to keep out very short enemies.*

Against the deep green hues of the mountain meadow and forests, the city stood out like a brilliant lighthouse on the edge of a green peaceful ocean.

Ajel pulled back to ride beside Gideon as they crossed the meadow toward the city.

"Sacred Heart was built by the Old Lords thousands of years ago," he began, once again explaining what Gideon never asked. "It is one of only three cities of its kind. The first, Noble Heart, lies between here and Phallenar. The evil king Palor razed the old city as a sign of his power and authority.

"The second, Broken Heart, was built near the coast of the eastern sea. It was lost in the Fall, for it now rests within the boundaries of the Deathland Barrens.

"This place, Sacred Heart, is the third and most powerful of the three cities. It alone remains, though it has been long abandoned."

"Why did the Old Lords build them?"

"They were for testing Initiates who wished to join the Lords of Wordhaven. Men and women whose hearts were set on becoming Lords of the Words had to be proven. Over a period of years, those who survived would progress from Noble Heart, to Broken Heart, and then to here, before finally reaching the title of Lord in Wordhaven."

"Those who survived?" asked Gideon.

Ajel grinned. "In that day, the quest for lordship was not one to be taken lightly. Anyone could seek it who willed. But only those with true, enduring hearts would survive all the way to Wordhaven."

"Huh," said Gideon.

As the riders drew closer to the city, Gideon began to realize why Ajel had warned Lairn that it would not be as he expected.

The city was, of course, deserted, its function having been lost with the passing of the Old Lords. But there was more. Its appearance reminded Gideon of scenes from the Mayan ruins in Mexico. The alabaster stone, proud and solid from a distance, was etched with cracks created by erosion and the prolific growth of vines. The vines writhed around everything and even totally obscured the walkways in many places.

Still, considering how many thousands of years it had been here and the harsh mountain weather, it seemed a miracle that it stood at all.

Donovan led the group to one of the spiraled gates into the city. "Prepare yourself, Gideon Dawning," he called from ahead. "You must pass under the gate."

"What's he talking about?" Gideon asked Ajel.

Ajel rode on in silence for a moment, his brow slightly furrowed. Finally, he said, "It is difficult to explain. But do not be afraid. The gates are not dangerous—except perhaps to your soul."

With that, Ajel prodded his horse forward, trotting toward the gate. Donovan had already passed through. His head was bowed now, his breathing heavy. Gideon stopped and watched as Ajel ran his horse under the archway. Instantly, the golden-haired man broke out in uproarious laughter, releasing the reins of his horse and lifting his arms to the sky. Laughter consumed him, it seemed, so much that he was unaware that his horse was running in circles or that he was very close to falling off.

"These people are clearly nuts," Gideon said under his breath. Tentatively, he prodded his horse slowly forward, approaching the brilliant archway as cautiously as a cat trying to sneak past an angry dog. "So what does that make me?" he added with a sigh.

Kair called out from behind Gideon, "It is better if you do not linger long under the arch, sojourner," she said.

Gideon didn't turn around, but grimaced in a way that he felt looked appropriate for the challenge and urged Orisoun to speed up to a light gallop. The last second before passing through, Gideon couldn't help closing his eyes.

Like an invisible waterfall plummeting from the sky, an immense weight forced Gideon's body flat against Orisoun's neck. Columns of thick water—but not water—held him down, forcing the air from his lungs, deafening his ears to any sound at all.

His vision blurred, and everything slowed down. Where once Gideon had seen Ajel laughing on the other side, now he saw something new—but something he almost recognized.

He is in a dark room where two figures stand in silhouette. One is large, the other much smaller. A muffled cry. It's coming from the smaller one. It is clearer now. A boy—frightened, confused. He would rather die than be in this room. He will die, kill himself, any way he can, just to stop the. . .

146

Gideon screamed. He grabbed his head, which was shaking violently. "No, get out! Get out! No, no, no more! Get out. No, no, no. . ."

Strong hands clasped Gideon's wrists, gently forcing them down. "It is passing, Gideon Dawning," said Ajel. "I am sorry."

Gideon opened his eyes. He was curled up in a ball on the ground, his horse grazing calmly some distance away. He was covered with grass and leaves.

"Let go," Gideon commanded. Ajel complied.

Without looking up, Gideon purposefully stood, then brushed his arms, legs, and tunic while Ajel watched him thoughtfully. Finally, after every small blade of grass was gone, Gideon ran his hand through his black curls and looked up. Ajel's face was, for once, free of expression.

"What the heck was that?" Gideon asked with mocking politeness.

"It is normally not. . .so bitter," offered Ajel. "You are indeed a mystery to us, sojourner."

Gideon clenched his teeth. "Was it a test?" he asked.

"No, not exactly," said Ajel. "It is. . .difficult to explain."

"Try real hard," Gideon hissed.

Ajel paused. "It is, or was, a preparation. A way of perceiving what was to come for those who made it this far, to this city. That is all."

Gideon took a deep breath and looked down at the ground.

"If I may ask, sojourner, your. . .experience troubles me," continued Ajel. "What did you perceive in the gate?"

Gideon's blue eyes glared up at the Wordhavener's own. "Nothing," he said flatly. Then he walked away.

Once everyone had gathered on the other side of the gate, Donovan led the group toward the horn-shaped mountain in the city center.

Suddenly, with a raised hand, Donovan stopped the travelers just outside the great stone's perimeter. With astonishing grace, he silently dismounted, gesturing for the others to do likewise. Calling everyone together, he spoke in a whisper.

"We are not alone in the city," he whispered. "There is another presence here."

"Guardians?" Gideon whispered.

Donovan didn't answer. Like a panther on the hunt, he stalked toward the great horn in the city's center. Ajel followed with equal, if not superior, grace, then gestured for the others to fall in behind.

With a stealth that made Gideon feel like an awkward child, Donovan and Ajel rounded one glistening structure after another, quietly making their way to the far side of the city—toward an area hidden by the great stone horn.

As they rounded the last cluster of buildings along the perimeter of the stone, Donovan pointed skyward. A wispy trail of smoke rose from the far side. Donovan pointed the group toward a diamond-shaped building that sparkled green in the light; a second later he made a silent dash for the spot he'd indicated.

The others followed one at a time until everyone was crouched next to the white diamond walls. As they moved around the building's edge, Gideon noticed a smoothness in the wall he couldn't explain. The sensation was similar to the feel of a wet bar of soap, though it was not damp at all. At one point, Gideon tried to dig his fingernails into the seemingly pliable surface. But when he did, the wall held firm, like steel against his fingers.

Just out of sight of the smoke, Donovan crouched and silently rolled out on his stomach into the tall grassy area that surrounded the building. One by one, the others followed suit, with Gideon rolling last. He'd never done that maneuver before, but managed to carry it out with passable, albeit clumsy, grace.

Once he rolled into the grass, Gideon tentatively lifted his head and stole a peek toward the fire.

A lone man sat quietly on a rock, his back to the group, stoking the flames of a blaze on which he was apparently cooking. He seemed oblivious to their presence, but rather concentrated on his meal as though it were his whole universe.

Not much could be told about the man from the back. He wore a black leather poncho with a white frock beneath it. On his back rested a large bow and a quiver of arrows. His hair was deep auburn and was gathered in the back of his head in a whimsical twisted fashion that looked almost clownish. He wore no hat nor any insignia that Gideon could make out.

Just as Gideon was about to look toward Donovan to see what they were going to do next, the man spoke without turning around.

"Welcome, travelers," he said in a jovial tone. "Come, and be refreshed. I have been expecting you."

CHAPTER 15

REVEL FOUNDLING

With all the attention given to the mysteries surrounding
Gideon Dawning, I now wonder why the Remnant
apparently gave such little thought to other mysteries that
had for years lived in their midst. For here was Revel
Foundling, an orphan child from an unknown land, raised
in the Remnant, but possessing abilities that they could never
teach, nor even begin to fathom. His adopted father, Laudin Sky,
once said that Revel came to the Remnant as a gift from the
wildness. It's curious to me that Laudin never asked why the gift
was given and what its purpose was to be. In retrospect,
I wonder if perhaps it was because he feared the answer.

—The Kyrinthan Journals, Musings, Chapter 4, Verses 6–7

The waning beams of the evening sun cast crisscross silhouettes of pines and aspen across the ground—and the stranger's red hair. He still did not move, despite Donovan's sudden shuffle to his feet and the quick steely sound of a broadsword, now drawn.

Gideon held fast to the ground, counting the seconds in his head, waiting for something to happen—a sword stroke, a dagger, an arrow, a Word—anything. But nothing did. The world had stopped, it seemed, just to watch these two men decide their fates.

Finally, Donovan's sword lowered perhaps an inch, and the black rage in his eyes lessened. He was still furious, that was sure, but the look was softer, as though the threat of immediate danger had somehow fled.

Now the stranger stood and Gideon turned to look at him. He had one hand clasped around the back of his neck. His head was down and his eyes closed. And he was apparently laughing.

"Revel Foundling." Donovan spit his words with a fury that beat the late afternoon air. "Is this the time for levity? I might have killed you!"

"Donovan, you underestimate your own heart," replied the black-cloaked man, chuckling. "You would not have killed me without knowing who I was. Besides, now is especially the time for levity."

"With that, I most certainly do not agree," replied Donovan flatly. "We have been through much these past days to give us cause to lay humor aside."

The man turned to look at Donovan and revealed to Gideon a most profoundly featured man, with a brow like a hawk and golden birdlike eyes that seemed intent on things other men couldn't readily see. His curly, auburn hair was long like Ajel's, though he kept it tied in a fanciful knot at the back of his head. He pursed his lips and furrowed his abundant brow, which only deepened his hawkish appearance. Slowly, he rose and approached Donovan, with his hands extended downward in front of him, the palms out. Just like Mara and Cimron had done, Gideon remembered.

With a cautious deliberateness, the man embraced Donovan.

"Rest easy now, kinsman," he said quietly. "I know much of what has happened to you, and I have no doubt that your heart has been up to the task."

"We have managed," was Donovan's grumbling reply.

Finally assured that the man was no Guardian or other enemy, Gideon stood to take a closer look. By standing, however, he announced his presence to the stranger, who turned to him with the calm abruptness of a raptor's swiveling gaze.

"Is this him, then?" the man asked Donovan, who nodded slightly in response. "Well, well," the man said and walked toward Gideon without shifting his eyes off him at all, not even to watch where he was walking.

Gideon stood frozen as though incapable of movement, though he didn't see any obvious reason why he should feel that way. This guy was not nearly as big as either Donovan or Ajel. He wasn't as big as Gideon, for that matter. But something in those strange gold eyes conveyed a wildness, like he was actually an animal who had only recently taken the form of a man.

Revel came to within two feet of Gideon, then stood and studied him with a freshly furrowed brow. On his forehead he wore a silver headband. From such close quarters, Gideon could easily make out the inscription: *Erit Endum Luvenndar.*

"Are you then the Kinsman Redeemer, my friend?" asked Revel, his gaze unaltered.

Gideon felt his face flush hotly, momentarily squelching his undefined fear of the man. "No," he said quietly, "and I'm not sure I'm your friend either."

Revel's furrowed brow quickly vanished, overrun by an expression that looked most like disappointment, though it was hard for Gideon to tell.

"The journey has been long, brother," Ajel broke in. "The sojourner has endured much, all piled upon learning the ways of a land he does not know. He is new."

Gideon wasn't sure whether Ajel's words were meant as an excuse or an accusation; but upon hearing them, Revel's abundant smile immediately appeared, though his eyes still looked alien in the descending sunlight.

"True," Revel said, his gaze still fixed on Gideon. "The land is proved by its ways. And I am confident your heart shall be proved by yours. One way or the other." As he said this, Revel grasped Gideon's shoulders, as though this might break the tension a bit. But it didn't. Gideon resisted the burning urge to knock his hands away.

Within moments, the last sunbeams of the day disappeared behind the nearby peaks to the west, and the air quite suddenly grew crisp. With the same hawklike deliberateness Gideon had noticed earlier, Revel turned away from him and motioned for the travelers to gather around the fire he had built. Roasting over the brightening blaze were the carcasses of several small game—like squirrels, perhaps, but larger. Whatever they were, the aroma was sweet and invigorating. How many days had it been since Gideon had eaten anything warm or, for that matter, filling?

To one side of the fire, Revel had gathered several fruits that looked something like pineapples, though they had no green crown. As everyone sat, he took each fruit and dug in it a hole with an arrow, then passed it to Ajel, who distributed the fruits to the others. Once each had a fruit, they drank from it together.

It tasted something like banana juice, but not as sweet. It flowed more like syrup than water and seemed to expand in Gideon's stomach. He swallowed it all.

By the time Gideon drained the fruit of its juice, Revel had passed out chunks of the freshly cooked game. Kair had held Gideon's portion on a large green leaf on her lap, apparently unable to get his attention off the fruit long enough to give it to him.

This too Gideon gobbled down furiously. It wasn't until after he tossed the bones into the fire that he realized that the others were each consuming their food with painstaking slowness, savoring each bite as though it might be their last. The entire time their gazes were intent on each other, not the food. It was quite the ritual, Gideon surmised—as though each were a mirror for the others in which great secrets of the soul could be discerned, if only one looked long enough.

Gideon shook his head, then lay back on the grass. He was beyond trying to figure out the oddities of these quirky people. In the beginning, he had tried not to offend them, but now he was almost past caring.

"Surely you have come for a greater purpose than to serve a meal, kinsman," said Donovan at last, wrapping small bones in his leafy plate and setting it in the fire. "Though the meal is welcome refreshment for us."

Revel picked up a stick and poked at the fire. "I am glad the meal pleases you," he said, glancing only briefly at Donovan. His gaze returned to the fire, and he said nothing more. Neither did Donovan, who continued watching the blaze as though the matter was settled.

Gideon sat up and leaned slightly toward Revel, waiting for him to say more. But the hawk-browed man continued to stoke the fire with his stick, his eyes once again intent on something beyond the blaze before him.

"So, why are you here?" Gideon asked at last, wondering if Donovan hadn't asked the question directly enough.

Revel looked up from the fire and confronted Gideon with a reproachful glare. Gideon met his stare, which was no easy feat, and smiled so as to look as innocent as possible. No one else looked up except Ajel, who looked at Gideon in the pitiful way a teacher looks at a student who seems inexplicably determined to fail.

At last, Ajel nodded at Revel, and Revel turned his gaze back to the fire. "I am sent from Wordhaven," he said calmly. "It is Paladin's wish that I guide you back safely."

"The way is known, brother," Ajel said. "And Donovan has guided us well all the way from Calmeron sounden."

"Our vigils have sighted three warcor in different parts of the range," said Revel. "One was sighted not two days from here. Our usual route can no longer hide us safely. I will guide you another way."

"Did the vigils see who leads the warcor?" asked Donovan. "Did they see how they were armed?"

"Borin Slayer leads the warcor farthest to the south," replied Revel. "It is not known who leads the others, though there were no signs of the Council Lords."

"That at least is a relief," said Ajel.

"As for your other question, the Guardian troops themselves were not seen directly," Revel continued. "The warcor are hidden in make-shift shelters and under the cover of the trees, apparently to hide their numbers."

Donovan only sat quietly at Revel's response, but his brow furrowed slightly.

"What is it, Donovan?" Ajel asked.

"Perhaps nothing," he said without changing his expression. "It is unusual to hide a warcor in this manner. I cannot reason why they would do it."

"Who knows what processes lend to their logic," laughed Revel as he poked at the fire. "Like children in the dark, they do not know what dangers they toy with."

"They may be in the dark, brother," said Ajel. "But they are far from children." He paused, catching Revel's eye, then added, "Songwill is destroyed."

Revel stared at Ajel, his smile slowly erased as his eyes narrowed. For an instant, those golden eyes seemed ablaze with rage, then just as quickly faded to sorrow. He shifted his gaze off Ajel's compassionate face and looked directly into the fire as it slowly consumed the dead-wood pine. The smell was pleasant and fresh, like the mountains themselves. But in its light, Revel's face looked horribly menacing.

"We must travel from this place before the light is fully gone," Revel said at last. "Paladin fears its discovery is at hand."

"Travel? Now?" Gideon asked. "Do you realize what we've been through already today? We don't have the strength to travel any farther, even if we wanted to, which, by the way, I don't."

Revel didn't look up.

"I fear Revel speaks true, Gideon Dawning," Ajel said. "At best, we have only an hour of light left to us this day. If a warcor is anywhere near Sacred Heart, we must be sure we are not."

Ajel turned back to Revel. "You have planned a way for us?" Revel nodded. "Then we must be moving soon," he continued. "Lairn and Kair will retrieve the mounts. Donovan, you and the sojourner make certain our passing here is not detected. I will speak with Revel about the way he has chosen for us."

Carefully placing what was left of their meals in the fire, Kair and Lairn rose and quickly disappeared behind the base of the great tower. Ajel took Revel's arm and led him some distance away, where they knelt in the grass and spoke in low tones.

Gideon sat still in the grass, fighting to contain the anger that boiled within him. Like a leaf in a storm, he was being blown by forces he could not control, and he felt increasingly bitter at those he blamed for it. Still, he had to admit, he had nowhere else to go. And Ajel had promised him they could help him return home.

He filled his lungs with the cool mountain air and listened to the crackling noises of the warm fire at his feet. For all the danger and pain he'd endured in this new land, Gideon had to admit it was, nevertheless, quite beautiful. For the first time, he found himself questioning whether "home" was a place he really wanted to go after all.

"Are you well, Gideon Dawning?" asked Donovan, leaning over him like a bear.

"Yeah, fine," Gideon replied and got to his feet. "What am I supposed to do?"

"Come, I will show you." The twosome disappeared around the dark stone in the center of the city.

CHAPTER 16

THE HEAVEN RANGE

As the eldest son of Mara and Cimron, Lairn was destined
to one day follow in his father's footsteps to become the High
Elder of Calmeron sounden. But even such an exalted title
as this was not enough for that ambitious youth. Lairn wanted
to make a difference on a larger scale, far beyond the borders of
Calmeron. So when he heard that Wordhaven was once again
accepting initiates from the soundens, he wasted no time in
telling his parents that he felt called to join their cause.
Like most youth, he was an idealist. He believed that he could
change the world, if only he was passionate enough in his faith
and willing to pay whatever price was required for success. And
it is in this faith that I find the most profound lesson of his life.
For, in the end, he was absolutely right.

—THE KYRINTHAN JOURNALS, CANTICLES, STANZA 23, VERSES 51–54

The way quickly grew steep for the horses, their great nostrils flaring as they strained their way up the slopes. Gideon's gray stallion, which had seemed unstoppable before, seemed to tire more quickly now. The visible snorts of his breath grew so fierce in the cooling air that he began to look something like a dragon, threatening to blaze away the overgrowth of greenery that pulled at them as they climbed.

After a time they came upon a small valley. Green carpet grasses covered the sloping floor, while thick blankets of trees and vines clung to the slopes all around them. The last light from the sun had faded now, and the shadows quickly moved in to claim the landscape, especially here in the valley where they rode. The air thickened slightly as the colder air of night flowed silently in from the west. Gideon shivered and pulled his cloak in more tightly.

Without a sound, Revel dismounted from his horse and waved for the others to do the same. Donovan quietly informed Gideon that they were not stopping but were giving the horses a brief rest while the ground was more level. Soon, he said, they would not be able to ride the horses at all.

Not half an hour later, Donovan stepped to the side and moved calmly past Gideon, pacing up next to Ajel and Revel. Gideon knew at once that something was wrong. His walk had been almost too relaxed, especially for Donovan. Almost instinctively, Gideon began scanning the trees and dark sky for signs of danger approaching.

A few minutes later Donovan returned and slowly resumed his methodical pacing behind Gideon.

"Please stop looking around so suspiciously, Gideon Dawning," Donovan implored quietly. "It is best for now that they do not know we suspect them."

"We are being followed?" asked Gideon without turning around.

"A group is tracking us from the west," Donovan replied. "They have been with us now for more than an hour, but they are maintaining their distance."

"An hour?" whispered Gideon. "Why didn't you say something?"

"I was not certain until now."

"Well, what are we going to do?"

"For now, they are only watching," responded Donovan. "So we shall watch them also, until Revel can find a path down which we can safely disappear."

"What if they're Guardians?" Gideon asked. "Couldn't they just yell down here and kill us all?"

"The Words lose force with distance," said Donovan. "Even if they are Guardians, they can do us little harm from so great a reach. Please now, be quiet. I must listen."

Gideon sighed and tried not to let his increasing anxiety show in his movements. The light was completely lost now, and the valley floor was cloaked in impenetrable shadows. Gideon unknowingly stepped closer to his horse as the group marched on into the darkness ahead.

The silence thickened as they traveled on through the valley. Having lost the ability to see the others clearly, Gideon found the lack of conversation unbearable. Only the mesmerizing crunch of the horses' hooves on the mountain grass seemed to offer any comfort of the others' presence. As much as he tried not to think about it, he couldn't help imagining the Guardians edging silently closer under the canopy of the moonless night, close enough now to speak and be heard, close enough to call out and tear into Gideon's flesh. Again.

Nervously, he reached under his bag and pulled out the almond wood staff. It was the only weapon he had—a fact that he never thought to consider before now. The staff felt well balanced in his hand and solid. It was smooth like glass, but not so slippery, and pleasantly warm from nestling up against the horse's side. Even so, he knew it was a pitifully weak weapon compared to the Words. And the warmth of the wood could not push back the cold that now bit at Gideon's fingers and throat.

Suddenly, almost as though waiting for the full night to fall, Revel and Ajel turned sharply to the right, away from the mysterious trackers. Not quite fifty paces to the east stood a great mass of trees and shrubs, which looked like a black cloud into which anything could disappear. Breathing a quick sigh of relief, Gideon tugged on his mount and followed the others toward the dark haven.

Relax, Gideon, relax, he reminded himself. *Maybe they won't even see us now.*

But they did. From out of the tree-covered hills to the west, black shapes oozed onto the valley floor like shadows stretching across it in a second, darker sunset. Their movements seemed liquid in the night, so much so that at first Gideon could not tell where one dark shape ended and the next began. The mass of them together swirled like black ants swarming toward their prey.

Revel and Ajel spun back toward the approaching force to get a better grasp on what they were up against. For a quick moment, they stood perfectly still next to their mounts, Revel sniffing at the air and Ajel's tall form standing like a stone in the night. Then Ajel stumbled back a step, and Gideon tensed. It was the first time Gideon has seen Ajel react to anything in fear.

"Merciful Giver," Ajel breathed. "It cannot be."

"Riftmen!" Revel yelled a second later, jumping up on his horse. "Quickly, this way!"

Revel reeled his horse around and charged toward the black cloud of trees to the east. Gideon awkwardly yanked himself up onto his horse, sliding the staff under his arm as he pursued his companions toward the hills.

Within seconds they were under the frail cover of the trees, and Revel pulled his horse off to the left toward a small ravine that creased into a large hillside. The rest followed instinctively, as if all individual thought were sacrificed in shared panic. The trees whipped past Gideon in a blur, and he instinctively kept his head down, all the while praying that Orisoun had better vision than he did. Without warning, the group broke out again into open air, and Gideon could see that the ravine they followed led up to nothing but the sloping side of a mountain. Revel slowed the group and danced his horse around the ravine bottom, looking as if for a snake in the rocks and sand.

"Curse the evil one," snapped Revel at the ravine floor. "We must find water. If there were even a stream, we could stand against them."

"There is no water," Ajel offered, almost soothingly. "There must be another way."

"Why water?" Gideon demanded, not willing to be led blindly any longer. "What good is water?"

"Please be silent, Gideon Dawning," said Donovan scoldingly. "We haven't time to explain."

"Why water?" Gideon asked again defiantly.

"The riftmen cannot bear the touch of water," Ajel answered. "Revel seeks a stream to cross to give distance to our cause."

"Who are the riftmen?" Gideon asked.

"No time for that," Revel snapped. "This way."

Revel urged his stallion up the ravine and onto the ever-steepening slope toward the mountain's peak. The horses huffed furiously at the task, but could not manage much speed at all with such uncertain footing. Gideon glanced over his shoulder. The darkness was everywhere, and every tree and rock to their backs seemed to be slithering toward them. Gideon shook his head to block out the confusing images and clung to his staff like a drowning man clings to a passing log.

"Revel, there." The voice was Ajel's, though Gideon could not make out which shape ahead of him had spoken. Gideon looked toward the only clear area ahead of them and could just make out a dark shadow nestled against the slope. It was surrounded by great stone slabs leaning against each other, like a fallen Stonehenge.

"It is a cave?" Revel's voice asked.

"Yes. Perhaps it is enough," responded Ajel. Then a shape ahead of Gideon turned and spoke to the group. "Leave the mounts here," Ajel commanded. "The riftmen will not bother them, and they may serve as a distraction for a time."

Gideon got off his gray stallion, still clinging to his almond wood staff, and glanced at the oozing shadows behind them. Then, with a panicked burst of strength that betrayed his exhaustion, Gideon raced up the hillside toward the dark blur Revel had called a cave. Not thirty paces from the opening, a pair of brawny arms engulfed him and sent him hard against the sloping rocks.

Dazed for only an instant, Gideon quickly struggled to free the arm that held his staff.

"Peace, Lord Gideon," a young voice whispered behind his head.

Gideon turned to see Lairn's fearful face staring back at him. Quietly, Lairn pointed into the night sky. Looking up, Gideon saw the faint traces of a black form, like a winged man, blocking out the stars.

"Dear God," he rasped. "They're demon-spawn!"

"He was upon you, Kinsman Redeemer." Lairn sounded apologetic. "I knew of no other way to divert his cause."

"Thanks," replied Gideon coolly, ignoring the reference to the Kinsman Redeemer.

Shuffling around to get a view of the cave, Gideon sighed mournfully. The opening was already surrounded by black, shimmering figures. A few paces deeper in the cave, Gideon could just make out the frantic forms of Donovan and the others, all of them fighting with Words and swords and arrows to keep the riftmen at bay.

Without warning, Gideon heard a soft crunch in the ground just a few feet away. "Come" was all Lairn said as he heaved Gideon to his feet and ran with him toward a standing of stone jutting out of the mountain near the cave. Gideon barely kept his balance and would have fallen if not for the helpful shifting of his staff and Lairn's strong arm on his. On his back, Gideon could feel a thick chill creeping upon him, like the slimy muck of cold oil spilled down his spine.

The pair reached the outcropping just in time for Lairn to throw Gideon up against the rocks behind him and turn to face the shadows that chased them. Over Lairn's shoulder, Gideon could at last see them.

They were manlike, but without distinguishable faces as such. Their skin resembled black, shimmering oil, their hands were clawed. If they wore any armor, it was not evident. Nor could Gideon see any eyes or a mouth. Like glistening shadows, their movement displayed a liquid quality, as though the forms they now held were by choice alone.

Gideon defensively raised his staff as the first of them reached Lairn. The young man's muscles strained as he embraced the shadowy beast and hurled him to the side. The riftman hit the rocks with a thud and for an instant seemed to conform itself to the shape of the stony surface. Then, just as quickly, it was up again and back upon Lairn.

With great effort, all apparently designed at keeping the riftmen away from Gideon, Lairn ripped and struck at the black shapes. But they were undaunted and, apparently, unharmed by Lairn's attacks.

Gideon stepped forward, staff in hand, but Lairn saw him, and with his one free leg, shoved the sojourner back.

"No, Redeemer," Lairn rasped above the choking sounds of the riftmen. "Away! Save the land."

The brief distraction Gideon caused was all it took. There was a blur and a scraping blow across Lairn's face. His scream was muffled by shimmering bodies as they engulfed him, smothering out his consciousness. Like ruthless hounds, they tore at his flesh, as if looking for a bloody treasure within his very body.

Gideon didn't know he was crying until he tasted the tears on his lips. *Not for me!* he screamed in his mind. *The boy shouldn't die for me!*

"It is a lie!" he screamed aloud at last. "Lairn, you fool! I am no Redeemer! You naïve fool!"

The sound of his words drew the riftmen's attention from Lairn's dismembered body. Their black sheen now bore red stains on their claws and chests. Gideon didn't even notice the blood, so consumed was he with the fury of guilt that blinded him. Lifting the staff like a mace, Gideon screamed at the approaching clawed forms with a rage so hot he felt he was on fire.

"Damn you, demon-spawn!" he roared. "Damn you to hell!"

There was a flash, like the sun itself had appeared for an instant and then vanished. Gideon's staff quivered, then glowed with a blue flame that traveled back and forth along its length. Gideon tried to throw it down, but his hand held fast, possessed by the mysterious

GIDEON'S DAWN

power that now surged through it.

In an instant, the staff was ablaze with the brilliance of azure flame. The riftmen backed away, and those at the cave mouth turned from their prey to see their judgment.

Against his will, Gideon's hand lifted the staff high overhead, and blue lightning struck out, searing through the chest of the closest riftman. From there, the shaft of lightning continued to the next black form and then the next. The riftmen, frozen in fear, watched as the blue flame wove a web through their bodies, so that their dead brothers were held standing by the sheer force of the fire.

Within seconds the web formed, and every riftman—several hundred strong—was pierced through the heart. As the last shadow let out a choking cry, the blue flame ceased, and the blue light that engulfed Gideon's staff shot at once into the night sky and disappeared.

As though in a strange and macabre dance, several hundred black shapes slumped together to the ground, and the stillness of the mountain night quietly returned.

Gideon fell, shaken. The dark form of the staff rolled quietly out of his now limp hand and rested on top of what was once Lairn. His deep blue eyes, wide from the horror he had just witnessed, blinked mechanically in the absence of any conscious thought. His eyes fell on the staff and on Lairn, or what was left of him. Without thought, he reached for the almond wood. Perhaps he wanted to get it away from Lairn, to somehow protect the boy from the strange power it encased. *I tried to help*, Gideon cried to himself. *My fault.*

"Gideon Dawning! No!" the voice was Donovan's, booming from the mouth of the cave as he ran toward the sojourner. His right arm had been slashed, yet somehow he managed the strength to hold on to his sword.

"The staff," Gideon said blankly. "It's on Lairn."

"Do not touch it," Donovan called. "The body is corrupted by the riftmen's claws. The foulness within will destroy any living soul that touches it."

Gideon drew back his hand and leaned back against a rock. "Why, Lairn?" he sighed, closing his eyes. "I'm no Redeemer."

Donovan stood quietly over Gideon's limp body and surveyed him for wounds.

161

"I'm fine, Donovan," he sighed. "They didn't get to me." He looked at the warrior, who dangled his sword at his side as though the hilt were glued to his limp hand. "Your arm," Gideon said. "It's bleeding."

"The poison is not as fast in me as it is in others," Donovan said. "Kair has great skill in matters such as this."

From behind the warrior, Ajel appeared. His tunic was ripped in several places, and his face was smeared with something black. But for all his weariness, he moved as regally as ever.

"Are you injured, Gideon Dawning?" he asked.

"No," Gideon returned, wincing inwardly at the thought of why he had been spared injury. With a composure that betrayed his inward horror and confusion, he stood up and was relieved to find his legs would support him.

Ajel looked at Lairn's remains. "It is a sorrow that we cannot mourn him properly. The riftborn have stolen even that honor from him."

"He did not leave without honor, kinsman," Donovan corrected him.

"You speak true, friend," Ajel said quietly. Then, abruptly, he called back to the cave. "Revel," he said, "bring wood for burning, many branches." Ajel turned again to the body and tore from the hem of his frock a large strip of cloth. With it he retrieved the staff, wiping it clean, then tossed the cloth across Lairn's marred face.

"You must be restored," Ajel said to Donovan. "Go now. I will call you when it is ready." Donovan nodded and turned back to the cave.

"You're not going to bury him?" Gideon asked. He felt strangely protective of Lairn's body, as though in death he could provide the aid that he failed to bring in life.

"The riftborn are corrupted souls," Ajel responded. "Their home is beyond the Black Gorge to the east. Their touch causes great ill. And their claws corrupt unto death. The poison resting on Lairn will spread to kill every living soul in this valley. To bury him would be to infect the land. Only the true fire purges the corruption."

"The true fire?"

"The fire of Life. The fire of *Dei'lo*."

Ajel moved closer to the sojourner. "Here is your staff," he said.

"No, I don't want it," replied Gideon, taking a step back.

"It is only a staff, Gideon Dawning, though it is like nothing in the land. It has no power apart from you."

"What are you talking about?" Gideon retorted, his head spinning from a distant sense of accusation. He fought to hold it at bay.

"The land is proved by its ways," Ajel said. "You have shown yourself, Kinsman Redeemer."

"That's a load of bull!" Gideon hissed. But just then Revel, Donovan, and Kair approached, each bearing an arm full of deadwood. Donovan's arm was still bloody, but Gideon could no longer see the wounds under the shredded sleeve. They carefully arranged the wood in a crisscross pattern around Lairn's remains. It was clear this was not the first time they had performed such an act.

When all the wood was in place, everyone gathered around the pyre silently. For a moment, Ajel looked around at the night sky. The darkness that had been so absolute only an hour before was challenged by the rising of the moon, which now tipped over a distant peak. The air was crisp and cool and emanated a peace that let Gideon know that the mountains saw nothing of the carnage that had occurred here. Or, if it saw, its greatness demanded that it still carry on, unchanged.

But there was no such peace in Donovan's face. His sorrow, masked only a moment before, was now clear. "I have failed, kinsmen," he said slowly. "Lairn was my charge, not only from his family at Calmeron, but also from Wordhaven itself. So I am doubly filled with sorrow at my loss, at our loss. He was to have been one of the first."

Ajel touched Donovan's shoulder, then motioned for the company to stand back. For a moment longer, he looked at what was Lairn. It was then that Gideon saw Ajel's tears. Until that night, Gideon had never known that a man's tears could be so beautiful.

"*Jeo pur'theron!*" Ajel said the strange words with surprising force. Instantly, the deadwood surrounding Lairn's body burst into a brilliant azure flame—a flame exactly like the one that had consumed Gideon's staff before. Gideon jumped back in shock, his eyes suddenly shifting to the staff, which Ajel had leaned against the rocks.

In a move that seemed almost too fast, Ajel came beside Gideon and placed a firm hand on his shoulder. "It is well," he said. "It is not a fire that destroys life—only the death within life."

"But the riftmen. . . ," Gideon stammered.

"That is a mystery," said Ajel. "The fire cannot consume a living soul, yet your fire slew the riftborn. Their bodies remain, but the fire cleansed them. They are dead, but harmless to the land."

"How do you know?" asked Gideon. "You said they were full of corruption."

Ajel stood silently for a moment, watching the blue flames. "I do not know how I know this, Redeemer," he said at last. "But I am sure of it. We need not burn them now. Your fire was enough."

"No," Gideon said, backing away. "I'm not your Redeemer."

"We must rest now." Ajel managed a smile. "We can talk more of this in the sunlight."

Slowly, the fire consuming Lairn's corrupted flesh began to fade, and Ajel directed the company to return to the cave, where they prepared for rest until the morning. No one said anything more to Gideon, not even Ajel.

The horses, wandering somewhere in the night, carried the bedrolls the travelers used. So Gideon and the others had to make do with their tunics and the rocky cave floor. Even so, the numbness of shock and the exhaustion of his body quickly carried Gideon to a dead man's sleep. His last fleeting thought was that he should get up and go sleep next to Lairn's remains. Somehow, he was sure, that would have been the right thing to do. But the thought quickly faded, and darkness came at last.

CHAPTER 17

THE PATH TO WORDHAVEN

*I have often wondered what it would have been like to have
known Gideon Dawning in those early days—before he knew
who he was, before greatness had been thrust upon him. By all
accounts, he was a bitter and distrustful man who cared little for
others and even less for the Words. In truth, if I had known him
then, I don't believe I would have liked him at all or seen any
quality in him that would cause me to think him extraordinary.
And I can't help but wonder what that says about me.*

—THE KYRINTHAN JOURNALS, SONGS OF DELIVERANCE, STANZA 2, VERSES 16–17

The morning announced itself softly, with cool, caressing breezes and
the sounds of mountain birds. The sun, white as though purged in the
night, broke over the eastern peaks like the watchful eye of God. And
the air was filled with the smell of. . .horsehair?

Gideon snorted at the tickling on his nose. Daring a peek through
the slits of his eyes, he saw only a horse's mane—a gray horse. The
earth was moving beneath his huddled form, and his feet dangled stupidly, numb from the awkwardness of his position.

He had fallen asleep on his horse. It was the sun that had awakened him, cresting the mountains to spill into his eyes. With a semi-
conscious frown, Gideon stretched the ache in his back and legs and
sat up. Revel rode alongside him holding Gideon's reins.

"So you are awake again," Revel said with a grin. "You have seen
two dawns this day already. It is no wonder you call yourself Dawning."

Gideon frowned again, this time directly at Revel, and said nothing. He found himself in a heavily forested region of the range, though
the vegetation was more appropriately alpine than the junglelike
growth they had to hack through to get here. The thick growth of
vines had been replaced by the smell of spruce and the crunchy sounds

of pine needles beneath the horses' hooves.

Ajel and Donovan rode ahead about a hundred paces. Kair stayed to the rear. Slowly, the memories of the morning became clear once again. They had awakened at dawn, located the horses, and rode out to the north amid the bodies of fallen riftmen. Gideon wasn't even allowed time to visit Lairn's remains, assuming there were some.

That had been several hours ago. Now the sun was at midmorning or so, and the terrain, though still mountainous, was distinctly different.

"Where are we?" asked Gideon.

"Far from danger now," Revel replied confidently. "The destruction of an entire warcor of riftmen has given our adversaries cause to rethink their strategies. They have not moved beyond the slaughter."

"No, I mean where are we?" repeated Gideon, wondering why Revel had to use a word like "slaughter" to describe what had happened.

"We should reach our destination by sunset," said Revel, turning his gaze on Gideon in that same birdlike way Gideon had noticed when he first saw the man.

"You mean Wordhaven?" Gideon asked.

"You were going somewhere else?"

Gideon didn't answer, and Revel smiled once again. Gideon checked his horse's packs to see if anything was lost in the chase the night before. Everything was in place, it seemed, including his almond wood staff. Seeing it caused a sudden chill to run down his spine.

"I placed it there," Revel offered nonchalantly. "You refused to touch it this morning, but I believed you were not yet thinking clearly."

"Thanks for your consideration," Gideon said, more or less under his breath.

"You are welcome, sojourner," Revel replied, missing the sarcasm. "Here now. Your reins," he added, holding them out.

Gideon took them without saying anything and prepared to move ahead to avoid any further conversation with Revel. But he moved too slowly.

"Are you well?" asked Revel. "How do you feel?"

Gideon clenched his jaw. He was never a morning person to begin with. And waking up on a horse increased the effect tenfold.

"Fine," he said.

"That is good, good," replied Revel. "Though it is also a wonder.

You seemed full of sorrow in the night."

"Did I?" Gideon said in a tone that made it clear he couldn't care less.

"Yes, sojourner," said Revel. "I am sure even the Guardians heard you moaning in your sleep."

At the mention of Guardians, Gideon perked up a bit. "What are you talking about?" he retorted. "There were no Guardians there."

"They were there, Gideon Dawning," said Revel. "Though we never saw them, they were watching."

"How do you know if you didn't see them?" asked Gideon.

Revel shrugged. "Well, I do have a special keenness that comes on me in forested lands," he explained. "But that is not how I know of the Guardians. The riftmen have no love for their own kind. They do nothing together unless they are forced. Only the power of the Council Lords could accomplish such a horror as we saw last night."

"Then why didn't the Guardians attack too?" asked Gideon.

"That is a mystery," agreed Revel. "I myself believe they had planned to follow their riftmen in attack, but halted in fear at your power. We are grateful for your actions, my friend. I do not think we would have lived through the night otherwise."

"Don't thank me," Gideon grunted sarcastically. "I didn't do anything."

Revel said nothing in response at first, but looked up at the peaks to the west, as though gauging the group's position in relation to the shadows from the sun. In a moment, his eyes rested once again on Gideon.

"Ajel has said that you still deny your calling," he said. "To be the Kinsman Redeemer is a noble thing. Why do you not accept it?"

Gideon snorted and shook his head. "You guys just won't give it a break, will you?" he asked. Revel didn't respond. Gideon shook his head again. "You're all set on making me fit into your little prophecy. Except I don't. I'm not from around here, and I don't know anything about your war with the Guardians. I'm not your savior. I don't know exactly what happened last night, but I do know I had nothing to do with it."

"I sense that you are confused," said Revel.

"Whatever." Gideon rolled his eyes. "Listen, if we have to talk, can we at least talk about something else?"

"Of course," replied Revel with a grin. "What would you like to talk about?"

"Nothing," Gideon said.

Revel laughed. "All right, then, I will choose. How did you acquire your staff?" he asked. "I know of every type of wood in the Inherited Lands, and I have never seen its like."

Gideon stammered awkwardly over his response. How do you explain you are from another world? "I. . .I don't know," he said at last. "I tried to use it to save myself from. . .I just had it when I came here, that's all. It wasn't on purpose."

"Then this wood grows freely in your land," said Revel, thoughtfully.

"Yes, in some places," replied Gideon. "Not in the mountains, though. That's why I went to look at it. It shouldn't have been there."

"Your home is in the mountains, then?"

"Well, no. I was in the mountains when. . .I came here."

Revel looked around at the peaks that surrounded them. "Tell me, where are these mountains you speak of?"

Gideon glanced around a moment at the deep green and blue that surrounded them. As beautiful as it was, something about this terrain seemed portentous, deep, and alien.

"It's not these," he said at last. "I don't know where they are."

Revel shrugged. "That is a sorrow. I too feel the emptiness of not knowing my home." Revel smiled. "I would like to visit your home, Gideon Dawning, if only to see the tree from which this wood comes. Lairn worked his skill masterfully on it, don't you think?" Revel leaned over from his horse and ran his fingers along the exposed part of the staff strapped to Gideon's mount.

The mention of Lairn's name made Gideon tense. He couldn't stop the flashes of scenes from the grisly night before. Lairn's strong arms and young face, ripped to shreds by the riftmen's claws.

"Tell me something, Revel," Gideon said slowly, without looking up. "Donovan said something last night I didn't understand. He said Lairn was to be 'one of the first.' What did he mean by that?"

Revel's hawkish features scrunched up pensively, as if pondering how best to answer the question. Finally, he asked, "Did Ajel explain to you the purpose of Sacred Heart?"

"He said it was like a training center for potential leaders at Wordhaven," replied Gideon.

"Yes," said Revel. "That and much more. The heart cities were constructed as centers of transformation for potential Lords of Wordhaven."

"Transformation?"

"Like when a caterpillar becomes a butterfly? It first goes into a cocoon. You understand?"

"I understand what a cocoon is," said Gideon.

"Well, the heart cities were 'cocoons' for transforming common people into Lords."

Gideon shifted his weight on Orisoun's back. "So what does that have to do with Lairn?" he asked.

"The heart cities have been abandoned for many centuries," Revel continued. "For that reason, there has not been a new Lord of Wordhaven in thousands of years. But now, Paladin Sky believes he has learned enough to open a training center again in the very heart of Wordhaven itself."

Revel paused a moment, then said, "Lairn was to be one of the first initiates in the training. He aspired to become one of the new Lords of Wordhaven."

"Oh," said Gideon, suddenly wishing he had never asked.

"Ah, I see we are stopping now," said Revel.

Looking ahead, Gideon could see Ajel and Donovan dismounting their horses and pulling several small bundles from their packs. Kair, prodding her mount to move to a relaxed trot, rode past Gideon and Revel to see if Ajel needed help with the food.

Gideon took in a deep breath. The thin air felt clean in his lungs, like breathing in pure oxygen. The noontime sun brightened the deep colors of the landscape, causing the forest evergreens to seem almost brilliant against the rusty backdrop of the rocks and clay. The grasses swished to and fro at the slightest breeze, playing freely with the mountain flowers that grew among them.

Despite such familiar signs of beauty, Gideon couldn't shake the feeling that it was all part of something quite unknown to him and deep in a way that seemed almost sentient. Perhaps it was the too-blue sky or the excessive richness of color in everything else. Or perhaps it was the haunting questions about what strange creatures might hide in the shadows of such tranquil scenery. Juron, riftmen, Guardians, and God knows what else. It looked like his earth, but everything in him told him that his earth was far, far from this place.

Gideon and Revel reached the others and dismounted to eat and rest. The rations consisted of the usual things—dried beef, leafy plants, and that strange, sweet juice Revel had served them the night before. Gideon greedily grabbed his bundle from Kair and plopped down on the grass. As hungry as he was, he found he was more relieved just to get off his horse. Absently rubbing his lower back, he promised himself he'd never fall asleep on horseback again.

"We must go on foot from here," Donovan said. No one responded, except for a nod from Kair. Gideon found that welcome news. He'd had enough of horse riding to last him for the rest of his life.

"Are you well, Gideon Dawning?" The voice was Ajel's. Gideon looked up to see the golden-haired tower of a man hovering behind him.

"Yeah, peachy," he said with his mouth full. "How much farther do we have to go?"

"It is not far, but the way becomes quite steep. We will reach Wordhaven before the sun sets."

"What's it like?" asked Gideon. "I mean, is it a castle or village or. . . ?"

Ajel smiled. "Wordhaven does not give itself easily to description. It is a hidden place. And you will find rest there."

Ajel walked away without further discussion and left Gideon with his usual frustration at the Wordhaveners' answers.

Just minutes later, Donovan signaled for the group to move on. The afternoon sun was warm, and Gideon noticed he had begun to sweat under his leather tunic. He still felt incredibly sore—his whole body ached from riding for so many days without a break. With a sigh, he stood up and adjusted his clothes to allow some air against his skin beneath the poncho. Absently, his hand brushed across his satchel, and he suddenly remembered the *ja'moinar* bread that Mara had given him at the start of his journey. It hadn't done him much good in the desert, but maybe it was worth a try now anyway.

"It's probably spoiled by now," he heard himself mumble aloud. Tentatively, he pulled the cloth-wrapped bread from his shoulder bag and looked at it closely. It smelled as fresh as the day he'd received it.

It was a wonderful aroma filled with honey and cinnamon. The very smell of it seemed to soothe his aching limbs, if only for an instant.

Gideon pinched off a tiny piece from the loaf and tasted it. It was sweet and seemed full of nuts, though none were visible. Gideon started to break off more when Donovan approached with Gideon's horse.

"Gideon Dawning, please stop!" exclaimed Donovan, his black eyes bright with alarm. "You must not waste the *ja'moinar* bread."

Gideon withdrew his hand, but held the loaf up to his nose. "Waste it? Mara said it was for strength on my journey, right? Well, this is my journey, and I'm exhausted. Besides, it will just go bad if I don't eat it."

"The *ja'moinar* will not spoil," Donovan countered. "And your need for it later may well be far greater than your need now. Please, do not eat it."

Ajel walked up as Gideon continued his argument. "Look, it's my bread, Donovan. I think I'm perfectly capable of determining when it's best for me to eat it."

"It is my fault," Donovan said to Ajel. "I did not explain the true nature of the bread."

Ajel smiled and placed his hand upon Donovan's shoulder. "The people of the Remnant have a saying, Gideon Dawning," he said. " 'If you have run with footmen and grown faint, how will you compete with horses?' I see that you are weary, and yet you are still standing, are you not? You are able to walk and even to argue quite effectively against Donovan. Remember your dream in the Plains? Who is to say that your *ja'moinar* bread is not intended for such a time as that?"

Gideon clearly wasn't moved. He just grinned at Ajel and chewed all the more sarcastically. "Come, kinsman," Ajel said to Donovan. "Let us go now. The sojourner must make up his own mind."

Just as Ajel began to lead Donovan back to their horses, Gideon felt a rush of fire and ice shoot down his body. He yelled aloud, frightened by the strange sensation, and quickly jumped toward his gray stallion to get away from whatever had struck him. But he jumped too far and actually slammed into the flanks of his horse. The startled stallion snorted and trotted away, and Gideon hit the ground with a thud.

Donovan ran over as Gideon shook his head to clear his vision. "What. . .what happened?" Gideon asked.

"You have taken the bread," Donovan said, with a hint of disgust. "You are truly wasteful, sojourner," he added, and with that, he headed off to retrieve Gideon's horse.

Still slightly dazed, Gideon stood and tested his limbs. To his amazement, the soreness was gone completely. He felt as if he had just slept for a week and awakened to swim in a warm bubbly pool. He even touched his skin to see if it was damp.

"Your mount, sojourner." Donovan spoke flatly as he returned with Gideon's mount. Luckily, it hadn't gone far.

Gideon took the reins from the big man, who walked past without saying another word. Gideon didn't care—he felt great, much better than he had since this whole wild trip began. He jogged after the others, who had already begun the hike up the steep slopes to the east. The afternoon sun, once oppressive, now felt like a warm massage on Gideon's shoulders. Carefully, he wrapped the *ja'moinar* bread in its cloth and placed it back in his satchel. If only a pinch made him feel this good, what would a whole slice do?

Traveling on foot made conversation much more difficult, since the horses were constantly bumping into the people and each other on the narrow trails. That, in addition to the thinning air, meant that not much was said for the remainder of the afternoon.

To fill the time, Gideon applied his observation skills to learning more about this mountainous land. Mostly, everything seemed quite normal. They had left the junglelike regions below and were now surrounded by canopies of pines and aspen broken here and there by granite outcroppings along the path. The air smelled of evergreen and damp earth, and the occasional sunbeam in the trees gave the area an almost holy aspect.

But there were oddities too. Gideon caught glimpses of strange animals—rabbits with long, bushy tails, white deer with black stripes, and birds with calls that sounded more like apes. It was all different, yet it was also basically the same—like a reflection distorted in an imperfect mirror.

In time, the afternoon sun turned to evening, and the canopy of trees shifted to allow the sunbeams to spill across them from the west. Abruptly, the path became level again, and the forest gave way to an expansive open meadow surrounding a small lake at the base of a jutting cliff of gray stone. The cliff faded into steep grassy slopes as it rose. Gideon could tell that the cliff before him was actually part of a larger mountain that curved out away from him in both directions. He couldn't make out the crest.

Crossing the grassy meadow, Donovan stopped on the banks of the lake and waited for the others. Gideon came to the water's edge and allowed his horse to drink. Just then, Ajel casually mounted his horse. Donovan did the same.

"Are we riding again?" asked Gideon.

"No," said Ajel. "It is easier to cross the lake on horseback."

"Cross the lake? Why?" Gideon asked.

"Look there, sojourner," Ajel said as he pointed toward the cliffs. "We are home. Beyond the lake are the gates to Wordhaven."

CHAPTER 18

WORDHAVEN

People have always thought of Wordhaven as a sort of paradise
on earth. And why not? Beyond question, it is more wondrous
than any destination in the Inherited Lands. But one must
remember that, first and foremost, Wordhaven was created
to be a fortress. And its defenses are as formidable as they are
mysterious, as inescapable as they are lovely.

—THE KYRINTHAN JOURNALS, MUSINGS, CHAPTER 23, VERSES 3–4

Before Gideon could form the question on his lips, Ajel was off, with
Donovan close behind. Moving some distance around the lake's edge,
Ajel abruptly stopped and turned his horse into the water, absently, as if
there were no water at all. The stallion trotted onto the lake's surface—
and did not sink. Donovan followed, his mighty black stallion prancing
across the water's top without so much as a downward glance.

Gideon only stared. He was past trying to figure out why things
like this kept happening, but he still couldn't help gawking, like a little boy watching a trapeze artist for the first time.

"Do not look so astounded, sojourner," Kair said curtly as she rode
past him toward the water. "It is not the feat it seems to be. Come."

Gideon didn't move. Not yet. He just watched her silently as she
rode to the lake's edge, waiting for her to repeat the miracle. He never
would get used to life in this place, however beautiful it appeared.
Perhaps alone he could. Over time. But mysteries lurked everywhere
here and were almost as difficult to explain as the people.

Kair stopped on the shore and waited as Revel stepped up beside
her. It was the man's laughter that finally jarred Gideon into blinking.
Revel was laughing at him, of course. It seems the man thought everything Gideon did was either funny or offensive in one way or another.
But Gideon couldn't see why his confusion would be funny. He had

grown weary of the monumental strain of never knowing what was going on. He ignored Revel, or pretended to at least, and prodded his own horse forward. By now, Ajel and Donovan had reached the opposite shore and were waiting for them on a wedge of earth that was only briefly level before shooting up toward the cliff.

Getting Gideon's attention again, Kair pointed to an indiscriminate spot on the water, then walked her horse out onto it. Her mount's hooves stood firm, just as the others had. But it wasn't until Revel stepped out also that Gideon saw it.

Just inches beneath the placid surface lay a stone pathway, stretching out from the shore into the center of the lake. It was only a few feet wide and blended so beautifully with the subtle reflections of the water and the silty bottom that it was nearly beyond perception. In fact, even as Gideon traced its faint outline, the image blurred and he lost all track of it, only to locate it again in a seemingly different place.

At last, a mystery that could be understood. Gideon sighed. It seemed a small comfort, all in all.

Revel laughed again as he watched the sojourner struggle to find the path, then prodded his stallion on across the lake. Kair turned slightly as she moved ahead.

"You need not be troubled with the path," she said. "The mount knows the way."

Ordinarily, Gideon would not have taken Kair at her word. After all, the woman hated him. He had little doubt that she'd swear an invisible bridge stretched over a canyon just to get him to step off the edge. But he was past caring now. Let her drown him, or push him, or snub him to death. He just wanted to be done with the journey.

Gideon relaxed the reins on Orisoun, who until then had seemed strangely anxious to move into the waters. Once released, the gray stallion bolted out onto the water's surface as giddily as he might charge across a familiar field. If not for the staff strapped to the horse's side, Gideon would have certainly lost his hold and plunged into the icy water.

The small lip of land next to the cliffs seemed barely visible from the far shore, though now it appeared quite clearly—boldly carpeted in rich grasses and flowers. There was a trail there, barely noticeable, leading out from the water's edge and directly into the rock wall of gray stone that shot up toward the cool blue evening sky. No one said anything, not even Ajel, who always seemed so full of helpful explanations; but they all moved quietly up the path to the rock wall. There, they turned and watched Gideon as he approached.

"What?" Gideon asked, tired. "What are you looking at?"

"Would you like to open the gates to Wordhaven, sojourner?" asked Ajel.

Gideon sighed. "Why?" he asked. "Is it here?"

"It is here." Ajel pointed to the stone wall next to him. "Come closer and you will see."

For a moment, Gideon hesitated again. He was tired of all the games, all the surprises, all the testing he didn't understand. He thought about just staying put, just saying no. But something in Ajel's eyes told him that would be a grave mistake. Something in those eyes told him that if he didn't get up there, they might kill him on the spot. It made absolutely no sense. But then again, what had? It was enough that he sensed it—or rather, that Ajel caused him to sense it. Somehow.

Gideon walked his horse slowly up to the cliff's base. As he approached, the rock walls seemed to shimmer, as though made of water. Stepping still closer, the gray stone in one part of the cliff flowed away altogether, like water pouring over a falls, revealing a door.

Or, really, a portal. Two brilliant slabs of silver stood imbedded in the rock. Together, they were over thirty feet high and almost as wide. On the panels was carved a regal lion standing within a sphere.

The lion spanned the width of the doors, with one mighty paw raised in defiance or salute. Across its shoulders flowed a magnificent mane. It was so intricately carved that the mane seemed to blow in the evening breeze.

Gideon grudgingly dismounted and walked up to the doors. He felt suddenly small, like a mouse on the doorstep of a giant's castle.

"Stroke the lion's mane," said Ajel softly. "The doors will open."

Gideon looked at Ajel, who gave him an oddly reassuring smile, then reached up and brushed his hand over the carving. The silver was cool and felt strangely fluid, as though the lion's image could be stirred with a finger, then resettle into another pose altogether.

Soundlessly, the doors parted, like mighty arms reaching out to embrace the mountains. Gideon stepped out of the way, pulling his horse along behind him. As soon as the doors had parted enough, Ajel entered, followed by Donovan and the rest. Gideon quickly mounted his horse and followed. No one spoke, but somehow he got the sense that everyone was suddenly quite relieved. *Why? Were they afraid the doors wouldn't open?*

The doors closed noiselessly behind him. To all the creatures concealed in the grasses and trees around the lake, it seemed the riders had strode right through rock and into the heart of the mountain.

And on the inside, once the doors shut, it was nothing but darkness. *"Adon ipel'far."* Ajel's voice echoed into the chamber. Slowly, golden lights appeared along the floor in a line tracing off into the distance. They weren't bright but gave enough light for Gideon to see that they had entered a smoothly carved tunnel. The rounded walls glistened in the pale glow like black crystal. Aside from the darkness, it reminded Gideon of a subway station or an underground hangar.

The highest point was at least forty feet up, with about that same distance between the two sides. The golden lights ran along the edges on either side, disappearing far ahead like a runway to nowhere.

Despite the urge to wait until his eyes adjusted to the dark, the rest of the group showed no signs of slowing down. Instead, they urged their mounts to a near full gallop. Gideon reluctantly followed, though he guessed that even if he had resisted, Orisoun would've taken to a run anyway.

For several minutes Gideon's senses were filled with nothing but the loud haunting echoes of horses' hooves and the ever-present golden lights that blurred together as they rode. Behind them, the lights faded to black soon after they passed, allowing other lights ahead of them to come to life. All of this seemed perfunctory at best to the horses, which seemed to know the way instinctively.

At last, the group rounded a turn—one of many turns they had rounded—and came upon a grand golden door similar to the first one. Ajel motioned for Gideon to open this door just as he had the other.

Like the first, this door was about thirty feet high and equally as wide. And, like the first, a lion was inscribed inside a sphere. But this lion was different. It was lying, of all things, on its back, its mighty forepaws playfully swiping at the clouds carved above it. Despite its still formidable ferocity, the great beast looked for all the world like a kitten toying with a ball of yarn.

Gideon dismounted and walked over to stroke the great mane, just as he had before. This time the door felt warm. The gold was soft on his fingers.

Silently, the doors swung away. No sooner had they begun to part than an avalanche of light tumbled into the chamber. They all had to shut their eyes from the strain, but Ajel led them forward anyway, allowing the horses to act again as guides.

This time, though, Gideon didn't follow. Holding his hand tight on Orisoun's reins, he waited until his vision had adjusted before moving forward. Maybe he was just feeling edgy because he was so tired. But he wanted to know what he was stepping into this time.

When his eyes finally stopped watering, Gideon got back on his mount and rode slowly forward out of the darkness—and into a place beyond anything he had ever dreamed.

An immense emerald valley stretched out before him like a single green jewel opening to the sky. Great gray cliffs, shining like silver in the evening sun, rose in sweeping slopes on all sides. Mountain aspen, spruce, and pine blanketed the lower parts of the slopes all around, ultimately giving way to the majestic rocky slabs that surrounded the valley like a stony crown.

The lowlands spread before them like a living blanket, dotted by fields and groves, flowered meadows, and rolling hills. Down the middle flowed a river, meandering through green meadows like a child on a playful run through the grasses. The flow drifted slightly off to the north as it neared the travelers, then disappeared into the trees—which, oddly enough, made the river seem to flow uphill toward the end.

The geologist in Gideon immediately recognized the place as a volcanic crater—a huge one, at that. He would've recognized it before they entered the tunnel if the cone hadn't been so big. But even though he could reason how a place like this could naturally form in these mountains, it took away none of the wonder he felt just sitting in the midst of its immensity and its beauty.

He felt renewed. No, more than renewed. He felt alive, truly alive—a man awakening from a tired dream. A man awakening from death. Every muscle, every movement, every thought resonated with the pulsing richness of life he sensed around him. He could suddenly feel the pattern of the pressed grass beneath the horses' hooves, taste the cheery sounds of birdsong riding on the breezes, embrace the intimate caress of his hand running through his hair. It was all connected. Everything was Life. Everything was one.

"I can feel. . .everything," he said.

Thoughts came flooding into his mind like mountain rivers emptying into an ocean. *It is rest here, sojourner. . . . Yes. . .here the truth comes to light, here we see what we have sought. . . . You know it, friend. . . . Now, Redeemer, consider the distance.*

Gideon's mind grabbed hold of the last thought, spoken, he was sure, in Ajel's voice, though not audibly, and reached with his mind to the full extent of the valley. Sensations invaded him, flooding his own thoughts away, leaving only peace. He could see the smallest cracks in the cliff walls, even those the light could not touch. He felt the steamy heat of dozens of geysers bubbling and spewing throughout the valley, felt the warmth they brought to the earth and air. He sensed a herd of horses prancing toward them from the northwest. They smelled Orisoun and the others and were coming to greet them. He smelled them too. He knew that if he wanted to, he could enter them, become them, be them. It was all in his choice.

But there was more to see, before that. The life. . .the life of the woods! It was spilling over like water, pouring out from the edges like sunbeams through the tree trunks. And the fields, rich. And the hills, like Scolding Wind, but with only gentle breezes. He could feel it all as though it were all just a handbreadth away.

Reaching farther, his mind stretched to the far wall of the valley. He saw the stronghold there, a black-golden fortress imbedded in the stone. He reached out and touched Wordhaven.

And someone touched back.

Spasmodically, Gideon's mind recoiled, racing to move away from the power that touched him. It was an unknown force, powerful and inquisitive. And its brief scrutiny made Gideon feel suddenly naked, a vulnerable soul without a body to hide in.

But Gideon did have a body. And although he didn't know how he did it, he retreated into it once more, shutting out the sensations, breaking his ties with the life that surrounded him. He willed himself to separate, willed his thoughts to be once more his own, and severed the tie that allowed his experience to be somehow linked to the others.

What am I doing? Idiot! They can't know my thoughts. If they do, they will control me.

Still, despite his best efforts, Gideon could not break the ties completely. He could no longer sense Wordhaven, or the woods, or even the approaching horses. But he could still feel the grass under Orisoun's hooves, and he could still sense the strong presence of those who surrounded him.

Gideon slowly opened his eyes. When had he closed them? The others had dismounted and unloaded the horses. They were all laughing, childlike, unconcerned—even Donovan.

But not Ajel. Ajel had moved away from the others.

He was dancing.

His outer clothing lay in a heap on the ground, along with his tunic. He wore only a sort of waistcloth, like a towel around his hips. And he danced, off in the grasses closer to the river. He spun with arms extended toward the sky. He ran and rolled in tumbles through the grass. He was laughing some too, now. And singing.

The herd of horses rounded a small knoll to the north and came upon the field where Ajel danced. Without missing a step, the man fell in route with them and ran alongside the thundering hooves. It was incredible. He ran like the wind itself, his golden hair streaming out behind him like the flowing manes of the horses. He spoke as he ran, it seemed, and each word added strength to his stride.

It was beautiful. And all Gideon could think of was how hot his envy burned.

"Why do you envy?" asked Kair, not quite scornfully. "It is his name from the Giver. If you had not closed yourself, you would know it and share his pleasure with him. We all walk in the light of our naming."

This last statement held a clear accusation. Lord Gideon. Truthslayer. Kinsman Redeemer. Gideon turned from Ajel and forced his mind to seal itself off from the land even more. Kair shouldn't have known what he was feeling. What else might she have seen in his head? There were secrets locked there that she could easily turn against him later, if she knew of them. He turned away from her, but not before his shoulders shuddered involuntarily under her stare.

Concentrating all his energy, he imagined thick, steel walls erecting around his mind. *It must not be*, he reasoned. He must not allow them to see. Nothing. No thought. He focused, making the walls thicker, more solid.

With his mind, he sealed the plates together and set a guard around the perimeter. He didn't know how he did it. He just did. Although, he noted, the process seemed oddly familiar and. . .comforting.

"Show them only. . .what. . .you want," he muttered under his breath, straining as he sealed the final bolts and welded on a thick steel ceiling and floor.

"Indeed," Ajel panted breathlessly, "no one shall see more than that." Gideon turned back to see Ajel kneeling on the grass before him, hands on his hips, his chest heaving heavily. He was still smiling. The horses had run past them, now joined by the groups' own mounts. All except Orisoun, who stood anxiously next to Gideon, waiting to be released.

"The mount must run, Redeemer," said Kair, with special emphasis on the last word. "The life demands it."

Suddenly aware that all eyes were on him, Gideon turned to unstrap his satchel and staff from the gray mount. His movements were purposefully paced and cool, just like they always were whenever he felt threatened or invaded.

Ajel bellowed in laughter again, falling backward onto the grass and stretching his arms toward the sky. Gideon wondered what was wrong with the man, what he was laughing at, and whether it might be him. Casually, Gideon sniffed and gripped the almond wood staff tightly in his right hand. Immediately, Orisoun galloped away in search of his friends.

"Ah, it is good to be home, brother," Ajel said, his eyes closed.

"You have been away too long," replied Revel.

Ajel sat up. "Yes," he said. "Yes." Without a word, he stood and brushed the grass off his chest and arms, then reached toward Revel, who held his tunic. "Come, sojourner," he said with a smile. "The others await our arrival."

Without realizing how he knew it, Gideon understood that the steel wall he'd erected to seal off his mind from the others was not welcome. In fact, he *knew* they despised it as an unholy thing, an abomination of sorts. One of them—or perhaps all of them?—had let him know that, just before the walls were sealed.

And yet now no one challenged him or drew any attention at all to his actions. They simply accepted it. Or at least that's how it seemed. He couldn't really tell. He let out a cynical chuckle as he realized that locking his own mind in also meant locking their minds out. Moments before, he could've read their every thought in an instant if he chose to. Now he saw only gray steel walls.

Maybe later I'll let down the guard, he thought, *perhaps while they sleep.*

The last leg of the trek, across the valley to the stronghold, was exhausting for Gideon. Beyond his weariness from the long journey, it took all his remaining strength to maintain the barrier he had erected to his soul. The grass, the river, the sky all pressed on his thoughts, seeking an opening, a way again of becoming one. The worst of it was that Gideon wanted it too. When he was a part of the valley, even for those few moments, he felt complete. His weakness was infused with the strength of life surrounding him. His mind was free to travel, to know and be known in ways he'd never imagined. It was a taste of belonging. Something he had never experienced.

But he couldn't risk it. Already he could sense the presence of the others around him, gently probing his defenses, even as they spoke with each other without words. On several occasions they would all laugh at once or smile and nod. It was unnerving.

"Would somebody tell me why it is this way?" Gideon could see enough into their minds to know they understood the question.

"It is Wordhaven, sojourner," said Donovan. "It is the way of this place. You will. . .adjust to it."

"No, I won't," muttered Gideon.

"Donovan knows better than any of us how you feel, Gideon Dawning," said Ajel. "When he arrived not many years past, his feelings were like yours are now. They passed in time, as I'm sure yours will."

"No." Gideon enunciated more sharply this time.

"As you wish, sojourner," said Ajel. "But your choice makes the way hard for the Seer if she is to help you locate your home."

"I am not liking the sound of this." Gideon shook his head and looked down at the ground. "Who's this 'Seer'?"

"She comes," said Kair.

"And Paladin Sky," added Ajel.

Gideon looked up to see two figures approaching in the distance, with the glossy black and gold castle fortress looming behind them. One figure walked with a staff, and they both wore simple but elegant ivory gowns. They were clearly elderly, but carried themselves well, as though their silver hair and wrinkled faces were merely a mirage to fool the unsuspecting.

Gideon stepped out in front of the group to get a closer look. For a moment, he thought the pair looked like Mr. and Mrs. Finch, the couple who owned his garage apartment back home. But then the woman lifted her hand toward him and reached out with her mind to enter his thoughts.

Suddenly something slammed him to the ground—flat. It felt like a sledgehammer against a steel wall. The ringing in Gideon's head sounded like words in a cathedral. "You hide. You hide. You hide." It was an echo in a prison cell.

Gideon screamed, but even that didn't drown out the echo. It kept reverberating off the walls of his mind like a wrecking ball against a steel building.

Hands gripped his head. Warm, wrinkled hands, small but powerful. His eyes flew open, and it was the old woman. Her face was kind, grandmotherly. But her voice beat against his thoughts like an evil inquisitor. "You hide. You hide. You hide."

Gideon grabbed her wrists, but he could not break her grip. The fingers sunk into his skull; her kind, soft eyes stabbed deep into his mind. "Open," they commanded. "Stop hiding." He felt his neck stiffen against the probing, his muscles tense with resistance. Fingernails like little knives dug deeper, along with the thoughts, the pounding. "Stop hiding. Stop hiding. Stop hiding."

Gideon felt his walls begin to buckle under the strain. He heard the creak of bending metal in his head, knew it was just a matter of time until she ripped his barriers apart. Her face was so kind, so tender. How could she be pounding him like this?

Sweat broke out on his forehead. Frantically, he focused his thoughts on shoring up the walls, reinforcing the steel, creating additional beams. The woman's eyes grew wide, and there was a hint of wonder.

Then she smiled, and the world came crashing in on all sides.

"You hide," said the voice. "You must not do this anymore."

Gideon screamed again, his eyes wide with terror and pain. Then another hand reached over his eyes, covered them. "Not now," another voice said. And everything went black.

CHAPTER 19

THE AXIS

In the time of Gideon Dawning's arrival, very little was known about the Deathland Barrens. Even today, our forays into the despoiled lands have been rare, and for good reason. The Word of Desolation that destroyed the Pearl at Gideon's Fall also corrupted the essence of every living thing that lay to the east of that cursed hill. Every tree, every plant, every insect and animal, and every human being. . .all hideously transformed into something that is not really life at all. For the Word of Desolation did something far more devastating than simply kill all life in its path to the sea. It robbed all life of hope and then cursed it to keep on living. There is no greater death than that.

—THE KYRINTHAN JOURNALS, CHRONICLES, CHAPTER 12, VERSES 40–43

Lord Lysteria Asher-Baal slowly sighed as she stood on the balcony outside the Axis, overlooking the city. Phallenar sprawled before her like a jewel in the desert—an oasis of commerce and life in the midst of an ever-advancing landscape of barren bleached rock and gritty sand.

It's so sad, really, she mused.

The land around the city used to be so green and lush, and there were all sorts of wonderful animals and birds. But that idiot Palor had made the mistake of building his capital on the edge of the Deathland Barrens and apparently never gave a second thought to the fact that the Barrens were *spreading.* If he'd had only half an ounce of wit, he would have known that the spoiled lands would eventually overrun the city. But clearly he didn't, because here they were, in the middle of a rotting landscape, with only the Words to keep the desolation from reaching the city walls. And they did a poor job of that at best.

And lately, she'd heard reports from the Guardians and her own *jalen* about how the Barrens were beginning to encroach closer than ever, poisoning the soil, providing warrens and nests for creatures that should not exist. At least, not anywhere near Phallenar. According to her *jalen*, the foundations of some walls were actually beginning to crack—as if such a thing were possible!—under the strain of certain acid-filled vines that sprouted from nowhere out of the desert floor.

Lysteria rapped her fingers on the marble railing. Well, that would have to be dealt with and soon. Most likely, she'd have to do it herself. It was a shame, really. No one in the Council seemed to share her concern for the city. But the truth of it was that she loved Phallenar. She'd lived here all of her life, and it had long ago become a part of her. She loved its buildings, its abundance of gardens, the sounds of commerce and family life that filled its streets on a daily basis. She loved the smell of the spices on market days and the reverent way the people grew quiet whenever they came near the Axis.

In many ways, especially in more recent times, she'd come to see the city as a metaphor for her life—a portrait of her own resilience against the many injustices she had endured. If this beautiful city could remain safe from the onslaught of the Barrens, well, then, she could keep herself clean and pure-hearted no matter how much evil was festering around her too.

She glanced across the horizon to the west, toward the Memorial Wall. In the afternoon sun, it looked just like a natural cliff, or very close to it, running the length of the city from one end to the other. Atop one small section of stone, she could just make out a tiny finger-like tower projecting above the Wall. It was the place where her daughter, Kyrintha, lived now, locked away under house guard. She clucked her tongue and shook her head just a little. *If only that foolish girl were not so stubborn!*

With a blink, she turned her face back toward the city and smiled. At least the city remained open to her, and she embraced it like. . .like she would a child. She smiled at that. Yes, a *second* child. She groomed it, trained it, made it her own. And it was hers. Not so much as a stone was moved from here to there within the city walls without Lysteria's personal direction. The High Lord may seize the whole land in his grip, but Lysteria would always be the Mother of Phallenar.

"Raug, my shawl," she said aloud, her eyes still locked on the city below. Large, dark hands gently brushed her arms as her shawl, laced with black and golden silk, came to rest on her shoulders.

She was late for the Axis, but that was by design. By Council law, they had to wait for her. She would enter in her time, take her place on the dais, make all the other Lords watch as she dawdled with the folds of her gown. They might be irritated; a few might even be furious. But it was good to do from time to time.

It's good for them, she told herself. They were good people, all in all, but power had a way of making even good people blind to their own arrogance at times. *You have to guard against such things, you know.* So she made it her business to knock them down a notch or two every so often. It kept them honest.

She absolutely hated dealing with people who were all full of themselves. Not that all the Council Lords were like that, really. But it was still a good idea, she thought, to keep things real. Showing up late was just the right thing to do every now and again.

Silently, she turned and glided through the golden doors behind her. Raug followed just a step behind, a giant of a man with arms the size of tree trunks. She required all of her Wordsworn to maintain a strict and strenuous physical regimen. She wanted hers to be the strongest of all the Lords' *mon'jalen*. Of course, in a real battle, their physical strength would mean little. The Words of *Sa'lei* she taught them gave them the real power to protect her. But their size was intimidating all the same. And in all her years on the Council, she had come to respect the value of making a good impression.

Under his breath, Raug spoke Words that would summon two more of Lysteria's *jalen*. Three *jalen* were required to enter the Axis with their Lord whenever the Axis was in session. In modern times, their presence was largely due to tradition, though at one time they were brought in as a deterrent for any Lord intent on assassinating another—something that hadn't happened in over three hundred years.

For all its power, the *Sa'lei* tongue did have some limitations. A Word of death, for example, could kill only the one soul it was targeted for. After the last assassination of a Council Lord, the *jalen* were brought into the Axis so that if one Lord were slain by another, the *jalen* of the fallen Lord could immediately retaliate by destroying the killer. That seemed to solve the problem. And over time the Council matured, became more civilized. Now, the *jalen* were hardly needed.

But Lysteria still liked keeping the tradition alive. She believed traditions were important.

Raug mumbled something again, this time presumably to alert the Axis chamber that Lysteria was on her way. The Words that Raug spoke sounded curiously awkward to Lysteria's ears, even after all these seasons of working with them. "They were words not meant for the human tongue," her mother used to tell her. "It is the language of the dead." Her mother, Baree, was a crazy woman who refused to learn the Words and, consequently, was denied a place on the Council. She was the first person in four hundred years to refuse the Raising. Imagine! Council Law was quite clear on such matters, as it should be, of course. And Baree was shut up in the Tower of the Wall until she died, old and alone.

A foolish woman, Lysteria thought. And now it seemed her own daughter might follow in Baree's steps.

Two more black-vested men silently fell in behind Raug as the Lord continued to glide down the marble hallways that led to the Axis. They were both as large as bulls. One was fair-skinned with red hair, the other a smooth olive brown. Raug, of course, was as dark as midnight. She liked her men. . .varied.

All of the *jalen* were corded to their Lords by the Words. Lysteria's were sworn to her protection and to her pleasure. When she was pleased, they felt at peace. If she were injured, all of them would know it instantly. If she died, so would they, each within a month of her demise. Such an arrangement pleased her. It made her *jalen* fiercely loyal. . .among other things.

Gliding awhile longer down the gold arching corridors, Lysteria came at last to a gray and white marble door that bore her image. Quietly, she grimaced. She had never liked that carving. The artisans had made her look much older than she really was and too thin besides. It was a disgrace! None of the other Lords' entrance doors looked so shabby—except for Varia's, perhaps, but with a face like hers, she could hardly expect more. In any case, she must remember to speak to the city's chief artisan after the Axis was closed.

With that, the doors swung open, and Lysteria floated in. Without a sound, she eased herself up the ramp that led to her dais and stepped onto the marble circle that bore her emblem—a dagger thrusting out of water toward a single star. She never so much as glanced at the other figures in the Axis, though she knew they were there, staring. With practiced slowness, she adjusted her shawl and smoothed the folds of her gown. Only when her *jalen* had taken their place on the wall behind her did she place her hands on the golden railing—the sign that she was ready to begin.

"So glad you could join us, Lysteria," a deep bearish voice spoke from the other side of the chamber.

Lysteria smiled pleasantly at her husband. Her voice, however, sounded formal. "My apologies, High Lord. I have been. . .occupied."

"Well, we mustn't make it a habit, though on occasion I suppose it's not to be avoided," the High Lord's voice rumbled through the Axis like a growl. But there was no anger in it. In fact, he sounded rather amused.

"High Lord, shall we get started, then?" asked another voice. The High Lord looked to his left to see Lord Baurejalin Sint looking at him innocently, with his eyebrows raised in a way that looked particularly and purposefully childlike.

"Yes, yes, Lord Sint, we should get right to it." High Lord Balaam Asher-Baal quietly chuckled as he spoke. "I know there is considerable trouble afoot, and we must deal with it. So, then. . ." Balaam briefly scanned the notes that lay before him on the dais. "What of the warcor? Lord Baratii, you have news?"

Lord Bentel Baratii nodded, then briefly adjusted his red cloak, revealing for an instant the single strand of pearls draped around his neck. He wore no shirt under the cloak, only a multicolored silk vest, with silk pantaloons. It was the current fashion of the city, and Bentel had always firmly believed in the importance of keeping up with the times.

In addition to his knowledge of fashion, Bentel also understood the art of war—better than any member of the Council, except perhaps his sister, Fayerna. The two of them had been given the task of deploying the four warcor to find the so-called "Stormcaller."

"Yes, High Lord, I have news," he said. "I am sad to report that following your instructions has led three of our warcor, well, nowhere in particular. They search in vain through the Heaven Range. I'm afraid they have little hope of finding the rebels there or anywhere else. Meaning no disrespect, of course, but I told you before that I don't believe such large masses of Guardians can effectively surprise our flighty misfits."

"You may be right, Lord Baratii," said the High Lord with a sigh. "You may be right at that." The room fell silent, but Bentel continued to smile silently at Balaam, waiting for the question he knew would come next. "Lord Baratii," Balaam said at last, "why do you mention only three warcor? I thought four were sent."

"Oh," said Bentel with a start. "I don't suppose you've heard the news. The rebels destroyed one of them."

"Impossible," said Balaam dismissively. "A warcor of over a thousand Guardians?"

"No," said Bentel. "Not *that* warcor."

"Speak plainly, sir, please." Balaam spoke with just a hint of agitation.

Bentel scratched his eyebrow with his little finger, then replied, "One of the warcor of riftmen was destroyed, near the Constance Valley. The Guardians who were there watched from a distance as. . . well, they called it 'blue lightning'. . .came down from the sky and consumed them all. More than a thousand, and not one left alive."

"Then the ground in that place will be like the Barrens," said Lysteria.

Bentel paused. Lysteria rarely spoke in the Axis, and her unexpected comment surprised him. "Apparently, Lord Lysteria, the lightning. . .cleansed them," he said at last.

"What are you saying?" asked Balaam. "Lightning that cleansed them? Unheard of!"

"The battle took place in the night," continued Bentel. "When the morning light came, the Guardians found a valley full of ordinary dead men and women. No riftmen at all."

"That is not possible," said Lysteria. "We have no such ability."

"Indeed, perhaps not, my dear mate," the High Lord said, "but we can make them riftmen again and make them dance like jesters even though they are dead."

"Oh, Balaam, don't be so morbid," said Lysteria. Balaam smiled at her, and she grinned, just a little, in response.

"All of this is beside the point," said Lord Fayerna Baratii, breaking into the conversation. Bentel's sister had been quietly waiting for Bentel to tell the whole story about the lost warcor. But it seemed he wasn't going to, so she felt obligated to step in. "High Lord, the rebels themselves did not destroy the warcor. It was the Stormcaller who did it, the one they are calling the Kinsman Redeemer."

Balaam's brows furrowed, and his voice lowered a bit. "How could one man destroy an entire warcor? A warcor of riftmen, even?"

"I don't know, honestly," replied Fayerna. "But that is what the Guardians reported. High Lord, I believe that this man, whoever he is, is our true threat. If we destroy *him*, these ridiculous rebels will return to the obscurity from which they came."

"What do you suggest?" asked Balaam.

She smiled. It was like a crack in steel. "My brother is right," she said. "We sent a bear to do a serpent's task. The warcor will not find them. I will."

"You would go?" asked Balaam.

"Withdraw the warcor. I will have the Guardians summon the *juron* from the mountains. They will take me, along with Bentel and Lord Sarlina, to the Heaven Range. Our *mon'jalen* will come, of course. But no others. This false Redeemer may have some ability against riftmen and a few frightened Guardians, but certainly not us.

"It is time we put out this fire, High Lord." Her eyes now seared into his across the Axis chamber. "The longer it burns, the more our authority is consumed."

Balaam laughed—so naturally that only his *jalen* could know he was not genuinely amused. "Our authority, Fayerna, is not in question," he said. "But how we wield it is. These rebels are terrorists and lunatics. They are not a threat to us, but they are a threat to our people. That is why we must stop them." He sighed, then added, "Very well, I grant your request. The three of you may go. But I expect regular reports. And I am especially interested in hearing how you plan to find this one obscure man in such a vast range of mountains."

"Of course. And we thank you, High Lord," said Fayerna.

"And one more thing," Balaam added after a pause, "you may not kill him. This 'Stormcaller,' I mean. Capture him alive and bring him to me in good health."

"But, High Lord," asked Bentel, "why go to such trouble?"

"Trouble?" asked Balaam. "I hadn't thought it to be any trouble at all. Is it beyond your powers, Bentel? Or yours, Fayerna?"

"That is not what I meant, of course," said Bentel plaintively.

"We will do as you ask," said Fayerna, without looking at Bentel.

"Yes," said Balaam, smiling. "Of that I have no doubt. You have my complete confidence. Now, I think you three should take your leave from us right away. The more quickly we deal with this the better. I will see to the recall of the warcor."

"Yes, High Lord," said Bentel. With that, he gestured for Fayerna and Sarlina to meet him outside the Axis.

As the three Council Lords turned quietly to leave, Balaam called out, "Good hunting, my friends!" And he laughed again. This time some of his *jalen* actually winced as they felt the dark, raging fear coursing through the High Lord's heart.

CHAPTER 20

SEER SKY

The Society of the Remnant was a clandestine organization within Phallenar whose members believed the Council Lords had indeed found the Book of the Pearl, but had not been able to destroy it. It was their sole purpose to infiltrate the government structure in order to discover the Book's whereabouts. Ultimately they hoped to retrieve the Book and use its language to overthrow the Council's rule.

One member of the Society, Laudin Sky (s.c. 2026—2139) was raised to the Council position of Chief Mentor, the highest rank among the Lords that anyone in the Society had yet attained. Although he did not learn the whereabouts of the Book, he did learn of the existence of Wordhaven, the fabled ancient seat of power in the Inherited Lands.

This discovery led to the Sky Rebellion, in which one hundred members of the Society fled Phallenar on a quest to find Wordhaven. After thirty-five years of running from the Guardians, Laudin and the others finally located the fabled stronghold. Although the Book of the Pearl was no longer there, many of the writings from the Book were recorded in other documents and tapestries within the Wordhaven archives. Since the time of their discovery, the Remnant began to study these artifacts in an effort to learn the Words and discover the final resting place of the Book they still sought.

—THE KYRINTHAN JOURNALS, CHRONICLES, CHAPTER 1, S.C. 1900–2100

"He should be awakened before we begin."

"No, Ajel. We will awaken him when the time seems right."

"We have never had a Facing in which the tested one was not allowed to speak in his own defense."

"He will speak, Ajel. In only a little while. But you must see that this is no ordinary Facing. We will not awaken him until the Facing begins."

Seer Sky listened to the conversation between the two men from around the corner where she could not be seen. Her brother, the Paladin, was right, as far as he went. Obviously, the sojourner should not be awakened before the Facing. She could see into his mind much more clearly without his conscious interference. But if she had her way, that stranger would never be allowed to wake up—not during the Facing or anytime after that ever again. He was too much of a danger to them.

She had told the Paladin that earlier, quite convincingly, she thought. But he balked at the idea, spouting some nonsense about respect for life and the heart of the stranger. No doubt the real reason was Ajel, who had become strangely attached to the man. He always had been a champion for the weak or the broken. Well, this stranger was certainly broken—that much was clear even from Seer's short glimpse into his heart. But weak? If Ajel only understood how truly powerful this sojourner was, he would bind the man in cords of light himself and speak a Word of sleep so deep that even those who came near the man would collapse on the spot.

But he did not know. None of them did. And it seemed Seer must pay the price for their ignorance.

"You should have allowed me to continue searching his mind when he was tired from the journey, Paladin," Seer spoke from around the corner, the sudden stillness telling her they were both still there and listening. "Now he has had many hours of rest; it will be difficult."

"You ambushed the man, Seer, just as you now ambush us." Paladin Sky smiled, but Seer couldn't see it. Nor could she see Ajel's frown.

"He is more threat than you know, Paladin. But you will know soon enough." With that, Seer turned and walked away, down the corridor toward the Servant Hall. "In some things he is a wise man," she muttered, "but in most a fool."

Slipping left down a second corridor, she entered the maze of hallways and interconnections that were the hallmark of Wordhaven. Seer made it her business to learn those passages; and she'd spent the better part of the last fifty years doing just that. She'd found at least three ways to enter any of the smaller chambers in the Stand; for the larger chambers, such as the Servant Hall, she'd discovered eleven, so far.

"Adon'i'far," she whispered, and a faint glow filled the passageway where she now walked. Sunlight reached almost all the chambers, halls, and passageways in Wordhaven—a fact that was an irritating mystery in itself—but in a few of the more obscure passages, the light became too dim to see by clearly. Even so, the air was always fresh, always like spring, even in the deepest parts of the massive structure. Seer knew that by experience, of course. She'd searched through every nook, or very nearly. And yet so far the mighty Wordhaven had revealed only a few of its secrets.

Essentially, the layout of Wordhaven's castle fortress—which the Remnant called the Stand—was quite simple: a perfectly circular edifice, half hidden in the heart of the mountain. The layout was divided into three massive rings, which were separated by three concentric passageways—the outer, mid, and inner halls. The halls each towered seven stories high and allowed daylight in from above—even at night and even in the parts of the hall encased in solid rock. At each level, railed walkways lined the great halls, with frequent arched bridges on the various floors connecting one side of the hall with the other. The walls were rich in carvings, statues, and tapestries that told the stories of ages and people long gone and long forgotten. The Remnant had been studying the artifacts for over sixty years, and they still had not even seen them all.

Beyond the great halls, though, Wordhaven became a maze of turns and narrow passageways and apparent dead ends. Countless rooms remained untouched and seemingly untouchable by the Remnant, but countless more had been gradually discovered over the years—including the most important room in Wordhaven, the Chamber of the Pearl located in the deepest heart of the Stand.

Seer wasn't headed to that Chamber just now, but to one near it. The Servant Hall, as the Remnant had named it, was one of four identical auditoriums that ringed the Pearl's Chamber. Each a perfect three-sided pyramid, the original purpose of these giant rooms remained a mystery. But one was used now as the convening room of the entire Remnant—a place for the Servants of the Pearl to plan, to argue, and to dream.

By the time Seer finally slipped through the triangular doors, the stranger had already been brought in. He lay on a stone table in the center of the room, still asleep. Next to him, Donovan stood in his usual stoic way, along with a dark-skinned woman from the Hinterlands who was well known as Donovan's most prized student. By now, Ajel was there too, arranging the stranger's arms so they weren't flopped across his body like a drunkard.

Always thinking of dignity, that Ajel. Seer snorted loud enough so Ajel could hear and stepped up behind the Servant's Call—a long wooden table where all seven leaders of Wordhaven sat. Moments later, Ajel joined her there, along with Revel Foundling, Teram Firstway, Katira Peacegiver, Saria Sky, and, of course, Paladin Sky, who entered last of all.

The rest of the chamber was gradually filled with members of the Remnant, both young and old, all seated in rows on wooden stands that filled more than half the room. When they first arrived at the gates of Wordhaven years ago, the Remnant numbered barely two hundred. Now, almost seven decades later, their numbers were ten times that, maybe more. But so many were still just children. So few of them truly understood the magnitude of the struggle into which they'd been unwittingly born.

Seer frowned. Well, they would understand soon enough.

Paladin Sky stood, and the room fell silent. "Who convenes here?" he asked in a surprisingly soft voice.

"The servants of the Pearl" came the booming reply, the voices of all those in the chamber speaking in unison. "Like the servants before us, our mothers, our fathers, our sisters and brothers, so we now serve. Like those of true heart who stood as Guardians on these grounds, so we now stand. Like those of noble wisdom who spoke as Lords in service to life, so we now speak, one heart in honor of one name."

"What name?" asked the Paladin.

"We speak in the name of the Pearl, in the memory, and the power. We convene in that name."

"Let our hearts, then, speak true, for the sake of the Pearl."

"For the sake of the Pearl," they echoed.

Paladin sat down. He looked down at Gideon with an unreadable expression, as though he couldn't decide which of his mixed feelings would be the most appropriate to display. He had often wrestled with his role as guide for the Remnant, trying to gauge just how much of his real perceptions he should reveal to the people who followed him. If he revealed too much, the people might lose heart in the cause; not enough, and they might come to doubt him as a person. The strange effects of Wordhaven complicated matters. Stray thoughts may be perceived as easily as one perceives the wind. It took constant discipline to direct the winds of his own thought without appearing to do so.

His eyes remained transfixed on the stranger for some time. Finally he spoke, though it was hardly a whisper. "Whether we choose it or not, I fear that I am looking at the instrument of our destiny."

Seer blinked, but said nothing. The people remained silent, almost frozen. "Ajel," Paladin said, "tell the story of the sojourner's arrival among us."

Ajel nodded. Then in his own calming, elegant way, he relayed the story of the sojourner's arrival from its beginning. Most of it was not news to the Remnant—but Ajel recounted the events with painstaking care. Only upon explaining the razing of Songwill did he falter, and then only slightly, just a small catch in his throat. But it was enough. Everyone at Wordhaven knew of Ajel's special love for Songwill and for the *Nissirei* who had been slain before his eyes.

While Ajel spoke, Seer's eyes never left the crowd. She picked up their thoughts easily, more easily even than Teram, though he was older and more practiced. There was fear, of course, and a touch of awe at the sojourner. That was to be expected. It wasn't until Ajel began to display the stranger's staff and describe the circumstances of Lairn's death that she felt the one emotion she was searching for: anger.

She would need the anger of the people behind her if she was to convince Paladin to turn the stranger away—even to deliver him over to the Council Lords. It was the only way to see their cause protected, their community kept secure. There would be a time to confront the Council, but it was too soon now. And keeping that man among them set them on a premature course that would lead to certain destruction.

Finally, Ajel finished. Now Seer would act.

Paladin Sky gestured to Donovan and Aybel, who stood next to the sojourner on the floor of the Hall. "It is time for the Facing," he said. "Awaken the sojourner."

Seer stood up and cried out, "He must not be awakened! In his waking, we are destroyed!"

"Be silent, sister," said Paladin sternly. "This issue has already been decided."

"No!" Seer pointed at him. "You have decided, Paladin Sky, not them. Not us!" Her arms swept about to include the crowd. "You say this foreign man holds our destiny, and perhaps I agree. But you act in haste. You decide what is not yours to decide, Paladin or no."

Paladin Sky stood up and fixed his now-piercing gaze on Seer. He said nothing and did not move. It was a simple gesture, but enough to make his point powerfully clear. Seer had moved past questioning; now she was challenging his authority, his place as Paladin.

Curse that man, she thought. She didn't want the confrontation to escalate to this level. Questioning a decision was one thing, but questioning the integrity of the man who had led the Remnant for the past forty years was quite another. *Curse me! I have stepped too far. Too far!* With a snort that could be heard throughout the room, Seer sat down.

Paladin's gaze remained fixed on his sister. "No doubt these events have toyed with all of our fears and our concerns about the future of life in the Inherited Lands. But I have always held to the truth that it is never right to do evil even in order to accomplish good.

"I will not deny this man his personal dignity, whoever we believe him to be. When one is lessened in this way, so are we all."

Paladin Sky turned back to Donovan and Aybel. "Awaken him."

CHAPTER 21

THE FACING

Forty years after Wordhaven's rediscovery, Laudin Sky,
the Remnant leader who was known simply as Mentor,
was slain during a fierce battle with the Firstsworn of the
Council Lords—a man by the name of Donovan Blade.
Donovan was also mortally wounded in the fight, but was
saved from death by a Dei'lo *Word of healing. The Remnant*
took Donovan prisoner and carried him back to Wordhaven,
probably because they did not know what else to do with him.
Naturally, the death of Mentor Sky was hard on the
people of the Remnant. He had, after all, been their leader
since the beginning. But in time they recovered from their
loss and continued their quest for the Book. Laudin's brother,
Jesun, took the reigns of leadership for the Remnant. Jesun
had never been a teacher and so refused to take the honored title
of Mentor in his brother's place. Instead, he chose another title—
Paladin—because he felt it better fit his abilities and his
newfound role as protector of the Remnant's dream.

—THE KYRINTHAN JOURNALS, CHRONICLES, CHAPTER 2, VERSES 348–354

The world felt tingly, like tiny shards of ice and crystal rock were prickling the cold, damp skin up and down his body.

It was like waking up, but deeper. . .from death, perhaps, rather than sleep. To Gideon, at that moment, death would have been preferred. Nevertheless, he groped at consciousness, as much from habit as anything else, and lethargically opened his eyes.

"Are you restored, Redeemer?" Ajel's ever-present smile was the first thing Gideon saw. He looked away.

"You must awaken now, Redeemer," said Ajel. "You must awaken."

"Gideon. . .my name is Gideon." His voice sounded raspy and dry.

And yet, though he barely spoke, his words resounded clearly off the walls. No one stirred.

"A name of treachery," mumbled Seer from her seat behind the Servant's Call.

"Hold that, Seer," said Paladin sternly. "It is not yet your time."

Ajel placed a hand on Gideon's chest. "Yes, you are Gideon Dawning, a sojourner in the Inherited Lands." He paused briefly, looking down at Gideon's face as though considering whether that face might belong to someone Ajel knew in the past—a long-lost friend from childhood. Finally he continued. "I fear you may not understand what we are about to do. But I believe you have some measure of trust in me, however slight. I must ask that you trust me now. Do not fight, Gideon Dawning. Fighting will only harm you."

Gideon shook his head and tried to sit up. Only now did he realize he was lying on a stone slab in a large auditorium. And that there were hundreds of people all around him, watching. "Wait. . .wait," he began. "What. . .What's going on? Ajel, what's going on? What am I doing here? Who are these people?"

"You are among the Remnant, Redeemer," said Ajel. "This is your Facing."

"My what?"

"Enough!" cried Seer. She was looking directly at Paladin Sky. "It is enough, Paladin. Our delays only build his defenses."

Paladin looked at his sister, then back at Gideon. His thoughts seemed calm to all those in the room, but a hint of anxiety creased his noble features. Silently, he nodded.

At this, Ajel turned and walked away. Gideon began to follow, but Donovan and the dark-skinned woman held him down. "Ajel, what's going on? Donovan. . .let go of me!"

Thoughts. Powerful thoughts. Crashing into his mind. They struck from above him, beside him, all around. "No!" Gideon screamed. "Stop it! Stop it! Get out of my mind!"

"Let me see!"

The woman! It's the old woman. Where is she? Why does she. . . There! Go away!

Seer climbed up the steps next to the table where Gideon lay. While Donovan and the woman still held him firm, she gently cupped her hands around his head and looked directly into his eyes.

"I do not wish to harm you or upset you. But I must see into your soul. We must know both who you say you are and who you are in truth. When you resist me, it only hurts you. I will see everything. I will. Relax. Let us go together."

No, you witch. You're a witch. Get away! I don't want you here. You may not know me. You may not!

Gideon screamed as a thousand steel spikes plunged into his brain. The iron walls he had constructed in his mind to keep her out before now fell like cards in the winds of a hurricane. Frantically, in his mind he rebuilt the walls again—thicker, stronger, with spikes and moats and catapults with fireballs. But still she advanced. Why was she doing this? What did she want?

The pain! It was like nothing he had ever felt. . . . No! He had known a pain this great before. Even greater. Many times. More times than he could stand to remember. But now he could remember, perhaps, just a little.

"Great Giver!" cried Seer. "The agony!"

"Are you well, sister?" asked Paladin Sky.

"Be quiet!" she commanded and gripped the sojourner's head more firmly than before. Gideon grasped her frail arms, his knuckles white with tension. He seemed about to hurl the old woman's frail body over the table, but then his screams abruptly stopped. His arms fell limply to his sides.

Seated behind the Servant's Call, Paladin Sky leaned forward. "Now the Facing truly begins," he mumbled and did not care that the whole assembly heard.

"What is this place?"

It was Gideon's bedroom, of course, from when he was a child in Jasper. It was a mess, as usual. But there was his baseball glove, his favorite bat, and his Reggie Jackson poster, all right where they should be.

But she shouldn't be here.

"You don't belong here," said Gideon accusingly. "This is not yours."

Seer ignored him as she looked around the room. "Your chamber, is it? Hmm. . .why here? Why are we here?"

"It's my room; that's why I'm here," snapped Gideon. "You're the one who doesn't belong. Get out!"

"Gideon!" The call came from somewhere else, perhaps the kitchen.

"Yes, Mother?" responded Gideon instinctively.

"Your father wants your help out in the shed," she called from the kitchen. Seer stood quietly by listening.

"No!" Gideon yelled. "I don't want to go out there!"

"Young man, I'll have none of that backtalk!" his mother replied. "Now you put your shoes on and go help your father."

"But Mom!" Gideon cried.

"But nothing, Gideon. This is your final warning! Don't make me come in there!"

Gideon lowered his head, then plodded over to the bed and sat down. Quietly, he began to cry.

Seer stepped forward. "What do you fear, sojourner?"

Gideon's head shot up. "You!" he yelled. "You don't belong here! Get out!"

Suddenly they stood in a forest, gazing upward as the pine spires broke the sunbeams into a thousand shafts of light. The breeze was gentle, warm, and full of the smell of evergreen.

"Sherwood," muttered Gideon in amazement.

"What is sherwood?" asked Seer.

Gideon spun around only to see the old lady examining a pinecone she had picked up off the pine needle floor. "What are you doing here?"

"What are you doing here?" repeated Seer.

Gideon looked around at the woods and took a deep, deep breath. "This is my hiding place," he said. "Here I can sleep without being afraid."

"Afraid of what?" asked Seer. "What are you hiding from here?"

"You don't belong here," Gideon said again with sudden coldness. "You'd better get out. I'm warning you. You don't know what I can do to you."

"Enough of this quibble," said Seer. "If you will not show me willingly, then I will see it for myself. Hold there."

Gideon suddenly felt his feet anchored to the forest floor. The old woman began to move toward him, her hand extended toward his face.

Gideon frantically tried to move, but he was frozen solid from the knees down. "Stay away from me," he said coldly. "I don't want you near me. Stay back!"

The scene suddenly shifted from Sherwood Forest to a bleak stony cliff. Lightning flashed across ashen skies, and winds blew rancid odors up from the darkness below. Gideon stood perched on the precipice, with Seer only a *few feet away. He still could not move.*

"What do you fear so, sojourner?" asked Seer.

"I'm warning you," said Gideon through clenched teeth.

Seer took one step closer. Gideon was now unable to move at all. He stood frozen on the cliff, but his teeth were still clenched in a sneer. "Don't. . . touch me," he said.

"Let me see." Seer reached out her hand and touched Gideon's forehead. Her eyes flew wide open.

Gideon sneered. "You asked for it. You got it!"

Seer screamed.

CHAPTER 22

TRANSITIONS

*The families within the Council at Phallenar established and
maintained their power in the Axis through the purity of their
bloodlines. The more bloodline connections one could make with
each of the original Council Lords, the higher standing he or
she had within the present oligarchy. What wasn't commonly
known was that multiple generations of inbreeding within the
ruling families had taken its toll. My own birth was considered
something of a miracle. Many of the women of standing were
already barren, and those that could still bear children often gave
birth to young with deformities, both physical and mental.
Those with obvious physical deformities were usually locked
away in the Wall or were sometimes killed if their deformities
proved too severe, while those with mental deficiencies were
typically tolerated, so long as their disability didn't prevent them
from appearing healthy to the public. This problem led to a shift
in the power structure of the Council. Women who could bear
healthy young took on a whole new level of authority within the
Axis. This perhaps explains why the Council tolerated my own
bitter defiance as long as they did.*

—THE KYRINTHAN JOURNALS, SONGS OF DELIVERANCE, STANZA 10, VERSES 22–30

When Gideon awoke, everything had changed.

The old woman was gone, along with Ajel and Donovan and the
rest of the crowd of strangers that had been so eagerly watching his
torture from the sidelines of the chamber. The chamber itself was also
gone, replaced by a peaceful-looking room of gray stone and dark
wood, with a large bay window on one side and a fire in the hearth at
the end. Sunlight streamed in from the window across his bed, which
was quite large and, he thought, overly soft. His body was covered with

several woolen blankets, which, in the morning heat of the sun, were just beginning to make him feel a bit too warm. Slowly, he shuffled the covers off of him and sat up on the edge of the bed.

Not everyone was gone, he suddenly realized. Gideon sensed another presence in the room, although he did not immediately see anyone around. Still, he knew someone was close by. And that it was a woman. And that she was angry. He had no idea how he knew this, but it was as obvious to him as if the woman were standing with clenched fists right in front of him.

And then she entered from around a corner of the room that he hadn't noticed before. It was only then that he recognized her from the Facing. She'd been the one standing next to Donovan, the one who helped him hold Gideon down while Seer raped his mind.

She was tall and young—younger than Gideon—and pretty in the way of most women her age. Her skin was a flawless nut brown and reflected the light like satin. Her eyes were dark, intense like Donovan's, but without the same disturbing effect. Despite her dark features, her hair was very nearly white—or was it silver?—and as short as a man's. Shorter than Gideon's, in fact.

Although she was stunningly beautiful, she dressed as though she thought her beauty to be a sort of personal nuisance, like something that got in the way of her duties, whatever those might be. She dressed like a man, in a gray tunic and black leather pants. Gideon even noticed how she tried to walk like a man too. But her undeniable femininity kept getting in the way.

"Greetings, Gideon," she said, stopping awkwardly about ten feet from the bed. "I sensed you had awakened, so I am here to see how you are." Her greeting sounded anything but warm.

"Who are you?" Gideon asked.

"I am called Aybel Boldrun. You may call me Aybel."

"Where am I?"

"In a chamber on the east side of the Stand." She glanced around the room absently as though she were talking to no one in particular.

"I'm still at Wordhaven?"

She looked at him coolly. "Is that not obvious?"

Gideon grinned in a sarcastic way that seemed almost polite. "I don't suppose it is, or I wouldn't have asked."

Aybel turned her back to Gideon and walked to a table next to the window. "Then yes, you are still at Wordhaven."

"What's got you so ticked off?" he asked absently, rubbing the back of his neck to relieve the tightness he felt there. He had no tolerance for her attitude this early in the morning. "I'm the one who just got mentally raped by that old woman."

Aybel visibly stiffened. Slowly, methodically, she began to arrange some fruit on a tray that sat on the table in front of her. Gideon noticed her anger—or, rather, sensed it—growing.

"What?" he said, actually amused that he'd gotten a response out of her.

Slowly, she turned to face him and planted her hands firmly on her hips. "I am angry, sojourner, because you have awakened and she has not."

"What do you mean she hasn't awakened?" he asked, more seriously now.

"What have you done to her?" Aybel demanded. "And you'd best speak the truth because I will surely know if you are lying."

Gideon folded his arms defiantly. "If you can tell when I'm lying, then you'll know I'm *not* lying when I tell you that I don't have the slightest idea what you're talking about. That old woman attacked me! I didn't attack her."

"The old woman's name is Seer," snapped Aybel. "And you would do well to pay her the respect of calling her by her name."

"Okay, fine," said Gideon. "I didn't do anything to *Seer*. I don't even remember what happened. Except that you were there too, holding me against my will."

Aybel just stood there, hands on hips, staring at Gideon for what seemed like several minutes. Finally, she grabbed the tray from behind her and carried it over to Gideon's bed. "Here is some nourishment for you, Gideon," she said, setting the tray on the bed. "You should eat it. You will need your strength."

"Thank you," he said curtly. "So. What happened? At the. . .thing."

"The Facing?"

"Yeah."

"We do not know." Aybel turned and walked back toward the window. "Seer had successfully bridged the gap between you, but then both of your minds were strangely sealed from us. Not unlike the way yours is now. Shortly after that, she collapsed." She glanced back at him over her shoulder and raised one eyebrow. "And *you* fainted."

"Huh," said Gideon, nodding as though anything she just said made sense. "So, is she all right?" he asked, not that he cared particularly. Well, maybe a little. She was an old woman, after all. A bitter old mind-raping woman.

"We cannot awaken her. We cannot reach her thoughts. We do not know what is wrong."

Gideon picked up a peach and took a loud bite. "Well," he said, "maybe next time you'll think about the consequences before deciding to invade someone's mind against their will."

Aybel turned once more to face him. "There are many unanswered questions, sojourner," she said sharply. "And you can be certain that we will pursue them all until we are satisfied with the answers."

Gideon tried to ignore her veiled threat and took another bite of the fruit, which he now realized was not a peach at all, but some other kind of fruit entirely. But it had the texture of a peach, and that was good enough for him.

"Where's Ajel?" he asked at last. "I'd like to speak to him."

"Perhaps you will see him later today. He has many responsibilities," said Aybel, turning her attention to some unfolded blankets on a chair next to the window. "I am to take you on a journey through Wordhaven. Perhaps we will cross his path."

Gideon stood up. "I'd like to see him now, if it's all the same to you," he said. "I have some questions of my own to ask."

"When it is possible, sojourner," replied Aybel flatly. "For now, just eat. You need your strength."

"You keep saying that," said Gideon. "Why do I need my strength? What are you going to do? Attack my brain again?"

Aybel snorted. "Nothing so easy as that, sojourner. I have been assigned as your trainer. With my help, you are to learn the Words of *Dei'lo*."

Gideon rolled his eyes. "Oh, really?" he said, incredulous. "And if I refuse?"

With a raised eyebrow, she said, "Then you will die."

"Balaam is a fool."

Council Lord Bentel Baratii said nothing, but only smiled as he walked beside his sister, Lord Fayerna, and Lord Sarlina Alli. Fayerna always had a temper, even as a child. And it had only grown more volatile over the years. He had learned long ago to give her a wide berth whenever her anger was stirred. Nevertheless, he secretly found it amusing.

Sarlina remained a pace behind the two siblings, her head tilted slightly down. She knew better than to speak now too. "How long will I have to endure that silly old man," continued Fayerna. "He is. . .well, he is weak! I'm sorry, but that's all there is to it. He's weak. Pathetic!" This last word she directed at her brother.

"He is hiding something," said Bentel plainly.

"Oh, you don't really believe that, do you?" snapped his sister. "I doubt very seriously that that old man could hide a scroll if it flew up his backside. He acted out of general pomposity, that's all. I looked. . .that is, *we* looked quite formidable in there; and he had to do something to try to assert his own ridiculous authority. That's the only reason he wants that petty little Redeemer to live until he reaches Phallenar."

"Maybe Balaam plans to kill the Redeemer himself and so make out like it was all his doing," offered Sarlina.

"Well, eureka," mumbled Fayerna. "The simpleton finally gets it."

Sarlina put her head down again. Bentel glanced back at her and said, "Now, don't feel glum, Sarlina. I'm sure my sister doesn't mean you harm. Certainly not after your fine performance last night."

At this, Sarlina's cheeks reddened slightly, and she smiled. What she did last night seemed embarrassing at first, but it pleased Bentel and Fayerna. She liked knowing they were pleased with her. All the other Lords tried to make her feel dumb with their snobbish looks and complicated talk. But Bentel and Fayerna actually liked having her around. She almost felt like an equal with them. They made her feel like a real Lord.

Bentel reached back and stroked her cheek with the back of his hand. "There, that's better," he said. "Now, how about let's go catch us a false Redeemer?"

"Stop joking around, Bentel," said Fayerna. "And you too, Sarlina. Summon two of your *mon'jalen* to the Prisidium Square at daybreak in two days. Bring minimal provisions—we will take only what we need, and we'll have the juron to hunt for us, besides. I'll have my *mon'jalen* summon the juron. It will nearly kill the beasts to fly here with no rest or food, so we will have to let them sleep and heal before we can leave."

"Just as we have already discussed, sister, so it will be done," said Bentel, smiling. "Has the Firstsworn returned from Calmeron sounden with the item we requested?"

"No," said Fayerna. "But I expect to hear from him before this time tomorrow."

"I hope he can find what we need," sighed Bentel. "Without it, I don't think we have the slightest chance of success."

"Oh, he'll find it, you pessimist," chided Fayerna playfully. She was clearly in better spirits now, which is exactly what Bentel expected. Her anger was fierce, but notoriously short-lived. Most of the time she was a perfect delight to be around. "I'm sure the thing we need is there, somewhere in that couple's cottage," she added. "If need be, I'll go there and get it myself."

⬡

Even though he knew his room was something of a prison, Gideon had to admit the view was stunning. The bay window, which was situated high on the northeastern portion of Wordhaven, afforded him an expansive view of the crater valley below.

He could see vast acres of alpine forests and deep green meadows filled with several bands of horses and other large creatures that he could only assume were elk, though he knew they might be something else altogether. The entire left side of the window's view was filled with steep slate gray cliffs, which stretched out of the trees below and up beyond where he could see without opening the window. Which, he discovered with surprise, he could.

The air was crisp and cool with the chill of morning and carried the scent of pine and earth from the valley below. He took in a deep breath and closed his eyes. Everything here was so invigorating and alive. With just the slightest effort, he could reach out and sense the strength of the trees, feel the warming hardness of the cliff face in the morning sun, touch the wild, strong life of the horses as they grazed on the crunchy grasses in the meadows. . . .

With a start, Gideon shook his head and stepped away from the window. He looked around the room. Aybel was long gone, of course. But someone else might be around, watchers who were waiting for him to open the door to his mind so they could peer into his thoughts. Tentatively, he allowed his mind to reach out beyond the walls of the bedchamber.

He really had no idea how he was able to do this, of course. Ajel had said it was a characteristic of Wordhaven; but that explanation, if you could call it that, was no help at all. Still, he implicitly knew that, if he wanted, he could open his mind to drink in the entire valley at once— becoming a part of all the life within it and it, in return, becoming a part of his. It was such an appealing temptation. But far too dangerous.

For now, he contented himself with a more limited exploration. By opening his mind just a little and focusing on the hallway outside his chamber, he could. . .go there, in a way. Experience it, really, in his thoughts. He could feel the dark stone walls, sense the light that came from unknown sources above, and touch the smooth marblelike floor that curved away in both directions.

There was no one there. He reached farther, down one direction and then the other, until he came to other hallways and a number of circular stairways. Still he sensed no one. A little farther, and he noticed how several of the passageways led to apparent dead ends, though he somehow knew they were not really dead ends at all. He began to touch on several other chambers that, for the most part, were very much like his own.

The more he allowed his mind to open to Wordhaven, the more he appreciated the vastness of the place and the more he sensed a sort of nebulous presence within it. Not a living soul, exactly. More like the echo of one—as though something once lived in these walls that was so grand and so powerfully alive that it left a permanent impression on everything it touched. The sense of its presence was pervasive, but not at all threatening. And so Gideon continued.

After expanding his awareness through several more hallways and chambers and stairwells and doors, his thoughts finally touched on something much larger. A grand passageway, massive and beautiful and full of light, which curved away in two directions like a vast wheel. The feel of it was almost musical, though he could sense no music specifically. It was lined with terraces and bridges and railings of gold and black and ivory stone. And the whole thing was full of art.

Greetings, Gideon Dawning. . . .

Instantly, Gideon recoiled his thoughts, withdrawing his reach like a man withdraws his hand from a flame. Within a second, his thoughts were back within the confines of his bedchamber, safely locked away behind the steel barriers in his brain. The effect was surprisingly shocking, like having all your senses switched off at once. Gideon immediately felt dizzy from the change and stumbled over to the bed to sit down.

But in that parting split second, just after the voice spoke to him in his mind, he knew it belonged to a guard and that the guard had been expecting him.

Aybel would be coming back soon. Did he pick that up from the guard's mind too? He didn't know. But he knew she was coming.

Strangely, as odd as all of this was, Gideon found none of it particularly troubling. Much to his surprise, in fact, he felt amazingly calm about his entire predicament. In the past twenty-four hours, he had been taken captive by his companions, subjected to an invasive mind probe, held in a chamber against his will, and threatened with death if he didn't comply with his captors' wishes.

And it didn't really bother him at all.

He chuckled in amazement. Maybe he really *was* past caring this time. Maybe it didn't matter what they did to him—if they really *could* do anything to him, that is, beyond making him fall asleep whenever they got the whim. Perhaps he was beginning to wonder if these "Wordhaveners" were really as powerful as they claimed to be. Maybe, just maybe, they were more afraid of *him* than he was of them.

Now *that* was something worth thinking about. With a carefree flourish, he plopped backward onto the bed and grinned. Maybe learning *Dei'lo* wasn't such a bad idea, after all.

CHAPTER 23

THE HALLS OF WORDHAVEN

Paladin Sky never considered himself to be like those who are
called to greatness. He often said he would have been content to
live out his days as a simple merchant in the streets of Phallenar,
doing good when he could but never doing much to stand out
from the crowd. Sadly, two misfortunes kept him from this ideal
life he sought. First, the misfortune of being born during great
and terrible times. Second, the misfortune of being a man of
integrity who saw the beauty of suffering. And so it was that
greatness would not leave him alone.

—THE KYRINTHAN JOURNALS, MUSINGS, CHAPTER 5, VERSES 50–51

"You're making this very difficult, Gideon Dawning," chided Aybel. "I
would that you were not so bull-headed."

"Am I?" Gideon replied, raising his eyebrows as though surprised
by her appraisal. "I'm not trying to be."

"If you would just open your mind, I could explain this much
more easily."

"I prefer it this way," he smiled. "Besides, I think you're doing a
fine job."

Aybel sighed and blinked her eyes tiredly. "Very well, let us
strive on."

She gestured toward the center of the large tapestry before them,
one of more than a dozen tapestries that hung on the walls within this
section of the great hall alone.

"The Tongue of *Dei'lo* is constructed on an inverted pyramidal
structure," she began. "This phrase," she pointed to a series of words
embroidered in the center of the tapestry, "when properly learned and
spoken, creates peace within your center. The first Word is the root, or
foundation, upon which the others are built. All power within the

Language flows from the root Word and is directed by the Words that follow it. . .are you listening?"

"Yeah, sure," Gideon lied; his eyes had momentarily drifted over the black and gold railing and down several stories to the floor of the hall below. He wondered how there seemed to be absolutely no shadows anywhere in the entire hall, especially since the only light source he could see came from the huge skylights above. He couldn't even make a shadow by cupping his hands together.

"What in the Giver's name are you doing?" asked Aybel.

"This can't be good for your eyes," Gideon commented as he cupped his hands together over his eyes. "There are no shadows in here at all."

"The light is Word-wrought," explained Aybel, clearly frustrated by Gideon's apparent lack of focus. "I have lived here for over thirty years, and it has never damaged my ability to see. In fact, I believe my sight is much improved over what it once was."

"Thirty years?" Gideon looked up from his cupped-hand experiment. "You're kidding, right? You can't be more than twenty-five."

Aybel's eyes grew a bit wider, and she lifted her nose. "Not that it is your concern, but I have forty-six years, thirty-five of those since my Naming. It would be unwise for you to disdain my instruction simply because I am younger than you are."

"No. . ." Gideon smiled incredulously. "You can't be forty-six. You look too young for that." Her face darkened. "I mean that as a compliment," he added hopefully.

Clearly, she didn't take it as one. "How old are *you*, then?"

"Twenty-eight, last time I checked."

Aybel laughed so loudly that the sound echoed off all the stone walls of the hall and carried down to the floor several stories below. A few people stopped and looked up to see what was going on. "Then you have certainly had a hard life," she said at last.

Gideon frowned. He saw no reason for her to be rude. Besides, he was fairly sure that he didn't look a day over twenty-nine. "Weren't you talking about the root words?" he said coolly, gesturing at the tapestry.

"Um, yes," she replied, clearing her throat slightly to regain her composure. "There are only three root Words that we know of. This one," she pointed again at the first word on the tapestry, "is the most common."

"How do you pronounce it?" asked Gideon.

"I am afraid I cannot speak it without releasing its power. Perhaps you could sound out the word yourself, and I'll tell you if it is correct."

"Wait. If you can't say it without it. . .doing something," Gideon gestured awkwardly with his hands, "then what if I say it right? Won't that knock down a wall or something?"

Aybel suppressed the urge to laugh again, and this time only smiled. "No, the Words are not learned in that way. Pronouncing them correctly is only the first step. And it is no guarantee that the Words will ever become yours."

"How do they 'become yours,' then?" he asked.

Aybel looked down and nodded thoughtfully, as though recalling something from the distant past. "You must know their meaning, of course, but that too is just the beginning. You must meditate on each Word as though it contained a treasure locked up within its letters. For, in truth, it does. And when that treasure is opened to you at last, you must receive it." She raised her eyebrows and looked toward Gideon. "That is the most important part," she added. "Believing in its message."

"Its message?" Gideon repeated. "I don't understand."

"The language of *Dei'lo* carries a power that is rooted in truth," she continued. "But it is a truth that cannot be proven in ordinary ways; it must simply be believed. If you cannot believe the message of the Words, then you cannot know them. And their power is lost to you."

Gideon shrugged. "So what's the message of the Words?"

She stood there a long time, looking at Gideon, thinking about his question. Finally, she said, "I think you must discover that for yourself."

"Oh. Naturally," said Gideon. "I would hate for anything you people say to be obvious or clear." He shook his head and couldn't resist the urge to smile just a little at his own joke, even if Aybel didn't get it at all. "Okay, well, tell me this then," he continued. "Why does it seem so important to you that I learn these Words? What difference does it make to you?"

Aybel nodded as though the answer were obvious. "Because of what I have just explained, sojourner," she said, a little impatiently. "You cannot learn the Words unless you believe them. And you cannot believe them unless your heart is true. If your power is borne from truth, then the Words will pose no hindrance for you. But if your power is borne from falsehood, then you will not be able to learn *Dei'lo* no matter how hard you try, because the Language of Death is already rooted within you."

"So this is all a test," said Gideon grumpily, waving his hand absently toward the tapestry. "To see if I'm your 'Kinsman Redeemer'?"

"No," she replied simply. "I think that has already been shown."

Gideon snorted and shook his head. "You just don't give up, do you?" he mumbled.

"We are more interested in discovering what sort of Kinsman Redeemer you will be," she continued, "and, if we can, sway you toward a path that is good, the path of *Dei'lo*." She gestured toward the tapestry.

"Or kill me if you can't, right?" Gideon said coolly.

"It is also for your protection, sojourner, that you learn the Words," Aybel went on, ignoring his question. "If the Council Lords have realized who you are, they will want to capture you and use you for their own dark purposes. If you can learn the Words, they will not be able to easily turn you to their cause."

"I don't see what difference it makes either way," said Gideon. "Either I get used by them or I get used by you."

Aybel shook her head. "I do not think—"

"You know, you are all hypocrites," Gideon broke in. "You go on and on about the 'evil' Council Lords and all the horrible things they would do to me, and you seem totally blind to the fact that you are doing the very same things." Gideon pointed his finger at her. "You have threatened to kill me if I don't learn these Words. How is that any different from what these Council Lords would do? You are more like them than you want to admit."

"We are nothing like them," snapped Aybel, loudly enough for the people seven stories below to hear her. "What we do, we do for the good of the Inherited Lands. We may err in our ways, Redeemer, but our hearts are true even in our missteps. This is nothing like the Council Lords! Have you so quickly forgotten about your dream on the Plains? You do not see anyone here locking you in a cellar and releasing vermin to eat your flesh, do you? But that is what awaits you in Phallenar."

Gideon felt a rush of anger sweep over him at her mention of the dream in the Plains. He supposed it didn't surprise him that she knew about it, but it angered him all the same. "I don't even know if that dream means anything," he snapped. "Why should I believe what Ajel said about it? It wouldn't have been the first time he lied to me. As far as I'm concerned, it was just a dream."

"Then you are a fool," she said, planting her hands firmly on her hips.

"And you are a liar," he said coldly. "I don't even know why I'm listening to this." He turned his back to her and began to walk away.

"Where are you going?" Aybel demanded.

"For a walk," he called back.

"You must stay here, Redeemer," she said. "We are not finished yet." Gideon didn't respond. "Hold there, Redeemer!" she demanded.

"Why don't you just put me to sleep?" he yelled back without turning around. "That's what you people do, isn't it?"

Aybel opened her mouth in preparation to say something else, but then she thought better of it and let out a long sigh instead. She watched him storm away for a moment, considering her options. And then, with a frustrated shake of her head, she took off down the great hall after him.

———

"Aybel is having trouble with Gideon Dawning."

Paladin Sky glanced up briefly from his stool next to Seer's bed. But his hand continued to gently stroke her forehead. "I know," he said, looking back down at Seer's face, who lay there asleep and as still as death. Paladin closed his eyes briefly and shook his head. "I cannot reach her, Ajel. She is beyond my ability."

"It is not your fault, uncle," said Ajel gently. "None of us could have foreseen what would come of the Facing."

"She might have," corrected Paladin. "She probably did. And she tried to warn me, but I would not listen."

Ajel shifted uneasily as he stood across the bed from his uncle, but said nothing. Paladin Sky had never been one to doubt himself, and the fact that he was doing it now made Ajel uncomfortable.

Quietly, Paladin Sky grinned, just a little. "Peace, Ajel," he said. "I am not falling apart just yet."

"I will speak to the sojourner," said Ajel, changing the subject. "He must know something of what has happened here. He trusts me, a little at least. Perhaps I can learn what he is hiding."

"Aybel says he is not hiding anything," said Paladin. "Not about that anyway. She would know if he were lying."

"He has proven himself to be. . .surprising in many ways," countered Ajel. "He hides his thoughts from us with more success than even Donovan ever could. Aybel may not be capable of sensing his falsehood."

"Then you think he is lying about his remembrance of the Facing?"

Ajel sighed. "I do not know. But perhaps if I speak to him—"

"No," Paladin said. "I will speak to him. I think it is about time I got to know this Redeemer of ours."

Ajel shook his head. "He is dangerous, Paladin. He is far more powerful than he knows. And there is a brokenness within him that only adds to the danger. I do not think you should expose yourself to him—especially now."

Paladin Sky stood and engulfed Seer's hand in both of his own. He looked at her for several long seconds before speaking. "Remain with Seer," he commanded quietly at last. "I will return before nightfall."

Paladin gently laid Seer's hand back on the bed and smiled. Then he spoke a Word quietly under his breath and disappeared.

CHAPTER 24

◄ THE CLIFFS OF WORDHAVEN ►

The prophecies of Endimnar never mention Jesun Sky—
the younger brother of Laudin who came to be known as
Paladin. It was Laudin Sky whom the prophecies praised . . .
the author of the Sky Rebellion, the founder of the Remnant,
the discoverer of ancient Wordhaven. The prophecies never speak
of another man who would step in after Laudin is slain. A man
who would take the reigns of leadership and, in the taking,
forsake all that he ever was or ever wanted to be. A man who
would willingly lose even his own name and relegate himself to
live forever in the shadow of his brother's legacy. And he would
do all this for the sake of a dream that was never his—for no
grander purpose than his belief that it was the right thing to do.

—THE KYRINTHAN JOURNALS, MUSINGS, CHAPTER 5, VERSES 55–58

A cool wind blew in from the cliffs to the west and momentarily countered the heat from the sun, which beamed down pleasantly on
Gideon's shoulders. Although the volcanic thermals kept the air within
the massive crater comfortably warm, the high cliffs that surrounded
the valley on all sides limited the amount of direct sunlight Wordhaven
received each day. So, though it was now already midmorning, large
parts of the valley floor still lay in shadows. From his present viewpoint
on a wide rocky path that hugged the side of the western cliffs, Gideon
could trace the great line of the sun's shadow from one end of the valley to the other and even watch the line shift inexorably eastward, opening more and more of the valley life to the brilliant sun.

The infectious life within the valley below him continued to press
against his mental barriers like a child who wants to play and won't
take no for an answer. But, despite the beauty of the invitation, Gideon
kept his mind locked away from his surroundings. *You can look, but*

don't touch, he warned himself sarcastically. This was certainly no time to let down his guard.

The old man they called Paladin Sky walked just ahead of him and so far had not explained what this little hike was about. Gideon had been eating with Aybel and a few others in a large chamber that the Remnant used as a dining hall when a guard came in and announced that Paladin Sky wanted to see him. With a little coaxing from Aybel, Gideon begrudgingly agreed to leave his meal and go with the guard, who led him through a series of confusing passageways and stairwells until they came at last to the grand entrance of Wordhaven, which Gideon hadn't seen before. It was a massive circular room of white stone and silver, with a huge exquisite-looking pearl sculpture gracing the center.

And there, next to the imposing pearl, stood Paladin, looking very prophetlike with his white, flowing robes and matching white hair and carrying Gideon's almond wood staff as though it belonged to him. Once Gideon approached, the old man simply said, "Walk with me," then he turned and strolled out past the massive black stone doors, which opened silently as he approached them.

That was almost an hour ago. Now here they were, hiking along a wide stone ledge that looked as though it followed the cliffs around the entire valley. And Gideon still didn't know what all this was about. So he just kept following the old man, not quite sure why he was doing it, but content for the moment just to get outside and stretch his legs.

He would never have admitted it to Paladin, but he was thankful for the quiet. Aybel had been jabbering at him for days about the Remnant and Council and the Words and the Pearl and, of course, the Kinsman Redeemer. He'd tolerated it well enough. He'd even found some of it interesting, though he tried not to let Aybel see that. For some reason, he actually enjoyed antagonizing her. He wondered if he secretly liked her and didn't want to admit it, even to himself. Or perhaps the taunting was just his passive-aggressive way of protesting his imprisonment.

In any case, it was nice to get away from his "studies" for awhile and take in the beauty of the valley below them without the distraction of having to talk—even though he did wonder why the leader of the Remnant, a man who had barely spoken ten words to him before today, had suddenly demanded to see him, only to hike with him in silence. Of course it made no sense. But that was nothing new.

For another half an hour or so, they continued in this way, hiking along the precarious ledge, with each of the men, for his own reasons, content to keep the silence. Eventually they came to a wider section of the ledge, where the path leveled out and the greater part of Wordhaven itself was clearly visible, shining like a black and golden jewel in the morning sun.

Paladin Sky slowed his pace and walked to the edge, then planted Gideon's staff into the rocky soil with a sort of finality. Gideon stopped as well, wiping the sweat from his forehead and secretly glad for the chance to catch his breath. Despite the strenuous hike, he noticed that, unlike himself, the old man wasn't breathing hard at all and had scarcely broken a sweat.

As for Paladin, he never even looked at Gideon, but kept his dark eyes focused on the valley below, which he scanned slowly back and forth in a way that let Gideon know that he was doing far more than simply looking at the life that flourished beneath them. He was becoming a part of it.

Gideon stood behind the man for awhile, wondering whether he should be worried about what the Remnant leader might be planning to do next or just angry at being led around like a prisoner, which he knew was exactly what he was—even with his apparent freedom to roam Wordhaven at will. But he was surprised once again to discover that he really didn't feel strongly one way or the other. In fact, he didn't feel much of anything at all.

"You have my staff," Gideon said at last. He didn't really intend it as an accusation, but that's the way it came out.

Paladin Sky briefly looked down at the staff that he held in his left hand, but then looked back out on the view before him and let out a slow breath. After a few more seconds of silence, he said, "You know, I come up here often. It's a good place. It's solid, silent. A man needs a place like that. It clears the head." He tapped his temple with his index finger. "And I think the hike does me some good as well." He laughed quietly and turned his head toward Gideon, who did not respond.

"Join me, sojourner, please." Paladin Sky gestured to a spot next to him on the cliff's edge. Gideon automatically stiffened a little and did not move. "Don't worry, sojourner. I don't intend you any harm. Perhaps I should be worried that you will push me off the cliff, though, yes?" He smiled when he said this, but Gideon didn't believe the comment was intended solely as a joke. Paladin shrugged. "As you wish, then," he said. "But the view is better from here."

"I can see fine," said Gideon shortly. "Why did you bring me here?"

Paladin Sky turned to face him. "Because I need your help, and I don't know how to get it."

This time, Gideon was the one who laughed. "You need my help?" he asked incredulously. "You've held me prisoner for weeks now. You've invaded my mind. And now you want my help? How do you think I'm going to answer that?"

"I fear that my sister is dying," said Paladin Sky. "And I do not know the cause. Something happened to her in her link with your mind. And I fear that you're the only one who might be able to help her."

Gideon thought for a moment. "Fine," he said. "Let me go. And I'll promise to do what I can." *Which is a whole lot of nothing*, he added to himself.

Paladin Sky lifted Gideon's staff and ran the fingers of his right hand down its length, testing the smoothness of the gilded wood. "It's a fine staff," he said. "Well gilded. The wood is. . .unknown to me. What is it?"

"It's from an almond tree."

Paladin furrowed his brows slightly. "I'm unfamiliar with that wood. Still, it's a solid work. It has no power, you know, apart from you."

Gideon blinked his eyes tiredly. "So I've been told."

"You don't believe it."

"I have no reason to believe anything you tell me."

Paladin nodded thoughtfully. "Perhaps not. Perhaps not. But you cannot deny the reality of the life power that surrounds us here." He gestured to the valley below. "Even though you have sealed your mind from us, I know you sense the life here is true."

Gideon shifted his weight uneasily. "I don't see what that has to do with you or the others."

"It has everything to do with us," said Paladin softly. "This place is why we exist. That and what it represents. We are a part of the life you sense here. Every tree, every leaf on the tree, every wind that touches the leaf, every breath that creates the wind is connected in the trueness of life. This is the gift of the Pearl. You cannot be untrue and know this place." He considered Gideon for a moment, then added, "But you do not know this, for your mind is closed."

"I prefer to keep my thoughts to myself," said Gideon.

"Yes. But I think you keep them *from* yourself as well."

"Look," said Gideon, "do you have a point?"

Paladin Sky suddenly looked sad and furrowed his brow deeply. For a moment it seemed to Gideon that he was on the verge of tears. But then he stepped toward Gideon and extended the staff. "Here," he said. "Take this." Gideon hesitated. "It's yours," Paladin Sky added. "Take it."

"Why?"

"You do not trust me, yes?"

"No, I don't."

"Then take your staff. And strike me with it."

"What? No!"

"Please." Paladin gently laid the staff at Gideon's feet, then stepped backward toward the edge of the cliff. "I am at your mercy."

Gideon shook his head. "This is crazy."

"I assure you it is not, sojourner," Paladin said gently. He spread his arms out from his sides. "You do not trust us because we hold you against your will. Here is your chance to be free of us. We are here alone. I have commanded that we not be disturbed. As you have no doubt sensed, this path leads around to the gates of Wordhaven at the far end of the valley. You will have to run, but you can escape if you wish. You already know how to use the gates. I am unarmed, except with Words, and I give you my solemn oath that I will not use them in my defense. Strike me, and I will fall to my death. And you can be gone."

"Why?" asked Gideon. "Why would you do this?"

"I need you to trust me, sojourner." Paladin's voice grew deeper and more commanding as he spoke. "I need you to help me—to help us. And I can think of no other way to show you that our intentions are true."

Slowly, cautiously, Gideon reached down and picked up the staff. Paladin Sky closed his eyes, but otherwise remained perfectly still, with his arms extended from his sides. Still wondering whether it was some sort of trick, Gideon raised the staff defensively before him and quietly took a step toward the old man. Paladin Sky did not move.

Strangely, Gideon felt numb. The entire scene seemed unreal. Was he really thinking of striking the old man dead? What about going home? If he did this, he would shut out all chances of these people ever helping him get back. Didn't he want to go home?

In the heat of that moment and in the strange calmness of his thoughts, the answer became obvious. He really didn't *want* to go home. There was no life for him back there. Just a cat, an estranged brother, and a mother who could get along just fine without him. Maybe she'd even be better off. Maybe they all would be.

This was a strange land, he admitted. A weird land, with confusing people and mysterious powers he could not begin to understand. But it was also *new*. Even with the numbness that dominated his soul, he could sense that newness stirring a distant feeling deep within him. A feeling he believed had died years before. *Hope.* He felt *hope*. Hope for something different, something new. A second chance. The possibility of starting over. And maybe, just maybe, having a genuine life again.

He took another step toward Paladin Sky. Still, the old man did not move. Slowly, Gideon raised the staff over his shoulder and mentally targeted his arc to swing around and strike the back of the old man's head.

He wouldn't try to kill Paladin, of course. He was no murderer, even though part of him thought the old man deserved it. But he would not strike to kill. He could just give the man a good whack on the head, enough to knock him unconscious. Enough to give him time to get away.

Silently, he raised the staff a little higher, gauging the distance between the wood and Paladin's waiting head. But then, quite suddenly, he thought of Lairn. Perhaps the way he held the staff now, extended over his head like this, sparked the scene of Lairn's grisly death. He wasn't sure. The boy had believed in him so unquestioningly, so completely. His faith had been so absolute that he willingly died to save Gideon's life. And for what? *So I could clunk this old man and prove Lairn wrong? Is that all that the boy's death meant?*

And what about all the people at Songwill? And the little girl at Calmeron? Both of Cimron's children are now dead because of me. Because they believed I was something that I'm not. Something I could never be.

It's all a lie, Gideon thought. *It's all a lie. And I'm the only one who knows it.* But the thought of Lairn watching him now, with the staff held high ready to strike this old man, made his stomach churn. He couldn't do that to Lairn. Even if it was a lie.

At last, Gideon lowered his arms and dropped the staff to the ground. "Why don't you just let me go?" he asked with a sigh.

Paladin Sky opened his eyes. And smiled. "I knew you could not do it," he said.

Gideon looked up at the clouds. "Yeah, well, that makes one of us."

"You will help us then? We have an understanding, you and I."

Gideon lowered his head and rubbed his temples. "No," he said under his breath. "No, no, no!" He looked up and glared at Paladin Sky. "We don't have an understanding. We've never had an understanding. There hasn't been any understanding since I got here!"

Gideon took a step toward Paladin. "Listen. Just. . .let me. . .go. I am not who you think I am. I am not your 'Kinsman Redeemer.' I don't know what happened to your sister, and I don't have any idea how to help her. Okay? I don't remember. Heck, I don't understand half of what's going on around me, and I'm tired of trying to fight off a title that clearly doesn't belong to me. Why can't you just believe me? I'm no good to you. I'm not the long-lost savior of the world, and I can't help you win your war. So why don't you just let me go?"

"You are right, of course," said Paladin sadly. "It was wrong for us to hold you and to force you to endure the Facing. We have allowed our fear of what you may be to cloud our respect for who you are. And it seems we will bear the punishment for our error—both in your mistrust of us and in my sister's ailing condition. I take responsibility for our actions. I am sorry."

Gideon met Paladin's gaze and held it for some time. But he said nothing.

"You are free to go, sojourner," continued Paladin Sky solemnly. "But you are also free to stay. I only ask that you give me—give us—a little time that we might show you who we truly are and help you understand the cause for which we fight. Then, if you still wish to go, you will at least know what you are rejecting and what you are choosing to embrace."

Gideon stood and glared silently at the old man. *Did he even hear what I said?* Gideon asked himself. *He still believes I am this 'Redeemer.' This is crazy! But at least he's willing to let me go. And I could use some time to think about what I want to do next. . .where I want to go. . . .*

"All right," Gideon said at last. "I'll stay for awhile—as a *guest*." Paladin Sky nodded his agreement. "But I have one condition."

"What is it?"

"Nobody calls me 'Kinsman Redeemer' or any derivative thereof—ever. And nobody tries to convince me that I am the savior of the world."

"As you wish." Paladin smiled.

CHAPTER 25

PRISIDIUM SQUARE

*Under Council rule, class distinctions have always been strictly
defined and just as strictly enforced. For example, it was forbidden
for a peasant to bond with a commoner or a merchant with a
jalen. The only exception, as seen in my circumstance, was the
encouragement of bonds between Lords and underlords, as that
was the means by which the Council passed its authority from one
generation to the next. Despite this strict segregation of classes
within the city, however, daily life in Phallenar was surprisingly
free from conflict or any open expressions of prejudice.
The Council always attributed this to their governing policies,
which did allow people a surprising amount of personal freedom
within certain boundaries. Most historians today, however,
attribute this apparent harmony to the citizens' collective fear of
the Council Lords themselves. Conflict of any sort within the city
drew the Council's attention. And the last thing any citizen of
Phallenar wanted was to be singled out of the crowd.*

—The Kyrinthan Journals, Chronicles, Chapter 15, Verses 71–74

The light of the sun had not yet reached the floor of Prisidium Square
in Phallenar, but already many of the merchants were fussing around
their shops and carts, cleaning and preparing them for the crowds of
people who would be arriving within a few hours. Other city workers
were sweeping the vast limestone-paved square, which glowed with
an orange hue from the sunlight reflected off the Great Wall to the
west. A few others were busy watering the clusters of green trees and
grasses that dotted the area here and there. Another day of commerce
was about to begin.

Council Lord Bentel Baratii was surprised to see that the Sea Folk
had already brought in their morning's catch all the way from Silence

Sound. He wondered if they had arrived the evening before or had traveled through the night to get here at this early hour. By the fishy smell that wafted his direction, he guessed it was the former. That was understandable, naturally. Only a fool would travel the Gorge at night. The Black Gorge might be the only waterway between the Sound and Phallenar, but it was not the sort of place anyone wanted to go without considerable protection, even during the full light of day. A few Guardians always traveled with the Sea Folk, by order of the Council. But even with their protection, the Gorge still managed to claim more than a dozen lives every year.

With all their bustling about, the Sea Folk and other merchants made a good show of not noticing the Council Lords who graced the Square this morning or even of the six huge juron that stalked around in circles in the center of the Square as though confined to a cage. Bentel found their caution amusing, even if he didn't quite understand it. *Some people just fear authority*, he guessed.

Bentel never let himself get caught up in class distinctions like that. *People are all made from the same stuff*, he reasoned. *They just happen to have differing abilities and levels of intelligence*. He never chose to be a Council Lord, just as the merchants probably never chose to be common. Each person simply filled the role in society that matched his intelligence and ability. For that reason, he always made a point of treating commoners with respect, even more respect than was really their due. Just because he'd been born with more intelligence didn't mean he had to be arrogant about it.

Bentel turned his attention from the merchants to the other Lords who had gathered there this early morning. Fayerna was busily organizing their supplies into three equal piles, while Sarlina was doing her best to help however she could, which generally resulted in Fayerna repeatedly asking her to step to one side or the other so she wouldn't be in the way. Despite their constant bickering, though, Bentel knew that his sister genuinely cared for the girl. Fayerna always had a soft spot for the less fortunate, even though it seemed that they caused her unending frustration. Sarlina had been one of those "borderline" Lords—almost too stupid to make it to the Council level. But Fayerna had rallied for her acceptance and even taken it upon herself to train the girl so she wouldn't be an embarrassment. Bentel had to admit she'd done a good job. Sarlina knew how to look regal when she needed to, and she never spoke to another Lord without first checking with Fayerna or him. And, of course, she never spoke with a commoner for any reason whatsoever.

The big surprise of the morning had been the arrival of the High Lord himself, along with Lysteria, who came with their *mon'jalen* bearing gifts and random supplies for the journey. Fayerna had greeted them warmly, of course, and thanked them for their gifts, but then immediately set about repacking all of their supplies with a frustrated look etched on her face. Bentel left her to it, knowing better than to get between the woman and her obsession with organization. He only wished Sarlina was smart enough to get out of the way as well.

"We don't really need these blankets," Fayerna mumbled absently as she tried in vain to squeeze them into one of the satchels.

"We Worded them ourselves," said Lysteria, gesturing softly toward Balaam. "They'll keep you comfortably warm whatever the weather is like. I hope they're not any trouble."

"Oh, no," countered Fayerna pleasantly, realizing she'd been overheard. "No trouble at all, really. I'll just take out a few of these other things we don't really need." Her brows furrowed as she sorted through her own supplies, shaking her head at each one as she set it on the ground.

"So, what route will you be taking?" asked Balaam. The question was directed at Bentel.

Bentel turned his full attention to the High Lord. "We'll be flying west over the plains to the sight of the massacre in the Heaven Range. From there we'll track the rebels' route whichever way they went."

"You won't stop to rest before reaching the Range?" asked Balaam.

"Well, we hadn't intended to," explained Bentel. "We thought it best to get there as quickly as possible."

"You shouldn't push yourself so hard," said Balaam.

"I would hate to see you have to face those rebels without being rested," cautioned Lysteria.

Bentel smiled graciously. "Well, perhaps we should stop on the way, then. But, honestly, I don't really expect the rebels to be that much of a problem to us."

"Perhaps not, young man," said Balaam. "But you should not underestimate these people. Fanatics like these have been known to do ruthless things in the name of their cause."

"But they don't even have the Words, aside from a few pathetic phrases of ancient *Dei'lo*," offered Bentel plaintively.

"Even a Lord can be vulnerable to an arrow or a sword if he isn't careful," countered Balaam. "You watch yourself out there."

"Yes, High Lord."

"We want you back safe and sound," added Lysteria, trying to soften Balaam's tone.

"As do I, Lord Lysteria," answered Bentel with a deferential nod.

"Well!" said Fayerna, brushing the dust off of her traveling pants. "That about does it, I think."

She walked toward the other Lords with a smile. "Oh, Lok," she called over her shoulder, "you three can load the bags on the juron now. And don't worry, they won't bite you."

The three *mon'jalen*, who until now had been talking quietly in a huddle to one side, immediately stopped their whispering and marched toward the piles of bags and began to haul them over to the juron, who growled at their approach but did nothing more.

"Silly *mon'jalen*," said Fayerna with a smile. "You have to keep reassuring them about every little thing." She tucked a bit of wayward red hair behind her ear. "I have to say, we're so delighted that you came to send us off. You really shouldn't have gone to all the trouble."

"Nonsense," said Balaam with a wave of his hand. "We may have our differences, Fayerna, but we're still all serving the same cause. We wanted you to know that you have our full support and that we wish you fortune in your task."

"Why, thank you, High Lord," said Fayerna.

"Yes, to both of you, thanks," echoed Bentel.

"*Oooff*. . ." Bentel and Fayerna turned around to see one of the *mon'jalen* flat on his back with an overstuffed satchel lying on his chest. One of the juron had apparently spread its wings and knocked the wind right out of him.

"Oh, Sanchi," scolded Sarlina, looking clearly nervous that her *mon'jalen* had disrupted the Lords' conversation. "Why did you do that? You're a bad *mon'jalen!*" She smiled sheepishly at the other Lords, then stormed over to Sanchi and slapped him on the head. "Get up! Get up!"

"It's all right, Sarlina," said Fayerna tiredly. "He just got knocked over. He'll be fine."

Sarlina smiled sheepishly again and nodded, then quietly walked back to where she was standing before, next to the bags. She continued to glare at her *mon'jalen*, though, until he got up and got back to work.

"I must say, dear," Lysteria whispered to Fayerna, "I wonder if taking Sarlina along is such a good idea."

"She'll be fine, Lord Lysteria," replied Fayerna in a normal voice. "She can be troublesome at times, but she's really very good in a fight."

"Really!" replied Lysteria, as though such a thing could never be true.

"Oh yes," Bentel broke in, "Sarlina can be a vicious little cat when she's cornered. Not unlike my dear sister, here."

"I'm more like a juron, I'd say," corrected Fayerna, brushing some wayward dust off her shoulder. "Only far, far more deadly." She smiled, and Bentel laughed.

"Well, you must be off," said Balaam suddenly. "You have a long journey today, and I see that the sun has already reached the square."

"Yes, we really do need to go," agreed Fayerna, glancing back at the sunlight that now bathed the entire square in a brilliant white.

Bentel bowed slightly toward Lysteria and the High Lord. "Thank you again for coming out. I'm sure we'll return soon with our wayward Redeemer in hand."

"I'd expect nothing less," agreed Balaam.

Bentel and Fayerna bowed again, slightly, then turned to go.

"Oh, about that. . . ," said Balaam. The pair stopped and turned around. "I'm curious," he continued. "How do you plan to track the rebel?"

Bentel started to speak, but Fayerna broke in ahead of him. "If it please you, High Lord, we'd prefer that to be a surprise." She smiled with as much pleasantness and innocence as she could muster.

Balaam stared at her a moment, then smiled and nodded. "Well played, Fayerna," he said. "A surprise it shall be, then." With that, he offered Lysteria his arm and they turned to go.

Bentel and Fayerna watched them walk away in the direction of the Axis. Once they had gone far enough, Bentel turned to his *mon'jalen*, the only female of the three, and asked, "Kyrva, are the juron ready?"

"Yes, m'Lord."

"Then let's be gone. Fayerna, you have the item?"

Fayerna grinned as she pulled a small bundle of cloth out of her vest. As Bentel approached, she laid the item in her palm and began to carefully unwrap the folds.

"Did the Firstsworn have any trouble finding it?" asked Bentel.

"My, I should say yes!" said Fayerna. "Why, from the way he talked, you'd think the ordeal cost him his right arm." Fayerna pulled back the last layer of cloth to reveal a smaller, white piece of cloth, covered in rusty-brown stains.

"He's sure that's the Stormcaller's blood?" asked Bentel as he scrutinized the stained cloth. "How do we know it's not somebody else's?"

"Oh, it's his," replied Fayerna. "Borin gave me his personal assurance."

"Well, how does he know?"

Fayerna sighed. "Well, if you must hear the story. . .he went to Calmeron and found Cimron and his bondmate—they're those troublemakers that nursed the rebel back to health, you remember? Anyway, after some persuasion with the Words, Borin compelled them to supply him with a sample of the rebel's blood. And here it is." She held it up to Bentel's face like a prize.

He wrinkled his nose at it. "I am truly amazed. How did you know they would have something like this? I would have thought that they would have burned such a disgusting thing."

"You just don't know enough about the ways of these soundenors," said Fayerna. "They have a keen affection for collecting mementos and such, especially things that remind them of important events or important people. You must remember, many of the peasants firmly believe this rebel is the Kinsman Redeemer."

Bentel shook his head and rolled his eyes. "Myths," he said. "Backward beliefs for backward people."

"Come, let's go," said Fayerna. She turned from Bentel and walked toward the juron, who seemed unaware of her approach. She stepped up to each one in turn, held the bloodstained cloth in front of its nose, then spoke a few Words into the beast's ear. As she did this, each juron became noticeably agitated and began flapping its wings excitedly. As she finished the last one, Fayerna turned and called to the others, "Get on!"

The *mon'jalen* immediately complied, each climbing up the wing of his or her beast, then shuffling forward so that their legs straddled its neck. They grabbed the thick black mane with their gloved hands and waited. The three Lords followed, each duplicating the *mon'jalen's* movements with equal, if not superior, grace.

Once everyone was in place, Bentel glanced at each rider one last time to make certain everything was set, then he called out to the air above the group, *"Demoi shataris!"* Instantly, the juron looked up and, upon seeing the sky for the first time that day, spread their wings and took flight. They headed west, of course, following the faint scent of Gideon's blood, which, thanks to Fayerna's Wording, now obsessed them.

CHAPTER 26

THE STREETS OF PHALLENAR

*Both languages of power contain Words that allow the speaker
to transport instantly from one location to another. However,
in each language, there are strict restrictions: A speaker can
transport only to a place that he or she has been before and
knows extremely well. This created a problem whenever a
Council Lord or member of the Remnant needed to go someplace
new or not well known to them, for it required them to travel
there physically first and spend considerable time in that
place, before they could transport there using the Words.
It is true that High Lord Balaam found a way to overcome this
restriction, though no one has ever learned how he did it. The
Remnant, on the other hand, simply got around this problem by
using a different Word—one that allowed them to see, in their
spirits, a place to which they dreamed of going. Sa'lei has no
counterpart for this ability, though we can only guess as to the
reasons why. Some scribes have suggested that the language of
death cannot deal in dreams because dreams are a part of the
process of creation. Perhaps that is so. But I tend to think it is
because dreams require faith and hope in order to exist. And the
language of death cannot traffic in qualities such as these.*

—THE KYRINTHAN JOURNALS, THE LANGUAGES OF POWER, SECTION 3, VERSES 22–23

Lord Lysteria Asher-Baal and her bondmate, the High Lord Balaam,
watched from the shadows at the edge of Prisidium Square as the
three other Council Lords and their *mon'jalen* mounted the powerful
juron, who spread their massive black wings and took flight into the
morning skies.

All of the merchants, who had previously been pretending to
ignore the Lords' presence, now stopped their busy work and openly

gawked at the impressive spectacle. It was a rare thing for them to see a wild juron at all, much less six of them all together at once and each with a human master on top of that. It was little wonder that the commoners feared the Council Lords so much, mused Lysteria. To them, they were the creators of miracles.

"Well, I hope they can do it," said Balaam, watching the juron fly out of view to the west. He still held Lysteria's hand in the crook of his arm and patted it absently as he spoke.

"I'm certain they'll do their best if for no other reason than to strengthen their standing in the Axis."

Balaam nodded. "True, they are ambitious. Especially Fayerna. It's a good trait. But too much will kill you."

"Oh, you're one to talk!" Lysteria slapped him gently on the wrist.

Balaam said nothing, but grinned slightly.

They stood there in the morning shadows for a few more moments, silently watching the merchants as they put the finishing touches on their carts and storefront displays. A few of the early shoppers had already begun to trickle in from the city. Within the hour, the entire square would become a sea of hustling bodies, chaotically surging here and there in their bright-colored clothing and filling the square with the unmistakable roar of a thousand people haggling at once.

Lysteria loved the sounds and smells of the market, although she didn't visit it very often, at Balaam's insistence. Her presence in any marketplace had a way of disrupting the flow of commerce. And good commerce was important to the Lords for several reasons.

"Shall we go?" asked Balaam.

Lysteria nodded. "Can we walk? It's still early. Not many people are out."

Balaam glanced at the sun. "All right," he said. "For awhile."

Still holding her hand in his arm, Balaam led Lysteria down a narrow but straight limestone-paved roadway that shot off diagonally from the square. Half of the street was still in shadows, and the twosome huddled toward the darker side to avoid the already hot morning sun and to make themselves a bit less conspicuous in this public setting. Their two *mon'jalen* followed silently at a discreet distance behind them.

Not that they needed to worry about crowds at this time of day, really. Not many people were on the streets. . .a mother and her daughter here, a tradesman on a mount there. And they chose to ignore the Lords in like manner to the merchants in the square. But the sounds of morning life were everywhere, echoing out of the open windows that lined the street above their heads. . . .

". . .you'll want sounden bread with that. . ."

". . .not until you wash that face. . ."

". . .come help me with this, Jorda, would you. . ."

Lysteria swelled with pride as she listened to the sounds of life in the city. Happy people. That's what she heard. And that made her proud, because it meant that her city, her beautiful city, was running smoothly, just as she intended it to do.

"Do you think they noticed?" asked Balaam, suddenly breaking Lysteria's train of thought.

"What's that, dear?"

"The blankets. Do you think they noticed?"

"Well, I don't see how they could," said Lysteria. "They could tell the cloth was Worded, of course, but I already told them as much. I don't see how they can tell all that the Wording is capable of doing."

"I suppose not," sighed Balaam. "I suppose not."

"Are you really sure it will work?" asked Lysteria. "It sounds so dangerous to me, appearing inside a rolled blanket like that. What if the blanket is folded up or stuffed in a bag? How could you appear in something that small?"

"It will still work, Lysteria," said Balaam, a little shortly. "I tested it myself several times. I Worded the cloth so that I can sense when the blanket is free from restriction and whether there are people nearby."

"Then you just imagine yourself wrapped up in the blanket and speak the Word of Transport?"

"Yes."

"Very clever, dear, I must say." Lysteria patted him on the arm. "I would have never thought of such a method for transporting somewhere you've never been before."

"Of course not, dear," smiled Balaam. "Such a method would mess up your hair too much."

"You watch yourself, High Lord," she snapped. But she squeezed his arm to ease the reprimand. "Why do you want to spy on our lordly friends anyway?"

"I don't see how they can possibly track that one rebel in those vast mountains without some kind of outside help. They're hiding something, and I'd like to know what it is."

"Are you afraid they may be betraying you?" asked Lysteria.

Balaam nodded. "I wouldn't put it past them. They may have raised a following among the soundens. I'm not ready to call them traitors yet, but I have my suspicions."

"They do always present a united front in the Axis," observed Lysteria.

Balaam nodded. "And if they can capture this troublemaker and bring him back alive, I fear it will only strengthen their standing among the other Lords."

"Well, then why in Palor's name did you let them go?" Lysteria looked at him incredulously.

"I had little choice," replied Balaam simply. "You saw the way they played their hand in the Axis. Besides, I've been waiting for them to make their move. Now that they have, I have something tangible to work with."

"Is that why you required them to bring the rebel back alive?"

Balaam nodded. "In part, yes. I made their task more difficult. You know how hard it is to use the Words to capture something without killing it."

Lysteria gave her bondmate a sidelong glance and grinned. "But that's not the only reason, is it?" she asked. "You've got something else going on up there." She pointed at Balaam's bald head. "Don't you?"

Balaam reached up and enfolded her hand in his. "Always, my dear," he said with a grin. "Always. But I'll save that for another time."

"You don't trust me?" asked Lysteria incredulously.

Balaam gestured toward the sky. "I don't trust the air," he said.

Upon hearing this warning, Lysteria looked up and tried to sample the atmosphere around them with her thoughts. Distantly, weakly, she could sense in the air the telltale vibrations that emanated from anything that had been Worded. She wondered who among the Council Lords might be trying to listen in on their private conversation.

"A mite, Lord?" The beggar appeared in front of them out of a narrow walkway leading into one of the buildings. She looked fairly young, though it was difficult to tell under all the grime that coated her face. Her rags, made of burlap, identified her as a widow mourning her dead husband. At least that's what she wanted people to believe, suspected Lysteria.

"A mite, fair mistress?" She cupped both hands out in front of her. "For a forsaken widow?"

"I'm sorry, dear," replied Lysteria, "I haven't got a coin on me. Good day then."

"Thank you, m'lady," the beggar said as the twosome walked on past. "The Giver bless your day."

After they walked a few more steps, Balaam snorted, "She didn't even recognize who we are."

"Raug!" Lysteria called behind her.

Her *mon'jalen* immediately ran up beside her master. "Lord?" he said.

"See that that filthy troublemaker is put out of the city."

"Yes, Lord."

"And make certain she can't get back in. Take her to the Barrens."

"Yes, Lord." Raug slowly faded back to his place next to the other *mon'jalen.*

Lysteria leaned her head toward Balaam. "You should talk to Varia about this," she said. "Isn't she supposed to be in charge of caring for the impoverished?"

Balaam nodded. "You should talk to her," he said.

"Humph," Lysteria snorted. "She's as rude as she is ugly. She never pays attention to anything I suggest."

Balaam smiled. "She's just threatened by your beauty."

"Stop trying to change the subject."

"Was I?" Balaam looked surprised.

"Will you speak to her? I can't bear the thought of beggars in our streets."

Balaam patted her hand. "I'm sure you can handle it just fine, dear."

Lysteria shook her head. After a few seconds, she said, "You can be so cold at times."

"How do you think I got to be High Lord?" replied Balaam, still smiling.

CHAPTER 27

WORDHAVEN

In each generation, a High Lord was appointed as the Batai,
or Right Hand of the Pearl. The Batai served the Pearl exclusively
and acted as its representative in all matters of rule and
instruction. Throughout the Endless Age, all of the Batai were
proven men and women of noble heart who endured decades of
testing and training before they were called to carry the Staff of
Truth. Anyone who aspired to the call of Batai forsook all other
interests for the sake of that one aim. No Batai ever took a mate or
pursued any other interests of a personal nature. The Batai's entire
existence was committed wholeheartedly to the service of the Pearl.
Before his soul was corrupted, High Lord Gideon Truesworn was
widely esteemed as the greatest Batai of the entire Age. His devotion
to the service of the Pearl surpassed even that of his predecessors.
The Wordhaven records describe how he often committed himself
to long seasons of solitude with the Pearl, even going so far as to
refuse food or drink for days on end, so that he might focus his full
attention on gaining more of the Pearl's wisdom. His renown as a
leader extended even beyond the borders of the Inherited Lands so
that nobles from other lands made yearly sojourns to Wordhaven
simply to receive his counsel in matters of governing and life.

—THE KYRINTHAN JOURNALS, CHRONICLES, CHAPTER 2, VERSES 30–37

Gideon strolled along the open-air walkway of the Great Hall, casually looking back and forth across the massive atrium for any sign of Aybel.

Although it was only an hour or so past dawn, the light within the Hall was annoyingly bright, as it always was, prompting Gideon to squint to keep his eyes, which were not yet fully awake, from watering. Actually, it wasn't the brightness that bothered him so much as the fact that the unseen light source within the Hall mysteriously obliterated every shadow. This had the effect of making most everything in the grand chamber—including his skin—appear to be glowing. It was beautiful in its way, but he also found the phenomenon disturbing.

"Let's see. . . ," Gideon mumbled to himself, "Inner Hall, third level, along the inner wall. . ." He squinted harder as he mentally gauged the degree of curve in the corridor's walls. So far, that was the only way he'd found to distinguish one Great Hall from another—but it didn't always work. Since the three circular Halls were laid out concentrically, the Inner Hall was naturally smaller than the other two, and, therefore, the curve of its walls should be more obvious. But all three Halls were incredibly massive, so recognizing any curve at all took considerable focus. So even after more than two weeks of exploring the three Great Halls of Wordhaven, he still found it depressingly easy to get lost.

He blinked. "Well, I think this is it."

Some days before, after getting lost on the way to yet another training session—this one with Donovan and Aybel in a large chamber called the Training Hall—he had asked Aybel to provide him with a map of Wordhaven so he could navigate the corridors more easily. She seemed shocked at his request and promptly told him that such a thing was not permitted. The Remnant, she added, had learned their way around Wordhaven by following the tapestries, which were each unique and chronologically arranged, more or less. So that's what he should do too.

The problem with this idea was that there were literally thousands of tapestries lining nearly every wall in Wordhaven, and each one was an intricate mosaic of images and symbols that often ran together in such a way that isolating just one image out of a single tapestry took effort. So the very thought of having to study them well enough to use them as guideposts seemed to Gideon both exhausting and hardly worth the trouble.

On this particular morning, Gideon was to meet Aybel at the "tapestries of the Pearl," which she said were located on the third level of the Inner Hall, along the face of the inner wall. Although Gideon believed he was in the right general vicinity, he of course had no idea what that particular set of tapestries looked like. So he contented himself with looking for Aybel instead, which was easier to do, as she generally stood out in any crowd, with her telltale cropped white hair and chocolate-colored skin.

Even at this early hour, dozens of people were already milling about the Great Hall, busily attending to their daily tasks and assignments. Gideon still couldn't decide if Wordhaven was more of a commune or a military installation. In truth it was a mixture of both, he supposed, with a considerable amount of a tribal mentality thrown in for good measure. There was definitely a hierarchy of authority here, but there was also an unmistakable bond of familial affection. He had yet to hear anyone speak ill of another member of the Remnant, even jokingly.

Two levels below him, on the floor of the Great Hall, a company of Wordhaveners gathered piles of supplies into bundles and began stuffing them into large canvas sacks. They seemed to be preparing to go somewhere on an extended journey. Curious, Gideon paused and leaned over the black and gold railing to get a better view.

"Greetings, sojourner."

Gideon involuntarily jumped upright and spun around. There before him stood Ajel, smiling in that intimidating-yet-innocent way that he had, but otherwise looking quite different from the seasoned horseman and traveling companion Gideon had come to know during the trek from Calmeron. He had exchanged his brown leathers for pearly white robes, which looked very much like his uncle's, and made the man seem even taller and more regal, if that were possible. His long blond hair no longer hung about his shoulders, but was pulled back in a tail behind his head, which now sported a silver headband just like the one Gideon had seen on Revel some weeks before. But the eyes were still the same; that piercing, too-blue color that matched the grand skies of this strange land and made Gideon feel just as insignificant.

"Oh, Ajel. Hi," he said.

"My apologies, sojourner," said Ajel with a slight bow of the head. "I did not mean to startle you. Wordhaven is normally a difficult place for one to move in stealth." He grinned politely.

Gideon gave a mock smile in return. "Yeah, well, I'm not quite as in touch with my surroundings as some."

Ajel glanced over the railing to the floor below. "What were you seeing?" he asked.

"Oh, I was just watching those people down. . ." Gideon stopped short as he looked to the floor below and saw absolutely no one and no supplies. "Huh. . .that's funny," he mumbled. "There were a whole bunch of people down there just now," he said to Ajel. "I don't know how they got out of here so fast."

Ajel nodded, but offered no explanation of his own. "I am told you were to meet Aybel this morning," he said.

Gideon looked up from the spot where the people had been and glanced around the Hall. "Yeah," he said, "um. . .I'm supposed to meet her at the tapestries of the Pearl, I think."

Again, Ajel nodded. "I am here to tell you that she will not be joining you today. She has been called away with Donovan on a matter of some urgency. She asked if I would meet with you in her stead."

Gideon shrugged slightly. "That's cool," he said, trying to sound nonchalant. "So where'd she go?"

"I believe the tapestries you mentioned are this way," said Ajel, gesturing down the walkway to his right. With the slightest of nods, he invited Gideon to follow as he began walking down the corridor. "They have gone to Calmeron sounden to attend to Cimron and his bondmate, Mara," he continued. "They have been injured."

Gideon felt his heart race at the mention of his former hosts. . .and the thought of their two children, who were dead because of him. "What happened to them?" he asked slowly, forcing his voice to sound neutral.

"We have learned that Borin Slayer returned to Calmeron almost a fortnight past. He came to them searching for some sign of you."

"Of me?"

Ajel nodded, furrowing his brows slightly. "A piece of cloth, a boot, anything you might have handled during your stay there."

"Why would he want that?"

"I cannot fathom why." Ajel shook his head.

Gideon grimaced. He expected Ajel to have an answer for everything. Well, nearly everything, anyway. "Did he get it?" he asked at last.

"Yes," Ajel nodded, "a bloodstained fragment of cloth. . .but not before nearly bringing both Cimron and Mara to death themselves."

Gideon swallowed. "They're going to be okay?"

"We will know in a day or two," said Ajel with just a hint of sorrow in his voice. "Kair is with them. She is very skilled in the healing Words."

Ajel added nothing more, and Gideon found he did not want to ask about the nature of their injuries. The pair continued in silence for awhile, Gideon keeping his eyes absently focused on the walkway in front of him. That family had been so kind to him. . .and they had paid dearly for it. And now they were continuing to pay, even after Gideon was long gone from their home. It seemed that everyone around him always ended up suffering because of him. Everyone who really cared about him, anyway. Then a disturbing thought rose unbidden in his mind.

"Do they know. . .about Lairn?" Gideon asked Ajel.

Ajel nodded. "They have known for some time."

"How did. . .how did they react to the news?"

Ajel kept looking straight ahead. "They are resolved," he said.

Gideon looked back down at the floor. They probably hated him now, he realized. And who could blame them, after all the pain his presence had brought on their lives? He shook his head angrily. It's probably best that they hated him anyway, he decided. Maybe that way he wouldn't cause them any more grief.

They should just forget about me and get on with their lives. That is, if they even are still alive. He blinked to stop the burning in his eyes.

"Ah, I believe these are the tapestries Aybel wanted you to see."

Ajel made a sweeping motion toward several large woven tapestries that lined the wall. They were each identical in size, six feet wide and about twice as high. They were filled with images of a pearly-white orb set on the end of a long golden staff. The scenes around the orb on all the tapestries were varied and intricate in both detail and style and had a way of flowing into one another so that it was difficult to tell precisely where one scene ended and another began. Gideon wondered how long it must have taken to weave masterpieces like these and, really, how such amazing detail could be accomplished in a weaving at all.

Ajel pointed toward the panel closest to them. "This particular tapestry chronicles the details of the Pearl's destruction." He turned to Gideon. "Is this what Aybel wanted to show you?"

Gideon shrugged. "I guess so. I don't know. We've looked at a lot of these."

Ajel looked at Gideon a moment, as though considering Gideon's response. Then he turned back to the tapestry and pointed toward the top. "As with most of the historical tapestries in Wordhaven, the chronicle moves as a spiral from the upper left corner there, until it ends here in the center, where you can see the depiction of Gideon's Fall. If you wish, we can go through this tapestry together so you can better understand how the Inherited Lands came to be in their present state."

Gideon nodded halfheartedly, not sure he wanted to sit through another lecture just now, not after hearing about Cimron and Mara. In the last few weeks, he'd studied at least a hundred different tapestries, each of which dealt with a different aspect of history or wisdom or the use of *Dei'lo*. He even practiced learning the Words—quite unsuccessfully—with at least a dozen different people and explored so many "significant" engravings about this or that within the various chambers and rooms of Wordhaven that he'd lost count. All of this, he was told, was a part of Paladin Sky's attempt to help him understand why the Remnant existed and why they opposed the Council Lords. But his own cynical nature wouldn't let him shake the feeling that they might be trying to brainwash him, giving him a one-sided view of their history so that he would feel compelled to join their cause.

In truth, he had actually learned a great deal. And it interested him more than he would ever openly admit, especially to Ajel or Aybel. Still, he remained wary, forcing himself to continually question why any of it should matter to him at all.

Absently, he rubbed his eyes as Ajel continued.

"As you no doubt already learned, for many millennia prior to the events depicted here, the Pearl was the sole source of authority and power within the Inherited Lands."

"A living orb," Gideon interjected. "I still don't get that."

Ajel frowned slightly. "Yes, a living orb. The Pearl was not a talisman or any sort of magical device. It was a living being whose teachings and benevolent rule shaped and prospered all life within our borders. Did not Aybel already explain this?"

"Yeah, she did. It's just hard for me to think of a glowing ball as a living thing, I guess."

"Life takes many forms," said Ajel. "At times the most beautiful of these is also the one we least expect, the one that challenges our reason and our understanding of the world."

Gideon shrugged. "Well, okay. But how could they be sure it was alive? Why couldn't it have been a transmitter or just a power source of some kind?"

"The people recognized the life of the Pearl in the same manner by which I recognize life within you or you within me," replied Ajel. "Wherever life is present, it is undeniable. The Pearl, however, was more than simply alive. The Pearl was the embodiment of life."

Gideon was unconvinced. "Well, where did it come from?"

"From the Giver," said Ajel simply.

"How did it get here?" asked Gideon. "Did it just appear out of nowhere and say, 'Hello, I'm a white ball and I'm your new leader'?"

Ajel laughed. "It came as any good gift comes, sojourner—unexpectedly and without conditions. The Pearl never demanded authority. The people chose to follow it for they recognized what it was."

"Which was what exactly?" asked Gideon.

"It was the answer, of course."

"The answer to what?"

Ajel smiled. "To every question that matters."

CHAPTER 28

THE TOWER OF THE WALL

*I always knew I was destined for the Tower, from the time I was
quite young. For early on, while still a child, I could already see
the corruption that festered beneath the polished grandeur of the
Axis. I cannot say how or why I could so plainly discern what
was hidden to most of those around me. But I could see the
twisting effects of Sa'lei on the human soul, the darkness of heart
and conscience that came with their continued use. I saw this in
my parents most of all. Over the years of my childhood, I
watched the Words slowly choke their souls, then blind their
minds from realizing they were dead. And so I came to despise
Sa'lei and swore that the Words would never touch my tongue.
All this occurred before my tenth year, and even then I knew what
my hatred of the Words would bring me. So I prepared for my
imprisonment. I built alliances among the Guardians, the ser'-
jalen, the merchants, even a few of the other underlords. I nurtured
these friendships as though they were my life and hope—for, in
truth, they were precisely that. As a result of my efforts, by the time
I was imprisoned, my network of friends and spies extended as far
away as Morguen sounden and as high as the Axis chamber itself.*

—THE KYRINTHAN JOURNALS, SONGS OF DELIVERANCE, STANZA 1, VERSES 1–10

Underlord Kyrintha Asher-Baal looked up from her scrolls just as the
sunbeams of dawn spilled into her dark, silent chamber from the east
and frowned. She usually loved the view of the sunrise from her prison
home in the Tower, but not when it sneaked up on her like this, as it
had too many mornings lately.

She had been at it all night again, she realized, and would no
doubt bear the marks of her enterprise in the form of dark circles under
her eyes. No matter. She had no one to look beautiful for anyway.

She covered a yawn with the back of her hand as she stretched, then slowly and begrudgingly rolled up the scroll on the desk before her. Ten others just like it lay strewn on the floor or piled in her lap. A few were of the boring sort, detailing the multitude of tedious laws and regulations effected through the Council over the last several hundred generations, but most—the black scrolls—were records of the prophets from the Gray Ages—their teachings, their personal histories, and of course their prophecies. All of them were powerfully captivating and completely forbidden by Council edict.

They would have been destroyed centuries ago, she knew, if not for the Wording of *Dei'lo*, which protected them. Anyone trained in *Sa'lei* could not even bear to look at them, much less study what they said. So they had been locked away deep within the catacombs beneath the Axis, far removed from curious eyes. But, obviously, not far enough.

For the thousandth time, she smiled as she thought of what her mother would do if she knew. At times she thought of telling her, just for the pleasure of watching her go into a fit like a riftman. But she knew she could never tell. Not because she was afraid; her parents could do nothing more to her than they already had. But they would take the scrolls away if they knew she had them; and without them, she was quite sure she would go completely mad.

She blew out the flame of her reading lamp, then silently rose and padded across the chamber to her vanity, absently removing her night robe as she went. She plopped down unceremoniously before the mirror and scrutinized her image to see what damage another sleepless night had wrought in her face. The circles under her bright green eyes were noticeable, but thankfully not so severe that they couldn't be covered with a little cream. Her fine blond hair was tossed haphazardly around her head as though it had been tousled repeatedly for hours on end, which, in truth, it probably had, though she didn't recall doing it.

Everyone in Phallenar had always called her beautiful, but she was certain they would retract that claim if they could see her now. Not that she had ever believed their flatteries in any case. As the daughter of the High Lord himself, what else would they say? What else would they *dare* to say? She was to be their next High Lord. Her bloodline guaranteed it. Or it had, anyway, before she refused to bond with that arrogant fool Stevron and so was locked away in the Tower of the Wall until she saw the error of her stubborn choice.

That was three years past, almost to the day. They never thought she'd last this long, especially her mother. "Such a slight little thing you are," her mother had told her on the first day of her imprisonment. "I think you'll quickly tire of this whole ridiculous affair and return to the Axis where you belong. You have a destiny to fulfill, and your father and I will see to it that you do just that."

Obviously, her mother never knew her well enough to presume.

She retrieved a brush from the vanity and began the painstaking task of combing out the knots in her wayward locks. She couldn't fault her mother, really, for not understanding her that well. After all, she didn't understand her mother either. In truth, they had nothing in common, were nothing alike. They didn't even look like they came from the same family. Lysteria was tall and dark, with a pleasant yet some-what bony face, and ample breasts, which she displayed as proudly and frequently as her office allowed, even now in her advanced years.

Kyrintha, however, was a slight young woman, barely five feet tall on her best day, with smooth porcelain skin and soft, narrow features. She was not so ample in the breast as her mother, a fact for which Lysteria continually berated her, as if she could do anything about it. The truth was Kyrintha didn't favor either of her parents. Rather, she looked a great deal like her grandmother on her mother's side, a woman whom Lysteria loathed with poisoned disgust. Secretly, Kyrintha be-lieved this was the most probable cause of her mother's hatred toward her and the reason why Lysteria never took the time to learn much about who she really was.

This latter fact actually worked in Kyrintha's favor now, and she knew it. Her parents did not keep a close watch on her in the Tower, simply because they saw no reason to. They would never imagine that such a frail little wisp of a girl was capable of building her own network of spies within the Axis, a few from within the ranks of Lysteria's own *jalen*. Or that she could manage to secure the services of at least a hundred servants, merchants, Mentors, and Guardians throughout Phallenar, all of whom were devoted to her cause, even without the Word ability to bond them to her. But that was exactly what she had done, all from the confines of her small, isolated chamber.

Replacing the brush upon the vanity, she rose and walked to the wardrobe, where she pulled out the nicest of the three gowns she had been permitted to bring with her three years before. Laytren would be coming with her breakfast soon, and she wanted to look her best. She had decided this would be a day of celebration, albeit guardedly so. For the first time since her imprisonment, the news from her spies in the Axis was actually good or, at least, was the sort of news that could be turned to her advantage.

By the time she had bathed and donned her gown, there was a knocking at the door. "You may enter, Laytren," she said as she smoothed out the last stubborn wrinkles in her old, but well-kept, dress.

A clinking sound echoed from beyond the thick wooden door, then it slowly swung open and a gray-haired man in black Guardian's garb entered with a tray of food in his hand. "Underlord," said Laytren with a bow as he hung the door keys back on his black belt. "You look radiant today, m'lady."

"Oh, stop lying, Laytren," quipped Kyrintha. "I hardly slept at all last night, and I'm sure it shows."

"Studying the scrolls again, ma'am?" Laytren glanced briefly at the disheveled piles of parchment strewn on the floor and desk.

"Of course, of course," Kyrintha sighed. "What else is an underlord to do to pass the time?"

"Quite, m'lady," Laytren replied with a smirk. "But you should get your rest. I'd hate to see a face so lovely as yours get all bagged and wrinkled before its time."

Kyrintha gave him a stern look, which he disregarded. "I'm only telling you the truth, m'lady," he said. "With your parents so busy with governing, someone has to step in to watch out for you. I figure I can do the job as well as any."

"Thank you, Laytren," said Kyrintha with just a hint of affection, "but, really, I'm hardly a child anymore."

"There is truth in that, to be sure," said Laytren. He marched across the chamber and set the breakfast tray on the desk between two piles of scrolls. "I'm assuming you heard the news, ma'am," he said as he turned to face her.

"That depends," replied Kyrintha. "What news do you mean?"

" 'Bout the Lords, ma'am," he gestured loosely toward the ceiling, "the ones that flew over the Wall on those black-hearted beasts a few days ago."

"What about them?" asked Kyrintha, wondering if Laytren had heard something that she didn't already know.

" 'Bout why they went, m'lady," said Laytren, surprised at Kyrintha's apparent ignorance, "to capture that one they call Stormcaller and bring him back all in one piece."

Kyrintha moved to the desk and scrutinized the breakfast offerings on the tray. "Oh, yes, I know about that," she said. "Mentor Spriggs informed me of it yesterday."

Laytren nodded. Whatever information didn't come from him would naturally come from Spriggs. The two of them were her closest advisors and collectively managed her spy networks within the Axis and the Guardian Host.

"Your pardon for askin', but why do you reckon they're doing that?" Laytren rested his hand absently on the hilt of his sword, which he never went anywhere without and which Kyrintha had not seen him unsheathe even once in the three years she'd known him.

"You mean why are they bringing the rebel here instead of simply killing him?" she asked. Laytren nodded. "I don't really know," she said, furrowing her brow a little. "I do know it's my father's doing, but I'm not sure why he wants the man alive. I presume he wants something from him, but what, I couldn't say."

She pinched off a corner of a biscuit and placed it gracefully in her mouth, then chewed it slowly, habitually keeping her eyes fixed on her plate in the manner all the underlords were taught. She swallowed daintily, then continued, "Whatever his reason, I am glad for it, for it gives me hope that I may yet find a way out of this dreary Tower."

"You planning something?" asked Laytren with a hint of a smirk.

Kyrintha smiled. "Naturally. I'm going to take his prize from him," she said with a nod.

"How's that? You going to kill the Stormcaller to keep him from your father's hand?" His tone was incredulous.

"No, Laytren, of course not!" Kyrintha exclaimed. "Leave it to a Guardian to think that killing is the answer for everything!" She sighed. "Besides, I need the rebel alive."

Laytren gripped his sword hilt more tightly. "Why that?"

"Because my father wants him alive, of course. And for more than that. I want him alive because he knows the way to Wordhaven."

Laytren's hoarse laughter filled the chamber. "Wordhaven's a myth, lady. Surely you know it!"

Kyrintha grinned patiently. "Every Lord on the Council knows of Wordhaven's sure existence, Laytren. . .though not one of them knows where it is. And even if they did know, I doubt very much that they could enter it." Her grin quickly vanished. "That makes it the perfect place for me."

"You would go there, m'lady, a place that exists nowhere but in children's fables?" Laytren shook his head disapprovingly. "I cannot see the soundness of such thoughts."

Kyrintha locked her gaze on the Guardian with a calmness that belied the passion of her words. "There is nowhere else for me to go," she said simply.

Laytren looked unconvinced, although she knew it was out of concern for her safety rather than doubt of her intelligence. The old Guardian had been assigned to her chamber since the day she entered the Tower; and during the past three years, she had come to love him as a father, and she knew he loved her too as the daughter he never had. They had never voiced their feelings, of course. Such familiarity was not permitted between an underlord and a Guardian—even a Guardian like Laytren, who had never mastered the Words. But his feelings were clear enough without the need to voice them. She could see it in his actions and in the way he looked at her sometimes, like now.

"Look at this," Kyrintha said, gesturing to the stacks of scrolls littered around her, most of them black. "Why do you think I've been poring over these records for years?" She picked up a black scroll and thrust it toward him like a sword. "Why do you think I've read everything there is to read about the Kinsman Redeemer, which is who these rebels believe this man to be? I have learned things, Laytren. Wonderful things. Terrible things. Truths that have been locked away for generations to keep us ignorant and blind. It's all here, in the scrolls. That's why these writings are forbidden, because they know the knowledge contained here would be their undoing! The Council, my parents, they don't want us to know that Wordhaven exists because they fear it. But it does exist, Laytren. It does! And that's just the beginning of the things they don't want us to know."

"But you are an underlord, m'lady," said Laytren plaintively.

"Surely these secrets are not revelations to you?"

Kyrintha laughed mockingly. "You know better than that, Laytren. They don't tell the underlords anything. We are not even permitted to learn the most basic of Words until we are raised to full Lordship. We are bargaining chips in the game of power, bartered back and forth among the major houses for our capacity to breed. Nothing more."

" 'Tis a shame to see such bitterness in one so young," quipped Laytren with a frown.

"I prefer to think of myself as a realist," replied Kyrintha evenly. "I will never allow my parents to force me to marry against my will nor to raise me to a Council that I abhor. So I will remain locked away in this Tower the rest of my life, just as my grandmother did before me, unless I can flee to a place where the Council's power cannot reach me. And you know full well there is no place like that in all the Inherited Lands—none except Wordhaven. And so, that is where I will go. . .or die in the trying."

"Then I will do all I can to help you, m'lady," said Laytren with a slight bow of the head, "even if I think it's mad."

"I'm counting on that," replied Kyrintha. Then she smiled softly. "Thank you."

"How then will you capture him?" asked Laytren. "And right under the Lords' noses at that."

"In a bit, Laytren," she said. "Fetch Mentor Spriggs and bring him here. When you return, I'll tell you both what must be done. Until then, I believe I'd like to finish my breakfast, if you don't mind. I've had a very exhausting night."

Laytren grinned as he bowed. "Underlord," he said. He then turned and marched out, carefully forgetting to lock the door on his way out.

CHAPTER 29

THE HEAVEN RANGE

*The Council Lords believed they were the immutable masters
of their Language and, therefore, the natural rulers of
the world. They never realized the truth of it, that they were
slaves and not Lords, captives of the Tongue that mastered them.
Such is the nature of Sa'lei. It consumes your soul so slowly
that you never realize it is slaying you until it is too late.
And by then you are too close to dead to care.*

—THE KYRINTHAN JOURNALS, SONGS OF DELIVERANCE, STANZA 10, VERSES 17–19

The huge black beast lay motionless on the grass, its shallow, rapid breathing the only sign that it still lived. Owl-like eyes were sealed in exhaustion, and its dry black tongue hung loosely from its jaws, which lay gaping open in a final snarled grasp at life. Without food or water, it would be dead within the hour. But Bentel did not have time to save it and wasn't sure he cared to in any case.

"*Demoi blassht.*"

In an instant, the beast erupted in flames. There was no time for it even to flinch before the white heat of the Word ended its tortured life and reduced its massive bulk to ash. Seconds later, all that remained was a circle of blackened earth and a pile of gray ashes, which immediately began to swirl in the mountain winds around them, rising into the air like a menacing cloud.

Lord Fayerna coughed harshly as she waved her hand in front of her face. "Bentel!" she snapped between coughs. "You could have warned us!" The ashes of the juron swirled around her like a maelstrom, coating her black leathers with fine gray dust and sprinkling her face like a fresh set of freckles, which she of all people did not need.

"Sorry, sister," Bentel replied. "I didn't want to see the beast suffer any longer."

"Foolish," snapped Fayerna, still coughing and trying desperately to brush the ash out of her fine red hair. "It could have been saved. We may still need the beasts to follow the trail."

"Three are dead already, Fayerna," said Bentel calmly, "and the remaining two are barely alive. They are of no use to us now. Your Word has sealed their fate."

Fayerna coughed again, then glared at her brother. "How was I to know the Word would compel them so strongly? Even a Worded beast should be smart enough to know it needs to eat and sleep from time to time. I won't be blamed for their lack of sense!"

Bentel raised his hands in a submissive gesture. "No one is blaming you, sister," he said. "We all know how difficult it is to keep the Words from destroying. There was no way any of us could have foreseen that the Word would drive the beasts mad with compulsion. But there is no harm done, really. Look where we are!" He made a sweeping motion with his arm. "They stayed alive long enough to lead us here."

"We are still a long way from Wordhaven," Fayerna said coolly.

"Perhaps not," replied Bentel. "It could be over the next ridge."

"Or a thousand leagues from here," Fayerna retorted.

Bentel laughed and shook his head. "It doesn't matter," he said. "The trail is clear enough to follow, so long as we stay on the ground. We do not need the juron anymore."

"But we may need them later," snapped Fayerna.

"Then we'll call *more*," exclaimed Bentel. "These two that remain are too weak to do us any good now. You should release them from the Word and let them hunt. Perhaps they will survive to serve us another day."

"I never kept them from hunting," she said.

Bentel sighed. Sometimes his sister could be so unreasonable. "Fayerna. . . ," he said.

"Fine!" she yelled. "I'll release them. But if we're to go traipsing through this mountain jungle, I will not be carrying a single one of those bags!"

"Is that what this is about?" snapped Bentel. "The *mon'jalen* will carry the bags. Really, Fayerna, this attitude is beneath you. What is the matter with you?"

Fayerna took a deep breath and closed her eyes. When she opened them, they were full of anger. "Isn't it obvious, *dear* brother?" she said. "I'm tired, I'm hungry, and now you've covered me in the ash of a filthy dead animal!"

She angrily slapped away the ash that coated her trousers as she spoke. "We've been hard at this for more than two weeks, with no sign of it letting up any time soon. And now we've lost the juron, which from your attitude I clearly gather is all my fault, and so we've lost the one means by which we can track this stupid little man, a faceless commoner about whom I care less and less each day."

She glared at Bentel a moment longer, as though trying to think of something more to add, then, when she couldn't, shook her head in disgust and turned her attention to the task of brushing the ash off her shoulders.

Bentel watched her coolly for a moment longer, then said, to no one in particular, "We'll make camp here. A night's rest will do us all good."

Upon his word, the three *mon'jalen* jumped to action and began the task of setting up camp. Lok began clearing a patch of flat ground to make room for their shelter, while Sanchi marched off into the trees in search of wood for a fire. Kyrva, meanwhile, began sorting through the bags, separating those that contained food for supper and blankets to ward off the evening chill, which was already evident in the late afternoon sun.

Sarlina, apparently sensing that the moment of tension had past, slowly ambled back toward the siblings from her hiding place at the edge of the trees, where she had fled at the first sign of their anger. Bentel watched her out of the corner of his eye as she approached and couldn't help but chuckle to himself at her timid manner. She was very much like the dog he had in his youth—so easily frightened away at the slightest sign of displeasure, yet so desperately anxious for approval that she always came back, even after he'd beat her fiercely for some stupid thing she'd done.

Yet for all her submissive loyalty to him, he knew he would never be Sarlina's true master. That honor fell exclusively to Fayerna. Sarlina worshipped his sister above all else. She modeled everything she did after Fayerna's example—from the way she walked and talked right down to the way she styled her dull brown hair. Even her outfit mimicked Fayerna's in every detail, right down to the golden sword and snake pendant that Fayerna wore as the sign of her house. It was not Sarlina's family sigil, of course, but that didn't seem to matter.

Bentel turned from Sarlina as Fayerna came up behind him. "Did you release the juron?"

"Oh, yes!" Fayerna said in mock excitement. "They flew away like sweet little birds." She flitted her hands through the air sarcastically. "It will take days to call more, you realize."

"I think I shall get a drink," said Bentel, forcing a smile. "Would you care to join me?"

Fayerna paused. "That does sound good," she agreed cautiously. "This day has been too tiresome. Where's Sarlina?"

"In your shadow, as always," replied Bentel. Fayerna turned to see Sarlina not six paces behind her, standing perfectly still and watching them in silent awe. *Just like a good pet,* he couldn't help but think.

Fayerna extended her hand toward the younger Lord. "Come, Sarlina," she said. "Let's be done with this day."

Sarlina danced out of the shadows and took Fayerna's hand. "Can I drink too?" she asked hopefully.

"Of course, my dear." Fayerna smiled. "You are a Lord. You can do whatever you want."

Bentel knew that was a lie, especially for Sarlina, but he smiled at her anyway and followed the two ladies to the table Lok had quickly set up outside the shelter. "Kyrva, bring us drinks," he called into the night air. Immediately she appeared, seemingly from nowhere, and rushed to do just that.

By the time they'd had several drinks, the sun had dipped behind the peaks to the west, and the warming light of the fire basked their faces in a dancing golden glow. The aroma of the roasting meat was enticing and made Bentel's mouth water in pleasant anticipation.

"I don't get to drink wine much, you know," said Sarlina mischievously. "My Mentor would be angry."

Bentel raised his cup. "Well, your Mentor is a fat, ridiculous woman. And she doesn't understand the way of Lords. You're among equals now, and you can have as much wine as you want."

"True, true," agreed Fayerna, lifting her cup.

Sarlina beamed, delighted by their approval. "My Mentor *is* fat," she agreed, then took a deep drink from her cup.

"Not so quickly," cautioned Fayerna. "You must sip it, like this." Fayerna demonstrated the proper form for drinking wine, and Sarlina watched with riveted attention, then mimicked her motions precisely. "Good, that's better," said Fayerna.

"Kyrva, more wine," commanded Bentel. "And when will the food be served? We're all famished."

"It awaits your command, m'Lord," said Kyrva from the shadows behind him.

"Well, then, by all means, the command is given," Bentel retorted. "We'll need more than wine to regain our strength."

"As you say, m'Lord," replied Kyrva, who was already pulling the meat from the spit on which it roasted over the flames. Placing the meat upon a carving board, she whipped a small blade from a sheath strapped to her thigh and began to slice it in thin strips, the way her Lord preferred it. Bentel breathed deeply, filling his nostrils with the rich aroma of the roast, and let his eyes fall lazily closed. There was nothing quite so satisfying as a tasty meal at the end of an exhausting day, he thought, even if he did have to eat it out here in the wilds like a common vagabond.

"So what do you think our Lord Balaam is scheming?" he asked Fayerna absently as he reclined. "Why does he want the Stormcaller alive?"

"I really couldn't guess," Fayerna quipped. "And right now I really don't care." She looked toward the fire. "Kyrva, stop dawdling with that roast. Can't you see I'm hungry?"

Bentel opened his eyes and looked across the table at his sister. Her pitch-black eyes looked hard and bitter even now, as they always did, despite the softening effects of the fire's pleasant glow. He looked away and swirled his wine under his nose. "It's clear he wants something from the rebel, but what? What could a rebel have to offer a Lord?"

"You already said it once before," replied Fayerna absently. "He wants to slay the trophy for himself. What else?"

Bentel sighed and took a drink. "Then why send the warcor first? They all had orders to kill the Stormcaller on sight." He shook his head. "No, something has changed. He's learned something about the man that makes him more valuable alive than dead."

Kyrva appeared next to the table and quietly placed platters full of roasted meat and freshly cut fruits before each of the Lords in turn. She then faded back into the darkness as silently as she came.

"You think his *ser'jalen* have discovered some secret about the rebel that ours have not?" asked Fayerna.

"Though that is possible, I doubt it," said Bentel. "Our *ser'jalen* are better trained than his. Always have been." He speared several pieces of meat on his fork and shoved them hungrily into his mouth.

"I saw the High Lord reading scrolls," sputtered Sarlina as she chewed an overly large chunk of meat. A little juice dribbled down her chin as she spoke.

"Sarlina, for the love of the Words, don't speak with your mouth full!" snapped Fayerna. She reached across and wiped the juice away with her thumb. "A Lord never forgets her manners."

Sarlina quickly swallowed hard, nearly choking herself in the process. She let loose a hacking cough, turning her head first—thankfully, thought Bentel—then fixed her eyes down on her plate. "Your pardon, Lords."

"That's quite all right, Sarlina," said Bentel. "Now, what do you mean you saw him reading scrolls?"

"One day, before we left, I was walking with my cats on the high balconies of the Axis. They like the view from way up there, and they're not at all afraid of the height, so long as I am there too to keep them safe. They depend on me, you see, and I don't ever let them go too close to the edge. Anyway, I was there one day when one of my cats ran off down the hall, without my permission. So I went after it, me and Sanchi, I mean. We had to chase it a long way. I would have used the Words, but I was afraid I might kill it. . . ."

"Get to the point, dear," said Fayerna.

Sarlina frowned. "Well. . .I didn't mean it to do anything wrong, but it just ran right into the High Lord's chambers, into his *study*, right past his *mon'jalen*. And before I realized where I was, I was there too. The High Lord was very angry. I was afraid he would kill my cat. But he said he wouldn't so long as I didn't tell."

"Tell what, dear?"

Sarlina shrugged timidly. "That I had seen him there. . .or mention anything about the scrolls. He told me to just forget the whole thing, like it never happened. I thought that was nice of him. So I took my cat and left. She was a bad cat that day, but she doesn't know any better. She needs me to protect her."

She lowered her head and furrowed her brows worriedly. "You're not going to kill my cat now, are you?"

"No, Sarlina," said Bentel soothingly. "No one's going to hurt your cat. And if anyone tries, I will personally see to it that they are punished." Sarlina's face brightened noticeably at that. "Now, please, tell us about the scrolls. How many did you see? What kind?"

Sarlina's eyes grew wide. "There were dozens of them. Hundreds! Laid out everywhere. I'd never seen so many in one place before."

Fayerna reached across the table and laid a hand on Sarlina's arm. "Dear, now listen. This is important, so try to remember. Were any of the scrolls black?"

Sarlina nodded eagerly. "Most of them were black. With silver writing. I remember because they were so pretty. But they made me feel sick inside."

"Forbidden scrolls. . . ," Bentel said, nodding.

"How could he even touch them?" asked Fayerna incredulously.

"He has some *ser'jalen* without the Words," said Bentel. "We all do. No doubt they were there as well, opening the scrolls so he could study them."

Fayerna scoffed at that. "He could not read them, Bentel! The pain would be unbearable."

Bentel shrugged. "Perhaps. Or perhaps he had the *ser'jalen* read them in his stead, aloud so he could hear."

Fayerna daintily wiped the corners of her mouth. "The very notion sickens me," she said. "Even Balaam would not stoop so low."

"He might, if he thought there was power in it."

"It makes no sense!" exclaimed Fayerna. "He cannot learn the other Tongue. The attempt alone would kill him. And what would be the point? *Dei'lo* is the weaker language."

"That may be so. But it can do things that *Sa'lei* cannot. Call a Storm of Deliverance, for example. Or purge the riftmen of their plague. As you know, this rebel has accomplished both of these feats, or so we're led to believe."

"All the more reason for him to die," said Fayerna. "He is an abomination."

Bentel nodded. "An abomination that Balaam may intend to harness for himself."

Fayerna pushed her plate away. "Ridiculous! He cannot harness the power of the other Tongue. Council Lords have tried for generations without the slightest success. It cannot be done. There must be another explanation." She covered her platter with a napkin and rose abruptly from the table.

"Are you not going to finish your meal?" asked Bentel.

Fayerna closed her eyes. "I'm afraid this conversation has made my stomach churn. I'm going to walk a bit." Gracefully, she glided off toward the trees, with Lok automatically falling in behind her.

"Is Fayerna angry?" Sarlina whispered to Bentel.

"No, my dear Sarlina," replied Bentel with a smile. "Talking about the forbidden Tongue has this effect sometimes. Don't trouble yourself. She will be fine. Finish your food. We have a long hike ahead of us tomorrow."

Sarlina nodded quietly and turned her gaze back to her platter, which was nearly empty now. Bentel's platter, by contrast, was still quite full. He too, it seemed, had lost his appetite and even felt a subtle churning in his gut.

"Curious," he said, then stabbed another piece of meat and forced it in his mouth. Nauseous or not, he was smart enough to know he needed to keep up his strength.

Perhaps it was the disturbing aspect of the conversation or just his own growing weariness that caused Bentel not to notice the telltale vibrations of the Words as they sifted through the air behind him. Neither was he aware of the cold black eyes that stared at him from behind a pile of blankets at the edge of camp, watching as they ate, listening to their every word. And all the while revealing nothing of the thoughts that lurked behind them.

CHAPTER 30

THE TRAINING FIELDS

Before Donovan came to the Remnant, little was known of
the powers and limits of Sa'lei, beyond what could be obviously
observed. But Donovan's conversion brought with it horrible
revelations of the nature of the Tongue of Death. As the
Firstsworn of the Guardian Host, Donovan's knowledge of
Sa'lei was nearly as complete as any Council Lord's. He knew
what those who spoke the Tongue could do and the few
but important things that they could not. But he knew more
than only this. He also knew the heart and soul of every
Council Lord. This was to become his lifelong curse and the
Remnant's blessing. For he had been corded to all the Council
Lords for most of his days. He knew their cravings, their anger,
their secret hatreds and darkest fears. Collectively, they became
the nightmare from which he could never awaken.

—THE KYRINTHAN JOURNALS, SONGS OF DELIVERANCE, STANZA 8, VERSES 13–17

The two warriors circled each other warily, their focus staffs held
before them like wooden shields as they stepped smoothly and silently
around an invisible centerpoint on the grass.

The woman, clad in the brown fighting leathers of the Remnant,
moved with a cat's grace and stealth, never shifting her gaze for an
instant from the imaginary line of attack drawn between her staff and
opponent, watching his lips for any sign of a whisper.

But as much as her style matched that of a cat, the man, by contrast, moved like a lion. His steps were equally silent, but also ponderous in their way, as though each swath of grass on which he stepped
was claimed as his to rule. He moved with the assurance of a hardened
champion, one who had rarely, if ever, lost a fight. His nut-brown hair,
pulled tight in a knot behind his head, only added to his intimidating

ferocity. But nothing could equal the utter coldness of his gaze—from eyes as black as midnight, seeing everything, revealing nothing.

Like the sounds of quiet breezes in the trees, Gideon listened intently as their whispers began. He could not understand the Words, but he had been told some of what they did. Words of strength and health, stamina and courage. And, most important of all, Words of peace. Without peace, they had told him, a warrior could not hope to win.

Then, like lightning, Donovan struck. Whispering the Words under his breath, he leaped high into the air, swinging his staff in a wide arc as he flew across the circle bearing down on Aybel's head. It all happened in a flash. But, as fast as thunder answers lightning, Aybel rumbled her response, leaping straight up in the air, matching Donovan's height, then disappearing from sight.

Donovan countered, raising his staff back to focus level, but it was too late. The blow struck him in the small of his back, sent him flying twenty feet at least before he hit the ground. No sooner had he landed, though, than he also vanished.

For a time, the fight went on like this, invisibly. Gideon heard the shuffling on the grass, the heavy breathing of fighters in the throes of battle, and the sounds of staffs colliding in the air or near the ground. Then Aybel appeared as she fell to the earth, her face momentarily wincing from the sting of Donovan's unseen blow. With a speed that defied comprehension, she rolled to her feet and regained her stance with the focus staff before her, between her and her unseen foe.

With no time for thought, she spoke a Word, and a wind like a hurricane went out from before her, seeming to come from the staff itself, though Gideon knew that was not really the case. Frantically, Gideon gripped the rock on which he sat and shielded his eyes from the blast, which pressed against her unseen opponent, striving to hold him at bay until she could discern his precise location.

Above the howl of this new wind, Gideon could just make out the sound of Donovan's voice, somewhere to his right, yelling things he could not understand. Then he appeared in the center of the gale, standing upright and calm, apparently wholly untouched by the winds that whipped fiercely around him. With a whisper, Aybel stopped the wind and disappeared again, this time instantly reappearing directly behind Donovan. With staff held high, she took aim and swung for the small of his back a second time. But with a speed impossible to follow, Donovan spun and thrust his open palm into her solar plexus, sending her flying backward several feet onto the grass. Her staff sailed gracefully out of her hand, landing several feet from where she lay gasping for the breath his blow had stolen from her. In another instant, Donovan was on her, holding the end of his staff to her throat.

"Ground?" he asked.

Aybel nodded, still gasping as she tried to cough out her submission. Quickly, Donovan knelt beside her and spoke a Word of healing. Her breathing eased at once, but when she stood up, she still rubbed the place where he had struck her.

Once he could see that she was restored, Donovan turned and walked toward Gideon, who had been watching the battle from the relative safety of his rock. As Donovan approached, Gideon immediately noticed that the big man did not look well at all. His dark face had turned a ghostlike white, coated with a sickly sweat that glistened on his forehead and dripped from his cheeks. His breathing was heavy and uneven. For all intents and purposes, he looked like a man about to throw up.

Which is exactly what he did. Right there on the grass.

Aybel rushed up behind him, but Donovan raised a hand that stopped her cold. "It will pass," he said, still bent over and breathing deeply.

Gideon rose and walked over to them, being careful to avoid the mess Donovan had spilled on the ground. "What's wrong with him?" he asked Aybel.

"The Words are hard on him," Aybel replied. Abruptly, Donovan wiped his mouth with the back of his hand and stood. "The Words were harder on you, Aybel," he said, still pale. "You depended too much on the staff and forgot that I could also use my hands. A warrior must keep all of his weapons at the ready."

Aybel nodded, touching the spot where he had struck her. "I will not make that mistake again."

"Is this because he used to know *Sa'lei?*" asked Gideon, pointing at the vomit on the ground.

Aybel nodded, but it was Donovan who spoke. "You see my eyes. I still bear the marks of that dark Tongue. It is rare for one to turn from one to the other, and the way is fraught with difficulties. There is still much of the darkness of *Sa'lei* in me, and it rebels against the speaking of *Dei'lo*."

Gideon understood. From what Ajel had told him, following his conversion, Donovan had nearly died trying to learn *Dei'lo*. And that was after the years it took for Paladin and Seer to break the cording that had linked Donovan as Firstsworn to all of the Council Lords. That too had nearly killed him. And that was just the first step of his "redemption," as they called it, for it didn't even begin to address the darkening effects of *Sa'lei* itself, which Donovan had spoken since his youth and which still infected his soul on levels that Seer and Paladin could not reach.

It had been a hard road for Donovan, and it was still far from over. Once you travel down the path of *Sa'lei*, Ajel had said, it's very hard to *unlearn* the way. Still, Donovan stoically pushed himself mercilessly to learn the Words of Life, for some time never knowing whether learning *Dei'lo* would kill him or save him. He was past that point now, of course, but *Dei'lo* apparently still caused him great pain. With each use of the Words of Life, the Language rooted out another bit of the dark residue left behind by *Sa'lei*, allowing Donovan to forget another piece of the terrible knowledge of who he used to be. Maybe someday it might even restore the natural color of his eyes, which had turned pitch black years ago from the continual use of *Sa'lei*.

Despite his initial mistrust of the man, Gideon had come to respect him, even if he still fell short of saying he actually liked him all that much. For one thing, learning about Donovan's struggle with the Words made Gideon's "healing" back in Calmeron all the more profound. Donovan had used the Words to heal him from the Guardians' wounds and, from what he'd been told, made himself deathly ill in the process. Either Kair or Ajel could have done it in his place, but Donovan would not allow it. At the time, he feared that Gideon was a Guardian spy and therefore refused to let Ajel or Kair be exposed to the potential danger. That, Gideon thought, was a noble gesture, even if it was extremely misguided.

And then there was the story of Ajel's friendship with Donovan, which to Gideon seemed far beyond miraculous. While he was still the Firstsworn of the Guardians, Donovan had slain Ajel's father with a brutal Word of death, with Ajel right there, looking on. What motivated

Ajel to forgive Donovan of such a crime was beyond Gideon's comprehension. But Gideon had come to respect Ajel a great deal in the time he'd spent at Wordhaven. And if Ajel could choose to befriend Donovan after the man had murdered his own father, then Gideon was willing to lay aside his own doubts about the warrior and at least give him a chance.

After taking a break, Donovan and Aybel returned to the training field to begin another round of sparring. Gideon had come to enjoy these times of watching them and others battle with the Words. It was more than simple entertainment, though there was that. It was also. . . profound, even beautiful in its way. The battles were intense and the blows were real; even so, it seemed to Gideon more like a dance than a fight. The movements were so graceful and flowing and, well, peaceful, as odd as that sounded. Gideon felt an undeniable calm settle over him every time he visited the training fields.

He'd also learned a great deal about the Words in the process. Like what the Words could do and some of what they couldn't. They could make you fly over short distances or make your skin as hard as granite. They could hide you from your enemies and even allow you to instantly transport to places you'd been before. The powers of *Dei'lo* were awe-inspiring, even at the rudimentary level, which Aybel claimed was all that any of the Remnant knew.

They'd given up trying to teach him the Words, of course. He'd learned to pronounce a few of them, but the elusive "message" of the Words, the meaning from which their power flowed, seemed beyond his ability to grasp. Aybel said, repeatedly, that it was because Gideon stubbornly refused to open his mind to Wordhaven's effects. Maybe that was so. But Gideon still couldn't tolerate the idea of letting other people freely poke around his thoughts and feelings. There was too much that Gideon didn't want others to know about and some he didn't want to know himself.

For that reason, he contented himself with watching from the side, listening to Words he couldn't understand, but feeling their effects all the same. Perhaps that was why he'd stayed on at Wordhaven for so many weeks, even after they'd given him back his freedom. He liked the feel of the place, the way it calmed him. He hadn't had a rage for weeks, nor even a hint of one since he'd arrived at Wordhaven. Perhaps it had been even longer than that, though he now suspected he might have had one, or even two, during his stay at Songwill sounden.

Twice on that occasion, he'd awakened after being put to sleep by the Words—something he now understood was impossible without the use of *Dei'lo*. But perhaps the rage had been enough to break the Words' effects. That was the only explanation he could think of. Not that he had ever asked Ajel about it, of course, or mentioned it as a possibility. Besides, the way he felt now—under the calming influence of Wordhaven—it didn't matter much anyway. With any luck, his rages were now a thing of the past.

Gideon turned his attention back to the battle. Aybel and Donovan were circling again, quietly whispering their Words of strength as they held out their staffs before them. The staffs, Gideon had learned, weren't really necessary in a battle like this, since the real power came from the Words. But the Remnant fighters used them to help them focus their thoughts and to direct their Words with greater accuracy. Even so, he'd seen both Aybel and Donovan strike some serious blows with those things. Even with the Words, he reasoned, it never hurt to carry a big stick.

Suddenly, Gideon was shocked to find Revel Foundling sitting beside him, appearing out of nothing. Instinctively, he jerked back in surprise.

"Where'd you come from?" asked Gideon.

Revel smiled, which did nothing to soften the piercing effects of his golden eyes. "The Chamber of the Pearl," he said. The Chamber of the Pearl was in the heart of the Stand, at least a twenty-minute walk away.

Gideon sighed and shook his head. "I'll never get used to you people doing that."

"My apologies, sojourner." Revel smirked in a way that showed he wasn't apologetic at all. "I am sent by Ajel. He bids you come to the Chamber of the Pearl at once."

"What for?"

"He has found the Book," he said.

CHAPTER 31

THE TRUE SIGHT

*Lord Kih's was the last of the great Sojourns of the New Age,
dating from around s.c. 810 to 867. The Sojourn ended in
that final year with Lord Kih's death at the hands of an assassin
near the cliffs of what was then Prottell sounden. The day before
his murder, Lord Kih summoned a tapestrer and a mapmaker
and commissioned them to create a tapestry detailing the
Sojourn's journeys, giving special emphasis to their precise
location on that particular day. Some believe that Lord Kih
did this because he had discovered the Book of Dei'lo and hidden
it somewhere nearby to prevent the enemies who stalked him
from stealing it. Should anything happen to Lord Kih, the
tapestry, these historians believe, was intended to lead other
Sojourners to the place where he had hidden the Book away.
As it happens, Lord Kih was slain the very next day. The
tapestry was never followed, however, and now hangs on the
wall of Wordhaven's Middle Hall. The inscription at the bottom
of the tapestry reads, "Life sleeps in the heart of the Inheritance."*

—THE KYRINTHAN JOURNALS, CHRONICLES, CHAPTER 2, VERSES 231–247

Nothing seemed out of the ordinary as Gideon walked next to Revel
down the floor of the Inner Hall. Wordhaveners bustled here and
there, popping in and out of corridors carrying food or scrolls or some
other odd thing, performing the regular daily tasks that were essential
for running a complex as big as Wordhaven.

One cluster of relief workers to his right was busy packing sacks of
food and other supplies, preparing for another "transport" to Songwill
sounden. The Words allowed them to travel there instantly—at least
those Wordhaveners who'd spent considerable time there at some point
in the past. The Remnant had made almost daily trips there since the

sounden's destruction to help Borac and his people rebuild their homes and replant the fields that had been razed by the Guardians.

Gideon forced back a wave of guilt as he watched them. Once he had learned of the relief effort, he'd immediately offered to go and help, even though, for him, it meant a physical journey back through that God-awful desert that nearly killed him. He thought it was the least he could do after all the trouble his visit there had caused them. But Paladin refused his request, saying it would be too dangerous for everyone, especially Gideon himself. The sounden's refusal to bow to Phallenar had saved his life. But they had done it for the sake of the Remnant and their own honor—not out of any love for him. Some of them probably still thought he was the Kinsman Redeemer, but that was now overshadowed by the new title he'd earned at Songwill—the Bringer of Death.

"Has Ajel told anyone else about the Book?" Gideon asked Revel as they walked.

"Paladin knows. That is all."

"Why does Ajel want to talk to me?"

Revel grinned. "I will let my brother speak for himself."

Gideon frowned. He couldn't think of any reason why Ajel would want to tell him about the Book's discovery, especially not in person. . . unless it had something to do with him being the Kinsman Redeemer.

"You and Ajel are pretty close, aren't you?" asked Gideon.

"We are brothers," Revel said simply.

"You grew up together?"

Revel nodded. "Mentor Sky was the only father I ever knew. I was just a child when the Remnant found me, hiding in the trees outside of Morguen sounden."

"How'd you end up there?"

"I was owned by the Roamers—a traveling sounden of merchants," he explained. "We had traveled to Morguen sounden at the wheat harvest, as we did every year." Revel shrugged. "There was a Guardian raid, and my owners were slain. I ran to the woods," he laughed, "not realizing at the time that I was on the edge of Strivenwood. I stayed there for some time, I'm not sure how long. The Remnant came after the raid to help the wounded. That's when Mentor found me."

"You were a slave?" Gideon asked.

Revel smiled and nodded. "I don't remember much of those times.

It seems like. . .another life."

"Huh," said Gideon. "I know exactly how you feel."

Abruptly, Revel turned to the right and headed down a narrow passage off the main Hall. Gideon followed, noticing immediately the drop in brightness and the sudden appearance of shadows beneath his feet.

The passageway was oddly curved, flowing like a river to the left and then the right, with arched doorways marking the distance from time to time. Some of the doorways led down other passages and some to rooms or circular stairs. A few even seemed to lead nowhere at all, opening to nothing but a wall as black as Donovan's eyes. But somehow Gideon sensed that there was something behind the wall or perhaps that the wall wasn't really a wall at all. He followed Revel down the curving passage, looking through each doorway for some clue as to where precisely they might be.

That was when he saw her.

Through a doorway to his right, in a room with walls that glistened like mother of pearl, she was lying on a bed as still as death. Her gray hair had been arranged around her head beautifully like a fan; her hands were folded neatly across her chest. Paladin Sky knelt beside her, head bowed, whispering.

Despite himself, Gideon stopped. He hadn't seen the old woman since the day she'd ripped his mind apart. At that time, she had looked soft and plump, even grandmotherly. But what he saw now was just a shell of her former self. Frail, with sagging skin that barely clung to her protruding bones. Her closed eyes sank deep into her skull, and even from this distance he could see her breathing was shallow and labored.

Just as Paladin looked up and saw him standing there, Revel reached back and gently, but firmly, pulled him down the passageway. The scene of Paladin and Seer quickly disappeared behind the corridor walls. Gideon did not resist Revel's lead, though he wasn't sure why. All he knew was that he felt stunned by what he had seen. He had no idea she was so close to death.

No one had mentioned Seer for weeks, not since Gideon's strange conversation with Paladin on the cliffs. He wasn't sure why he never asked anyone about her. He'd just assumed that she was all right, recovering somewhere in the Stand. Perhaps he didn't want to think about it or talk about that day when she invaded his mind. Maybe he was still bitter about what she had done.

Revel continued to drag him gently by the elbow ever deeper down the curving corridor. Logically, Gideon didn't believe he should feel guilty about Seer. After all, she was the one who had attacked him, and he didn't even understand how their struggle had sent her into a coma. It was not his fault, he was sure. Even so, he could not help feeling deeply responsible for her condition, as though somehow he had caused it, just by being who he was.

It was a feeling that he continually struggled against these days on more levels than he cared to think about. It all began with the little girl in Calmeron, Cimron and Mara's daughter, whose name he still did not know. Would she have died if he hadn't tried to save her? And then there was Songwill. . .an entire village destroyed because of him. He didn't know how many lives had been lost there. He really didn't want to know.

The worst guilt of all, however, sprung from Lairn's terrible demise. Such a naïve and innocent young man, the kind of boy Gideon wished he could have been, now dead—because he believed in Gideon. Because he believed Gideon was someone he could never be. And now, Seer.

It wasn't his fault.

None of it was.

But somehow that didn't make it any easier to deal with. People had died because of him, and he realized that isn't the sort of thing you just "get over." His father had always told him he was a mistake, that he should have never been born. He never wanted to believe it. But now, after all the pain his life had caused, he wondered if his father might have been right after all.

By the time Revel led Gideon up to the solid gold portal that led into the Chamber of the Pearl, he felt completely numb. He barely noticed when Revel grasped his shoulders with both hands and looked intently at his face. And after Revel stretched his body up and kissed him on the forehead, several seconds passed before he realized what had happened.

"Ajel awaits us inside," Revel said. "Are you ready to go in?" His hands still gripped Gideon's shoulders.

"Why'd you do that?" Gideon asked, with just a hint of anger.

Revel shrugged. "Your sorrow is deep. I wanted only to offer what comfort I could. Tell me, is your sorrow for Seer?"

Gideon shook his head. "Don't kiss me again."

"As you wish. Are you ready?"

Gideon shrugged Revel's hands away. "Sure, I'm ready," he said, his tone suddenly light. "Why wouldn't I be? Let's go in."

Without another word, Revel turned and led him through the double golden doors.

The scene inside defied description. It was like looking at the entire world from the inside of a diamond. The walls were like liquid crystal, faceted into multiple planes that continually shifted, opening and closing windows to places both far and near, alien and familiar. Mountains, valleys, cities, people, animals, oceans, islands, storms, deserts—all of these appeared in different facets of the chamber, each of them flowing from one liquid panel to another, changing as they went from grand-scale panoramas to scenes with minute detail.

He saw people dressed like soundenors, eagles with silver wings flying over too-blue lakes, and merchants in a white city square selling their wares under the heat of an oppressive sun. And when he blinked, it all changed. He saw Remnant teams on patrol along the cliffs of Wordhaven. He saw an island like a jewel, set in a vast emerald ocean. He saw a single massive mountain rising like a temple in the desert—a desert without storms and without life.

The chamber was vast and roughly shaped like a dome or a pyramid—with all the shifting images, it was hard to tell exactly. The aisle on which he and Revel stood flowed gently downward toward the center. There, in the middle, was a Ring of Bright Water and beyond it, a fountain. Or perhaps it was a crystal statue. He really couldn't tell. It *was* glowing, that much he knew.

Kneeling there beside the Ring of Bright Water was Ajel, who looked up and smiled when he saw them.

"Hail, Gideon," he said, his voice echoing off the crystalline walls. "My thanks for coming."

Gideon was speechless. He kept looking around the chamber at the scenes as they flowed past and only hobbled forward toward Ajel because Revel prodded him gently from behind.

Ajel, noticing Gideon's astonishment, smiled knowingly at Revel, who grinned in response. "You remind me of my first visit to the Chamber of the Pearl," Ajel said to Gideon. "It is truly a wonder, is it not?"

"What is it?" Gideon asked blankly, still looking at the scenes around him, noticing for the first time the prismatic effects of the light that poured through the walls.

"A seat of rule," replied Ajel. "The heart of Wordhaven. A place where all of the Inherited Lands could be overseen and protected. It is from here that the Pearl governed."

"These images." Gideon pointed. "They can be controlled?"

"With the Words, yes," said Ajel, "though we do not know them all."

Gideon was startled to realize he had reached Ajel, who now stood next to the Ring of Bright Water, which flowed like a river moving in an endless circle around the chamber's center.

"We do not really know all of what the chamber can do," added Revel, who moved to stand next to Ajel. It was only now that Gideon noticed that they both wore their silver headbands, which were unlike any he'd seen other Wordhaveners wear. They reflected the light from the crystalline panels in a way that made them seem to glow.

"This place is awesome," exclaimed Gideon quietly. Then he looked at Ajel. "Thank you for showing it to me."

Ajel nodded. "I want to show you something," he said.

"The Book?" Gideon asked.

"Yes," Ajel replied. "There are Words that allow us to visit places in our spirits. Places we wish to go, places we dream of. This Chamber magnifies the effect of this so that you too can see what my spirit sees."

Gideon nodded. "So this is how you found it," he said, gesturing to the walls. "You can see any place you want from here."

"Since we learned the Words, we have never stopped searching for the Book," said Revel. "Until today, its location had eluded us. But now our hope is born anew."

"But why show me?" asked Gideon. "Why tell me first?"

"First, let me show you," replied Ajel. "Then we will explain."

Gideon frowned suspiciously but said, "Okay."

Ajel smiled, then turned to face the object in the center of the room, which Gideon could now see was a fountain after all, a single flowing column of water rising several feet into the air. Ajel bowed his head and whispered something quietly under his breath. A rumbling like thunder rose beneath his feet, and a sound of a melody filled the Chamber air. The song was unfamiliar to Gideon but bore the same stringed tones and lightness of the songs he'd heard at Songwill.

As the music danced upon the walls, the panels changed and grew ominously dark. What was a range of mountains transformed into dark foreboding stone. What was an island on an emerald sea shifted into dust and darkness. One by one the panels changed, creating from the dozens of images only one.

It was a cave. Or perhaps a mineshaft so deep under the earth that no light could reach it. But there, in the center of the darkness, was a single shaft of light, bearing down upon an ornate book covered in dust, resting on a flattened stone.

It was Revel who explained. "This place is deep beneath the streets of Phallenar, directly beneath the Axis. The mines go on for miles. It was only a few years ago that we discovered them. Since that time we have continually explored these tunnels, hoping for this." He pointed to the Book. "The chamber in which the Book rests has only one entrance, which is blocked by wards and other obstacles. To reach it would require great cunning and strength and even greater courage."

Gideon nodded. "And no doubt there are a whole bunch of Guardians blocking the way."

"Not just Guardians," corrected Revel. "*Mon'jalen*, who are nearly as formidable as Council Lords themselves."

"You're going to try to get it," said Gideon.

Immediately, the scene vanished, and the Chamber was flooded with the light of a hundred different scenes, flowing into one another as before.

"Yes," said Ajel. "Of course we must. It is why the Remnant exists." Slowly, he turned to face Gideon. "And I humbly ask that you go with us."

Gideon's eyes grew wide. "What?" he asked incredulously. "Me? You want me to go with you?"

Ajel bowed his head. "I know I am asking a great deal. But we would be eternally in your debt if you would consent to go."

Gideon couldn't help but laugh. "Ajel," he chuckled. "I am the last guy you want with you on a trip like that. I mean, let's face it, I am hardly what anyone would call a good luck charm for you people."

"I am more at fault than you for all that has transpired, sojourner," said Ajel softly. "And much of it may have been destined in any case. Please, allow us time to tell you all of what we plan for the journey ahead. Then you can make your decision."

Gideon shook his head. "But why? Why do you want me to go with you?"

Again, Ajel bowed his head. "My apologies, sojourner. I do not mean to offend. We have been instructed not to speak of the Kinsman Redeemer in your presence, but there is no other word I can use to explain our motives. You do not believe you are the Kinsman Redeemer. But the question for us remains an open one."

Gideon sighed. "Oh boy. . ."

Ajel continued. "Even if you are not, the fact remains that unparalleled acts have come by your hand. An entire warcor of riftmen purged. A Storm of Deliverance. . ."

Gideon raised his hand. "Look, Ajel, please. Don't start this."

"Again, I do not mean to offend," said Ajel. "But my belief demands I speak of this. . .possibility."

"Well, my belief demands I stop you," replied Gideon. "Hasn't there been enough carnage, enough death, for you to realize that I'm not this savior you're looking for?" He lowered his voice to a whisper. "Ajel, people *die* when I'm around. Is that what you call a Kinsman Redeemer?"

Revel laid a hand on Ajel's shoulder. "Brother, please. . . ," he said, then he looked at Gideon. "If you will not consider going as the Kinsman Redeemer, will you at least consider going. . .as our friend?"

As your friend? Gideon thought. *You really consider me a friend?* The idea was shocking. Sure, he'd come to respect Revel and especially Ajel and could even say he liked them both. But he never let himself think of them as friends. He never imagined they could feel friendship for him, not after all the horrible things that had happened because of him.

No, they don't think of me as a friend, he thought. *They're just desperate for me to join them because of their crazy beliefs.*

Even so, as he looked at their sad and desperate faces, he couldn't bring himself to say no. Not right away. Finally, he let out a long sigh and said, "I'll think about it."

Ajel smiled. "We could ask no more."

"Once the plan for our journey has been set, we will meet together with Paladin," said Revel. "He will answer any questions you may have."

"Okay," said Gideon with a hint of resignation. "Until then, I do have one question about this room."

"Yes?" asked Ajel.

"Can you. . .could you see my home from here?"

"I do not know your home," said Ajel sadly. "I do not know how to dream of it. Perhaps if *you* knew the Words. . ."

Gideon waved his hand. "Nah. . .forget it," he said dismissively. "It's not that big a deal. I was just curious."

"Do you still long for your home?" asked Revel.

"Not really," Gideon replied, shaking his head. "I just wonder sometimes, you know, what's going on back there."

Revel nodded. "The first time I came to this room, I asked my father the same question you asked of Ajel. I too wanted to see the home I had lost. I still do. Perhaps you and I are more alike than we first believed." He grinned slightly.

"Perhaps." Gideon grinned in return. "Were you able to see your home?"

"I do not remember it," Revel replied. "As Ajel says, I. . .I cannot dream of it. Whenever I have tried, I see only trees."

"Why trees?" asked Gideon. But Revel only shrugged.

"I will guide you back to the training fields, if that is your wish," said Ajel, gesturing for the door. Gideon, suddenly realizing that Ajel wanted to leave, nodded. He doubted he could find his way back to the entryway on his own. "I'm actually starting to get hungry," he said.

"Then we will pass the kitchens on the way."

The threesome strolled out through the ornate golden doors and back into the river-winding passage, with Ajel and Revel in the lead and Gideon following behind. The brothers continued to talk as they walked, seeming to forget that Gideon was there at all. But that was fine with him. He had a lot to think about and didn't feel like talking anyway.

"What of our people in Phallenar?" Revel was saying. "Have any of them tried to trace your spirit's steps?"

"Only to a point," replied Ajel. "We know the path from the Wall to the first of the iron doors."

"Who tracked that?"

"Myren. The old cook who works within the Wall."

"He is a noble man," said Revel. "A good friend of Father's, I have heard."

Ajel nodded. "When I was a child, he used to work within the Axis itself. He and Father were dear friends, as were our families. I remember Myren used to sneak me into the Axis with him sometimes, in the early hours long before dawn, and I would help him bake the morning bread."

"You baked bread for the Council Lords?" asked Revel, sounding a little shocked.

"What of it?" replied Ajel with a mild shrug. "Father was their teacher. He ate at Balaam's table more than once in his time. After the rebellion, Myren fell out of favor with the Lords, since they knew of his friendship with Father. They transferred him to the Wall, where he became a cook for the miners who created the network of tunnels spreading under Phallenar."

"What is the tunnels' purpose?" asked Revel.

Ajel shrugged. "We do not know. But I do have a theory."

"Naturally," joked Revel.

Ajel chuckled. "I believe the Council Lords carved the tunnels in search of the Book."

"In search of it? You think the Book was already in the cavern before they got there?"

"Yes." Ajel nodded. "There is evidence in the tapestries and scrolls to suggest the Book may have been hidden in a cavern near the Gorge by Lord Kih more than a millennia past. I have not yet had time to research that possibility in depth. But there are other reasons for my thoughts as well. First, the tunnels themselves are random and reckless, suggesting they were hewn without any clear destination in mind. They follow no particular vein of ore or precious metal, nor do they provide passage to any other place, besides the cavern of the Book. When Myren finally got word to us of the tunnels' existence, he made it clear that their purpose was unknown. As far as he knew, nothing was ever mined from the tunnels."

"But why expend so much effort to find the Book and then just leave it where it lay untouched?" asked Revel.

"If my theory is true," Ajel replied, "then I believe the Council

Lords fully intended to destroy the Book upon its discovery, but found that they could not. In fact, it is my suspicion that they cannot even approach the Book without considerable discomfort."

Revel nodded, and the two walked quietly for a moment. Then Revel said, "You know, Father would be proud of you, brother."

Ajel rested his hand on Revel's shoulder. "And you as well, brother. As am I."

Just then, Gideon was distracted from overhearing the conversation by a doorway on his left. He recognized it as the one he had passed earlier, the one that led to Seer's bedchamber. The two brothers did not notice as Gideon slowed his pace and gradually came to a stop beneath the arched doorway leading into Seer's room. Within a few seconds, the twosome vanished behind another curve in the passage, their voices trailing behind them.

Gideon let them go. He just stood there, looking at the old woman, wondering why he had stopped and why it had seemed so automatic.

Paladin was no longer there, and that at least was a relief. He didn't want to have to explain why he had stopped here, especially since he really didn't know himself. Slowly, cautiously, he stepped into the room, toward the bed where Seer lay unconscious.

Her face seemed even gaunter than before, like a skull with wrinkled skin draped over the bones. If it weren't for her shallow breathing, he would have thought she was already dead. The coma was slowly draining her life away. In fact, Gideon imagined she would have already died by now if not for the Words that somehow helped sustain her dehydrated, starving body.

Gideon found a stool next to the bed and sat down. Why had he come in here? What could he hope to do for her? Was there something he wanted to say, to make his peace with her before she died?

He honestly didn't know. His thoughts were disconnected and unclear, as though his brain had gone on autopilot.

"Well, here we are," he said at last, whispering the words as though his voice might awaken her. Then, tentatively, almost fearfully, he let his hand reach across the bed toward hers.

Perhaps he just wanted to hold her withered hand, he thought. To let her know he bore her no hard feelings anymore, that he had forgiven her. But just as his hand drew close to hers, her bony hand flashed out and gripped his wrist with cold fingers as hard and unyielding as rusty iron hooks. He began to pull away, but just as quickly felt himself grow dizzy and weak.

A second later, his eyes rolled back into his head, and he slumped forward on the bed, unconscious.

CHAPTER 32

SHERWOOD FOREST

Shikinah is now one of the most highly esteemed prophets
from the Gray Ages, though this was not always so. Her
prophecies foretold of the coming of a second High Lord
of the Pearl, who would be betrayed as the Pearl was and
hung to die on a Great Wall in Phallenar. So great was the
public reaction to this prophecy that several factions in
Songwill demanded she retract it. When she would not,
Shikinah was forcibly taken to Castellan Watch, beaten, and
hung on a great tree there to die. Oddly, just as her spirit faded,
she looked toward the sky and laughed, saying, "It is torn!
The heart is torn! At last I understand!"

—THE KYRINTHAN JOURNALS, CHRONICLES, CHAPTER 3, VERSES 34–35

When Gideon opened his eyes again, he found himself standing on a mound
of pine needles in the middle of Sherwood Forest. The smell of sweet pine
carried on the breeze, as did the airy dust, which danced nimbly through the
sunbeams of late afternoon.

He was not dressed as Robin Hood and carried no bow. He wore the
leathers of the Remnant and carried nothing, not even his staff. This was no
dream, he realized, for his thoughts were still locked in the conscious world—
of that old woman on her deathbed and of the frightening bony hand that
reached out from death to pull him here.

But where is here?

Slowly he stepped off the mound and walked into the forest, making certain to step lightly on the crunchy forest floor. He did not know why he was
here, or where she was, or what she wanted. But he had stopped her once
before and would stop her once again. . .once he found her. She was, after all,
nearly dead.

After several hundred steps, he saw his first dead animal. He could not
tell what it had been, a squirrel perhaps, sliced open and spread wide against

a tree, its limbs and eyes held firmly to the bark with tiny silver nails. The birds had pecked its nose away, and the stench of rotting flesh enveloped it like a cloud. What had been blood, he guessed, was now dark brown crust, and its skin seemed to have grown brittle.

He did not know why, but he looked at the corpse for a long time before moving on. It didn't make him nauseous, and that was unexpected. At last, however, he did walk on, turning his attention back to finding the old woman. He hadn't walked ten steps, however, before he saw another dead animal. And then another and another. Soon he was surrounded by death. Birds, cats, dogs, squirrels, and chickens. . .all ritualistically killed, displayed like sacrificial lambs on trees or over rocks. The smell of death and rotting flesh was everywhere. And everywhere he looked, dead and hollow eyes looked back. It was like a cemetery with no graves. And no respect for life.

"You did this." The voice came from behind him. . .a woman's voice, smooth and alluring. Gideon spun around and saw a breathtaking young woman with long golden hair, lips like honey, and eyes blue like the morning sky. She looked so beautiful, so out of place here, surrounded by the stench and old dried blood of death.

"Who are you?" he asked.

"I was not always old and gray, sojourner," she replied in a voice as smooth as silk. "You know full well who I am."

Gideon tensed slightly. "You're dying," he said. "Why are you inside my head again? Why now?"

"I never left," she said flatly, as though it were something he already knew. "You sealed me here behind the wall of this great forest, where you hide all your secrets. The Facing never ended."

Suddenly shaken, Gideon took a step back, away from her. "You're lying," he said. "You haven't been in my head all this time. I would've known."

The woman smiled sadly. "Like you remember this?" She gestured toward the dead animals that lay strewn all around them. "You locked me away beyond the places of your conscious thought. I have been as hidden as all of these things are."

Gideon's voice took on an edge. "What are you saying? That I killed these animals?"

Seer nodded. "You remember now, don't you? Your search for me has brought you here behind the wall you built so long ago. Now you can remember."

And, suddenly, he did. The image of the knife held in his childlike bloody hands came flooding back to him like a wall of rage. His bloody clothes, the ones he hid under the mound in the forest, he put them on like priestly robes every time he came to do the deed. He never really wanted the animals to die; he was always sad when they did, because it meant the end of the ceremony and the coming of the shame. He wanted them to live and suffer, filleted alive with cries of pain. The sacrifices gave him power, gave him dignity again, told him what he needed to hear—that he was not a weakling little boy. He had power too.

Gideon grabbed his head from the shock of these horrific memories flooding back into his conscious mind. How could he have done this? Was he a monster? Was he mad?

A wave of nausea surged through his gut as image after image of cruelly murdered creatures flashed before his eyes. And yet, the grisly scenes also enticed him, and he lingered for a time over the memories, remembering how they had made him feel.

"I understand," the sweet voice said. "It was your only outlet, I think. The only way you could manage the injury to your heart. And it speaks well that, in all of this, you never harmed a human soul. Except yourself, I mean."

Gideon shook his head, already feeling emotionally drained from the revelation of his secret childhood. "What are you talking about?" he said tiredly. "What injury?"

Seer pointed to her right. "That one," she said. Gideon followed her hand's direction until his eyes came to rest upon an old, dilapidated wooden shed nestled in the trees. He heard the sounds of hammering, of clanging tools and electric saws coming from behind the old but solid, oil-stained door.

"Gideon. . ." The voice was not the woman's now. It was his mother, calling from the house, which he now saw just off to his left. "Go help your father in the shed. Dinner will be ready in an hour and I don't want him to miss it."

"Mom, no. . . ," said Gideon weakly, but he knew it was no use arguing. When Dad called him to the shed, there was no getting out of it. Ever.

A feeling of stark terror quickly rose in Gideon's throat. He felt a pain stab through his chest, the sinking dread of someone trapped with no hope for rescue. Mechanically, against his will, he took a step toward the shed. And then another and another. As he walked, his thoughts went blank, and then he felt his heart grow numb. And finally, he felt nothing at all, the glorious comfort of nothingness.

"*You must not detach your soul from this,*" *said Seer's sweet voice from the trees to his right.* "*You must see this for what it was. Only then can you be free to grieve.*"

"*I don't want to feel it.*" *The words came hollow out of Gideon's mouth, but he didn't know who spoke them.*

"*You must,*" *she said.* "*Do not fear. The Giver is greater than any challenge to your heart.*"

And then he was there, at the door. . .reaching for the old rusty handle. . . opening it. . .hearing the creak of hinges as they swung. The man within was wearing a mechanic's uniform, gray-blue and stained with oil and grit. At the opening of the door, he turned.

"*Get in here, boy,*" *he said. Gideon entered.* "*You been out there playing sissy games again, ain't 'cha?*" *the man asked as he turned to face him.*

"*No, sir,*" *said Gideon, but it sounded weak and frail.*

"*Yeah. . . ,*" *the man said.* "*I see it on your girly little face. You ain't nothin' but a sissy, boy. And you know what a sissy like you needs, don't 'cha?*"

"*Daddy, please, I wasn't playing sissy games. I was just exploring. . . .*"

"*You even talk like a girl,*" *said the man, shaking his head.* "*I'm gonna have to teach you a lesson again, 'bout what it means to be a man.*"

Gideon backed himself up against the wall, and his father smiled as he unzipped his coveralls. Instinctively, Gideon closed his eyes. . . .

Later, Gideon lay on the forest floor, curled up in a ball with his head between his knees. The beautiful woman knelt beside him, gently stroking his black curly hair.

"*I grieve for you, sojourner,*" *she whispered.* "*I grieve for you.*"

"*Go away!*" *Gideon's muffled voice snapped.* "*Leave me alone!*"

Nodding, Seer stood. "*The wall is down, and I am free to go,*" *she said.* "*But so are you, sojourner. Remember that. You must not hide this anymore. It is a part of you, and it deserves to be grieved.*"

"*Get out!*"

She smiled sadly, then turned and walked slowly out of the forest.

Gideon awoke to the sounds of wailing. Deep, guttural sobs that surged in waves from a core of grief too deep for words. His stomach ached with soreness from the bitter groans that rumbled unbidden from his gut. His eyes burned with the heat of a thousand tears. . .that until now had been shut up in a prison for years behind a wall within his soul.

But there were no walls now. The dam had burst, and every ounce of pain and rage poured forth from him like a torrent. And he found he was afraid—terribly, terribly afraid—that the raging current of his grief would drown both his sanity and his soul.

Between the surging waves of sorrow, he became dimly aware of others in the room and in his thoughts. He was still in Seer's bedchamber, he knew, but that was now irrelevant. What mattered, a little, was that Seer was awake, her thoughts still with him, trying to comfort his pain even as she lay nearly dead in her own struggle for life.

Despite himself, he laughed at her attempt to help. His sorrow could not be comforted, could never be helped, could never be undone. The dam had burst, and now, most assuredly, he would drown in its flood.

Another voice broke through his thoughts and then a third and a fourth. Ajel, Paladin, Revel, Aybel—all of them were present, and he knew somehow that they knew everything. Whatever barriers he had built to keep his thoughts away from them had crumbled. Wordhaven itself flooded its awareness into his bitter soul, even as the sorrow flooded out.

Peace, sojourner. . .let it come. . . .

We are here and will not leave you. . . .

You did not deserve this horror. . . .

Pity? Was it pity now they offered him? Pity for the poor, poor boy, too weak to stand up to the coward of a man who had abused him? Too weak to say no, even when he knew he was old enough to run away.

He screamed out a string of curses, not knowing if he was yelling at his father or himself. And now, his shame was laid bare for everyone to see, to gawk at, to judge. And why not? He had judged himself years ago.

It was not your fault, sojourner. A child cannot be blamed for the abuses of the parent.

"I was weak!" he screamed. And then the screams turned into sobs. "A sissy."

No, you were strong. . .are strong. You did not let him steal your soul. You kept it hidden in the forest of your dreams.

He did not win. . .you did. . . .

But Gideon felt weak, helpless, even now. He hated that they were there, free to roam his thoughts, free to see the ugliness of his soul. But he could not stop them anymore. All his strength had been washed away in the torrent of his father's crime. "How could he do that to me?" he whimpered. "How could he?"

But there was no answer. And, with his father dead and gone, he knew there never would be.

In time, exhaustion overcame his tears; and in his weakness, he allowed them to lift him to his feet. He leaned on them heavily, Ajel on one side and Revel on the other, as they half-walked, half-carried him down the beautiful corridors of Wordhaven to his private chamber.

There they laid him gently on the bed and somehow convinced him to eat some small bits of bread and drink a few sips of water before he finally collapsed into a deep and dreamless sleep.

CHAPTER 33

THE GATES OF WORDHAVEN

Among the more practical revelations about Sa'lei *that
Donovan brought to the Remnant was that, unlike* Dei'lo,
*the dark Tongue is incapable of any truly creative act—that is,
it cannot create something from nothing. Rather, it can only
twist or alter what is already present in any given object, person,
or circumstance. Because of this limitation, the Words of* Sa'lei
cannot, for example, heal sickness or injury in the way Dei'lo
*can, for that requires creating health or wholeness where it does
not currently exist.* Sa'lei *can, however, mask the pain of illness
and numb the mind to even the most grievous of wounds, so that
a sick or injured person can continue functioning as though
nothing were wrong and even believe he is totally healthy
and strong right up to the point of final collapse.*

—THE KYRINTHAN JOURNALS, SONGS OF DELIVERANCE, STANZA 8, VERSES 18–22

"Clever. . ."

Lord Bentel Baratii poked a stick down into the water of the small lake, feeling out the edges of the hidden stone path that lay just beneath the surface.

"Can't we go around?" Fayerna sat on a stone several feet from the water's edge. Her black leathers still looked surprisingly sharp, despite the weeks of hard travel they had endured. The lines on her face, however, showed that the journey was taking its toll in other ways.

Bentel squinted off into the distance. "No," he said, "the cliffs on the far side prevent it."

"Well, it's too far for us to fly across," she snapped. "If only we still had the juron." Bentel smiled amiably back toward her. The trip had also taken a toll on her attitude, a fact that had grown more painfully obvious in the last few days.

"We are almost there, sister," Bentel said soothingly. "I'm confident the entrance lies somewhere in those cliffs."

Fayerna sighed heavily as she looked across the mountain lake toward the gray cliffs on the other side. "I don't see anything remotely resembling a gate. . .not even a cave."

"Why would they build a hidden stone path that leads nowhere?" asked Bentel. He tried very hard not to let his voice carry an edge.

Fayerna sighed again, glancing briefly at Sarlina, who sat contentedly at her feet picking blades of grass. "How deep is it?" she asked at last.

"Probably no more than three feet at the deepest point, but I will have Kyrva walk it first to be sure."

"Well. . . ," said Fayerna with a hint of resignation, "I suppose we have no choice then. Lok, go with Kyrva."

The *mon'jalen* nodded silently, then set the bags on the ground and headed toward the water's edge. Kyrva fell in silently beside him.

"Step here," ordered Bentel, pointing with the stick to what seemed like a random spot on the water. "You'll have to feel for the edges as you go. I don't think you'll be able to see it at all."

Without hesitation, the two *mon'jalen* waded into the water with Lok leading the way. With cautious steps, they waded out toward the center of the lake, never sinking more than a few feet beneath the surface. If the water was cold, they showed no sign of it. Several minutes later, they reached the far side and stepped out onto the shore.

"The path is firm," announced Kyrva, calling back toward the Lords. "But the water feels to be near freezing."

"Wonderful," muttered Fayerna, glancing toward the sky. "At least the sun is out today, for once."

"Sanchi can carry you, if you like," offered Sarlina. "He's very strong."

"I will not be carried," scoffed Fayerna, obviously offended by the implication that she was a weakling or, worse, overly heavy. Sarlina smiled innocently, immediately sensing she had said something wrong.

"Let's leave the bags for now," said Bentel. "We can send the *mon'-jalen* back to get them once we've explored the other side."

Fayerna said nothing but rose and walked to where Bentel stood, absently brushing some dust off her sleeves as she went. "Here?" she asked, pointing to the water's edge.

"No, here," Bentel replied, pointing toward a different nondescript region of the water. "I can go first."

"I will go," Fayerna said flatly. With that, she grabbed his arm for stability and stepped into the water. "By the Words, it's cold!" she snapped at no one in particular. But then she plodded into the lake, apparently determined to get this over with as quickly as possible.

Bentel and Sarlina followed close behind, with Sanchi bringing up the rear. Aside from a few mumbled curses from Fayerna as she stumbled along the edges of the path, the foursome made it across without much trouble. Upon reaching the other side, Bentel immediately gestured for the *mon'jalen* to follow him as he plodded up the shallow hill toward the gray cliffs jutting straight up from the grassy floor. Fayerna and Sarlina followed, after first shaking out the ice-cold water from their boots.

For a time no one said a word as all six walked along the cliff face in different directions, scanning the rock for signs of some sort of entrance. After half an hour, they still had not found a thing.

"Maybe there's nothing here," said Sarlina, looking plaintively toward Fayerna.

"Oh, it's here, dear," Fayerna replied, feeling the warm rock with her hand as she walked. "At least, it had better be, for Bentel's sake. Just keep looking."

"What am I looking for?" asked Sarlina.

"M'lord!" Lok called from a point along the rocks not far from the edge of the water bridge. "Something seems strange here."

Bentel and the others converged on the *mon'jalen*'s location as he pointed toward a particular section of the rock face. Bentel squinted as he looked to where Lok pointed. "What? What do you see?"

"It. . .shimmers."

And then Bentel saw it. For a brief moment, the rock face seemed to waver in the sunlight as though it were an image reflected on water. Bentel stepped closer, then closer still. With each step, the rock wall seemed to ripple in the light until it looked almost as though a waterfall were spilling over the stone. Finally, the waterfall appeared to wash away the rock completely, revealing a massive set of silver doors, emblazoned with a lion more than twice as large as any he had ever seen.

"It's beautiful," said Sarlina, who had come up behind him without him noticing. "It looks so real." Before Bentel could stop her, Sarlina ran up to the door and stretched out her hand to touch the carving. But in the instant her fingers touched the gate, blue fire shot out from the silver and enveloped her hand.

She screamed, yanking back her arm in pain and waving it wildly in the air. "It hurts! It hurts!" she cried, running here and there toward nothing in particular.

"Sarlina, come here!" ordered Fayerna. "Let me see."

But Sarlina did not hear her. Instead she turned back toward the door with fury in her eyes. "Bad lion!" she screamed through gritted teeth. "Bad!"

Then, without the slightest warning to the others, she let out a barrage of Words at the silver doors—Words to burn them, then to break them, then to hurl them to the sky. Fire and wind appeared from nowhere, blasting toward the gate with palpable malice. Black lightning shot out from her chest and stabbed repeatedly at the lion's heart. The Lords and the *mon'jalen* instinctively dove away from the attack, rolling on the ground to avoid the lightning, sparks, and shafts of flame. But when her anger was fully spent and all the smoke had finally cleared, the silver gate remained untouched.

When Sarlina saw the door was unharmed, she started to cry. "Bad lion," she whimpered and fell to her knees, still cradling her badly seared hand in her arm.

Fayerna, her leathers now badly stained with grass and mud, struggled to her feet and angrily brushed her disheveled red hair out of her eyes. From this distance, she couldn't see whether the gate was destroyed. But she could see Sarlina, and that was all she cared about right now. Without a word, she stormed toward the younger woman, who still knelt in the grass, sobbing and unaware. Upon reaching her, she raised an angry fist and prepared to swing.

"Fayerna, no!" Bentel yelled. At that same instant, Sarlina's *mon'-jalen*, Sanchi, leaped into the air from his crouched position several feet away and came down directly beside his Lord, immediately assuming a fighting stance toward Lord Fayerna. His eyes, normally docile and subservient to any Lord, now burned toward Fayerna with an almost arrogant malice.

"How dare you," she whispered, shifting her icy gaze toward the *mon'jalen*. Sarlina looked up, suddenly surprised to find Fayerna and Sanchi standing next to her.

"Fayerna, back off!" Bentel barked angrily as he stormed toward her. "Sanchi is only doing his duty. He believes you mean to harm her."

Fayerna's eyes flashed toward Bentel. "She nearly killed us all, and you tell *me* to back away?" She whipped her gaze back to the *mon'jalen*. "You step away from me now, or you will die where you stand." Her whisper carried a cold, steel resolve.

But so did Sanchi's whispered response. "You first, m'Lord," he said.

By now, Sarlina realized she was in danger and, as quietly as possible, began to crawl awkwardly away from the conflict, still cradling her injured hand and looking anxiously over her shoulder as she went.

"Fayerna. . .sister." Bentel tried to speak more softly now. He had to try to quell his sister's anger. Attacking any Council Lord—even Sarlina—was absolutely forbidden by Council Law and instantly punishable by death. If she so much as laid a finger on Sarlina in anger, Sanchi would be duty-bound to kill her or die trying. "This is getting us nowhere. You do not really want to harm Sarlina."

"She is an insolent child and deserves to be punished!" Fayerna snapped. "Look at me!" She gestured toward the stains on her leathers. "I am lucky to be alive after that. . .that simpleton's ridiculous tantrum."

"And what would you call what you're doing now, hmm?" asked Bentel. "A tantrum, perhaps? Look at her! She's terrified."

At that, Fayerna shook her head in disgust and stormed away from the *mon'jalen*. "It's not a tantrum, Bentel," she snapped. "The girl must learn to control herself."

"As must we all," Bentel countered.

She spun toward him. "Do not compare me with her." Her voice was quiet and cold. "I was not going to use the Words, unlike our dear Sarlina here."

Sensing that the immediate danger had passed, Sanchi relaxed his stance somewhat, but still moved to stand between Fayerna and his Lord.

Frustrated, Bentel slowly shook his head and sighed, mentally sorting the things that he could say from the things he wanted to. "Well," he said at last, "I agree that Sarlina must learn control. But she *was* injured for her lack of discretion. And I'm sure she feels very badly about it all. Don't you, Sarlina?"

With tears still in her eyes, Sarlina nodded, clearly afraid to say anything at all.

"Besides, she has inadvertently done us a favor," Bentel continued. "We now know that the Words can do nothing to harm the door." He smiled at Sarlina. "And that we should not touch it. Now I suggest we move on and look at our next option. Sanchi, I think you should begin by looking toward your Lord's injury."

Sanchi nodded, glancing briefly at Fayerna before turning his attention to Sarlina, who still sat huddled in the grass. Her right hand was blackened and seemed somewhat shriveled as she held it out to her *mon'jalen*. Sanchi gently helped her to her feet, then led her down the hill toward the water's edge, probably to try to cool the burn in the icy waters of the lake.

Fayerna watched sullenly as they walked past. "What options do we have now?" she asked Bentel. "There's nothing here but solid rock and a gate we cannot touch."

Bentel thought for a moment, then said, "In all of our studies, we've never heard of Wordhaven being incased in rock. As I recall, it is said to be an open and airy place."

"What of it?"

"Then I suspect that, if we cannot reach it through the gate, perhaps we can reach it from the sky."

Fayerna glanced up at the cliffs. "You mean, fly over this mountain. You think it's on the other side."

"Of course it's on the other side," said Bentel. "Why else would there be a door here?"

Fayerna looked at him for a moment, then heaved a tired sigh. "You're right, of course. Thank the Words that at least one of us knows how to keep his wits about him."

Bentel grinned. "In truth, I wanted to smack her too. You just happened to get there first."

Fayerna smiled sadly. "I'm sorry, Bentel. I don't know why I can't control my temper."

"Your temper serves you well. . .most of the time," he replied.

"Well," she brushed a patch of mud off of her thigh, "I'll need to summon more juron, then."

Bentel nodded. "I will see to the camp. I think we should set up in the trees across the lake. We wouldn't want them coming out of those doors and catching us unawares."

"Whatever you think is best," she said, still brushing flakes of mud and grass off of her leathers.

Bentel headed toward the lake, then stopped and turned back toward his sister. "And, Fayerna," he said, "you might consider checking on Sarlina before too long. Her hand looked pretty bad."

"I will," Fayerna sighed. "I will."

CHAPTER 34

A NEW JOURNEY

"How could they have let him go? Were they vain enough to
believe they did not need him anymore?"
I answer this critique with a question of my own: What good
could come from making him stay? For the help they so desper-
ately needed from him was the sort that must be freely given.
That kind of sacrifice can never truly be coerced.

—The Kyrinthan Journals, Musings, Chapter 10, Verses 12–13

"May I enter?"

The grandmotherly voice came from outside the door of Gideon's bedchamber. But even before he heard it, he knew who it was.

"Yes, come in, Seer," Gideon said without turning around. He was busy packing up the satchels with clothes and supplies for the journey ahead. He found it amusing that he was packing more things for Orisoun than for himself and was amazed to realize how little he actually needed anymore to feel satisfied and content. Definitely a big shift from his days before he came to the Inherited Lands—and he thought he was living frugally *then*.

"You know why I have come." It was not a question. Gideon turned toward the Wordhaven elder and grinned. She looked as fit as she had the first day he met her, with her white flowing hair and her grandmotherish face—a remarkable recovery in only a few days' time. But then, that was to be expected with the power of the Words, he supposed. She did walk with a staff for support, but he had heard she did that even before the Facing.

"You've come to try to convince me not to go," said Gideon pleasantly. "I could have guessed that even without your thoughts arriving ten seconds before you did."

Seer nodded. "I was wrong about you, sojourner," she confessed, then quickly raised a defiant finger. "Not about everything, of course. I was right about most of it, truth be told. But I was wrong to believe your heart was evil. I saw the signs of evil in your soul, but they did not come from you."

Gideon smiled awkwardly. He still hadn't gotten used to having his sordid childhood laid out in plain sight for everyone at Wordhaven to see. He doubted he ever would.

"I'm not so sure about that, Seer. I'm not sure about anything anymore. Not really." He shrugged. "But I do know I need to leave."

"That is precisely why you must stay." Seer took a shaky step toward him. Perhaps she wasn't quite so recovered as she appeared. "You are not ready to be alone. We can help restore you, to undo the effects of the injury to your soul. You must allow us to help you."

Gideon shook his head. "I appreciate your concern. Really." He paused and looked at her a moment, then sat down heavily on the bed. "I need to be alone with my thoughts," he continued, looking straight into her sky blue eyes. "I can never do that here. Not anymore. I can't get away from the mental bombardments from everyone around— including you—that continually peg me as the Kinsman Redeemer. It's hard enough to have to try to figure out who I am now, after learning the truth about my past. . .without having to deal with that too."

Seer nodded, and Gideon knew she understood, even though she didn't want to. "There are still many enemies out there, outside yourself, who wish you harm," she said. "At least stay until you learn the Words. Then when you go, you will at least carry that protection with you."

"Seer, please," he broke in, "you know I can't learn the Words. And you're not going to change my mind, no matter what you say. I realize you genuinely care, and I'm thankful. But I also know part of your concern is rooted in the belief that I am your Kinsman Redeemer. You must understand that I can't deal with that right now."

Seer frowned. "In truth, I do not know whether you are the one or not. I was once convinced. But now I am no longer sure."

"After being in my head, I don't see how you could even entertain the idea." He looked away from her, out the window. "I am without a doubt the most screwed up person I know."

She took another step toward him. "True greatness is born from our weakness, sojourner, not our strengths."

Gideon shrugged slightly. "I don't see how," he said.

Seer shook her head and rapped her staff upon the gray stone floor. "You are as stubborn and bone-headed as ever," she said.

"It has served me well," he said with a laugh.

"In some things, perhaps," she retorted, "but not in this."

She plodded awkwardly toward the window and seemed to purposefully lose herself in her own thoughts as she gazed down on the forest below them. Gideon looked down sadly at the floor, feeling her frustration.

He had brought nothing but trouble to the Remnant, especially to this old woman whom he had nearly killed in the Facing. Just the thought of that made him wince. And, of course, conjuring the mental image of Seer on her deathbed immediately sparked the litany of other dark memories. . .the little girl on fire, the destruction of Songwill, and that terrible night of Lairn's death.

I am the bringer of death, he thought. *The bringer of death. . .the bringer of death. . .* The words echoed bitterly in his mind. Determinedly, he forced his attention back to packing the satchels.

"Paladin tells me you have refused an escort," Seer said, still looking out the window.

"Yep," said Gideon as he tested the weight of the water bags. It was by far the heaviest thing he had to carry.

"You know he will have you followed, despite your wishes."

Gideon raised his eyebrows. "Really? Huh," he said, then shrugged. "I guess he'll do what he thinks he must."

"I tell you so you will know, sojourner," she said. "Help will not be far away, should you need it."

"May I enter?" Aybel's voice echoed through the room as she walked in, not waiting for a response. "Seer." She nodded toward the woman respectfully, then turned toward Gideon. "Your mount is ready, Gideon."

"Thanks, Aybel," Gideon replied. "I'm all packed up here."

"I will help carry your things," she said, then walked to the bed and started hefting the travel bags over her shoulders, including the water. Gideon still marveled at how strong she was, even after seeing her demonstrate it time and again.

"Thanks," he said. But before he gathered the remaining satchels, he paused to look at Seer, who still stood looking out the window. Awkwardly, he stepped up behind her, unsure of how to express what he wanted—*needed*—to say.

"I want. . .to thank you," he said at last, surprised by the shakiness in his voice.

"What for?" she said, turning to face him. "I have convinced you of nothing."

"Not for that," said Gideon. He paused. "I want to thank you for. . .helping me see the truth." He wanted to look into her eyes when he said it, but found that he could not. "I mean, after all that's happened to you because of me. . .after all you've seen, in my head. Well, you have every reason to despise me. I mean, *I* would despise me. But you don't. I know you don't. So, thank you. That's more than I deserve."

For a moment, Seer's eyes softened, and she smiled with just a hint of sorrow. "You are no worse than any other human soul," she said softly, "especially not mine. We all carry great darkness in our hearts, though very few will dare to face it. In that way, your heart is nobler than most. How then can I hate you, unless I also hate myself?"

Gideon smiled, unsure of what else to say. Finally, he turned and grabbed the bags off of the bed, then headed out the door with Aybel.

"Sojourner." Seer's voice stopped him, but he did not turn around. "I believe you could now learn the Words, if you wished," she said. Slowly, Gideon nodded, then walked out of the room.

Gideon started down the hall after Aybel, still thinking about Seer's parting words. To tell him he could learn the Words was a great compliment, perhaps the greatest she could offer, for it meant that she believed his heart was pure. Her words provoked an ache deep in his gut, a feeling, a longing for something out of reach. Despite himself, he chuckled at his reaction. The very idea that a part of him actually wanted to believe her. . .well, it was just sad enough to be funny. To hope that it might be possible for him to regain his innocence.

Now that's hilarious, he thought bitterly. *That's a real knee-slapper.*

But now was not the time for idle fantasies of what could never be. He had faced his darkest nightmare and admitted it was real. And after he had seen it in all its ugliness, he was still standing. That at least said something good about him and made him realize that it was no good pretending that he was okay anymore.

He was definitely not okay, had never been okay, would most likely never be okay again. That was the truth—the sad, undeniable fact of his existence. His father's abuse had left a scar so deep that it could never be erased. That man had raped not only his body, but also his soul. *When you finally accept that*, Gideon realized, *any notion of purity and innocence becomes hopelessly intangible and utterly irrelevant.*

Gideon glanced at Aybel and wondered why she hadn't said anything since they left his chamber. Despite the bitterness of his thoughts, he couldn't help but feel the warm flush rising in his cheeks as he looked at her. She was so beautiful, much more beautiful now than when he had first met her. For weeks he had tried to deny his attraction. He had kept his distance, forcing arguments between them at every opportunity to hold her at bay. Privately he told himself he was just lonely, that it was only lust he felt. But he knew it was more. That was really why he tried to make her hate him, he realized now. He wanted to protect her from his own flawed and broken love.

Even now, he tried to not allow his thoughts to go down that path, but he found he could not stop them, even knowing he could never love her in the way that she deserved. If only things were different. If only he were a different man, a whole man, perhaps there could have been something between them.

Suddenly, Aybel shook her head and let out a long, frustrated breath. Gideon stopped walking. "What?" he asked tentatively.

Aybel also stopped, then turned to face him. Her dark eyes looked angry. "Gideon, stop this!" she said.

"Stop what?"

"If you must wallow in despair, at least try to do so without proclaiming your thoughts to all those around you."

Gideon gasped. Had she really heard his thoughts? Did she know? "Um. . .sorry," he said at last. "I was just. . .daydreaming."

Aybel stared at him a moment, then shook her head. "You mistake yourself," she said. "And if you took the time to look somewhere outside your own dismal appraisal of your heart, you might actually see that you are not the only one who feels." Gideon glimpsed the tears that filled her eyes just before she turned and stalked down the hall.

Idiot! he yelled at himself. *Of course she heard my thoughts! And now look what I've done.* He ran down the hall after her.

"Aybel, wait," he said just as he reached her. But she did not stop, and so he fell in beside her, walking quickly. "I'm sorry," he said. "I–I don't know what to say."

"There is nothing to say, then," Aybel replied. "You are leaving. What else could be said?" She stormed on without looking at him.

"I shouldn't have thought those things," said Gideon, picking up the pace to match hers. "It was disrespectful, and I'm sorry."

Aybel snorted, but said nothing.

"Look," said Gideon. "I don't want to leave like this. I do care about how you feel. It was just a stupid fantasy, that's all."

"A fantasy?" Aybel snapped, still not looking his direction. They came to the entrance to the Outer Hall, and Aybel stopped under the threshold, then turned to face him. "It is only a fantasy because you will not let it be more than that, Gideon," she said angrily. "You feel love. I know, I have seen it. But you have selfishly judged yourself incapable of love, so you deny it is real. So tell me, Gideon, what is the true fantasy? The hope that you can love or the stoic conviction that you cannot?" Fresh tears welled in her eyes as she spoke. "It is a selfish pit you dig for your heart, for you are not the only one who pays a price for your decision not to love." She wiped a wayward tear from her cheek, but kept her eyes fixed on his.

Gideon's eyes widened as he began to realize what she was saying. She loved *him?* But how could she love *him?* It didn't make any sense. He was no Ajel, or Revel, or even Donovan. He didn't even qualify as a real man. At best he was a broken, bitter imitation of a man.

Surely what she felt was really pity, he thought, and she had mistaken it for love.

"I didn't mean to hurt you," he said at last.

"No," she replied coolly. "You only mean to hurt yourself, to finish the task your father began. But you are too selfish to see that in punishing yourself, you injure those around you as well."

"Then I guess that's another good reason for me to leave," Gideon snapped back, feeling suddenly hurt by Aybel's harsh tone. With that, he turned and headed into the Outer Hall.

"That's not what I meant," she said quietly.

"No, it's for the best," he said, still walking away from her. *Because*

I can't bear the thought of hurting you, he added silently, this time hoping she would hear his thoughts.

After a moment, she followed after him, but stayed a pace or two behind and didn't say anything more. Gideon could hear her footsteps, but did not stop or turn around. Instead, he just kept walking, trying to listen to her thoughts the same way she had heard his. For some reason, though, he could not. Probably because his own cloud of guilt and anger was too thick to allow anyone else's thoughts to reach him. *That would figure*, he thought sarcastically. *Something else I somehow managed to screw up.*

They walked down the Hall, past a dozen people or more who waved or nodded, past a hundred tapestries, past another hundred doors to nowhere, all without saying a word. When at last they came to the grand atrium that marked Wordhaven's entrance, Gideon felt as though his head was going to explode. What was she thinking? Did she really want him to love her? How could she want that?

And now he knew that just beyond those big gold doors, the rest of the Wordhaveners would be waiting to say good-bye. He hated good-byes—always had—but now with this new development with Aybel, all he wanted to do was run away without saying another word to anyone. Or, more to the point, thinking another thought. He paused a moment and observed the massive statue of the Pearl situated in the center of the atrium floor.

I don't know what you really were, he said to the statue in his thoughts. *But I wish you were still around. Maybe you could tell me what to do.*

Aybel walked to the door, then paused to look back to where Gideon stood. He looked back at her and was surprised to find no anger in her face. But what did he see? Sorrow. . .just sorrow. "The others are waiting," she said. "We should go."

Gideon smiled, a gesture that seemed trite even as he did it. Then he coughed awkwardly and followed as she walked out the massive doors.

As he suspected, Ajel waited for him there, along with Paladin and Revel and Donovan, and even Kair. Next to them stood Orisoun, who glanced nonchalantly in his direction as he approached. When he stopped before the Wordhaveners, Aybel stopped beside him, and he couldn't help but wonder if the rest of them could feel the tension between them.

It was Paladin who spoke first. "This is a sad day for us, sojourner," he said. "I understand that Seer was not able to convince you to stay."

Gideon smiled, trying very hard to look more pleasant than he felt. "It's time for me to go," he said, "but I will come back, I promise. . .as soon as I can."

"Then know that you will always be welcome in the Stand," said Ajel. "It is my hope that your sojourn will bring you the answers you seek and lead you back to us soon."

"And in one piece," added Revel with his characteristic grin.

"Oh, I'm sure you're ready to be rid of me for awhile," Gideon joked, trying to sound upbeat. "You have to admit I've been a lot of trouble."

"Allow me to assist in preparing your mount," Donovan broke in, stepping forward as he reached for the satchels draped across Gideon's shoulders.

"Uh. . .thanks," said Gideon, glad to have the weight off his shoulders. He then watched as Aybel followed Donovan to Orisoun and began to strap the bags upon the horse's flanks.

"It is a good mount," said Revel. "He will do you well."

"I appreciate you offering him to me," said Gideon. "And for all the supplies." He gestured toward the bags.

"Oh yes," said Paladin, "I nearly forgot." He reached behind him and retrieved Gideon's staff, which had been lying unnoticed on the ground. He held it out toward Gideon. "Your staff."

Gideon reached out and took it, nodding his thanks to Paladin. It was the only remaining piece of his life from before, and he was glad to have it in his hands as he journeyed alone in the Inherited Lands, which still felt strange and alien to him despite the months he'd spent here. The gilded almond wood felt warm to his touch, simultaneously soft, yet hard as steel. It was comforting.

"Thank you all," Gideon said, "for your hospitality, your kindness. And most of all, for your. . .patience." He forced a grin. "I have learned a lot. . .maybe more than I wanted to know. But I must try to find a way through this on my own now."

As he spoke, he purposefully looked at each of the Wordhaveners in turn, fighting the constant impulse to look away, trying not to think about the fact that each of them knew everything about his darkest secrets, even those he had spent years hiding from himself. But he wanted them to know his gratitude was sincere, and so he forced himself to look at them and smile at each in turn.

"Well, I guess I'd better be going," he said finally.

"Revel and I will go with you to the gate," offered Ajel.

"No, thank you," said Gideon. "I'd rather go alone from here."

"Very well, as you wish." Ajel nodded, almost sadly.

Gideon smiled again, awkwardly, then headed toward Orisoun. Donovan and Aybel had finished preparing the mount and now stood stoically nearby.

"Thank you, Donovan," said Gideon. "I will always try to remember to duck, just like you taught me."

"The Guardians will not leave you be," said Donovan, ignoring Gideon's attempt at humor. "You must be careful."

"I will."

"And keep your head covered," added Aybel.

"Oh, yeah," said Gideon, touching his head. "Black hair, right. I'll do that."

"And, for when you need greater strength, perhaps you can make use of this." Donovan pulled a small loaf of bread from the folds of his tunic and held it out toward Gideon.

"Oh, I couldn't, Donovan," said Gideon. "You've given me enough already."

"It is a great affront to refuse a gift freely given," said Donovan flatly.

Gideon grinned apologetically. "Then I accept it, of course." He took the bread from Donovan's hand. Its unnatural weight confirmed that it was *ja'moinar*, the same bread Mara had given him for his journey to Wordhaven. Gideon slipped it into the folds of his poncho. "Thank you."

"May you never have need of it," said Donovan.

"I probably will," quipped Gideon pessimistically. Then he grinned. "But I'll use it wisely this time, Donovan. I promise."

He glanced toward the others momentarily, then said, "Well, I guess this is it." He patted Orisoun on the neck and prepared to mount, but then turned awkwardly to Aybel. "Good-bye, Aybel," he said. "I hope. . .to see you again."

"May your sojourn be fruitful, Gideon," Aybel replied. "Perhaps we can talk again, when you return."

"I will look forward to that very much," he replied, feeling a wave of hope wash over him. Maybe there would be a chance for them. Someday.

He patted Orisoun again, then grabbed the mount's gray mane and swung himself up easily to his back. His riding pants instantly gripped the gray coat, making him feel snug and secure. He grinned, despite himself. Maybe he was a failure as a human being, but at least he had learned how to ride a horse.

With a parting wave, he turned Orisoun away from Wordhaven and headed toward the golden gate on the far side of the valley.

As he traveled down the smooth stone road that split the valley's center, he let his thoughts reach out and join with the richness of life that surrounded him. He felt the breezes to the north dancing through the pines, heard the whistling songs they made from several miles away. He sensed the heat held in the stones of the western cliffs and touched the fierce and fragile heartbeats of the birds that nestled in its crevices. The deer, the elk, the curious squirrels with raccoon tails, he knew them all, felt their breath as their life force mingled with his, becoming one.

The effect made him feel both insignificant and grand. It was pure splendor, and for a time it dulled the sorrow of his heart. In that union, his only lingering grief was that he had spent so much time here fighting to hold all this life at bay—determined, out of stupid shame, to keep himself apart, alone. How could he have been so arrogant? No wonder the Remnant viewed his mental isolation with such contempt.

He continued slowly down the road, knowing that once he passed through the gate, the link of intimacy with the land would fade. He did not know how long it might be before he would experience Wordhaven again or even if he would ever return, so he wanted to make it last as long as possible. Orisoun seemed to be in no hurry either, content to clip-clop down the road at the lazy pace Gideon had set. The other horses called to him from the grasslands to the southwest. Somehow they knew that he was leaving and might not come this way again.

Some time later, the golden doors came into view, and Gideon sighed. *This is it,* he thought, not quite sadly. *From here on out, I'm on my own.*

Danger, Gideon, danger!

The thought came crashing into his mind, and he knew at once that it was Aybel. Feeling the panic in her thoughts, he frantically looked around to find the source of her concern. But he saw nothing but the green grasses of the meadow, felt nothing but the peace that emanated from the life around him.

Above, sojourner. . . came the thought, this time from Ajel, whom he knew was now running toward him from the Stand. Gideon looked up, seeing nothing at first, but then noticed the movement of a dark bird soaring against the backdrop of the cliffs to the south. And then he saw a second bird, and then a handful more. His heart began to pound when he realized they were not birds at all. He felt them, sensing their great black strength, feeling their rage at being driven and controlled against their will.

"Juron," he whispered, even as he felt a wave of nausea in his gut.

Return! Ajel yelled inside his head. And instantly, Gideon obeyed the command, turning Orisoun back toward the Stand and willing him by thought to run with all his might to safety.

It was then he sensed more than the juron sweeping down upon him from above. He sensed the people riding on their backs. He reached out to them with his mind, but found he could not touch their thoughts, could not determine who they were. They were shielded somehow from the land's effects, with walls far more dark and strong than any Gideon had been able to construct.

What he *could* feel was the juron, swooping ever closer, flying faster than Orisoun could ever hope to match. Instinctively, he grabbed his staff from the holder at Orisoun's side. He felt Ajel running in the distance, faster than any man could run. But even with the Words empowering his pace, he knew that Ajel would not reach him in time.

With all his will, he clung close to Orisoun's mane and begged the horse to run faster. But it was no good. Within a moment's time, he saw the first winged shadow on the ground, whipping past him as it turned to circle back for a strike. Despite the terror rising in his throat, he forced himself to look up again and saw the juron swooping toward him from behind, not thirty feet above the ground. There were six of them, he knew, flying in two separate groups. The first three, he could see, were mounted with soldiers dressed in black.

Guardians.

He wondered how they could have found him here and if this meant that Wordhaven itself was under attack.

"Demoi barrucht!"

No sooner had he heard the grating Words than Orisoun stumbled and tumbled heavily to the ground. The horse's fall sent Gideon flying. He landed with a painful thud upon the grass beside the road and watched the world spin by as he tumbled several more feet before finally coming to a stop.

Driven by panic, he jumped to his feet, his head still spinning from the fall. Orisoun had fallen on the road but thankfully was already up as well, though hobbling toward Gideon with a noticeable limp. Instantly, he felt the horse's pain but was relieved to know the injury to his leg was not severe.

Looking up, he saw three Guardians swinging around in formation, adjusting their flight to match his new position. He looked around, hoping for some cover, and saw nothing but open meadow all around him. Suddenly, he spotted the staff not ten feet away and ran to retrieve it. Snatching it up, he held it out in front of him like a shield, the way he'd seen Donovan do a thousand times in practice. He knew it was a futile gesture, but he did it anyway.

He felt so helpless. He didn't know the Words, couldn't defend himself in any way that mattered. But even so, it would not be like Calmeron again, not this time. He would not let them take him down without a fight.

Suddenly, he felt a shaking beneath his feet and heard a sound deep like a growl rumbling from the cliffs. He glanced toward the Stand in the distance, and his mouth dropped open in shock at what he saw. The gold inlaid in Wordhaven's walls was glowing. It radiated heat and light like molten rock, creating waves of distortion in the air.

A strong emotion, like resolve, but far more deep and strong, filled his mind. He knew somehow that feeling came from Wordhaven itself, though he could not guess how that was possible. Just as the three Guardians approached the ground on which he stood, golden ribbons of light more fiery than the sun poured out from Wordhaven's walls. They saturated everything—the air, the trees, the grasses on the meadow—until all of these things seemed to disappear in the brilliance. Despite himself, Gideon fell to his knees and covered his face. He heard fire and screams and the ghostly howl of juron. An instant later, the golden rays had faded. When Gideon opened his eyes, he saw three juron on the ground not fifty feet away. They were dead. And next to them lay three bodies, two of them charred beyond recognition.

How full of fury is the justice of love.... The thought was Ajel's, and Gideon turned to see the man running down the road, just a hundred feet or so away. Others followed behind him on horseback, and for the first time he allowed himself to think he might just get out of this alive.

Then he heard a scream echo from behind him and turned to see one of the remaining three juron bearing down on his position. A young woman sat atop the beast, and even from this distance he could see the wild rage on her face as she screamed into the wind. Immediately, Gideon felt his body being lifted off the ground and hurled through the air away from Ajel and the others.

Instinctively, he gripped the staff more tightly, tensing every muscle in his body in fear of the impact that was sure to come. He landed some three hundred feet away and was surprised to find, when he had struggled to his feet, that he was still uninjured. He looked back toward Ajel and the Remnant who had joined him, but his attention was quickly diverted to the skies above them, where the sky was suddenly filled with thousands of jagged fiery spears—or what looked like spears—hurtling toward the ground. He watched in horror as one Wordhavener, then two and three, collapsed in lifeless heaps, their chests run through and pinned cruelly to the earth by solid fire.

He fought the flood of agony rising in his mind as he watched Ajel spread his arms and speak a Word into the sky. And then a luminescent shield appeared like a dome of light covering them all. And the spears, which still hurtled down in droves from above, bounced off harmlessly. Another Word, and Gideon saw the juron's wings grow limp and watched as it fell, almost in slow motion, from its height down to the road. The woman atop the beast fell too and screamed. Then, with a dull thud, it was over. Both juron and woman lay motionless on the stone, both dead.

The action around the Remnant distracted him enough so that he failed to notice the remaining two juron as they noiselessly swooped in behind him. He had just begun to turn around when the larger juron of the two snatched him off the ground with its great jaws, gripping the leather of his poncho like a vise. Without thinking, he took his staff and swung it madly at the juron's head. But it did no good. He watched in quiet horror as the ground fled beneath him, hearing nothing but the thunderous beating of the juron's wings as they headed out of the valley toward the utmost ridges of the southern cliffs.

The last thing he saw, or felt perhaps, was Ajel's face, widening in horror.

Peace, sojourner. . .we will not rest. . . .

*No. . .*said Gideon in his mind. . .*don't come for me.*

I am already dead.

CHAPTER 35

THE EDGES OF STRIVENWOOD

For all the obvious courage of the Sojourners from the New Age,
only one of the Great Sojourns ever dared cross into the borders of
Strivenwood in search of the Book—that of Lord Natel in s.c.
672. That Sojourn numbered over three thousand strong, and
Lord Natel believed he could use their numbers to thwart the
Worded effects of the forest. Beginning in Morguen sounden,
Lord Natel had the Sojourners form human chains by linking
themselves with rope; then they made parallel forays into the forest
like spears, always keeping an anchor of seven people outside the
Strivenwood boundary. At first, the technique seemed successful, as
hundreds returned from the Wood claiming to have seen the Book.
But, for an assortment of reasons, no one was ever quite able to
reach it, and so the chains grew longer and the forays went deeper,
until at last the Sojourn was forced to form one single chain over
two miles long and plunge into the darkness of the forest.
Only one person survived that day, Lord Natel's firstborn son.
He was the final anchorman for the massive line. Several hours
into the foray, the mass of people inexplicably surged forward
with such force that the seven anchors were dragged forward
with them against their will and one by one disappeared into
the Wood. At the last moment, when it was clear that he would
be dragged in as well, Lord Natel's son cut the rope. Over three
thousand people disappeared that day, never to be heard from
again. Lord Natel himself was first among them.

—THE KYRINTHAN JOURNALS, CHRONICLES, CHAPTER 4, VERSES 55–61

She sat on the ground with her head between her knees, her red, disheveled hair cascading down messily like a mop, covering her face and arms. The trickling music of the small stream flowing next to her seemed to offer no comfort, if she even noticed it at all. Neither did she seem aware of the ominous moans that, on occasion, floated in from the darkness surrounding them in nearly every direction.

The only light, in fact, came from the direction of the great river, which they had followed from above after leaving the Heaven Range and which now flowed by them somewhere to the south, not far from their camp. Without the natural light filtering in from that direction, no one would have been able to see anything at all.

Gideon didn't know how long she'd been sitting there like that, all wrapped up in her own little world. Actually, he would have known, except he lost count some time ago on account of a particularly ominous moan from the woods, which distracted his thoughts for several minutes. He'd given up trying to keep track of the minutes after that.

Not that there was much else to do at the moment. Upon their arrival here, they had bound his wrists and ankles in some sort of Word-wrought cords, stuffed a gag in his mouth, and dumped him unceremoniously at the base of a massive tree. The man also took the *ja'moinar* bread Donovan had given him and smiled cruelly as he slipped it into his tunic. Since then, they had all but forgotten about him. The man took off here and there, using Words to clear the space of clutter, send the juron to hunt for food, and even hew a large chamber right into the trunk of one of the trees nearby. And the woman, well, she went straight to the edge of the stream, plopped down with her head between her knees, and hadn't stirred since.

By now Gideon had decided that these two were definitely Council Lords and not just Guardians. It wasn't because of anything they'd said since his capture, which hadn't been much in any case. It wasn't even because of anything they'd done with Words, as terrifying and impressive as their abilities obviously were. It was really the way they carried themselves. For all their apparent prowess in battle, they still didn't move like soldiers. There was something more regal about both of them, more refined, and perhaps more arrogant. They had the air of royalty, even with dirty faces and smelly clothes.

The other thing that struck Gideon was the way they treated each other—with strained deference and a familiarity that was different from the comradeship of soldiers. They acted more like siblings or perhaps lovers. Even now, he was busy pulling wood together for a fire, the look of frustration obvious on his face as he glanced at her with impatient regularity. Yet he said nothing and did nothing to express his anger, except perhaps throw the wood on the pile with a little more force each time he collected another load.

Gideon blinked. Definitely not the behavior of soldiers. Ultimately, of course, it didn't matter whether they were Guardians or Lords. Both were equally capable of killing him any instant they chose. But it did give him something to think about other than his own imminent death.

"Demoi sler blassht."

The pile of wood erupted into flames, but then the fire just as quickly disappeared so that only the outer edges of the wood were immediately consumed. Within a few seconds, the flames returned, more slowly this time, and the pile began to burn like a normal campfire. Gideon watched the event with interest, then tried to swallow as he morbidly imagined what would happen if the same Words were used on him. Such a death would no doubt be torturously slow and excruciating, designed to torment and not just to kill.

"The juron will return soon with food," the man said to the woman.

She didn't respond. He looked at her for a few moments in silence, then turned to the fire and began poking at it with a stick while he absently spoke a series of Words. Gideon heard a great cracking sound from above. Then, seconds later, a log several feet long floated down into view, freshly ripped off the heights of one of the great trees. It drifted noiselessly until it came to rest on the ground directly behind the man, who promptly sat on it.

"You shouldn't use the Words so much here." The woman said this without turning around or even lifting her head. Her voice sounded muffled and tired.

"Why not?" asked the man.

"Strivenwood is Worded in ways we don't know," her muffled voice replied. "It might react to *Sa'lei* like that awful fortress did."

"I've set wards all around. We're safe enough, I think."

Just then, two juron stalked right past Gideon and padded silently into the camp. He jumped, amazed that he hadn't heard any sound of their approach. Both carried prey in their mouths, some type of small antelope from what Gideon could tell. But he caught only a glimpse of the creatures before the man grabbed each animal in turn, right out of the juron's mouth, and flung it into the air, speaking Words over each one as it flew.

What followed was a gruesome and macabre dance, as each animal's hide was sloppily ripped away from the flesh and vaporized in midair. Bones snapped in rapid succession as the skinless antelope flopped and twitched like tortured puppets. The sound of tearing flesh and sinew followed, as piece by piece the creatures were savagely dismantled into consumable chunks. The smell of wet flesh permeated the air, and Gideon did not think he would ever eat meat again. If he lived long enough for it to matter.

Some of the meat dropped in front of the juron, who tentatively picked it up in their jaws, dragging it off into the darkness as their glowing owl-like eyes stayed fixed on the man, who ignored them. His attention remained focused on the remaining hunks of meat. He directed them to the fire, floating them there above the flames in slow rotation. He spoke continuously throughout this morbid display, mostly under his breath, his expression dull, as though he found the whole thing tedious.

Finally, he turned his attention from the fire and looked back toward the woman, who still sat motionless on the banks of the small tributary several feet away. His gaze then swung briefly toward Gideon, who stared back at his black eyes in amazement, not only at the curious resemblance he saw to Donovan in the man's eyes, but also at the unveiled hatred that emanated so nakedly from his gaze.

"I've been thinking, sister," the man said, turning back to the fire. The woman stirred a little but did not look up. "Why should we return this fool to Balaam? He has cost us far too much for us to just hand him over with no recompense for our trouble. I think we should keep him awhile, until we can discover whatever secrets he holds that have caused Balaam to salivate so."

"And then?" the woman asked.

The man poked the fire with his stick. "Then I think you should kill him. . .for Sarlina's sake."

A few moments later, the woman lifted her head and pulled her hair tiredly away from her eyes. Using water from the stream, she rinsed her face, then tied her hair into a loose knot behind her head. When all of this was done, she stood and sighed, then turned and walked toward the fire.

"It is a stupid idea, Bentel," she said, extending her hands toward the flames to warm them. "Balaam would hunt us down and have us killed for treason."

The man laughed. "It is risky. But not stupid. We have lost much on this little errand, Fayerna. Sarlina, our dear Sarlina, is dead, murdered by the cowardly act of a rebel. Our *mon'jalen*, slaughtered by that cursed fortress. . ."

"I do not need to be reminded," the woman said icily.

"But look at what we've gained," continued the man. "We know where Wordhaven is." He leaned toward her. "We *alone* know this, Fayerna. We know something of its defenses now. And we have the 'Great Stormcaller,' bound like a helpless kitten, ready to reveal to us whatever secret he holds, to tell us why exactly he is so valuable to Balaam alive."

The woman stared into the fire a moment, then spoke. "I can't believe she's gone. That foolish girl never could keep her peace." The woman looked at the man. "It was because of Sanchi, you know. Just a *mon'jalen*. . .but she flew into that rage of hers when she saw him dead. And now she's gone."

The man looked at her determinedly, then said, "She *is* gone. Because of the rebels. Because of him," he nodded toward Gideon, "and because of Balaam. Fayerna, Balaam knew there would be trouble; he knew it would not be as easy as everyone believed to capture this fool. He did not want to risk his own precious skin. So he sent us, his greatest adversaries on the Council, knowing full well that we might perish. Perhaps even hoping we would.

"He couldn't lose either way, you see. We return with his prize, and he basks in the glory of whatever secrets he reveals about this scum. Or we perish in our attempt, and he is rid of the greatest threat to his power on the Council."

"I was the one who suggested we go on this journey, Bentel," she said.

"We have been played for fools, woman," he replied. "No doubt Balaam orchestrated the entire affair, from the warcor to this very moment. Did we not all wonder why he wanted to send a warcor of riftmen and not Guardians? He knew what would happen to them! I don't know how, but he knew. He knew this rebel would destroy them somehow. And he knew that we would see it as a misstep on his part and move in to take advantage."

"You are attributing a great deal of intelligence to our High Lord," quipped Fayerna. "I do not like to think of myself as a mere pawn in his game."

"Is that not what we have been until now?" he asked. "We might as well admit the truth. That is why I think we should not go back to Phallenar and hand Balaam his prize on a silver platter. I think we should stop playing the pawn and turn the game upon the player."

"Just what are you suggesting, Bentel? That we raise an army and march against Phallenar? You know we wouldn't stand a chance."

"Nothing so grandiose as that, sister," said the man. "We need only to stay out of Balaam's grasp long enough to uncover whatever secrets this rebel holds, to learn exactly why this man is so important to Balaam alive."

"What good will that do?"

"If we can prove that Balaam knowingly withheld vital information about this man from the Council, information critical to the safety of the Lords, then we can have him immediately dismissed. Not only would he be removed from the Council, but his tongue would be cut out and he would be banished from Phallenar. Nothing would stand in our way."

The woman shook her head briefly, then reached out and snatched one of the chunks of meat floating above the fire. She spoke a Word to cool it down a bit, Gideon guessed, before she took a bite out of the flesh.

She carefully chewed and swallowed before continuing. "I can't begin to list the suppositions you are making," she said at last. "But I suppose I must try. First, you suppose that Balaam wants this man alive for some intelligent reason and not just because of the rather more obvious motive of making a trophy out of him in Phallenar. And even if there is an intelligent reason in Balaam's head, you suppose that reason to involve some manner of secret that Balaam is keeping from the Council—a secret vital to the Council's safety. And even if both of those things were true, you suppose that this stupid-looking rebel also knows this secret, whatever it is, and that we can discover it by probing his mind with Words. And then, presuming all of that is true, you suppose that we can present these revelations to the Council in a way that will be believed and in a way that Balaam will not be able to counter with lies."

The man looked increasingly angry the longer the woman spoke. By the time she finished, his face was red from more than just the fire-light. Abruptly, he stood and hurled his stick into the fire. "Are you saying we should just give him what he wants? Play along with his game because, when it all comes down to it, we are pawns after all, and there's nothing to be done for it? Is that what you want?"

"Of course not, Bentel," she said evenly. "I'm simply saying we don't have enough information. . .not yet." She offered him a piece of her meat, which he took, somewhat angrily. "In truth, I have every reason to believe you are correct. The fact that Balaam has wanted us out of the way for years is no secret to anyone. And his decisions in the matter concerning this rebel have been clearly suspicious. But if we want revenge—and believe me, I do—then we must make certain we do it intelligently, lest we fall unwittingly into another of Balaam's traps."

"What do you suggest, then?" asked the man.

"We will send word to the Council that the rebel has been captured, but that Sarlina has been lost and that I have been injured. We will tell them I am too weak to travel or use the Words, and so we have gone into hiding for a time while I recover, for we fear we are being pursued by a rebel hoard. That should keep Balaam's eyes off of us for a time, and it will turn the Council's attention toward this alleged rebel army, which we will suggest is somewhere far to the south.

"Then we will disguise ourselves and go to Morguen sounden. It is not all that far east of here, correct?" The man nodded. "We will go there and discreetly summon a few of our *ser'jalen* and set them about the task of uncovering whatever secrets Balaam may be hiding in the Axis. Sarlina saw him reading the forbidden black scrolls. We need to discover what he was reading and why. Meanwhile, you and I will dissect this rebel's simple mind, piece by piece. If there are any secrets locked inside that black-haired head of his, we will uncover them."

The man nodded, listening intently. "And what about Wordhaven?"

"What about it?" the woman replied. "It presents no immediate threat to Phallenar. As far as I can see, the Council does not need to know that we have found it. . .not right away. I think we should wait to reveal our discovery until a time when the revelation serves us best."

The man chewed the meat thoughtfully for a moment, then smiled. "I am delighted that your grief has not dulled your thinking."

"Not grief, brother," she replied. "Hatred. There's nothing quite like hatred to focus the mind."

CHAPTER 36

CHAMBER OF THE PEARL

We often forget how little was known of the Words of Dei'lo
*in those days. Communication in the Tongue was rudimentary
at best, even among the eldest of the Remnant. Most of what
they could say would sound today like the fumbling speech of
children. It was many years later before it occurred to them
that there might be more than one way to say a thing and that
some variations of Words carried more weight than others.
That was why not many Words worked when they drew near
the Deathland Barrens—not because the Deathland Barrens
were too strong, but because their Words were too weak.*

—The Kyrinthan Journals, Musings, Chapter 12, Verses 12–14

"I thought I would find you here."

Ajel forced a smile as Revel walked through the gold portal leading into the Chamber. He knew his brother would come looking for him, but he'd hoped it would take him longer to discover his whereabouts. He wasn't really of a mind to talk to anyone right now. But, if he had to talk to someone, he supposed that Revel was better than anyone else.

As if in response to Revel's arrival in the Chamber, the multifaceted walls altered momentarily, shifting to view deep green forests all over the Inherited Lands.

"That's right, it's me, the tree man," Revel said to the walls with a wry grin as he walked down the golden aisle.

"I do still wonder why it does that," said Ajel, glancing at the forest views surrounding them. The views in the Chamber didn't shift for everyone, but they did sometimes for some and nearly every time Revel entered the room. They often shifted for Ajel as well—only in his case they would focus on high places, like mountain peaks and plateaus. He had no idea why. "Do you come from the Servant Hall?"

311

"Yes," replied Revel. He plopped down next to Ajel, who knelt on the floor at the base of the Ring of Bright Water.

"What words from the *mon'jalen*?"

"It's no good," said Revel, touching the water momentarily with his finger, watching the wake it created as the water flowed by. "We got his name out of him, but little more. Apparently, he belongs to the Council Lord that perished. Seer says he is corded to her, so he knows he's going to die soon. His thoughts are filled with nothing but revenge."

"No doubt his thoughts are of me, then," said Ajel, copying Revel's motion in touching the water. "It is a good thing Aybel gagged him the moment she realized he was still alive."

It had been Ajel's Word that caused the Council Lord to fall and break her neck. He saw no other option at the time, but the act of killing another human being shook him deeply nonetheless—even if she was a Council Lord. "What is his name, then?"

"Sanchi. I believe that's what Seer said. He's originally from Arameth, across the Eastern Ocean."

"Seer got that from his mind as well?"

"No." Revel shook his head. "Donovan believes he may have met him once, years ago while he was still in Phallenar. Besides, his eyes are Aramethian."

Ajel pulled his wet finger from the waters and touched it to his forehead. For a moment, he closed his eyes and let the coolness of the water calm his troubled thoughts. Finally, he said, "I suppose the plan will not be changed, then, since the *mon'jalen* will tell us nothing."

Gently, he felt the warmth of Revel's hand rest on his shoulder. "I know," said Revel. "I don't want him to go either."

Ajel shook his head slowly. "Paladin's place is here at Wordhaven," he said. "I really do not understand it, brother. Most any other time I would be glad to let the others take the lead. But this one time when I truly want my voice to be heard, no one listens."

"They listened to you," countered Revel. "They just listened to Paladin more."

"That is the sorrow of it," Ajel said. "They are so used to listening to him that they have lost the ability to think for themselves. Paladin's judgment is clearly skewed in this. Why will they not see it?"

"You say that as if you cannot be wrong," said Revel. "As for me, I can understand why Paladin must go with us to Phallenar."

Ajel glanced at Revel's piercing eyes, saw the simple logic there, and quickly looked away. "I certainly cannot," he said. "Or, if I am wrong, then perhaps I do not want to."

Revel pulled his hand away so gently that Ajel barely noticed. "Finding the Book has been his life's aim," said Revel. "We can't expect him to sit here while someone else goes off to retrieve it."

Ajel shook his head. "The Book is not his quest to own. It belongs to all of us. And now Wordhaven is discovered, or at least that is what we must assume. A full attack from Phallenar will likely follow soon enough. This is not the time for Paladin to leave."

"Precisely why Donovan has chosen to remain, Ajel," replied Revel resolutely. "And also why we are going, along with Aybel and Kair, to make certain Paladin is kept safe. Of course, you know all this. You were there in the Servant Hall the same as me. It's not like you to fret over a decision once it's made, even if you disagree with it."

With a sigh, Ajel shifted his position on the floor and leaned back on his hands. "You're right. There is more to it than just Paladin's choice to go."

"Like what?"

Ajel frowned. He held no secrets from Revel; he never had. Yet he was unsure how much he wanted to tell his brother right now. A few of his concerns seemed petty, even to himself. And yet they nagged at his thoughts relentlessly. For example, he did not like the fact that Aybel and Kair were chosen to go with them to Phallenar. They were fine fighters and as well versed in *Dei'lo* as any in the Remnant, which was woefully little, truth be told. But neither had ever been to Phallenar nor traveled along the Whey River—so neither could use a Word of transport to any spot along that route. Because of that, the group would have to travel by mount and raft all the way to Morguen sounden—a dangerous and lengthy trek, even in less volatile times.

He would have preferred to go with Revel—and no one else—by Word to Morguen sounden, then continue by foot to Phallenar. But the others would not hear it.

"I suppose I'm troubled that my voice was so easily dismissed," Ajel said at last.

"They did not ignore you totally, did they?" said Revel. "You and

I are going ahead to prepare the raft. That was your idea, if memory serves."

Ajel grinned cynically. "In part, I suppose," he admitted. Seeing that Paladin would not back down in his desire to go, Ajel had then suggested that he and Revel be allowed to go on ahead to Phallenar—to make preparations and see if they could learn where Gideon was held. But the others would not allow that either, stating it would defeat the point of traveling together for safety.

In the end, they did finally agree to allow Ajel and Revel to transport by Word to the old raft, which was hidden along the banks of the Whey River at the base of the Heaven Range, to make certain it was seaworthy and to stock it with provisions. With that accomplished, however, they were to return to Wordhaven and disembark with the rest of the group on foot. It was not even close to the arrangement Ajel had wanted. He shook his head.

"If I had truly won my case," Ajel said, "you and I would be going to Phallenar alone—by Word of transport and not on foot."

"You never asked for that," said Revel. "You know full well we cannot transport to Phallenar. I have never been there, for one thing. And the Word of transport does not work so close to the Deathland Barrens in any case."

Ajel grimaced. "You know what I mean."

"So you are simply pouting because you did not get your way?" asked Revel.

Ajel shot an angry glance at Revel, then caught himself and quickly softened his expression. He knew his brother did not mean to provoke him. He was simply being Revel—utterly guileless and therefore unswervingly blunt.

"Well?" Revel tilted his head curiously and tried to look in Ajel's eyes.

Ajel chuckled, despite his angst. "Apologies, brother," he said. "Truth be told, I suppose I am mostly troubled by our lack of commitment to the Kinsman Redeemer."

"We are to rescue him if we can," said Revel hopefully.

"Yes," Ajel nodded gravely. "But it is not our primary aim. We are to retrieve the Book. With that as the goal, I fear that the Redeemer will become little more than an afterthought."

Revel shrugged. "It carries a certain logic to me. Our chances of saving the sojourner will improve tenfold if we can first recapture the Book."

"If he lives that long," countered Ajel. He turned to look his brother in the eye. "Revel, if he is the Kinsman Redeemer, we must not allow the Council Lords to cut off his destiny. I fear that the Book may mean little to us if Gideon is not allowed to become what he is destined to be."

"And what exactly is that?" asked Revel. "Even Seer now doubts whether he really is the Kinsman Redeemer."

"Seer has been wrong before," said Ajel somberly.

Revel sighed, then smiled broadly at his brother. "Then I suppose you'll have to put your trust in the Giver. If the sojourner truly is the Kinsman Redeemer, the Giver will see to it that he fulfills his destiny, Council Lords or no."

"That seems a simplistic answer," scoffed Ajel.

"Faith *is* simple," Revel replied. "It's just not easy. Do you really think the future of the Kinsman Redeemer depends on us?"

Ajel looked away. "I know what faith is, Revel," he said coolly.

"Sounds to me like you may have forgotten."

"I have not forgotten!" Ajel stood abruptly and walked along the edge of the water, away from where Revel sat.

Revel stood as well. "All right. Then what is it?"

Ajel looked down at the water as it flowed past, water that glowed without the need for glowood and flowed without the need for gravity. "I don't know," he sighed. "I don't know."

"Perhaps you are looking too deeply for an answer, Ajel," said Revel. "It's obvious that you care for the sojourner. Perhaps it is only that."

"We all care for the sojourner, brother. . .including you."

Revel smiled. "Yes, but not as you do. I can sense your guilt."

"Guilt?" Ajel listened as he spoke the word aloud, mulling it over in his mind. "Yes, I suppose there is that," he admitted finally.

"You take too much upon yourself. You cannot hold yourself responsible for the sojourner's path."

"Can't I?" asked Ajel softly. "I was the one who pressured Donovan to bring him to Wordhaven. I was the one who promoted him as the Kinsman Redeemer, putting him in harm's way before the Gathering at Songwill. I have tried to force his destiny because I was so convinced he was the one."

"Was? You no longer believe he is?" asked Revel.

"I don't know. What if I am wrong?" Ajel knelt and touched the water with his hand. "Then I have killed a man because of my misplaced faith."

"We each walk in the light of our convictions, brother," offered Revel soothingly. "Who is to say you are not right? Besides, the sojourner is not dead yet."

"Yes, he is," countered Ajel quietly. "In his own mind, he is."

CHAPTER 37

◄ MORGUEN SOUNDEN ►

*The Trusts bound the soundens together in a rich tapestry of
culture and industry. The knowledge of each Trust was
complementary rather than competitive, creating a society in
which each sounden contributed equally to the success of the others.
It was an easy symbiosis, but one that could be maintained only
so long as each sounden played its role and guarded its Trust
with diligence. Which, as we know, is not what happened.
Most of the Trusts are now lost to us. They were lost, or rather sold
off, during the first part of the Black Ages, when the majority of
the soundens bartered away the secrets of their special skills in
exchange for favors from the Council Lords. As a result, the special
knowledge of the Trusts became diluted and over time dissolved
into little more than meaningless fragments of folklore. This
degradation was most clearly seen at Morguen sounden, whose
proximity to Phallenar eroded its culture and purpose so quickly
and profoundly that it not only lost all knowledge of its Trust, but
actually became an abomination of the glory it once held.*

—THE KYRINTHAN JOURNALS, CHRONICLES, CHAPTER 4, VERSES 100–108

Gideon reached up to tuck a wayward tuft of hair back under his
hood, then remembered that his hands were still tied beneath his
robe. He sighed.

Concealing his hair had become something of a habit since his
arrival in the Inherited Lands, but it was becoming nearly impossible
now that his black curls had grown so long—not to mention the black
scruffiness of his growing beard. It didn't matter anyway, he supposed,
since he was captured. But he still didn't care to advertise the fact that
he was different, especially in this crowd of strangers.

He looked down at his disguise and grunted. The robe they wrapped
him in was ugly, he thought, all brown and shiny like cheap satin.

"Benny" had called it a mentor's shift or something like that, not that it mattered or that he cared. He hadn't eaten in days, not since before his capture, and had not slept much either, thanks entirely to the fact that Benny and Fay would not allow it. Something about preparing his mind for dissection.

A couple of regular masochists, these two. It didn't matter, anyway. He couldn't hope to get a proper night's sleep with his hands and feet tied and with a gag stuffed halfway down his throat.

He shuffled along behind his captors through the crowded floor of Morguen sounden, trying to keep from tripping on the edges of his robe. He didn't want to follow them, but found he could not help himself. It had been that way since morning, when Benny had thrown some *Sa'lei* gibberish in his direction as they neared the sounden. Now he just tracked along behind them like a dog on a leash, unable to disobey the Council Lord's command to follow. He thought about turning and making a run for it. He willed it so repeatedly. But it was no use. It was as if his body didn't belong to him anymore.

His thoughts were still his own at least, such as they were. And he supposed his speech was still under his control as well, or else they wouldn't have bothered to keep him gagged as he was, especially with the disguise. They'd wrapped a scarf around his mouth to hide the gag, which he thought just made him look all the more conspicuous.

A hooded monk with a scarf wrapped around his mouth, stumbling through town in the heat of the day. Yeah, that's *a good cover.*

To his surprise, though, no one seemed to notice him at all. Nor did they pay much heed to the other two travelers, who had used the Words to give themselves new faces and expensive-looking clothes. Or was that just an illusion?

Who cares? he thought. It didn't seem to matter to the soundenors either way. They bustled past the trio without so much as a glance, busy going about their sounden business, which, offhand, seemed quite extensive. And decidedly strange.

Then again, the whole sounden was strange. When Fay first said they were approaching the sounden's edge, he thought she was nuts—okay, *more* nuts. There was nothing to be seen but grassy plains and the foreboding trees of Strivenwood. But then there it was, sprawled before them like a man-made canyon in the middle of the plains—an entire city carved right out of the earth. It looked something like an archaeological excavation site, only it was vibrantly alive with color and people and the frenzied buzz of activity.

On a grand scale, the sounden gave the impression of a massive amphitheater, shaped something like an eye, with spiraling streets that criss-crossed hypnotically as they wound their way down toward the bottom several hundred feet below. Adobe buildings of all shapes and sizes lined the roadways, jutting out from rough clay walls like unfinished sculptures trying to escape the earth. Only the centerpiece of the sounden was made of stone—one massive granite stone to be exact, smoothed to form a perfect dome, which rose out of the sounden's floor like the eye of a god, looking up upon its people from deep inside the earth.

Gideon had never seen anything like it before. For some reason, though, it reminded him of the Floor of Songwill sounden and, to a lesser degree, the towers at the base of Calmeron where he'd first appeared. He couldn't say exactly why and was too tired to think about it much.

As they passed below ground level, he stepped right through an odd and totally irritating wall of sound. Walking down the spiraled street was like wading into a cacophonous sea of voices, which rose in relentless waves from the sounden floor below.

At first he couldn't tell what all the commotion was about; but as they drew closer to the floor, the reason became clear. The entire base of the man-made canyon was covered end to end with one gigantic flea market. Colorful booths and wagons of every conceivable shape and size filled the space around the dome. And in the cracks between them flowed an endless chain of buyers and sellers of all creeds and colors, scurrying like flamboyant ants preparing for war.

The sound grew more deafening as they descended, until it felt just like a thousand people were screaming directly into his ear. He screamed back in irritation, but it only made him cough on the gag. When he and his captors finally reached the bottom, they were instantly swallowed in the melee, with voices and hands reaching out to them from every direction.

"Fresh *ja'moinar*, m'lady? Delivered just this morn from Calmeron. . ."

"Heading north? I've got pondari for your journey. No finer beast for carrying heavy loads. . ."

"Diamonds, m'Lady? Emeralds perhaps? Smuggled from the forbidden reaches of the Raanthan Plateau. . ."

Oddly, the sound of the crowd was more tolerable once they reached the floor. Something to do with the natural acoustics of the place, he supposed. Adding to his relief, the hoard of merchants surrounding them ignored Gideon completely, preferring instead to hurl their sales pitches toward his captors, especially Fayerna, who was clearly seen as the primary target of their wiles. But she just waved them away without a word and walked past. She ended up having to wave her way all the way through town. Gideon found that amusing, despite his weariness. . .or perhaps because of it.

After shuffling along behind them for what seemed like an hour, the Council Lords led him up another street, which, like every street here, spiraled up from the sounden floor. Within minutes, they came upon a fairly large adobe structure with a heavy wooden door. Above the door there was a dark wood sign that read "Haven's Rest" swinging idly in the hot breeze. The two Lords entered, and Gideon silently trailed behind.

It took a moment upon entering for Gideon's ears to stop ringing and his eyes to adjust. He hadn't realized just how bright it was outside and decided the glare must be due in part to the sounden's utter lack of grass and trees to diffuse the sun's harsh light. Why anyone would design a town in such a dismal and irritating fashion was beyond him. It was like an open grave, a barren dustbowl of noise. Even though the sounden was situated close to a river and surrounded by verdant plains, the place was like a desert once you entered it.

Finally, Gideon's eyes and ears adjusted, and he saw that they had come into a pub of sorts. Tables dotted the wood floor haphazardly, surrounded by wooden stools, some of which where filled with people drinking and talking or having a meal. There was a fireplace in one corner, though Gideon couldn't imagine why they'd ever need one here, and a long window on the far end that opened into the kitchen. A tiny barrel of a woman scooted back and forth between one fire or another, minding pots and turning slabs of meat on an open grill. Every so often she dropped a plateful of food or drinks upon the windowsill and yelled, "Marteef!"

Marteef, apparently, was the little pencil of a man who wore an apron and scurried to the window every time she called that name. Neither of them took notice of the Council Lords at first, who still stood in the entry as though trying to decide whether the place was too repulsive to their refined tastes. Gideon didn't mind the waiting, though. It gave him a chance to still the ringing in his head and breathe in the heavy aromas of grilled meat and stew that wafted from the kitchen through the room. His captors might not let him eat, but they couldn't keep him from enjoying the smell.

Finally Fayerna stepped toward the little man as he walked past with two clay mugs filled with something that looked suspiciously like beer. "My good man," she said, "where would we find your lodge mistress?" Even her voice sounded different now.

"See tha' door?" The man bobbed his head toward a passage near the fireplace. "Thas the way to the rooms. But I say we are mos' full up, what with the merchants' fair. Only the richest room be free."

"Quite," said Fayerna with a condescending grin. "I'm sure we would not be comfortable in less. Even your best may be. . . ," she raised an eyebrow as she quickly scanned the room, ". . .suspect."

The thin man seemed unperturbed. "See for yourself," he said, then shrugged and walked away.

Gideon followed the pair through the doorway into a smaller chamber that contained another window, which opened to yet another room next to it. Through the window sat a younger woman at a desk with her eyes closed, leaning heavily on her elbows, her face all scrunched up between her hands. She was quite asleep.

"Are you the lodge mistress?" asked Bentel, loudly. The young lady bolted upright at the sound of his booming voice.

"Yes, yes, what?" she said, blinking as she looked around. "Oh yes. Apologies, I must have dozed. Hardly get a wink with all those blasted merchants about, screaming all the day and carousing half the night. Oh. . .you wouldn't be merchants, would you? I mean no disrespect, o'course. . . ."

"We require a room," intoned Fayerna, slowly and with irritation.

"O'course, ma'am," the lodge mistress replied. "I fear all we have is the master lodge. It is our finest, and none better you'll find here in the sounden. Two golds a night. . .meals included, o'course."

"We'll make it three on this condition," said Bentel, "that our presence here remain a private matter. Our business here is. . .delicate, and we do not want our competitors to learn our whereabouts. Is that agreed?"

"Without doubt, sir," the lodge mistress replied. "Your business is your own, to b'sure."

"That is, of course, assuming that we like the room at all," Fayerna broke in, "and that there aren't any bugs."

"It's a fine room, ma'am, you'll see," she replied, glancing over Bentel's shoulder as though noticing Gideon for the first time. "Fine mentor, will you be wanting a room of your own as well?"

"The mentor is not feeling well, I fear," said Bentel, as he patted his own throat, "a problem with his voice. He will stay with us so that my bondmate may restore him to health."

"At your word, then," said the lodge mistress. "It's a good thing, anyway, as we haven't another room to offer. The one you have is plenty grand. It has two chambers, plus a bath. Oh, and a balcony overlooking the Dome. Quite grand, yes."

"I'm sure it is," said Fayerna. "If only we knew where to find it, we could visit it ourselves."

The lodge mistress blushed. "Oh, oh, oh. Apologies, ma'am. Some days I lack the sense of a pondari. The stairs are here, around the corner." She pointed toward a small opening to her left. "Yours is the only door at the top."

Bentel slapped three gold coins on the windowsill. "If the lady likes it, we may be staying many days. If that is so, I'll pay the next week in advance."

The woman positively beamed at that. "Why, that would be wonderful, sir. Truly a gift from the Giver, that."

"As long as our stay remains private, our stay will do good for your business," warned Bentel. "Otherwise. . .well, you wouldn't want your business to take a fall, now would you?"

The woman's eyes grew suddenly wide, but Bentel turned and stalked away before she could say anything. Compelled to follow, Gideon ambled up the spiral staircase behind him.

The rooms themselves were really quite nice, which was a surprise even to Gideon. The walls were of adobe and wood, the furnishings colorful and smelling of flowers. The two rooms were of a size, bordered by a heavy red curtain, very much like those Gideon had seen at Calmeron. Each room held a bed, a table, and a few lamps; and one room even had a couch. The balcony extended the full length of both rooms, which opened to them through two large glass doors, covered in red curtains like the first. Gideon realized this was the first time he had seen glass windows outside of Wordhaven. Neither Calmeron nor Songwill had panes in their windows, although he scarcely noticed the fact at the time.

Funny what you remember about places, he thought.

"Will this do for you?" asked Fayerna.

Bentel shrugged. "I am not particular. The real question is whether it will do for you."

Fayerna sniffed the air suspiciously and ran a finger along the table to check for dust. "It will suffice, I suppose. Though only just."

Bentel grinned. "My *ser'jalen* often use this place when they have cause to come here. It is neither the best nor worst the sounden has to offer, but the owners know how to keep their mouths shut."

Fayerna didn't respond, but continued her examination of their new quarters.

"What about him?" asked Bentel.

Fayerna glanced toward Gideon, who still stood motionless behind Bentel. "Put him in the other room, I guess. Against the wall."

Bentel turned toward Gideon and grinned. "I'll set him up nicely," he said, then added, "come."

Gideon surged forward against his will and followed Bentel dutifully into the adjoining room. Once there, he roughly shoved Gideon against the wall next to the glass doors leading out to the balcony.

"It will hurt less if you don't struggle," Bentel said tiredly, "not that I care. *Demoi cordit learon bartuk, si valent lak pise enferon.*"

Everything happened in a blur. Gideon felt his body slam against the wall. His scarf and robe ripped away, as well as the brown leathers he wore underneath, and flew idly across the room. The black cord that bound his wrists dissolved, only to be replaced by two that secured each wrist separately to the wall. His boots flew off, and his ankles were likewise fastened to the wall. Finally, his gag lurched out of his mouth so hard it ripped a tear in his dry, chapped lips. He felt a string of blood drip down his chin.

"I told you not to struggle," chided Bentel amusedly, noting the blood.

Slowly, Gideon tried to lick his lip. His tongue felt like sandpaper on his tender skin, and his jaw ached from being overstretched for days.

"I suggest you don't try using the Words," Bentel added casually. "I've warded the space around you to flame at the first syllable of *Dei'lo*."

Gideon forced a grin and felt his lips rip even as he did it. "Don't worry, Benny," he said hoarsely. "I don't know any *Dei'lo*."

"Tsk, tsk," Bentel replied, shaking his head. "I had hoped you would not start with lies. This does not bode well for you, I fear."

Gideon lowered his head and surveyed his bonds. The black cords couldn't be seen directly, he had learned, but only with peripheral vision. And even then they looked fuzzy, like worm-shaped strands of darkness wrapped around his wrists and ankles. He was stripped naked, save for the small clothes covering his privates, and he looked thinner than he remembered. He could see every rib. But still, he was unafraid.

I am already dead, he thought.

"What do you want from me, Benny?" he asked coarsely.

"My, but you are stupid," said Bentel in a bored tone. "You fail even to recall my name. I am Lord Bentel Baratii. My name is not Benny, fool."

"Uh-huh," said Gideon. "So what is it you want?"

Bentel stepped toward Gideon until they were nose to nose. Gideon met his black-orbed gaze unflinchingly, despite the chills shooting down his spine.

"You should not be in such a rush to find out," Bentel whispered menacingly. "For when you do, it will be pain like you have never known." He smiled.

Gideon said nothing in response, but fixed his gaze on the Lord's black eyes. Finally, Bentel frowned and shook his head. "By the Words, you stink!" he exclaimed and turned toward the other room, waving his hand before his face as he went.

"I'm not the one who stripped me naked," Gideon said.

Bentel spun around and glared. "You mind your tongue, rebel," he snapped. "You know I could kill you with a Word."

Gideon laughed, but it sounded more like a cough. "Yeah, I know that. . .Benny." He looked toward Bentel's back and grinned.

Bentel flashed him an angry look, then slowly softened it to a smile. "You know, this may actually be fun after all," he said. With that, he turned and left the room.

CHAPTER 38

THE AXIS

*I never really knew my grandmother, Baree. From the earliest
days of my youth, I knew only that she had been locked away in
the Tower of the Wall, but no one would ever tell me why. It
was not hard to discern, however, that my mother hated her; and
for me, that was reason enough to meet this woman for myself.
When I was only seven, I sneaked into the Tower under cover of
night and stole my way into her private chambers, terrified at
the thought of what sort of monster I might find. What I found
was no monster at all, but a gray-haired woman with gentle
hands and soft of voice, who hugged me without hesitation the
moment I appeared. She spoke to me of many things that night,
some that made me laugh, but more that made me cry. It was the
only conversation we ever had, but it forever changed my life.
For the moment I walked out of that chamber, I swore to myself
that I would never, ever let them raise me to the Council.*

—The Kyrinthan Journals, Songs of Deliverance, Stanza 1, Verses 40–43

Lord Lysteria Asher-Baal gracefully rested her delicate hands on the
railing as the line of Lords plodded reluctantly into the Axis. It was
scarcely past dawn—clearly too early for the taste of some, she noted.
She frowned slightly as she watched them shuffle up the ramps dramatically as though every step were torture.

We've grown too soft, she thought, *too comfortable in our power.*

The Council had been the unchallenged authority in the Inherited
Lands for nearly six hundred years. The power of the *Sa'lei* tongue was
absolute and irresistible. That's what they'd always believed. It was
beyond comprehension that anyone could challenge the Lords' power
or that anyone would dare to try, for that matter. But that would all
change today, in a moment, once Balaam told them that one of their

own had been slain by a rebel's Word.

Despite the gravity of the news, Lysteria couldn't deny a certain thrill of anticipation at what was about to transpire. She had prior knowledge, naturally. Balaam had told her all about it a few days past, and, admittedly, the revelation had shocked her to the core. But she'd had time to let the information settle in her mind, time to let her rage rise to focus her nerves. Now she stood on the other side, still angry, but resolved, determined, sure of the path. Not like these others, who still basked in the innocence of their ignorance. She looked forward to seeing the blinders ripped from their eyes.

Lord Varia Desa-Rel entered through her portal, with her weasel of a bondmate, Mattim, at her side. Her taste in clothes seemed even worse today than usual, Lysteria noted, if that were possible. Her gown was orange—actually *orange*—with white and gray lace bordering the sleeves and bodice. Not that there was much bodice to speak of, naturally. Varia had few physical charms and absolutely no sense of style. But she did have large breasts, and she made a point of spilling them out of whatever garment she wore.

Well, so be it, thought Lysteria. *Perhaps she flaunts her bosoms to draw attention from her unfortunate face. It would certainly be reason enough.*

Her dislike for Varia was no secret on the Council. The woman had made a play for Balaam some years back, hoping no doubt to supplant Lysteria's position of power at the High Lord's side. It was an attractive proposal, truth be told, despite Varia's lack of feminine beauty. A Lord bonded for power, after all, never for love or physical attraction. Varia's house was powerful, arguably more powerful even than Lysteria's. It could have served Balaam well to break bond with Lysteria and join with Varia, politically speaking.

Balaam, however, had laughed at her advances and even went so far as to call her a fool to her face. His choice was both unwise and foolhardy—even Lysteria saw that—but there it was. Following that encounter, he made it known in the Axis that he *loved* Lysteria, and he wasn't going to trade her in for a more politically advantageous mate. Such ethereal motives were frowned upon in the Council and were even considered heretical by some. But Balaam's actions won Lysteria's heart. And she had loved him truly ever since.

Varia never forgot that slight, however, and from that day her lifelong goal became seeing Balaam fall from power and Lysteria right along with him. She went on to bond with Mattim, a man of strong bloodline but questionable intelligence, and quickly turned his heart against them as well. Together, they formed a most dangerous alliance— one that Balaam watched with more vigilance than they would ever guess.

It wasn't only Varia and Mattim that Lysteria would be watching on this day, however. She wanted to watch them all, see their faces go wide in fear when Balaam told them the news, see them look sheepishly to him for leadership in the face of genuine crisis. She wanted to gloat over their admission that they actually *needed* Balaam after all— that all their years of nitpicking and gossip about his lack of character had been petty and shameful.

It wasn't as though she hated them, really. Not all of them. A few she even liked, after a fashion. There was Lord Baurejalin Sint, for example, a solid, pragmatic man who wasn't given to flattering talk. He said what he thought, usually without hesitation—a fact that made him an excellent advisor to Balaam and equally assured that he would never rise to the position of High Lord.

And there was rickety old Lord Maalern Fade, who had taken to using a cane in recent years. He was the oldest Lord on the Council, but he looked much older than his 143 years. Most of the Council Lords seemed prematurely aged, truth be told. Lysteria's mother had always claimed it was from speaking too much *Sa'lei*, but Lysteria naturally dismissed her crazy ranting out of hand. *Sa'lei* didn't affect anyone that way—not unless you meant it to. If anything, the Council Lords aged more quickly than commoners because of the immense weight of rule that rested on their shoulders. And who could expect less? It was just one of the many sacrifices borne by those called to govern.

Lysteria watched sympathetically as Lord Fade scowled up at the dais in front of him before starting the long hobble up his ramp.

Poor old man, Lysteria thought. *He's just wasting away. His mind is still sharp, though*, she reminded herself, *if a tad too bitter*.

He knew the Tongue better than most and would just as well knock you through a wall as look at you, especially if you tried to keep him from something he wanted. Like dinner, for instance, or his afternoon nap. He once incinerated a *mon'jalen* just for waking him accidentally.

But he liked Lysteria. She thought he fancied her as something of a daughter, since he had no children of his own. And she received his gruff affection warmly, even if she thought it a bit misplaced.

It wasn't long before the rest of the Lords reached their respective dais and placed their hands on the railing as a signal of their readiness to begin. By tradition, no Lord spoke before the Axis commenced, not even to their *mon'jalen*. Even idle chatter among those who speak *Sa'lei* had a way of making others nervous.

As they settled into place, some of the Lords finally noticed the presence of a stranger among them. Stevron Achelli stood on the dais that had belonged to Sarlina, his hands resting confidently on the railings. He wore a silk longcoat of brilliant white, with a purple sash bound at the waist, and a padded breastcloth embroidered with the sigil of his house—a gold ram on a field of purple. His golden hair hung free about his shoulders, accenting the strong, square lines of his jaw. Lysteria thought how nobly his eyes would set off his handsome features once the orbs turned black.

Stevron was an underlord of high standing in Phallenar, the promised bondmate to their daughter, Kyrintha, and Balaam's personal ward. At the first word of Sarlina's death, Balaam had raised Stevron to full lordship and spent the last several days putting the final touches on his training. Balaam had even given him several fully trained *mon'-jalen*, whom he had already managed to cord.

Under normal circumstances, such a raising would be done by consensus of the Council as a whole. But these were hardly normal circumstances, and Balaam rightly saw the need to raise a Lord as quickly as possible. Of course, the Lords did not know that Balaam had hand-picked Stevron years ago to be his true successor, once it became clear that Kyrintha wanted no part of the Words.

Under Balaam's watchful eye, the youth had secretly studied *Sa'lei* in silence since he was a child. Balaam rightly believed the language of *Sa'lei* would never reach its full power until it was spoken as a native tongue. He intended Stevron to learn *Sa'lei* side by side with the common tongue, even though he could not speak it often for risk of exposure from his eyes turning black. Still, only by learning *Sa'lei* from childhood could he be truly fluent, Balaam argued—and, as a result, more powerful than any Lord before him. And Balaam intended him to be the most powerful High Lord the Axis had ever known.

The boy was to be his greatest legacy, he often said in private, the child Kyrintha never was. Through Stevron, Balaam planned to raise the power and glory of the Council to the height of heaven itself and extend its rule beyond the borders of the Inherited Lands, perhaps to encompass the entire world.

And now his time had finally come, though sadly without much fanfare, since no one in the Axis could be allowed to suspect the truth. To them, he was just an underlord, devoid of Words, here in the Axis to observe, perhaps, or perform some minor task for Balaam. In time, they would learn otherwise.

Finally, Lord Fade reached his dais and laid aside his cane to grasp hold of the railing. At this, Balaam stepped forward and began.

"Noble Lords, I appreciate your willingness to come at this early hour. We face grave matters this day, and I thought it best to alert you of them as soon as possible.

"I'm sure you've noticed the presence of Stevron Achelli. He is here, in Lord Sarlina's place on the Council, because of the sad news I must bring to you now. Lord Sarlina Alli is dead."

The Council Lords stood silent, apparently in shock and disbelief. Lysteria glanced toward Lord Rachel Alli, who stood in stoic silence on her dais. There was no reaction from her, no apparent grief or shock. Not that Lysteria had expected any, really. Rachel was Sarlina's elder sister, but there was never any love between them. They had hardly spoken since they were children. From the beginning, Rachel had loathed her sister for her mental flaws, just as she loathed everything that fell short of her prickly standards of perfection and order.

"I know the news of Lord Sarlina's death comes as a shock, but that is not the end of it. I must further report that Lord Sarlina died of unnatural means, by the *Dei'lo* Word of a rebel."

That news brought a gasp, followed by a moment of stunned silence. Then the questions began to fly from the Lords' mouths all at once.

"How do you know this, High Lord? Where are Lords Fayerna and Bentel?"

"How could it be *Dei'lo?* We have the Book! Surely this was a Word of *Sa'lei!* A rebel *mon'jalen*, perhaps? A fight between the Lords?"

"This does not explain why this underlord is present, High Lord. He has not been raised to Lord Sarlina's post, surely, without our consent?"

"Where did this happen? Does the murderer yet live?"

With a calming strength, Balaam raised his hand to silence the barrage. "I am as shocked as you are, my friends," he said once the chatter died down. "And I will answer all of your questions as I am able. Let me begin by relating to you the events that led up to this convening.

"Early yesterday I received a personal visit from Lord Bentel Baratii. He informed me that several days past, he and his party were taken unawares by a large detachment of rebels moving down the slopes of the Heaven Range. A battle of Word and sword ensued, in which he says our fellow Lords and their *mon'jalen* fought bravely and without fear. They inflicted heavy casualties on the rebel mob and sent them retreating to the south toward Dunerun Hope. However, he reports, our Lords also incurred several losses in the fight. He told me that all of their *mon'jalen* were slain by Word or sword. And Lord Sarlina fell at the Word of one of the rebel leaders. Both Lords Bentel and Fayerna were close enough to hear, he says, and are certain it was a Word of *Dei'lo*. He further reports that Lord Fayerna was also injured—in her case by sword. Her injury, he said, is not life threatening, but is severe enough that she remains unconscious and therefore unable to transport herself back to Phallenar. Consequently, he told me that he and Lord Fayerna have spent the last several days in hiding, camped along the base of the Heaven Range. He came to me as soon as he was certain he knew their location well enough to return there by Word."

Balaam paused to scan the faces in the chamber before continuing. "Having said this, I am sad to tell you that most of Lord Bentel's report is a lie."

A wave of murmurs floated through the Axis. Balaam continued, "Prior to Lord Bentel's visit, I learned from my own sources and to my great sorrow that Lords Bentel and Fayerna have plotted treason against us. It is true that they encountered a rebel force of some sort. It is also true that Lord Sarlina and all of their *mon'jalen* perished in the battle that ensued. What Lord Bentel did not report was that they successfully captured the Stormcaller in that fight and that they intend to uncover for themselves the secret of his power so that they might use that power against us."

"All due respect, High Lord," Lord Varia broke in, "but doesn't this sound more than a little preposterous? Surely our fellow Lords cannot be so simple to believe that acquiring a few Word-wrought tricks from this Stormcaller could possibly make them strong enough to defy the entire Council! Forgive my bluntness, but I must say your story lacks the smell of truth. It smells more like an opportunity for personal vengeance."

"With reluctance, I must agree, High Lord," added Lord Mattim, with no reluctance at all. "You cannot expect the Council to accept your word on this without first hearing from Lords Bentel and Fayerna ourselves."

"I understand your concerns," replied Balaam smoothly. "In your place, I would carry the same suspicions. The fact that these Lords have opposed me for years is no secret. Yet this matter goes far beyond the petty bickering of Council politics. Besides, what you suggest is impossible. I tell you true that Lords Fayerna and Bentel have rebelled. They will not submit to return here for questioning—not by you or me or anyone else. I fear we will not see them again except on the field of Words. As High Lord of this Council, my word on this matter will have to suffice."

"I'm afraid it does not," scoffed Varia. "You may be High Lord, but you are not beyond questioning. We will not condemn our own on your word alone."

"High Lord, if I may speak," said Lysteria, right on cue. "Perhaps Lord Varia is right in this. This matter is too grave for there to be any doubt as to the truth of it. Perhaps, High Lord, if you would expose your *ser'jalen* and allow their evidence to be examined by the Council. . ."

That took everyone off guard, just as Balaam hoped it would. For her to side with Varia in anything was beyond rare. And to challenge Balaam openly, especially to go so far as to ask him to expose his *ser'jalen*, would give them reason to believe that she knew his story to be true.

A Lord's *ser'jalen* were sacrosanct. The network of spies took years to build and was by definition absolutely secret. *Ser'jalen* were shadowy figures, operating in the hidden background of every level of government and every aspect of common life and commerce. They were information gatherers, propagandists, and assassins. Their true identity was known only to their Lords. It had been that way for generations.

Of course, Lysteria knew full well that Balaam had uncovered the rebel Lords' plot on his own, without the help of his network of spies. He had used the Worded blanket carried by Lords Fayerna and Bentel to secretly transport himself to their location regularly so that he might learn of their plans firsthand. But the rest of the Council would never suspect that. Neither would they suspect that he had already selected a few of his lesser *ser'jalen* to be questioned and compelled them by Word to claim that they had heard the rebel Lords plot their treason with their own ears.

Of course, the Council would use Words of their own to probe the veracity of the *ser'jalen*'s claims—something they were not permitted to do to Balaam himself. But the High Lord had done his work with this in mind. The Words he used on his *ser'jalen* went deep, but they were also subtle. The Lords would not discover his deception unless they probed in exactly the right obscure location within the *ser'jalen*'s minds. And even if they did get so lucky—which Balaam highly doubted—the *ser'jalen* would die before uttering a sound.

The irony of the scheme was not lost on Lysteria—that they must use lies to convince the Council of the truth. But Balaam knew from the outset of this travesty that they might not believe his report. They would, however, believe the *ser'jalen*. Especially once their probing Words failed to uncover the slightest hint of deception.

Balaam frowned. "That is unprecedented, Lord Lysteria," he said, with convincing irritation. "A Lord's *ser'jalen* are his own private matter. What you are suggesting would compromise a network that has served this Council for more than a hundred years."

"Don't you mean 'served *you*,' High Lord," intoned Lord Varia, not without spite. "As you say, this matter goes beyond the petty bickering of political rivalry. If you want the Council's trust, you must allow us to question your *ser'jalen* ourselves."

Balaam's face grew visibly red with anger. But after a moment, his feigned rage subsided, and he shook his head and sighed. "If you will not believe your High Lord in any other way, then so be it," he said, but his voice still sounded defiant. "But I am appalled at this spectacle of mistrust. How petty we have all become! I do this only for the sake of the Council, which is more than I can say for your motives."

He glared openly at Varia and then at Lysteria for added effect. "I will arrange a meeting once the Axis is dismissed. In the meantime, I trust you are willing to grant me the benefit of the doubt so that I might continue my 'alleged' explanation of the facts."

"Of course, High Lord," intoned Varia smugly. "Please, do continue."

Balaam took a deep breath. "The *ser'jalen* that you will question will also tell you this—that Lord Fayerna is not injured and that she and Lord Bentel are not camped at the base of the Heaven Range as he reported. They have hidden themselves in Morguen sounden, under the guise of traveling merchants, with the Stormcaller masking as their mentor companion. They intend to remain there in hiding until they can extract the information they seek from the rebel and discern how they might turn it against us."

"Not to be seen as siding with Lord Varia," said Lord Baurejalin Sint tentatively, "but even if their plot is treason, what real power can they hope to gain from this common rebel?"

"I cannot be sure," replied Balaam, "but the fact that he holds powers foreign to us is beyond question. Our own Firstsworn witnessed him calling the storm in Calmeron, which in minutes slew more than a hundred of our finest Guardians. And other Guardians watched as he dispatched a full warcor of riftmen with that gilded staff of his. Word of these feats has spread throughout the soundens. Even in the streets of Phallenar I am told that many quietly hold him as the promised Kinsman Redeemer."

"Pah!" snapped Maalern Fade. "The prophecies of imbeciles. No one heeds those children's fables anymore."

"They most certainly do, Lord Fade," corrected Balaam, "and even if the rebel Lords cannot master the Stormcaller's power, they can still use his fame to raise rebellion against us."

"Pah!" said Maalern Fade again, but with less certainty this time.

"All right, all right," broke in Baurejalin Sint, "let us assume all this proves true for the moment. What are we to do about it? And what does all this have to do with the presence of this underlord?"

"An underlord no longer, Lord Sint," said Balaam bluntly. "May I present Lord Stevron Achelli, raised to the Council as successor to Lord Sarlina Alli."

"By whose word?" Lord Varia asked coldly.

"By mine," said Balaam.

"You have no right!" snapped Varia.

Balaam slammed his fist upon the railing, his face suddenly red with rage. "I will have no more of this insolence!" he yelled, his booming voice echoing like thunder off the chamber walls. "You know full well that I have every right as High Lord to act as I see fit for the good of this Council. There is no time for debating who should be raised in Sarlina's place—not in a crisis like this! Stevron is a good choice—an obvious successor to Sarlina, and every one of you knows it."

He paused a moment, allowing the ponderous silence to have its effect. "I have listened to your questions," he continued icily. "I have noted your concerns. I have even gone so far as to expose my *ser'jalen* so that you might believe the truth. But there is a limit to my tolerance, and you have reached it!"

The Axis fell silent. Lord Varia looked suddenly uneasy and fumbled nervously with the folds of her gown. "Now I will tell you what we will do," continued Balaam, his voice stone cold and resolute. "You will each question my *ser'jalen* this very day. You will not eat or sleep or perform any other task related to your duties until this is done. When you are convinced, and you *will* be convinced, we will assemble a warcor of Guardians to march on Morguen sounden. We will surround the sounden and seal it so that no one may transport by Word in or out. Then we will move in, building by building, closing the net until we flush out these rebel Lords and capture them alive. Then we will bring them back here to face trial before this Council."

"And what of the Stormcaller, High Lord?" asked Lord Sint quietly.

"If they have not already killed him by the time we arrive, then we will capture him as well. And I will deal with him myself."

At that, the Lords fell silent, clearly afraid to say anything more. Lysteria couldn't help but smile.

CHAPTER 39

◄ THE RIVER WHEY ►

And he shall come before the struggling trees.
He shall anoint their branches with his tears,
And on their roots his blood will pour.
He will be humbled there,
His heart will tear asunder,
A tear will rip his breast.
Then he will see the Giver's face,
At the hour of his choosing.

—FROM THE WRITINGS OF THE PROPHET BARI, IN THE YEAR S.C. 1250

Kneeling, he touched the water gently, reverently, and meditated on the rippling patterns of current that danced around his fingers. Diamonds made from sunbeams on the water danced as well, away, always away, from his probing touch. He could never reach the diamonds, he knew, no matter how gently he might try. There were some things that could never be known. But it did not make the longing go away.

Still, the coldness of the crystal flow freely offered its embrace, shooting tingles of awareness up his arm, into his soul. He breathed a quiet prayer of thanks for the mystery of rivers, for the beauty that could be touched, and the fringes of the glory that could be seen but never known.

The journey down through the forests of the Heaven Range had been a delight, refreshing to his heart. Revel loved Wordhaven, but he had always known it could never truly be his home. His place was in the trees, the forests, and glens. He felt a part of them in a manner that even the mystery of Wordhaven could never match. He *was* a part of them, in fact, though he knew not why or how. For in the wood, the trees became his eyes and ears and sense of touch. As long as branch touched branch, so far could he extend his senses to know what lay beyond his human sight, what sounds were heard beyond his human ears. It was a glory no other in the Remnant shared. And a mystery that none of them had ever solved.

He was sad to leave the wooded lands, when at last the team emerged upon the northwestern edges of the Plain of Dreams. It was always like that, leaving the forests. . .like leaving the greater part of yourself behind. But at least he could now feel the throbbing pulse of Strivenwood at his back. And from that he took some comfort.

Ajel was with him too, and there was solace in that as well. He could bear long times away from wooded lands so long as his brother stayed close by. He felt connected to Ajel in the same way as the trees. He knew his thoughts, felt the great weight of the burdens on his soul, and the strength of his shoulders, which were more than able to bear them. He could not explain the connection with his brother any more than his link with the wood. So he didn't try. He knew only that it was. And that was enough.

Without looking up, he knew that Ajel was currently busying himself on the raft, directing others to shift supplies here and there, making sure everyone had a place to bed and knew where everything was. The raft had been in some disrepair when he and Ajel had come earlier to stock it for the journey. After all, it hadn't been used in decades, not since the Remnant first arrived at the base of the Heaven Range. But it had weathered the years well enough, and within a few days the two of them had it ready to sail again. Then they transported back to Wordhaven only to leave again, this time with the others. Ajel, of course, believed that whole arrangement was a waste of precious time. But Revel embraced the journey with delight for reasons that even Ajel would never fully understand.

A golden leaf of aspen floated peacefully down the edges of the flow, and Revel marveled how such a simple thing could touch the diamonds so effortlessly. It was the dawn of fall. The waning heat of summer would soon give way to winter snows within the Range. Where they were going, of course, he would not see them. It was always summer near the Deathland Barrens.

"Are you sad to leave the forests?" Ajel's voice came drifting down the river current as his feet crunched softly on the grass nearby. Revel wondered why he did not sense his approach.

"I was. But Strivenwood is close. I can almost touch it."

"Strivenwood is not like the other forests," Ajel observed.

"It's different," agreed Revel. "Dark and Worded. But it's still a wood. I can still know it if I get close enough."

"I pray you never do." Ajel knelt beside him. He plucked a stem of grass from the ground and placed it on his lips.

"Did you get everyone settled?"

Ajel nodded, sucking absently on the grass. "We're ready to launch. We have some hours of sunlight left, and I'd like to get as far downriver as we may before dark."

Revel touched the water gently one more time to say good-bye. "Well, so be it," he said, standing. "Let's go then."

Ajel nodded, and the two of them headed back upstream along the northern bank to the place where the raft was moored. As they rounded the bend, the raft came into view, bobbing its ugly head at them like a tired leviathan too old to care that it was still alive.

In truth, it was a large, cumbersome beast, blocky and misshapen from years of patchwork repairs and awkward additions to its bulk. It was by habit alone that they still called it a raft, for it had long since grown from those humble beginnings into something larger and far more complex. The old hull was still in place, a single hollowed trunk from Strivenwood, gilded stem to stern. But to that two more had been added, along with two more sails, and such an assortment of odd-shaped wooden shacks and slanted decks that the whole thing looked like a floating pile of dark wood cubes assembled by an idiot. There really was no name for what it had become, and so "raft" seemed as good a name as any.

Despite its queer appearance, the raft had proved itself a sturdy vessel and long-lived. It was this same boat that carried the original members of the Remnant up the River Whey some eighty years before on their sojourn to find Wordhaven. Back then, it had truly been a simple raft at the start; but as new members joined their cause along the way, the craft had been expanded to accommodate their numbers. By the time it reached the Heaven Range, it held well over two hundred souls, though not comfortably, to be sure. For the five of them, however, it would be more than room enough.

Three masts sprung up from the decks like barren sentinel trees, their wood dark and gilded like everything else on board. The sails had been stowed away, as they would likely not be needed on the journey downstream. Revel felt their absence made the beast look strangely naked and only added to its fearsome aspect. He hoped the winds would favor them so that at least the tired beast might at some point later have the honor of its clothes.

As he stepped onto the plank that led up to the deck, he heard a mournful sound behind him, like the distant moan of an old man, weeping in the wood. Ajel heard it too, for he turned around and flashed his blue eyes toward the wall of Strivenwood. "You hear that?" he asked.

Revel nodded. "It is the wail of the lost ones." He had heard the sound once before, as a child, when he had run to Strivenwood to escape the Guardian raid upon the Roamers at Morguen sounden. It was there that Paladin had first found him, after the Guardians had slain his owners. "The Roamers called it such. They say it is the cry of all those who have wandered into Strivenwood over the generations. They say that once you go inside, you can never leave and never die."

Ajel shrugged. "Who knows what it truly is," he said, apparently unconvinced by Revel's explanation.

"Perhaps the Book will tell us." Paladin appeared upon the deck, smiling broadly and looking as strong and fresh as the day they left Wordhaven. Revel marveled at the strength his uncle had displayed thus far on the journey. Despite his 160 years of life, he was more fit and able-bodied than most men half his age. He claimed, of course, that it was just the blessing of *Dei'lo* at work—that the language kept him young in heart and body. But Revel suspected it was more than only that. He was driven by his passion to find the Book—to finish the task his elder brother had undertaken so many years ago. It was that quest that kept him strong.

"Are we all aboard?" asked Ajel as he stepped onto the deck.

"Just waiting for my wayward nephew," replied Paladin, grinning slightly at Revel. "I suppose you've been off staring at something again, yes?"

Revel hopped onto the deck behind Ajel. "I went to greet the river," he said, smiling back at his uncle.

"Pull in the plank, then, and let's be off," said Paladin. "Aybel, Kair, release the moorings. Ajel, if you would take the helm."

Ajel nodded and promptly climbed a makeshift ladder to an upper deck, then crawled into a windowed shack that sat higher than the rest. It was there that Ajel's father had long ago installed controls for the raft's two simple rudders.

"It seems your brother is in great haste to leave," said Paladin, once Ajel had left.

"He is concerned for the sojourner," agreed Revel, nodding.

"The lines are secured," called Kair from stern.

"We are away," responded Ajel from the helm.

Revel watched the shore slowly recede as the great bulk of the raft turned ponderously toward the center of the current's flow. The River Whey was not so wide here as it would be later on, which made the flow in this part a tad more treacherous. But it was plenty deep, even here, so there was little chance of them striking hidden boulders. As the raft pulled out into the main part of the channel, Revel could already sense the acceleration beneath his feet. He frowned slightly as he watched the trees of Strivenwood drift silently away.

"I fear he may be disappointed," said Paladin.

"Who. . .Ajel? About what?" asked Revel.

Paladin blinked. "The sojourner. I doubt that he is still alive. Or if he is, that he will be for long."

"You believe they would slay him so quickly?"

"Quickly?" said Paladin. "It has been almost two weeks since his capture. If I know the Lords, they will have already dissected his mind, extracted what secrets they could, and tossed his body's husk into the Gorge."

Revel frowned sadly. Ajel would not like hearing Paladin talk like this. "You know the Lords better than any of us," he agreed, "but I think we should hold onto our hope as long as we may. We cannot really know what has become of the sojourner as yet."

Paladin chuckled lightly. "Always the one to hold out for proof, aren't you, Revel? Well, I hope you are right. But even if the sojourner does yet live, I do not think we will be able to offer him much aid. If he is to live, it will be by his own wit and the Giver's good will."

"You do not mean to try to rescue him at all?" asked Revel, troubled by the finality of his uncle's words.

"I mean to find the Book," said Paladin flatly. "That is the most important thing."

Revel furrowed his hawkish brow, which had the unfortunate effect of making him look murderously angry. "Have you shared these thoughts with Ajel?"

"He knows," said Paladin. "He does not like it. But that cannot be helped for now. He will see the rightness of it in time." Abruptly, he laughed and slapped Revel on the back. "Besides," he added jovially, "who can say what we will find in Phallenar? Perhaps we will be able to rescue him after all."

If it is convenient, added Revel, but he didn't say it. "I hope we do," he said instead. "He is a strange one, but I rather like him."

They said nothing more for awhile; and in time Kair and Aybel joined them on the foredeck, and each found a quiet place to sit and watch the shore go by.

It was a sun-filled afternoon, with no sign of rain ahead and hardly a cloud to be seen to the south over the plains. In these conditions, the raft could no doubt be clearly seen from miles away upon the plains or from farther down the river's edge. But Revel knew that they were in little danger of discovery. There were no soundens between Morguen and the Heaven Range. Even the Roamers rarely traveled this route.

At one time in the distant past, perhaps, the river had been a rich highway of life and commerce, but no more. With the Plain of Dreams on one bank and Strivenwood on the other, this otherwise beautiful land had long ago become an unwelcome and dangerous place. People never traveled on the Whey, especially not this close to Strivenwood. It had been that way since the time of Palor Wordwielder.

The current slowed a bit as the hours passed, and the river gradually widened in a yawn that stretched for half a mile or more from bank to bank. Paladin and Kair fell asleep right on the deck, while Aybel stood like a sentry at the center bow of the raft, watching the water suspiciously as though at any moment a serpent might emerge and bare its mighty fangs at them.

Ever Donovan's disciple, noted Revel with a grin. *Trusting nothing, testing everything.*

Both Aybel and Donovan saw almost nothing for what it was, it seemed, but rather looked for how everything might be used as a weapon or what it might conceal. To Revel, it sounded like a horrible way to live. Knowing that, he couldn't help but wonder how Aybel felt about the sojourner, especially now that he was captured—and most likely dead, if Paladin were right.

While at Wordhaven, the stranger had somehow managed to over-come her considerable suspicions about him. Did she come to *love* him? That's how her feelings came across to Revel whenever he stood near her in the Stand. But here, away from the intimate effects of Word-haven, he could only guess how she might now feel about the man.

Was she sad? Bitter that he left her? Or, like Ajel, resolved in the hope that they would find him alive and save him from the Council's grasp? He would have to remember to ask her about it sometime when they were alone.

From the distance, Revel heard another long and mournful wail, echoing over the waters from the depths of Strivenwood. This time it sounded like an old man's howl, weeping horribly, like one whose chil-dren had been slaughtered before his eyes. The words came after, float-ing thinly across the river. *I know you! I know you!*

The voice was unnerving, even for Revel, who never had cause to fear anything in a forest before now. He watched as Aybel turned her head toward the sound and scanned the shore nervously. *She heard it too*, he realized. *I wonder what her suspicious mind will do with that.*

The voice troubled Aybel enough that she left her perch at the ship's center bow and joined Revel along the port side. "You must ignore the cry," she said to him matter-of-factly. "It is a deception."

"Truly?" asked Revel, surprised at just how deep her suspicions could go. "How can you tell?"

"I was taught of it while still a child, living in my father's house." She knelt upon the deck next to him, her short white hair rustling in the breeze. "The Hinterland, where I am from, borders Strivenwood on its southmost reach. My people know this call. It comes whenever the wood senses a curious soul near its borders."

Revel smiled grandly. "And I am that curious soul, I suppose."

"Do not take this lightly, Revel," warned Aybel. "That Wood has taken many of my people over the generations. Here it is called Strivenwood, but my people named it Soulsbane. That Worded forest can probe your soul and find the one temptation it can use to draw you in. There is no coming out again."

Revel scoffed. "There is no Wood like that. The trees do have souls of their own kind, I admit, but they are not evil, and they know nothing of human hearts."

Aybel tilted her head curiously as she looked at him. "You sense the souls of trees, do you not? It is part of your gift?" Revel nodded. "Then who are you to say these trees may not be gifted too, to sense *your* soul and find the thing you long for most?"

"Then use it to tempt me to my death?" Revel cut in. He paused to ponder the idea. "Perhaps, I suppose it is possible," he admitted at last. "But this is not the Deathland Barrens, and these are not the Fallenwood. I sense no evil from these trees. Wording, yes. But no evil."

"The Wording of *Sa'lei is* evil, Revel," Aybel said, as if that explained it all.

Revel shrugged. "I spent several days hiding in the edges of Strivenwood as a child. I heard the mournful cries. But I never heard a voice calling to me, and I never felt tempted to go deeper in the Wood."

"Perhaps back then you were not so curious about the Wood," she said, "as you are now."

Revel sighed and turned his gaze back on the shore. He saw no point in talking further along these lines. He knew more about the forest—*any* forest—than Aybel ever could. But he could see he would not sway her from her beliefs.

Suddenly, he felt the warmth of Aybel's hand resting on his arm. "Heed my warning, Revel," she said quietly, but with a sternness in her voice. "Even you are not above deception on this matter."

"Of course, Aybel. Thank you." Revel smiled. Then she turned and walked away.

I wonder if she's off to warn the rest as well, he thought. *Or did she believe the voice was calling only to me?* Quietly, he chuckled at the notion, then turned his gaze back to the darkening line of trees across the water.

CHAPTER 40

THE DARK WOOD

Like an infant returning to the womb of dreams,
So will he be swallowed by the womb of darkness
that conceals the light of Life.
The wanderer will stop his wandering,
His wanderlust will be no more.
When he hears the whisperings of the wood,
He will know his hour has come.

—FROM THE WRITINGS OF THE PROPHET BARI, IN THE YEAR S.C. 1250

Revel lay awake on the foredeck, his hands cupped beneath his head, his eyes wide open and unblinking toward the night sky.

He usually preferred sleeping outside, under the light of the stars and sometimes moon, with the sounds of crickets and bullfrogs singing in the night. But not this night. Tonight the stars seemed dull and ominous, despite the absence of clouds. And there were no crickets, no bullfrogs singing. They were too wary to sing tonight, because of the desperate wailing of the lost soul in the wood.

Help. . .

It had begun in earnest soon after the others had gone to bed below deck. Ajel stayed up top with him, but he preferred the hammock to the hardwood of the deck itself and so had set up his bed near the stern. Revel couldn't see him, but he knew his brother was fast asleep, oblivious to the haunting cries.

The wailing voice brought no rest to Revel, however. Since nightfall, the old man's calls had grown more frequent and more. . .directed, it seemed. As though the man trapped within the trees could actually *see* him lying on the deck and so had turned his full attention to begging him for help.

I know you. . . . I know you can help. . .help. . . .

Of course, he could not know me, Revel thought.

In all probability, the man wasn't even real, but rather just some aberration of the Worded Wood. It's said that the trees of Strivenwood sing in the winds as do the grasses of the Plains, only the trees make words in their branches.

Hollow words, he told himself. *The cries of ghosts long dead.*

Yet if that were so, where then was the wind? The air had been as still as death since sunset, when the team stopped for the day and moored the raft on Strivenwood's shore.

At least it's not too muggy, he observed absently.

You are. . .You are. . .I know. . .I know. . .

For a time he tried to focus on more peaceful sounds, like those of the river current gently brushing the mossy edges of the hull; but it was no good. When the voice called, it captured his thoughts more each time, it seemed, until at last he gave up sleeping altogether and rose quietly from his blanket to sit along the railing close to shore. His golden hawklike eyes saw in the night as clearly as most men do the day. But though he scanned the trees intently, he could see only darkness in their depths.

The voice then came once again, closer than ever this time. And what he heard it say ran a shiver down his spine.

You. . .I know you. . .foundling. . .come. . . .

He sounded only fifty feet away or less, just behind the curtain of black beyond the first row of trees. And he *was* watching him, Revel knew that now, calling to him as if he knew exactly who Revel was.

"Who are you?" he called into the trees, not caring if the sound awakened Ajel or the others.

Who are you? the voice echoed in return. *I know. . .I know. . .*

"Who am I, then?" Revel called.

Come. . . , the voice said. *See. . .and help me. . . .*

"I cannot help you," Revel responded to the Wood. "You are nothing but a memory, beyond my reach."

Help you. . .I can. . .foundling. . .of the Kah. . .

The Kah? thought Revel. *But the Kah are no more.*

He'd read some about the Kah in the records of Wordhaven. They were an ancient race of castellans, sworn to the service of the Pearl, whose sole purpose was to guard the entrance to Castel Morstal, the ancient prison of the evil one. It was from them that Castellan Watch got its name. When the evil one escaped its mountain keep millennia ago, it was believed that the Kah stood to restrain him and were all destroyed. No one really knew for certain what had happened to them, of course. But there had been no sign of living Kah for a thousand generations.

The Kah. . .you are. . .I know. . .you can help. . .help!

Could it be the voice of a Kah? wondered Revel.

They were known to live deep in wooded lands, far from the traffic of common life. For all he knew, perhaps there was once a tribe of the Kah living in Strivenwood before it was foully Worded.

Kah. . .can help. . .I can. . .

Before he realized what he was doing, Revel climbed up on the railing and leapt nimbly to the grassy bank along the river's edge. *I just want a closer look,* he told himself. *I won't go in. I only want to glimpse this aberration.*

Quietly, he stalked along the river's edge to the place in the trees from where the voice had come. His eyes, well accustomed to darkness, glowed like red burning coals in the night. But he could still see nothing beyond the first line of sentinels in the giant wood.

Fear not. . . , the voice said, seeming now mere breaths away. *You are Kah. . . .Come and see the truth. . . .*

Suddenly, he saw the form of a man dressed all in white ambling through the trees. Within a second, he disappeared behind a massive trunk.

"Wait!" he called, but heard no answer.

Cautiously, he touched the bark of the outermost tree and extended his senses through the forest. Instantly, he felt the man's realness there, not thirty feet away, and he knew the man felt him too.

"I know," the voice said. "I know you."

Carefully, he took a few steps into the Wood, still keeping his hand against the bark. Looking back, he checked the raft's position and noted the clear and easy path between him and the shore. *Just a few more steps,* he promised to himself. *Just that much more and I can see him.*

He took one step, and then took two. On the third, the form that was Revel Foundling melted into the darkness.

Morning came quietly and without much alarm. Revel was often known to go off by himself, especially at sunset or dawn, so Ajel did not think much of finding Revel's blanket unoccupied when he arose as the first rays of sunlight hit the deck. It was not until an hour later, when the entire team had broken their fast and was prepared to leave, that Ajel felt the sense of worry deepen in his gut.

At first, he said nothing to the others, blaming his concern on his own overprotective nature. But when Aybel told him of her conversation with Revel the evening before, his fear took root in earnest.

"You do not really think he would go into the Wood?" asked Paladin, incredulous after hearing Ajel's concerns. "The man has more sense than that."

"It is not his sense I question, uncle," replied Ajel worriedly. "You know the Wording of this Wood is foul beyond measure. Even some of the Lords of old could not resist its call."

"It called to him, of that I am sure," added Aybel. "That Wood reads hearts as easily as men read scrolls. I fear it must have found the one temptation he could not resist."

Paladin scoffed at that. "What could it possibly say that would tempt him to such a foolish act?"

" 'I know you,' " replied Aybel simply.

At that, Ajel sighed heavily and lowered his eyes. Slowly, he nodded. "If there were a temptation that might beguile him to enter, that would be it."

"To me it is a strange temptation," said Aybel. "Why would Revel be drawn by a simple phrase?"

"Revel's sole and greatest dream has always been to learn his true heritage. . .where he came from. . .who he is." The sorrow in Ajel's voice grew weightier with each word. "If he believed the voices in that wood knew something of his true past, it might be enough to draw him."

"If that is so, then we must find him," said Paladin resolutely. "And soon. The danger of the Wood increases the deeper in you go."

Within moments, the raft became a hurried rush of activity. Ajel raced below deck and pulled long cords of rope from the stores. These he passed to Aybel and Kair, who knotted them together in a line, then anchored one end firmly to the moorings on the raft.

While they did this, Paladin called a gentle breeze from the south to help carry his voice into the trees. He climbed to the highest point on deck and turned to face the Wood. From there he yelled out Revel's name repeatedly, pausing between each call to listen for some response.

Meanwhile, Aybel and Ajel tied the far end of the rope around their bodies, then made repeated forays into the trees while Kair stood watch at the Wood's outer edge and fed the rope their way. At its full length, the chain of rope stretched several hundred feet. But each of their incursions to the Wood revealed nothing.

The only surprising thing to Ajel was how ordinary the forest appeared. The *bian'ar* trees, like the peaceful giants of Castellan Watch, shot regally toward the sky; while on the ground the wildlife common to such wooded lands scurried busily around them, apparently unconcerned by the strangers' intrusion into their homes. The gentle breeze that Paladin called wove a calming path around the monolithic trunks and lightly rustled some of the man-sized leaves that had fallen from the heights and long ago turned brown and crisp. If he were not so fearful of his brother's fate, Ajel would have thought it beautiful.

The woods, however, were as dark as they were lovely. The light that filtered down from high above was dim at best and in some places nonexistent—especially in the deeper reaches where they probed. Ajel was undeterred by this, however. His eyes were not as good as Revel's in the dark, but they were better than those of most men. Even in the darkest reaches, he could make out shapes and movement and knew that he could recognize Revel's form if it moved anywhere nearby.

However, after several hours of nothing but stillness and silence, he at last began to question if his effort might prove futile. For the first time, he considered untying the rope that bound his waist and continuing deeper on his own into the dark.

"You mustn't think of untying yourself," cautioned Aybel as if she'd read his thoughts. "The Wood is lying to us now. It is not half so innocent as it appears."

"I may have no choice, Aybel," Ajel replied, his voice anguished. "I must find him."

Abruptly, Aybel turned back toward the forest's edge and pulled heavily on the rope to drag Ajel backward, away from the blackness ahead. "We must go back now," she commanded. "The Wood has begun to beguile you."

Surprised by her alarm, Ajel quickly dug in his heels and stood his ground. "It is not beguiling," he said, forcing a smile. "It is only my lost brother that compels me."

Aybel wrapped the rope around her wrist and pulled it taut between them. "If you undo that rope, I promise you *will* hear Revel's voice everywhere around you. But you will never find him."

Ajel felt his anger flare, but kept his expression calm. "Aybel, I do appreciate your concern. But I do not think you can understand. He is my brother. I cannot leave him here."

"We're not leaving anyone, Ajel!" Aybel exclaimed. "We will not leave him here! But you must not be unwise, lest your fate be the same as his."

Ajel listened to her words and knew at once that they were right. But he still found himself reaching to untie the knot around his waist. "You can keep me in sight," he said, fumbling with the knot. "Revel could be injured, just a dozen feet away, and unable to answer us. I just want to go a little farther. I have to."

The next thing Ajel knew, Aybel was upon him. She launched herself into his chest like a stone from a catapult, wrapping her arms around him as they tumbled to the ground. "Forgive me," he heard her whisper in his ear as she locked her hands behind his back.

And then he heard her speak the Words, and all his world went black.

CHAPTER 41

THE WALL

*During the New Age that followed Gideon's Fall, only two of
the Great Sojourns to find the Book ever dared invade the
Deathland Barrens. The first was led by Lord Basreal in s.c.
165. He led an army of five thousand Guardians and Lords
across the Black Gorge from a point due east of Calmeron
sounden. Three months later, Lord Basreal washed up on the
banks of the Silence Sound, a thousand leagues to the north.
Though nearly dead from hunger and loss of blood, he mustered
his remaining strength to warn his rescuers of the unimaginable
horrors he had seen and begged them not to send another soul
into that barren hell.*

*Two hundred and fifty years later, after the fervor of his
warning had long faded from memory, another Sojourn
dared to cross into the barrens. It was a larger force by far,
ten thousand strong, and led by High Lord Marin, arguably
the greatest High Lord of the entire New Age.
Not one soul of that great company was ever heard from again.*

—THE KYRINTHAN JOURNALS, CHRONICLES, CHAPTER 3, VERSES 263–280

*Aside from the pondarin and their sound cannons, they all look very much
like ants.*

Lysteria's eyes roamed back and forth across the warcor as it formed
below her on the sandy plains. Thirteen hundred black-clad Guardians
scurried here and there, hauling supplies to wagons, securing reins on
juron, or forming rectangular companies around the pondarin. About a
dozen of the smelly beasts rose out of the sand like sluggish hairy islands
in a sea of haste. They were yoked in pairs, with massive turrets centered
across their backs. From these the sound cannons rose higher still, proud
and elegant, like metal-skinned serpents preparing to strike.

She could not see him from her small balcony that jutted out from the western Wall, but somewhere down in that ordered confusion, Balaam walked among the fray with the Firstsworn at his side. He would play the general now, encouraging the common troops, assuring them of their victory ahead. That would be no easy task this time, Lysteria noted with some worry. The Guardians were used to being the favored force in any fight. They had never been asked to battle against a full Lord, much less two. Though the warcor's might was considerable, their victory in this case was far from certain.

Absently, Lysteria flicked open her fan and fluttered it lightly beneath her chin. The heat of the sun had not yet reached the Wall's western side, but the midmorning air was nonetheless thick and oppressively still. She considered summoning a breeze to cool herself, but then thought better of it. The speaking of Words might distract Balaam, and the Word of winds was sometimes difficult to control in any case. Without the proper vigilance, a simple breeze could quickly swell into a windstorm.

"No Words to cool the air, Mother?" asked Kyrintha, nodding slightly toward the fan that now fluttered at Lysteria's chin. The Lord blinked, but didn't respond.

"I'm sure your Lord mother knows the power would be sensed by those below," advised Lord Stevron Achelli, who stood at Lysteria's right, the place of highest honor. "She would not want to raise alarm among the warcor. You will come to appreciate such nuances of *Sa'lei* once you are raised to Lord yourself."

"You mistake yourself, Stevron," said Kyrintha coolly. "I have no intention of being raised."

"You will address Lord Stevron with proper respect, daughter," Lysteria said sharply. "He is a Lord now."

"Is he?" asked Kyrintha innocently. "I hadn't noticed."

"Kyrintha. . . ," warned Lysteria.

"I would think a *Lord* would know that simple Guardians cannot sense the power of the Words as *Lords* do," Kyrintha continued. "Even I know that."

Lord Stevron's face flushed noticeably. He opened his mouth to speak, but Lysteria calmly raised a hand to silence him. "Your jealousy is unbecoming," she said to her daughter. "Lord Stevron is not to blame for your stubborn ways. That he was raised ahead of you is no one's fault but your own."

"If I am stubborn, it is only because I've had such excellent examples to follow," Kyrintha quipped matter-of-factly.

Lysteria sighed. She knew it was a mistake to include her daughter in these proceedings, but Balaam had insisted.

"I will not argue with you now, Kyrintha," she said. "This is neither the time nor place. Your father asked you here to stand as his daughter and nothing more. The least you could do is handle the task with a little grace. Now be silent."

"My father stands me here as a showpiece for the masses and nothing more. Stevron is his true daughter now."

"I said be silent!" Lysteria whispered in a hiss. Her sudden flash of anger unsettled the *mon'jalen* behind her, who automatically stepped forward protectively. "It's all right," she sighed, waving her *mon'jalen* back in place. "I have nothing to fear from my own daughter."

Only because she does not have the Words, she added silently and with more than a little spite. *At least no one but Lord Stevron can hear her*, she reminded herself in an attempt to calm her nerves.

No other Lords had come to see off the warcor, apparently in some feeble attempt to demonstrate their disdain for the strong hand Balaam had wielded over them in recent days. Even Lord Sint had declined to make an appearance. Only Balaam's protégé came as requested.

She had to admit she'd come to like Stevron more and more in recent months and could even now admit she bore him some small affection as a son. He had always enjoyed Balaam's fatherly approval, of course, since the very day he was orphaned as a child. But Lysteria was much more hesitant to accept him—at first as Balaam's protégé, then later as Kyrintha's chosen "replacement" on the Council.

It took Balaam many years to sway Lysteria from the hope that her daughter might yet repent and change her foolish ways. But who could fault her for clinging to a hope like that, however weak and frail it seemed? No other mother would blame her, certainly. They would understand. A mother can never give up on her children, not completely, though in every outward way it may appear that she has. Lysteria was no different. In the deepest places of her heart, she held onto that small possibility of redemption for Kyrintha. She had no choice about her feelings. . .though only another mother would understand why.

"I understand that Morguen sounden has already been sealed," Lord Stevron commented.

"Yes, that's true," Lysteria replied. "Lord Sint saw to it himself. Among the Lords, he is the only one who has spent any time there. He says it is a filthy place, all dust and the stench of sweat. Personally, I can't see why anyone would want to go there. But he claims it is an excellent spot for trade and hearing gossip."

"But if it is now sealed, the rebel Lords must know that they are discovered," said Stevron.

"Perhaps," Lysteria replied, "but only if they attempt to use the Words to transport out of the sounden. And even then, they will only know that their Word has failed. It may take some time for them to realize the cause."

"But surely they will be suspicious," countered Stevron.

"Of course. . .I'm sure they will," agreed Lysteria. She failed to see the point of critiquing the action further. What was done was done.

"And what of their *ser'jalen?*" Stevron continued, sounding a tad bolder now. "What if the Lords are forewarned of the warcor's coming?"

Lysteria flashed a disdainful glance his way. "If I did not know better, Lord Stevron, I would say you doubt the High Lord's tactics."

Stevron bowed his head slightly. "I only ask that I may learn, good Lord."

"Yes," Lysteria replied, not quite convinced. "Well, you can be assured that whatever *ser'jalen* once served our rebel Lords are now dead or otherwise detained."

Stevron raised an eyebrow in surprise. "Impressive," he said with a slight grin. "How did the High Lord uncover their identities?"

Lysteria gave Stevron a purposely reproachful look. *You presume too much, young man,* she thought. The boy was bright and clearly ambitious, but far too arrogant for his own good. He had to learn his place.

"Well," added Stevron, somewhat awkwardly. "I only asked to. . . well, I mean. . .clearly, I have much to learn."

"Best you keep that in mind," advised Lysteria. "Such a perspective will serve you well."

Kyrintha let out a sarcastic grunt, but Lysteria chose to ignore it.

Just then a distant cry drifted up from the fields below. Lysteria turned to see a wayward juron leap into the sky, apparently reacting to some unknown threat perceived nearby. The rider had been taken unawares by the beast's reaction, it seemed, as she was now dangling like a puppet from its belly, restrained from plummeting to her death by a single leather strap, which had apparently gotten tangled around her ankle.

On the ground, a cluster of the antlike soldiers rushed toward the spot from which the juron fled—a spot which Lysteria suddenly realized was now occupied by a vile and horrid beast, twice the size of any juron, and most of that a gaping pinkish mouth. The rest of the bulk seemed all coils and fangs and translucent scales, which blended so perfectly with the terrain that she could not quite discern the edges of its form, except when it moved.

"Riftborn," said Stevron idly. "From the look of it, a viperon. The Sea Folk have complained about them for years. The larger ones are known to burrow, but I have never heard of one hunting so far from the Gorge. It is rather beautiful in its own way, don't you think?"

Lysteria fanned herself all the more furiously. "Certainly not," she snapped. "It's repulsive. And so close to the city. Do you mean to tell me that *creature* burrowed all the way from the Deathland Barrens, *beneath* Phallenar?"

"Perhaps." Stevron smiled amicably. "But it's more likely that it wandered inland from somewhere north or south of the Wall. Most likely it just lost its way and has now found itself here quite by accident. The Sea Folk say the creature much prefers the soft muds of the Gorge."

"Well, this one apparently prefers drier earth," she said with obvious disgust.

"Too bad for it," Stevron replied, nodding toward the field.

The air around the beast erupted brightly into flame. For a fleeting moment, its writhing form turned brilliant orange as it stretched its great bulk high above the plains, as if it meant to fly away from the attack. But then it was gone. Only a wide circle of blackened earth remained to mark its passing.

Meanwhile, the dangling rider had somehow managed to regain her place upon her wayward beast. She glided nimbly to the ground not far from where the whole episode began.

"Well, what's a send-off without a little excitement, eh?" said Stevron lightly. Lysteria, however, was far less pleased about the intrusion. It was one thing to tolerate the presence of riftborn vines along the edges of the city, but to allow this sort of abomination to roam so close to Phallenar? She would not have it! And as soon as Balaam returned to the Axis, he would hear her outrage.

Oh, he would balk and call it a small matter; but in the end he would give in and do as she demanded. Even if it meant scourging with fire the whole of the Deathland Barrens, she would see to it that vile perversions like that beast would never be permitted near her city again.

"May I ask a question, Mother?" Kyrintha's voice interrupted her thoughts. She had almost managed to forget her daughter was still standing at her side.

"If it is a proper one, then yes."

Kyrintha smiled sweetly. "The warcor will not slay the rebel Lords, will it? They will be brought here to trial?"

"That is what the High Lord commanded," Lysteria answered.

"Will they also capture the Stormcaller, then? Or will they simply slay him?"

"The High Lord wants him brought back alive if possible," she explained, "though by the time they reach him, I think it will be too late."

"Why do you say that?" Kyrintha asked.

Lysteria sighed in annoyance. "Because, my dear, by then the good and kind Lords Fayerna and Bentel will have already ripped apart his mind."

"Oh," replied Kyrintha, trying to sound unconcerned. "How sad for him."

A trumpet blasted in the distance, and the vanguard of a dozen juron took to the air, their black-clad riders almost unnoticeable upon their imposing shoulders. They circled the entire warcor in formation as the ground troops began their northward march. The pondarin followed suit, albeit languidly at first, as they were prodded forward with the Words. Soon enough, however, the entire company was underway, on march toward the certain battle that awaited them in the north.

Thirteen hundred hardened fighters to capture one mysterious rebel and two wayward Lords, Lysteria mused worriedly. *For Balaam's sake, I hope it is enough.*

CHAPTER 42

◀ THE CHAMBER OF THE PEARL ▶

*In retrospect, Lord Sarlina Alli's death proved to be something of
a mixed blessing for Ajel Windrunner and the Remnant. On the
one hand, the fact that Ajel had slain a Council Lord using* Dei'lo
*and that her death had come so easily certainly emboldened the
Remnant's courage and fortified their faith in the Words. But it
also caused them to dangerously underestimate the real power of
their adversary. Lord Sarlina, after all, was really just a simple-
minded girl, who was slain as much by her own reckless rage as
by any Word from Ajel. More than that, her defeat occurred
within the protected valley of Wordhaven, where the power of*
Sa'lei *is heavily restricted. Had that battle been against any other
Lord or in any other place than Wordhaven, the outcome would
most certainly have been quite different. Unfortunately, the
Remnant did not come to realize this fact until it was too late.*

—THE KYRINTHAN JOURNALS, MUSINGS, CHAPTER 8, VERSES 73–77

Donovan burst through the golden doors and marched impatiently
toward the fountain in the center. "You asked to see me?" he said.

Seer scanned the crystalline panels as he approached. The scenes
did not shift for Donovan as they did for others. It was as if the chamber did not see the former Firstsworn at all or did not want to.

"Yes," she replied. "I want to show you something." She stood
along the edges of the Ring of Bright Water, leaning heavily on her
weathered staff. Though almost fully recovered from her encounter
with the sojourner, she found that she grew tired more easily than she
once had. And she had been at her work for many hours now.

"I am quite occupied just now, Seer," said Donovan quickly. "The
preparations are barely begun."

Seer waved her hand idly. "You've had thirty years to prepare

Wordhaven for attack," she said. "A few moments with me won't make any difference."

Donovan frowned, but said nothing.

"Besides, the news I bring will change your plans, I think," she added.

"What news?" he asked, his tone still impatient.

"It's best I show you," responded Seer. "Best you see it for yourself. Come, come."

She waved a withered hand at him, beckoning him toward her. With some reluctance, Donovan complied. She knew he felt uncomfortable in the Chamber; he always had. Almost as uncomfortable as he felt with her. But that was to be expected, she supposed. His own Facing was over thirty years past, but it had been none too gentle. And he still wore the memory of it like a scar upon his soul.

"Don't worry, I won't bite," admonished Seer sarcastically, beckoning him farther forward to stand within her reach. "But there are things you must see, and I know only one way to show you."

"I have no time for soul-searching now, Seer," snapped Donovan. "The entire Stand is in my care."

Seer furrowed her wrinkled brow at him. "This is not about you, Donovan, though it will affect what you will do. Now turn around and look at the panels."

"Seer. . ." He hesitated.

"Do it!" she snapped. "Or I'll hound your presence from dawn 'til dusk until the Book is found. You wouldn't want that, would you? The Giver knows *I* wouldn't."

Reluctantly, he frowned and did as he was bid. *How one so bulky could be so timid,* thought Seer incredulously. *And with a little old woman at that.*

"Now, look." With blue-veined fingers, she gripped the back of his neck and spoke the Words of summoning. Immediately, the crystalline panels shifted like mirrors in the sun, then slowly coalesced into a single scene upon the plains.

"A warcor!" Donovan exclaimed. "With fighting juron and sound cannons. Is this the present that we see?"

"Of course it is!" Seer snapped impatiently. "Their march began just one day past."

"Then they are coming," he said with resolve.

"No, no, no!" Seer replied, irritated. "Can't you see the angle of the sun? They march north from Phallenar, not toward us at all."

"But why?"

"Be quiet!" she commanded. All his jabbering made it difficult for her to concentrate. "I'll show you all I know. Just listen and watch."

Donovan obeyed, and Seer closed her eyes to help focus on her thoughts. Quietly, she whispered another phrase in *Dei'lo*, and the images in the crystal changed again, shifting northward along the course the warcor followed. In moments, the scenes arrived at Morguen sounden.

"I cannot say with certainty," she said, "but if they do not change course, their march will bring them here in two days' time."

"Why there?" asked Donovan. "Morguen is no threat to Phallenar."

"I do not know," Seer confessed. "But there are two more things that I must show you, which may help discern their cause." She gripped his neck more tightly. "But be warned, Donovan. What I do now is wrought from deeper Words than those that conjure simple images. I could find them in no other way."

"Find who?" he asked worriedly.

"The sojourner," she answered. "And your fallen kinsman on the Whey."

"You speak of Ajel?" Donovan asked. But Seer had already begun to whisper.

Suddenly, the paneled scenes shifted once more, but this time they did not move toward different scenes, but instead revealed only colors—black and white and the crimson hue of blood. Slowly, almost reluctantly, the colors began to shift and merge, until a shape that looked something like a face emerged. It was the sojourner. And his eyes were bleeding.

Donovan cried out at the sudden thrust of pain that stabbed his temples and burned like fire in his eyes and throat. Thoughts, foreign and unbidden, came rushing through his mind like the ramblings of insanity.

There are no rats, no rats, no rats. . .no dungeon. No dungeon! It's Fay and Benny, not the other. No old hag. It's not time for me. No no, no no. They won't get to me. They won't. I'll make it. Just breathe. Breathe, breathe.

Searing pain, like daggers stabbing his ears, knocked Donovan to his knees. But he still felt the grip upon his neck.

"Hello, Gideon," the voice spoke, slicing through his brain like a sword through butter. "Curious name you choose. A hero's name. A name that carries power."

No no, no no. You already know I don't know anything. I don't. . .

"Where is the power that you hold, Gideon?" the voice asked sweetly. "Where are the Words you know, hmm? Where have you hidden them? Show me, and I'll stop all this horrible pain."

No Words, don't know. Don't know! I have no Words. Just a. . . stranger. . .here.

"Oh, but you do," the voice said pleasantly. "Remember the staff? You called lightning with this staff. I'm holding it right now. Don't you see it? No, of course you don't, your eyes are filled with blood. Well, perhaps if I let it touch you, you will remember."

The blow knocked Donovan to the Chamber floor, wrenching him from Seer's grasp. With the connection broken, his own thoughts returned to him, though the sting of the blow from the staff remained. When he opened his eyes, the Chamber was still dark and red, and he saw Seer sprawled upon the floor beside him, her bony hand held weakly against the side of her head.

"Seer, are you injured?" he asked, shuffling awkwardly to her side.

"No more than you," came the feeble reply. Slowly, she fumbled to her knees and, with some effort, turned her head to look at him. She thought she was ready to feel the sojourner's pain a second time this day, but it was far worse this time than before.

"We are not finished," she said tiredly.

"The sojourner is near death," interrupted Donovan. "Where is he?"

She shook her head. "I do not know. But he is right in one thing. He will not die at his captor's hands. He has yet to face the dungeon rats he saw in the Plain of Dreams. I fear that dream alone is all that keeps his hope alive now."

"A sad hope at best," said Donovan. "But what does he have to do with the warcor?"

"I told you I don't know," she snapped. "Now help me up. There is one more thing I must show you."

"Is it Ajel? Or is Paladin in danger?" He reached down to help her to her feet.

"Those two are well for now," she said, grunting as she stood. "Though not for long if they resume their trek to Morguen."

"Resume?" asked Donovan, surprised. "They have stopped?"

"Yes," she said, "to search for Revel. He was lost to Strivenwood a few days past."

"What? Why did you not tell me?" Donovan demanded angrily.

"I only learned of it this morning," she replied. "And quite by mistake. I was searching for the sojourner, but found him instead."

"Is he all right? Can he be rescued?"

Seer sighed as she leaned heavily on his arm. "You ask too many questions, Donovan. Be quiet. And I will show you what I know while I still have the strength."

Slowly, she laid her free hand on his neck, just beneath his rocky jaw. As she spoke the Words this time, she leaned heavily on his arm.

The panels shifted once again, this time to dark and mossy swirls of green. Slowly, Revel appeared within the confusion, sitting idly in the branches of a *bian'ar* tree.

"What's he doing?" Donovan asked.

"Wait."

Another rush of power plowed through Donovan's thoughts, but it was different this time. . .confused and alluring.

"We know who you are! You don't, but we do!" Donovan turned to find the voice's source and saw a little boy dancing nimbly on a limb nearby. He wore green leathers from head to toe, with a bow and quiver strung across his back. His hair was brilliant red, and his eyes. . . his eyes were golden, like Revel's.

"I tried, but I'm too small!" he said excitedly. "Not like you. You are big and powerful. You can defeat them."

Defeat who? Revel's thoughts echoed through his mind.

"The trees, my son." Donovan spun around and saw an old graybearded man, dressed in the ancient robes of Wordhaven Lords. He clung to the branches of a nearby tree as if in terror of letting go. "I cannot fight it for long. But when I felt you near, I had to. . .just once more."

Fight what?

"The enticement of the trees, Kah warrior. You can overcome it. You must, for all our sakes."

"I know! I know! I know!" yelled the boy, laughing hysterically.

But I feel no enticement. They are only trees.

"Believe that, and your soul is already lost," the old man said. Suddenly, a horror filled his face. He let out a pitiful scream, hopeless and full of sorrow. Then in an instant, he transformed into an orb of light and flew away.

"I know, I always know!" yelled the boy. "I keep the truth hidden away where they can't find it. That's how I found you, you know. Take me, take me!" he screamed as he danced along the limb.

Take you where?

Suddenly, though, the boy tripped and lost his balance. Quiet terror mixed with resignation filled his eyes as he tumbled silently down through the canopy to the forest floor below. Donovan watched as he struck the ground, unsure if what he saw was real. No sooner had the boy hit bottom, however, than another *bian'ar* tree, older and more grand than any he had ever seen, appeared close by, rising from the very spot where the boy had fallen.

But they are only trees, he heard Revel think. *They do not worry over human souls. So grand. . .so peaceful. . .*

Donovan felt a gentle tingling in his hands. He looked down just in time to watch his arms transforming into branches.

"No!" he yelled, suddenly jumping away from Seer. Without his strength to hold her, she promptly collapsed to the floor. The chamber's multifaceted panels swirled a moment longer, then reformed into a dozen different scenes from places far and near across the Inherited Lands.

"Great Giver, forgive me!" Donovan muttered under his breath as he saw the old woman sprawled on the floor before him. He rushed to her side and gently slipped his arms beneath her bony form.

"Seer, are you hurt?" he asked worriedly.

"Help me up, you timid ox," she said weakly. "Why are you so afraid?"

Gently, he lifted her frail body up off the marble floor. She felt no heavier than a bundle of rags. "You should not push yourself so," he said.

"Don't tell me what I should not do," she snapped. "I do what must be done, as do we all. As *you* will do, now that you see the danger. Put me down!"

"I will carry you to your chamber," he offered.

"I'm old, Donovan, not dead," she said shortly. "I just need to catch my breath."

Grimacing, he set her softly to her feet. She wobbled a bit at first, but gripped his arm for stability. Once she caught her breath, she looked up sternly at his face. "So now you know what you must do, don't you?"

His face hardened at the question. "My place is here at Word-haven, Seer. I am charged with its protection. I cannot leave."

Seer frowned. She was afraid he would react this way. "You must go to them!" she explained, frustrated. "Surely you can see the plan has soured. A warcor no doubt waits for them in Morguen. One of our number has already been lost, and if they reach that sounden, they will all share a fate as bad or worse!"

"You make too many assumptions, Seer," Donovan said softly. "We do not know with certainty that the warcor is bound to Morguen. And with Revel lost in Strivenwood, Paladin will surely stay and search for him. He may yet abort the quest for the Book with no word from us to persuade him."

"Bah!" she scoffed. "For a great war leader of Phallenar, you are as daft as a pandori! Have you not considered that the warcor goes to Morguen to set an ambush for *us?* I tell you Paladin is walking into a trap!"

Donovan's face flushed red with anger. "I am no longer of Phallenar, Seer. You know that. And as to your question, of course I see that it could be a trap. But I do not believe it is. If Balaam knew Paladin Sky was coming to Phallenar, he would not send out an army against him. He would wait and set a trap within the city Wall."

"How can you know that? You think you know Balaam so well as to read his thoughts?" she scoffed.

"I do," said Donovan gravely. "You of all people should remember that."

She waved her hand as though to banish the notion. "Well, it will make little difference even if you are right. By the time Paladin reaches Morguen, the warcor will already be there. Once they discover him, it will not matter why the warcor was sent. They will slay him and all the rest as well."

"Surely Paladin will not abandon Revel to Strivenwood," Donovan countered. "It is his nephew we speak of."

"And my nephew as well, lest you forget," said Seer. "But Paladin *will* leave him. Not right away, not without a thorough search. But once it seems clear that Revel cannot be rescued, he will go on."

"How can you be certain?" he asked.

"Because he is my brother, and I know him every bit as well as you know Balaam—perhaps better. The Book compels him. Now that he knows where it is hidden, he will not stop until he has it in his grasp. That matters more to him than anything—even the life of his beloved nephew. He is not a bad man, Donovan; but he is obsessed with fulfilling Mentor's dream. Yet if we allow him to go on to Morguen, he will perish before the search even begins."

Donovan gazed down at her with black, unreadable eyes. "We can send someone else to warn him."

"He will not listen to another, you know that. You must go."

"I doubt anyone could reach him in time," Donovan countered angrily. "If he does continue with the quest, as you say he will, they will be to Morguen before any of us could even reach the waters of the Whey."

"That is why you must leave now, before he gives up his search for Revel and moves farther downstream. There is still time, but not much."

Abruptly, Donovan spun and marched toward the door. After several steps, he stopped and simply stood there, silently watching the scenes around him as they shifted by.

"Well?" Seer demanded.

After a moment, he took a deep breath and lowered his gaze to the floor. "I'm sorry, Seer," he said without turning around. "I cannot go. Wordhaven is discovered. I must see to its protection. . .whatever the cost. I believe that is what Paladin would have wanted."

"But they will all die!" she yelled.

"They are in the Giver's hands now," he said calmly. "We must trust that." And with that, he marched out of the room.

CHAPTER 43

MORGUEN SOUNDEN

Not a Word from their mouth can be trusted;
Their heart is filled with destruction.
Their throat has become an open grave,
And with their tongue they speak illusions of deceit,
Leading many to the pit where scream the dead,
"We are alive!"

—FROM THE WRITINGS OF THE PROPHET MIKAIL, IN THE YEAR S.C. 1103

Gideon awoke to the pungent odor of feces and urine and the smell of old sweat.

He had long ago lost track of the days since he had been locked away in this little room—or the number of times he had struggled back to consciousness after being interrogated to the edge of insanity.

His body hung like a carcass from the center of the room, suspended on nothing but Words. The light from the windows had been blocked out, though he didn't know how, and a single brilliant light had taken its place. He couldn't say precisely where the light was, because it seemed to be everywhere and nowhere in particular. No matter where he looked, it assaulted his eyes, following his gaze wherever it turned. A single spike of tortured brilliance in a world of empty black.

Luckily, the lighting problem lessened considerably once his eyes began to bleed—a side effect from the Words they used, or so they told him. It wasn't long before his eyelids crusted shut from all the blood, which reduced the painful glare from the horrid light. Now all he saw was a field of red, which he found preferable.

Nothing could compare, however, to the torment of the interrogations themselves. During his "sessions," they spoke to him only in *Sa'lei*; and even though his ears couldn't comprehend the language, his mind somehow understood every grating Word. The questions they

asked burned through his brain like wildfire with such merciless ferocity that he fully believed he would surely go mad. The Words invaded
his thoughts, burrowed into his memories, and laid siege to his secrets
with more bestial force than even Seer could have imagined.

But it was not enough. He had told them nothing.

He discovered their Achilles' heel early on, when he first realized
that they didn't actually know what he was thinking. Their Words acted
like hot pokers in his brain, torturous probes that demanded answers to
specific questions. But for all their twisted power, he found his torturers
could not actually step into his mind the way Seer had, nor could their
Words compel him to reveal the secrets he held there. Theirs was the
power of torture and pain, nothing more. And enduring pain in silence
was a skill he had spent years perfecting.

Of course, he knew nothing of the Words they sought, which is
what they asked about most often. But they asked him other things as
well—about the layout and defensive capabilities of Wordhaven, or
about various members of the Remnant, and most especially Ajel,
since he was the one who had killed the other Lord. But he would give
them nothing.

Really, he found it wasn't all that difficult to resist their burning
probes, once he stopped trying to fight the pain of their Words. He
already thought of himself as dead in every way that mattered, anyway—his hope, his love, his dream of any sort of normal life, all murdered by his father's twisted drives. The physical pain these new
torturers inflicted was nothing more than the instrument that would
kill his body too and so finish the job once and for all. Once he realized that, the pain actually became something of a welcome friend.

Unfortunately, though, he did not die as quickly as he would have
wished and soon began to question whether he would ever be allowed
to die at all. For reasons he couldn't explain, his body fought to stay
alive despite his wishes otherwise, as if his tortured bones possessed some
secret knowledge of a purpose he had yet to fulfill and so wouldn't agree
to let him go.

Still, perhaps it was not so metaphysical as all that. It might simply
have been that they didn't torture him enough. Not physically, anyway. Despite being stripped and strung up like an animal, they hadn't
really done that much damage to his body. After all, it was his mind they

wanted. They beat him sometimes, of course—especially Fayerna, who had developed a fondness for using his staff like a club. But for the most part, they ignored the more overt aspects of physical torture and allowed his body to suffer through sheer neglect. He couldn't remember the last time he had moved, or tasted food, or had even a sip of water.

But that was just as well. The lack of nourishment had also stopped the flow of other processes in his body. The stench was terrible as it was; he certainly didn't want it to get any worse.

In part, it might even have been his own cruel logic that kept him from death's grasp. Whenever Fay or Benny would torture him, he would inevitably think about the dream he had in the plains—the dream of rats and dungeons—and Ajel's prophetic assurance that the dream would come true. He couldn't die today, his mind would argue. The dream hasn't come true yet.

I dream of torture yet to come, and that's *what keeps me living through the torture today.* He would have laughed at the pathetic irony, but his throat was far too swollen and dry.

Whatever reason for death's elusiveness, the torturous sessions would eventually end with his body still quite alive, albeit weakened and frail. And after a time—hours or days, he was never sure—his rebellious body would somehow force his mind to make the slow mental crawl back to the waking world.

For him, that was the worst part of this whole ridiculous abuse—waking up. Realizing he had to wait at least another day to die.

As his thoughts cleared, he became aware of voices arguing in the next room. He immediately recognized them as Lords Fayerna and Bentel. But there was another voice as well—far weaker and much more afraid. It was a woman, one who sounded like she was close to death herself.

"They are *all* gone?" screamed Fayerna. "Not one of my *jalen* remains alive?"

"As far as I know, I am the only one," the voice said weakly, "for you or for Lord Bentel."

"Impossible," Bentel said defiantly. "There is no way Balaam could uncover all my *ser'jalen. I* don't even know who some of them are!"

"I tell you, Lord, and I tell you true," the woman pleaded between her struggled gasps for air. "I don't know how, but the High Lord has uncovered them all. All of my contacts, all of the *mon'jalen* I report to, they are all dead. Everyone in my family was also slain, and none of them even knew that I served you."

"I can't believe this," said Fayerna.

"But, my Lords, what is more important is that they are coming!" The woman's voice seemed to weaken even as she spoke.

"He *cannot* know where we are!" snapped Fayerna. "The old fool believes we are headed for the Barrier Mountains. Surely he sends the warcor there!"

"No, m'lord," the woman said plaintively. "They are nearly upon the sounden as we speak. You must flee now!"

"You say they are near the sounden?" asked Bentel.

"M'lord," said the woman, "when last I spotted the warcor, it was no more than three leagues away. That was more than one hour past."

"Then they are here!" exclaimed Bentel. "Fayerna, we must transport away from here at once. . .perhaps back to the wooded place where we stayed for a time."

"No, m'lord," the woman heaved. "You cannot. The High Lord has sealed the entire sounden and its environs so that none may use a Word to transport in or out."

"I'm not leaving without the rebel, in any case, Bentel," said Fayerna coolly. "I have not yet learned from him what I want to know."

"Forget him, sister!" Bentel said heatedly. "What matters now is our survival. The idiot would only slow us down. I doubt he's even still alive."

Don't I wish, thought Gideon sardonically. *I'm not quite dead yet, no thanks to you.*

"I am not finished!" Fayerna repeated emphatically. "I will not leave without him!"

"Then you will carry him!" Bentel yelled back.

"M'lords, please," implored the feeble voice. "You must flee!"

"Be quiet!" yelled Bentel. "Do you know a hidden way out of this sounden?"

"Not as such, Lord," the woman replied. "But all the roads are crowded this time of day. I'm sure that you could. . ."

"Then your work is finished," Bentel broke in. "And by the looks of your wounds, so is your life. Would you like me to slay you?"

"No, m'lord!" pleaded the voice.

"Then I will leave you to die at your own pace," he said. "Remain here, and do not try to follow us. If I see your face anywhere outside these walls, I will burn you on the spot."

"Of course, m'lord," she said feebly.

Everything grew silent for a moment then, with the exception of the clattering sounds of footsteps and the occasional murmur of low voices. Then, quite suddenly, the curtain dividing the two rooms flew open, and Fayerna's form stood silhouetted in the frame. Her mouth and nose were covered with a scarf.

"*Demoi esset limpion chi,*" she said with a muffled voice. "*Ma prisht!*"

Instantly, Gideon fell to the floor and into a pile of his own waste. With shaky hands, he rubbed the dried blood from his eyes and was relieved to find the torturous spotlight was gone. Though his legs felt like lead to him and despite the considerable pain of moving after days of being locked in one position, he quickly struggled to his feet and stumbled toward the pile of clothes in the corner of his room.

It was more than just a desire to be clothed that provoked him to this action. He felt *compelled* to dress himself, much in the way he had felt compelled to follow Bentel through the streets of Morguen sounden. He didn't fight it, though. It was pointless to resist.

Within moments they were on the spiraling streets of Morguen sounden, plowing frantically up the crowded path toward the rim. Bentel led the way, with Fayerna and Gideon close on his heels. When they left the lodge, he could barely stand, much less walk at such a pace. But Fayerna had issued some command in *Sa'lei* at him, and he felt a surge of strength flow through his bones, though something in his feelings told him this too was a lie. Nevertheless, he had no trouble keeping pace and couldn't help it anyway, since Bentel's Word once again compelled him to follow.

Aside from the occasional gasp at his stench or the remaining crusts of blood on his face, the crowds didn't pay them much attention. They bustled about as they normally did, unmoved by the threesome's urgent pace and apparently unaware of the warcor's approach. He imagined Bentel would see that as a good sign, for it likely meant the warcor had not yet reached the sounden rim.

"We'll go north," he muttered to Fayerna, "toward the Sound." Fayerna nodded in agreement, but said nothing.

At the next crossroads, they turned right onto a smaller path that was less heavily traveled by the locals. Once the road had cleared a bit, Fayerna pulled a scarf out of her cloak and held it over her mouth and nose.

"You should have let me take a bath, Fay," said Gideon in a gravelly voice. His throat felt like sandpaper.

"Be silent!" barked Fayerna. She raised his staff, which she carried in her free hand, and whacked it hard against his head. Spots formed before his eyes, but he felt no pain from the blow. Obediently, he bowed his head and fumbled silently along behind them.

Nothing seemed unusual when they reached the north rim. There were no signs of activity anywhere along the sounden rim beyond the usual convoys of traders' wagons and travelers from Phallenar or the Silence Sound. The plains south of the rim were as empty and vast as Gideon remembered them, filled only with an undulating ocean of singing grasses. Their peaceful song echoed lightly over the chasm in the breeze, even as the trees of Strivenwood loomed like silent sentries behind them to the west and north.

"Do you sense something?" asked Bentel suddenly.

"Yes," Fayerna replied, scanning the horizon. "Someone nearby speaks *Sa'lei.*"

"Perhaps it is only the seal placed over the sounden," suggested Bentel. But he did not sound like he believed it.

"Perhaps," said Fayerna, sounding equally unconvinced.

The three headed east along the rim, following a deeply rutted road that stretched toward the horizon and disappeared.

"Where are we going?" asked Gideon before he remembered that he wasn't supposed to speak.

In a blur, the staff swung high and struck him again, this time across the jaw. It drew no blood, but left his ears ringing like church bells. Still, he felt no pain.

"We head to Silence Sound," replied Bentel casually, ignoring Fayerna's violent reaction. "The warcor will not follow us there."

Just then, out of the corner of his eye, Gideon thought he saw a large black shape arcing through the skies to the south. But when he turned to look at it directly, there was nothing there. He grinned sardonically.

Great! Now I'm seeing things!

Fayerna, however, must have seen it too. She stopped cold and glared up at the sky. Seeing nothing there, she turned to scan the southern rim in the distance. "They are here, Bentel," she said. "Veiled."

"You are certain?" asked Bentel. She nodded in response. "Well, if they are still veiled, then they likely are not ready to attack."

"Or they're setting an ambush," Fayerna snapped. She shook her fist at the sounden. "Curse the seal on this place! Would that we at least had mounts!"

"You think the warcor lines the southern rim, then?" Bentel asked, ignoring her temper. She nodded angrily, and he turned to scan the view across the chasm of Morguen sounden. "If that is so," he said with a frown, "then it is too late to make an escape. Even if they haven't recognized us yet, they will before we can get too far."

Fayerna quickly inspected the area around them. It was largely flat and open, with short grasses and a few scattered bushes a stone's throw to the north. One side, of course, was taken up entirely by the sounden rim, which from their present location dropped off dramatically for at least two hundred feet before reaching the roofs of the highest houses. "You mean to fight from here?" she asked Bentel. "We are hopelessly exposed."

Bentel shook his head quickly. "Visibly perhaps, but if you are right, then the sounden's canyon sits between us and the warcor. Their Words won't travel far enough to do us harm."

"What if they have sound cannons?"

"If so, I think I can destroy them. But we must act quickly!"

After a moment, Faynera nodded her agreement and turned toward Gideon. "What of him?" she asked.

Bentel glanced his way, then spouted something in *Sa'lei*. Immediately, Gideon plopped down to the ground like a puppet whose strings had been abruptly cut. "He will behave," Bentel said. "Although I would still prefer him dead."

Fayerna ignored the comment and walked to the edge of the rim. "Get ready," she said. "Let's see who Balaam sent to greet us." After scanning the sounden for a moment longer, she cupped her hands around her mouth and screamed down into the canyon.

"Demoi vacht erisht!"

At her Words, the air before them shimmered briefly, then shot off in a gust of fury down the canyon wall. Gideon felt a rush of wind at his back, as though all the air around him were being sucked into the vacuum left by her cry. For a moment, he realized he couldn't breathe. Within an instant, however, more air rushed in to fill the void created by her Words—just in time for her to speak them again. Three times she repeated the harsh *Sa'lei* phrase, each time shifting the angle of her voice to shoot congealed waves of air along slightly different courses down the chasm walls.

From his position on the ground, he couldn't see what was happening below them nor understand why she was apparently attacking the sounden instead of the hidden warcor on the plains. Moments later, though, her intentions became clear.

When the wall of wind wrought by her Words collided with the far rim of the chasm, large portions of it immediately shattered, sending shards of earth and stone exploding up into the sky. A great cloud of orange dust billowed up around the impact, obscuring a large portion of the plains from view. But as the dust began to settle, Gideon suddenly saw a sea of black-garbed soldiers where once there had been only grass.

"Surprise!" said Bentel toward the distant soldiers, smiling in that sarcastic way of his. "Welcome to your death!"

CHAPTER 44

THE BATTLE OF MORGUEN

The children of Morguen are shattered;
Their young ones wail their questions to the winds,
"Why has the destroyer come to ruin?
Why have we become death this woeful day?"
"Because you have become an open grave," replies the Giver.
"Because you were dead long ago and would not turn and see it."

—FROM THE WRITINGS OF THE PROPHET SILMAR, IN THE YEAR S.C. 1320

The warcor shifted toward them in slow motion, like a tremendous black snake slithering along the far rim of the sounden.

Behind that black line, rising out of the plains, stood several yoked pairs of a most unusual-looking beast, tall and hairy and looking something like giant sloths. Each team of animals bore on its back a sort of monstrous cannon, a weapon that actually resembled a tuba, but far more serpentine and ornate in design. Packs of Guardians swarmed around the beasts frenetically, hastily prodding and pushing the slow-moving creatures ever closer to the rim.

In the air above, a dozen juron soared in winged formation along the southern rim. Their riders looked like black dots upon the creatures' backs, and Gideon wondered why they were not turning to attack.

As if in answer to his question, the juron broke formation. The beasts re-formed in groups of three, then turned and soared out above the canyon toward the northern rim. Just then, great pillars of fire shot up on either side of the warcor and began to circumvent the rim, leaving mighty walls of flame in their wake. The pillars rushed onward at a maddening pace, like fiery tornadoes bent on devastation.

"They mean to hem us in," said Bentel with a casualness that belied the obvious danger of the situation. No sooner had he said this, though, than Fayerna barked out something in *Sa'lei*, and the three of them were instantly enclosed in an object that Gideon could best describe as an oily sphere that was at once transparent, yet also black as midnight. At that same moment, the world around them fell deathly silent—as if they had been sealed within a chamber where nothing but their own voices could be heard.

To Gideon, it felt as though he'd been cut off from the world and was now watching the entire scene played out before him on a movie screen without the benefit of volume. Perhaps because of this, he didn't notice at first that he was no longer on the ground. The oily sphere had lifted them some twenty feet above the rim. He could still feel the ground beneath his legs, although he could plainly see it wasn't there. And when he looked toward the rebel Lords, they too seemed to stand on nothing at all.

At that point everything began to happen at once. The pillar of fire crossed angrily to their rear, leaving in its path a wall of flame rising at least fifty feet high, blocking any hope of an easy exit. Although the flames lapped at them from only feet away, he heard no sound of it, nor did he feel any of its heat.

When he shifted his gaze back toward the rim, the juron were already upon them. A line of fire shot out from the foremost rider, and for a moment the entire space around the trio was coated with an eerie, silent flame. It didn't penetrate the sphere, however, and after a moment its menacing dance dissipated into the air. Despite the ineffectiveness of the attack, Fayerna was nonetheless enraged at the affront. She hurled Gideon's staff toward the juron and cursed them with a scream. . .just before she spoke a Word that blew both the rider and his beast to tiny bits.

The two remaining riders wisely veered away, while other teams flew in to take their place. More fiery blasts were hurled at them, all of them equally ineffective; and Fayerna continued her rampage of retaliation, alternately exploding her attackers or setting them ablaze. Bentel, by contrast, seemed completely unfazed by the barrage of fire and had focused his attention instead on the warcor in the distance, while occasionally glancing toward the sounden below.

When it seemed a plan had formulated in his mind, he turned his full attention toward the ground directly beneath them and yelled out a string of Words at the top of his lungs. The ground responded to his command, forming waves of solid earth that rolled away from them in both directions, following the same course on which the pillars of fire had come and growing ever larger as they went.

Although Gideon couldn't hear anything outside the sphere, he imagined the Guardians' screams at the sight of Bentel's creation, for across the chasm he saw them scurry like rats toward the center of their ranks. They were not fast enough, however; and within seconds the mighty tidal waves of earth and stone reached their outer lines, then quickly plowed through the midst of them in a cloud of angry dust. In their path, black-garbed men were tossed like toys into the air, flinging their arms madly as they flew and no doubt screaming as they were hurled into the canyon by the hundreds or buried under angry tons of rock and earth. Absently, Gideon wondered if that was how he must have looked when his students watched his own encounter with an earthquake.

Once the dust had cleared, the warcor seemed to be in shambles. Hundreds of dead Guardians lay strewn in clustered piles, while those who remained alive rushed madly back and forth, apparently unsure of what to do or where to go for safety. Behind the massive piles of broken earth, however, the hairy beasts were yet untouched. All six of the strange contraptions on their backs still gleamed brightly like brass trumpets in the sun.

This fact apparently displeased Bentel considerably, for this time it was he who cursed and pounded a fist into his thigh in anger as he glared at the creatures across the way. Fayerna, distracted by his outburst, turned momentarily from her carnage and glanced at him questioningly.

"The sound cannons," he barked in response to her silent question. "We must destroy them."

Fayerna nodded, then quickly looked down into the sounden, searching. "Those buildings," she said at last, pointing beneath them toward a nondescript cluster of adobe structures. Bentel looked to where she pointed, then furrowed his brow a moment, as though trying to gauge the distance between them and the sound cannons in the distance.

After only a few seconds of calculation, he spoke. *"Damonoi fleur et puverot obre talcht!"*

He yelled this toward the buildings. Soundlessly, one of the larger adobe structures broke free of its foundations and hurled itself toward the warcor. Fayerna mimicked his Words, and another building, equally large, followed the first. Out of one of the windows, Gideon could see a woman, waving her arms pathetically and screaming toward the ground. Within seconds, she hurtled out of view.

In rapid succession, the buildings reached their targets and smashed heavily to the ground, pulverizing two of the sound cannons and the beasts that carried them. In frantic response, the remaining Guardians scrambled toward the four other cannons, apparently to move them close enough to fire back at their attackers.

Already, though, two more buildings hurtled through the air, responding to the Lords' *Sa'lei* commands. Below them, Gideon watched as panicked soundenors raced after the flying structures, helpless to rescue their friends and loved ones who were trapped inside. He stared in horror at the silent masses below him and then at Fayerna and Bentel themselves. Even he had not thought them capable of such heartless destruction.

That was when he noticed his staff lying on the floor of air at Fayerna's feet. Before he had a chance to think, he lurched toward the almond wood, dragging his useless legs behind him. Despite his disability, he closed the distance rapidly and snatched the staff away without either of his captors noticing.

Gideon didn't know why he wanted it. So long as he was crippled by the Words, he lacked the strength or stance to strike either one of them with any force. But it felt good holding it all the same. The wood's strange warmth brought reassurance and helped to still the pounding of his heart.

Even before the second wave of buildings struck, a third was airborne and then a fourth. At the last minute, the Guardians turned the beasts away and tried to flee, but it was too late. The second two buildings hit their mark with malicious precision, exploding as they struck the ground. The final two were close behind.

Meanwhile, a few juron still flew around their protective sphere—those that had not yet been vaporized by Fayerna's wrath. They no longer attacked, but kept their distance as they circled timidly above or below, apparently unsure of what they should now do. Occasionally Gideon could see the faces of the riders as they sped past. Most of them looked terrified, and a few looked angry. But all of them looked lost.

Suddenly, Gideon was distracted by a brilliant explosion in the distance. At least, he thought it was an explosion, until he saw the red-hot wave of fire charging toward them across the chasm. A second later the final building crushed the last of the sound cannons, but it was one second too late. The wave turned white-hot as it sped across the gulf, racing toward them like an angel of death.

"The juron. . . ," was all Bentel could manage to say before the wave of fire hit. The air shuddered with the impact, and the oily sphere instantly began to crackle under the heat. He heard a sound like breaking glass; then, a second later, the sphere exploded into a thousand shards and fell like snowflakes toward the earth.

Gideon fell too, along with his captors, even as the sounds of fire and wind and the cries of a thousand pained voices below rushed in to fill the void the sphere had made.

This is it, he thought in relief and clutched the staff close to his breast as if to draw some final drops of comfort from its warmth before he died.

What happened next seemed like a dream. Everything around him slowed, and once again the sounds of both life and death faded away. All he could hear were the voices of Fayerna and Bentel speaking in *Sa'lei*. Despite the harshness of the Words, their tone was oddly calm and almost reverent, like one might say a prayer.

In this strange slow-motion state, he watched two juron glide beneath them just as their Guardian riders fell gracefully away, like dead leaves carried idly by the wind. Bentel landed lightly on the back of one of the beasts just as it arced and flew away. Then he was aware of Fayerna's face, looking at him as if he were a toy she could not decide whether to keep or throw away. There was a swirl of motion, as though the world was spinning in a fog of feathers and fur. The next thing he knew, he was being lifted out of the canyon, carried by a juron's claws, which dug heavily into his shoulders. And still, there was no pain.

Beneath him, the sounden rim gave way to fields of stubby grasses and then to the mighty trees of Strivenwood. The only sound he could hear was wind and the throbbing drumbeats of the juron's mighty wings. He was surprised to find the staff still in his hands, though it could do him little good in his current state, hanging helpless as a rag doll four hundred feet above the ground.

He couldn't see much of what was going on above him, but it seemed that Fayerna was having trouble controlling the beast, for it flew haphazardly, shooting left, then right, then up, then swooping down so close to Strivenwood that he could almost touch the treetops with his feet. It wasn't until he heard Fayerna screaming in *Sa'lei* that he realized they were still being pursued.

A fireball flashed to his right, followed by another, which passed below. He saw Bentel briefly swoop into his field of view, his mouth agape and screaming something at the air. The sky thundered in response, followed by a brilliant flash, and then Bentel's juron soared up again and out of sight.

It must be those last few juron riders, he thought. *They must have pursued them out of the sounden.*

Another bolt of fire, and Fayerna's juron arced sharply down away from the blast. She screamed some response, but he couldn't tell if her Words had hit their mark. Her juron now skimmed the forest, so close that a few of the branches struck his Word-crippled legs. He watched them flop and dangle lifelessly from successive impacts. But he felt nothing.

He had no time to think about his numbness now, however. For in the dark branches below he saw, for the first time since his capture, an opportunity for escape.

The trees were huge, with massive leaves the size of a man and branches as thick as ordinary tree trunks. He thought the chances good that he could survive a fall into those woods. All he had to do was land on one of the upper branches. There was no guarantee he would, of course, especially given his crippled state. But it was a risk he was more than willing to take, given the alternative. Still, he had to act quickly, before Fayerna flew the beast too high above the trees.

The juron's claws were all that kept him from the fall, so at first he tried pummeling the beast's forelegs with his staff. From his present position, he found that he could muster quite a powerful upward swing. But the juron didn't even seem to notice his assault, much less react by loosening its grip.

Seeing the fruitlessness of his efforts, he wondered if he could strike Fayerna instead. It could be done, he thought, provided he swung high enough and in the right direction. With careful thought, he gripped the staff with both hands at its smaller end, then formed a mental target in his mind. He had seen enough juron to know approximately where she sat; and if he could gauge her height well enough, he might be able to strike a blow directly to her head. He would have only one chance, though. If he missed, she would no doubt kill him instantly with Words.

Still, even that sort of death would be better than enduring any more of their torturous interrogations. And the opportunity for escape might not present itself again.

His heart began to pound anew as a fresh burst of adrenaline flooded through his veins, masking for a time the terror in his heart. Without a moment's hesitation, he dropped the staff down low beneath him, then swung it quickly high and hard over his left shoulder so as to miss the juron's head.

The staff struck something solid, though what at first he did not know. When nothing immediately happened, he quickly snatched the staff back down again and prepared to make a second desperate strike.

That's when he saw the blood, glistening darkly on the gilded wood. And then he saw Fayerna, falling limply through the air to his right. Her eyes were closed as if she were asleep. And her face looked almost peaceful, but for the ugly bloodstain on her temple. Silently, she disappeared into the leafy trees as if absorbed into a dark green cloud.

Before he had a chance to realize what he'd done, the beast above him seemed to go mad. The juron writhed and jerked and flapped its wings indiscriminately, as if suddenly terrified to find itself flying. Screeching out its owl-like roar, it flung Gideon's limp body from its claws—perhaps unsure of what he was or how he got into its grasp.

Like a rag doll, Gideon fell, tumbling toward the forest below— toward freedom or toward death. As a final act of emancipation, he spread his arms to welcome the trees. Whether they brought death or escape, it was all the same to him.

CHAPTER 45

STRIVENWOOD FOREST

Who was it that appeared before Gideon in Strivenwood?
The spirit of some great Lord of old? A Raanthan, perhaps?
Or was it just a madman's dream, as Gideon claimed at
the time, a dream that was somehow warped to life by the
Worded effects of Strivenwood. In truth, we may never know
the answer. Toward the end of Gideon's days with us, long after
the event had passed, I asked him if he really knew what he
had seen that day. He assured me that he did, but added
that he would never tell another living soul. When I asked
him why, he would say only this: "Because it is a private love."

—THE KYRINTHAN JOURNALS, CANTICLES, STANZA 12, VERSES 13–15

The forest was soundless and still.

Gideon knew it was full day, but he could find no sun. The trees, awesome spires, jabbed into the sky's heart like spears, their leaves acting as canopies to make the forest floor dark and damp.

There were no signs of animal life. No bird, no insect. Only Gideon. And he walked, looking about him like Alice in Wonderland. He was fleeing from something. . .what? He couldn't remember. But he walked, waiting for his mind to clear, waiting to remember.

Gideon looked down at himself. He was wearing white—all white. It was an outfit like a priest or a judge would wear. On his breast there was embroidered the emblem of a sunrise, with bright spectrum-color beams shining from his shoulders to his waist. But the sun was not a sun. It was more like a pearl, woven from silk. And he was still walking. . .looking. *Looking for what?*

"Do you know why you are here, Gideon Dawning?"

A Voice. Terrible. Terrible. Booming. Where did it come from? Gideon saw no one. Only the trees. *They must be over three hundred feet tall.*

"Do you know why you are here, Gideon Dawning?"

"No!" Gideon yelled, covering his ears. "What do you want? And how do you know my name?"

One that looked like a man stood before him. His eyes were fire. His hair was whiter than any white Gideon had ever seen. He wore a robe like Gideon's, but it was torn. It was torn across the chest.

"You are here to die, Gideon Dawning. Indeed, you have already died that your life may be saved. This land will die too that it may also live again."

"Die?" Gideon stepped away. "But I don't want to die. Not really. Not now. Who are you? I don't want to die."

"I will not kill you, Gideon Dawning. But you are here. Do you know why you are here?"

Gideon tried to dash behind a tree and run away, but his feet would not move. "No. I mean, I don't understand. What are you talking about?"

"You are a sojourner in a land that is not your own, Gideon Dawning. You always have been. But now you have come here to make a way for me. Speak pure, and you will not fail."

"Fail? Fail at what?"

But the light from the stranger's eyes faded slowly into the distance, rising ever higher into the trees until all that remained was a tiny shaft of sunlight breaking through the canopy above.

"What the. . . ?" he muttered as he scanned the tangled mesh of leaves and branches high above. But there was nothing. He closed his eyes and breathed a heavy sigh, wondering if the man had been a figment of his mind and why the whole exchange had seemed so sad and so familiar.

And then it came to him.

"The dream!" he said aloud and was at once surprised to hear the strength of his voice echoing through the trees.

The dream, he repeated silently. *The dream I had in Providence, Colorado—it seems like years ago.*

But it had not really been that long, he realized. It was the night before the earthquake on the mountain, when he was so afraid of having a rage in that old hotel, afraid of everyone finding out. *That was the man in my dream. . . . In fact, that* was *the dream!*

Immediately, he looked down at his clothes. There was the white robe, with a brilliant silken sphere embroidered on the breast and richly colored rays shooting off it all around.

"I'm still dreaming," he whispered, listening carefully to the words to test how real they sounded. Then, quickly, he remembered that he had said something like that too—before, in the hotel room, because he. . .

Cautiously, he sniffed the air. *Honey! I smell honey!*

"I must be completely mad," he muttered. Anxiously, he rubbed his eyes and tried to think of something real, some real memory of where he was and how he got here. But all he could think about was the man.

Fail at what?

It wasn't until several minutes later, when he saw the staff, that he finally remembered. It was lying on the ground not far from where he stood, under the fringes of a bush; and even in the shrouded light, he could see the bloodstain gleaming darkly on one side. One glimpse of that dark token of his desperation and every detail of his recent days flooded back into his conscious mind. The juron's claws lodged firmly in his shoulders. . .the desperate blow that sent Fayerna plummeting into the wood. . .the juron's crazed reaction and his own fall toward the trees. He remembered and shuddered.

But his memory seemed to stop there, frozen in time. He could not recall anything after that. Had he collided with the trees? It did not seem so. And yet, here he was standing on the forest floor.

And what about his clothes? He was in a Mentor's shift before; but now when he looked down, he saw only the brilliant robe. There was no stench about him either, nor any stains of filth and crusted blood upon his skin. It was as though someone or something had scrubbed away all evidence of his torture, fitted him with clean garments, and then just left him standing there, without the faintest clue as to why.

More troubling still was the apparent fact that he was standing at all. Bentel had spoken a Word that crippled his legs—hadn't he? Yes, he remembered that much clearly. So was he now deluded, only imagining he could stand? And what about his other wounds, the juron's claws embedded in his flesh, the bloody blows upon his head? What of the *Sa'lei* Words that for days on end had tortured his body and ripped his mind apart?

Fayerna had spoken something that made him feel impervious to pain, but what he was experiencing now was clearly more than only that. He felt. . .*well*. No injuries, no soreness, no swollen tongue. . .not even any pangs of hunger!

Tentatively, he reached down and retrieved the staff from its place beside the bush. Its calming warmth spread gently through his hand, just like it always did. "I must be mad," he said quietly. *The impact of the Council Lords' torture must have finally made me crack. How could it be anything else?*

For a long time, he just stood there staring at the gilded almond wood, trying to recollect his thoughts into some reasonable order of sanity. Once again he had found himself in a circumstance that made no sense at all. And he searched his thoughts in vain to find some way to determine whether the circumstance was real—and simply unexplainable—or just the product of his quite deranged and shattered mind.

Eventually, though, he realized the task was quite impossible. For if he had truly gone insane, how could he trust any explanation he might give himself for why he was no longer crippled, why his clothes had changed, or why it seemed he had just *lived* a dream he once had in Colorado?

And then of course there was Strivenwood itself to consider. Ajel had told him long ago the Wood was Worded in some unknown way and deadly to all who entered it as a result. Well, now he *had* entered it, and so death was no doubt lurking somewhere around the next tree, like a lion ready to pounce. It seemed death was never far from him anymore; and yet, until now it stubbornly refused to come close enough to finish him off.

Of course, maybe it *had* come, and he was just too much in shock to realize it. Maybe he was really lying unconscious on the ground somewhere, still crippled from the Words and quite delusional and dying from the fall.

Maybe. But he didn't feel like he was dreaming. So, in the end, regardless of whether he was alive or delusional and nearly dead, he decided he might as well go have a look around.

Walking far beneath that awesome canopy felt something like passing through a dark and long-abandoned grand cathedral. He felt obligated to step quietly and to whisper, if he spoke at all, as if the open spaces between the trees were host to some unknowable presence, some distant holiness, that commanded an attitude of reverence from lesser beings like himself.

It was awesomely quiet. In the distance, sometimes, he thought he could hear a sound like moaning, but it never lasted; and he assumed it must simply be the wind spilling through the upper branches several hundred feet away. As for wind upon the ground, there was none. Only vast curving walls of chocolate-colored bark, separated by large undulating stretches of damp black dirt—and all of the space between filled with the strong and too-sweet smell of honey hanging everywhere he breathed.

There were few bushes, no grass, and no animals that he could see or hear. The only sign of any life at all was from the trees, which covered the black ground with their fallen, curled, enormous leaves. At first these gave the landscape the appearance of little rolling hills, but the illusion was broken once Gideon collapsed a few of the mounds under his feet. Although the leaves were as big as bedspreads, they were still fairly thin and brittle and crumpled up as any other dead leaf would.

Aside from its obvious alien qualities, Gideon decided that Strivenwood was really a fairly peaceful place and seemed neither deadly nor even all that dangerous in any tangible sense. Of course that could have been just another part of the hallucination, so any conclusions about the Wood had to be viewed with appropriate suspicion. But his current experience was all he had to go on at the moment.

Eventually his wanderings began to take the form of a straight line, or what seemed to him to be a straight line, toward what he believed to be the edges of the forest. He could not see the edge, of course, and had no reason to believe that he knew where the edge was—nevertheless, he felt confident that he was going the right way to get him out of Strivenwood. He realized that this too was most likely a product of his delusional state. But he had nothing else to go on and so saw no reason to resist the unexplainable urge to walk in a particular direction.

He continued on this way for several hours, until it grew too dark for him to see. Then, without the faintest sense of fear at being lost in such a grand and dark place all alone, he lay down upon a giant dying leaf and fell asleep.

When he awoke the next morning, Revel Foundling was sitting beside him.

He sat cross-legged on the forest floor, his hands cupped nervously beneath his chin, with his abundant red curls dangling loosely over those curious golden eyes. He wore the same black leathers Gideon had last seen him in, and his forehead still sported the same silver headband, which bore that odd inscription in some language Gideon didn't know. He seemed calm enough, yet his face revealed a tension that Gideon couldn't explain. He waited until Gideon sat up and took a good look at him before he spoke.

"Hail, sojourner," he said at last. "You see me, then?"

"Of course I see you," Gideon replied, irritated at the stupidity of the question and at being spoken to at all before he was fully awake. "Why wouldn't I? You're sitting right in front of me."

Revel tilted his head in that strange birdlike way of his and blinked his golden eyes. "You know who I am?"

Gideon sighed and looked him over suspiciously. "Well, you look and sound like Revel. . .but you're probably just another product of my delusion."

"You fear you are deluded?"

Gideon laughed sarcastically. "Well, let's see. I'm apparently in Strivenwood, though I don't remember exactly how I entered it. I'm wearing a white robe that I don't remember putting on. I'm *not* injured, which makes absolutely no sense. And Revel Foundling is suddenly sitting next to me. Yeah. I'd say I'm delusional."

"I am no delusion, sojourner," said Revel firmly. "It is I."

Gideon shook his head. "I really can't see why I would imagine *you*, though," he muttered to himself, ignoring Revel's comment. "But then, I guess you make about as much sense as the robe." Absently, he brushed fragments of dead leaf off his sleeves. "Still can't explain why I'm not injured. Or why I don't at least stink." He sniffed his robes suspiciously.

"I tell you I am real, sojourner," Revel repeated, "as is your garment, though I cannot say how you came to wear it. It is just like the robe of Lord Natel."

"Who?"

"One of the lost souls of Strivenwood. It was he who lured me to the Wood in hope that I might save him." He shook his head somberly. "But I could not."

Gideon covered his face with his hands, then slowly ran his fingers through his hair. "Oh. . .this makes no sense."

"I am confused as well," admitted Revel. "Thoughts are difficult to hold here in the Wood. Perhaps it would help if you told me how you came to be here—what you *do* recall, I mean."

Gideon breathed heavily. "All right." He sighed in resignation. "Why not?"

Beginning with his capture at Wordhaven, Gideon related to Revel—or rather, this *illusion* of Revel—all of the events leading up to his present circumstance, including his strange encounter with the man with eyes of fire. When he had finished, Revel just sat there quietly for several minutes, apparently trying to absorb the meaning of all that Gideon had said.

At last, he spoke. "I cannot explain what has happened to you, sojourner. But it seems that we are both subject to powers and a purpose that is beyond our knowing. I am glad I was at least able to find you, though I cannot say it will help us escape from this place."

"Okay, okay." Gideon rubbed his eyes again, then buried his face within his hands. "This is too weird," he said tiredly. *I can't make sense of this.* He got to his feet and brushed the remaining leafy fragments off his robe. *His* robe.

The man with fire in his eyes. The dream that was not a dream. And now Revel, appearing out of nowhere, in the middle of a vast and empty forest. "I'm either dead or crazy," he concluded. There was simply no other explanation.

"Just because you do not understand a mystery does not mean you should not believe in it," offered Revel.

"But how can I know what's real?" Gideon retorted. "It has to make sense somehow, doesn't it?"

Revel shrugged. "Sometimes the only way to know a thing is real is to trust it."

Gideon waved his hand dismissively. "That's a circular argument." He snorted with a grimace.

And yet, upon reflection, he had to admit that something about it sounded true. Since his arrival in this strange land, he'd had to let go of a lot of his suppositions about what was real or possible. He'd seen more miracles than he could count, had even been healed on more than one occasion, and had more recently been subject to a litany of supernatural horrors that he could not begin to comprehend and did not care to remember. If all of that were true—and real—was his present circumstance any less believable?

"All right," he said at last, turning to Revel. "How did you find me here?"

"In wooded lands, my senses extend as far as the forest edge," Revel replied. "The effect is not unlike that of Wordhaven, I suppose, though it is not of the Words. It is an ability unique to my people. I felt you the moment you entered the trees. Though it required much effort, I finally managed to find you."

"Your people?" asked Gideon. "I thought you didn't know anything about where you came from?"

"I did not," said Revel, "until Lord Natel told me. He is one of the Old Lords, from a time long ago when my people still roamed some forests of the Inherited Lands. In his time, he led one of the Great Sojourns into this very Wood in search of the Book. But the Wording of the Wood entranced him, and he has been striving here ever since. He recognized me even from beyond the forest and used what little strength he had to still the madness long enough to call me."

"He's still alive?"

"In a sense, yes, though his spirit perished long ago. The Word that cursed this Wood has that effect. As best I can tell, it lures you with the promise of whatever ecstasy you crave, then consumes your soul in striving after that very lust—a lust that you can see, but never quite reach. Eventually, your spirit fades away to death until only the lust itself remains. The Lord Natel I met was just a shadow of the man that once lived, though he did not know it."

"Huh," said Gideon, considering the implications. "But if that's true, then why aren't we affected by the Wood?"

"In your case, I do not know," Revel replied. "As for me, I am affected and mightily so. Even now the Wood beckons me, enticing me to offer it my dreams. The things it offers me in return are wondrous. . .and vile. . . ." He seemed to lose himself a moment, as though listening to some alluring song that only he could hear. Abruptly, he shook his head. "It takes all of my ability to resist the call," he added finally. "I must remain connected to the trees. They alone serve to keep my sanity firm."

Gideon shrugged. "I don't feel anything like that. It's just a forest." He looked around. "Big and. . .empty."

Revel stood and brushed the dirt off of his leathers. "If that is so, then the power that surrounds you is even greater than we knew. Tell me, sojourner, does all this clear evidence still not convince you of who you are?"

Gideon stiffened involuntarily. "I know exactly who I am," he said coolly. "And who I'm not."

Even as he said the words, they felt awkward on his lips. Did he really know who he was anymore? Had he ever really known? "Don't you think we should be leaving?" he asked abruptly.

"Yes," Revel admitted as a sudden weariness washed over his face. "I would be most thankful to be free of these woods. But my abilities are quite confused here. I fear I cannot tell which way will lead us out."

Gideon frowned suspiciously, then retrieved his staff from where he'd laid it the night before.

"Then I'll lead." All of a sudden, he felt very anxious to get moving and to get away from Revel, though he was not sure why.

Revel gestured toward the shrouded trees around them. "There is no way to know which way is true," he said sadly. "Since I first entered, I have tried to leave, to get back to Ajel and the others, but I cannot. The Wording affects my sense of the trees in a way I cannot overcome. To me, every direction seems right and yet not right."

He sighed tiredly. "In truth, I am amazed I even found you."

"Well, I know the way," said Gideon flatly. And, with no more explanation than that, he started walking that direction.

As if afraid to be left behind, Revel fell in quickly beside him. "How do you know this?" he asked urgently.

"I don't know." Gideon shrugged impatiently. "I just do."

Despite the obvious strain in his face, Revel managed a grin. "I have to say, I would not be surprised if you did."

Gideon didn't want to know what that meant and so made no further comment, and the two of them continued through the Wood for some time in silence. Revel would at times mutter feverishly under his breath and shake his head violently, as if arguing with demons Gideon couldn't see. But Gideon thought it best not to ask what was really going on, and Revel didn't seem interested in talking about it, anyway.

And so they simply walked, both of them consigned to the purely irrational belief that Gideon actually knew where he was going.

CHAPTER 46

PRIVATE CHAMBERS

A Word is heard weeping in the plains,
"Make way for the Pearl!
Make clear the path of the Staff of Life!"
He wears a crown of black upon his head
And on his shoulders a mantle of deliverance has been laid,
For the sake of the Refounding Age
That he is called to preach as herald, as witness,
as the maker of ways.
In the Giver's time, the Waymaker will make his way
to the house of Sa'lei Lords,
but not before his mantle is made true.
At the core of Noble Heart,
he will bear the burden of proof.

—FROM THE WRITINGS OF THE PROPHET SHIKINAH, IN THE YEAR S.C. 1600

"So there are none left? None at all?"

Lord Lysteria Asher-Baal produced a handkerchief from some-where within the abundant folds of her gown and patted it delicately to her neck and brow as she spoke. It wasn't that Balaam's chambers were too warm, really, but the proximity of the forbidden scrolls he kept here always made her skin go damp—not to mention making her stomach clench like a fist.

"Oh, there are a few." Her bondmate waved his hand idly without turning around. "Stragglers, nothing more."

The High Lord stood stoically with his back to her, staring out his chamber window as he sipped a hot mug of mint tea. Lysteria had given up on hers and set it aside on the table next to the couch where she sat. The tea was supposed to help settle the queasiness in her stomach, but as far as she could tell, the sweet heat of the liquid only served to aggravate it. The only real solution, she knew, was to get away from those cursed black scrolls. But this was the only place in the Axis that was sufficiently warded so they could be certain they were not being overheard.

"And what of our dear Lords, then?" she asked.

"Both escaped, as far as we know," said Balaam with a snort. "And the Stormcaller as well, apparently." He took a sip of tea. "There was one report of the rebel falling from a juron into Strivenwood. And then another one of Fayerna doing the same thing. But none of the *ser'jalen* could confirm it either way."

"Well," said Lysteria, lightly dabbing the nape of her neck, "I just can't understand how an entire warcor could be wiped out so simply, even against two Lords. It sounds as if the Guardians hardly put up a fight."

"I don't know how," said Balaam, "but Bentel and Fayerna must have been warned ahead of time. That's the only explanation."

"How could they have been?" Fayerna asked incredulously. "You had all of their *jalen* slain."

"I said I don't know, didn't I?" Balaam snapped. Lysteria pursed her lips at the affront, but said nothing. "I suppose one of their *jalen* must've eluded me," he added with a bit softer tone. "But they had to have foreknowledge of the warcor somehow, or else they would not have been able to catch the Guardians unawares as they did."

"Well, what will we do about them now?" Lysteria asked.

"Bentel and Fayerna? I haven't a notion," Balaam replied with a bitter chuckle. "I don't even know where to look for them. I've got *ser'-jalen* flying all over the region in stealth, but there's no sign of them anywhere."

He turned from his perch next to the window and ambled slowly toward his desk. "They did find one curiosity, however," he continued, "a group of those Wordhaven rebels traveling down the River Whey on some Word-awful contraption that barely passes for a boat."

Lysteria's eyes widened. "More rebels? Coming this way?"

"Not exactly." Balaam shook his head. "They seemed to be headed for Morguen sounden, albeit slowly. I think they somehow discovered where the Stormcaller was being held and were on their way to rescue him. Too late, of course. As usual."

"Are we going to destroy them, then?"

Balaam frowned and shook his head. "Why waste the time?

They're not important enough to worry over. At this point, I'm much more concerned about the Stormcaller than a wayward handful of *Dei'lo* extremists."

"You mean Fayerna and Bentel," she corrected.

"I said what I mean," replied Balaam, a little too sharply. He turned his attention to the *ser'jalen* seated at his desk, who until that moment had been trying very hard to seem as though he wasn't there. "Haven't you found it yet?" Balaam snapped.

The *ser'jalen*'s shoulders twitched involuntarily in surprise at being addressed directly. It had been more than an hour since Balaam had so much as looked his way.

"I believe I have found the correct scroll, High Lord," he said with a shaky voice. "But it will take a moment to locate the passage you requested."

"Well, be quick about it!" Balaam commanded. "Can't you see the lady is beginning to feel ill?" He gestured toward Lysteria, who frowned even as she quickly patted a bit more of the perspiration off her brow. Truth be told, she thought she was handling the presence of the horrid black scrolls a fair bit better than Balaam, who was clearly far more agitated and pale and sweaty and obnoxious than she was.

Just like a man to use a woman as an excuse for his own weakness, she thought bitterly.

The *ser'jalen* who sat behind the desk, however, didn't seem to notice the hypocrisy in Balaam's comment at all. He only looked at Lysteria with wide, sheepish eyes, then began shuffling the pile of black scrolls on the desk before him with even more furious determination than before.

Lysteria slowly cleared her throat before speaking. "You are more worried about the Stormcaller than the rebel Lords, then?" she asked, trying to sound as casual and at ease as her roiling stomach would allow.

"Yes, of course I am," replied Balaam.

Lysteria raised an eyebrow questioningly. "But why?" she asked. "He's just another rebel lunatic."

Balaam shook his head angrily. "No, he's more than that, though no one realizes it yet. Including him, I hope."

"You don't mean you believe all the gibberish about this man being the Kinsman Redeemer?"

"What?" said Balaam. "Kinsman Redeemer? No, of course not. Those Wordhaven rebels were fools to even suggest it. But what he really is may prove just as bad."

"Your pardon, High Lord, but I think I've found it." The *ser'jalen* looked up hopefully and with more than a little fear in his eyes.

"You think?" said Balaam shortly. "You better know!"

The *ser'jalen* swallowed. "It is the right passage, High Lord. I'm certain of it."

"Well, then read it."

Lysteria started to rise. "Balaam, do I have to stay for this?"

"Sit down, please, dear," said Balaam. "I want you to hear this."

Lysteria grimaced, then relaxed back into the chair with a sigh. "If you insist."

"I do," said Balaam firmly. "You're not the one who's had to endure these scrolls for weeks, as I have," he added. "Listening to a few lines won't kill you."

Lysteria rolled her eyes dramatically. As far as she was concerned, Balaam's obsession with those scrolls was repugnant and more than a little heretical, if she were truly honest about it. But she thought it best to hold her tongue on the matter. No amount of arguing the point would have made any difference in his behavior. Once he made up his mind about something, there was no changing it, however reasonable her objections might be. He was terribly bull-headed that way.

"Well, get on with it, then," she said.

The *ser'jalen*, taking this as his cue, leaned closely over the black scroll before him, focusing his attention on a short block of silver writing. "Here it is," he said, by way of warning.

*"In the Giver's time, the Waymaker will make his way
to the house of Sa'lei Lords,
but not before his mantle is made true.
At the core of Noble Heart,
he will bear the burden of proof."*

"Shall I continue?" asked the *ser'jalen*, looking worriedly toward Balaam, who was leaning heavily on the edge of the desk and gripping his stomach as though he'd just swallowed a knife.

"No," gasped Balaam in reply, wincing in pain. "That is enough."

Tentatively, Lysteria swallowed, trying to force back the bile that had been steadily rising in her throat as she heard the words. The sound of them bore into her skull like nails into a coffin and set her head to spinning like a top. She felt very much like throwing up or fainting or both, but she was determined not to show weakness—not in front of Balaam and *certainly* not in front of a mere *ser'jalen*. She patted her brow lightly, then folded her hands slowly across her lap before she spoke.

"I'm afraid I still don't see the point," she said carefully, forcing every word to sound far more calm and even than she felt.

Balaam straightened and took in a deep breath, then exhaled slowly, momentarily closing his eyes as if to stop the room from spinning. When he opened them again, they looked far angrier than before.

"It's right there, Lysteria," he said coldly. "The prophecy tells us where we will find him."

"Find whom?" she asked, irritated.

"The rebel!" Balaam shouted, then winced at the effort. "He is not the Kinsman Redeemer, but someone far different, and in his own way, perhaps far worse. That's what no one realizes—apparently not even you, I'm disappointed to say. And he is going to Noble Heart."

Now it was Lysteria's turn to look angry. "Well, how am I supposed to know what the scrolls say he is?" she snapped. "I haven't been reading these black documents day and night for months as you have—for reasons, I might add, I can't begin to fathom—and I can hardly be expected to give credence to what they say, in any case. They're horrid things, Balaam. Heretical fantasies that some charlatan prophet scribbled on parchment generations ago. Even thinking about them makes me ill." She patted her forehead furiously to emphasize the point.

"He's going to Noble Heart," Balaam repeated flatly.

Lysteria waved her hand dismissively. "Everybody knows Noble Heart doesn't exist anymore."

Balaam slammed his fist down on the table. "Don't be dense, Lysteria! It doesn't become you. The *ruins* of Noble Heart still exist. And he's going there."

How dare he! Lysteria shot to her feet, ignoring the churning effect the motion produced in her stomach.

"Of course, High Lord," she said with icy coldness. "Please, forgive my insolence. I shall endeavor to be less 'dense' in the future. Is that all you wished to share with me?"

For a moment, Balaam just stood there, silently rubbing his eyes as he leaned once again on the desk for support. Finally, he said, "I'm sorry, dear. It's the scrolls. The irritation of them makes it difficult to remain civil."

Lysteria's eyes softened a bit, but she kept her silence.

"This rebel is dangerous," he continued. "If I am right about him, then his presence may be the undoing of all that we believe in. That's why I need him alive. It's the only way I can make certain the prophecies never come true."

"I didn't know you were one to believe in foolish *Dei'lo* prophecies, Balaam," Lysteria said coolly.

"I'm not sure I do," Balaam replied. "But I'd be a fool to ignore the possibility. That's why I'm sending our *mon'jalen* to the ruins of Noble Heart. If this prophecy is right, then we won't have to go searching for the rebel at all. He will come to us."

"My *mon'jalen* are at your command, as always, Balaam," said Lysteria. "I'll tell Raug to make any arrangements you desire. May I leave now? I *am* feeling rather tired of this."

Balaam looked anxiously in her eyes. "Of course, of course," he said, waving his hand toward the door. "We will talk again a bit later, yes? Once we are away from these cursed scrolls."

Not likely, she thought angrily. But she said nothing and only pursed her lips into a sort of half smile before abruptly turning and stalking out of the room.

CHAPTER 47

◤ THE RIVER WHEY ◢

*Since its inception, the Remnant had always carefully held and
maintained a reputation for presenting a united front to the
world. One cause, one voice. But one should not think this meant
that the Remnant was actually unified in all of its affairs. It was
not without the petty jealousies and divisive controversies that
are common to all such organizations of its size, though almost
all of these were carefully veiled from the view of outsiders.
The coming of Gideon Dawning, however, quickly began to
unravel this delicate veil of uniformity. Within the halls of
Wordhaven, there were some who resolutely believed that the
Kinsman Redeemer was a corrupt and powerfully deceptive
figure who would worm his way to power as Palor had done,
only to usher in a second and far more pestilent Age of Slaughter.
For this reason, these factions naturally believed the Redeemer
must be stopped from fulfilling his dark call, preferably by
slaying him on the spot. To these passionate believers, it made
no difference that Paladin had offered to protect Gideon
Dawning from harm. For they believed the sojourner was the
fulfillment of their most dreaded prophecy. And that he must die.*

—The Kyrinthan Journals, Musings, Chapter 5, Verses 1–10

Another dawn had come and gone before they reached the final stand
of trees. And when at last they did, the experience seemed oddly anti-
climactic—to Gideon at least. Of course, he could only guess what
was going through Revel's battered mind when the river finally came
into view. To be honest, he wasn't even sure at first whether Revel
believed the river was real at all. He just stared at the sparkling current like it was just another mirage concocted by his torturous dream.

It was to be expected, Gideon supposed. The entire trek had been a never-ending nightmare for the Wordhavener. He seemed lucid enough at first, but Gideon couldn't help but sense the unseen tension weighing heavily on the man, even when he smiled and tried to make out as if everything was fine.

By the second day, however, even the smiles had faded. And so did any lingering confidence that the golden-eyed man would be able to withstand the Wood's influence long enough to reach its border. As the journey progressed, Revel's face took on a tortured aspect that only grew more severe the farther they traveled. His crazed ramblings became more frequent and more intense.

In the beginning of their trek, Gideon had noticed how he would occasionally pause to place his hands upon the trees they passed. But by the end, this strange communion with the trees had turned into a frantic obsession. Not a single tree was passed untouched; and the space between them was bridged by one mad dash after another. Eventually, Gideon was forced to lead Revel by the hand from tree to tree along the route he believed was right for fear that the man would charge off toward some tree that wasn't in their path and lose his way altogether.

Despite the slow progress imposed by Revel's madness, Gideon wasn't at all worried about getting lost. He knew the way, as clearly as if he'd walked it a thousand times, though—like everything—how he knew it remained a mystery. He did, however, grow increasingly worried about Revel. He could do nothing for his companion beyond coaxing him patiently onward from tree to tree. He only hoped they'd reach the border before the strange effects of Strivenwood pressed the Wordhavener so deep into madness as to lose all hope of return.

When at last they emerged from the final stand of trees, Gideon expected Revel to raise a triumphant shout of victory or at least breathe a sigh of relief. But he did nothing of the sort. In fact, neither of them said anything at all to mark the event beyond marching stoically to the river's edge and filling their empty, growling stomachs with the cool, clear waters of the Whey.

Shortly after that, Revel collapsed in exhaustion on the grassy bank and fell right to sleep. For awhile, Gideon lay back silently on the grass beside him, content simply to rest his tired legs and take in the rediscovered vastness of the early morning sky. But soon his own weariness got the better of him, and, banishing all thought of where they were or what they should do next, he too fell asleep.

Sometime after noon, Gideon was startled into consciousness by a sudden commotion nearby. Opening his eyes, he saw Revel standing upright and peering intently up the river's meandering course.

"What is it?" Gideon asked, alarmed by Revel's sudden apprehension.

"They're coming," he said, without diverting his gaze from the water's course.

"Who's coming?"

"It is Ajel," he muttered after a pause. "They search for me along the edges of the Wood not far to the west."

Gideon leaned forward and scanned the water's course where Revel had been looking. He saw nothing but an empty river, glistening brightly like a flowing carpet of jewels under the morning sun. "Revel, are you feeling all right?" he asked dubiously.

"They must have realized they could not come in after me," continued Revel, still looking upriver. "And so they search along the forest's edge in the hope that I am able to come out." He flashed a smile at Gideon. "Their search would be in vain, if not for you, sojourner. You have my deepest thanks."

Gideon frowned suspiciously. "You're not making sense, Revel," he said, still scanning upstream. Maybe Strivenwood was still warping the Wordhavener's perceptions. "From what you told me, it's been at least five days since you entered the Wood, more than two since you found me. We've spent almost all that time *walking*. There's no telling where we are in relation to them now."

"They are coming, sojourner," Revel insisted. "The trees tell me they are close. It seems that for all our walking, we have not traveled far downstream."

Gideon stood to face his companion. "I don't need to remind you that those trees nearly killed you!" he said emphatically. "It's stupid for you to believe whatever they might be telling you now. It's just another illusion from Strivenwood, Revel, can't you see that? Ajel and the others are probably miles away by now."

Revel shook his head impatiently. "I am no longer trapped within the Wood, sojourner. My senses are clear; and I tell you they are coming."

Gideon frowned worriedly and scanned the waters once more. Finally, he said, "Revel, listen to me. There's no one there. I don't see anything."

But then it appeared, floating idly into view from around a distant bend along the river's course, looking for all the world like a discarded pile of wooden boxes bobbing slowly in the current.

Revel smiled. "Do you see something now?" he asked jokingly.

"Is *that* them?" Gideon asked, squinting to get a clearer view.

"It is indeed," Revel replied. "Why did you not believe me?"

Only because you've been teetering on the brink of insanity for the past three days! he thought sarcastically. Instead he said, "I just didn't see anything, that's all."

"You should not put so much confidence in your eyes, sojourner," Revel advised judiciously. "They rarely see the whole truth in any circumstance."

"Forget it, Revel." Gideon sighed tiredly. "Let's just let them know we're here."

"They already do," he replied confidently. "Ajel has sensed my presence."

"What?" asked Gideon incredulously. "Are you two, like, mentally linked or something?"

Revel responded to the question with a look of surprise, then blinked curiously. "Aren't all brothers?" he asked.

Gideon snorted. "Not hardly," he said, as images of his own brother, Jacob, came flooding unbidden to his mind. A pang of sadness shot through his gut as he pondered the seven years of silence that stood between them like a wall that had grown thicker and more ominous with each passing season. He wondered how his brother was doing and whether he would ever have the chance to speak to him again. . .if he even wanted to.

"That is a pity," said Revel as if he had overheard Gideon's thoughts.

Gideon frowned slightly. "Let's go," he said. "The sooner we get on board, the sooner we can eat." The water he had used to fill his empty stomach had long since lost its effect.

"As you wish," said Revel. "Though I think I would prefer sleep now more than anything."

Gideon shrugged noncommittally. A few more hours' sleep wouldn't be too bad, at that. But first he had to eat something. He grabbed his staff and walked past Revel toward the ship, which was now close enough for him to see a cluster of people huddled on the bow, waving.

He wondered how they would react to seeing him again, especially dressed as he was now, in robes like those of their Old Lords. He didn't relish the thought of having to explain how he had found himself in these strange new garments or really any other detail of the last several days. But he figured the task was unavoidable. Even if he refused to tell them anything, he knew Revel would.

As they drew closer, he began to make out their faces. And the recognition of one in particular formed an immediate knot in his gut.

"Aybel is with them?" he asked Revel, trying to sound nonchalant.

"Yes," said Revel, "along with Paladin and Kair and Ajel of course. They are all well, or were when I last saw them."

"Uh-huh," said Gideon. *As if I didn't have enough to deal with as it is!*

Still, he was relieved to know that she was all right, that she wasn't injured in the Council Lords' attack on Wordhaven. And a part of him, a part he didn't want to admit was real, was thrilled at the thought of seeing her again. It was foolish for him to think that something might work out between them. He knew that. But he also couldn't help but hope.

Moments later, the odd-looking craft diverted from its course down the center of the flow and glided peacefully toward their position on the bank. And all the while the water's gentle churns and chops, which echoed from the hull, were interrupted by Ajel's shouts of "Hail! Hail!" from some unseen place on board.

Lines were tossed and anchors set, and soon the two wayward travelers were on the deck, enduring, in Gideon's case, the abundance of hugs that awaited them.

"Great merciful Giver!" Paladin exclaimed repeatedly as he constrained Gideon in a great bearish embrace. "A miracle that you are both safe and alive!"

"Thanks," said Gideon awkwardly, his arms pinned to his sides.

"You are welcome on the raft," echoed Ajel, who had come bounding out of his hiding place the instant they were aboard. "Welcome,

welcome indeed!" he repeated, hugging Revel with such force that the weary man could hardly take a breath.

Once Paladin's bulk had finally released Gideon and stepped aside, he saw Aybel standing behind him, looking somewhat tired and oddly vulnerable, with Kair beside her, looking the way Kair always looked whenever he was around.

"Greetings, Gideon," said Aybel quietly. "It is the Giver's gift that you are safe and have found your way to us again."

Gideon took a tentative step toward her. "Hello, Aybel," he said. "It's good to see you."

"Fortune certainly seems to be with you, Redeemer," said Kair, with her standard dose of suspicion.

Gideon nodded. "Kair," he said, ignoring the unwelcome title.

"How did you come upon these robes?" Paladin broke in with his characteristic bluntness, reaching across Aybel to sample the soft white fabric of Gideon's sleeve.

Revel promptly laid a hand on Paladin's shoulder. "That will be a great story to hear, uncle," he said with a grin, "and I'm certain the sojourner is anxious to tell it." He quickly winked at Gideon. "But our friend here brings news of more immediate concern."

"Oh?" said Paladin. He looked at Gideon expectantly.

Gideon sighed. He really didn't want to get into this now. All he wanted to do was put some food in his rumbling stomach, take a nap, then, after that, maybe talk to Aybel alone. . .after he'd had a chance to think about what he wanted to say. But there was no avoiding Paladin's stare.

"Revel tells me you're heading for Morguen sounden," he said. Paladin nodded. "Well, I just came from there—a few days ago anyway—and I don't think it's the kind of place you want to go right now."

Paladin blinked. "Why not?"

"It's a war zone," said Gideon. "Benny and Fay were attacked by a whole warcor of Guardians along the sounden rim. The whole place is in shambles. Buildings were destroyed. Lots of people were killed, although I think most of them were Guardians."

Paladin looked puzzled. "Benny and Fay?" he asked, looking to Revel for help. "Who are Benny and Fay?"

"Those are the sojourner's pet names for Council Lords Bentel and Fayerna Baratii," explained Revel, clearly amused at the idea.

Gideon grinned, slightly. "That's kind of how I got here, actually. Fay and Ben—uh, Fayerna and Bentel—hijacked some juron and tried to get away, but a couple of Guardians pursued them, I think. I couldn't see it that well. Anyway, in all the fighting, one of the juron ended up dropping me into Strivenwood." It wasn't exactly the whole truth, but it was all he cared to say about it at the moment.

"Strivenwood!" Ajel broke in, all of a sudden looking at Gideon as though he were a ghost. "How did you escape it?" He looked at Revel. "How did you both?"

Gideon rubbed his eyes. "You know, I'd really like to tell you all about it, but I'm really hungry. Do you think I could eat something before we continue?"

Suddenly, Paladin grabbed hold of Gideon's arm and slapped him heartily on the back, which hurt. "Of course, of course," he announced loudly. "My apologies, sojourner. Ajel, Kair, would you prepare some food for our lost kinsmen?"

Paladin abruptly herded him down the deck, apparently toward whatever galley this haphazard ship of theirs might contain. Ajel and Kair rushed on ahead of them, disappearing into one of the dozens of wooden doorways that spotted the ship. Aybel was suddenly nowhere to be found.

Moments later Paladin led him into a fairly spacious room in the aft section of the craft, where he promptly seated him and Revel at a large, weathered table. After much bustling about and the clattering of dishes and pans, Kair emerged from an adjacent room with a tray of food in one hand and a stack of dishes in the other. She quickly laid out the wooden plates before them. Ajel followed with two skins of water and a small loaf of bread. Gideon's mouth immediately watered in hope that the bread was *ja'moinar*, like the loaf Mara had given him. His hopes were dashed, however, once he took a bite and realized it was just an ordinary loaf. But the tray that Kair had brought contained a variety of fruits and nuts that all looked very good, as well as a substantial pile of the usual dried meat, which Gideon had grown to like quite well during his time at Wordhaven and which he was careful never to ask too much about.

Once the food and drink were served, the entire group sat down.

Without hesitation, he shoveled some food onto his plate, then into his mouth, ignoring the fact that his haste would likely offend the Wordhaveners, who always consumed their meals with excruciating slowness. While still at Wordhaven, he'd asked Ajel why they ate that way and was told that it had to do with showing reverence for the moment and giving thanks, or something like that. But at this moment Gideon just couldn't care about any of it. He only wanted to eat.

Lucky for him, Revel showed less interest in the food and so was more available to answer Paladin's questions, which he kept shooting out at them in fiery succession. While Gideon chewed, Revel replayed the story of Gideon's torturous experiences with the Council Lords, as best he knew them anyway, as well as the major highlights of their battle at Morguen and Gideon's subsequent escape into Strivenwood.

From time to time, Paladin would look to Gideon for confirmation of Revel's account, and he would nod furiously before quickly taking another bite. As long as he was chewing, he figured, he didn't have to say anything. The only part Revel left out—intentionally, Gideon surmised—was that of Gideon's encounter with the fiery-eyed man and the subsequent realization that he was no longer injured and that his clothes had been changed. He guessed that Revel thought it best for him to tell that story himself.

"And so you see why we must not go to Morguen," Revel was saying. "Many of the Guardians are no doubt still there, and with the sounden in such confusion, we could not hope to pass through it unnoticed. And then there are Lords Bentel and Fayerna to consider."

"You mean just Lord Bentel," Paladin corrected. "Did you not say Lord Fayerna fell to Strivenwood?"

"That is the sojourner's account," nodded Revel. "But I never sensed her enter the forest."

"Could you have missed it?" Paladin asked.

"Perhaps," said Revel. "But I do not think so."

I watched her fall! thought Gideon indignantly. But his mouth was too stuffed with food to say anything.

For a moment, Paladin furrowed his brow and stroked his chin thoughtfully. At last he said, "What you have told me explains much. I see now that the Lords who attacked Wordhaven have somehow defied Balaam by their actions. But I cannot yet discern what they could have done to bring the Council's wrath upon them."

Gideon quickly forced himself to swallow. "It's because of me," he broke in hoarsely. Paladin looked at him questioningly. "Bentel and Fayerna were supposed to take me to Balaam," he continued. "But they were angry about that other Lord dying, and somehow they blamed Balaam for it. . .well, him and Ajel. Anyway, they decided to keep me to themselves, to try and figure out why Balaam wants me so much, I guess so they could use that information against him."

"I see," said Paladin. "I assume the Lords used the Words to probe your mind, then."

Gideon nodded, but purposefully said nothing more. He had no desire to recount the details of his torture to anyone, especially himself.

"And what did they search for in your mind?" Paladin asked, pressing the issue.

Gideon took another bite of meat to give himself time to consider how he wanted to answer the question, if at all. Finally, he swallowed and said, "They wanted to know what I knew about *Dei'lo*, mostly. And they wanted to know some things about you and about Wordhaven."

"About me?" asked Paladin.

"Well, all of you," Gideon explained. "Especially Ajel, since he was the one who killed that other Lord."

Paladin nodded thoughtfully in response, then asked, "And what did they learn from you?"

"Nothing," said Gideon flatly. "Not a thing." He knew his tone sounded more than a little prideful, but he didn't care.

"I do not mean to question your word in this," Ajel interjected, "but how can you be certain they did not gain the knowledge you hold."

"Because their Words don't work like that," Gideon replied confidently, secretly pleased to be in a position of teaching *them* something about the Words for a change.

"Actually, I guess I have Seer to thank for helping me perceive the difference. They weren't able to enter my mind the way she could. Really, they couldn't enter my mind at all, not directly." He fumbled for the words to explain what he was trying to say. "Their Words acted like. . .a computer virus or a probe, which tried to pull out specific answers to their questions. It was kind of like a truth drug, I guess, but a lot more painful."

What are you saying, Gideon? They don't know what a truth drug is. Or a computer virus, for that matter!

"How did you resist it, then?" asked Paladin, apparently understanding enough of the explanation to continue.

At this, Gideon smirked. "I guess I'm pretty good at forgetting what I don't want to remember," he said. "It's a talent I never thought I would be glad to have. Anyway, they didn't get anything out of me. Not even your names."

There was a moment of silence. Gideon took the opportunity to grab a handful of nuts and toss them in his mouth.

"Your resistance on our behalf speaks well of your heart, sojourner," said Ajel at last. "You have our deepest thanks." After he said this, he glanced thoughtfully at Kair, who quickly looked away.

"You still have not told them how you came to wear the robes," Revel interjected.

But Paladin waved his hand commandingly. "There will be time for that later," he announced in a tone that was at once weighted with authority. "Kair, do we have a map of the Inherited Lands?"

"I believe so, Paladin," she replied.

"Then bring it," he commanded. "We must discern a new route to our goal." She immediately rose from the table and disappeared through the door.

"It would seem, sojourner, that you are destined to travel with us whether you wish to or not." Paladin smiled as he said this, but his tone was anything but light.

The statement took Gideon by surprise. He hadn't really thought about what he might do next. For the past several days, just getting out of Strivenwood was all that mattered. "What do you mean?" he asked finally.

"I mean that you must stay with us if you wish to stay alive," replied Paladin. "It was dangerous enough for you when only Guardians were pursuing you. But now it seems that Balaam himself has taken an interest in you. I know him, sojourner. Believe me when I say that there is no more ruthless or powerful man in all of the Inherited Lands. He will not rest nor even tire until he finds you. And when that happens, you will not want to be without our protection."

Gideon shook his head. "I don't know," he said suspiciously.

Paladin's explanation sounded honest enough, but Gideon couldn't help but feel some kind of veiled threat lurking beneath the words.

"More than that," Paladin continued, "if you speak true, then you have slain a Council Lord. That makes you a marked man. A hunted man. If you choose to continue your sojourn on your own, you will be slain on sight by any Guardian or Council Lord within a thousand leagues of where you sit."

"But I *can* still leave if I want to," Gideon asserted, his tone suddenly full of challenge and suspicion.

Paladin nodded. "Of course, of course. But only if you wish to perish. It would seem a waste to struggle so valiantly to stay alive these past difficult weeks only to throw it away now."

Gideon grimaced. He didn't care to tell Paladin that he hadn't really tried to stay alive at all. If anything, he had invited death to come and take him, to end the ridiculous and twisted story of his life once and for all. But it was death, and not Gideon, that had resisted.

Before he could offer any reply to Paladin, however, Kair appeared in the doorway grasping a large furled scroll in one hand. Paladin waved her in as Revel and the others quickly removed the dishes and the food, apparently not even thinking to ask whether Gideon was finished, which he wasn't.

A moment later, the scroll was unfurled on the table, revealing a map of the entire Inherited Lands. Gideon surveyed the various regions with great interest, astonished to discover how many places he recognized. Toward the bottom, he saw Calmeron sounden, situated next to the massive forest they called Castellan Watch. North of there was Songwill, nestled in the center of the Scolding Wind Hills. Beyond that he could see the Barrier Mountains, the Dunerun Hope, and the impressive breadth of the Heaven Range, which he now realized extended far north and east of the part he had seen, until it butted up against a vast plateau that covered the entire top portion of the scroll.

But there were also places on the map he didn't recognize. Places with foreboding names like Black Gorge, Deathland Barrens, and Fallenwood. And in the middle of it all sat Phallenar, the city he had heard so much about and had already learned to hate, even though he'd never seen it.

A sudden chill ran down his spine, however, when he looked just north of Phallenar and saw his name.

"What's this place?" he asked, pointing to the lone small hill drawn upon the map.

"Gideon's Fall," answered Ajel. "We have spoken of it many times at Wordhaven."

"Oh yeah," said Gideon, remembering. "I guess I just didn't expect to see it included on a map."

"It is the place where the Pearl was slain," Kair broke in coolly. "Why would we not mark it?"

"I don't know," said Gideon defensively. "It just surprised me, that's all."

"We are here," interrupted Paladin, pointing to a spot along the River Whey, not far from Morguen sounden. "I had hoped to enter Phallenar from the north, here, under the guise of merchants from Morguen. But with a warcor in the area, this entire route is compromised. We dare not try to reach the Gorge anywhere along the path where the Guardians may be traveling."

"We could try to enter through the Wall, here," offered Revel hopefully, pointing to the center of what looked to be a massive manmade structure bordering Phallenar's western side.

Paladin shook his head. "Almost all the Guardian host are garrisoned within the Wall. It would be too dangerous." He ran his finger to the structure's southern end. "I think our best hope will be to enter from the south, away from the Guardians' eyes."

"Then we would have to leave the river," Ajel observed.

"Yes," Paladin agreed. "I think that is the only way for us now. At first light tomorrow, we will make a southern route through the Plains," he followed the course with his finger, "then turn east once we have cleared the Wall."

"That course will leave us fully exposed," cautioned Kair.

"Yes. There is that," Paladin agreed. "But we have the advantage of being unexpected. The Council does not know that we are coming and so will not be looking for us. And their search for the sojourner will keep them focused here, near Morguen and Strivenwood. They will not likely think to look to the south."

"What of the raft, then?" asked Ajel. "We cannot leave it moored here in the open, lest the Lords uncover our trail."

Paladin sighed. "I fear there is no choice in that. We must sink it."

"Paladin, Ajel and I brought enough supplies on board to last for several months," objected Revel. "Must we lose them all?"

"We will take what we can carry," said Paladin. "The rest will feed the life within the river."

"The sinking of the raft will be no easy task," said Ajel. "She is a sturdy craft."

"Then I will leave it to you to discern how it will be done," said Paladin, grinning slightly. "As for the rest of you, there is much else to be done in preparation for our departure. Revel, as you know most about what supplies there are on board, you can assist Kair and Aybel in pulling the items we will need and dividing them into packs. We will each carry a share of the burden." He looked specifically at Gideon as he said this last part, to which Gideon shrugged apathetically.

"I have no problem with carrying a pack," he said.

"Then you have decided to remain with us," said Paladin, making it sound a little like a question.

"I guess 'if I want to live,' I don't have much choice," he said with some sarcasm. "But I'm not at all sure about going with you there." He pointed on the map to Phallenar.

Paladin smiled. "There will be time to consider that decision on the way."

I'm quite decided on the matter already, thank you, he said silently. But aloud, he said nothing.

After waiting a moment for Gideon to respond, Paladin continued. "Then let us begin the work. Revel, once you have helped us find the supplies that will be needed, you should take your rest. More than any of us, you need to regain your strength for the journey ahead." He turned to Gideon. "You should rest too, sojourner."

"No argument here," Gideon agreed. "Just show me where I can bed down, and I'll be out of your way."

"Kair will show you," said Paladin.

At his word, Kair rose again from the table and nodded curtly for Gideon to follow. As they passed through the rickety old door into the growing coolness of the late afternoon air, Gideon couldn't help but wonder once again where Aybel had gone.

CHAPTER 48

ACROSS THE PLAINS

By the time the Gray Ages were fully established, the only vestige
of Dei'lo *that remained was a diluted and broken form of the*
language, which came to be known simply as the High Tongue.
It was mainly spoken in ceremonies or by the prophets of
Songwill, who used it to record their prophecies, always on
the rich black scrolls of Valoran sounden with silver-laden ink.
Though it was not Dei'lo, *it was still close enough to wield*
some power in its speaking and to have some effect on those
who heard it, especially those who knew its opposite, Sa'lei.
It was perhaps this fact, more than anything, that kept the
scrolls from destruction once the Council took control. The new
Lords respected power over all else, even power wrought
from Dei'lo. *And though they loathed the scrolls' effects, they*
recognized the value of keeping them intact, against such a
time when their power might prove useful.

—THE KYRINTHAN JOURNALS, CHRONICLES, CHAPTER 5, VERSES 48–51

He found her the next morning, just as the first rays of morning were
spreading like a carpet over the plains. He was surprised to find that the
ship had been moved to the opposite side of the river during the night
as he slept, in preparation for the group's journey south into the plains.
Aybel was kneeling next to the gangway, which had also been moved,
and was busily sorting a few last-minute supplies that Ajel had suggested they include in the packs.

"Where were you last night?" he asked by way of greeting.

Aybel glanced briefly in his direction, then quickly returned to her
task. "I was watching the stars," she said matter-of-factly. "I was not
needed in the galley and so preferred to enjoy the night air."

"You were missed," said Gideon.

"Really," she said. "By whom?" Her tone was noticeably harsh.

"Well, by me, I guess." Gideon shifted his weight awkwardly.

Aybel huffily tossed a blanket into the pack before her. "You guess?" she said, turning to face him. "If you are not certain of your own heart, Gideon, how can I be? We are not in Wordhaven any longer."

"What's Wordhaven got to do with anything?"

"It was easier to speak with you there," she said. "I could discern your feelings, even those you seem unaware of. Now you are completely closed to me."

Gideon shrugged. "I'm completely closed to myself half the time."

"Yes, I know," said Aybel. There was a hint of pain in her voice. "And that is what makes you untrustworthy." She turned back to her work.

"Untrustworthy?" Gideon asked, a little hurt by the suggestion. "How am I untrustworthy?"

"Is that not clear?" replied Aybel, as she shoved one pack aside and pulled another toward her.

"Not to me," said Gideon. *Or I wouldn't be asking the question, would I?*

Aybel paused, but did not turn around. Her head dropped slightly before she spoke. "Because you do not know what is in your heart," she said slowly, sadly. "When you say how you feel, you speak on behalf of a stranger living inside you. You do not know yourself—not your true self. Therefore, nothing you say can be trusted."

"I know what I feel," said Gideon angrily. "You make it sound like I don't know myself at all."

Aybel turned to face him. "Do you? I am not so sure."

He looked into her ebony eyes and saw her fear and vulnerability there, pouring out at him in a way that was so unguarded, so innocent and lovely. "I know that I care about you," he said softly.

She searched his eyes with an intensity he found at once unnerving and attractive. Then she said, "Perhaps that is true. And in truth I care for you as well. But that alone is not enough. There is still much within you that you do not know. And much more that you may see but do not hold as valuable or true. Until that changes, I cannot trust you."

"So that's it then?" Gideon asked, flipping his hand in a gesture of finality. "You've done your analysis, drawn your conclusions, and now you've passed your judgment on me without so much as a word from me?"

Aybel turned back to her work and began sealing packs. For a moment, it seemed as though she wasn't going to say anything more, but then she stood and turned to look him squarely in the eyes. "I have not passed judgment on you, Gideon. You have passed judgment on yourself—a wrong judgment. *That* is the problem."

With that, she picked up the closest pack and walked away.

I have judged myself? What's that supposed to mean? He considered pursuing her to ask the question, but then thought better of it. If she was done talking with him, then why make the effort? She'd clearly already made up her mind about him, anyway.

But she said she cares about me, didn't she? Does that mean there's still hope?

"Clear the deck!"

The voice was Revel's, calling down from the upper reaches of the boat, where he stood next to the center mast with a saw in his hand. Without waiting for anyone to respond, he began sawing furiously at the base of the pole, preparing it to topple off the ship into the river. Quickly, Gideon moved toward the gangway along with the rest of the Wordhaveners. They shuffled onto the shore in a line.

Ajel had suggested they cut down the masts because he didn't think the boat would sink deep enough to conceal them from view. The other two masts had already fallen and were winding their lazy way down the river's course. Once the third one was down, they would offload the rest of the packs, then set about punching holes in the hull. Revel had found some sledgehammers and spikes to accomplish the task, which came as a surprise to Gideon, who couldn't think of a good reason for storing items like that on a boat.

Within minutes, the great center mast screamed out one long, final creak as it toppled heavily onto the deck, then bounced like a baton a few times before plunging heavily into the current. It only narrowly missed the packs that Aybel had been working on, which irritated Gideon for some reason. He wondered why no one thought to remove them before they started hacking away at the bones of the ship.

With the last mast disposed, the rest of the Remnant returned on board, hurrying in clusters toward the packs on the deck or climbing below with hammers and spikes in hand. Gideon felt pretty useless in the midst of all this activity, but he generally felt that way around the Remnant, even when they were short-handed and there was an abundance of things to be done, like now. They hadn't asked him to do much of anything since he came aboard, beyond carry an item or two from here to there. For all his alleged familiarity with these people, he realized with some sorrow that he was still an outsider to them. And the stinging conversation with Aybel had only heightened his awareness of their imposed isolation.

Perhaps out of defiance, then, he rushed to pick up the last two packs from the deck, just managing to get to them ahead of Revel, who had come bounding down from his perch as the final mast hit the water. Gideon snagged the packs out of Revel's reach, then, with a curt nod to the man, carried them awkwardly down the gangway to shore. Kair was waiting there and nodded in greeting, albeit begrudgingly.

Gideon ignored her. He had enough to think about without trying to figure out what he had done to make Kair loathe him so utterly. He dumped the packs on the ground, then moved to stand some distance away where he could watch the boat sink in peace.

Paladin emerged from the bowels of the ship and came bounding down the gangway, loudly instructing everyone to stand back. There were two lines holding the raft in place, and Paladin untied one of them and wrapped it around his wrist, then instructed Kair to retrieve the other. Gideon just stood there, wondering again why they never asked him to do anything and trying not to conclude it was because they didn't trust him for all the reasons Aybel had explained.

"Ready!" Paladin yelled into the air.

Immediately, Gideon heard the hollow muffled thuds of sledgehammers pounding in unison against the inner hull. Aybel and the others would have to race off the boat once the water started flooding in, he suddenly realized. His concern for Aybel heightened as he considered this, and he began to worry that Ajel and Paladin had not really considered the danger of what they were doing.

"Will they be all right in there?" he called to Paladin, who was standing some distance away.

"Do not worry, sojourner," Paladin replied. "The raft will not sink quickly."

You hope, thought Gideon cynically, but he said nothing more.

A moment later, though, the sounds of muffled sledgehammers ceased, and Ajel and Revel emerged from below deck with Aybel on their heels.

"Now!" Ajel yelled as he ran down the gangway. Paladin and Kair tossed their lines onto the deck, then jumped straightway into the water and leaned heavily against the hull. The other three quickly joined in, pressing their weight against the dying leviathan to give it one final push into the main flow of the current.

By the time Gideon moved in to help, the job was already done. The group waded back toward the dry grasses of the plains as the lumbering beast floated noiselessly toward the channel's center, picking up speed and losing some height as it went.

"Are you sure that thing will sink?" asked Gideon as they stepped sluggishly back onto shore. "It's all wood."

"Gilded wood," Revel corrected. "That sort does not float in water."

"It's not all gilded," countered Gideon.

"Enough of it is, I think," said Ajel, "though some parts of the upper raft may break off and remain afloat, I agree. It is a risk we cannot avoid. We could not burn it for fear of drawing attention to our presence."

They watched the raft awhile, slowly sinking ever deeper into the waters as it drifted downstream. No one made a sound, except for Paladin, who grunted occasionally to himself as the craft slowly vanished from view. Gideon sensed within the group a certain sorrow that he could not readily explain except to assume that the dilapidated old boat had somehow meant much more to them than anyone had cared to say.

After a moment, though, Paladin retrieved his pack from the ground, which everyone took as a signal that it was time to leave. Gideon grabbed the pack nearest to him and threw it heavily onto his back. It really amounted to nothing more than a canvas bag with two shoulder straps sewn in one side, and it was heavy—probably at least sixty pounds. The straps would have been horribly uncomfortable if not for the extra shoulder padding provided by his white robe.

He was glad now that he hadn't exchanged his mysterious garment for something more common—like the others' brown traveling leathers—though he still couldn't explain exactly why he had made the decision. Originally, he had every intention of disposing of the robe; but when it actually came down to doing it, he found that he couldn't. Or, rather, that he didn't want to.

Gideon was certain it had something to do with the dream in the forest, which now he realized wasn't really a dream at all. And with what the man he saw there had said:

"You are a sojourner in a land that is not your own, Gideon Dawning. But now you have come here to make a way for me. Speak pure, and you will not fail."

The words had been ringing in his head all morning, just as they had every morning since he first heard them, pressing against his thoughts like a puzzle demanding to be solved or, far more alluring, a calling waiting to be fulfilled. He didn't know what they meant. But something about them, something about the tone in which they were given, filled him with an unexpected and unexplainable sense of hope. It was as if all the years of broken and meaningless abuse that had come to define his life might eventually be brought to bear in some vast and unknowably good purpose—if only he could stay the course and complete the task that would be set before him when the time was right.

This is a ridiculous train of thought, he told himself. *The fantasy of an idiot.*

But in the weeks since the revelation of his father's abuse, he'd become so starved for hope—hope of *any* kind—that he didn't care if it was nonsensical. This was a land of strange and miraculous things. Who could fault him if he chose to believe that one more miracle might be possible—a miracle that would tell him that his life was not the mistake he thought it was? And so he kept the robe, hoping that it might actually come to mean something.

Before long, the little company's hike southward through the plains had fallen into a comfortable rhythm. They formed a rough line through the singing grasses, with Paladin and Ajel leading the way and Gideon to the rear, followed only by Kair, who seemed to prefer the back-most position. There wasn't much talk, as there was little need for it, and it only distracted from the reedy music that floated lightly on the winds. The grasses were much higher here than they had been along the edges of the Barrier Mountains. Or perhaps it was just that

Gideon was no longer on a horse. But all that he could see of the group ahead were their heads, bobbing up and down above the grass like balls floating on a lake of gold and scarlet water.

He saw Aybel's head up there, standing out from the others because of her brilliant white hair, which more than compensated for the fact that she was a bit shorter than the rest. There was more he wanted to say to her, though he doubted now whether she would even submit to listen. Mostly, he wanted to tell her about the dream, about the man's words, and about the crazy hope that made him keep the robe instead of throwing it away. He couldn't explain why he wanted to tell her specifically, since he certainly had no desire to tell the others anything about it. He guessed perhaps he just wanted her to see that he did know something about his heart after all and that he did believe in some of what he saw there. At least a little.

"I am surprised that you still wear that robe today." Kair's words broke through his private reverie with such force that he actually jumped.

"Pardon, Redeemer," she added coolly. "I did not mean to frighten you."

Gideon instantly frowned, but didn't turn around. *Why does she insist on calling me that?*

"I'm not frightened," he said. "I was just enjoying the quiet."

She apparently ignored the hint, for she continued. "You have not yet told us how you came to possess it."

"Possess what?" he asked.

"The robe," she answered.

"I guess there hasn't been time," he said idly.

"There is time now."

Gideon rolled his eyes, though she couldn't see it. As much as he wanted to tell Aybel about the robe, it was the last thing in the world he wanted to share with Kair.

Thinking fast, Gideon said, "I have a better idea. Why don't we talk about you?"

"About me?" she asked, clearly surprised.

"Yeah," Gideon said. "I mean, you seem to be involved in everything that goes on with the Remnant. But during my time at Word-haven, I never saw you more than once or twice. And even then, I never heard you say a thing. So," he absently shifted the weight of the pack on his shoulders, "I'd like to know about you."

A moment of silence followed, then she said, "There is not much to tell."

"Oh, come on, sure there is," Gideon chided her. "Like. . .what do you do in the Remnant? What's your role?"

"I am Paladin's assistant," she said simply.

"And what does an assistant do?"

"I assist him."

She clearly wasn't going to make this easy. But if she was going to insist that they talk, then he was determined it would not be about him.

"So how did you get the job?" he asked. "How did you join the Remnant?"

"I was born at Wordhaven," she answered. "I have known no other place."

"Are your parents still there?"

"No," she answered. "They were both slain."

"Oh." That surprised Gideon. "I'm sorry."

She said nothing.

"So. . . ," he continued awkwardly, "were they also born in the Remnant?"

"No," she replied. "My mother was from Calmeron sounden and my father from Songwill. They met at Wordhaven and later bonded."

"Oh," said Gideon interestedly. That at least explained her unique combination of red hair and blue-gray eyes. "That's surprising, in a way. You didn't seem too comfortable in Calmeron or in Songwill for that matter."

Again, she did not reply.

Guess I hit a nerve, Gideon thought. *Good. Maybe we can stop talking now.*

But after a moment, Kair spoke again. "There is no great love between the people of Calmeron and those of Songwill," she explained tersely. "They do not exchange with one another in bonding. Because of this, I am. . .somewhat of an outcast in either place."

Gideon was surprised to hear such an honest and even vulnerable response. He softened his tone. "Well, if it's any help," he said, "I know how it feels to be an outcast."

Another pause. Then she said, "It is not as though I am a sojourner without a home, Redeemer. Wordhaven is my home and always will be." Her words sounded almost defiant. "And more than that, I have something of my heritage, from my father's side at least. He raised me in the Songtrust, a gift that taught me many things. . .including many things about you."

"About me?" Gideon laughed. But he felt the tension rising up his neck.

"You play the part of an ignorant fool so well that even Paladin is convinced," she said calmly. "But I know your treachery, Redeemer."

Gideon was stunned as much by the harshness of her words as by the icy calmness with which she delivered them.

"My treachery," he repeated. He stopped momentarily, then turned to face her. He was surprised to find the look of fear on her face.

Why is she afraid?

But he said, "I really have no idea what you're talking about." Shaking his head, he turned back to the trail and continued walking.

"I have sung the prophecies since I was a youth," she continued. "They are a part of my blood; they are my life. My heart knows their meaning well. I see well enough who you are, and I know what you mean to do. I am not so fooled as some may be."

The steely calmness of her tone made Gideon shudder, but he tried to make it seem like a shrug. "Huh," he said, without stopping or turning around. "Let me guess. I'm the Kinsman Redeemer. And for you, that's a bad thing."

"So you admit it freely."

"No!" he replied sarcastically. *Why do I keep having to deal with this?* "I've already told you I'm not the Kinsman Redeemer. In fact, I've said it repeatedly since the moment you first met me. How can I make it any clearer to you than I already have?"

"Your very actions betray you, Redeemer," she replied. "You claim the name of our betrayer. You use the power of *Sa'lei* to slay your enemies, then claim no knowledge of how you did it. And now you wear the robe of the Lords of Old, a robe of authority and power. And yet you claim no desire to rule? You are a fool to think we cannot see through this."

Gideon felt his face flush hot with anger. "We?" he said mockingly.

"Are you trying to tell me that Ajel or Paladin or the others here believe as you do? I really don't think so!"

"I am not alone in my beliefs," she replied, her voice still calm and even. "If you strike me down, there will be another. And another. And another. Until you are stopped."

Gideon spun to face her, and she froze in her tracks. "Until I'm stopped?" he asked incredulously, trying to ignore the fear in her eyes and in his own heart. "Now you're threatening me?" He shook his head, as much in confusion as in anger. "Kair, you are nuts!" he added, not quite yelling. "You need help. And I'm done talking about this!"

He turned and stalked down the trail, away from her accusations and toward the relative safety of the rest of the group, which now hiked some distance ahead. He walked as quickly as he could without breaking into a run and made the conscious choice not to turn and see whether she was following close at his heels. Within a few minutes, he had caught up with Revel, who was merely strolling along in comparison to his frenzied gait.

"Sojourner!" said Revel, surprised by Gideon's sudden appearance next to him. "Are you well?"

"Peachy," snapped Gideon. "Just peachy."

Thankfully, Revel said nothing more, but merely raised his eyebrows curiously for a moment, then turned his attention back to the path.

They walked on together for some time, passing through the afternoon hours in silence, with only their breathing and the sound of the musical grasses to keep them company. Gideon didn't turn around anymore that day, nor did he allow himself to think about the implications of what Kair had said or the threats she had made. There was too much spinning through his mind already—questions that loomed so heavy and ponderous that they threatened to crush him under their collective weight.

Who was the man in the dream?

What was he trying to say?

Why did he give him this robe?

Was there really a purpose behind this whole insane experience—all the torture, the confusion, the revelation of his abusive past? If so, what was it?

What was he *really* doing here, in this strange and dangerous world?

And yet one question overshadowed them all like a thick, impenetrable fog. It was the one question Gideon never imagined he would be forced to ask himself, the one thing he was always certain of, and never doubted, until he had come here. He could never have predicted that asking it again, after so many years, would provoke such fear and turmoil in the deepest caverns of his soul.

Who am I?

As afternoon pressed onward into night, the waning sun dipped silently below the grassy horizon, and the light that had been brilliant yellow faded to a mixture of majestic oranges and purples. If Gideon had looked behind him then, in those evening hours, he would have seen Kair walking silently with leering eyes not ten paces back. But more than that, he would have seen another face, farther back but far more cruel. It was a face he would have once recognized with fear, but which had now become so twisted with dark, vicious rage that it barely even qualified as human.

And it was following him.

CHAPTER 49

NOBLE HEART

The Path to Lordship through the hearted cities required
postulants to advance through three distinct levels of training—
Novitiate, Novice, and Apprentice. Novitiates were the exclusive
realm of Noble Heart and in a typical year numbered close to
ten thousand strong. Most of these progressed within a year or
two to Broken Heart, where they were named Novices, and
entered into what all regarded as the most difficult phase of
their training. Most Novices did not make it past the first year,
and many that did remain died. Only handfuls survived the
ordeal and were extended an invitation to travel to Sacred
Heart as Apprentices. The danger did not end there, however.
For in as much as the tests of Broken Heart could slay the
body, those of Sacred Heart could imperil the soul.

—The Kyrinthan Journals, Chronicles, Chapter 3, Verses 300–303

They spent the night out on the open plains, under a canopy of brilliant and unfamiliar stars, and dreamed of places they had been, were now, or would be someday.

It was perhaps the most peaceful night of sleep Gideon could remember having since he was a child. It was, in fact, a scene from childhood of which he dreamed, a rare and happy time when his parents took Jacob and him to see the Grand Canyon. The only part that didn't seem real was the music, which played soothingly in the background through the entire experience, tickling his ears like a gentle lullaby. He didn't remember hearing music in the Grand Canyon of the past; and when he awoke, he realized he had been listening to the wind upon the plains in his sleep.

There had been no talk of using *Dei'lo* to block the plains' Wordwrought effects the night before. In fact, no one had mentioned the

Wording at all. Not even Ajel, who had been so adamant about putting Gideon to sleep by other Words the previous time they crossed the plains. But by the time they stopped their hike, Gideon was too tired and perhaps too jaded to worry over it one way or the other. He'd already survived one nightmare on the Plain of Dreams. What possible difference would another make?

Luckily, though, the dream didn't turn out so badly this time.

They rose just as the first rays of the sun scattered over the grasses, and Paladin swiftly announced that they would head for the ruins of Noble Heart, which lay somewhere to the south. Gideon vaguely recalled Noble Heart as being the first of the ancient centers for new novitiates into Wordhaven. Sacred Heart, which he had already visited, was the third and supposedly the most resplendent of the three. With detached resignation, he wondered if this new place would also have an arched gateway, as Sacred Heart had, and whether it too would force him to relive dark memories of his abusive past.

He shared none of these questions with the others, however, preferring the quiet as they ate their dried fruits and meat, packed their things, and embarked once again on a trek across the plains. No one seemed bothered by his silence—in fact, no one else was saying much either. Only Ajel talked, or rather whispered, with Paladin as they hiked along. But even their exchanges lacked their usual animation and fervor. As for the rest, they plodded on in a contemplative haze, apparently content to remain lost for awhile in dream-inspired memories of the past or unsettling visions of the future.

The day passed uneventfully and without much comment. Even Kair, who had been so insistent in expressing her opinions to Gideon the day before, now seemed pleased to keep her distance from him, walking as she preferred to do, far to the rear of the others. Aybel kept her distance too, a fact that bothered him, though he tried to make himself believe it didn't. She'd made it clear that she didn't want anything to do with him. So why should he care what she did?

It wasn't until late in the day, when Paladin announced that they had arrived at the ruins, that he felt like saying anything at all. And that was just to ask what seemed to him an obvious question.

"What ruins?"

It was Ajel who turned to respond. "Noble Heart was razed by

Palor Wordwielder during the time of the Slaughtering," he explained. "I fear there is not much left of it to see."

"Well, I don't see any of it," he responded tiredly. He scanned the region all around and saw only the same unchanging landscape he had observed all day—shoulder-high grasses blowing idly in the breeze for miles in every direction.

"It is here, Gideon," Aybel added unexpectedly and with a touch of irritation. "Why would we mislead you in this?"

"That's not what I meant," Gideon explained defensively, but Aybel had already walked away.

"Here, sojourner. Come and see."

The gruff voice was Paladin's, though Gideon had lost sight of him somewhere in the grass ahead. Following the direction of the sound, Gideon soon found him in a small clearing, seated on the ground and leaning against the smooth remains of what was once a stone wall. Standing barely five feet high, it was composed of pinkish granite blocks hewn into decidedly impractical shapes—triangles, parallelograms, and such—yet fitted together with such precision that they required no mortar at all. The remnants extended some ten feet or so in either direction from where Paladin reclined.

"This was once a mighty fortress," he explained, "with six walls as smooth as glass, the legends say, standing nearly one hundred feet above the plains. Though, I confess, it is difficult to imagine it as such now." He brushed the stonework absently with his fingers. "Still, the workmanship is without compare, would you not agree? Except perhaps at Wordhaven."

"It's very. . .impressive," Gideon commented in a tone that showed he didn't care one way or the other.

Ajel and Revel appeared behind Gideon, emerging like ghosts out of the green and purple wall of grass. "We will rest here tonight," continued Paladin. "At first light, we will turn east toward the Wall. We should be within sight of it by evenfall tomorrow."

"Should we not continue on in the night, uncle?" asked Revel. "Surely it would be best to approach the Wall under cover of darkness."

"I have already discussed that matter with Paladin, brother," interrupted Ajel. "We must stay here."

"And why is that?" asked Revel. Then, turning to Paladin, added,

"Did you dream something, uncle?"

Paladin ignored the question and instead hopped quickly to his feet. He was an amazingly agile man, especially for one so advanced in years. "We had best make camp before the sun sets," he said. As he strolled off into the grass, he called behind him idly, "Revel. Walk with me."

Revel promptly followed, and Gideon couldn't help but get the feeling that there was something they weren't telling him. Again.

He didn't pursue the matter, however. Truthfully, he didn't have the energy to care. The constant bombardment over the past several weeks of strange events and tortures and struggles and revelations and feelings he didn't want to feel were beginning to take their toll. He felt completely overwhelmed by it all, exhausted by the sheer intensity of his experiences.

Even the present—and quite perilous—reality that he was here, in the middle of this grassy sea, with a band of rebels heading toward a city where all he could reasonably expect to find were rats and dungeons and most probably death—all of that only barely registered as real or important in his conscious mind. He knew he should be apprehensive, or excited, or afraid of what was happening. He knew he should have been thinking about ways to protect himself, ways to remove himself from the path of inevitable harm ahead. But there was no more room left within him for such trivial things. It was as if all of his natural mechanisms for self-protection had shorted out, and all that remained was hollowness. . .and one small, disconcerting speck of hope.

He'd considered giving up many times before—at Calmeron, in the Dunerun Hope, and especially after the Facing at Wordhaven. But what he felt stirring in him now was not like any of those exactly, though it shared some similar traits with the notion of surrender. He didn't know really what to name his feelings, since he had never experienced anything like them before. All that he knew, all that he was certain of, was that he had to pursue the mysterious course that had been laid before him to its end, whatever the outcome or personal cost.

Speak pure, and you will not fail.

He was aware that his choice would serve only to confirm the others' suspicions about him—that he really was their Kinsman Redeemer. And even though he knew he was not and could never be that sort of man, he didn't care what they believed anymore. It was enough that he knew what he really was—a miserable fool who'd fallen through the cracks of common life into a world that mistook him for someone that mattered.

The truth of it was that most of his life had been built on lies—and the majority of those were ones he told himself. But somewhere between the Facing and Aybel's all-too-calm rejection of his heart, the last vestiges of that pretense had at last fallen away.

Now there was only the hollowness and that irritating bit of hope lodged like an abrasive grain of sand within the crevice of his heart. It had been planted there by that crazy dream in the Worded forest. Only he knew that it was not a dream. And that was why he could not let it go.

He had to know whether the hope he had was real. . .and if it might be strong enough to rescue his life from pointlessness.

It wasn't long before the camp was set, and someone had started a fire with Words, and everyone sat peacefully gnawing on sticks of dried meat, watching the bluish flame dance around a mound of grass without consuming it. Gideon hadn't seen that particular trick before, but he made no comment about it. It almost made sense, actually. Ajel had once told him the blue fire of life didn't consume living things, but only the death within them. So that would explain why the grass was not being consumed. But, then, how could the fire burn at all unless the grasses themselves were somehow tainted with death?

Gideon placed his mat out on the ground next to the ruins, then took an open spot before the fire between Ajel and Revel. Revel passed him a portion of dried meat and one of the applelike fruits they'd brought along with them, which Gideon received with a nod of gratitude. He ate in silence for awhile, glad for once that the Remnant didn't like talking during their meals.

After some time had passed and the meal was mostly eaten, Ajel finally broke the silence. "As Paladin has mentioned, sojourner, we head tomorrow for the Wall," he said. "If it is not your intent to join our quest, I think it would be best for you to leave from Noble Heart on the morrow. There are soundens to the south of us where you can find provisions and lay whatever plans you may have for the remainder of your sojourn."

Gideon stared into the fire, chewing idly on one end of the meat as Ajel spoke. When he had finished, Gideon casually replied,

"I'm going with you."

Kair looked up from the fire, her eyes glaring garishly at Gideon through the blue flame. He grinned back at her.

"I am surprised to hear it," Paladin said cautiously, "though certainly pleased."

"I too am startled, I confess," added Ajel. "Tell me, sojourner, why have you decided this?"

Gideon glanced at Revel, wondering whether he had told them yet about the dream. But the golden-eyed man only grinned in that mischievous way of his, revealing nothing, and took another bite of meat. Shaking his head, Gideon finally said, "It would take too long to explain."

"You know we will face great danger," said Ajel. "And you do not have the Words."

"I know," said Gideon.

"He has his staff," offered Kair, all of a sudden sounding oddly kind, "and the robe."

"Ah, yes, the robe, the robe," Paladin mused. "If your heart is truly set on joining us, then we will need to get you other garments. That robe will never do in Phallenar."

"Nope," said Gideon flatly. "The robe stays."

Paladin chuckled a little nervously. "You jest with me, sojourner," he said. "You stand out like a beacon on a hill at midnight wearing that."

"I'm not kidding," Gideon replied.

Now Paladin frowned. "Any soul in Phallenar who sees you dressed this way would think you a religious fanatic and report you to the Guardians. And as for the Guardians. . .well, I don't have to tell you how they will react."

Gideon shrugged lightly. "I guess I'll just be a fanatic, then."

"Paladin," Kair broke in, "if he wishes to keep the robe, then we must let him. Have you not said yourself that we must let the Redeemer choose his own course?"

"Yes, I have affirmed that," replied Paladin, clearly chagrined. "And I do not mean to tamper with it now. But any of us with history in Phallenar knows full well that to wear a robe like that within the city boundary would be seen as open defiance of the Council's rule. The common folk will not know what it means, perhaps. But the Guardians might, and the Council Lords certainly would. He would be slain on sight. And likely all of us with him."

"Still, he must choose his own path," repeated Kair. "Who are we to say whether his choice is unwise?"

Gideon had to admit it felt peculiar to have Kair, of all people, defending his position. But he saw through her motives easily enough. She wanted him to wear the robe precisely because she wanted him to be killed. The realization was unnerving, to say the least. Still, for the moment anyway, her words served him.

"She's right," Gideon affirmed. "I must choose my own way."

"Are you wishing for your own death?" asked Paladin harshly.

But Gideon only smiled. "Oh no," he said. "I've moved way past that now."

All of a sudden, the fire in the center of the camp exploded with a violent deafening crack. What was blue flame turned instantly to white, then consumed the mound of grasses in less time than it took to blink. The faces all around fell into shadow as the bitter scent of burning ash permeated the air.

"Shields!" commanded Paladin from somewhere in the sudden dark. Gideon had barely enough time to grab his staff from the mat behind him before Ajel's hands, like vise grips, descended on his shoulders.

"Over the wall, quickly," he whispered. "Out of sight."

Gideon didn't need to be told twice. Whatever these "shields" were, he knew he didn't have one or couldn't create one with the Words, and so the wall seemed a natural second choice. He quickly scrambled over the granite barrier with staff in hand and dropped more or less noiselessly down the other side.

Just then, another crack split the air—as acrid and electric as any lightning bolt, but void of any distinguishable light. Gideon heard someone grunt, not so much in pain as in the strained effort of resistance.

"Who attacks us?" Paladin demanded, calling into the night. But he was answered with yet another bolt of blackness, cracking like a whip upon the ground beside him.

"*Adon'i'far celo abri*," Ajel called loudly from somewhere in the dark. In an instant, the black of night transformed to day as a sphere of silver light appeared above their heads. It had the look of a tiny sun, though far more pale and delicate. Still, it blanketed the region all around in a silver glow, enough to lure Gideon to hazard a peek over the wall.

The Wordhaveners had not moved an inch from their positions in the camp. They sat or crouched low to the ground, and around each of them twinkled a silver glassy sphere, barely noticeable at all but for the shimmering reflections of the tiny sun above. Not one of the Wordhaveners looked particularly afraid as they scanned the perimeter of the camp. There was a practiced sureness to their movements, a sudden cold and calculating determination in the aspect of their eyes. They looked so different from the peaceful travelers that had been seated next to him only moments before. Now they looked like soldiers, trained for battle and ready to kill. Or to die.

He knew what they were looking for. A face, a foot, the flurried movement of an arm—anything upon which they could focus and to which they could speak with Words. But there was nothing but a wall of grass and the showering of black bolts streaming out of unseen places in the sky.

A sudden rally of jagged jet black lines stabbed at the silver sun, and it quickly exploded in a hiss. Darkness shrouded the onslaught once more, as unseen bolts of death struck against the Remnant's shields like black vipers gone mad with rage. The Wordhaveners groaned under the strain of it, whispering frantically to themselves and to the shields that were their sole defense against the attack. In the midst of the barrage, Ajel somehow managed to speak again the Words to light the sky. But not long after the tiny sun appeared, it was quickly lashed to nothingness by a second flurry of black lightning.

While there was light, however, Gideon noticed something interesting. The rain of bolts that struck the camp was not hurled randomly, but with precision, assailing each of the Wordhaveners in turn. Gideon had learned a thing or two about the limitations of *Sa'lei* during his captivity with Fayerna and Bentel. He knew that, like *Dei'lo*, the Words of *Sa'lei* could not function without a focus—a line of sight between the speaker and the object spoken to. Given the circumstances, that could only mean that their attackers must be somewhere within view, shrouded in the grass, of course, but close enough to target their victims. And if they were close enough to see, then they were close enough to be seen.

Another spread of bolts rained down, this time on Kair. Gideon knew this only because of the sudden scream that echoed from her position and the dull thudding sound of her limp body falling to the ground. A shuffling followed; and when Ajel once again created the sphere of light above them, Gideon saw that Kair lay crumpled next to Revel, with his shield now extending over the two of them like a fragile bubble. He couldn't tell if she was breathing.

While the light remained, Gideon took the opportunity to scan the wall of grass. His present height advantage afforded him a more extensive view of the surrounding plains. If he could pinpoint just one attacker's face, he could draw attention to it, perhaps allowing the others to aim their Words at some particular target.

In the last moment before the light was vanquished, Gideon saw it. A face, clearly contorted by madness and filled with more dark rage and hate than he had ever seen or believed possible within one man. But despite the disfigurement brought on by his insane fury, Gideon instantly knew who he was. And what he wanted.

An angry knot clenched in his stomach. With a rush of instinct, he gripped his staff with such ferocity that his knuckles turned immediately white. He felt its heat beneath his palms, felt it grow hotter as his own rage rose burning in his chest, mingled with an unexpected surge of fierce determination.

He thought of calling out to the others, but quickly realized it would do no good. They would never be able to see their attacker from where they sat, even in the brightest light. But the madman, standing as he was, could see them, which made them all-too-easy targets of his malevolent rage. Gideon had to think fast. He needed some way to draw the man into plain sight. Even if he could just get him to say something aloud, that might be enough for the others to pinpoint his position.

Suddenly, he heard himself yell into the darkness, "What do you want now, Benny? Haven't you had enough of me yet?" His words dripped with mocking sarcasm.

Immediately, the lightning ceased. A hush of quiet fell over the plains, leaving only the hollow melodies of breezes echoing in the distance. Gideon took a breath and wondered why he didn't feel afraid.

"C'mon, give it up, Benny boy," he yelled. "I'm not worth your trouble. You've got bigger problems to worry about, so I hear. Isn't that right, Benny?"

"You. . ." The malicious whisper resonated through the air from all directions, as though the wind itself were speaking to him. "You slew her. Now I will slay you." The words skittered through the dark like shadows, sending chills down Gideon's spine.

"Fayerna's not dead, Benny," Gideon lied. "I survived the fall, didn't I? And I don't even have the Words; you know that. Fayerna's much stronger than me. She's probably waiting for you right now at the campsite, wondering why you haven't shown up yet."

"Dead. . . ," the hollow whispers replied. "You will pay. . . ."

The rage in Gideon's breast grew hotter still, and, for the first time in his life, he found that he didn't fear it. Instead, he welcomed it, inviting its embrace like an old friend he thought he'd never see again. He felt the heat of its protection flood his bones, filling his heart with its strength, its boldness, its conviction to act. "I've already paid you all I'm gonna pay, Benny." His voice sounded hard and sure. "You had your time with me. And failed. Now make like a good little lord and go away."

"Where. . .are you. . . ?" The words hissed like snakes upon the breeze. "I will slay them. . .to find you. . . ."

Instantly, the earth beneath him began to rumble and quiver. Remembering the sound of thunder in the ground, Gideon instantly knew what was coming. But there was nothing he could do. A second later, a wave of liquid earth rolled through the camp, tossing bodies carelessly through the air like puppets. The swell of earth exploded with terrific force against the remnant wall; but much to Gideon's shock, the ancient barrier only shuddered a little under the impact and stood firm. The wave promptly toppled to a lifeless heap against it.

The Wordhaveners, however, didn't fare so well. Gideon could hear several of them, in random places all around, moaning or whispering frantically in distress. He wished that he could see more clearly to know how badly they were injured or whether they were strong enough to re-form their shields.

Frantically, he strained to hear Aybel's voice within their midst, but found no sign of her. He couldn't say if that was good news or bad. But the very fact that she was now in danger of her life *because of him* only served to fuel his rage. By sheer reflex, his thoughts jumped back to Lairn, lying in a bloody heap at his feet—all because he had been too afraid to do anything. . .or too afraid to believe he *could* do anything.

Well, I'm not afraid anymore, he told himself, realizing it was true. *And I won't let it happen again.*

"You have no issue with these people, Benny," he said coldly to the dark. "Leave them alone!"

A hissing filled the air, something like a mocking laugh, but far less human.

"I'm warning you, Benny!" Gideon said. *I won't let this happen again. Not like Lairn. Not to Aybel!*

"Die, die, die, die. . . ." A chorus of laughing whispers echoed spitefully around his ears.

Then, just as quickly, another barrage of black lightning bolts rained down upon the Wordhaveners from the dark canopy above. Gideon strained to identify the dark crumpled shapes of his companions under the storm. He watched as a few of the shadowy figures scrambled away from the blasts. But most of the dark bodies he could discern didn't move at all, but only lay motionless on the ground like helpless targets. He couldn't tell whether they were merely unconscious or already dead. Not that it mattered. If they didn't move soon, they were as good as dead anyway.

It was the thought that one of them might be Aybel that pressed him to the brink of rampage.

What had been mere fire in his breast now flamed to an inferno, searing white with passionate rage. And before he knew what he was saying, he screamed to Bentel through the night.

"Stop!"

The lightning instantly died away, leaving only the crinkly sound of burning grasses crackling in the unexpected stillness. The caustic fumes from Bentel's mad assault seared his eyes. But he didn't notice. His only thought, burning white and pure at the center of his fury, was this: *No more!*

Suddenly, another whisper came upon the wind. "What. . .did you do. . . ?"

But Gideon didn't pay it any heed. Instead, the fire in him yelled, "I will *not* let you hurt them, Bentel! You won't hurt anyone anymore. It stops here. And now."

". . .puny. . .nothing. . .a Word and you are gone. . ."

"Enough, Bentel." His voice was cold as ice and hard as granite. "It's time for you to see what you've become."

Blue flame descended from the sky, enveloping both Gideon and the staff in an aura of righteous fury. Far brighter than the sphere of Ajel's Words, it lifted Gideon silently into the air, shedding a blue and eerie light across the grasses of the plains. Through the piercing glare of that new sun, he saw Bentel—a small, blackened shell of what was once a man—and wondered why he ever feared him at all. The little man had long ago ceased to be alive in any way that mattered. All that remained of him was just a shadow, a play of the darkness to trick you into thinking he was real. But there was nothing substantial about him. And all it took was a pure, shining light to expose the truth for what it was.

In that blue ball of hovering fury, Gideon felt a whisper forming on his lips. With a gentleness that belied the passion coursing through his soul, he said simply, "Behold the Light."

A surge of blue fire screamed through his bones, then exploded toward Bentel in a shaft of blinding radiance. A moment later, the horrified shadow that called himself Lord Bentel Baratii was gone.

Gently, the sphere of blue flame floated Gideon to the ground. Then, just as quickly as it had appeared, the fire retreated back into the stars in a stream of brilliant blue. And it was gone.

The campsite and all the fields for miles around fell eerily silent under a blanket of stillness, as though the land itself had gone mute in shock from the power it had witnessed. Not even the wind blew anymore.

Like the land, Gideon too felt stunned. What had just happened to him? What had he just done? Was it real? Was it *him*?

Suddenly, a frail and pain-filled moan shook him from his bewilderment, shocking his heart into racing once again. *Aybel!*

Ignoring the numbness of his limbs, he leaped up onto the remnant wall and squinted worriedly down into the camp. "Aybel, where are you?"

No sooner did he speak the words, however, than a rush of black forms burst into the campsite from every direction. They each spoke something as they came, but he could not understand the Words. Instinctively, he vaulted back down off the wall to retrieve his staff, which he had inadvertently dropped when the blue fire left him.

The blow came out of nowhere, striking hard as stone against the back of his skull. In that instant, he crashed heavily to the ground, unconscious.

CHAPTER 50

THE PATH TO PHALLENAR

*The Barrier Wall of Phallenar, more properly known as The
Memorial Wall of Palor Wordwielder, stands today as perhaps
the most mysterious legacy of Palor's reign. Constructed over a
period of sixty years, it spans more than five leagues from end
to end and rises one thousand feet off the floor of the plains—
large enough to conceal all of Phallenar behind its ponderous
mass. Touted at the time as a grand symbol of Palor's benevolent
protection of the Inherited Lands, its true purpose was more
likely that of military defense. But defense against what?
That pivotal question remains unanswered—and, in the
final analysis, may be unanswerable. Whatever secret terror
compelled Palor to construct the Wall perished along with
him on the shores of the Delving Ocean. We may never
know the Wall's true intended purpose or name the
unseen foe it was designed to thwart.
It is ironic, then, that the Wall has in fact become the perfect
memorial to Palor Wordwielder, though not in the manner
he intended. For, like the Wall, Palor himself remains an
enigma to us, a jumbled confusion of genius and arrogance
whose true intentions may never be resolved. And ultimately,
in my opinion, he was just as much a waste of space.*

—THE KYRINTHAN JOURNALS, MUSINGS, CHAPTER 12, VERSES 120–125

"The High Lord will have your head, Muriel, I'd wager it," the voice
snapped hoarsely.

"What for? I got the rebel, did I not?" a woman's voice answered.

"You bludgeoned the fool with a stone! He is likely dead by now.
And so will you be, come the morrow."

"He was breathing well enough when I tossed him with the rest.

Just ask Raug if you doubt it."

"Why not simply use the Words? There'd be no question of his dying then!"

"There's no guarantee of that, Malcus, and you know it full well! In any case, I did what I did for good reason. You saw him slay the Council Lord, did you not? He is no ordinary man, that one. He wears the robes of the Old Lords and carries their power too. I could not be sure *Sa'lei* would work against him. Besides, the stone did the job just as well."

"For your head's sake, I hope so."

"You know full well it's your head you're worried about, Malcus. Not mine. But you need not trouble yourself. The Stormcaller is alive. And when you get your commendation, you'll have me to thank."

Gideon rolled his head away from the sounds of their voices and groaned. At that moment, he would have gladly relinquished the ability to hear just to have a few more hours of unconscious bliss. But the insistent clatter of the conversation pulled him unwillingly from his stupor. He was awake and none too happy at the fact.

His head positively throbbed. Without opening his eyes, he gingerly reached back to feel the spot where he'd been struck and winced upon finding the telltale swollen lump near the base of his skull. At least he felt no crust of blood, no broken skin, which he took as a good sign. Unfortunately, the discovery did nothing to diminish the roaring pain between his ears.

He lay there a few moments longer, listening to the world around him from behind his shuttered eyes, waiting in vain hope for his head to clear. Beyond the banal prattle of harsh and unfamiliar voices, he heard other more intimate sounds—the flowing, haunting melodies of the reeded grasses of the plains. But knowing he was still within the Plain of Dreams proved a small comfort. Something had gone horribly wrong the night before, and now—he realized with disgust—he was once again a prisoner. But of whom and for what purpose only the voices could tell.

When at last he summoned the courage to move, he twisted cautiously onto his side and slowly, painfully pushed himself into a seated position. It wasn't until then that he realized his head had been resting on Aybel's lap. She was sprawled haphazardly next to him, eyes closed, as still as death. But when he quickly held his hand up to her nose, he felt her breathing. It was light, but steady enough to calm the sudden shock of fear that shot through his chest. She was alive.

One glance around told him the rest of the Wordhaveners were all present, slumped against one another like so many sacks of grain, all unconscious. . .or possibly dead. *What happened?* he wondered. *Where are we?*

Then, for the first time, he noticed they were all floating in midair. Instantly, his heart sank like stone as he recognized his strange—and disturbingly familiar—surroundings.

They were sealed inside an oily, translucent globe, floating ten feet or so above the plains. It was the same creation that Bentel and Fayerna had used to shield themselves from the warcor's attack at Morguen. Only this one wasn't soundproof at all, as far as he could tell. He could still hear the fluttering wind-borne music dancing across the grasses. And there were those other voices, laughing together in a raucous and guttural manner that bored like drill bits into his temples.

It didn't take him long to find the source of all the banter. Beneath him, several feet beyond the edges of the sphere, he saw them—every one bearing swords and each wearing uniforms as black as midnight.

Guardians!

There were ten of them, some men and some women, cutting a straight path through the tall grasses of the plains while the sphere floated lazily in their midst. They were jostling with one another in the rough manner all soldiers do after a particularly successful mission and seemed unaware that Gideon was awake. In fact, they paid no heed to the sphere at all.

At the sight of the Guardians, a jolt of panic once again pierced Gideon's gut, causing him momentarily to forget the throbbing agony in his skull. Forcing back the rise of nauseous bile within his throat, he purposefully turned his attention to his fallen comrades and began the grim task of determining which of them aside from Aybel were still alive.

Despite the Guardians' seeming indifference to the sphere, Gideon stayed crouched on his hands and knees to avoid drawing their attention as he shuffled awkwardly over the motionless bodies of his companions. Beginning with Ajel, who was closest, he systematically checked each one for signs of breath and pulse and was relieved to find they were all alive. Beyond these passive indicators, however, they remained as motionless and unresponsive as corpses. In spite of considerable shaking and face slapping—as much as he dared, given how little he knew of their injuries—he couldn't rouse so much as a groan from even one of them. Eventually, he gave up and slumped heavily against the side of the sphere, exhausted from the effort and the resounding ache within his skull.

"Stormcaller! Looking for this?"

Gideon bolted upright in surprise, then just as quickly let out a painful moan as the sudden movement sent shockwaves through his head. After a moment, as the throbbing began to ease, he shifted his weight, slowly this time, to locate the source of the guttural voice that had startled him.

He found one of the Guardians standing beneath him in the grass, thrusting a gilded, wooden staff tauntingly into the sky. Gideon's staff.

But this wasn't just any Guardian. The man was absolutely huge! Easily as large in frame as Donovan on his best day and twice as muscled. His sleeveless black vest revealed glistening ebony arms the size of tree trunks, which rippled as he shook the staff like a helpless snake he meant to strangle. His mocking smile revealed a mouth full of white gleaming teeth, which stood in stark contrast to the midnight black of his shaven head and the even blacker emptiness of his whiteless eyes.

"If you want it back, why don't you come down here and get it?" The Guardian spat the words in a deep gravelly voice that was nearly as intimidating as his imposing size. Without waiting for Gideon's response, he laughed hoarsely at his own jest, and the other Guardians quickly fell into laughing with him. Clearly, Gideon wasn't the only one who felt intimidated by this mountain of a man.

"Where are you taking us?" Gideon demanded, trying not to sound as fearful as he felt.

But the brute seemed not to hear him, for he cupped his free hand behind his ear and leaned in mockingly. "What was that, Stormcaller? Speak up! I could not quite make it out."

"Where are you taking us?" Gideon repeated, this time yelling loud enough to reignite the throbbing between his ears.

The Guardian threw back his head and laughed. He laughed so heartily, in fact, that he hurled the staff to the ground and clutched his massive hands against his stomach. All the other Guardians laughed right along with him, trying very hard to match his fervor.

"Did you see?" the Guardian barked between guffaws. "The little Stormcaller is trying to speak to us!" He laughed some more, thoroughly entertained by the thought, though Gideon had no idea why he found such a simple question so amusing. He was still chuckling when he finally bent down to retrieve the staff from the ground. "He is not only captured," the Guardian added with an abundant smile. "He is stupid!"

More jeering laughter followed.

Now this is getting ridiculous, Gideon fumed.

Beast man or not, this guy was quickly wearing on Gideon's nerves. "What's so freakin' hilarious about asking where you're taking me?" he screamed, hurling the words at the Guardian like daggers through the barrier of the sphere. But the man only laughed again, even more heartily this time, if that were possible.

"How could one so slow of wit slay Lord Baratii with such ease?" the Guardian asked finally with a sarcastic grin. "Don't you realize that none of us can hear a word you speak? You're in a Stilling Sphere, rebel *idiot*. Scream all the Words you want. There will be none to feel their bite but you and those slumbering fools with you."

A Stilling Sphere?

Gideon frowned as he once again examined the translucent boundaries of their floating cell. It looked exactly like the sphere he'd been trapped in once before with Fayerna and Bentel. But that sphere allowed no sound beyond the boundary to penetrate within. *This* sphere must be the opposite of that one, he reasoned. He could hear everything beyond the barrier, but no one outside could hear him. An effective prison, he realized grimly, for anyone who fought with *Dei'lo*...or *Sa'lei*, for that matter.

"You'll have plenty of chances to be heard soon enough, rebel," the Guardian said, this time with no humor in his voice. "As you can see, we have reached the Wall, and my Lord Lysteria Asher-Baal will be very anxious to speak with you."

Gideon had been so intent on the Guardians, he hadn't even noticed it. But when he looked eastward, the sight of the Wall literally took his breath away.

To call it a Wall was like referring to Mount Everest as just another hill. It was colossal, monstrous in its dimensions, and altogether forbidding. It rose imperiously from the plains like some dark and imposing god, eager to crush any ignorant soul who strayed beneath its shadow. The brightness of the late afternoon sun beat down upon its mottled face, but the stony expanse seemed barely to notice, as though the foreboding force of its presence was mighty enough to deny even the sun from touching it.

Unbidden chills danced down Gideon's spine as he struggled to comprehend the size of the man-made obstruction that spread before him. Its length alone seemed immeasurable, stretching as far as the horizons both to the north and south. Its height was equally impressive, but could at least be estimated, especially by a geologist, who was used to gauging the dimensions of cliffs and other outcroppings by sight alone. After some quick mental figuring, Gideon reckoned the upper rim to be at least a thousand feet above the plains and possibly more. He could only imagine how thick the Wall must be to make it reasonably stable.

But stable it was, or seemingly so. Though it was clearly man-made—formed of dark granite blocks the size of houses—it resonated with permanence, as though it were an eternal thing, greater and more powerful than any mere mortal could create.

Its surface was far from featureless, despite the dross of gloom that seemed to coat it like a permanent shadow. There were massive balconies protruding from its skin, visible by the dozens upon even a single glance, dispersed along the Wall at various heights like baleful eyes leering ever westward across the plains toward the unseen mountains far away. And along the bottom, at ground level, there were doors—massive arched stone gateways that would rival those of even the most imposing fortress. There were far fewer of these than there were balconies, but still enough to give the impression of menacing teeth, which sank hungrily into the plains as though intent on consuming them.

It was an ominous sign of things to come, this Wall. For behind its monstrous blocks, he knew what was waiting for him. A dungeon full of ravenous rats anxious to tear out his flesh. And a woman in a purple gown who would make certain he would not die too quickly.

He took a deep breath and sighed in resignation to his fate. Or perhaps he should call it his destiny, though he failed to see what difference it would make. Either way, he was resolved. He would see this through to its end, whatever that end was. He had to. He had to learn the truth about himself, whatever the cost.

He sighed again, this time with a sarcastic smirk smeared across his face. *It's not as though you have much choice about it now anyway, Gideon,* he joked silently. *You've been captured, remember?*

He looked despondently toward Ajel, who somehow managed to appear graceful and at peace even slouched clumsily as he was against Revel's shoulder.

If only he were awake, Gideon thought wistfully, *he might know what to do.*

A guttural bark from below jolted Gideon from his reverie. Turning toward the sound, he saw that they had already arrived at one of the arched portals to the Wall, and the Guardians had taken to dashing purposefully about, attending to the various ponderous iron crossbeams and grates that guarded access to the heavy wooden doors. Far different from their earlier affability, the Guardians moved now like trained soldiers, as a single organism, under the iron-fisted direction of the hulkish black man, who still clutched Gideon's staff like some newfound symbol of his authority.

Gideon savored his last few moments of restful quiet, even as the Guardians quickly dispatched the last of the crossbeams and unlatched the final lock that separated him from the severe world that awaited him. This would be his final moment of undisturbed rest, and he knew it. Once he passed through those doors, all hell would break loose. Both for him and his companions. He looked across the sphere to where Aybel rested, it seemed, in blissful peace on a blanket of nothing but air. "Why did you have to come with us?" he whispered sadly. "Why you, of all people?"

Suddenly, Gideon heard a woman's bitter howl, followed by a flash of heat and light. He turned to see the big black Guardian crouched low to the ground, surrounded by a glistening smoky sphere, baring his teeth like a leopard preparing to pounce. Another burst of flame erupted and then two more in rapid succession.

One by one the Guardians vaporized before his eyes, consumed by white-hot flame to piles of ash before they could so much as flinch in pain. It happened so fast that Gideon couldn't tell where the attack was coming from. But the flames were clearly the work of *Sa'lei*, not *Dei'lo*. The bursts were too identical to the ones he'd witnessed in Songwill sounden—and the one he experienced intimately, when the little girl was burned to ash in Calmeron, even as she clung to his neck for protection.

Mere seconds passed, and it was over. Nine piles of gray ash dotted the ground where nine of the Guardians had stood just moments before. Only their leader remained, still protected within his spherical shield and smiling broadly like a man crazed with the lust for blood. Abruptly, he scanned the perimeter for any further signs of life, then turned his soulless gaze toward Gideon, who flinched under the stare of those baneful, dead black orbs.

Then, in a flash, the shield around the Guardian disappeared, and he stalked toward Gideon menacingly, still clinging to the staff like a talisman that made him impossible to kill.

He stopped mere feet from Gideon's stoic face and stared into his eyes, as though considering which type of death he preferred to inflict. Then, in a perfectly deadpan voice, he said, "We must hurry. There is little time."

CHAPTER 51

WITHIN THE WALL

*Looking back, I am far from proud of what I did to Gideon
Dawning. In fact, nothing brings my heart more shame than
the memory of my misdeeds against him and many others on
the day of his arrival at the Wall. I was desperate, true, but I
cannot offer that as an excuse. All that I can say, all that I will
say, especially to my accusers, is this: You were right. It was my
arrogance, my selfish will to live, that in large part sparked the
fiery rain of death that fell upon the Remnant that day. And
you must know that the realization of that singular fact has
been more bitter to my soul than anyone can fathom. I have seen
the darkness of my heart. And all that I can hope for now—
the one thing to which I cling in my most desperate faith—
is the unreasonable hope that mercy triumphs over judgment.*

—THE KYRINTHAN JOURNALS, SONGS OF DELIVERANCE, STANZA 13, VERSES 5–9

Gideon's head whirled, and not just from the throbbing pain. "What
do you mean there's little time?" he said. "Are you saying I have little
time or that we have little time?"

The distinction seemed a critical one to Gideon, for obvious reasons. But there was no answer. The mammoth Guardian had already
turned away and was now walking determinedly toward the open portal of the Wall, dragging the sphere behind him by some Worded
means that Gideon couldn't discern.

Oh yeah, Gideon remembered suddenly, *he can't hear me,* slapping
himself on the forehead in frustration at his sluggish reasoning—and
immediately regretting it as spikes of pain once again ricocheted
through his skull.

Ah! Stupid! he yelled in silence at himself, pressing his palms against
his eyelids in an attempt to calm the storm he had aroused. Within a
few seconds, however, the mental hurricane began to fade, and he felt

stable enough to open his eyes again.

To his immense surprise, he found himself kneeling on real, hard earth, no longer floating ten feet above the ground. The Stilling Sphere was gone, and the Wordhaveners now lay dispersed randomly on the clearing behind him like so many discarded rag dolls. Before him, just a few feet away, stood the Guardian—all muscle and teeth and the smell of sweaty leather. If he looked imposing from above, he was absolutely terrifying from ground level.

"Get up, Stormcaller," he commanded. "Help me carry these sleepers inside. The longer we remain out here, the more likely you are to die today."

Gideon didn't need to be told twice. Truth was, this guy could have told him to stand on his head and sing "The Eyes of Texas" and he would've done it without so much as a blink. He wasn't the sort of man you said no to. Not without expecting to die.

He hopped to his feet, ignoring the rush of pain in his skull, and quickly strode over to Aybel and bent down to collect her in his arms. He rose and turned toward the Wall only to see the Guardian hefting Revel and Ajel at the same time, effortlessly tossing one over each shoulder. The big man disappeared inside the Wall, then reappeared a moment later, empty-handed.

Following his lead, Gideon carried Aybel through the impressive portal doors and entered an antechamber of dark, rough stone, dimly lit by two torches set in floor-mounted stands. Three large corridors shot out from the chamber, one in each direction of the compass except west, where the portal doors opened to the plains.

Gideon scanned the chamber for signs of where the Guardian had put Ajel and Revel, but he saw nothing except empty stone floors in every direction. Suddenly, from out of the hallway to the north two young men appeared, wearing tan canvas tunics with matching white undershirts and white sashes tied around both of their waists.

They were fresh-faced, about college-age from the looks of them, though Gideon doubted they'd ever seen a classroom. Despite their youth, they seemed careful to maintain the humble demeanor of servants, not ever letting their eyes meet Gideon's as they approached. Without a word, they bowed slightly toward him, then lifted Aybel right out of his arms, as if it was the most natural thing in the world anyone would do. Then, without so much as a nod, they turned and headed back into the shadowy corridor from which they had emerged.

"Wait," Gideon called after them, suddenly realizing what just happened. "Where are you taking her?"

"You will see soon enough, Stormcaller." The Guardian's voice positively boomed behind him, bouncing off the stony walls like thunder in a canyon. Gideon turned to see him holding Paladin and Kair—this time with one over the shoulder and the other under his arm. He wasn't grinning at all now and, in fact, seemed strikingly calm—a sharp contrast to the madman who had made fun of him on the plains.

The question is, which version is really him?

"What's your name?" asked Gideon finally.

The big man scowled at the question, but he answered, "I am Sovereign Raug al'Teth, Lord Brother of Edenhedge and sworn inheritor of the Stone Crown," he proclaimed, proudly sticking out his thickly muscled chest as he spoke and seeming unaware that he was still carrying two full-grown bodies in his arms. "I am of the Hinterlands," he continued. "Captured as *jalen* by the Council Lords when I traveled here many years ago as the emissary of my people. My strength belongs to Lord Lysteria now." His lips twisted slightly as he said her name. "But not my soul. That is still mine." He spat the last words bitterly.

Gideon drew in a nervous breath. "Well!" he said awkwardly. "Good. Good for you." He tried to force a smile and failed. "My name's Gideon. Gideon Dawning. Thanks for. . .um. . .not killing us."

"The day is not over, Stormcaller," Raug replied flatly.

Gideon nodded uncomfortably for a moment, unsure whether he should say anything more. But Raug just stood there, staring at him. So finally Gideon said, "Okay, point made. What now?"

Raug made a quick gesture with his chin. "Walk that way," he commanded.

So Gideon did. Right down the dark corridor where the other two men had taken Aybel. Raug followed close behind, the heavy footfalls of his boots pounding the stone floor with rhythmic thuds. There was little light, just the occasional freestanding torch. The farther they ventured down the cavelike hall, the more it stank of mold and rotting earth. But the floors were dry, for the most part. And there weren't any rats. Well, only a few.

After what seemed like a quarter mile or so, Raug grunted and used Kair's head to nudge Gideon toward a set of stairs to the right, which plunged quickly toward a sea of absolute blackness below. He had no wish to see where those stairs might lead, as thoughts of putrid dungeons filled his mind. But a nudge was a nudge, particularly when it came from a beast like Raug, and so with the slightest of shrugs, Gideon headed down the stairs, being careful to step slowly so he didn't slip on a patch of mold or wayward rat.

Please don't let there be more rats down there!

Down and down they went in total darkness. Perhaps they descended five flights, perhaps six—it was hard to tell as there was no light, and the stairs seemed to follow an irregular, almost irrational course. But when they'd reached a certain point, Raug grunted again, and Gideon felt another nudge against his back—*Paladin's feet this time?*—urging him to turn to his left.

Moving totally on faith or perhaps fear of Raug's wrath, he stepped in the direction Raug had indicated. Within a few seconds he found himself slamming heavily into a splintery door. At Raug's urging, he fumbled for the doorknob, which turned out to be some sort of iron handle, and yanked it downward with a loud clang. Once the latch was released, the weighty door swung open away from him on its own accord, although not without its rusting hinges issuing a loud complaint at the strain. Gideon was forced to blink as light spilled through the door into the dank hallway.

With a sigh of gratitude, he stepped back into the world of light— well, the world of torchlight at least—and into a square chamber about twenty feet across. His friends were all there, still out cold and sitting propped against the walls as though they'd all just settled in for a collective nap. The only difference was that every one of them was now bound and gagged with long strips of burlap strapped tightly across their mouths and binding their wrists behind their backs.

Raug followed him in, slamming shut the door behind him with his boot, then effortlessly plopped Paladin and Kair to the floor. In a flurry of movement that belied his size, he reached under his belt and whipped out two strips of burlap, which he promptly secured around each of their mouths. He didn't seem to be hurting them, exactly, but Gideon still found the rough procedure unsettling. It was as if the

Guardian didn't treat Paladin and Kair as people at all, but rather as a pair of pigs he was preparing to slaughter for the evening meal.

Suddenly, Gideon heard a shuffle behind him and spun to find a young woman standing next to one of the torch stands, quietly appraising him with her eyes as one might appraise a horse before placing a bet.

She wore a gown of deep green or perhaps black. . .it was difficult to tell in the flickering torchlight. But it was elegant and beautiful, as was she. Though barely five feet tall and unadorned with diamonds or crowns, she nevertheless carried the look of a princess, with a perfect round face and the most enchanting green eyes Gideon had ever seen. Her hair, the color of sunlight, was elegantly arranged in a sort of French twist around her head. She held her delicate hands lightly clasped beneath her bosom, as though they were designed to do nothing more than carry a bouquet of fresh flowers.

But there were no flowers in her hands at the moment. And if her beauty gave the impression of fragility, the stern expression on her face quickly convinced Gideon that she was far more resilient and determined than her appearance might suggest.

"Who are you?" Gideon asked, not sure if he sounded more awed or confused.

But it was Raug who answered. "You are addressing the honorable Underlord Kyrintha Asher-Baal, Stormcaller. See that your next words carry more respect." There was no mistaking the threat concealed in Raug's warning. And no doubting that the threat was genuine.

Gideon bowed slightly toward Kyrintha. "I'm sorry. I meant no disrespect. I'm just a bit confused about what's happening here."

Kyrintha stepped toward him, her movement as graceful and noble as that of any queen. "What is happening here, Stormcaller, is that I have rescued you and your companions from the hands of my parents. I have done so at great cost to myself, perhaps even the cost of my own life. I would think you would show more gratitude."

"Well. . .yes, of course. . ." Gideon fumbled. "I mean, I *am* grateful. Very grateful, actually. Um. . .thank you."

Kyrintha seemed unimpressed. "So you are the mighty Stormcaller." Arching an eyebrow, she sniffed disdainfully. "In truth, you do not look like much of a Redeemer to me, despite the robe of Lords you have donned."

"I am no Redeemer, ma'am."

"Though I must confess I've never seen such a peculiar head of hair before," she continued, ignoring his comment. "Is it truly black, Raug? I cannot tell in this dismal light."

"Yes, Underlord," the Guardian replied. "And though he is puny, he is more trouble than he appears. This past night I watched him slay Lord Bentel Baratii single-handedly with naught but a Word and that staff there."

She raised both eyebrows this time. "Is that so?" She turned and stepped momentarily into the shadows behind her, then returned with Gideon's staff, holding it cautiously in one hand away from her body, as if she feared it might turn into a snake at any moment and bite her. "With this?" she asked, eyeing it circumspectly.

"Yes, Underlord." Raug shifted his weight impatiently. "Underlord, begging your pardon, but there is little time. The Axis will soon realize that something is amiss, if they have not already."

Kyrintha continued to eye the staff circumspectly, pretending not to hear him. Then, with a sigh, she said, "Yes. You're right. Let's get to it, then." She glided to the wall and leaned the staff against it. "Awaken them," she commanded.

Raug jumped into action. Moving with the quick precision of a seasoned soldier, he marched from body to body, grasping each head in turn like a melon and barking some Word roughly in each ear. It seemed out of place to see a commanding figure like Raug stoop to such subservience, especially toward such a slight and fragile-looking woman as this underlord. Clearly, there was much more to her than met the eye.

Within a few brief moments, the task was done. And one by one, the Wordhaveners began to stir, albeit slowly.

"As I understand it, the *Sa'lei* Word of sleep brings no true rest to the body. Is that so?" the underlord asked.

"That is true, m'lady," Raug replied. "They will be as weary as if they had not slept at all these past two days."

The underlord clicked her tongue in annoyance. "Well," she sighed. "I suppose we'll have to do something about that. We can't have them too weak to fight."

"To fight?" asked Gideon. "Fight who?"

"*Whom*," corrected Kyrintha with annoyance. "Fight *whom.*

443

Hopefully, no one. But it is a dim hope at best. I assume you cannot offer them some Word of *Dei'lo* to bring them strength, can you?"

"Um. . .no," Gideon replied, for some reason a little embarrassed at the admission. "I don't know any *Dei'lo*."

"I had heard as much," she quipped. "I suppose we'll have to risk removing the gag from one of them." She scanned the Wordhaveners' faces as though contemplating which one looked the least threatening or defiant. Most of them, however, had as yet barely summoned the strength to open their eyes, much less attain anything close to a menacing glare. After a moment, however, she pointed abruptly toward one of them and said, "That one."

It was Kair. Raug immediately strode over to her and, in a careless movement, whipped the gag off of her mouth, causing her head to whiplash painfully against the wall. The underlord frowned briefly at the Guardian, but said nothing.

Instead, she turned her attention to Kair. "Before you speak, you should know that Raug here is *mon'jalen*. If any unseemly Word comes out of your mouth, he has orders to slay you on the spot—and all of your companions as well. It would behoove you, then, to choose your words carefully."

Kair said nothing, but only stared suspiciously—not at the underlord—but at Gideon.

Why is she glaring at me? I'm not the one holding her captive!

Suddenly, his eyes widened in shock as he perceived what she was thinking. Incredulously, he blurted, "C'mon, Kair, you don't actually think I'm in cahoots with these people?"

But she only stared at him all the more accusingly.

"Get up," commanded Kyrintha, ignoring the exchange. "Use your Words to heal your comrades. We have little time."

Kair sat there, considering for a moment, then slowly rose to her feet to comply with the underlord's request. Gideon could tell that she herself was in considerable pain, though she did her best to conceal it.

"And don't touch the bindings," Kyrintha added as an afterthought.

Despite her own impaired condition, Kair made short work of the task, whispering the Word of healing in each ear in turn. Gideon never had figured out why the Wordhaveners tended to whisper the Words rather than speak them aloud. Perhaps it was simply to keep their enemies from knowing how much *Dei'lo* they actually knew. *Or perhaps*, he thought, *how little.*

In less than a minute, the job was done, and Kair returned to her spot and slumped heavily against the wall again, quickly closing her eyes and whispering quietly to herself.

"Stop it! What are you speaking?" demanded Kyrintha.

Kair paused and opened her eyes tiredly. "I am merely healing myself, Lord. Your henchman was somewhat less than gentle."

Raug grunted angrily, but the underlord held up a hand to silence him. "We don't have time for gentleness, woman. By now the news of your escape has reached the Axis. It won't be long before the entire length of the Wall will be crawling with Guardians. If you are to survive at all, we must act quickly."

Kair eyed her suspiciously. "You are not a Lord, are you?"

"No. But that is hardly. . ."

"And yet this *mon'jalen* serves you," continued Kair. "How can this be, if you are not corded?"

"Enough questions," snapped Kyrintha. "I will explain everything—to all of you." Her eyes danced across all their faces as if to make certain they were all fully awake and paying attention. "But you must be quiet."

"Okay," Gideon interjected, with more than a little suspicion of his own. "We're listening."

The underlord smoothed the ruffles in her gown briefly before she spoke. "My name is Kyrintha Asher-Baal," she said, "daughter of High Lord Balaam and Lord Lysteria Asher-Baal and the sole true heir to the High Lord's seat on the Council. But I have no desire for the title. My reasons for this are my own, and I will not explain them further to you, so do not waste my time by asking. All you need to know is that I would rather die than embrace the title of Lord.

"I know you have to come to Phallenar in search of the Book of *Dei'lo.*" She paused a moment, waiting for the revelation to sink in. Once she was satisfied, she continued. "Do not be alarmed. The Axis remains quite ignorant of your quest. I gleaned your secret entirely through means of my own—means of which my parents know nothing.

"I have stolen you from my father's hand and brought you here to offer you a proposition. I will help you get the Book you seek. In exchange, you will take me with you back to Wordhaven." Her words didn't sound much like a proposition at all to Gideon. More like a command.

Kair glanced at Paladin, who could only look back at her somberly, then she said, "And if we refuse?"

"Then Raug will go immediately to the Council and tell them that your Redeemer here accomplished your escape at the portal to the Wall. He will report that the Stormcaller slew all the Guardians with the power of his staff, save Raug himself, and that, after a difficult and harrowing pursuit, Raug finally managed to subdue you all here in the bowels of the Wall and has you tied up and gagged like helpless kittens in this very chamber."

"You may not know *Sa'lei*, Underlord, but your heart is clearly full of corruption." Kair spat the words with disgust.

Surprisingly, the underlord smiled. "How you judge my heart is irrelevant. That is the offer. You may either take it or refuse it. But decide quickly."

"Underlord," Raug broke in. "Lord Lysteria has summoned all of her *jalen* to the Wall."

"Are you summoned as well?" she asked quickly.

"No, m'lady," he replied. "I think she believes me slain."

"You are corded to Lord Lysteria!" exclaimed Kair accusingly. "Surely we now can see your offer is nothing but a trap!"

Gideon looked perplexed. "What do you mean by corded?" he asked Kair.

"He is a prisoner of *Sa'lei*," she snapped, "sworn to obey his Lord's slightest whim."

Raug shifted his great bulk menacingly toward Kair. "That she can compel my obedience, that much is true. But she has no sway over my thoughts or what I know to be true."

"But you are *mon'jalen*," Kair shot back, spitting the words like venom. "You speak the language of death! What do you know of truth?"

Raug stepped ominously closer, his eyes radiating black fury. "Donovan Blade was once as I am and worse. Is that what you say to him as well?"

"Stop it! Both of you!" commanded Kyrintha. "We don't have time for this. I need your answer now."

"We'll do it," Gideon blurted before Kair had a chance to respond. "You help us get the Book, and we'll take you with us."

"No!" yelled Kair. "You have no right to speak for us, sojourner. Only Paladin can say what we will do."

"We don't have a choice, Kair!" Gideon replied. "It's our only option."

"I will not be a pawn in your betrayal," she said coldly.

"Fine!" Gideon yelled. "Have it your way." He stormed angrily toward Paladin, who merely looked up at him with an almost eerie calm. "What do you say, Paladin?" Gideon asked. "Do you agree to her terms?"

Almost without hesitation, he nodded slowly—first to Gideon and then to Kyrintha.

"There!" Gideon said angrily, looking at Kyrintha. "You saw it. We agree. Now, take off their gags."

Kyrintha eyed Gideon a moment, suspicion clouding her gorgeous green eyes. Finally, she waved her hand idly toward the *mon'jalen* and said, "Do as he says."

Suddenly, the chamber door burst open and in rushed a gray-haired man garbed in Guardian black, his face awash in panic. At his heels came another man, even older, with long tangled locks of abundant gray hair flying wildly around his face. The second was not dressed as a Guardian, however, but wore a shiny brown hooded frock that covered his form from neck to toe.

"M'lady," the older Guardian exclaimed, "*jalen* have entered your chambers. They know you are missing, and they are now headed this way in search of you."

"I hope you have not led them to me, Laytren," she said heatedly.

The Guardian looked as if she'd just speared him in the chest. "By the Words, I would not do such a thing, m'lady."

"We managed to slip away before they could find us, Underlord," explained the other man. "But it will not be long before they come here on their own accord. You and your new friends here must be off—quickly!"

"I would not yet call them my friends, Mentor Spriggs," she quipped. "But I think we do at least have an agreement."

"Indeed, Underlord. We do." The voice was Paladin's. And when Gideon turned to see him, he was already standing. His hands, now unbound, were folded neatly at his waist. And his face exuded a strange mixture of serene calm and unbending determination.

Gideon breathed an audible sigh of relief. The rest of the Word-haveners—Ajel, Aybel, Revel, and, of course, Kair—were all standing too, and each had an expression similar to Paladin's own. Whatever doubts or suspicions they may have carried about the veracity of Kyrintha's offer seemed washed away by Paladin's singular nod of acquiescence.

"Underlord, if you'll permit me, I have an idea of how we may proceed," said Paladin stoically.

"A moment, please. . .Paladin," she replied, holding a single finger in the air to emphasize the command. She then turned quickly back to the two older men. "Laytren, you will go immediately to my mother in the Axis and tell her that I have escaped my chambers and that I was spotted fleeing the city through the north gate. Tell her I am traveling under the guise of a Roamer merchant and that you believe I have found shelter within one of their bands on its way to Morguen sounden. You will demand permission to lead the charge for my recapture." She swung her finger toward him and shook it forcefully. "You must be very angry, Laytren, or she will certainly not believe you."

"Anger I can manage, m'lady. What with those cursed *jalen* defiling your chambers, I'm angry enough to tear the head off a slanther as it is."

"Good," she replied satisfactorily. "Use that. And you, Mentor Spriggs. Get word to my network about everything that is happening. Ask them to create whatever diversions they can to keep the Guardians from us. . .and the Council Lords as well. Do you understand what I am asking?"

"Yes, Underlord," the Mentor replied, a look of sadness on his face. "I'm afraid that I do."

"Then go, now!" she commanded. "And do not worry for my safety. I will keep Raug here to protect me."

The two men immediately bowed and, without so much as glancing toward anyone, dashed out of the chamber as quickly as they had come.

"Now, Paladin," Kyrintha continued, turning gracefully to face him. "What is this great plan of yours?"

Paladin nodded slightly, then asked, "Underlord, what hour of the day is it?"

"It is a few hours past dusk, I suppose. . . ."

"Good, then," said Paladin. "We will have darkness as our ally." He took a casual step toward the underlord, and Raug immediately tensed.

"It's all right, Raug," Kyrintha said calmly. "We have now thrown our fates together. There is no turning back now for either of us. Paladin knows that as well as I."

"As you say, m'lady," Raug replied obediently, returning to a more relaxed stance—but he still kept a wary eye focused on the Remnant leader.

At that, Paladin calmly raised his hand to summon everyone's attention; the chamber fell instantly silent as all eyes riveted on his face. It was as though the man had just stepped into the room for the first time, as his carriage and demeanor assumed a wholly different and more authoritative bearing from that of a few moments before. As if by a single decisive thought, he had stepped once again into himself and was at once every inch the wise and seasoned leader of the Remnant—a man who was all too familiar with fighting against the odds.

"Despite the change in our circumstances, I believe we can still follow the plan as Ajel and I laid it out before we left Wordhaven."

"Wait a minute," Gideon interrupted. "What plan? I didn't hear about any plan."

"There was no need to tell you of it, sojourner, until we knew with certainty that you would join us," explained Paladin calmly. "And by then, obviously, there was no time."

Gideon frowned. He didn't like being kept in the dark, even if the reasons for it were perfectly logical. "Okay, then, so what's the plan?"

"We will form two groups," Paladin continued. "One will delve into the tunnels to retrieve the Book, while the other travels over ground through the city to the Sea Folk Wharf to make a way for our escape. We have some friends among the Sea Folk. We will need to find them and book secret passage from the city north toward Silence Sound.

"As I am more familiar with the city than any of you, save the Underlord, of course, I will lead the group that will head for the wharf. Kair, you will accompany me. And Underlord, if it please you, I think it would be best if you would travel with me as well."

"I would have suggested the same," agreed Kyrintha. "I have had some practice at traversing the city unnoticed. But what of Raug? He can see to our protection if we are discovered."

Paladin shook his head gently. "Stealth will be our greatest asset in the city streets. A *mon'jalen*, especially one of such. . .considerable proportions, would be difficult to conceal. Besides, I do not believe his protection will be needed. The Lords will have their attention diverted elsewhere."

"The other group," Kyrintha offered, almost as a question.

Paladin nodded. "Ajel has studied the tunnels extensively. He knows the way to the chamber where the Book is held. The rest of you will accompany him. But you must be watchful and alert. The tunnels are dangerous. In all likelihood, the Lords have set many Worded traps and wards along the route. These will be difficult to discern, though perhaps the *mon'jalen* can be of some help in that."

The Guardian nodded cautiously.

Paladin continued. "Once Balaam and Lysteria realize that we are no longer in the Wall, they will naturally assume that you have all escaped into the tunnels. You will be pursued. But the advantage will still be yours, for the Lords have no reason to suspect that you will know where you are going. They will have no reason to believe the Book is in danger of discovery, as deeply hidden as it is. Not until you retrieve it will they realize what has happened."

Gideon held up a hand to interrupt. "Paladin, I've seen the cave where the Book is kept. There's only one way in and one way out. If we're being pursued, how will we get out of there? Not all of us can use the Words to transport back to Wordhaven, you know."

"Using the Words to transport out is not an option, sojourner, for any of us," replied Paladin. "The boundaries of Phallenar are sealed against certain Words, both of *Dei'lo* and *Sa'lei*. It is impossible to transport by Word either in or out of the city. We must carry the Book beyond the northern confines of the Wall. Only then can we transport it home."

"I did not know that," said Kyrintha, clearly amazed that she could have been ignorant of so important a fact.

"Not far from the entrance to the chamber is another tunnel," continued Paladin, "one that leads to the alcazars of the Axis. Ajel will show you the way. It is a minor tunnel, rarely used by the *jalen*. Ajel believes you will encounter little resistance along its route. Once you reach the alcazar, you will make your way to the docks, where we will be waiting for you. By the Giver's help, we will be out of the city well before dawn."

A moment of silence followed Paladin's words. Then Kyrintha said, "I agree to your plan, Paladin. And in so doing, I place myself in your hands."

Paladin nodded, offering the underlord the faintest of smiles.

"And when this is over," she added, "I shall be interested to hear more of the secrets my parents have neglected to share with me."

"Just so," agreed Paladin, his expression somber. "When this is over."

"We must move now, m'lady!" boomed Raug suddenly. "The *jalen* approach!"

"Where are they now?" asked Kyrintha in a tone much calmer than his.

"I cannot be certain," said Raug. "Perhaps four levels above us now. They are descending."

"How does he know that?" Gideon asked quietly, nudging Revel lightly with his elbow.

Revel only looked at him quizzically, as if the question might have been a joke. Finally, he said, under his breath, "You should retrieve your staff now, *Lord* Gideon. You may need it." He smiled mischievously.

For once, Gideon didn't react foully to being called "Lord." He *was* wearing the robes, after all, by his own choice. He could hardly blame someone else slapping on him the title that went with it. Besides, Revel was right about him needing the staff. Gideon didn't have the Words and was—at *best*—merely competent in basic self-defense. His only real weapon was the staff, if he could call it a weapon at all. And as for the mysterious power that had enveloped him on the plains. . .well, he couldn't depend on that happening again anytime soon. Ajel had said that the staff had no ability of its own, that the power really came through Gideon himself. But the distinction hardly seemed significant. Either way, he had no idea how to make it work.

"The hour is upon us, kinsmen," said Paladin. "May the Giver grant us favor in our quest."

"Spoken true," the Wordhaveners echoed in unison. The next few seconds were filled with quick hugs and white-knuckled handshakes, and Gideon took the opportunity to collect his staff, which still leaned against the wall on the far side of the chamber. No one noticed this except Raug, whose eyes immediately locked on Gideon in a particularly threatening glower. Thankfully, though, he didn't move to interfere.

A moment later, Ajel distracted Gideon from Raug's fierce stare with a warm and gentle hand on his shoulder. "It is time, sojourner," he said quietly.

"Let's do it," Gideon quickly replied, flashing Raug a quick defiant grin. The big man didn't even blink.

Paladin was already at the door, with Kair and the underlord at his heels. Pausing only briefly, he turned and said, "We will see you at the docks." With that, they vanished into the darkness of the musty hall.

"The entrance to the tunnels is not far from here," said Ajel, looking to Raug. "You know it?" Raug nodded. "That is where our journey begins."

Ajel glanced at all the faces in the chamber, then let his eyes linger briefly on Gideon. "Follow close," he added, then gracefully turned and strode out the door. Gideon followed with the rest, close at Ajel's heels, stepping from the torchlight of the chamber into the dismal blackness of the hall. And Gideon couldn't help but wonder where and when the rats would come.

CHAPTER 52

BENEATH THE WALL

"Jeo pur'theron atmiron rundi."

Ajel whispered the Words furtively into the darkness, his hand resting lightly but firmly on Gideon's shoulder. A fist-sized orb of light coalesced before them, floated idly in the corridor, casting the wet stony walls in an eerie bluish hue.

"Thanks," Gideon said dryly.

He was just about to ask Ajel how he knew where the heck he was going in the black soup of this subterranean maze beneath the Wall and was relieved that he didn't have to bother. Apparently the great Ajel did have *some* limitations after all, he mused smugly—absolute darkness being one of them. Of course, the fact that Gideon himself couldn't even see the nose on his face seemed beside the point.

He couldn't say the same for Raug, however, who had barreled on ahead of the group as soon as they cleared the chamber door into the corridor. Half-muttering something to Ajel about securing the path to the mines, he disappeared into the darkness ahead as though there were no darkness at all.

He knows these passageways, that's all, Gideon told himself. *That's the only reason he's gone on ahead.* And he wanted to believe it. But his private reassurances were halfhearted at best.

Still, Ajel didn't seem distressed in the least by the hulkish Guardian's rapid exit, even when the pitch-black of the corridor all but paralyzed their own progress down the hall only a few dozen steps from the torch-lit chamber where they'd begun. Gideon held his tongue. . .but also gripped his staff a bit more tightly.

With the Word-conjured light, of course, came some clarity of their surroundings, though still not nearly as much as Gideon would have liked. What had been pitch-blackness now revealed a cramped passage of rough-hewn stonework and rotting wood beams, like something between a hallway and a subterranean sewer. Similar passageways shot off the hall at odd intervals, heading off to unknown regions.

Within a heartbeat Ajel was on the move again, confidently guiding the group ever deeper through the veinlike roots of the maze beneath the Wall. Just how deep below ground they actually were was anybody's guess. Maybe Ajel knew; he certainly seemed to, at least. But all Gideon could tell with certainty was that they were definitely headed *down*.

The farther they groped toward the ever-receding darkness ahead, the steeper their descent became. Coupled with the thickening layers of muddy slime beneath their feet and the almost insane twists and turns of the hallway itself, it wasn't long before Gideon began to question if they were still in a corridor at all, but had inadvertently managed to stumble into the mining tunnels without him noticing.

He never got the chance to ask the question, however. At that moment the monstrous form of Raug suddenly appeared before them, materializing out of the darkness ahead like an ominous demon standing guard over hell itself. The blue light of Ajel's orb glistened wetly on his flesh, giving the *mon'jalen*'s skin a purplish, inhuman aspect. What alarmed Gideon most, though, were his teeth, which glowed maniacally in the darkness like *Alice in Wonderland*'s Cheshire Cat. The lunatic smile was back.

"Is it safe?" asked Ajel with a calmness that made Gideon wonder if the Wordhavener had actually noticed the crazy man's beastly sneer.

The Guardian shrugged rapidly. "There were some Guardians watching the entrance to the mines," he rumbled, still grinning like a madman. "They are no longer a problem."

Ajel nodded matter-of-factly, as if the Guardian had just told him the walls were wet, then glided closer to the *mon'jalen*, with the orb tracking neatly beside him. "Then lead on," he said to Raug. "But once we enter the mines, you must allow me to take the lead. I alone know the way to the chamber we seek."

"Just so," the Guardian replied with a quick nod, then he whipped around and disappeared into the darkness once again.

"An interesting protector, would you not say?" asked Revel, whose face suddenly appeared next to Gideon.

Gideon shook his head sarcastically. "The man is insane, Revel," he whispered, then added, "that is, if you can call him a 'man' at all.

He's more like a Sasquatch."

Revel arched his hawkish eyebrows as if confused by Gideon's suggestion. He seemed about to ask a question but then merely shrugged instead and said, "He is not so different from how Donovan once was, in the beginning."

"Donovan? Like *that?*" Gideon asked incredulously. He snorted. "You've got to be kidding."

"No," Revel replied calmly. "The *mon'jalen* is torn, waging a war within himself between what he is and what he knows he should be. Attempting to break free of *Sa'lei*'s hold can force a man to madness. Donovan fell prey to insane violence many times before he finally mastered it."

Gideon shot him an alarming look. "Are you telling me this brute we're following really *is* insane?"

Revel returned the look with a grin. "Perhaps," he said. "But who better to unleash upon our enemies than a lunatic beast?"

"He doesn't *have* a leash, Revel," Gideon quipped. "That's what scares me."

"Be silent!" Ajel commanded, stopping dead in his tracks. Gideon stopped short, nearly sliding into Ajel's back before he could regain his footing on the mud-laden floor. "Aybel, what do you hear?" Ajel whispered over his shoulder.

Gideon glanced over his own shoulder to see Aybel standing as motionless as a statue behind them, her ears perked toward the ceiling as though expecting the stones to speak to her. After a moment, she whispered, "Footfalls. Perhaps seven men. . .descending on stairs."

"How near?" Ajel asked.

Another moment, and then, "I cannot tell. Perhaps a quarter league."

Ajel sighed lightly; Gideon couldn't tell whether it was from relief or worry. Then he said, "It is good that we are nearly to the mines. We must hurry. But move as quietly as you are able." With that, he turned and glided onward, as silent as a cat.

It was hard enough just to stay upright on the slippery downsloped walkway, much less do it quietly; but Gideon took the warning to heart and tried his best to keep his boots from slurping in the mud as he walked, while lifting the edges of his robe to better see his steps. Though it had been his choice to wear the Ancient Lords' garment, he still couldn't help but feel a bit like a woman in a dress at times—like now. His only comfort was in the knowledge that none of his companions nor anyone in this whole land as far as he knew would think it strange to see him "hike up his skirts" or "smooth out the folds of his gown." Even so, it felt ridiculous to do either, and he wasn't very good at it besides. The fringes of his white robes had already turned brown from the muck on the floor, despite his fumbling attempts to keep the fabric from brushing the ground.

Thankfully, he didn't have to hike up his skirts for long. Within a few minutes the group reached the entrance to the mines. Or at least Ajel identified it as such, though it was little more than a charred hole in the corridor wall—the consequence of certain explosive Words of *Sa'lei*, according to Revel, who also discouraged Gideon from touching the tunnel's rough-hewn walls, though he didn't say why.

Suddenly, Raug emerged from the mine entrance, a feat that seemed completely impossible even as Gideon watched it happen. The *mon'jalen* was easily as big around as the entrance to the caves—bigger, really—but he swept out of the opening with a fluidity of motion that belied his considerable bulk and managed to avoid so much as brushing against the dust clinging to the tunnel walls.

"The way is clear for the first quarter league," he reported stoically. "Beyond that, I cannot say."

"I am grateful, Raug, for your help," Ajel told him. "I can see clearly that your heart is true."

Raug stiffened at Ajel's comment at first, but then slowly relaxed into a smug and surprisingly sane-looking grin.

Maybe he's only half-crazy, Gideon quipped to himself as he watched the black man. *I just hope the sane part is the one in charge.*

Ajel turned toward the others, the blue orb spinning with him like his own personal moon. "Once we enter, you must remain behind me at all times. The way is Worded in places, though we cannot know precisely how. Raug, you will follow close behind me and use what skills you have to aid me in detecting and countering whatever wards are set against us. Revel, you and the sojourner will follow behind Raug." He paused only briefly, then added, "Remember your charge, brother." Gideon saw Revel nod quickly in response.

What charge? Gideon wondered. But he suspected he already knew. *Protect the Redeemer.*

He grimaced at the thought, fighting off the sudden feeling that he was nothing but a liability on this quest—a weak and ignorant "civilian" who had to be protected because he was helpless to protect himself. Only that wasn't true, was it? He had proved otherwise in the Plain of Dreams, hadn't he?

I protected them *against Benny that night*, he thought indignantly, but then bit his lip hesitantly. *If only I knew how I did it.*

"Aybel, as always, will stand as rear guard," Ajel went on. "We are being tracked by Guardians, possibly *mon'jalen*. And there may be more on the path ahead. So be wary. The Giver be with us."

With a swirl of his cloak, Ajel stepped through the opening into the mines, his blue orb following close behind. The rest of them moved toward the opening obediently—first Raug, then Gideon, Revel, and Aybel—in the order Ajel had prescribed. A moment before reaching the shaft, however, Gideon accidentally stepped in a particularly thick mound of mud, which immediately cemented its hold on his boot like a basin of sticky black tar. Hiking up his robes even more than usual, he alternately jostled and tugged on the boot for several anxious seconds in an attempt to free it from its viscous prison, but it was no use. He had about decided he'd have to go on without his boots, when Raug abruptly turned and reached down, engulfing Gideon's ankle within his massive hands, and gave the boot a quick yank. With a loud slurpy moan, the boot popped free of the mass, knocking Gideon severely off balance in the process. He would've fallen if not for his staff, which he instinctively jammed against the rocky wall for stability.

Raug released his leg as quickly as he had grabbed it and, of all things, chuckled when he saw the thick layer of tar still clinging to Gideon's boot. As if the whole episode wasn't embarrassing enough!

"Curse the Guardians," Raug rumbled with a mischievous grin. "Even dead, they will not leave you be."

Gideon quickly examined the tarlike coating on his boot more closely, then looked again at the black pile of muck that had trapped him. There were six other mounds just like it, he observed, dotting the area surrounding the entrance to the mines.

Gideon swallowed and stared at his boot. "I stepped in a *Guardian?*"

he asked, cringing at the thought. Raug didn't answer, but only sauntered noiselessly into the mines. Gideon swallowed again and shook his head. "I stepped in a Guardian," he repeated cynically, this time to no one in particular. "That figures."

Without another word, he followed Raug into the mines, with Revel and Aybel close at his heels.

"Stay close," Ajel whispered from ahead, his blue orb of light casting ghostly shadows across his determined face. "And be silent!" He almost sounded angry this time.

Gideon opened his mouth to protest, but then thought better of it. He needed to focus on the task at hand and stop worrying over whether he was an asset or a liability to the quest. Paladin had asked him to come along, hadn't he? He glanced down at the silken sphere emblazoned across his chest and breathed heavily. Besides, he had his own reasons for being here, he reminded himself, reasons that no one else could fully understand. Not Paladin. Not even Ajel. He couldn't turn back now. He had already passed well beyond the point of no return.

Hardening his face into a scowl, he gripped his staff determinedly in both hands and set his gaze squarely on the bluish light ahead. Whatever he had once been to the Remnant, he would *make* himself an asset for them now. That was all there was to it. He would not let his doubts get the best of him—he could not now, with so many depending on him. Instead, he would use his anxiety, channel it, remold it into rage, and hurl it at anyone or anything that tried to hurt him or his companions, especially. . .

Surreptitiously, he glanced over his shoulder. Several feet back, Aybel's gaze quickly shifted to meet his, her expression curious, and he reflexively looked away. He could not deny the feelings that rose like fire in his chest whenever he looked at her any more than he could pretend that she shared them. Not exactly, anyway. Not in a way that mattered. Perhaps, if he could prove himself to her somehow, earn her respect, then maybe. . . His thoughts ambled off, and he shook his head in frustration.

Focus, Dawning! He chided himself irritably. *This is no time for daydreams about a romance that will never happen. She's made that abundantly clear.*

Banishing the useless train of thought, he forced himself to focus again on the narrow path ahead. The tunnels were not unlike the corridors of the Wall, though there were some distinct differences. They were smaller, for one thing—barely wide enough for two men to stand abreast—so long as one of the men wasn't Raug, that is. The stone was different too. Gray rather than black, and chalky. Calcium carbonate most likely, he reasoned. Probably an old reef deposit, not that it mattered. Absently, he tugged at one of the smaller rocky masses jutting out of the wall. It broke off easily in his hand and crumbled to the tunnel floor.

"Silent!" cautioned Ajel again, casting a warning glance over his shoulder. But it was too late. The tunnel walls began to moan as though crying in sudden anguish; and before Gideon could so much as gasp, Revel was already upon him, engulfing the sojourner with his body like a shield. In that same instant, Raug flung a massive fist against the tunnel wall, hissing a litany of unnatural-sounding Words at the chalky stone through angry clenched teeth. The ground rumbled angrily back, then there was a sound something like thunder, and Gideon suddenly realized the tunnel was collapsing around them.

In less than a second, the air was choked with blinding dust. Gideon instinctively buried his face in the sleeve of his robe to keep from gagging. The thunder echoed for a few seconds longer, and then it was over.

The passage fell silent as a tomb. And when the dust had finally cleared, Gideon could see that was exactly what the narrow channel had become.

A tomb.

CHAPTER 53

THE STREETS OF PHALLENAR

Kyrintha crouched as best she could beside the shadowed curtains of the sedan chair, squinting down the cobbled street for some sign of Paladin.

If she'd been thinking, she would've selected a different dress for this escapade, but it was obviously too late for that now. The skirts were ample enough for running, if the need should come, but the bodice was entirely too restrictive to permit anything approaching an effective crouch. It was all she could do just to stoop without utterly gasping for air.

She clucked her tongue irritably at the oversight and, in a larger sense, at her own rash decision to go along with Paladin's plan in the first place. *She* was the captor in this scenario, after all. She was the one who had been laying plans for years—not *him*—plotting and preparing her every step toward freedom with such meticulous caution and forethought. And yet, despite all this, she now found herself skulking through the back alleys of Phallenar at this forsaken hour of night— quite the opposite of her desires. If she had her way, she and the rebels would already be long gone—westward, into the Plains, and far away from the Wall.

And yet she had no one to blame but herself. She had assented to Paladin's authority as meekly as a schoolgirl. Just like that. It was completely unlike her, and she definitely did not like the worrisome sensation it lodged in her stomach.

She kept her agitation well hidden from Kair, naturally, who knelt beside her silently in the shadows, looking far more comfortable and at ease than was reasonable under the circumstances. The woman was almost as small and fragile-looking as Kyrintha herself, but the under-lord was hardly fooled by that. There was a fire in the rebel's gray-blue eyes that was every bit as obvious as her abundant red curls. Whether it was the fire of passion or hatred, Kyrintha didn't know. But the impact of it was formidable all the same. It made her wary.

The fact that the woman hardly spoke didn't help things either. She hadn't breathed a single word to Kyrintha since they left the holding cell within the Wall. And when Paladin finally appeared from around a distant corner up ahead and waved for them to follow, the redhead only thumped her roughly on the back before dashing silently down the path to join him.

Swallowing irritably, Kyrintha followed, her skirts whisking noisily against her legs as she half-ran down the cobblestone path behind the red-haired rebel. When the time was right, she would have words with this Paladin. She didn't mind the danger inherent in their quest—she had faced worse several times since her imprisonment. But there was something that prickled her thoughts like a splinter wedged under her skin. Something about this plan of theirs.

The strategy had seemed sensible enough when Paladin presented it to her in the Wall. But now, here in the foreboding streets of Phallenar, the whole idea seemed grossly optimistic. How could they really expect to sneak all the way across the city undetected—what with the scores of vigils that patrolled the byways each night?

She had traveled the streets at night many times since her imprisonment, of course. But she had never attempted to traverse the full width of the capital. They were certain to be discovered. . .unless they were very, *very* fortunate. Regrettably, she didn't feel particularly lucky this night. If anything, she felt a foreboding sense of dread.

Kyrintha gave her head a quick shake to banish the troubling sensation. This was no time to let her misgivings take hold of her—and it was far too late for second-guessing the plan anyway. If there were problems, she'd just deal with them as best she could when the time came—the same way she always had. She just hoped there'd be time to deal with these particular problems before they killed them all.

Paladin smiled down at her when she reached the corner where he was waiting. Well, she thought it was a smile—it was somewhat difficult to distinguish one expression from another in the moonless night. But she smiled back in any case, as much to reassure herself as anything.

Because of the dark, they had thus far managed to advance well into the city without so much as an alleycat noticing their presence. But that advantage quickly dissipated once they reached Palorsfall Road, the main artery connecting the Barrier Wall with the Axis Tower.

The roadway was lined on both sides with stately glowood pillars, permanently gilded in water and glass so they glowed continually year round. The expansive street was swimming in their golden light, from the corner where the threesome stood all the way to the Axis Tower in the distance. The effect was made all the more dramatic by the many gold, silver, and crystalline monuments that graced the center of the road at nearly every intersection along the way. In the daytime, they were startlingly impressive works of art. But at night under the light of the glowood pillars, they took on an ethereal life of their own. Even the memorial depicting Palor's Fall, for which the street was named, had more than once brought tears to Kyrintha's eyes when she gazed down upon its entrancing beauty from the Wall at night. And she *hated* the man.

Kyrintha didn't have to tell Paladin that it was folly for them to travel openly on this road. The presence of the glowood pillars made that obvious. But what was not so obvious and what troubled her far more was the absence of something that they should have seen along this route, but didn't. She looked into Paladin's eyes and realized he'd noticed the omission as well.

"Vigils," he whispered hoarsely, his eyes sharp with consternation. "Where are the vigils?"

Kyrintha shrugged uncertainly. The vigils were Guardian sentries who patrolled the streets of Phallenar throughout the night. Usually traveling in teams of two or three, it was their charge to keep the peace, which in the Council's interpretation meant arresting any citizen who roamed the streets past midnight. The vigils worked every single night of the year; there were no exceptions. At least, Kyrintha had never heard of one, and she was in a position to know, having worked so diligently over the past three years to learn their patterns so as to avoid them any time she herself stole into the city after dark.

And yet on this night there were none. Not one, on the entire length of Palorsfall Road.

"Could your Mentor Spriggs have done this?" whispered Paladin quickly.

Kyrintha shook her head worriedly. "No. My network might create distractions for us, nothing more."

"Then we must tread all the more cautiously," warned Paladin. "Something is not right."

Following Paladin's lead, the threesome fell back into the shadows away from the lighted road and began a meandering course through the darker gutters and alleyways toward the east. It was difficult to see much of anything as they plodded along. Kyrintha was occasionally too late in discovering a filthy pool of used water or, worse, a fly-ridden pile of discarded food and animal parts. After only a few unlucky slips, however, she learned to use her nose as well as her eyes to guide her steps, and so avoided the worst.

Despite the unseen hazards of the alleyways, it wasn't long before the Wall no longer towered behind them like a dark curtain of night, and the Axis loomed over their heads like a menacing spear stabbing into the heavens.

The Axis was a marvel of architecture; everyone said so. But Kyrintha had never liked it. Its glistening white ramparts reminded her of bleached bones, and the pointed bronze tower thrusting out of its center looked like the weapon used to slay whatever beast it once was. Still, it did hold a certain beauty at night, especially with the glowood-lined waterfalls that poured rather gracefully down its sides. It was as if the beast, though dead, still bled its golden blood, flowing down to feed the verdant gardens that ringed the Axis perimeter.

There was still no sign of vigils anywhere, but they gave the Axis a wide berth all the same, traveling far around it to the south before heading eastward once again, toward the Sea Folk Cliffs.

The absence of the vigils worried Kyrintha deeply. The only plausible explanation she could think of was that they had been called away on some emergency. But the only emergency urgent enough to require them all would be an invasion of the city itself. Or, perhaps, a clandestine attempt to steal the Book of *Dei'lo* from its secret chamber deep underground.

She shuddered at the thought. If the other Wordhaveners had been discovered, then it wouldn't be long before she and her companions would be exposed as well. If they were captured now, any hope of escaping this Giver-forsaken city would be lost forever. And, she knew, that would not even be the worst of it.

The gutter ways and alleys seemed endless after awhile, and

Kyrintha began to worry whether Paladin actually knew where he was going. It'd been a long time since he'd lived in the city, after all. Things had changed considerably in the years since he roamed its streets. The way he rambled back and forth through the byways—so haphazardly, it seemed—only served to confirm her worst doubts.

She was just about to suggest that she take the lead from him when they rounded a corner and came upon the borders of Prisidium Square. The sight of it shocked her. She was certain they were somewhere farther west, near the Bankers Row, perhaps. Sniffing the air in consternation, she paused to smooth the folds in her soiled gown and silently chided herself for not paying closer attention to their route. Still, if Paladin's circuitous path had managed to make her feel disoriented, perhaps it would have the same effect on their pursuers—if there were any.

Having now regained her bearings, she saw that they were nearly to their destination. Prisidium Square was nestled in the northeast corner of the city. Their goal—the stairways to the docks—lay just beyond it to the east.

Unlike Palorsfall Road, the Square was sparsely lit at night, with only four freestanding torches arrayed around its center. Even so, they huddled close to the borders of the Square, hugging the shadows of the buildings that lined its perimeter as they made their way to the eastern side.

It wasn't until they almost reached the Square's far edge that Kyrintha heard a familiar grating voice call to her from the dim shadows of the torchlight. At first, she thought it was just her frenzied nerves playing tricks on her imagination. But when at last she turned to look, she saw the unmistakable silhouette of her mother's regal form—like a nightmare in the waking world, strolling idly toward her.

"Why, daughter," Lysteria laughed stiffly, "what a surprise to find you here."

CHAPTER 54

BENEATH PHALLENAR

"You are. . .well, sojourner?" rasped Revel hoarsely between coughs.

Gideon was coughing too. They all were.

"Yeah," he rasped finally. His voice sounded rough, like sandpaper. As gently as he could, he pushed Revel off of him and turned to look behind him. "Aybel, you all right?"

"I am unharmed," she answered. He couldn't see her in the dust, but her voice sounded shaky.

"Thank the Giver," said Ajel quietly. His voice too carried a nervous edge. "Raug, I presume we have you to thank for our survival."

Raug grunted roughly in response. Or perhaps it was more of a snort. Then he said, "This cursed stone is Worded. I did not perceive it until it was too late. I countered the effect, but I do not think my Words will hold for long."

"Then we must move on quickly and for more reason than the stones," Ajel replied. "The sound of the collapse has no doubt revealed our location to the *jalen*. They will not be long in coming. Aybel, see if you can discern how much stone lies between our pursuers and us. We need a sense of how large a barrier there may be. The rest of you, help me clear away the stones ahead."

"There isn't time for that," Raug barked. "The walls will not hold that long." Abruptly, he grabbed onto Ajel's leather tunic and jerked him unceremoniously away from the wall of stones ahead. "Stay back there," he said. "I will clear the way."

Ajel raised his hand to protest, but Raug had already turned away. Focusing on the fallen stones ahead, he began to rumble coarse phrases in *Sa'lei* under his breath. The Words sounded unnatural and twisted, sputtering bitterly off the *mon'jalen's* tongue, as if he disliked the taste of them as much as Gideon did their sound.

Even so, the effect was immediate. A few of the larger boulders began to tremble violently, hissing and cracking under the strain of whatever power Raug's Words brought to bear. Fine fissures formed within the stones like spidery webs, cracking their surface like eggshells. And then, one after the other, they simply imploded, collapsing upon themselves like tiny black holes, until there was nothing left but a trace of black powder so fine as to be nearly invisible.

Once in the flow of the Words, Raug seemed oblivious to everything else. Like a bitter mantra, he chanted the *Sa'lei* phrase again and again, each time more feverish than the last. The rocks reacted with equal fervor, imploding more rapidly than at first, hissing their defiance even as they collapsed one by one into dust. The big man's face began to perspire even as the broad smile of insanity crept once again across his lips. If Gideon didn't know better, he would have thought the man caught up in ecstasy—a rapturous fervor of strain and delight. It had all the traits of a religious experience, Gideon noted worriedly. And more than a few signs of a stark raving lunatic.

With his focus riveted on the stones ahead, Raug didn't even flinch when the wall of rocks behind them began to quiver. By the time Gideon turned to see what was happening, the pile of stones to their rear had begun to shimmer with a menacing red glow.

"They are here!" exclaimed Aybel, leaping away from the barrier. "We must move now!"

Within seconds, the Remnant's would-be tomb grew oppressively hot. What was a red glow turned fiery yellow, and the stones seemed to waver as though veiled behind a curtain of water. Only there was no water here, save the sweat on Gideon's face, which now dripped heavily down his nose and forehead, stinging his eyes. Aybel pressed against Revel in an attempt to flee from the heat, forcing Revel in turn to lean into Gideon. But there was nowhere to go. Raug had blasted away more than a ton of fallen rock, but there was still no sign of a break to the tunnel ahead.

"Raug, you must work faster," Ajel commanded loudly, gripping the big man by the arm. But Raug seemed not to hear him at all. Gideon doubted it would have mattered if he had. The *mon'jalen* was already spitting out *Sa'lei* at a feverish pace. Gideon doubted he could speak any faster without sprouting another mouth.

"It burns! It burns me!" Aybel shrieked, madly hurling her body against Revel and Gideon to get away from the rocks, which now glowed as bright as any lava Gideon had seen. She bore the brunt of the heat, he realized despairingly. Revel was shielded somewhat from the blast by her body, and Gideon himself was more protected still.

Without thinking, he dislodged himself from between Revel and Ajel and flung his body like a blanket over Aybel, tossing his hood over his head in the process. The robe might catch fire immediately so close to the heat, he realized, since it was made of cloth and not leather, like the others'. But it might also provide more insulation than leather could; and if it didn't catch fire, it might give them the extra time they needed.

At that same instant, Ajel shot his hand out toward the heat and spoke, his blue eyes intense and glowing with panic. Hot air swirled around them in response, and then a shield appeared, translucent and blue, between Gideon's back and the melting wall of stone. If it made any difference at all, however, Gideon couldn't tell. The radiant heat from the rocks still burned through his garments, searing the skin on his back and legs like a hundred hot irons.

"It opens!" Revel yelled. But Gideon wasn't sure which barrier he was referring to. Glancing up through his cowl, he saw the man's hawkish face staring back toward the molten wall, anger reflecting in the red heat of his eyes. Shifting his skin against the heat of the robe, Gideon risked a brief glance over his shoulder. There, in the center of the wall of melting stones, an opening had formed. It was no bigger than a fist, but it was growing, expanding, and through it emerged a spindly, clawed arm, swiping at the heated air as though blindly trying to locate its prey. It looked like a skeleton of some creature long dead. Only the skeleton was made of molten stone.

Just as the smell of burning cloth reached Gideon's nostrils, he heard Raug's deep voice growl up ahead. "It is enough," he told them. "Go now."

Forcing himself to turn away from the groping claw behind him, he looked toward the pile of stones ahead and breathed a quick sigh of relief as he saw a small opening in that wall as well. It was big enough for only one man to pass through, but it would do. Without hesitation, Ajel shoved the *mon'jalen* toward the opening. Raug, however, did not budge.

"You go," Raug said. "I will collapse the tunnel behind us."

Ajel nodded quickly and moved toward the opening, with the little blue orb tracking closely behind. He turned briefly to wave the others forward before he scrambled through.

As if I needed any encouragement, Gideon thought dryly.

Shoving Aybel and Revel forward, they quickly crawled into the opening one at a time, with Gideon following. Even before he could make it halfway through, however, he felt Raug's beefy hand latch onto his hindquarters. The shove that followed launched him clear of the hole and sent him sprawling face-first onto the hard tunnel floor beyond.

Gideon grunted as his chest thudded against the ground. Ignoring the sting of the impact, he flipped onto his back and glared angrily back toward the big man, who was just emerging—with some difficulty—from the opening.

"What was *that?*" Gideon demanded "Are you trying to kill me?"

"You are too slow," Raug grunted dismissively, fumbling awkwardly to his feet. Abruptly then, he knelt down and peered back through the opening. Light from the molten wall spilled over the *mon'jalen's* face. Even from this distance, Gideon could feel the heat radiating through the hole. The heat didn't seem to bother Raug, though. He just smiled—that crazy, maniacal smile—and barked some command in *Sa'lei.* As the sound of crumbling stone echoed through the walls, he whipped his head around and locked his eyes on Ajel. "We can go now," he told him. Then, looking down at Gideon, he added, "And do not touch the walls."

Keep your crazy hands off me and I'll think about it! Gideon thought bitterly. But once he scrambled to his feet, he was careful to stand well away from the tunnel walls.

"This way," Ajel commanded, a moment before launching once more toward the darkness ahead. Raug followed obediently, pausing only briefly to shoot a condescending smile at Gideon before stepping ahead. Gideon did his best to ignore the slight, quickly snatching his staff from the ground before plodding after the big man. Revel and Aybel said nothing, thankfully. Well, Revel grinned a little. But he was always doing that.

With the *jalen* close on their heels, Ajel picked up the pace considerably. He no longer stopped periodically to make sure everyone was all right. In fact, he never even turned around. He just kept going, half-trotting when the space allowed it and slowing to a quick march the rest of the time. Gideon followed determinedly, keeping his eyes focused on the glowing blue orb several feet ahead, watching as it darted left and right along the course of the tunnel or occasionally dashed through an opening in the wall, only to reveal another tunnel identical to the one in which they currently traveled.

If anything happens to Ajel down here, he thought grimly, *there's no way we'll ever find our way out of this maze.*

He kept his mouth shut, however, deciding it would be useless to voice such concerns at this point, and focused his attention on the tunnel walls, which he had avoided fastidiously since the cave-in, even after he saw Raug bump against the rocks several times. Nothing happened when *he* touched the walls, of course.

A few times weird things did happen, however. . .like the tunnel suddenly coming to a dead end or turning straight up toward the surface like an elevator shaft. But these were minor hindrances compared to what they'd already been through, and Ajel quickly dismissed them as illusions to be ignored and passed right through them as if they weren't even there, which, as it turned out, they weren't.

If anything, Gideon was worried that the way had become *too* easy—as if someone had purposefully removed the most dangerous wards so they could pass unhindered. But why would anyone do that—unless they were being lured into a trap?

He finally suggested as much, whispering his concerns to Revel, who had been hovering irritatingly close to him since their escape from the *jalen*.

"Good, sojourner," Revel whispered in reply. "I'm glad you see it is a trap. Ajel knows it as well, I assure you. But he also knows we must keep going, all the same. All we can do is be wary."

"Why is that, exactly?" Gideon whispered, sounding a little harsher than he intended.

"The way is blocked behind us," Revel replied quietly. "The only other exit is near the chamber where the Book is held. And so it seems we must go forward to see what trap the Council has laid for us. Besides, once you know a trap is there, it's not really a trap anymore, is it?"

Gideon didn't say anything to that, though he found Revel's logic dubious at best. Still, they *couldn't* turn around, that was sure. So he guessed Revel was right, after all. All they could do was be wary—and hope that they were able to sidestep whatever sort of snare the Council had set. . .before it killed them.

CHAPTER 55

PRISIDIUM SQUARE

"Mother! Wha. . ."

With a dexterity that seemed too fast to be human, Kair tumbled through the air from her position ten feet away and landed deftly in front of Kyrintha, blocking her from her mother's view. Instantly, a luminescent shield of blue sprang up around the two of them. From beneath her leather frock, Kair produced a small wooden rod and positioned it defensively before her, her gray-blue eyes riveted defiantly on the gray-haired matriarch of the Council Lords.

"This one is our captive, Council Lord," snapped Kair. "Perhaps you would like to negotiate for her release?"

Lysteria smiled condescendingly. "How impressive—all that jumping about. It's very intimidating. You must have practiced many months to perfect such a skill." She lifted an eyebrow mockingly. "And the sphere—very nice. I wonder, though, what class is it? *Ja'doul?*" She frowned skeptically for a moment, then said, "Don't know? Well, I suppose it won't matter in the end. I do wonder about that stick, however. Do you intend to swat me with it?"

"What are you doing here, Mother?" Kyrintha demanded angrily.

Lysteria seemed not to hear her, however. She'd turned her attention to the shadows behind them and was scanning them inquisitively. "Where is the other one?" she asked quietly, as though speaking to herself. Abruptly, she focused her gaze back on her daughter. "There were three of you," she sniffed. "The other one was a man."

"Do you want to barter for your daughter's release or not, Council?" Kair growled.

Lysteria's eyes shifted to the Wordhavener and laughed. "Barter? By the Words, my dear, no! What a droll notion. I can't imagine what you could possibly have to offer me in any case."

"I offer you her life!" Kair exclaimed.

Lysteria smiled again and this time looked directly into her daughter's eyes as she shook her head. "My, but you rebels are fools, aren't you?" She clucked her tongue in annoyance. "Let's stop this play acting, shall we, daughter? We all know you are not their captive. Quite the opposite in fact, as I understand it." She frowned slightly. "Now, let's see to your other companion."

Briefly, Lysteria turned her attention away from the two shielded women and scanned the region for signs of their missing comrade. Apparently, it was the opening Kair had been waiting for. With a flick of her wrist, she aimed her shortened staff directly at Lysteria's head and blurted out the Words at the top of her lungs—"*Jeo di'!*"

As though struck by lightning, the air around Lysteria blossomed into a cocoon of brilliant red fire. Streamers of red flame blasted out from the orb in a dozen different directions, momentarily blanketing the square in a hellish blood-soaked glow. A moment later, the reddish hue dissipated as quickly as it had appeared. The cocoon around Lysteria also vanished. She herself, however, was still standing. And she looked anything but pleased.

"Why are you trying to force me to kill you so quickly?" Lysteria snapped at Kair. "You are an impertinent fool. . .I dare say more of one than my own daughter. . .if that were possible," she added with a grimace.

Kair, however, didn't seem to notice the Council Lord's verbal tirade. In truth, she didn't seem to notice much of anything at all. Her eyes only stared blankly at the Council Lord. Her mouth hung limply open as though she had forgotten what she wanted to say. Finally, though, she muttered rather numbly, "You did not fall."

Lysteria waved her hand dismissively. "Not all shields are visible, my dear girl. None of the really important ones are."

Suddenly, Kyrintha stepped in front of Kair, who barely seemed to notice the switch. "Let her go, Mother," Kyrintha demanded. "She's useless to you. It's me you want, after all. Just leave her alone, and I won't resist."

"You *always* resist, my dear," her mother quipped. "I very much doubt you could choose any other way. And contrary to your contention, this rebel redhead is far from useless to me. I see a spark in her. Something. . .unexpected. She may prove very useful indeed."

Gathering her skirts, Kyrintha deliberately stepped through the protective sphere Kair had created and took a few brazen steps toward her mother. Outwardly, she projected an attitude of fury and arrogant defiance. Inwardly, however, she breathed a sigh of relief. Until she'd taken that first step through the shield, she'd had no idea whether she could pass through the Worded barrier at all, much less do so without inflicting considerable damage upon herself. For all she knew, Kair's Worded sphere might have flooded her body with an electric shock or burned hot blisters into her skin. She passed through the barrier unhindered, however, feeling only a slight tingly sensation wherever the bluish light of its surface grazed her skin.

With all the regality she could muster, Kyrintha ambled casually across the square—not exactly toward her mother, but not away from her either. Her intent was not to get away—there was little hope of that now—but rather to distract her mother's attention away from Kair so as to give the Wordhavener an opportunity to escape.

"That's the only way you can see people, isn't it, Mother?" she said indignantly. "As objects to be used for your selfish benefit. How you have managed to maintain such a myopic, small-minded perspective of the world for so many years is an implacable mystery that I think I shall never solve. You may bear the title of Lord, Mother, but there is nothing noble about you at all."

That got Lysteria's attention. With rage in her eyes, she swung her gaze fully on her estranged daughter, who had now managed to "stroll" at least twenty paces away from Kair. The Wordhavener, however, still seemed lost in shock at her failed use of *Dei'lo* against the Council Lord. She remained huddled within her protective sphere, utterly motionless and clearly too bewildered to realize that Kyrintha was providing her an opportunity to get away. The underlord couldn't help but grimace.

Well, she thought, *at least Paladin had the good sense to run.*

"How dare you speak to me that way!" Lysteria hissed under her breath. "You have been a thorn in my heart from the day I gave you breath. I tried to love you. I gave you all that you could want—and more! I had so much I wanted to share with you. So many treasures I wanted to give you—things I never got from *my* mother. But you would have none of it! Everything I laid before you, every jewel of wisdom I offered, you spat upon like filth. You rejected your own mother—your own mother!—in favor of a crazy old hag who didn't have the sense to tell a diamond from a dunghill. And she has made a dunghill out of you!"

That's it, Mother dear. Let it all out.

"Baree was three times the woman you'll ever be, Mother," Kyrintha retorted bitterly. "If you had listened to her instead of following your own greed, perhaps you might not have become such a perversion of nobility. You're a sad woman to behold, Mother. A prisoner of *Sa'lei*. And the saddest thing about it all is that you don't even realize you are in chains."

Lysteria gave out a hearty laugh, but there was no humor in her voice. "Me, a prisoner? And this from a wisp of a girl who's been locked away in the Tower of the Wall for the past three years! I am not the prisoner here, Kyrintha. You are clearly more delusional than I had believed."

"Walls don't make a prison, Mother," Kyrintha said coldly. "Even if you seal me in that Tower for the rest of my days, I will remain far more free than your vile heart has ever been."

In fury, Lysteria stomped her foot on the smooth, flat cobblestones of the plaza. The echo carried across the square like a hammer falling on a gavel. "I have had enough of your insolence, child," she growled darkly. "Your little game is over. Balaam and I will decide what to do with you once these rebels are in hand."

Kyrintha took a bold step forward. "You can't dismiss me that easily, Mother. Not anymore."

"Oh, but I can," Lysteria replied with a mocking grin. *"Demoi bracht!"* The blast from the Words knocked Kyrintha flat on her back—some twenty feet from where she had been standing. It felt like getting horse-kicked in the stomach—and Kyrintha had no doubt that the injury itself was equal to the sensation, if not worse. The stabbing throb within her gut made her want to curl up into a ball and cry, but she found she could not. Despite the spasms of wrenching pain, her legs wouldn't obey her command to bend. Frustrated, she willed her arms to push her body onto its side, but they only twitched a little in response to her command and then fell limp.

Oh well, she thought, resigned. *It's not so bad in this position, I suppose.* And, in fact, it wasn't. The cobblestones felt curiously soft against her back. Truth was, she barely felt them at all. And as for her head, well, it actually felt comfortable, strangely warm against the stone. And wet. . .definitely wet. . .

"Jeo carim venuta ris! Je' sharim ris!"

The Words came screaming through the night air toward Lysteria as fast as Kair herself, who was suddenly hurtling toward the Council Lord from twenty feet in the air, her feet aimed solidly at Lysteria's head. The blue light of the rebel's protective sphere crackled and sparked as she flew, matched only by the fire of mad fury glaring from her eyes.

The move took Lysteria somewhat by surprise. She'd assumed the rebel's spirit had been completely broken by the failure of her precious *Dei'lo*. Apparently, the girl had more courage than she let on. Luckily, the rebel's obnoxious Worded scream alerted Lysteria of the attack in plenty of time to invoke her own defensive shield against it. Kair's feet slammed harmlessly into a second, larger invisible sphere surrounding Lysteria, and she promptly dropped to the ground with an unceremonious thud.

"You are a tiresome little gnat, you know that?" Lysteria snarled. But Kair only glared up at her in contempt, silently cradling her foot in her hands. The blue light of her own defensive sphere still crackled angrily around her.

Surprisingly, however, Lysteria's expression suddenly softened. Her face took on an almost motherly aspect—soft and gentle and full of sweet compassion. The transformation was nearly profound enough to make Kair forget she was a Council Lord. She smiled down at the injured Wordhavener.

"You're terribly misunderstood, aren't you, dear?" she said soothingly. "Never quite belonged anywhere, yes? Not even with these. . . rebels." Her smile broadened even more, giving her skin the fragile appearance of crinkled paper. "Well, my dear, *I* understand. I do, truly. And I'd like to help you, if you'll let me."

Without warning, a blow plummeted down on Lysteria from above. The Council Lord crashed heavily to the ground, landing roughly face forward on her elbows. The shock of the blow sent her head bobbing in recoil and managed to dislodge the singular gold pin she used to contain her abundant gray hair within its tight bun. With the pin gone, her hair very nearly exploded from its bonds, cascading down around her face like a waterfall breaking through a dam.

"*Jeo pur'theron*," the masculine voice resounded across the plaza.

Once again, the invisible sphere around Lysteria erupted into existence as mighty arms of blue flame reached out from around to seize her. The sphere responded with serpentine flames of its own—fiery red and full of dark fury. As she struggled to her knees, tentacles of red and blue flame coiled around one another, each like a blazing python attempting to strangle its opponent. None of the flames reached the Council Lord's skin, however; and as she flung her wayward hair away from her eyes and looked up to find her attacker, she still managed a cynical smile.

A man stood before her—his own body encased within a sphere of bluish flame. He wore the brown leather garments of the Remnant, but that wasn't what immediately captured her notice. It was his face. It was a bit older than she had remembered. More weathered, perhaps, and harder. But she thought she recognized it all the same.

"Mentor Sky," she growled with contempt. "I had thought you were dead."

"Have your eyes grown so feeble, Lysteria?" Paladin replied mockingly. "Or is it just your memory that fails you? Mentor Sky *is* dead. It is his brother who speaks to you now."

Lysteria laughed derisively. "Oh yes, of course! The younger brother, trying to fill your elder's shoes." She looked him over dubiously, then shook her head in disappointment "You're not very good at it, though, are you? Now that you mention it, you don't look like half the man your brother was."

This time it was Paladin who smiled. "Perhaps not. Then again, I'm not the one on the ground, my lady."

Lysteria shook her head in annoyance—even as the red and blue flames continued to writhe around her in their strangled dance. Slowly she began to struggle to her feet—not an easy task, she realized, considering the bulkiness of her abundant silk skirts.

"If you do not wish to die today, I suggest you remain on the ground," Paladin advised. "I want only to collect my friends and be on my way."

She paid him no heed, however, and continued to gather her skirts around her. "You should have waited a little longer," she chided arrogantly, not even looking at him. "Another few moments, and my physical shield would have dissipated completely. I would be unconscious now. . .perhaps even dead. As it is, you only managed to scrape my arms. . .and make me angry."

"Jeo ventim ru!"

The *Dei'lo* scream came not from Paladin, but from Kair, who was still huddled in a semipanic on the ground next to the Council Lord. Still clutching at her injured leg, she made no attempt to move away even as the gale of wind she invoked exploded against the Council Lord's shield.

"Kair, no!" yelled Paladin, but it was too late. Lysteria had already turned toward the fallen Wordhavener, her face immediately twisted in fury.

"Damonoi' insetchin fearan ama ta'ine!"

From behind her own protective sphere, Lysteria spat the Words at Kair like venom from a snake. Instantly, the sphere surrounding Kair shifted from blue to red—and just as quickly melted into nothingness. Kair screamed in terror as the red flows of Lysteria's Words re-formed into spindly glowing strands that entwined themselves repeatedly around Kair's mouth and eyes. Within seconds, her screams had stopped, and she collapsed into a heap, whimpering.

A whisper spilled from Paladin's lips, and in a flash he rose into the air and disappeared—blue sphere and all. The useless wind that Kair had summoned quickly died away, while at the same time the last of the blue strands of flame that assailed Lysteria's shield were choked out of existence by her own red arms of fire. Their task complete, the dark red flames disappeared as well and, along with them, any visible sign of the protective sphere that encompassed the Council Lord. It was still present, however. Just as Paladin was, though for the moment, at least, she couldn't see him.

That fact hardly troubled her, of course. She knew he had not actually fled—he was too stupidly arrogant to be so sensible. And she could force him into the open any time she wished. Awkwardly, she stood to her feet.

Let him think he's hiding, she quipped to herself. *It will give me a chance to catch my breath.*

Idly brushing the dirt from her gown, she whispered quietly under her breath, summoning additional spheres to secure her own defenses. It had been foolish to let down her guard against physical attacks. Balaam would certainly rebuke her harshly for that—if she ever got around to telling him, anyway. But she wouldn't make the mistake again, in any case. With her new shields firmly in place, she would be safe from any further assaults. Even if this Paladin went so far as to hurl an entire building at her, she wouldn't incur so much as a scratch. Not that she believed he was capable of something so formidable, of course. But it never hurt to be too careful.

Brushing her hair away from her face, she calmly took in her surroundings. The rebel girl was still huddled at her feet, whimpering like a tortured rabbit. And several feet away, her daughter still lay sprawled out on her back, as still as death. She clucked her tongue in irritation.

I hope she doesn't die too quickly, she thought. *That would be more than she deserves.* She sighed. The girl always was disappointingly frail. Just like her grandmother.

She could fret over her daughter's condition later. There were more immediate concerns at hand. She glanced up toward the sky and blinked. "Trying to discern what to do next, are you?" she said. "Don't tell me you've exhausted all of your *Dei'lo* tricks already!"

"You will not succeed in the end, Lysteria." Paladin's voice resonated across the square—rising, it seemed, out of the stones themselves.

"I've already succeeded, you foolish man," she replied sharply. "And you have already failed. You think I came to Prisidium Square by accident? I think even you know better than that. And you must also realize that your friends beneath the city have also been revealed. My bondmate goes to meet them even now." She smiled smugly. "No, my dear *Paladin.* I do not think this night will go well for your ridiculous cause. Now come out of the shadows and show yourself. *Demoi uncuvrat shin ak aerat.*"

Waves of shimmering black billowed outward from Lysteria like the ripples on a pond. They radiated along the ground and upward toward the dark night air. As the waves reached a point about thirty feet up, the air in one section of the sky began to crackle and spark with lightning spears of brilliant blue. A few seconds later, Paladin's defensive sphere materialized, hovering in the air like a second, smaller moon. Floating within its center, Paladin stood, his eyes wide open in surprise and alarm. His hiding place revealed, he quickly whispered more *Dei'lo* to the air. Suddenly, there were two Paladins, floating side by side. Then three, then seven, then twenty, then fifty or more, all locked within their blue shining spheres and enveloping Lysteria on every side, joining together sphere to sphere, like a dome of bluish light.

Then, all of the Paladins spoke at once. "You cannot succeed, Lysteria. *Dei'lo* is the stronger Tongue. It has always been so."

"You show me tricks, Paladin," Lysteria sneered. "But I know power! If *Dei'lo* is as strong as you claim, why then was your precious Wordhaven abandoned so completely and all its Lords reduced to nothing more than dust-laden memories? Your archaic language lost its power centuries ago. And it is only your ridiculous faith that keeps you from realizing it."

The voices echoed in response. "You cannot destroy the Book, Council Lord. We know you cannot. What does that say of your 'power'?"

Lysteria shrugged noncommittally. "A trifle of semantics, nothing more. The Book's destruction calls for a particularly complicated phrasing of *Sa'lei*. Frankly, we haven't thought it worth the bother."

"For a Council Lord, you do not lie very well," the Paladins replied.

"I grow weary of this, rebel," Lysteria spoke into the air. "I'm afraid your attempt at intimidation has not done much to impress me."

The Paladins smiled. "It seems we are at a bit of an impasse, Council Lord. You can only use your Words on one of me at a time. The question is, which one is real? We could be here all night finding out. It's far too tedious a task for someone of your importance, don't you think? Hardly worth the trouble."

Lysteria shook her head. "For as little as you know of your own language, rebel, it seems you know even less of mine. *Damonoi sepracht cuerat ak quintavet!*"

As soon as the last Word of *Sa'lei* spilled from her lips, Lysteria lifted her head to the sky and screamed. It was a scream of agony and pain, filled with pure black malice. Paladin watched in horror as the scream turned visible, spewing from the Council Lord's mouth like a vile river of filth, unfathomably dark and full of hate. The river spilled into the air, swirling around the space beneath the dome of Paladin's spheres, and slowly began to coalesce into a series of human forms. One by one, the forms took shape, becoming solid—becoming *her*. Within seconds, the air under the dome was filled with duplicate Lysterias, one to match each of Paladin's creations. They floated through the space until each one faced a single *Dei'lo* sphere, and there it remained, staring into Paladin's faces, until the scream of agony finally faded into silence.

Lysteria—the *real* Lysteria, who still stood on the ground at the dome's center—wavered briefly from the exhaustive drain of the Words, but then comported herself and drew in a second breath. When she spoke again, the Words resounded in a chorus through the mouths of each of her creations.

"Damonoi saberk slicurat ak deraka!"

Crescent-shaped sabers dripping red flame appeared before each of the Lysterias in the air, hovering for one split second before slicing maliciously into the radiant blue light of Paladin's spheres. Fire and lightning erupted from the impact, filling the air with crackles of heat and putrid blue smoke. One by one the blue spheres winked out and, along with them, the illusionary duplicates Paladin had invoked. . .until only one human form remained, dangling tenuously ten feet above the ground.

Like a puppet whose strings were cut, Paladin collapsed to the cobbled ground with a muffled thud. His brown leathers, charred black from the heat of Lysteria's Word, radiated faint lines of smoke in the night. His face and hands were swollen, glistening wetly with blisters from the fire of the saber's blow. His shield was gone. He seemed hardly lucid as he fumbled awkwardly back and forth upon the cobblestones, as though trying in vain to shift his weight to some part of his body that was not burned.

Lysteria sniffed the air and frowned. There was nothing quite so vile as the smell of singed human flesh. She waved a hand in front of her face to disperse the stench. "Well," she said at last, "you hardly seem the grand warrior of the Remnant now, do you?"

Paladin coughed weakly. Through swollen, smoke-burned eyes, he searched for her; and when at last he found the place where she stood, he forced his head up higher and met her condescending gaze. Even in this broken state, he still managed to look defiant.

"I am not important," he gasped hoarsely. "The Words. . .the Pearl. . .are all that matters. Against them, you will not prevail."

"You idiot," Lysteria spat derisively. "Haven't you heard? The Pearl is dead. And so are you. *Damonoi blassht.*"

Red flames emerged on Paladin's skin, racing across his body like wildfire on the open plains. To Lysteria's alarm, however, he was not immediately consumed. Above the hissing sound of the flames, she could hear his anguished voice, crying into the air the somber tones of *Dei'lo*. How he found the strength to speak, she had no idea. Instinctively, she invoked a defensive shield, which flashed into existence around her.

But the Words he spoke were not for her, it seemed. Even as the flames danced along his skin, he fumbled to his knees and then miraculously rose slowly to his feet. He didn't look at her. In fact, he did not seem to care that she was present at all. But lifting his face to the night, his anguished cry rose up toward the stars.

"Jeo erit mein fuergan yin mein rey'demtoriam! Mein papatreim, mein papatreim!"

Raising his arms to the sky, he screamed his declaration to the night, even as burning skin and flesh hung dangling from his bones. He proclaimed the Words, even as melted garments fell like scales from his charred flesh. He maintained his cry until the fire finally consumed his lips and only teeth remained. Then, in a flash of red, all that was left of his body turned to dust.

Lysteria watched the gruesome spectacle in silence, aghast at the intractable defiance of the man she had just slain. She could not comprehend what she had witnessed, why the man—why *any* man— would war against the inevitability of a Word of Death. It was insane. *He* was insane. No other line of reasoning could make sense of it. There could be no other explanation.

Nevertheless, she stood there for a time, staring at Paladin's ashes as though it was a puzzle she needed to reason out. Eventually, though, her thoughts were distracted by the frail sounds of a woman weeping. Turning, her eyes fell once again upon Kair, who was still huddled on the ground, utterly blind and mute and tormented by the Words the Council Lord had spoken to bind her. She would not realize that her leader had been slain nor that her new comrade, Kyrintha, lay dying not thirty paces away. All Kair knew was her own hate—the very hate that Lysteria had sensed in her earlier. The hate Lysteria would now turn to her own advantage.

She glided toward the fallen rebel, then stopped short as she glimpsed her daughter's silent form lying on the stones beyond. For a moment, she considered walking over to see if Kyrintha still lived, but then quickly decided against it. By every right, she should no longer harbor even an ounce of affection for her rebel child. But for whatever reason, she could not stomach the thought of watching her die. It's just the nature of a mother's love, she supposed. She could not bring herself to hate her daughter completely, not even now, after such an obscene and bitter betrayal.

Let her die in peace, she told herself piously. *It is a better gift than she has ever given to me.*

Turning her attention back to Kair, she knelt beside the rebel's crumpled form and laid a bony hand upon her head. "Now, my dear," she cooed soothingly, "you and I have some matters to discuss."

CHAPTER 56

THE CHAMBER

Gideon crouched still as a statue and perked up his ears to listen. Nothing. *What are they doing up there?*

Just a few minutes before, Ajel had ordered everyone to stop while he and Raug went to investigate yet another anomaly up ahead. A minute later, the blue light of Ajel's floating orb silently winked out, and everything went black as pitch. Gideon had never been particularly claustrophobic—in fact, he rather enjoyed the few occasions when he'd gone spelunking as a part of his geology coursework at the university. But then, he'd never gone caving in Worded tunnels like these before— and never with a hoard of murderous *jalen* pursuing close at his heels. Under these circumstances, the inability to see his hand in front of his face was more than a little unnerving.

He could still sense Revel and Aybel's silent presence hovering somewhere to his rear. Or at least he thought he could. The darkness had a way of playing tricks on a guy's perceptions. But, if they *were* still there—and he hoped to God they were—neither one was making so much as a whisper of noise.

What if they've gone ahead to see what happened?

They were both certainly stealthy enough to sneak past Gideon without him knowing. In fact, they'd been silent as cats since the moment this harrowing trek began.

All of a sudden, Gideon felt the warm breath of a whisper next to his ear. "This is it, Gideon Dawning. The chamber is just ahead."

Gideon very nearly jumped out of his skin. Quickly, a hand came gently down on his shoulder. It was warm, with just enough firmness to hint at a strength that went beyond common. Immediately, Gideon relaxed. He'd recognize that touch anywhere.

"Ajel?" he whispered. But it wasn't really a question.

"Come," came Ajel's whispered reply. "And be ready."

Ready? Ready for what?

But it was too late for questions. In all likelihood, Ajel wouldn't know the answer anyway. All he knew, all any of them probably knew, was that there was a trap waiting for them somewhere ahead. Cynically, Gideon recalled his earlier conversation with Revel. *If you know there is a trap*, Revel had told him, *then it isn't really a trap anymore, is it?* Well, maybe. But at this moment, nothing sounded more untrue.

It's not a trap only *if you know how to beat it*, Gideon countered darkly. If they lived through this, he'd make a point of subjecting Revel to a much-needed lecture in critical thinking.

Gripping his staff firmly in both hands, Gideon inched his way forward, relying totally on memory to tell his feet which way to step. The *last* thing he wanted to do now was bump into the tunnel walls again and bring the stones crashing down on their heads. Or something worse.

He didn't hear Ajel again, nor any of the others, for that matter, and so he forced himself to assume that they were right there next to him, keeping pace with his painfully slow progress down the narrow passage. He didn't dare whisper to find out if it was really true, of course. If they *had* moved on, he certainly didn't want to know it. A fact like that might let his fear get the better of him and leave him too terrified to move at all. He couldn't afford to let that happen.

Thankfully, it wasn't long before a dim light appeared up ahead. It wasn't much, just the faint reflection of an unseen light source spilling through an opening some fifty paces away. But it was enough to reveal the fuzzy outlines of his fellow Wordhaveners and Raug. Especially Raug, actually, whose hulkish swaying form all but blocked the light from view with every ponderous step.

As it turned out, it was Raug who reached the opening first. Gideon watched as the *mon'jalen* carefully probed the space surrounding the rock-hewn aperture, checking, he assumed, for *Sa'lei* wards or other traps. Only when the big man was completely satisfied did he throw Ajel a weighty nod, then disappear through the stony portal. Ajel went in next, followed by Revel, then Aybel, and finally Gideon himself.

The chamber struck Gideon as something of a disappointment. He'd seen it once before, of course. . .well, in a way he had. Ajel had used the mystical powers of the Chamber of the Pearl at Wordhaven to show him this room. But that rather ethereal tour of the Book's chamber had seemed so dreamlike and, well, more than a little dreary.

Gideon had just naturally assumed that the real thing would somehow be more impressive.

But it wasn't. The chamber was about forty feet across and dome shaped. It had one door, which they had just used and which was really more like a rough hole than a proper door of any sort. The rest of the space—the floor, the walls, the domed ceiling—was just dust-covered gray stone, roughly cut as though whoever made this room was in a great hurry to get it done.

The chamber's sole distinguishing feature was a small stone table rising out of its center, about four feet high and as many feet across, and looking oddly out of place—like a piece of the room that the builders forgot to chip away. Gideon might have thought that was exactly what it was if not for the item that rested upon it.

The fabled Book of *Dei'lo*.

Or so Gideon assumed, since no one had actually said what the Book looked like. But from the looks on their faces, it seemed a pretty sure bet. Ajel, Aybel, Revel—they each stared at the thing like a legend come back to life. In many ways, he guessed that's really what it was. . .to them. To Gideon, however, it was just a book and not a very impressive one at that.

It was big, at least. Easily twice the size of the cumbersome Gutenberg Bible he'd seen in a museum a time or two. But there was no gold binding on its spine, no ornate lettering on its brown leather cover. In fact, there was nothing on the cover at all except the embossed image of a sphere resting atop an elaborately carved staff.

There was, however, a shaft of light pouring down upon it from above. What made that particularly interesting to Gideon was that the shaft lacked any identifiable source. When Gideon looked up, he saw only the chamber's domed ceiling. No torch, no spotlight. Just light, appearing out of nothing and cascading down on this one spot. On this *Book*.

Curiously, no one approached it. The team quietly spread out along the wall near the door, with their eyes riveted on the Book like it was a living thing—an extremely dangerous living thing. Ironically, this was especially true of Raug, who pressed his bulk against the stony wall as though trying to merge with it. It was the first time Gideon had actually seen fear on the *mon'jalen's* face. And more than just fear. What was it—pain? Guilt? He couldn't tell. But whatever it was, it had the monstrous man looking as sheepish as a schoolgirl.

As for Gideon, the Book evoked no such fear or apprehension. It was just a book, after all. But he had learned to pay attention to his companions' reactions to things, even when he didn't exactly understand them. So he kept his distance as well, contenting himself to wait for Ajel to make a move.

He didn't wait long. After gesturing for the others to stay put, the golden-haired Wordhavener moved toward the light, whispering to himself with each cautious step. He hadn't taken more than three steps when everything suddenly changed.

In the blink of an eye, five white-robed figures stood before them, lining the wall on the opposite side of the chamber. They held no weapons, but there was murder in their eyes. Horrible pitch-black eyes—like Donovan's and Raug's. Like Fayerna and Bentel. Like anyone who spoke *Sa'lei*. Gideon barely had time to notice that only three of the figures were men before the one in the center absently flicked a finger at his side and hurled Ajel backward through the air, slamming his body hard against the chamber wall. He landed with a heavy thud that sent a cloud of dust spiraling up from the rocky floor.

After that, everything seemed to happen at once. Blue crackling shields sprung to life around the Remnant even as Ajel jumped back to his feet. Just as quickly, the man whipped his icy gaze toward Gideon and began to chuckle. Seeing the danger, Revel dove toward Gideon to protect him from whatever was coming. But he was too late. Smiling, the man spat out something in *Sa'lei*, and Gideon had the sudden impression that he was falling—only he wasn't falling *down*; rather, he found himself falling *toward the man*, as though gravity had somehow been turned on its head, and he was now plummeting toward the wall behind the man who spoke.

He landed hard against the stone and felt the instant warmth of blood pouring down his forehead. The impact knocked the staff out of his hand, and it bounced woodenly against the rock before coming to rest against the wall a few feet away. He lay against the wall as well, flat on his stomach with arms outstretched, and immediately found that he couldn't move. His body felt as if it weighed a thousand pounds. It took all of his strength just to turn his head, and even then he couldn't see much of what was going on behind him.

What he could see, though, wasn't encouraging. Ribbons of fire erupted from the chests of the white-robed figures, slashing through the chamber like leather whips, flailing against the Wordhaveners' shields like fists of molten lava. The Remnant's shields sparked and sizzled under the blows; and in response, the Wordhaveners began to bounce around the room like players in a pinball machine, alternately flying and leaping from floor to wall in an attempt to outmaneuver the thrashing snakes of fire. Occasionally, Gideon could hear Ajel or Aybel or Revel screaming out something in *Dei'lo*, and one or two of the robed figures would stumble momentarily, as if slapped on the face, and their fiery strand would weaken. The effect didn't last long, however, and soon they would stand tall again, their flaming attack unbroken.

One of the five, however—the same one whose Word hurled Gideon against the wall—didn't participate in the fighting, nor did he pay it much attention. If anything, the whole exchange seemed to bore him. He was much more interested in Gideon himself. Turning his back to the battle, he focused his black-orbed eyes on Gideon's face and smiled—the way a zookeeper might smile at a rambunctious monkey who'd finally been recaptured after causing considerable mischief on the grounds.

"Who are you?" Gideon growled hoarsely. His words came out slurred under the pressure of the Words.

"High Lord Balaam Asher-Baal," Balaam replied smoothly. "The real question, however, is who are you?"

"No one that matters," came Gideon's strangled reply.

Balaam grinned amiably. "Your rebel friends seem to think otherwise," he said softly. "More to the point, so do I."

"Leave them alone!" Gideon spat, trying to sound threatening, and failing.

"I will," Balaam replied, "once they're dead."

The High Lord's last word was cut off by a blood-curdling scream. It was Aybel. Forcing his head to turn a few inches more, Gideon strained to see what had happened to her. Out of the corner of his eye, he saw her huddled against the wall, her hands upraised defensively before her face. Her shield was shattered, and she looked on the verge of total collapse.

Seeing the opportunity, one of the white-robed women—a Council Lord, Gideon now realized—stepped toward the fallen Wordhavener with her mouth agape, as though deciding which form of death she would inflict on the injured rebel. Before the Words formed on her tongue, however, Raug leaped in front of her, instantly encasing Aybel within the bounds of his own fiery red protective sphere.

A scowl of heightened rage, combined with the look of surprise, enveloped the Council Lord's face. Clearly, she didn't like having her art interrupted so flagrantly—especially not by some lowbred malefactious *jalen*. With a hiss that sounded far too much like a snake, Words spewed from her mouth—and millions of vermin like slimy black maggots materialized upon Raug's shield, instantly covering it so completely that both Raug and Aybel disappeared from view, replaced for a time by a squirming ball of poison-filled life.

For a moment it seemed the shield would hold, but soon the voracious worms began to take their grisly toll. Ill-shaped holes appeared along the surface of the writhing ball, bordered by threads of vivid red and sparks of fire. In mere seconds, Raug's sphere all but disintegrated, consumed by the insatiable mass that fed upon it. At the last moment, Gideon heard the big man's guttural yell from within the prurient mound, and what little remained of the sphere exploded outward in a flash—and along with it, the charred remains of the abomination evoked by the Council Lord's Words.

It was enough to draw Balaam's attention—and not only his. The rest of the Council Lords took notice as well and turned their full focus on the rebellious *mon'jalen*. If their faces had been angry before, they were mad with fury now. To be defied by common rebels was odious enough, it seemed, but for a fully trained and trusted *mon'jalen* to turn on his masters—that was an abhorrence that could not be endured.

Aybel, still barely conscious, huddled weakly on the ground behind Raug's feet. But she was not the target this time. Words echoed through the chamber, and lightning, black as midnight, burst out from the Council Lord's chest—and into Raug's. There was no shield to protect him this time, and without it, he erupted in black flames. He was dead long before the lightning bolts released their hold. . .long before his black, putrid remains fell like sticks of charred wood to the chamber floor.

During the frenzied onslaught, Ajel had somehow managed to

pull Aybel clear. Or at least it seemed so, though Gideon could barely turn his head enough to see. A moment later, however, he caught sight of her again, crumpled in a ball on the ground by Ajel's side. Revel was there as well, the three of them now encased in a single and seemingly more formidable protective sphere—though why the sphere seemed stronger, Gideon could not exactly say.

Quite suddenly, the battle ceased. The room fell silent but for the lingering hisses and pops from Raug's lifeless form, which still smoked darkly from the blast. In all of this, the Book remained untouched and seemingly untouchable. Even the foul smoke, which now filled the chamber, did not dare trespass into the steady shaft of light that hovered over the sacred tome.

Slowly, almost casually, Balaam stepped forward. And, as if in deference to the act, the other Lords retreated toward the walls. If any of them were still shielded, Gideon couldn't tell it. But perhaps Ajel could, for neither he nor Revel made any attempt to speak.

Instead, it was Balaam who spoke, in the common tongue. "Which one of you is the leader?" he asked simply.

"Our leader is Paladin," Ajel replied proudly, "brother to my father, Laudin Sky, whom you once knew as Mentor."

Balaam shook his head patiently. "Paladin, as you call him, is dead," he said flatly. "I want to know who leads here."

For a moment, Gideon was stunned. He didn't know what to make of Balaam's placid declaration that Paladin had been killed. Was he telling the truth? Perhaps he just said it to throw Ajel off balance. He hoped that was the case, at least, for Ajel's sake.

"I am called Ajel, the Windrunner," came the reply. "I lead here."

"That is your given name?" the High Lord asked, somewhat incredulously. "How strange." He shrugged. "Well, I assume you have come for this." He gestured disdainfully toward the Book. "And I assume by now you must realize you will not get it. Your rebellion has been long and at times, I confess, well fought. But it has now reached its end. Your leader is dead; you will soon follow. And what remains of your 'Remnant' will quickly be accounted for as well."

"You presume too much, Council," Revel said defiantly. "You do not know how this will end. Perhaps you will yet die before the morning dawns."

"You hardly seem in a position to utter threats, rebel," Balaam spat. "Especially against a High Lord."

"Let me slay them, High Lord." A younger white-robed man stepped forward, looking all too eager. "We need not endure any more of this."

But Balaam raised a hand to silence him. "Patience, Lord Stevron," Balaam replied, somewhat irritably. "Watch. And learn." Bowing his head, the younger Lord quickly skulked back into the shadows.

"I offer you a deal," the High Lord continued. He gestured toward Gideon. "You see I have 'acquired' here your acclaimed Redeemer. I plan to slay him, naturally. But I am willing to forego his execution in exchange for your cooperation."

"How can we cooperate with you?" asked Ajel brazenly. "We are of two different worlds."

"Perhaps," agreed Balaam thoughtfully. "But what I ask is not too much. I want to ask you a few questions—simple questions, nothing complicated. In exchange for your honest reply, I will let him live. Simple as that."

"Gideon Dawning is not yours to slay, High Lord," said Ajel. "You have no power over him."

Balaam smirked blandly. "It would seem that I do."

"Touch the Book," Ajel demanded, pointing to the volume between them.

"What?" Balaam spat.

"Prove your authority over the Redeemer," Ajel said. "Touch the Book, and we will do whatever you command from this day forth."

Balaam waved his hand dismissively. "You are insane."

"And you are a pretense," Ajel shot back. "You *cannot* touch it. You cannot even approach it without exposing your weakness. Even standing this close makes your stomach boil, does it not?"

"It is an abomination!" shouted Balaam.

"No, High Lord," retorted Ajel. "*You* are the abomination. You and all those like you, going back to the time of Palor himself. It is you who have poisoned the Inherited Lands; *you* who have poisoned the souls of those who inhabit it. Sa'lei has blinded your eyes so that you cannot see what you have become. That is why you will not touch the Book, because it would force you to look at yourself as you truly are.

And you cannot bear the thought that you are nothing."

Ajel's words echoed through the chamber, gradually dissolving into silence. For a moment, Balaam only looked at him, his face red with fury. But when at last he spoke, his words were smooth and cold as ice.

"Do you really think you can goad me into touching that vile thing?" he asked quietly. "A pity. I had hoped you would not turn out to be so great a fool." Turning to his companions, the High Lord said, "I've changed my mind. These rebels are not worth questioning. I will get all I need from the Stormcaller himself." For one pensive moment, he turned to look at Gideon. Then, with a flutter of his hand, he issued the command. "Slay them."

As if with one collective breath, the four Council Lords launched their foul language at the huddled Remnant. Once again, black lightning erupted from the white-robed chests, striking against the Wordhaveners' sphere with crackling explosions of blue light and smoke. Ajel and Revel screamed their Words above the onslaught, focusing all their knowledge of *Dei'lo* on their defensive screen, while Aybel still lay helpless at their feet. But it did not seem to be enough. The shield wavered erratically under the force of the Council Lords' barrage, alternately swelling and receding as each new bolt of black struck at its all-too-fragile border. Fissures formed across the globe, only to be sealed by Ajel or Revel's quick Worded response. For all their stamina and obvious courage, however, Gideon knew the sphere could not hold up for long. And as soon as it collapsed, they would all be dead.

There was only one hope—and it was a slim one at best. If Gideon could reach his staff, maybe, just maybe, he could do something to help. He didn't know what; he certainly didn't know how. Still, he had no choice but to try.

The staff was at least in clear view, sealed against the wall as he was, only a few feet from his outstretched hand. But weighted under the intense pressure as he was, the thing might as well have been miles away. Nevertheless, with every ounce of strength remaining in his bones, he strained to shift his body sideward, toward the lifeless almond branch. He grunted with the effort, then suddenly stopped short for fear that Balaam or one of the other Lords had heard him. Fortunately, they were all quite occupied with their own efforts and didn't seem to notice him. Besides, the clash of sphere and lightning was so loud that they probably couldn't hear him even if he screamed.

Thankfully, they were so distracted, they didn't glance his way as the dingy-robed sojourner fumbled and scraped, inch by painful inch, along the coarse rock wall. Blood stains oozed into his robe as legs and arms scoured against the knife-sharp stones. But Gideon didn't feel it. His only thought, his one imperative, was to reach that staff.

Just as he heard Ajel's pain-filled scream echo through the chamber, his trembling hand at last clasped the warmth of the gilded wood.

In an instant, the wall released its hold, and Gideon dropped like dead weight to the floor. Turning quickly, he saw the final vestiges of Ajel's shield buckling under the strain of the Council's torrent of black death. As though on instinct, he whipped the staff before him and pointed it directly at Balaam's back.

Balaam must have sensed something, for he spun around. Gideon watched his eyes grow wide in shock as he saw the sojourner standing there before him, staff in hand. The High Lord opened his mouth to speak, but it was already too late. Once again, as had happened in the Plain of Dreams and in the mountains of the Heaven Range, blue light streamed down on Gideon's head and exploded in a wrathful ball of flame around him, enveloping him within its comforting strength. The black lightning stopped as the remaining Council Lords turned to see what was happening. No sooner had their eyes met his than his own lightning, blue and pure and full of light, erupted from his staff in five directions, striking at the heart of each Council Lord simultaneously.

Brilliant red shields exploded into life around them, crackling and hissing under the strain of Gideon's flow. He couldn't hear their words, but their mouths were moving at a frantic pace as they fought to fend off this strange new power that railed against them. He saw panic in their eyes, and then fear. Yet, for some reason he couldn't explain, he did not hate them. Instead, he pitied them. They were just hollow, empty shells. . .souls that at one time held treasures greater than even life itself. But they had traded that all away for the promise of absolute power. A promise that, at its heart, was just another lie.

A scream, and one of the fiery shields buckled and collapsed. A woman, still so young and fresh-faced, wailed in terror as the blue light pierced her. Instantly, she was enveloped. The lightning wrapped itself around her soul and almost gently tore it from her body. Her lifeless form dropped silently to the chamber floor, even as the light that had entwined her exploded through the rocks above and disappeared.

Gideon barely had time to look away before a second shield collapsed, this time from around an old and grizzled man who stood not far from Balaam. Within a breath, the same fate that had befallen the girl overtook him as well.

Suddenly, Gideon noticed that Balaam had moved. Like the others, he was struggling against the blue lightning of his staff, but there was no look of panic or fear in the High Lord's black eyes. He stepped toward Gideon, his face full of only hate and deep, dark rage. It was a look Gideon had seen only once before, in the face of another Council Lord a few days past. But Balaam's expression did not seem so crazed as Bentel's had the night he died. There was a coolness to Balaam's glare, a determined sense of purpose that would not be denied, not even by the power that now stormed so forcefully against him.

His lips moved briefly, and suddenly black lightning leaped at Gideon from out of Balaam's breast. It slashed at him, or rather at the power that encompassed him, flailing madly at the blue orb of fire, searching for an opening, a pinhole of weakness through which it might break in.

But it found nothing. Frowning, Balaam spoke again; and this time the lightning struck out not at Gideon, but at the stone walls of the chamber surrounding him. Instantly, Gideon saw the danger. Balaam might not be able to reach him directly, but collapsing the chamber on top of him might do the job just as well.

Suddenly, Ajel appeared at Balaam's back. He bore the Book in his hands, though Gideon had no idea how or when he'd managed to secure it or even how he could hold it at all, after all he had said about its unapproachable power. But hold it he did. Wielding the bulky tome like a club, he thrust it right through Balaam's shield and brought it squarely down upon his shoulders. With a scream and flash of brilliant light, the High Lord fell sprawling to the ground.

The remaining Lords looked on in horror as their leader struggled to his knees. The fabric of his white robe was burned away, revealing a mass of red and blistered flesh across his back. But before Ajel could back away, the wounded High Lord turned and spewed a barrage of Words against him, releasing from his outstretched hand a torrent of red flame so intense that Gideon could feel its heat even within his own protective sphere. The flame, however, passed through the Book as though it wasn't even there. And, miraculously, through Ajel as well. When the flames finally died away, not even the Wordhavener's hair was singed.

The look of shock on Balaam's face quickly overran his anger. He struggled awkwardly to his feet even as the blue lightning from Gideon's staff continued to assault his now weakened shield from behind. For his part, Ajel ran back toward Revel and Aybel and quickly motioned for them to place their hands on the Book. The act seemed curious to Gideon, but he didn't have time to think about it.

Turning to face the sojourner once again, Balaam spat another barrage of Words; but somehow Gideon knew these were not like the ones he'd spoken before. Hearing the sound of crumbling stone, the sojourner turned in time to see the rock dissolving behind him, creating a tunnel that disappeared into the distance. Suddenly, the entire chamber went strangely dark, as though blankets of shadows had been cast all around him. Like a fire starved of oxygen, his own blue sphere quickly sputtered and fizzled into nothing. Panicked, he turned to see what was happening to him. And the last thing Gideon saw was Balaam's laughing face, hurtling toward him through the air.

CHAPTER 57

THE SEA FOLK CLIFFS

As they began the long descent down to the Sea Folk Wharf, Ajel paused to check the position of the stars to the east. The night was still black, but the stars told him it would be dawn within a few hours. They needed to be clear of Phallenar before the first rays of morning struck the pinnacle of the Axis.

It had been a long night—a horrible night. The lengthy battle against Balaam and his puppet Lords had taken a considerable toll on their strength, and in the end it had resulted in a standoff of sorts and an appalling exchange. Balaam fled with Gideon Dawning as his captive, while Ajel and the others escaped the chamber with the Book. Ajel had no idea whether the sojourner yet lived.

At least the rest of them were still alive, Ajel thought, trying to comfort himself. If it hadn't been for the Book, there would not even have been that. It was an act of pure mercy from the Giver that Ajel realized the Book's invulnerability was transferred to anyone who touched it. It was quite an unexpected revelation, really. When Balaam summoned that storm of fire against him, Ajel rightly reckoned his life was at its end. But as the blast enveloped him, he felt nothing. No heat, not even wind. Curiously, in that surreal moment, the only thing he could think of was how beautiful it all was, like standing in the center of the sun.

The Book had done that—saved his life, as well as the lives of Revel and Aybel. It was just the first of many gifts the Book promised to bring the Remnant. Gifts that, in time, would surely remake the world.

Cautiously, he adjusted his leather poncho to better conceal the priceless treasure, which he nestled protectively against his chest. Scouring the array of rickety zigzagging stairs before him, he finally located the shadowy outlines of Aybel and Revel some one hundred paces below. He didn't realize he'd been standing motionless for so long. They were already halfway to the Wharf.

Hurriedly, he dashed down a set of stairs to his right. For all their squeaks and weathered railings, the stairs were still a marvel of engineering. Clinging to the precarious cliffs on Phallenar's eastern border, the extensive latticework of stairways extended some one thousand feet or more from top to bottom, connecting the markets of Prisidium Square with the Sea Folk Wharf that bordered the Black Gorge's western shore. What's more, the stairs supported more than a few merchants' shops, tucked into nooks and fissures along the strenuous route or built up along some of the more generous ledges. It was like a city unto itself in many ways—a vertically constructed village, where most of the Sea Folk built their homes. Those that deigned to live on land at all, that is. Most of them did not; they didn't trust in rocks and dirt—in the same way that other people did not trust the sea. But a few of them had managed to overcome their fear or else were forced to do so by the loss of a boat or the unavoidable necessity of trading with the people of the land.

Even at this predawn hour, many of the Sea Folk were already up and milling about. Most of the fishing boats, of course, had already departed, trudging their course northward to the Silence Sound, where they would coax their daily catch from those eerily silent waters. Some would be returning with the dawn—the fortunate ones, anyway—their holds filled with mantakrill and botsan and the occasional shrin eel.

A few of the boats were still moored at the docks, of course. Mostly the larger sailing vessels, commissioned by the Council to carry goods north to Morguen and several other smaller soundens along their route. It was one of these in particular that Ajel wanted to find— a ketch named *Endurant,* appropriately enough. Paladin had known the captain during his years as a merchant trader in Phallenar, and the two of them had been friends of a sort. Paladin remembered the stout little man as one who held no love for the Council Lords, and he had little doubt the fellow would help them. Still, friendship with the Sea Folk was a slippery matter even in the best of circumstances. And the present circumstance could hardly be called ideal.

After dozens more zigzags down the cliff, Ajel reached the Wharf at last and scanned the docks for signs of Revel and Aybel. The air was far more humid here and carried a malodorous stench that the Sea Folk staunchly claimed did not exist. The likely truth was that they could not detect it; the Sea Folk were known to have a feeble sense of smell, though no one ever said it to their face. It was just as well, Ajel realized. No one should have to endure the stench of the Deathland

Barrens for more than an hour, yet the Sea Folk made their home within clear sight of its borders. In truth, it was a blessing from the Giver that they could not smell it.

Suddenly, Revel appeared on the docks, emerging from the humid darkness like a ghost as he ran to meet his brother. He didn't look to be in danger, exactly, but the feelings Ajel sensed from him were troubling nonetheless. Something was amiss.

"What is it, brother?" Ajel asked as Revel closed the gap between them. It was then that Ajel saw the tears streaming down his face. "What has happened?" he added hastily. "Do we have passage?"

Slowly, Revel nodded, trying to control his sorrow long enough to speak. After a moment, he said, simply, "Paladin is slain."

Ajel immediately shook his head. "No, brother. Balaam only spoke that as a ruse to unsettle our hearts. I'm sure that Paladin is here, somewhere on the Wharf. We need only to find him."

Revel shut his eyes to block out the tears. "No," he said. "The word is not from Balaam, but from Kair. She waits for us on the *Endurant*, along with the underlord. . . . There was a battle, brother. Lysteria ambushed the three of them in Prisidium Square. She must have known they would pass that way."

An icy chill ran down Ajel's spine. He could not believe what he was hearing. "Lysteria?" he asked somberly. "But how could she have known?"

"I do not know," said Revel, with fresh tears rolling down his cheeks. "It doesn't matter how. She was there. And Paladin was slain by her Word."

The words pierced Ajel's heart like daggers. And yet, he could not cry. "What of Kair and the underlord? Are they well?"

"Both were badly injured in the fight. By Kair's account, the underlord was at the point of death herself. But, thank the Giver, Kair herself was well enough to speak a Word of healing—both for herself and the underlord—once Lysteria left them. But for Paladin, there was nothing she could do."

"Lysteria left them?" Ajel asked, suddenly suspicious. "Why did she leave them alive? Was she injured as well?"

A look of scorn flashed across Revel's face. "Why do you ask such a thing? Is it not enough that Paladin is slain, that you should question why the same fate did not befall the rest?"

"I am thankful that they survived, brother," offered Ajel soothingly. "But this is not a time for us to lose our wits to grief. If Lysteria was not injured, then she left for some other reason, perhaps only to set a stronger ambush for us here. Did Kair tell you why the Council Lord fled?"

Revel shook his head distressfully. "No. She said only that Lysteria left them after Paladin fell. She did not say why." Abruptly, Revel drew in a somber breath and made a quick attempt to wipe the tears from his face. When he looked up, however, his eyes still glistened in the darkness. "Perhaps Paladin's death was Lysteria's only aim. When that was done, perhaps she saw no need to trouble with the rest."

"Perhaps," Ajel replied tentatively. But the explanation did not sit well. Why would the Council Lord have left her daughter uncaptured—unless she believed Kyrintha was also slain?

"Whatever the case, we cannot tarry here," he said at last. "The most important thing now is to get the Book away from Phallenar. Only then can we use the Words to transport it back to Wordhaven. You say the ship has been secured?"

Revel nodded sorrowfully. "Yes. . .and you are right, of course. Unless the Book is made safe, Paladin's death will be for nothing."

"Take me there, brother," Ajel ordered bluntly. "Quickly."

Nodding once again, Revel turned and ran into the darkness. Ajel followed, clutching the Book all the more tightly to his chest, as much for comfort as to keep it safe. There would be time for grieving later, he told himself, once the Book was safe within the Stand at Wordhaven. Until then, his own sorrow would have to wait.

Still, he couldn't help but feel envious of Revel's tears. His brother had always been freer with his feelings than Ajel. But then, Revel didn't bear the burden of leadership as Ajel did. And now that Paladin was dead, the full weight of it landed all the more heavily on his shoulders. The truth of it was, for good or ill, Ajel was the leader of the Remnant now. He only hoped his heart was ready for the task.

When they reached the ship, Kair was standing on the gangway waiting for them. Her abundant red hair was clumped in reckless tangles around her head, but her expression was as calm and stoic as ever. Behind her stood the underlord, looking decidedly pale and considerably disheveled in her stained and tattered gown, but otherwise uninjured. In the darkness behind them, Ajel noticed two squat figures scrambling fore and aft along the deck, completely oblivious to the Wordhaveners' approach. He could only assume that one of them was the Sea Folk captain Paladin had once called friend. He felt the sudden urge to rush up the gangway to meet him. . .if only as a means to connect with the uncle he had now lost. Instead, he merely blinked and turned to smile at Kair.

"Peace unto the ship *Endurant,*" he said. "May we join you on the timbers?"

"Captain Quigly grants you peace," Kair responded dutifully. "His timbers are yours."

Ajel stepped across the gangway with Revel at his side. It was uncommon for a captain not to grant the right of passage himself, but the two Sea Folk on board were clearly in too much of a rush to bother with such formalities.

"Has Revel told you?" Kair asked suddenly.

Ajel nodded slightly. He didn't want to think about Paladin now. "Are you restored?" he asked. "I heard you had been injured."

"I am well enough," she replied stolidly. But her expression seemed strained, as though she did not quite believe her own words.

"And you, Underlord," continued Ajel, "are you fully restored?"

"I'll be all right, I suppose," Kyrintha replied. The sorrow in her voice was obvious, however. "I will be better once we are underway."

Ajel smiled, trying not to look too sad. "From what I can see of our hosts, we will not have long to wait." He paused, considering what he should say next. They were looking to him now for good or ill. They needed his strength, his assurance that everything would turn out for the best. If only he were certain it would.

Finally, he said, "Our hearts have endured much in the last few hours. There will be time to speak of it in detail, to share our feelings and our grief. But for now, I must ask that you steel your hearts and focus on the tasks that yet remain. What matters is that we carry the Book safely from Phallenar and secure it away from the Council's grasp. Once that is done, we will consider what has happened and what must happen next."

"What of the sojourner?" asked Kair.

"Only the Giver knows his fate," Ajel replied darkly. "Even if he still lives, we can do no more to help him."

CHAPTER 58

GIDEON'S DAWN

"God help me! My arms!"

Gideon desperately cried out in the hollow muck-laden chamber, but his words just echoed up the stony walls and into the darkness above. In the near pitch-black of the dungeon pit, Gideon could see only faint indications of other things moving in the chamber. The floor, which was covered in water, rippled occasionally from the sudden movements of slimy creatures that apparently thrived there. It looked and smelled of sewage. The walls were stone covered with wet growth built up from years of this cool, rancid dampness. The whole room reeked of waste and rotting flesh.

Gideon hung on a wall three feet off the floor. His body was suspended by chains bolted around his wrists that pulled his arms outward toward the corners of the ceiling—if there was one. Gideon couldn't tell. His legs were fastened to the wall, but he couldn't tell how.

Even in the cool of the chamber, his weakened body dripped from the humidity. His shredded robe hung like rags from his waist and limbs. They were covered in blood, though he knew somehow it wasn't his own.

They want me conscious, he thought. *They won't hurt me to the point that I might pass out. That's gotta be the only reason I'm not dead.*

Gideon momentarily pulled at the iron band around his right wrist, and immediately he screamed at the awful pain that shot up his arm. The bonds were bolted so tightly that they cut into his flesh. He gritted his teeth in agony as he felt the cold iron rubbing exposed tendons in his wrists. But there was no way he could ease the pressure. His arms and shoulders screamed under the pull of his own weight.

"God, help, I. . . ," he cried again, stopping short because of the pain. He winced as he took in another breath. Even the motion of his lungs dug the iron deeper into his limbs. Exhausted, he hung his head down to his chest and watched sweat slowly drip from his drenched black curls onto the putrid floor. He knew exactly where he was; he knew exactly what was going to happen. And, knowing, he prayed for unconsciousness.

In the distance, beyond the walls of the dungeon, he heard a sudden clanging, like the sound of great iron doors closing. Moments later, muffled footsteps, made from leather boots passing on dry stone, echoed in the chamber. Gideon raised his head and halfheartedly flipped his wet hair away from his eyes to try to see what he knew was coming.

Somewhere in the void of the dungeon, the creaking of a massive iron door echoed through the chamber. Oily ripples sounded all at once all over the room as whatever creatures were there scampered into the safety of the corners. For a moment all was quiet. Gideon squinted to try to locate the door that had opened to his hellish pit.

"*Demoi fleur blassht.*" A woman's voice echoed through the room. Immediately, a torch came ablaze and floated on its own into the air about the center of the chamber.

Gideon winced, his eyes seared by the sudden brilliance. He blinked repeatedly in an effort to adjust and slowly turned his head back toward the voice.

"Oh, you poor thing," she said sadly. "You poor, poor thing." She shook her head, then sighed. "Well, let me get a look at you."

Carefully, she leaned in and tapped her index finger on her chin, as though Gideon were a piece of meat she was thinking about cooking for supper. "Hmm," she said. "So, you are the great threat." She sounded disappointed. "Well, I just had to come see for myself."

As Gideon's eyes adjusted, he began to make out a face to match the coarse, pinched voice. Standing under the arch of a doorway some thirty feet away was an older woman. Her abundant gray hair was pinned up in a pile on her head—just as he remembered from his dream on the Plains. She wore a purple gown, possibly velvet or silk, that pulled tight around her thin waist, then flowed to the floor in cascading waves of material. The sleeves of her gown draped almost to the floor as well, causing her to have to bend her arms to keep the fabric off the slimy surface.

Around her neck hung a great red stone, like a ruby, in a gold setting, surrounded by countless diamonds. Her neck plainly showed the wrinkles and sags of age, but her bony face was pulled as tight as the hair on her head. Gideon saw no wrinkles there. Her pencil-thin lips grinned at Gideon. Her eyes, like black marbles, glistened emptily in the torchlight. If she hadn't been speaking, Gideon would have thought she was dead.

"Balaam has said that you could be the undoing of all we believe in," she said, folding her arms gracefully. "But from my view, you seem little more than a mouse caught in a trap." She chuckled lightly.

"What. . ." Gideon swallowed, trying to hide the pain in his voice. "What do you want?" But even as he choked out the words, he already knew what she would say.

She smiled warmly. "You mean, dear boy, why aren't you dead yet? Oh, don't you worry about that, young man. You will be soon enough." She paused, considering him a moment. Then she added pleasantly, "But not with Words. The Words would kill you too quickly, and we need you to talk to us before you. . .well, pass on."

From behind the woman appeared a hulk of a man, his pale brawny arms glistening wetly in the torchlight. He wore black, a sleeveless uniform similar to the one Gideon had seen on Raug. He was big like Raug too. He towered over the woman, but she seemed to barely notice him. She extended her hand, and he placed in it a wooden staff, polished so meticulously that it shimmered darkly in the torchlight.

"Young man, you do recognize this, don't you?" asked the woman.

Gideon forced his head up a bit more to get a look at the staff. "No," he said with effort, dropping his head again to his chest.

A fire lit in the woman's black eyes, but her tone remained pleasant. "Oh, come now, there's no reason to lie," she said with a wave of her hand. "It is your staff I hold, of course. The staff that collapsed that horrid chamber and very nearly ended my bondmate's life. My stars! I would just love to know how it works, you know. If you would just tell me that, then I'm certain we can get you out of this dismal room and into a nice hot bath. With dinner to follow. You'd like that, wouldn't you? So tell me. What Word is used to give this its power?"

"I don't know," said Gideon defiantly. "I don't know what you're talking about."

She waved her hand dismissively. "As I thought," the woman said. "You need a little coaxing. All right. I will return in a little while. But in the meantime, let me leave you with a little gift."

The woman turned to the pale-skinned man. "Bring the box," she said.

"Yes, Lord Asher-Baal," his deep voice groveled. Immediately he produced a wooden box about two feet square and set it inside the room next to the door. Once it was on the floor, he popped the lid and tossed it aside. Within seconds, large black rats began pouring out of the box and into the rancid mire on the floor. Gideon forced back a surge of bile rising in his throat.

"They're very hungry," said the woman with a smile. "And very good at smelling out food. When I return, perhaps you will be more willing to talk."

The woman looked up at the torch and opened her mouth to speak, but then stopped short. "No," she said. "I'll leave the light. It would be uncouth not to let you see what's coming."

Abruptly she turned and walked away, her regal gown flowing after her in waves of deep purple. The guard slammed the door and left Gideon alone to watch the black rodents, who were already sniffing their way toward him.

Well, at least the waiting is over, Gideon thought cynically.

Within minutes, the first few reached the wall upon which Gideon hung and sniffed the air. They smelled his flesh, but they weren't long enough to reach his feet, and the muck on the floor seemed to hamper their ability to jump.

Soon, however, other rats joined the few that had found him; and slowly, almost purposefully, they began to crawl on top of each other, rat upon rat, until they could just reach the tips of Gideon's toes.

The first bites felt like pinpricks, just as he remembered they would. But as soon as the first drops of blood hit the water below, the rats seemed to go mad. They clamored viciously over each other, latching their pointed teeth on Gideon's toes, then his feet. Gideon cried out at the pain and cursed the bonds that held him helpless against his attackers. Soon, some of the rats climbed up on his feet and began biting into his legs. The pain was nauseating, and Gideon screamed in horror as he felt small chunks of his flesh being torn away by the rodents' teeth.

"No!" Gideon screamed wildly, pulling at the bonds that tore into his arms. But the bonds wouldn't give, and all he heard in response to his call was his own echo coming back to haunt him.

Finally, overcome by pain and exhaustion, he willed his body to stop struggling against the stinging bites and hung his head in resignation to his fate. If he were lucky, maybe he would bleed to death before the woman returned.

"That's a better choice, I think." A voice suddenly echoed through the room. "Struggling will only make them bite more aggressively."

Numbly, Gideon lifted his eyes to find who had spoken. On a far wall, some forty feet away, a man hung from chains similar to Gideon's. Only he was like no man Gideon had ever seen. In fact, Gideon wasn't exactly sure he was human at all.

His skin was silver. Or perhaps gray. But it sparkled like crystal in the firelight. His hair, white to the point of seeming almost colorless, draped his front in long dry strands that hung wistfully all the way to his waist. His arms and legs were long too—much longer than a man's—and they bulged and strained against the shackles in a way that seemed un-natural, as if the structure of his long, sinewy muscles had been curiously rearranged. His hands and feet were unusually large, as were his eyes, which from this distance looked like glistening pools of molten bronze. His face was long and narrow, like his entire body, and he seemed to lack any mouth at all. But Gideon supposed he must have one, since he had just spoken.

His amazement at the man's peculiar appearance momentarily caused him to forget about the rats. To his surprise, when he looked down again, he saw that they were gone.

He blinked in astonishment. "The rats are gone," he muttered, almost phrasing it as a question. In his condition, he wasn't certain he could trust his eyes.

"They are," confirmed the. . .whatever it was.

Gideon sighed wearily, then momentarily winced from the jolt of pain the motion had provoked in his arms. His mottled legs were striped with blood, which flowed thickly from dozens of pockmarked wounds created by the rats' sharp teeth.

"It doesn't matter. I'm going to die anyway. If the loss of blood doesn't get me, the diseases certainly will."

"You will not die today, Gideon Dawning." The man-thing was suddenly standing right there before him, looking as stoic and unper-turbed as a glassy pond. He glanced down at Gideon's legs. "There will be some scars, however," he added. "And they will not be the last."

Gideon glanced at the wall where the man had been shackled. The chains and bonds were still there, hanging motionless as if they hadn't been used for years. "How did you get free?" he asked.

The man smiled. So he *did* have a mouth, slight though it was. "I have been waiting for you, Gideon Dawning," he said. "I am for you."

"Who. . .what are you?" Gideon rasped.

"I am called Telus," he replied evenly. "I am of the Raanthan. My people live on the high plateau north of Strivenwood Forest. I have been sent to assist you. I have been waiting here for quite some time."

"Waiting. . . ? Sent by. . . ?" Gideon shook his head in confusion. He was far too exhausted and in pain for this right now. "Oh, forget it," he muttered at last. "Listen, whoever you are, can you get me down from here?"

"I will do more than that," Telus replied. "We must leave. Lord Lysteria will return very soon."

"Just get me down," Gideon rasped painfully. "This is killing me."

With a curious nod, the Raanthan pressed an overly large hand against Gideon's chest, then wrapped the other around the bonds on one of Gideon's wrists. The iron bond unclasped easily, clanging lightly against the stone as Gideon's arm fell limply to his side. He did the same with the other bond and then with the braces on Gideon's ankles. Only when all the bonds were loosed did he gently relax the pressure on Gideon's chest, allowing the sojourner to slide, somewhat roughly, to the murky floor.

Surprisingly, Gideon didn't collapse under his own weight, despite the weakness in his legs. The coolness of the slimy mush actually felt good against his tortured feet and shins. He decided not to think about what the slime contained. There was nothing he could do about it, anyway.

Steadying himself against the wall, he glanced up to get a better look at his rescuer—and his jaw dropped. This. . .Raanthan, as he called himself, towered more than three feet over his head, looking down at him with eyes so saucerlike and liquid that they seemed anything but human. And yet there was something very human about him. Well, not human exactly, but. . .reassuring.

"Who sent you?" Gideon asked.

"Don't you know?" Telus replied.

Instantly, Gideon furrowed his brow in frustration. "How could I know?"

The Raanthan shrugged—a most peculiar-looking gesture on

someone so alien. "You will. When you must."

"What?"

"We must leave now, Gideon Dawning," the Raanthan continued, ignoring the question. "Close your eyes."

"What the. . .why do I need to close. . ."

"Close your eyes, Gideon Dawning," he repeated, a bit more sternly. "You must. Or I cannot act."

Feeling a fresh wave of frustration, Gideon raised his hand to rub his eyes, but stopped short as he caught sight of his injured wrist. Through the abrasive tears of flesh and crusted blood caused by the iron bonds, he could see white bone. He thought it curious that he felt no pain. . .and more than a little disturbing.

"All right, fine," he said at last. "I'll close my eyes."

And so he did. Telus's hand came to rest on his head, and the smells in the room began to shift. The stench of filth and rats and rancid mud faded quietly away, only to be replaced by other, more pleasant aromas—grass and moisture and the musty scent of earth. A quiet breeze began to waft across his shoulders and with it a distant melody, a chorus of woodwinds.

Telus removed his hand, and Gideon opened his eyes to faint purple ribbons of clouds coasting through the eastern sky, marking the distant approach of dawn.

"Where are we?" Gideon asked. Other than the dimly glowing clouds and a host of brilliant stars, everything was still quite dark. They were outside, that much was sure. And from the sound of the reeded music, they stood somewhere on or near the Plain of Dreams. But there was moisture in the air—too much for the plains, unless there was rain nearby. And the ground under Gideon's feet was far from grassy. It was lumpy and barren and felt as rough as hardened lava against his bloody feet.

"The place where everything began and where it will begin anew," Telus replied cryptically. Then, to clarify, perhaps, he added, "You stand on Gideon's Fall."

Gideon recognized the name immediately. He had first noticed it on a map Ajel and the others had used to plot their route to Phallenar. On the map, it was depicted only as a small black boil rising out of the plains, somewhere between Phallenar and the Silence Sound. Considering the black abrasive rocks beneath his feet, he figured the drawing wasn't far from accurate.

"More than two millennia ago, another Gideon stood on this very spot," Telus told him, "and from this place he fractured the world. *That* Gideon—the Truthslayer—became the herald of a dark power, a living being of shadows and seduction, whose name at that time was known only to a few. He does not care that you know his name, of course, only that you bow to his rule. It was he who created the Tongue of *Sa'lei*, he who used it to subvert the souls of your people through avarice and the lust for power."

The Raanthan looked down at Gideon. "You too are a herald, Gideon Dawning. That is why I have brought you here, for it is from here that your journey must begin. Do you understand what I am telling you?"

"Not even a little," Gideon replied. But really, he did—a little. "I suppose you're telling me that I'm the Kinsman Redeemer."

Suddenly, Telus threw back his head and let out a squeal that set Gideon's teeth on edge. It was like the sound of a dozen owls all screeching at once, only a good deal more irritating. It took several tense moments for Gideon to realize the grating sound was laughter. "You—the Kinsman Redeemer?" Telus squawked. "By the Giver, no!" He screeched again mirthfully.

"Hey look, *I* didn't come up with the idea," Gideon retorted, his pride more bruised than he wanted to admit. "I just keep hearing it so much that I naturally assumed that's what you meant. . . ," a pause, and then, "well, then what *do* you mean?"

Like flipping a switch, the Raanthan's demeanor grew serious once again. "You are not the Kinsman Redeemer, Gideon Dawning," he said. "But you are his herald. You are the Waymaker."

"The Way-what?" Gideon asked. Now *there* was a title he had yet to hear.

"The Waymaker," repeated Telus. "You have been charged to usher in the return of the Pearl, as the first Gideon did for Abaddon. Do you know nothing of the prophecies concerning this?"

Gideon frowned cynically. "There hasn't been much time for study lately," he quipped. "What with people trying to kill me and all."

"You will have to make time on the journey ahead," Telus replied matter-of-factly. "Regardless of the dangers we must face."

"What journey?" Gideon asked sharply. "And what do you mean by 'we'? Are you taking me somewhere else?"

"You are the Waymaker," the Raanthan replied simply. "You must make the way for the Pearl."

Gideon sighed irritably. "As I understand it, the Pearl was destroyed some two thousand years ago," he said. "On this very spot, as I recall."

"As you understand it, perhaps," Telus replied.

"Are you telling me the Pearl was not destroyed?"

Telus frowned—if you could call it a frown. For all Gideon knew, it could have been a smirk. "There is a mountain far from here," he said. "That is where you must take the Pearl. That is where ways will be mended and a way made."

"Take the Pearl?" Gideon said flatly. "But how do I find it?"

"You are the Waymaker."

"That doesn't answer my question."

"Yes," said Telus. "It does."

"No. . .it doesn't," replied Gideon mockingly. He sighed. "Look," he said, "I'm far too beat up for this right now. I mean, look at me."

He glanced down at his shredded robe and gave his bloody legs and wrists a once-over. He didn't want to look too closely, though. "I'm exhausted," he continued. "I'm bleeding. My clothes are tattered rags. I don't have any boots, and these rocks are cutting my already bloody feet. I'm clearly in no condition to go on another journey right now, not with you or anyone else. So even if you told me I was the Pope, it wouldn't make any difference! I need sleep." He paused, sniffing the air disdainfully, then added, "And a bath."

"There will be time," said Telus. "Your companions will be passing below us in the Gorge within a few hours. When they do, we will descend to join them. Their ship is large. You will be able to heal there."

"Who—Ajel? Aybel?" Gideon asked.

"All but one of your companions survived the night," said Telus. "The rest are coming this way, though they do not yet know that you still live. They carry with them the Book of *Dei'lo*."

Gideon was surprised. Well, at least *that* was good news. "But what about my friends? You say one of them was killed?"

"Yes."

"Which one?" Gideon asked, not at all sure he wanted to know.

"I must let the story tell itself," replied Telus, sounding suddenly pensive.

"How can you know all this, anyway?" asked Gideon suspiciously. "Weren't you in the dungeon the whole time—waiting for me, as you say?"

Telus nodded, but then added quietly, "I know some things."

"Really. . .how?" *And who sent you?*

"I must leave you now," the Raanthan announced abruptly. If Gideon didn't know better, he'd say he'd made the strange man uncomfortable.

"Why?" Gideon asked. "Where are you going?"

"There is something you will need for the journey ahead," explained Telus. "I must go and retrieve it for you."

"What is it?" Gideon asked.

Telus didn't answer. Instead he said, "I will return before your companions arrive. We will travel down into the Gorge together."

"And what am I supposed to do?" Gideon asked, more than a little frustrated despite his exhaustion. Or perhaps because of it. "Just stand here and bleed to death?"

The razor-thin lips on Telus's face formed briefly into a grin. "I suggest you sit," he said. And with that, he bounded off down the rocky slope and disappeared into the predawn darkness.

"Hey, wait a minute!" Gideon called. He tried to follow, but quickly found the porous rocks too painful to traverse on his wounded feet. In resignation, he fumbled back to the apex of the hill, then repositioned a few of the smoother rocks to make a place to sit.

Bunching what little cloth remained from his robes beneath him, he lowered himself onto the rocks and drew his blood-crusted knees up to his face. Seeing the bloody pockmarks on his calves and the torn skin on his wrists, he couldn't help but chuckle at the utter morbidity of his condition.

Idly, he thought back to the day when he had gashed open his own chest during a rage in his apartment back home. It seemed like a lifetime ago. He'd been so terrified then, so frightened—not only by the injury, but even more so by its cause. And that was just one cut, he realized grimly, one out-of-control incident on one very bad day.

"And just look at me now," he quipped aloud, scrutinizing his shredded wrists. "You've moved way past crazy."

But even as he said it, he knew it wasn't really true. He still struggled to make sense of this world, of all that had transpired since his fateful arrival in the Inherited Lands. But there was a certain rightness to it, all the same. . .an awareness that welled up to his conscious thought from deep within his battered soul and told him that this was how it was meant to be. That it was, somehow, *true* and *good*.

The life he'd known before coming here had been torn mercilessly away. But it hadn't been much of a life anyway. In fact, he realized grimly, little of it had been real at all. The truth seemed so obvious now, so simple and crisp, he wondered how he could have missed it all those years. Back home, his life had been a parody, a sad and ridiculous game of pretending to be real and hoping that in the pretending, somehow, he could make it so.

But now, as he looked down at his crazy tattered robe, his blood-streaked legs and shredded wrists, he didn't feel the pretense anymore and realized it had been burned away for good. In its place, he simply felt *alive*. The sensation flooded through his veins like liquid fire, commanding his senses to offer their respect to both its purity and its danger. And even though the feel of it frightened him, he had to admit its flavor was sweeter than any honey he had ever tasted.

Just then, the first rays of dawn broke out over the horizon to the east. Brilliant yellow sunbeams flooded the sky, turning it instantly from black to that now-familiar azure blue and illuminating the few white clouds that had been hiding in the stars. In the dawning light, miles and miles of verdant flatlands appeared before him in a misty yawn that extended eastward far beyond his vision.

So this is the place of new beginnings, he mused. *A new journey. And I am the Waymaker.*

He laughed. "Whatever *that* is," he quipped aloud. Still, he found that the mysteries of the path ahead did not disturb him anymore. They would unravel themselves in their sweet time. Eventually every mystery would tire of hiding the answers he sought. At least that's what he chose to believe. For now, he was content to know he was alive and that the fragile hope reborn within him through the dream at Strivenwood had not proved false. There *was* a reason he was here—a purpose that, though yet unclear, would prove his meaningless life had meaning after all.

There's no turning back now, he realized soberly. Now that he knew the truth—or at least a *part* of the truth—he would pursue it wherever it led him, pay whatever price it demanded of him, and embrace whatever titles seemed necessary to find its end.

So he would be their Waymaker, if that's what the course demanded. But in and through all of that, woven through the very heart of its fabric, he knew he would become something more as well. Something deeper.

And though he didn't really know what that "more" would look like, he took comfort in the calm assurance that it would be the most authentic and raw expression of life he had ever dreamed.

GLOSSARY

Abaddon (Ahb-bah-DAAN)—True name of the force of evil in the Land. His origin is not known. Millennia ago, the Pearl subdued him and locked him away in Castel Morstal. There he remained for thousands of years, guarded by the Kah and the powerful Words of the Old Lords. Nevertheless, at some point in the distant past, he escaped (it is not known how) and set his heart toward the destruction of the Pearl and the people along with it. After accomplishing that dark deed through Gideon Truthslayer, Abaddon's whereabouts became a mystery. Although he is no longer commonly believed to be an actual being, he is nonetheless referred to in most cultures as the legendary enemy of the Giver. In this present age, his common name is the "evil one," but in past ages he has been called Destroyer, Father of Ruin, Spirit of the Age, Corruption, Deathfear, and Pearlslayer.

Ajel Windrunner (AH-jil WIND-run-ner)—Son of Laudin and Danielle Sky, and nephew of Jesun (Paladin Sky), Saria, and Seer. A leading member of the Remnant.

Aybel Boldrun (AY-bel BOLD-run)—A member of the Remnant assigned to watch over Gideon and, if possible, teach him the Words of *Dei'lo*. She is an immigrant who journeyed from the Hinterlands after her brother was lost in Strivenwood.

Balaam Asher-Baal (BAY-lum Asher-BAYL)—High Lord on the Council of Phallenar, a man of great power and even greater ambition.

Barrier Wall, The—An expansive stone barrier on the edge of Phallenar built by Palor Wordwielder, supposedly as a memorial to his own greatness. Historians who have examined the Wall, however, suggest its purpose may have been as a defensive shield against some unknown force west of the city.

Batai (Bah-TYE)—From the High Tongue, meaning "Hand of the Pearl." In ancient times, it was a common reference for the High Lord of Wordhaven.

Baurejalin Sint (Bar-REJ-a-lin SENT)—Lord on the Council of Phallenar. A pragmatic supporter of Balaam, who sees himself as the natural successor to the High Lord. He keeps to himself when not in the Axis chamber or with his occasional love interest, Rachel Alli.

Bentel Baratii (Ben-TEL Bar-a-TEE)—A young, ambitious Lord on the Council of Phallenar. He and his sister, Fayerna, form a powerful team that only a few on the Council will openly oppose.

Bian'ar (BYE-an AHR)—From the High Tongue, meaning "the light of life." A white puttylike substance found as a solid layer between the outer bark and the inner hardwood of the trees in Castellan Watch. The *bian'ar* is harvested through a complex mystical process known only to the people of Calmeron sounden. The process collects the *bian'ar* while leaving the trees undamaged. *Bian'ar* harvested in any other way rots within an hour or two after it is collected.

Bian'ar eyes—Waking visions that sometimes occur after prolonged exposure to unrefined *bian'ar*. Although these visions, which can last for days, are often mysterious and difficult to interpret, they always indicate a major event looming on the horizon. The greater the magnitude of the event, the greater the frequency of *Bian'ar* eyes. These visions had so consistently warned the Calmeron soundenors of Guardian attacks, for instance, that the Guardians became convinced they had an informant in their ranks. The "eyes" also foretold Gideon's arrival and the death of Cimron's daughter in Gideon's arms (see Cimron te'Mara).

Black Ages, The—The period from the first year of the Slaughtering (S.C. 1605) to the present day. In S.C. 1650, the Council Lords forbade the use of the title "Black Ages," calling the times the "Council Age." This new title, however, is rarely used except in Phallenar or whenever the ears of the government may be near.

Black Gorge, The—A long, narrow, water-filled canyon that marks the major boundary between the Deathland Barrens and the rest of the Inherited Lands. Commonly called the Gorge.

Book of Dei'lo—A sacred tome containing the knowledge of *Dei'lo*, a language of power taught by the Pearl during its time in the Inherited Lands. Only those whose hearts are free of *Sa'lei* may touch the Book, open it, or learn the Words within it. Almost all others who try instantly perish. Immediately following the destruction of the Pearl, the Book disappeared from Wordhaven. It has been lost ever since.

Borac conMata (BOOR-ac con-MAAT-ta)—An elder of Songwill sounden and confidant of Elima conSeth. Elima chose Borac at birth to become the next *Nissirei*.

Borin Slayer (BOOR-ihn)—High Commander of the Guardians of Phallenar. Borin's official title is Firstsworn, to reflect the fact that he is "corded" to all of the Council Lords.

Broken Heart—The second in a series of ancient training centers designed to test Initiates who aspired to become Lords of Wordhaven. Now thought to be located somewhere in the Deathland Barrens.

Calmeron sounden—A village on the edge of the Castellan Watch. The soundenors of this village are the only people in the Inherited Lands skilled in harvesting *bian'ar*, which they use to create glowood or Worded breads that can be exchanged for goods they need to survive. They also regularly give the Worded breads as tribute to the Lords of Phallenar, in exchange for the Council's "benevolent protection."

Castel Morstal (kaas-TEL moor-STAL)—From the High Tongue, meaning "Death's Inner Chamber" or "Death's Breaking Place." A vast mountain keep created by the Pearl as a prison for Abaddon. Though watched over by the Kah for centuries, no mortal has ever entered it.

Castellan Watch—A great forest stretching from the Barrier Mountains in the west, to the Scolding Wind Hills in the north, and to Calmeron sounden in the east. It was named by the Kah, who, legends say, once lived in the heights of the great trees. The massive trees in the Watch are similar to those found in Strivenwood Forest, though it is not known whether the trees of Strivenwood also produce *bian'ar*. Other than the people of Calmeron sounden, few are willing to venture into the Watch for extended periods. Those who do often never return.

Chief Mentor—A title given to the scholar responsible for educating the Underlords at Phallenar in the ways of government and Council life.

Cimron te'Mara (SIMM-ron TE maar-ah)—An informant of the Remnant who lives in Calmeron sounden. Through the *Bian'ar* eyes, Cimron and his bondmate both knew of Gideon's arrival and foresaw that his appearance would mean the death of their daughter, Kira. Nevertheless, they chose not to interfere with the vision because they believed Gideon was indeed the Kinsman Redeemer. And without their daughter's presence with him, they feared that he would have been killed instead.

Cording—The practice used exclusively by Council Lords to bond their *jalen* to them using the Words of *Sa'lei*. Once corded, *jalen* become Wordsworn to protect their Lord from any injury. If their Lord is attacked, they are instantly aware of it. If their Lord is killed, they too will die within one month's time. Although it is possible for Council Lords to become corded to each other, their mutual distrust has thus far prevented it.

Council of Lords—The ruling body of the Inherited Lands, currently made up of thirteen Lords who have been granted the right of succession by their elders. Succession is granted only to direct descendants of the original twenty-five families whose members formed the first Council in S.C. 1610 (after the death of Palor Wordwielder). Although officially all members of the Council except the High Lord are equals, in reality those members who can claim ties to the greatest number of Council families hold the greatest power in the Axis. This ranking system has resulted in significant inbreeding among the Council Lords and has caused several serious medical problems to arise over the centuries. Not the least of these is barrenness. In the present

Council, all the women of child-bearing years are barren, and only a few of the female underlords are capable of bearing young. So far, this knowledge has been kept from the public.

Deathland Barrens—Commonly refers to all land east of the Black Gorge. This land became both desolate and dangerous as an immediate result of the Word of Desolation spoken in ancient times by High Lord Gideon Truthslayer.

Dei'lo—A powerful language that has in its speaking the capacity to transform both the physical and spiritual world and the individuals within them. The heart of *Dei'lo* is the power of creation.

Donovan Truthstay—Originally Donovan Blade, the former Firstsworn of the Council Guardians. Donovan was captured by the Remnant after he was mortally wounded in a battle with Laudin Sky (S.C. 2139). Not long after being restored to health, the Remnant severed his cording to the Council Lords and convinced him to abandon his former office and join the rebellion against Phallenar.

Elima conSeth (EL-leema con-SETH)—High elder of Songwill sounden. See "*Nissirei*."

Endimnar—A highly esteemed prophet from the Gray Ages. Endimnar prophesied the coming of a Kinsman Redeemer, a warrior-teacher who would reclaim the power of the Pearl and restore the hearts of the people in the Inherited Lands. He also foresaw the coming of the Slaughtering, calling it the starting point of a Black Age in which hatred would rule without mercy. Palor Wordwielder claimed to be the Kinsman Redeemer Endimnar had foretold, but his rule actually brought on the Black Age. Since that time, many people associate the coming of the Kinsman Redeemer with a second, more horrible Black Age, instead of the prosperity Endimnar foretold.

Endless Age, The—The period dated from the arrival of the Pearl in the Inherited Lands until the time of Gideon's Fall. The actual length of this age is not known.

Fallenwood—A corrupted forest located in the eastern part of the Deathland Barrens. Before Gideon's Fall, the forest supported several soundens established within its borders. Nothing is known about what became of them.

Fayerna Baratii (Fa-IR-na Bar-a-TEE)—Lord on the Council of Phallenar. Older sister to Bentel, who together share a common love interest, Lord Sarlina Alli. This threesome often works in concert to accomplish their own agenda on the Council.

Gideon Dawning—An unwitting sojourner in the Inherited Lands. A man of great wounding and great promise.

Gideon Truthslayer—Ancient High Lord of Wordhaven responsible for the Pearl's destruction and the creation of the Deathland Barrens. Originally named Gideon Truesworn, his devotion to the Pearl became clouded by personal greed. Seeing the opportunity to destroy the Pearl through the High Lord, Abaddon offered to teach him a Word so powerful it would destroy the Pearl and transfer its power into Gideon himself, thus making him the supreme force in the Inherited Lands. At a place now known as Gideon's Fall, the High Lord spoke the Word that destroyed the Pearl. The High Lord was never heard from again after that, but the resulting earthquakes and firestorms ravaged the land continuously for three days and three nights, resulting in the creation of the Black Gorge and the Deathland Barrens.

Gideon's Fall—The final act of High Lord Gideon Truthslayer, which destroyed the Pearl and created the Deathland Barrens. Also refers to the place where Gideon spoke the Word, a nobby blackened hill north of Phallenar along the cliffs of what is now the Black Gorge.

Gilding—A wood-treatment process that involves encasing wood in the sap that bleeds from the trees of the Castellan Watch. Once hardened, the sap forms a lightweight shield that has the appearance of crystal and prevents the wood from getting wet—and, thus, glowing.

Giver, The—Common name for the Creator, who sent the Pearl into the Inherited Lands to subdue Abaddon and establish the Endless Age. Although his ways are often viewed as mysterious, he is still believed to take an active part in the lives of the people.

Glowood—A common name for wood that comes from the Castellan Watch or any other wood that has been infused with *bian'ar*. Unprocessed *bian'ar* has the effect of causing the wood to glow when saturated with water. The effect lasts as long as the wood remains wet.

Gray Ages, The—The period from the end of the final Sojourn in S.C. 867 until the first year of the Slaughtering in S.C. 1605. It was during this age that Wordhaven was abandoned and eventually forgotten.

Guardians—In the present age, Worded soldiers responsible for enforcing the Council's will throughout the Inherited Lands. Though they are sworn to follow the will of any Council Lord, the wishes of the High Lord generally take precedence over all others. In ancient times, the Guardians were life-sworn servants of the Pearl whose primary task was carrying out the Pearl's wishes.

High Tongue, The—An ancient language derived from *Dei'lo*. Many remnants of the language remain in present everyday life, but the language's exact purpose and power has been lost.

Hinterland—A narrow strip of lush greenlands isolated between the Silence Sound and the Raanthan Plateau. Populated by a proud people called the "Kolventu."

Ja'moinar (ZHA-moy-NAR)—From the High Tongue, meaning "bread of those who live." Only the breadmistresses of Calmeron sounden are able to make this bread, using an ancient ceremonial process in which the women recite a litany in the High Tongue while mixing *bian'ar* with their own human tears.

Jalen (zha-LEN)—The common title for all personal bodyguards and spies belonging to a specific Council Lord. There are two orders of *jalen*, according to their primary function. *Ser'jalen* are information gatherers. Their task is to spy on other Council Lords or anyone else of interest to their masters. *Mon'jalen* are of greater importance. Their task is to act as personal bodyguards for their Lord. While *ser'jalen* are sometimes taught rudimentary fragments of *Sa'lei*, *mon'jalen* are trained in a full arsenal of Words, even more than Guardians. Because any Council Lord may kill another simply by speaking a Word, *mon'jalen* are sworn to immediately avenge any injury, however slight, that's inflicted on their Lord. All *jalen* are "corded" to their Lords by the Words of *Sa'lei*—so that in the instant any Lord is injured, his or her *jalen* will know it; and if any Lord is killed by unnatural means, all of his or her *jalen* will also die within one month's time. This delay before their deaths allows the *jalen* time to avenge their Lord's murder. As a result of this cording, all *jalen* tend to be highly motivated protectors and servants.

Juron (ZHUR-ON)—Black, winged lions that nest on the heights of the Barrier Mountains. Although naturally fearful of people, they can quickly become vicious if threatened.

Kah, The (KAH)—From the High Tongue, meaning "Watchers." A legendary race of tree-dwellers whose sole purpose was to stand watch over Castel Morstal to make certain that Abaddon could never escape. Legends claim that the Kah were endowed with mysterious talents and the ability to sense the movements and intentions of the evil one wherever he roamed.

Kair of the Songtrust (KYE-EYR)—A member of the Remnant whose mother is from Calmeron and whose father is from Songwill. Because of the enmity between these two soundens, she can claim neither as her home. She is especially adept at the healing Words.

Katira Peacegiver (Kah-TEER-ah)—Servant of the Pearl at Wordhaven. She and her husband, Teram Firstway, are among the last of the original Remnant who fled from Phallenar during the Sky Rebellion.

Kinsman Redeemer—A mysterious figure mentioned in many prophecies recorded throughout the Gray Ages. Some prophecies speak of the Kinsman Redeemer as a mighty warrior who will defeat the evil one and return the language of *Dei'lo* to the people as it was in the beginning. Other prophecies describe him as a champion of peace, who will be overthrown by evil authorities and sacrificed to somehow preserve the land. Since the time Palor Wordwielder claimed the title for himself, all people have associated the Kinsman Redeemer with tumultuous change—whether for good or for evil.

Kyrintha Asher-Baal—Underlord of the Council in Phallenar; daughter of Balaam and Lysteria. Though approved for succession onto the Council, she has rejected it. Therefore, according to Council law, she has been sealed up in the Tower of the Wall until she agrees to comply. So far, she has remained in the tower for three years.

Lairn conCimron (LAYRN con-SIMM-ron)—Teenage son of Cimron, who was to become one of the first real Initiates into Wordhaven in over two thousand years.

Laudin Sky—Instigator of the "Sky Rebellion" against the Council Lords in S.C. 2060. Once Chief Mentor of all the Underlords in Phallenar, Laudin later escaped with over one hundred companions in search of the fabled Wordhaven. After a thirty-five-year sojourn, he found it and became the first leader to sit within its walls in over one thousand years. Rather than equate himself with the ancient Lords of Wordhaven, however, he chose the title "Mentor," as a constant reminder of the bondage from which he had been freed. After he was killed by Donovan Blade in a Guardian ambush, the mantle was passed on to his younger brother, who changed the title to "Paladin" and now leads the Remnant at Wordhaven.

Lysteria Asher-Baal (Liss-TEER-ee-ah Ash-uhr BAYL)—Lord on the Council at Phallenar. Wife of High Lord Balaam. A great patron and fierce defender of the glory of Phallenar.

Maalern Fade (MAY-lern FAYD)—Oldest member of the Council Lords. He represents the last of his family line.

Mara ta'Cimron (MAAR-a TA SIMM-ron)—Bondmate of Cimron and a breadmistress of Calmeron sounden.

Mattim Dasa-Rel (Matt-TEEM Das-a-RELL)—Lord on the Council in Phallenar. Married to Varia Dasa-Rel.

Mon'jalen—See *"Jalen."*

Morguen sounden (MOOR-gwen sounden)—Located on the southern end of the Silence Sound near Strivenwood Forest.

Mystery—An obscure island located north of the Inherited Lands off the coast of the Raanthan Plateau.

New Ages, The—The period from Gideon's Fall (S.C. 1) to the end of the last major Sojourn (by Lord Kih, in S.C. 867). This period was marked by successive generations of lesser Wordhaven Lords, who launched mammoth Sojourns to try to locate the lost Book of *Dei'lo* and reclaim the glory of former days. So obsessed were they with finding the Book that they neglected to protect the knowledge of the Words they still retained. Consequently, the strength of their society steadily declined as the knowledge of *Dei'lo* and culture of Wordhaven were gradually lost. Not long after the end of this period, Wordhaven was abandoned.

Nissirei (Nis-seer-AYE)—From the High Tongue, meaning "first song of the people." The title belonged to the High Elder of Songwill sounden, who was handpicked from birth by the previous High Elder and raised solely to fill that role for the people.

Noble Heart—The first in a series of ancient training centers designed to test Initiates who aspired to become Lords of Wordhaven. Thought to have been located somewhere in the Plain of Dreams.

Orisoun (Or-iss-SOWN)—From the High Tongue, meaning "prayer to the Giver." The name of Gideon's mount.

Paladin—Title given to the First Servant of the Pearl at Wordhaven. Currently the title belongs to an old, strong man of fierce passion and piercing insight.

Palor Wordwielder—The only person who ever sought the title of king over all of the Inherited Lands. His attempt failed, but not before killing hundreds of thousands and shattering the soul of the people.

Palor's Finger—A point on the edge of the Delving Ocean where Palor apparently destroyed himself after failing to overthrow Songwill sounden. Legend claims Palor killed himself by summoning a mighty ocean serpent that dragged him out to sea.

Pearl, The—A fantastic living orb sent by the Giver to teach the people of the Inherited Lands the Words of *Dei'lo* and show them how to live in peace with one another.

Phallenar (FALL-en-NAR)—Capital city of the Inherited Lands, seat of power for the Council Lords for over six hundred years. Its founding by Palor Wordwielder led to the Slaughtering in S.C. 1605.

Plain of Dreams—A Worded plain of singing grasses that stretches from the Dunerun Hope to the outskirts of Phallenar. The region is Worded so that anyone who sleeps within the plains will dream of actual events from his or her past, present, or future. The origin and purpose for this Wording are unknown.

Pondari—A large slothlike creature with long reddish fur and a peaceful disposition. Though dull-witted and often stubborn, its immense size and strength make it a favored beast of burden for Roamers and other travelers carrying large loads. Though largely domesticated, wild pondarin can still be found in the Hinterland as well as many parts of the Heaven Range.

Prottell sounden—The original name of Phallenar. In ancient times, that sounden's Trust was the knowledge of interpreting prophecies and dreams. It is where Palor Wordwielder was born.

Raanthan (RON-thun)—From the High Tongue, meaning "to cover." A mysterious race who are said to live north of the Heaven Range in the Raanthan Plateau. Few facts about them are known, but legends and myths abound. Some of the more prominent beliefs are that Raanthans have no gender, can speak only in song, and are able to wrap their bodies in light like a blanket.

Rachel Alli—Lord on the Council at Phallenar. Occasional lover to Baurejalin Sint.

Raug (RAWG)—A *mon'jalen* guard corded to Lord Lysteria Asher-Baal. Originally from the Hinterland, Raug was forced into service while acting as an emissary of peace from his people.

Remnant, The—Originally called "The Society of the Remnant." A clandestine organization within Phallenar, whose members believed the Council Lords had indeed found the Book of *Dei'lo*, but had not been able to destroy it. The Remnant's sole purpose was to infiltrate the government in order to discover the Book's whereabouts. Their ultimate aim was to steal the Book and use its language to overthrow the Council's rule. After the Sky Rebellion, most of the Remnant fled Phallenar or were killed. Though the organization was thought to be shut down within borders of Phallenar over six hundred years ago, it does, in fact, still exist. (See "Sky Rebellion.")

Revel Foundling—An orphan boy adopted by Laudin Sky after a Guardian raid on Morguen sounden. His origins are a mystery, as are the source of his unique abilities, which come alive whenever he enters forested lands.

Rhema (REY-ma)—A little-known settlement on the northern coast of the Deathland Barrens. Home of the Cal'eeb.

Riftborn—Humans or other creatures born in the Deathland Barrens. Also can refer to any creature that's been mutated by the Barrens' effects.

Riftmen—Humans who have been perverted by the effects of the Deathland Barrens. Having no specific form, riftmen can assume any shape they wish and hold a human form only by choice. Their skin and body fluids carry the plague of the Barrens. One touch can cause serious illness; a scratch will cause death. So feared are they that contact is avoided at all cost.

Roamers, The—The common name given to nomadic soundens of traveling merchants. Essentially, they are smugglers, often stealing from one sounden in order to sell the goods to another. Their existence is officially forbidden by Council Law.

Sa'lei—A powerful language that has in its speaking the ability to pervert both the physical and spiritual world and the individuals within them. The heart of *Sa'lei* is the power of destruction.

Sacred Heart—The last in a series of ancient training centers designed to test Initiates who aspired to become Lords of Wordhaven. Thought to have been located somewhere in the Heaven Range.

Saria Sky (SAH-ree-ah SKYE)—The quiet eldest sister to Seer, Laudin, and Jesun (Paladin) Sky.

Sarlina Alli (sar-LEEN-ah ah-LEE)—Lord on the Council at Phallenar. Mentally disabled from birth, she relies on the guidance of Fayerna and Bentel Baratti and does whatever she can to please them.

Scolding Wind Hills—A Worded region of verdant hills stretching from the Barrier Mountains in the west to the border of the Deathland Barrens in the east. Named "Scolding Wind" because of the unique and terrible power they release against anyone who speaks a Word of *Sa'lei* within their borders.

Sea Folk, The—A race of squat, gnomelike people who make their home upon the seas. Also called the "Wondrojan," they instinctively distrust solid earth and prefer instead to live in floating cities out on the open sea.

Sed Kappan-Mati (SED KAP-an MA-tee)—Lord on the Council at Phallenar.

Seer Sky (SEE-ur SKYE)—Elder sister of Jesun (Paladin Sky). Especially gifted in the interpretation of dreams.

Ser'jalen—See *"Jalen."*

Seven Stays, The—Seven towering "sound chambers" constructed along the border of the Deathland Barrens south of Rhema. Day and night the priests of Cal'eeb cry out from the chambers the Words that hold the Barrens at bay.

Shikinah (Shi-KEY-na)—A highly esteemed prophet from the Gray Ages. Her prophecies foretold of the coming of a second High Lord of the Pearl, who would be betrayed as the Pearl was and hung to die on a Great Wall in Phallenar. So great was public reaction to this prophecy that several factions in Songwill demanded she retract it. When she would not, Shikinah was forcibly taken to Castellan Watch, beaten, and hung there to die. Oddly, just as she died, she looked toward the sky and laughed, saying, "It is torn! The heart is torn! At last I understand!"

Sky Rebellion—Named for its instigator, Laudin Sky, the rebellion was actually more of an organized escape from Phallenar. The rebels were all members of the Remnant, who fled the city on a quest to locate the fabled Wordhaven.

Slaughtering, The—A three-year war led by Palor Wordwielder and his armies of "New Guardians." During that time, many soundens were completely obliterated, their inhabitants killed or taken as slaves to Prottell sounden (now Phallenar). The war represented the first time the Words of *Sa'lei* were used in open combat. The war ended with Palor's suicide, which came at the end of an unsuccessful siege of Songwill sounden. Until recent events, Songwill was the only sounden in the Land that was still officially free from Council rule.

Sojourn—A private journey taken by individuals who seek spiritual renewal or intellectual enlightenment. Once a sojourn begins, it does not end until a person either finds the enlightenment he seeks or dies in the attempt. In ancient times, the Lords of Wordhaven led entire armies of people on sojourn together in search of the Book of *Dei'lo*.

Sojourner—A title of respect bestowed on any person who leaves home on a quest for spiritual enlightenment. In ancient times, the title referred to those who traversed the Inherited Lands in search of the Book of *Dei'lo*.

Songwill sounden—Located in the heart of the Scolding Wind Hills. Their original Trust under the Old Lords involved the power and beauty of music and art.

Sounden—A community of people within the Inherited Lands.

Stevron Achelli (STEV-RAHN ah-KELL-ee)—A Lord on the Council in Phallenar. Handpicked by Balaam and Lysteria to become husband to their daughter, Kyrintha—or, if necessary, take her place as Balaam's successor.

Strivenwood Forest—A vast forest stretching from the Heaven Range in the west to the Black Gorge in the east. The forest is Worded, though the exact nature of the Wording is unclear. All that is known is that anyone who enters the forest is lost forever.

Teram Firstway (TEAR-uhm)—Servant of the Pearl at Wordhaven. One of the few original members of the group that escaped from Phallenar in the Sky Rebellion.

Trevail Plains—A small region of land on the northern tip of the Deathland Barrens, inhabited by a people who call themselves the Cal'eeb, which in the High Tongue means "Standing Ones."

Trust, A—An endowment of hidden knowledge. In reference to soundens, a Trust is a unique application of the Words of *Dei'lo* known only to the people of the sounden to which it was given and to the Wordhaven Lords themselves. The Trusts gave each sounden its identity and purpose, and so naturally each sounden held its special knowledge in the highest esteem and guarded it with utmost secrecy. The knowledge of each Trust was complementary rather than competitive, creating a society in which each sounden contributed equally to the success of the others, thus binding the soundens together in a rich tapestry of culture and industry. It was an easy symbiosis, but one that could be maintained only so long as each sounden played its role and guarded its Trust with diligence.

Underlord—An honorary title given to a son, daughter, nephew, or niece of a Council Lord. Although underlords have no official authority nor any access to the Words of *Sa'lei*, they still manage significant influence in the affairs of the government in Phallenar.

Vallera Kappan-Mati (va-LEHR-ah KAH-pan MAH-tee)—Lord on the Council at Phallenar.

Varia Dasa-Rel—Lord on the Council at Phallenar. Married to Mattim Dasa-Rel. A thorn in Lysteria's side.

Visitation, The—A common reference to the prophesied arrival of the Kinsman Redeemer.

Warcor—A military unit of Guardians or other soldiers, consisting of exactly thirteen hundred fighters—one hundred for each of the Council Lords.

Wordhaven—Home of the Pearl and ancient center of power during the Endless Age. Except for the Remnant, no one knows its location.

Acknowledgments

I owe an enormous debt of gratitude to my editor and friend, Mike Nappa, whose resilient belief in my writing and consistent demand for excellence brought this book to life in more ways than I can name. My thanks also extend to the good folks at Barbour Books, whose diligence and skill helped shape the manuscript into the final form you now hold.

I am equally grateful to the many friends and fellow writers whose honest critiques and suggestions during the writing of this book were as invaluable as they were gracious. Among these great champions of my cause are Stephen Parolini, June Criner, Joan Schubart, James and Beth Frazier, Mark Furaus, Don Shipp, and several others to whom I owe my continuing debt of thanks.

And to my family—Don, Laverne, Gary, Brenda, Stephanie, and David—I owe the greatest debt of all. Without your faithful prayers and loving support over these years, I doubt I would have ever dared to write at all.

Finally, to those of you who have taken the time to share the journey of this book with me, I thank you. If you'd like to learn more about me and my writing feel free to access my Web site at www.MichaelWarden.com, or you are welcome to e-mail me at mdwarden@yahoo.com. I look forward to hearing from you.

ALSO FROM
BARBOUR BOOKS
An imprint of Barbour Publishing, Inc.

Time Lottery by Nancy Moser
ISBN 1-58660-587-9

After twenty-two years of scientific research, three lucky individuals will receive the opportunity of a lifetime with the Time Lottery—to relive one decisive moment that could change the course of their lives.

Operation: Firebrand by Jefferson Scott
ISBN 1-58660-586-0

Former navy SEAL Jason Kromer is appointed leader of Operation: Firebrand, a covert operations team specializing in nonlethal missions of mercy. Its first challenge: a winter rescue of orphaned children made homeless by Russian rebels.

Face Value by Andrew Snaden and Rosey Dow
ISBN 1-58660-589-5

Just days after Beth Martin's long-awaited facelift operation, she is found dead—and her cosmetic surgeon, Dr. Dan Foster, finds himself playing amateur detective after being framed for the killing.

Interview with the Devil by Clay Jacobsen
ISBN 1-58660-588-7

Journalist Mark Taylor has landed the story of his career—an interview with the coldhearted leader of a new terrorist network. Mark is taken hostage, tortured, and beaten. Now this Christian's only hope lies in God's sovereign hands—and in the heart of the terrorist's nephew, a devout Muslim man Mark befriended during the Gulf War.

Available wherever books are sold.